THE
DESTINY
OF THE
DEAD

'The guards are dead. We've done it, Nish. The pass is ours.'

'Not yet. Their reinforcements are on the way, maybe thirty. We'll have to try and take them down as they come.'

'No, we won't,' said Clech. 'There they are. Get down.'

He pulled Nish down flat. The running enemy were silhouetted in the dim light at the crest of the pass, and Clech roared, 'Fire!'

A fusillade of arrows whistled overhead from Nish's archers, who were already through the pass, and many of the enemy reinforcements fell. A second salvo took down more, whereupon the rest turned and ran.

'*Now* we have the pass,' said Nish, feeling a quiet satisfaction that they'd won it at so little cost. But how long could they keep it?

'Hold your fire!' said Clech. 'Archers, this way.'

As he and Nish headed up to the crest, a second rocket shot up from further down the mountain behind them, bursting with an ice-blue flare that cast a cold light on the enemy dead and the snowy peaks to either side. The last of the reinforcements were bolting down towards the western gate of the pass.

'That's Klarm's answer,' said Flydd, stepping out from behind a crag and wiping his blade on one of the fallen soldiers. 'He's on his way.'

By Ian Irvine

The Three Worlds Series

IAN IRVINE

A TALE OF THE THREE WORLDS

THE DESTINY OF THE DEAD

Volume Three of SONG OF THE TEARS

www.orbitbooks.net

ORBIT

First published in Great Britain in 2009 by Orbit
This paperback edition published in 2009 by Orbit

A CIP catalogue record for this book
is available from the British Library.

ISBN 978-1-84149-473-9

Typeset in Veljovik by M Rules
Printed in the UK by CPI Mackays, Chatham ME5 8TD

Papers used by Orbit are natural, renewable and recyclable
products sourced from well-managed forests and certified
in accordance with the rules of the Forest Stewardship Council.

Mixed Sources
Product group from well-managed
forests and other controlled sources
www.fsc.org Cert no. SGS-COC-004081
© 1996 Forest Stewardship Council
FSC

ACKNOWLEDGEMENTS

I would like to thank my editor, Nan McNab, and my agent, Selwa Anthony, for their hard work and support over many years and many books. Thanks to Laura Harris at Penguin Books, and Bella Pagan and Darren Nash at Orbit Books, for support, encouragement and assistance in so many ways. I would also like to thank everyone at Penguin Books and Orbit Books for working so hard on the eleven books of The Three Worlds series and for making such a success of them.

CONTENTS

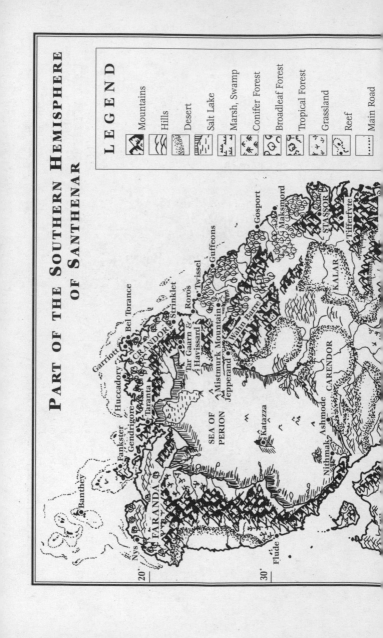

PART OF THE SOUTHERN HEMISPHERE OF SANTHENAR

LEGEND

Mountains

Hills

Desert

Salt Lake

Marsh, Swamp

Conifer Forest

Broadleaf Forest

Tropical Forest

Grassland

Reef

Main Road

Maps by the author

Part One

RUIN ON THE RANGE

ONE

'There's no way out this time, is there?' said Maelys, wiping the teeming rain from her eyes.

Nish glanced at her and managed a smile, for she was even grubbier than he was; her small figure was clotted with mud from head to foot. 'I can't think of one.' He rubbed his nose and winced. His battered face was so swollen that he was almost unrecognisable.

It was mid-morning on the Range of Ruin, and everyone had gathered in a ring around him, hoping for a miracle, but it wasn't going to happen. The enemy held the surrounding ridges, trapping them in a clearing in the forested valley; they had been ordered to take Nish and Maelys alive, and put everyone else to death. All their struggles over the past weeks, and all Nish's agony, had been for nothing.

He and his Gendrigorean militia had driven themselves to the limit of human endurance to climb the rain-drenched range and reach Blisterbone Pass before his father's army, and they would have succeeded had their treacherous guide, Curr, not led them astray. The pass was only a league away in a direct line, yet it was as unreachable as the moon, for the enemy's advance guard had beaten them to it and the rest of that monstrous army could not be far behind.

For supporting Nish and daring to oppose his corrupt father – the God-Emperor Jal-Nish Hlar – the peaceful little nation of Gendrigore was going to be obliterated and its men, women and children taken into slavery. Nish felt responsible, for the Gendrigoreans had not wanted to go to war; he had talked them into coming and now he bitterly regretted it.

Their situation was hopeless, yet he could not give in. During the lyrinx war they had snatched victory from defeat many times, and surely there had to be a way to do it again. But they could not win by force of arms, which left only the Secret Art.

'Flydd?' Nish said quietly. 'We really need your help.'

'What if you made another portal with the mimemule?' said Maelys, for Flydd had used that little mimicking device to create the portal that had brought her, Flydd and Yggur here.

Xervish Flydd, the mancer who had led humanity to an impossible victory in the war against the lyrinx ten years ago, swayed on his broad feet. Though he had regained some of his lost gift for the Art, he had never been the same after casting that terrible Renewal Spell upon himself almost six weeks ago.

It had replaced his aged and failing body with that of a bigger man in middle age, but Flydd was in constant pain and he seemed meaner, harder and . . . Nish resisted the thought for as long as he could – less trustworthy. A few minutes ago, Flydd had been gazing at the Profane Tears, Gatherer and Reaper, the source of the God-Emperor's power, as though he wanted to snatch them for himself.

'I can't!' Flydd said, clutching at his belly. 'Bringing so many people through that second portal took everything I had, and the *aftersickness* –' He doubled up as though he was going to vomit, gagged, and straightened painfully. 'I don't have the

4

power to use the mimemule again.' He looked around blearily. 'I don't know this place. What's our line of retreat?'

'There isn't one,' said Nish. 'We're in a valley shaped like a tilted oval bowl. It's a good league long and half a league wide, and the upper end runs up to the white-thorn peak, the mountain guarding this side of Blisterbone Pass.'

With his sabre, he gestured towards the towering mountain, barely visible through the blinding rain. 'The upper part of the valley ends at the cliffs; I don't think anyone could climb them. The enemy holds the ridges to either side of us and they're bare, rain-washed rock with no cover – we'd never fight our way up. They also guard the only way out, a gorge spanned by a natural arch of stone.'

He pointed downslope, though nothing could be seen in that direction save a wall of rainforest marking the lower edge of the clearing. 'The valley floor is covered in forest, apart from another clearing lower down, near the gorge.'

'Is it more defendable than this one?' said Flydd.

'I don't know. What do you think, Tulitine?' Nish said to the tall, striking woman to his left.

The old seer had used a Regression Spell to temporarily restore herself to a relatively young age, then made a desperate attempt to reach Nish's militia and warn them that they had been betrayed, but she had arrived just as the trap had been sprung.

Tulitine thought for a moment. 'I don't think so, for the valley narrows down there. The enemy archers could fire into the clearing from the stone arch, and from the nearby ridge.'

'Forget it,' said Flydd. 'We'll make our stand here.' He turned towards the river that ran down the centre of the valley; it could just be made out through the trees. 'Can they cross the river and attack us from behind?'

'I'm afraid so,' said Tulitine. 'It's partly dammed by fallen trees just upstream; that's how I got here.'

'Can you stop them crossing with your Art?' said Nish.

'I only know healing charms. Besides, the Regression Spell is already fading, and when it comes undone . . .'

Tulitine had hinted earlier at what it would do to her. The consequences were going to be horrific and there was nothing anyone could do to stop the spell failing. That left only Yggur, who towered to Nish's left, craggy as an ancient cedar and seemingly as indestructible.

'I know you've got power, old friend,' Nish said, 'and we've never needed it more. If you could create a concealing mist or . . .'

'Ordinarily, that would be the easiest of spells,' said Yggur. 'Especially here, where there's water everywhere . . .'

'But?' cried Nish. Yggur had been his last hope.

'Gatherer is watching everything I do, and the moment I try to draw power Reaper blocks me. I'm not strong enough to take on the greatest force on Santhenar.' Yggur rubbed his inflamed wrists. For seven years he'd been held prisoner by the Numinator, whose enchanted bracelets had continually drained him of his powers of mancery to bolster her own. 'Besides, I feel strangely hobbled in this place.'

'What do you mean, *hobbled*?' said Maelys sharply. She pressed a hand between her breasts, and frowned.

Nish had seen her make that unconscious gesture many times, and knew that she was making contact with her taphloid, the mysterious little device she'd worn around her neck since childhood. Touching it normally comforted her, but she seemed troubled now.

'I don't know.' Yggur's gaze flicked towards the red-hot caduceus, the height of a small tree, embedded in the centre of the clearing. Whatever uncanny force drove its internal fires, it was unquenched by the teeming rain. 'There may be a way to hide what I'm doing from Gatherer,

6

but . . . it will take time to find it.' He headed towards the caduceus, shielding his eyes from its glare.

Time we don't have. Nish could feel the radiance beating upon his bruised face. The caduceus, a winged shaft tightly entwined by a pair of open-mouthed serpents, was made of black iron forged from the heart of a meteorite and, when Stilkeen had hurled it down, its point had penetrated half a span of solid rock.

Hostage! For – white-ice-fire! that tormented *being* from the void had cried as it seized the God-Emperor and carried him off, but what had it meant?

Had Stilkeen meant that Jal-Nish was held hostage until it regained the chthonic fire – the force that had once bound its physical and spirit aspects together – stolen from it in ancient times?

Or did the caduceus signify that the whole world was Stilkeen's hostage? Either way, Nish had no idea what to do about it. No one on Santhenar had faced an immortal *being* before and not even Yggur, oldest of them all, knew how to deal with it.

'Then I'd better organise our defences.' Nish turned away, sick at the thought of the coming massacre. The professional soldiers up there were going to tear his rag-tag militia apart.

His eye fell on the ginger-haired cook's boy, Huwld, a cheerful, scrawny lad of eleven.

'What the blazes are you doing here?' Nish cried.

'Got better,' grinned Huwld.

He had suddenly appeared halfway up the range, as though the militia had been hiding him from Nish all that time. Nish had sent the boy back with the third of his militia who had contracted dysentery, but somehow Huwld was still here, and it made the coming battle so much worse. The boy was going to die, along with all his people, and Nish couldn't bear it.

The Gendrigoreans seemed to have no idea what an army was really for, or how brutal and savage warfare was. And why should they, Nish mused. No enemy had successfully crossed the Range of Ruin into Gendrigore in over a thousand years.

At first he'd thought of them as little more than carefree, pleasure-loving innocents, impossible to turn into a decent fighting force, but he knew better now. Inside, they were tough as the gnarled roots of an old tree.

Huwld had vanished again and, as Nish scanned the militia for the boy, he saw Aimee, a young woman so small and slender that she made Nish look tall. Whatever had possessed him, allowing her to join the militia? She was as brave as any warrior, but what use was she going to be when the fighting started? A heavy blow would break her in half.

Nish shook off the gloom and self-doubt before it became despair, and looked up. Above the western ridge, Jal-Nish's deputy, the dwarf General Klarm, stood spread-legged on a drifting air-sled the size of an emperor's bedroom. He appeared to be issuing orders to his troops, who were lined up along the ridge like pegs on a washing line. Nish estimated their number at a thousand, three times his militia, and they were big, brutal men, twice Klarm's height. The God-Emperor's white standard, mounted on a wooden pole at the bow, flapped high above him.

Nish still couldn't come to terms with the betrayal, for Klarm, who had been a friend and ally during the war, was one of the bravest men Nish had met. Yet after Jal-Nish seized power ten years ago Klarm had, inexplicably, taken service with him and was now his commander-in-chief, even trusted with the Profane Tears in his liege's involuntary absence. And because Nish's militia had refused to surrender, Klarm would show no mercy.

'They'll shoot us down from the edges of the clearing,' said Gi, a gentle, sturdy young woman, one of Nish's lieutenants and his closest friend in the militia. 'No need to risk their own lives.'

'The God-Emperor doesn't give a damn for his soldiers' lives,' said Flydd, 'but he would not risk his only surviving son's life, and neither can Klarm. They'll have to come on foot, and an agonising death awaits any soldier who harms you, Nish.'

Nish took no comfort from that, for no one could control the course of a battle, and in its chaos soldiers were often killed by accident, or even by their own people. Besides, he would sooner die in battle than be captured and see all his friends and allies slain.

'Take them!' Klarm's amplified voice rang out from the air-sled, and his troops began to move down the steep ridges towards the rainforest covering the floor of the valley.

'What if we run into the forest?' said Gi. 'It's dark in there. Some of us might escape.'

'They've ringed the valley and they hold the only exit,' said Nish. 'Klarm will make sure that no one escapes. We've got to stay together.'

He raised his voice. 'Form into a circle, facing out. Archers at the front, lancers behind them and swordsmen at the rear. Archers, when I give the order, fire until they're just ten seconds away, then fall back. Lancers, hold firm and make them come onto your spears. They won't dare fire at you for fear of a stray arrow hitting me or Maelys.' At least, Nish hoped they wouldn't.

The militia formed a tight circle, about forty paces across, surrounding the caduceus with their backs to it.

'What good will it do?' said Hoshi, a big, enthusiastic youth who had been an apprentice potter in Gendrigore. Nish had tried to train him in leadership but Hoshi had no head for it, his only tactic being to go straight at his opponent, whacking furiously.

Nish rubbed his scarred left hand, which was aching again. Many years ago, on the battlefield of Gumby Marth, his father had thrust Nish's hands into the tears in an attempt to control him, but the compulsion had failed and Nish's feeble, unreliable clearsight had appeared instead. Last month, in a cavern at the clifftop of Mistmurk Mountain, he had put his left hand into Reaper in a desperate effort to enhance his clearsight and find Flydd's lost Art, and had partly succeeded, though his hand had been hideously burned.

He kneaded the scars as he considered Hoshi's question. The poorly armed and untrained militia stood no chance in hand-to-hand combat with Klarm's crack Imperial Militia, but Nish's archers were skilled hunters and could do great damage if he used them well.

'From the edge of the clearing it'll take the enemy at least a minute to reach us through the mud, and our archers can each fire ten arrows in that time. If we can even the numbers, and delay them a minute or two, Yggur might be able to do something . . .'

'He'd better get a move on!' snapped Flydd, for he and Yggur had always been rivals and, clearly, Flydd felt his own helplessness keenly.

'I don't think you should use your Art so close to the caduceus, Yggur,' called Tulitine, who was standing a few paces from it.

'Why ever not?' said Yggur imperiously. He did not appreciate being told what to do.

Nish would have been cowed, but Tulitine was unfazed. 'If you do, it may go ill for you.'

'Death may go ill for us all,' said Flydd wryly.

The enemy were skidding down the wet slopes and

moving into the forest; they would reach the edge of the clearing in minutes. It was still pouring, Nish was sweating rivers in his sodden clothes, and the humidity was so thick he could have sliced it with his sabre.

'We can't get away,' said Tulitine. 'We've got to concentrate on saving *you*, Nish, so you can rebuild your forces and fight again.'

'I led my militia here,' Nish said, 'and I'm not running out on them now.'

'You must,' she said urgently. 'When your father took over with the tears, you swore to return, bring down his corrupt realm and restore freedom to Santhenar.'

'And I've failed,' he groaned. 'Again and again.' Nish deeply regretted that despairing vow after Jal-Nish had slain his beloved Irisis, for he was never going to fulfil his oath. The enemy was too strong.

'You've got to try harder,' said Tulitine. 'You gave hope to a million desperate souls – indeed, your vow has been the people's only hope over the ten years of your father's brutal rule, and you cannot let them down.'

'I can't do it, Tulitine.'

'You've got to try and get away. Even if you die in the attempt, striving valiantly to keep your word, you will become a beacon of hope for generations to come – just as Irisis's self-sacrifice has strengthened you.'

'What kind of a man escapes at the cost of his friends' lives,' said Nish, 'and the loyal militia that has followed him all this way?'

'A man who does what he has to do for the greater good,' said Flydd, 'no matter how hard it is.'

'Or a man who abandons his friends in their most desperate need,' Nish retorted. 'When Father returns, as I'm sure he will, he would call me a coward and an oath-breaker. How could *that* make me a beacon of hope?'

'It's a difficult choice, but you have to make it.'

'I've made it.' Nish turned and passed through the circular lines towards the centre. 'I can't stand in front of my troops and tell them I'm running away.'

'I'll tell them,' said Tulitine, 'because it must be done for the good of the empire.'

'No, you won't! I will not abandon my people.' He walked away.

'I can't bear it either,' Maelys said quietly, going with him.

'The waiting?' said Nish, glad she was there. Though only nineteen, and of a quiet, shy disposition, Maelys had an inner strength the equal of anyone here, and he felt better for having her at his side.

'The knowing that everyone else is going to die, while I'll live because of the possibility that I may be bearing your child.'

After an interval he lowered his voice and said, 'And are you?'

'Of course not,' she muttered, meeting his eyes. Hers were the colour of dark chocolate and showed nothing, though a pink flush spread across her pale cheeks. Maelys blushed easily, and rather prettily, despite the mud on her face. 'I made that story up to save our lives.'

She had told his father that she had gathered Nish's nocturnal seed months ago, while nursing him, and placed it inside herself so as to become pregnant. And Jal-Nish, desperate for a grandchild, had believed her.

'You did save our lives,' said Nish, 'so it was worth it.'

'It cost me my friendship with Colm. Afterwards, he looked on me as no better than a – a whore!' Her flush deepened.

'You can't be a virgin *and* a whore.'

'In Colm's eyes I was,' she said plaintively. 'I really liked him, Nish. He was good to me, in the early days.'

12

Nish restrained the urge to tell her just what he thought of Colm, who had lost his clan's estate in the war and would forever be bitter about it, as he was about a number of other injustices. Colm also resented the stain on his clan's name left by his distant relatives Karan and Llian, once heroes of the Time of the Mirror, who were now known as Karan Kin-Slayer and Llian the Liar.

Nonetheless, Colm had treated Maelys better than Nish had in the first month they had travelled together. But Colm was gone. He had accepted Klarm's offer of amnesty and was now their enemy; he and Nish could be fighting each other in minutes.

It was time to make amends. He put an arm across Maelys's mud-covered shoulders and drew her closer. 'I'm sorry it's come to this. And sorry for the way I treated you, after all you'd done for me. Can . . . can you forgive me?'

She looked up at him and her dark eyes were shining. How little it took. 'Of course, Nish. I – I wasn't honest with you in the early days; I should never –'

'They'll be through the forest any minute!' cried Flydd. 'Yggur, are you ready?'

'Not yet.' Yggur was walking in a spiral around the caduceus with his right hand upraised, the fingers hooked as if he were clinging onto a bar.

'What's he doing?' whispered Maelys, pulling away and turning to stare at Yggur.

Nish knew that she was fascinated by mancery. Maelys had been told that she had a gift for it, but she had never been trained and now she might be too old to learn.

'He's trying to find a point where Gatherer can't penetrate the *field* surrounding the caduceus,' said Flydd in grudging admiration. 'Yggur is taking an awful risk, but if he can find that point, he may be able to use his fog spell there without Gatherer instantly cancelling it.'

'Assuming that the caduceus doesn't cancel him,' muttered Maelys. 'I can *feel* the power radiating out from it. It's a horrible, alien thing and we shouldn't go near it.'

'Tulitine was right,' said Flydd. 'By its very nature, or the nature of the *being* that created it, the caduceus affects all spells done nearby.'

Nish was also afraid of it, but Yggur was their only hope now. Nish headed towards him and she followed but, as they approached, Yggur's hooked fingers clenched and the caduceus flared white hot.

Momentarily, Nish felt a throbbing pain behind his temples. One of the iron serpents around the shaft was displaying its forked tongue, while the other had its mouth wide open, baring two pairs of fangs. The upper ones were huge, the lower pair smaller and curved backwards to hold its prey, and in a flash of clearsight he noted that the serpent with the fangs had something burning at its core.

'Stilkeen is in pain,' said Maelys, wrapping her arms around her chest and squeezing hard. 'Terrible pain, just from being in our world.'

'Tell it to bugger off, then.' Nish turned away, for there was no more time.

He called his signallers and his four lieutenants – Hoshi and Gi, Clech the giant fisherman, and the dapper joker, Forzel – and they agreed on signal codes, both flags and horn blasts, in case Yggur succeeded and there came an opportunity to retreat.

'Chief Signaller Midge,' Nish said to the fuzzy-haired young woman whose size belied her name, for she was tall and solidly built, 'stay close to me. If Yggur manages a fog, we'll need to retreat at once.'

'How will we find our way?' asked Midge, wiping her muddy face on a yellow flag and turning it brown.

'Not on the signal flags, Midge, please.' Nish scraped the

mud off with his sabre and handed the flag back. In some respects they *were* like children, his loyal Gendrigoreans; he didn't think he'd ever turn them into soldiers. 'If we get a chance to retreat, we'll head downslope and gather at the lowest edge of the clearing. We can tell we're going downslope even in fog.'

'What then?' said Hoshi.

'How would I know?' Nish snapped. He thought for a moment. 'We'll go through the rainforest to the lower clearing and try to get out via the gorge.' There was still no sign of the enemy. He raised his voice. 'Lancers, ready your spears. Archers, fire the moment they come out of the forest, and again as they rush us. Keep firing until they're twenty paces away, then draw back so the lancers can meet their attack.'

The clearing, which was shaped like an egg, was about four hundred paces by three hundred. Running soldiers, even on this boggy ground, would not take long to reach the centre.

'How's Yggur going?' Nish said to Flydd.

'Do you see any fog?' Flydd snapped. He'd been really cranky of late.

'Isn't there anything *you* can do?'

'I've already tried. Curse this body. Why did I let Maelys talk me into taking renewal?' Flydd scowled at her.

'If I hadn't, you'd probably be dead by now,' she said quietly.

'At times like this, I wish I was,' Flydd muttered. 'I feel as though my new body is fighting me all the way; after all this time, it still doesn't *fit*.'

'I'm sure you'll get used to it,' said Nish.

'If I survive, you mean. And if I don't, good riddance.'

'Where are they?' said Maelys, standing on tiptoes and scanning the forest all around. 'Why are they taking so long?'

'They know we've no way of escape,' said Sergeant

Flangers, cleaning his purloined Whelm jag-sword with a clump of grass. His friend, protector and constant shadow, Chissmoul, was at his side. 'They're taking their time to make us sweat.'

'Still, it's wonderful to have you here,' said Nish.

Flangers, apart from being an old friend, was their only other experienced soldier, and a master of battlefield tactics, but he'd lost weight in his seven years of captivity and Nish wasn't sure he was ready for the rigours of warfare.

'It's good to have the old team back together, surr,' said Flangers. 'We showed the enemy a thing or two in the past, and we can do it again.'

'Of course we will,' Nish said unconvincingly. 'Archers, get ready –'

Maelys gasped, and all around, people were crying out and pointing.

Feeling the radiance beating upon the back of his head, Nish whirled; his head spun sickeningly and the pain behind his temples grew worse. The caduceus was keening, the note rising and falling, and it had brightened to white-hot again. The iron serpent with the fangs appeared to be staring at Nish, while the other snake was looking at Flydd, and Nish imagined, for one mad moment, that he saw its tongue flicking in and out.

'What's it doing?' Nish cried.

Maelys caught at her taphloid. Yggur threw himself backwards away from the caduceus, tripped and fell, sending out a spray of muddy water. Fog wisped up around him but disappeared at once.

'I don't know,' he said, scrambling out of the way, his frosty eyes wide. 'But we meddle with it at our peril.'

'At Santhenar's peril,' said Flydd. 'Do you recall the volcanic ruin wrought upon the world of Aachan not so many years ago? Fifty thousand Aachim fled through a portal to

Santhenar, and surely all those who remained behind on Aachan perished.'

'What of it?' said Yggur.

'Chthonic fire caused Aachan's ruin; the very fire Yalkara stole from Stilkeen in ancient times so her people could escape from the void. What dreadful forces might the caduceus contain?'

'Then why did Stilkeen leave it here?' said Yggur, scooping up handfuls of muddy water from a puddle and rubbing it all over his face, which was coming up in hundreds of little blisters. He winced, but turned back.

'Stay away from it,' said Tulitine. 'I think it's a trap.'

'I'm sure it is, but with Klarm using Gatherer to block my powers, the one place I can use my Art is next to the caduceus.'

In an open space, Nish noticed the three healers setting up their station. Closest was lanky Dulya, her chin marred by a large strawberry mark, and behind her, plump and palely pretty Scandey, one of the sisters of poor Tildy, the milkmaid who had been murdered by Vivimord in Gendrigore. After Scandey had seen Vivimord tried by ordeal above the Maelstrom of Justice and Retribution, and found guilty, she had been one of the first to join Nish's militia.

The third healer was Ghosh, a stocky youth with an exceptionally long body and short, thick legs. Unlike the other Gendrigoreans, he never smiled. He found his healer's duties too overwhelming.

Pulling his collar up to protect the back of his neck, Yggur backed towards the caduceus until his clothes began to steam, then stopped and raised his hands to try the spell again.

Nish's gut tightened. What if Tulitine was right? Was Yggur doing just what Stilkeen wanted?

'They're coming out,' Gi shrilled.

Nish ran out through the lines as the first of the Imperial troops appeared. Within minutes they had formed an oval ring around the edge of the clearing, surrounding the militia.

'Archers, pick your targets,' said Nish. 'Lancers, get into line; don't you remember anything you've been taught?' He turned, his head throbbing worse than ever, and noticed Maelys beside him. 'What the blazes are you doing out here – you're *unarmed*. Get into the centre of the circle.'

She ducked through a gap in the line, towards the little rise where the healers were getting ready to work on the brutal fruits of battle.

Nish faced the enemy and tried to prepare himself for what was going to be a massacre.

Two

Nish drew the black sabre which he'd taken from Vivimord's tent after the zealot's disappearance in the Maelstrom. The sabre was a magnificent weapon with an edge that never needed sharpening, though it was a trifle long for him. Whenever he held it, the pain in his left hand eased, which was curious.

'I don't like you using that weapon,' Flydd said to Nish dyspeptically.

'Why not?'

'It's an enchanted blade.'

Nish nearly dropped the sabre. 'Really? What kind of enchantment?'

'I don't know, but I'd be very careful with it. Go behind the lines. If they take you, they can butcher us at their leisure.'

The keening of the caduceus rose half a note, as if mimicking the song of the tears, and again the black eyes of the fanged serpent seemed to be on Nish. He rubbed his throbbing temples, then said coldly, 'I'm not cowering behind my friends while they die for nothing.'

'If the enemy takes you, their deaths *will* be for nothing.'

'You're talking like a manipulative scrutator, Flydd.'

'You've got to start acting like one if you hope to bring down your father. You have to do whatever it takes.'

It was a side of Flydd that had bothered Nish as far back as the time of the lyrinx war, but it had been more evident since his renewal. He seemed harder and more ruthless now and Nish rarely saw the kindly, warm-hearted side of him.

'I tried that once,' said Nish, 'and look where it got me. I'm going to defeat my father my way, or die trying, in which case my troubles will be over.'

'You have a higher duty –'

'How dare you lecture me!' Nish cried, for his headache was blinding now and there wasn't time for this. 'If you can't help me, get out of my way.'

Tightening his jaw, Flydd stalked back through the lines. Nish turned to face the top of the clearing and swished his sabre through the air. Though he was skilled with a blade, he was a small man and would be at a disadvantage fighting the tall Imperial troops. On the other hand, they could not afford to harm him.

They did not wear armour, for no man could have endured it in the heat of the tropical lowlands, and neither had they carried their huge, cumbersome war shields up the precipitous mountain paths. It gave Nish's archers the advantage, though they would only have ten arrows each to capitalise on it.

The enemy were armed with short lances and long swords; they wore iron helms and carried small oval shields that only covered their torsos. They stood silently around the edge of the clearing, at least eight hundred of them, awaiting Klarm's orders. The remainder held the ridges to either side, to cut down anyone trying to escape and, even if they lost hundreds to Nish's archers, the end could be in no doubt.

'Why don't they attack?' said Gi, trembling. She had never

been in a battle before – hardly any of the militia had seen warfare.

Nish put a steadying hand on her shoulder and she looked at him gratefully.

'They're trying to unnerve us,' said Tulitine.

'They're succeeding,' said Nish, though he was icily calm now, for during the war he'd been in dozens of battles. There were only two possible outcomes for anyone – you lived, or you died – and, ultimately, anyone's survival came down to chance.

In Tulitine's serene and beautiful face it was hard to see the old woman she'd been before. How long did she have before the failing Regression Spell took its savage toll? 'I wish you'd go inside the circle,' he said.

'But you're not game to order me about,' she said, smiling. 'I'm standing with you, Nish, and if it comes to it I'll fall with you. I've had a good life – for the most part – and a long one, and it would be a blessing to die while I still have my health and my looks.'

'I never thought of you as vain,' he said absently, waiting for the enemy to move.

'I'm human. Who would be old and feeble when vigorous youth and beauty were on offer, even for a few days – ah, here he comes.'

The air-sled came zooming down the ridge, then lifted and shot above the tops of the trees before curving in an elegant arc around the clearing. General Klarm stood mid-centre, legs spread and cloak flapping.

'He appears to be enjoying the ride,' said Nish.

'Klarm has command of the marvel of flight. And with the tears, he has only to wish for something and he can have it. Who would not enjoy that?'

The question sounded like a test, and Nish did not reply. The air-sled side-slipped towards the troops at the pointy end of the clearing and hovered soundlessly in the heavy air. Klarm raised his hand and the teeming rain stopped.

'Can he even control the weather?' said Gi breathlessly. Few Gendrigoreans knew anything about mancery and they were superstitious about it.

'For a moment, evidently,' said Tulitine, 'though if he holds back the rain now, later it must fall all the harder. Weather is driven by forces beyond our understanding, and if one changes it there is always a consequence. And a cost.'

'Come back into the line where we can defend you, Nish,' called Hoshi, the apprentice potter. 'Don't make it easy for them.'

His Gendrigorean troops never called him surr, only Nish. He'd been irritated by their lack of discipline at first, until he appreci-ated that it was just the way they were. He moved back through the archers and the wavering line of spears, eyeing the enemy. 'They're covering their bodies well with those oval shields. We're not going to take many down.'

'We could aim for their heads,' said Gi, raising her bow.

'Not at this range.'

'The legs, then. It's a tough man who can fight with an arrow through the leg.'

'They're tough,' said Nish. 'Archers, take aim.'

His hundred and fifty archers drew back their bowstrings. The enemy army lifted their spears.

'Advance,' Klarm said softly, yet his amplified voice came clearly to every part of the clearing. 'Cut Cryl-Nish Hlar and Maelys Nifferlin out. Leave no . . .' His voice faltered; he had been a decent man, at heart, and clearly still had trouble with his orders, but Klarm had sworn to the God-Emperor and would follow orders to the letter. 'Leave no one else standing.'

A shaft of sunlight broke through the churning clouds, illuminating the caduceus and the mud-caked militia surrounding it, and the sodden ground steamed. Nish scratched his backside. He hadn't washed since Boobelar's treacherous attack several days ago, and he itched all over.

The Imperial troops took a step, then another. No one spoke; the clearing was silent save for the keening of the caduceus. The hairs on the back of Nish's neck lifted, then fell.

'Nish!' said Gi. 'I've had an idea.' She put her mouth to his ear.

Nish studied the line of the enemy, then nodded. 'Well done! Why didn't I think of that?' He lowered his voice, 'Archers, turn halfway to your right and take aim at the body of the enemy you are then facing. Pass the word around.'

The archers turned and, instead of aiming at the soldier directly opposite, each took a bead on a man forty-five degrees around the oval ring, for the soldiers' small shields did not protect them from arrows slanting in from the side. It was a fundamental weakness of Klarm's encircling position. He should have formed two lines and crushed the militia between them.

'Fire!'

The archers let loose a ragged volley, smoothly reached for their second arrows and nocked them as Nish counted five seconds. 'Fire!' He watched the arrows to their targets, counting under his breath, and a good number of the enemy fell, more than he had expected. But not near enough; not even all those who had been hit. He squinted at the soldiers, wondering if they were protected by sorcery.

'Fire!'

More soldiers fell. The survivors whipped their shields around to cover their left sides, exposing their chests to frontal fire, and charged.

'Face forwards,' roared Nish, 'and now fire at the man directly ahead. Hold fast, lancers. They're taking a lot of casualties and they'll be exhausted when they get here. We can beat them.'

Gi fired, drew another arrow, then gasped.

'What is it? Are you hit?' He hadn't seen the enemy fire, but Klarm might have battle mancers among his troops, attacking with unknown Arts. 'Fire!'

'My arrow went right through its target,' she said in a tight voice, struggling to control her terror, 'and the soldier didn't even check. He just kept on.'

Her teeth were chattering, her eyes darting this way and that, but she forced herself to hold firm and he admired her all the more for it. That first, terrifying experience of battle – even without mancery – could break the strongest soldier.

Klarm must be using the tears to undermine the morale of the superstitious Gendrigoreans. '*Fire!* I think some of the enemy are illusions.'

The enemy were ploughing through the mud. 'W-we're going to die, Nish,' said Gi.

He thought so too, but he had to pretend otherwise. 'Hold firm, Gi – illusions can't fight. We can beat the enemy. We'll come through this yet, you and I.'

The lie sickened him, and especially telling it to sweet, gentle Gi. Why, why had he allowed her to come?

'How can we tell which is which?' said Gi, firing again.

The leaders were less than a hundred paces away when Nish noticed that not all of the soldiers were struggling in the mud; some were moving easily through it with not a trace of muck splattering from their boots. 'Fire!

'Watch their feet – half the soldiers are phantoms, *illusions*,' he roared, 'and they can't touch you. Klarm hasn't got the numbers.' Yet even with half their number, the enemy were a superior fighting force.

The air-sled drifted his way, about twenty spans above the ground. Its metal frame was slightly bent from where it had crashed earlier, and a clump of grass dangled from a kink in one of its runners.

'Should I bring the dwarf down, Nish?' said a red-haired, balding man, one of Nish's best archers.

Nish hesitated, but only for a second; Klarm's death could swing the odds their way, and it was kill or be killed now. 'Have a go.'

The archer swung, aimed and fired in one fluid movement. The arrow streaked towards Klarm's throat, but the dwarf's head whipped around, his hand reached for Reaper, and a moment before the arrow reached the target it burst into splinters.

The caduceus shrilled; Nish's head screamed and, momentarily a red mist obscured his vision. It cleared; in another flash of clearsight he saw the churning core of the caduceus again, then a vibration shot from Reaper towards the red-haired archer, a tube of vapour condensing in its wake, and struck.

The archer's bow shattered first, then his hand; the vibration propagated up his arm, tearing it to pieces in a stinging spray of blood, tissue fragments and shards of bone.

The archer was splattered with the pulverised remains of his arm, as was everyone around him, and blood was pumping from his shoulder. He had not made a sound, but he was so pale that the freckles on his fair skin stood out like moles. His eyes were fixed on Nish as if to say, 'Why did you tell me to shoot?'

Gi let out a moan that made Nish's skin creep, and many others echoed it. The superstitious Gendrigoreans could face death in battle with fortitude, but the uncanny Arts terrified them, and if they panicked the battle was lost.

Then, oddly, Klarm cried out in pain, the air-sled dipped sharply, recovered and shot away.

Tulitine reached the bleached archer as he collapsed and

pressed her fingers against his spurting arteries, but Nish knew the man could not be saved; not up here. The healers Dulya and Ghosh ran out, bearing the stretcher.

Nish turned away; they had their job to do, and he his own, and one second's inattention could prove fatal. 'Hold, hold!' he roared to the nearby rabble. 'We're beating them. Aim! Ready? Fire!'

Fortunately, most of his militia were too far away to have seen what had happened. The archers fired, but Nish did not see many enemy fall. The real soldiers laboured across the boggy soil, churning it to mud.

Nish caught his breath. Ten seconds until they struck. 'Fire!' He rubbed his eyes, for his vision kept going in and out of focus and the headache was worse.

'Fire! Archers, fall back.' They could do no more. Effectively, half his militia was now useless.

The illusory soldiers disappeared; the real ones kept on and struck, driving through the lancers' spears with ruthless efficiency, catching the spearheads on their shields and hacking through the shafts with their swords.

Before his lancers could recover, the enemy were attacking the front line, smashing a lancer's shield aside with one blow, taking him in the belly or throat with the next, then shouldering the sagging body out of the way to attack the next man, and the next.

Even with only half their expected numbers it was terrible, bloody slaughter, as sickening as anything Nish had ever seen in war. In ten more minutes, the Imperial forces would butcher the lot of them, and it could not be borne. Neither could he do anything to stop it.

Three soldiers were converging on Gi and Tulitine, grinning. Nish came out from behind them, sprang forwards and thrust his sabre through the ribcage of the nearest man, who died with an astonished look on his swarthy face.

He had not seen Nish coming. The Imperial troops were well trained but there had been no war in ten years and they were not battle hardened the way Nish had been. He whirled, struck upwards and slew the second man with a slash that took his head off, then turned for the third.

The soldier was out of reach, and Gi was defending furiously with the heavy sword that had been her grandfather's, but even had she been trained in sword fighting she could never match this man. He was toying with her, feasting on her terror, delivering a minor cut to the shoulder, another to the thigh. Nish tried desperately to reach him but the soldier saw him coming and laughed as he thrust his blade into her heart.

Loyal, gentle Gi, who had been Nish's closest ally since he'd arrived in Gendrigore, fell on her back into the mud. Her eyes met his, she looked puzzled, then their light faded and she was dead.

No time to grieve; no time for anything. Nish ran and, with a wild swipe, hacked through the soldier's side. He screamed and fell on top of Gi's body, thrashing. Nish heaved him off and put him out of his agony with one swift thrust. After a last look at her compact, bloody form and her pretty, bewildered face, he shook his head and turned to survey the battlefield, which had descended into the chaos of hundreds of individual melees.

'The cause is lost,' bellowed Flydd from not far away. 'Yggur, if you're going to do anything, do it now! Nish, this way.'

'I'm not going anywhere,' said Nish. He had led his faithful militia here and nothing could induce him to run out on them now.

On the circling air-sled, Klarm was peering around the steamy clearing, searching for him, and Nish felt an urgent need to hide. He slid in behind Tulitine but Klarm touched

27

Reaper and Nish's head felt as though it were bursting – as if the dwarf had used the same spell on him as he had on the red-haired archer.

Every nerve fibre sang and his scarred hand shrieked with pain. The scars took on a bright, silvery glow, like a reflection of the mercuric shimmer of the tears, and even when he slipped the hand inside his shirt, its glow could still be seen. He'd never hide now.

He raised a fallen spear in his shining hand; the caduceus shrilled, his headache faded and his vision cleared suddenly, as if he were seeing the world through a diamond lens – his clearsight had switched on, as it sometimes did when things were desperate.

From the corner of his eye he made out an aura swirling around the caduceus; high above them, the Profane Tears roiled menacingly. And, to his surprise, something pulsed within the blade of the sabre – Vivimord's enchantment?

It was no use to him; he had no idea how to use it. Catching a movement from the corner of his eye, Nish whirled; a giant of a warrior was heading for him. Over his back was strapped a span-long sword, and he carried a weighted net whose cords had a faint aura, no doubt linked to the tears. On seeing Nish's shining scars, the giant raised the net. Once he threw it, it would be impossible to evade.

THREE

Nish had no time to think – clearsight suggested that the giant would toss the net to the left, so he hurled himself to the right and prayed that he was not mistaken. He wasn't; the net missed save for its weighted edge, which settled over his calves, burning like the touch of the tears, and he began to lose feeling from the knees down.

Biting back a gasp, he tried to squirm free, no longer able to feel his feet. He heaved his right leg to one side but the edge of the net felt as though it was searing through his left ankle.

The giant flicked the net into the air to envelop Nish completely and, unable to escape, he transferred the sabre to his glowing left hand and hacked at the soldier's knees.

He missed; the tip caught in the net and he braced himself for another jolt of agony. Instead, his hand brightened, the enchanted sabre sang and sheared through the net as if it were cotton.

From on high, over the fighting, Nish heard Klarm's anguished cry. Had the spell he'd used to light up Nish's scar backfired on him? Could the enchanted sword have something to do with it? Nish didn't understand what he'd done, but he planned to keep doing it. Hacking the net to pieces, he lunged for the giant, who snatched at the sword on his back. Before he could bring it over his head, Nish had opened his belly with the sabre.

The giant clutched at his entrails with both hands, trying to stop them from sliding out, but they spilled through his fingers and he fell. Nish ducked behind him to survey the scene.

. Dozens of his militia lay dead and more were dying by the second. As he stood up, tall, dapper Forzel, who had somehow contrived to look immaculate even in this mud bath, was beheaded, his head landing face-down in the muck. Forzel the joker would laugh no more.

The air-sled, which had been wobbling through the air not far above, recovered and shot upwards. A signal horn rang out.

'What's the dwarf doing?' said Beyl, a short, darkly tanned woodsman who was better than most with staff or sword.

At forty-three, he was one of the oldest of the Gendrigorean militia. His frizzy grey hair, hacked short with a knife, covered his head like a grey carpet and he wore an earring shaped like an ear of corn.

'He's calling down the troops he left guarding the ridges,' said Stibble, a burly blacksmith covered in black hair. He did not carry a sword, but wielded his long-handled hammer with deadly efficiency. 'We're beating him.'

'Nah,' said Gens, a little gnome-like shoemaker whose fingers were stained brown from leather dressing. He wasn't much of a swordsman but he was hard to hit, being so small and nimble, and his knife work was craftsmanlike. 'He's just making sure of us.'

Zana, a stocky cutler with cropped hair and a flat nose, said nothing at all. She carried the biggest sword of anyone in the militia, and used it with a surgeon's precision.

Two soldiers came at Nish, one from the left swinging a cudgel, the man on the right raising a mallet. They had to take him alive but they weren't bothered about breaking bones, and he couldn't fight them both at once – or could he? With clearsight singing along his nerve fibres, maybe he could . . . if he were game to trust it.

Nish ran between them – normally a suicidal move – then turned away from the tall soldier with the mallet and slashed at the more dangerous opponent, the thickset fellow with the cudgel. He swung a horizontal blow at Nish, who ducked: he'd *known* what his opponent was going to do.

Sensing that the man behind him was about to strike, Nish swung the sabre up and over his left shoulder and felt it hit something hard, the soldier's forehead. He fell away and, as the man with the cudgel took a second swipe, Nish leaned backwards and, striking up at an angle, took him down.

'I think I've got something,' cried Yggur over the clamour.

Nish wove back through the fighting, towards the caduceus. Yggur carried a jag-sword but had not drawn it, for none of the enemy had dared go that close to him. He was not only a tall, powerful man and a fine swordsman, but also a mancer of mystery who had lived for more than a thousand years. No one knew where he came from, and few people understood his Art, which had stayed with him even when the destruction of the nodes had robbed most other mancers of their Art.

He stood with his back to the caduceus, long legs spread, arms held in a vase shape above his head, chanting.

'What is it?' Nish panted. More soldiers were converging on him, and even with the benefit of clearsight he could not hold them all off.

'I don't know . . .' Yggur turned towards Nish but did not appear to see him. 'I'll have to try it.'

'Make it snappy!' bellowed Flydd.

Yggur strained until the hairs on his upraised arms began to smoke and a tenuous mist formed around him. People cried out; Nish recognised Klarm's voice among them. He felt waves of heat and the caduceus brightened until it resembled a rod of molten lava welded to the earth, so bright that it burned.

The pouring rain turned to steam clouds which were whipped into a spiral around the caduceus, spinning ever faster until they formed a miniature tornado that was plucking grass and mud up with it. The grass flash-flamed to char and was whirled up the funnel of the ever-growing tornado, out of sight. The clash of sword on sword stopped as friend and foe stood side by side, staring.

Yggur sagged, his eyes wide and fearful, and he was not a man given to exposing his emotions. 'It feels as though the caduceus is feeding on me,' he rasped. 'Drawing the very essence out of me.'

'Get on with it,' said Flydd, pushing through, jag-sword in hand. Shreds of bloody uniform were caught between the jags, and what looked like a man's thumb. 'We need that mist.'

He glanced towards the air-sled, which was drifting sideways across the battlefield. Klarm clung to the pole flying the God-Emperor's standard as if he could barely stand up.

'The runt isn't looking so bold now,' sneered Flydd. Again his yearning eyes lingered upon the tears.

'The caduceus hurt him through Gatherer, but he'll soon recover,' said Yggur.

'Try again.'

Yggur put up his arms, gave Nish another of those blank stares, then set his jaw and forced hard. Nish's scarred hand burned anew, but its silvery glow faded a little. As he took the sabre in his left hand, which sometimes helped to ease the pain, a mist sprang up, thickened and whirled in towards the caduceus.

There came a sound like thunder, save that the echoing boom was at the beginning and the whip crack at the end; spectral figures wisped into being above the caduceus, but vanished again; allies and enemies cried out, all at once. The air-sled wobbled and this time almost fell out of the sky.

'Yggur has no idea what he's doing, has he?' said Nish to Flydd.

'Not a clue,' said Flydd. 'Yet if he can gain us a breathing space –'

The sky turned yellow, darkened to the purple of a bruise and slowly went black. Had it not been for the uncanny red radiance coming from the caduceus, Nish would not have been able to see at all. The whirling wind was chilly now and blowing right through his sodden clothing, but it suddenly died and the moisture in the saturated air condensed into fog so thick that he could not see his silver-scarred hand on the hilt of the sabre.

The clash of weapons stopped again, for no one could see to fight. The groans of the wounded rose in pitch. A woman was crying, 'Don't leave me,' over and over; a man sobbed, 'Please, please, put me out of my misery.'

As Nish groped through the dark, he could not help remembering other battlefields littered with the dead, and the maimed comrades who, too badly injured to walk, had been left to die because nothing could be done for them. One war ended and another began. Would there ever be peace? And what was the point of fighting when there was no hope of victory?

His sodden shirt flapped as the whirlwind picked up

again, and momentarily the bright caduceus pierced the fog like a lighthouse beacon – but was it offering shelter, or luring them to destruction?

The fog had thinned fractionally; he could just make out his feet now. Time to retreat. 'Chief Signaller?' he yelled. 'Midge?'

She did not reply, and he was cursing her for not staying close, as he'd ordered, when he trod on her shoulder. Midge lay face up in the mud with a broken spear through her chest. She was not yet eighteen.

Shaking his head at the waste, Nish heaved the signal horn out from under her, shook the bloodstained mud from it and blew three ringing blasts followed by two short ones – the signal to retreat to the lowest point of the clearing.

Was there really any chance? Wherever he led them, the enemy would follow once the fog cleared. And yet, while they lived, while they were free, a tiny hope remained, and Nish had fanned the embers of such meagre hopes into flame before today.

Another clap of inverted thunder echoed forth and he heard the air-sled whistling across the sky.

'Come down, you treacherous little flea!' Yggur roared.

The air-sled made a grinding sound; Nish heard a monstrous *splat*, the sound of mud spattering in all directions and steam belching up. The dwarf cried out, 'The tears, the tears!'

He must have dropped them during the crash but there was no chance of seizing them – Nish would never find them in the fog. Besides, even without them, Klarm was a powerful mancer who still had his knoblaggie.

After blowing the signal again, Nish moved down the slope. Distantly, other horns repeated the message. The fog was slowly thinning – he could see two paces now – and he made out several of his militia moving in the same direction.

'Get a move on,' he said, afraid that the fog would clear suddenly and the enemy would resume the attack.

One of Klarm's soldiers appeared in front of Nish, staring the other way. He stabbed him in the back and pushed him aside. It was kill or be killed now.

He had not gone far when lightning flashed from the direction of the caduceus, turning the fog orange. Flydd bellowed in pain, his cry oddly muffled, and then the rain Klarm had held back could be restrained no longer. Tulitine the seer had seen truly.

The skies opened in a deluge like nothing Nish had ever felt before – not in Gendrigore, the wettest place he had ever lived, nor on the Range of Ruin, which was even wetter. This was solid rain, so heavy that his knees bent under the weight of it, rain that hissed and steamed away from the red-hot caduceus and flowed ankle-deep down the slope, tugging at his feet.

Even if the fog cleared, no one could fight in such weather. The enemy would put their shields over their heads, hunker down and wait it out. They knew that the militia was on its knees and, even if they ran through the fog, where could they run to?

'Come on,' he shouted to Tulitine, who had appeared to his left. He had to shout or she would not have heard him. 'A downpour like this can't last long.'

The fog thinned a little more and Nish saw Hoshi. 'Where is she, Nish?' he said anxiously.

He must be looking for Gi, who had been more than a friend to him, and Nish could not bear to tell Hoshi that she was dead. He did not want to think about her, for the look in Gi's soft eyes as she'd died had reminded him of other friends, other deaths, and one especially – the best friend he'd ever had.

'This kind of rain can last for ages, up here,' said Tulitine.

Nish was thinking fast. 'If it keeps up, it'll flood the valley floor –'

'The low-lying parts, certainly.' Her eyes were on him. 'And that won't take long.'

'What if we head for the lower clearing?'

She understood at once. 'It would flood first, since it's right by the river. Come on.'

Nish took the bow and quiver from a fallen archer and slung them over his shoulder. He must have died early on, for his quiver was nearly full. Nish had used both javelard and crossbow during the war, and had been a good shot with both. He was not an expert with the longbow but at close range he did not have to be.

The glimmerings of a plan were forming. 'We can't climb the ridge in this, but we might scramble through the gorge over the boulders on the right-hand side.'

'We'd better be quick. These mountain rivers rise fast.'

'And the gorge will soon be impassable . . . Tulitine, if we can get through quickly, the rising river might stop them from following. They'd have to climb out over the ridge, and by that time we could be anywhere.'

He tipped water out of the horn and sounded the signal again then, with a last glance around the battlefield, headed down.

'Where's Gi?' cried Hoshi, grabbing his arm.

He had to be told. 'I'm sorry. She died in the first assault.' It was impossible to put it gently when Nish had to shout to be heard.

'Where did she fall?' Hoshi shook him. 'She might still be alive.'

Not with a sword through the heart. Nish pointed up the slope, mutely, and Hoshi splashed through the mud, crying out her name.

Nish turned away, never hating war more than he did at

36

that moment. He felt sick at the thought of leaving her body behind, to say nothing of the many wounded, but he could not do anything for anyone who could not walk unaided. He had to save those who were still on their feet and had little time to do it.

He skidded down the slope, sounding the signal over and over, and in a couple of minutes reached the eaves of the rainforest, where the fog was thinner, with the last of the survivors. They numbered two hundred at a rough count, which meant that a hundred and sixty had fallen.

He could not bear to think about the bloody, useless slaughter, the waste of young, precious lives, nor about those lying wounded on the battlefield who might, in other circumstances, have been saved. Nothing could save them now and even the walking wounded had little chance in this climate, where a scratch could turn septic in half a day. He had to become iron-hard and think about nothing except saving the able-bodied.

It was almost as noisy in the forest, with the rain hissing and rattling on the leaves high above, and just as wet. The ground squelched underfoot and the rain fell in cascades.

Everyone gathered around in a ragged, gasping circle. He saw Maelys on the far side, blessedly unharmed, along with Tulitine, supporting a tall, muscular man between them, though it took a few moments before Nish recognised him as Yggur. What had happened to him? Nish could not see any obvious wounds but Yggur seemed barely able to walk. And, being the only mancer still able to use his Art, he was the key to their survival.

'Clech,' Nish said to the huge fisherman, who was propping up a tree, panting, 'can you bring Yggur? You're the only one strong enough.' Though not even Clech could carry him for any great distance.

Clech heaved Yggur over his shoulder like a net full of fish and grunted, 'Which way?'

'Down through the forest, across the lower clearing and through the gorge – if it's still open.'

Flydd stumbled out of the fog, bent double and holding his belly.

'Xervish?' said Nish. 'Are you –?'

Flydd straightened up painfully. 'When the lightning flashed from the caduceus, it felt as though I was being torn in two.' He peered into the foggy clearing. 'What's the plan?'

Nish explained. Flydd frowned. 'Any hope is better than none, I suppose.'

'I reckon they lost two hundred up there,' said Nish, 'mainly to our arrows. And if half their troops were illusions, that means Klarm only had five hundred, not the thousand we thought –'

'It still leaves them with three hundred crack fighters to our two hundred novices. If they get among us, they'll massacre us.'

'They're coming,' someone yelled.

The downpour had not abated but the fog was clearing to ground-hugging patches of mist, between which Nish made out a dark mass moving down the clearing. 'This way.'

He pushed further into the forest. The tangle of vines and creepers made it impossible to run except to his left, where deer had opened a winding trail wide enough for two people to move abreast.

Behind him, bowstrings twanged as his archers fired. He felt a trickle of hope – for the moment, he had the advantage. His troops could fire on the enemy from cover, while they could not fire back for fear of hitting him or Maelys. It would help to even the odds, and gain vital seconds. He began to jog on the slippery path.

Maelys slipped in beside him, wearing a huge knife in a

scabbard on her right hip. He was pleased to see that she was armed, though she could be killed as easily as Gi had been, and he could not bear to think about that possibility.

'I've never seen such rain,' she panted, her breasts bouncing as she ran. 'I didn't think the sky could hold so much water.'

'The Range of Ruin is the wettest place on Santhenar – and the *really wet* season is yet to come.'

Could this be the beginning of it? If it was, every gully would become impassable and they would be trapped here until it ended five months later – or, rather, until they starved to death.

She picked a leech off her forearm and flicked it aside, the puncture ebbing a thin trail of blood. 'I reckon this rain has something to do with Yggur's spell – and the caduceus. What if they're feeding on each other?'

'Mmm.' He did not have time to think about that, though he felt sure the same interaction had temporarily heightened his dormant clearsight.

'How far is it to the gorge?'

'Half a league, I'd guess.'

As they hurried along, they brought each other up to date – what Nish had been doing since Vivimord had carried him to Gendrigore through the portal nearly six weeks ago, and where Maelys had been with Flydd and Colm. She told him about her visits to the Nightland; her encounter with Emberr and his tragic death, for which she felt responsible, though she did not say why, and her relentless pursuit by the Numinator and Yalkara.

Nish said little, for there was little he could say, but when he put an arm across her shoulders he sensed that it was a comfort to her.

She stopped for a moment, looking up at him as if she wanted to tell him something important. 'Nish?'

'Yes?'

Maelys gnawed her lip, flushed, then looked away. 'It doesn't matter.'

They ran on. 'So did you find it?' he said. 'I expect you didn't, or someone would have told me.'

'Find what?' said Maelys absently.

'The antithesis to the tears. That's what you went to the Tower of a Thousand Steps for.'

'I asked the Numinator but she didn't know anything about it.'

The path curved to the left, he heard the river roaring not far away and they broke out of forest onto a long, narrow and sloping strip of grassy riverbank. The torrent, to his left, gnashed at the bank, which had partly collapsed up ahead, leaving just a crumbling rim of earth five paces long but less than a pace wide. The narrow strip of undermined bank, along the vine-tangled wall of the forest, was only held together by tree roots.

Maelys stopped, for the grassy river bank to either side of the collapse was saturated and nearly as dangerous. 'Put one foot wrong and we'll end up in the river. We've got to find another track.'

'There isn't time,' he said roughly. 'Go across and scout out the lower clearing. If the enemy find a faster path through the forest, we're finished.'

'What about you?'

'I'm going to set up an ambush. Run! See if the gorge is still open.'

She edged along the riverbank, hanging onto the looping vines. Nish closed his eyes, afraid for her, then turned back to warn the leaders, who were close behind.

'After everyone crosses,' he said, 'I want ten of our best archers to take cover on the far side and ambush the enemy as they try to cross. But if they're getting across under fire, the archers must retreat. I'm not losing another man if I can help it.'

The word was passed back and Nish hauled himself along the quaking riverbank. Maelys was out of sight. His worn boots could not grip the wet grass and without the vines he would have slid straight into the river.

Several dozen lancers crossed, a group armed with swords, then more lancers. The best part of a hundred of the militia had made it without loss, but there was no sign of the archers yet. Most would be at the rear, since they had been firing on the enemy who, judging by the approaching clamour, were close behind. A band of his swordsmen came pounding down the track and onto the grassy riverbank, but stopped at the edge of the collapsed section.

'Come on!'

They came on, looking back fearfully, for they were exhausted, panicky and many were weaponless.

'Where are the archers?' said Nish, starting to sweat.

'They're coming,' gasped a red-faced, yellow-bearded fellow whose name Nish could not remember. Yes, he was Avigg, a carpenter.

'All of them, Avigg?'

'Except the last dozen. They got cut off. Enemy came through the forest.'

And the rest must be low on arrows. Nish began to worry that he'd have to do the job for them. He had to gain a few minutes or the enemy would run them down before they reached the gorge.

He fitted an arrow to his bowstring, but did not draw it back. 'Go on,' he said to Flydd and Tulitine, who came next. 'Follow the path. I sent Maelys to the lower clearing to see if the gorge is still open.'

'What if it isn't?' said Flydd, who looked worse than before.

Nish waved him on without answering, scanning the forest for a place where he could shoot from cover. Half a dozen lancers crossed, then Clech appeared, red in the face and staggering under Yggur's weight.

'He'll have to cross by himself,' said Nish. 'I don't think the bank will take the weight.'

'He can't,' said Clech, 'and if I put him down I'll never lift him again.'

Which would mean that Yggur was lost. 'All right, but go carefully.'

Clech peered over the edge at the thundering waters. 'Don't worry! I'm not washing my filthy feet in there. You'd better not stay here long, Nish. The bank can't last.'

Nish did not need to be told. The rising water was flowing so furiously that it was carrying small boulders with it, and if anyone fell in, they had no hope of survival. But there was no hope if the enemy caught them, either.

With a *whoomph*, a curving section of bank collapsed a third of the way across and was swallowed by the water, leaving an even more precarious passage across a suspended network of tree roots.

'Climb through the forest,' said Nish. 'You'll never get across there.'

'I'm a fisherman. I'm used to slippery decks.'

Clech clambered across the roots, holding Yggur over his shoulder with his left arm and hanging onto the vines with his right. Nish couldn't bear to watch, but when he looked again Clech was over and onto the grass.

Not everyone was so lucky. Three of his precious archers, clinging onto the same vine, were lost when the first one slipped and his weight pulled the vine down over the edge. It did not break, but none of the men had the strength to haul themselves up the wet vine and, one by one, they fell into the river and were pulled under.

Another group of archers appeared. 'Go across and find an ambush site,' Nish said. 'Fire on the enemy as soon as they appear. We've got to gain some time.'

The leading archer held out his empty hands. 'Sorry, Nish. All our arrows are gone. The next group might have a few left.'

Nish cursed. 'Run to the lower clearing. I'll wait for them.'

They had no arrows either, and nor did the band after that. They'd emptied their quivers firing at the enemy from the forest.

Nish cursed them black and blue. 'What kind of fools use up their last arrows with the enemy close behind?'

'We saved some arrows for last,' said Lym, a short, stocky woman who had to shoot with her bow held horizontally, since it was longer than she was tall. 'And then, *last* came, and we had to use them. Sorry,' she said anxiously.

He waved her across, knowing she was right, and followed. Even if his archers had carried a hundred arrows each, that number would only last ten minutes in battle. Readying his bow, he withdrew into cover on the downstream side, and waited.

The rest of his stragglers managed to cross the quaking root-path, save for the final group of six, four archers and two lancers, who burst out of the forest just ahead of the enemy. They might have made it along the dangerous strip of riverbank had they gone at once, but they baulked momentarily, and the enemy rushed them, forcing them over the bank at spear-point into the torrent, where they were driven with bone-smashing force against rolling boulders.

Once, Nish had almost been inured to the horrors of war, but this casual slaughter of men and women so dear to him stiffened his resolve to tear down the world his father had

43

created, and replace it with a better one. I will do whatever it takes, he thought. I will *never* give in.

But first he had to win the war; no, first he had to survive this battle. Nocking his arrow, he fired and took the leading soldier in the throat.

Three more fell before the rest of the Imperial lancers scrambled back into the forest, but Nish's plan was in tatters, for he could not ambush hundreds of men by himself. He moved further into the forest gloom. He had to try and hold them off, yet if he stayed here long they would hack paths through the jungle to attack him from all sides. But if he could delay them for another minute or two, the militia might just reach the gorge first.

He didn't see the little wisp-watcher globe drifting though the canopy high above, nor the one that came after, but their spoked irises contracted at the sight of him. One stayed on watch; the other drifted back the way they had come.

A soldier appeared at the far end of the grassy bank. Nish shot him and ducked backwards under a liana as thick as a giant python. As he did, three arrows struck the vine in a tight group at chest height, where he had been standing, and others sang through the vines to either side. They had been waiting for him to fire. Clearly, they did not expect Nish to be here in person, but their arrows could kill him just the same.

He slid around the next tree and sighted through the gap between its twin trunks, but no one else appeared. Were they cutting a path to bypass him? With the roar of the river in his ears he'd never hear them, and he could not afford to wait much longer.

A minute passed. What were they up to? I'll give them another thirty seconds, he thought, and if they don't come out I'll go.

The thirty seconds were nearly up, with no further sign of the enemy, when something round and hard dug into his lower back and a deep, familiar voice rumbled, 'Drop the bow, Nish, and raise your hands.'

How had Klarm got so close, without a sound? There would be no getting away from him.

Four

Maelys had seen battle before, from a distance, and it had been a haunting experience, especially the hours she had served in the healers' tent with Tulitine, trying to repair the maimed and broken bodies. And afterwards, escaping past those huge piles of corpses – thousands of fresh young lives turned to the reeking dead – had been even more scarifying. If she closed her eyes she could still see them. And they had all died for nothing!

But this had been far worse, for she had been right in the middle of the fighting, and no matter which way she'd turned there had been violent, bloody death in front of her. Spears had fallen all around her, one flying past her stomach so close that it had torn her clothes; another time, an enemy's wild backswing had nearly taken the top of her head off, though the soldier hadn't known she was there.

Whatever Yalkara had done to the taphloid the other day, it seemed to be protecting Maelys from deliberate attack. The soldiers could certainly see her, but then their eyes would slide away as if diverted, and they would turn aside.

She shuddered at the memories and ran faster, splashing along the forest path away from Nish, but still worrying about him. She had wanted to tell him about lying with Emberr, and that she might be pregnant, but had felt too embarrassed.

Could she be expecting? It would change everything if she was, but there was no way of telling, since it had only happened a few days ago. She wouldn't know for weeks – assuming she survived that long.

Maelys dismissed the distracting thoughts and kept running until she reached the lower clearing, then peered out. It formed a ragged circle extending for several hundred paces along the river to the point where it ran into the gorge, though the rain was so heavy, and the air near the river so full of whirling spray, that she could barely see the gorge.

The clearing rose steeply to her right, like a tilted saucer, up to the right-hand ridge of the valley, and she began to trek across the slope. The valley was narrower here and she had been told that the encircling ridges were connected via a natural arch of stone spanning the centre of the gorge, though she could not make it out. To her left the saucer's rim formed a gentle lip up onto the river bank, and a curving pond had formed there. Further on a narrow gully ran into the river.

She plodded across the slope of the clearing, below a long, curving rock outcrop over which runoff poured in little cascades, towards the entrance of the gorge. It was hard to see through the spray from the roaring river, though on the right side a jumble of boulders the size of elephants *might* be negotiable.

Maelys gulped. She had never been adventurous – her idea of a perfect day was sitting by the fire reading a book – and the passage through the gorge looked extremely dangerous. The river's torrential flow was grinding boulders together in its bed and flinging spray up a good three spans, while waterfalls cascading over the sides of the gorge would deluge anyone trying to pass through.

It might be possible to leap from one huge boulder to the next, though they appeared to be covered in moss and would be horribly slippery. We'll lose a lot of people getting through, she thought, and I'll probably be one of them. The Gendrigoreans were outdoor folk, used to climbing and naturally dexterous, but Maelys was not. Her knees went wobbly at the thought.

Not to mention that, at the rate the river was rising, the lowest point of the passage could be closed off by the time the militia arrived. She looked back, and through waves of driving rain made out the first of them entering the clearing. She splashed back.

'There's the gorge,' she said to the huge militiaman carrying Yggur, whose eyes were closed; his arms and legs flopped with every movement. 'It's going to be difficult to get through, though, with the water rising so fast . . .'

'And the longer we wait the more difficult it will be,' the militiaman rumbled. His voice was even deeper than dear Zham's, who had given his life at the top of Mistmurk Mountain so Maelys, Nish, Flydd and Colm could escape. 'My name's Clech.'

'Maelys,' she said, shaking a paw the size of a pumpkin leaf, but his grip was gentle around her little hand.

He set Yggur down in the mud and looked at her inquiringly, as if awaiting her orders, which was absurd.

'Are the rest of the militia close?' she said.

'I don't know. Do you want us to go through the gorge?'

She was not used to giving orders and had no idea what Nish would do. Was it better to send most of the militia

48

through even if the stragglers were cut off, or should they wait until everyone was here? Either way, her instructions, made in ignorance, would be condemning some people to death.

'I suppose so,' Maelys said, then felt a powerful instinct that it was the wrong decision. 'No, wait until everyone gets here. I'm sure Nish would want us to keep together.'

Gnawing a knuckle, she scanned the ridgeline and the edges of the clearing, knowing the enemy could appear anywhere and attack without warning. Maelys had never been a leader, nor had she any desire to be one, and she had no knowledge of battlefield tactics.

He broke into her panicked thoughts. 'You and Nish are old friends.'

'Er, yes.' She did not want to go into their differences since she'd helped to rescue him from his father's prison, months ago. 'We travelled together for a long time.'

'He was very pleased to see you, when you came through the portal.'

Was he? Nish had treated her badly in their early days together, partly because Maelys, to her shame, had tried to use him to fulfil an obligation to her family. However he had softened after his father caught them at the top of Mistmurk Mountain, and Nish had certainly changed during the time they had been separated.

Our experiences, and especially our choices, make us what we are, she thought, and I'm not the naïve girl I was when I met him, either.

More of the militia straggled in, men and a small number of women. Some were weaponless while the rest carried broken lances or notched swords. Most of the archers were out of arrows, and Maelys shook her head in dismay. Even if Nish had been the greatest leader in the world, he could do little with such a rabble.

Tulitine appeared, hobbling and supporting a staggering, feverish Flydd, but neither of them could relieve Maelys of the burden of command.

'What's the matter with Xervish?' she said.

'When the caduceus blazed up, it also hurt him badly, but he's getting better.'

Flydd didn't look it. 'Are there many more to come?' asked Maelys, scanning the circle of faces. People were hard to identify, being covered in mud, but she did not see Nish anywhere.

'A dozen at most,' said Tulitine hoarsely, rubbing her arm as if in great pain.

'Where's Nish?'

'He stayed behind to ambush the enemy.'

'All alone?' Maelys cried.

'I don't know.'

'What are we supposed to do now?'

'I don't know,' Tulitine repeated. 'I can't think.'

The militia were standing around, staring at Maelys. 'What do you want us to do?' said Clech.

She couldn't send them through the gorge without Nish. 'Go up there and get ready to defend yourselves.'

She indicated the waist-high outcrop of brown stone she'd passed earlier, near the top of the clearing. It curved across the slope for some thirty paces, and the two-hundred-odd militia might just cram in behind it, though it would be cramped to defend.

It was the only cover available, though if they had to run from there to the gorge they would be exposed all the way. Still, if the gorge became impassable, as was looking increasingly likely, they could retreat up into the narrow band of forest below the rocky ridge.

Maelys rubbed her forehead, trying to think like a commander. From there they might scramble over the ridge, which was no longer guarded, but then what? Klarm would hunt them down; he would never give up.

'I'll go along the track a bit and wait for Nish,' said Maelys. 'I'm sure he'll be along any second.' She had to keep up the pretence, for her own sake as much as theirs.

Clech was heading for Yggur when he sat up and said in a shaky voice, 'I'm all right now. I can walk.'

Clech nodded and led the militia up the slope. Tulitine said quietly, 'You can't go unprotected.'

'I'm not going far,' said Maelys.

'Wait!' Tulitine put her hands over her eyes, stiffened and her head lolled forwards. 'The pieces are moving into alignment,' she said in her lower, whispery seer's voice. 'The next few days will determine not just the fate of this obscure militia, but all Santhenar, and the choices of these two matter most.'

Flydd's head shot up; Yggur forced himself to his feet, swaying. '*These* two?' said Yggur. 'Nish and Maelys?'

'That's how I read the future.'

'Then she must stay with us, where she can be protected,' said Flydd.

'You're not listening,' said Tulitine. 'Our time is nearly done; Maelys must make her own decisions.'

'But I haven't the faintest idea what to do,' said Maelys. She was fed up with being the focus of obscure foretellings and could not bear the responsibility laid on her. 'I can't do it.'

'Your choices are still vital,' said Tulitine, 'whether you accept the responsibility or reject it. Come here; we may be able to improve your defences a little.'

'What do you mean?'

'Show us the taphloid,' said Flydd. 'Yggur, we might need a hand.'

Yggur lurched across. 'What is it? You'll be lucky to get anything more out of me today.'

'We need to heighten the shield in Maelys's taphloid. Can you – ?'

'Her what?'

Yggur had never seen the taphloid, for the only time Maelys had used it in his presence, at the Tower of a Thousand Steps, she'd kept it hidden. She held it out.

Yggur glanced at it without interest. 'What is it?'

'A device my father, Rudigo, gave me when I was little,' said Maelys.

'I've a vague memory of having seen one before, though I can't say where. So many years, and so many devices – they all blur into one another.'

'Father told me to wear it always. It's designed to hide the aura created by my gift, though it's been behaving oddly ever since we ended up here.'

'What gift?' Yggur said sharply. 'I didn't know you had a gift for the Art.'

'I don't know what mine is, though some people in my family could locate the God-Emperor's wisp-watchers, or hide from them. My little sister, Fyllis, has the strongest gift. She fooled all the watchers in Mazurhize, and Gatherer too, and got Nish out of prison all by herself,' Maelys said proudly, 'though she was only eight.'

'Remarkable,' said Yggur.

He did not seem overly impressed, but then, he must have known thousands of people more gifted than her, including the greatest mancers of all. 'But I've never had any training,' said Maelys, 'and apparently I'm too old to start now.'

'Very possibly.' He held out his hand.

She lifted the taphloid over her head, more reluctant than usual to take it off. 'Be careful. It's set to protect me, and it's hurt everyone who's touched it – at least, everyone with a gift for the Art.'

'I'm not *everyone*,' he said curtly, closing his big fingers around the egg-shaped, yellow-metal taphloid. It had no apparent effect on him, and he closed his eyes as if thinking.

'Yggur?' said Tulitine shortly.

He shook himself and handed it back to Maelys, shaking his head in puzzlement. 'It felt as though it belonged in my hand, like an everyday object from long ago suddenly found again, though how can that be? I don't remember ever having one. Put it on, Maelys. It doesn't just hide your aura; it also makes you harder to see, a considerable advantage on the battlefield.'

'That must be Yalkara's doing,' said Maelys. 'To protect the child she thinks I'm carrying.'

'Hmm,' said Yggur. 'Well, I've done all I could to increase the protection, though I don't think I made much difference.'

The taphloid seemed heavier, and warmer, and every so often it gave a little shudder, as though something inside it was wobbling like an off-centre spinning top. It had been doing that a lot since she'd come through the portal from the Tower of a Thousand Steps, and Maelys was afraid it was breaking down.

She set off without looking back, for five precious minutes had been lost and, though another fourteen stragglers had arrived, Nish had not. They were the last, they said, and they had seen no sign of him.

Maelys crept along the track with the rain pouring down as heavily as ever, increasingly afraid that Nish had been captured, or . . . or *killed*. She could not bear to think about that, for he had been a part of her life for too long.

As a little girl she had hero-worshipped him from the time she first heard, then read and re-read, the tales of his mighty exploits during the war. She no longer had any romantic feelings for Nish, thankfully, but she would always care about him.

She dragged her thoughts back to the present. If she went on, she was bound to run into the Imperial army and be captured; the taphloid would not hide her from their direct sight, but returning to the militia also felt wrong. No, she must keep going – if anyone could find Nish, she could.

Nifferlin Manor had been torn down by the God-Emperor's troops when Maelys was still a child, but the family had remained in the ruins, for they had nowhere else to go. The estate had been searched a number of times and she had quickly learned how to find the best hiding places, and how to move silently through forest and across moor. The scriers had never found her.

She slipped into the rainforest, weaving between the huge, buttressed trunks festooned with vines of all sizes, some thin as string, others as large around as her waist. There was no danger of a stick snapping underfoot to give her away, for the ground was like a sponge made of rotten wood and dark brown humus like peat, and all was covered in ankle-high moss, downy ferns and huge, extraordinary fungi. Many of them were a luminous green or blue in the dim light, with suggestive or vulgar shapes and unpleasant odours.

She hadn't gone far when she heard soldiers running down the track. Maelys slid behind a phallic fungus taller than she was and peered around its oozing side. The troop splashed past, only a few paces away, led by a burly, toad-faced sergeant.

Another squad followed close behind, and finally a smaller figure clad in sodden brown robes and dripping hood, moving with a sliding, slithery stride. A battle mancer? Maelys froze.

Even worse; far worse. The unblinking iris of a little wisp-watcher was mounted on the man's head, a shimmering loop-listener clamped to his left shoulder, and as he drew near she caught a whiff of burnt bones – scrier! She feared scriers more than any of the God-Emperor's other servants, for they had hunted her family many times, and twice they had almost caught them.

He stopped, raised his flared nostrils and began to sniff the air. His head rotated left and right like an oiled piece of machinery; now he was staring at the stalk of the fungus. Could he make her out in the gloom? The huge wisp-watchers could see in the dimmest light but a little one might not be so keen-sighted. She dared not move, not even to clutch her taphloid.

Though the rain was almost deafening, Maelys scarcely dared to breathe in case the loop-listener could detect it. A scrier's spying devices could be linked to Gatherer, and if he did hear her, Klarm would soon be told about it.

The scrier reached up with a long-nailed hand and caressed the loop-listener, which rotated back and forth before pointing at her hiding place. Behind the stalk of the toadstool, Maelys slid her hand down to the big knife on her hip, not that it would be any use against a scrier. He would call in the troops, then torment her while they held her down.

Don't see me, she thought, as if that could make a difference. *I'm far away and, the longer you waste here, the less chance you have of finding me.*

The taphloid warmed slightly. The scrier turned away, looked back, then shook his head and moved on. More troops ran by, and more. Once they'd gone, Maelys shivered and crept away, now really anxious about the time.

The best place for Nish to ambush the enemy was the dense forest at the nearer end of the partly collapsed path next to the river. She struggled through the dripping jungle beside the track, fretting about how much time she was taking, but if she went further into the forest she was likely to get lost.

Another squad of troops ran by. The enemy would soon be in a position to attack, and they would quickly overwhelm the militia sheltering behind the outcrop. She had to go faster.

Maelys only just stifled a cry as another scrier came slithering around the bend, just paces away on the track, and for a second he was looking right at her. She tried to blend into the forest, hoping the mud all over her would help.

The scrier stopped abruptly and squinted between the trees, nose up. She stared at him, restraining the overwhelming urge to bolt. He moved the iris of his wisp-watcher back and forth, but it was pointing slightly away from her. She took hold of the taphloid and, after a few seconds, he too headed on.

She was approaching the collapsed section of path now – Maelys could just make out the dangling roots through the trees. There seemed to be far more exposed than before, and the river was a lot higher, which explained why the enemy had been so far behind; presumably they'd had to hack their way through the tangled vines.

The ground shook then heaved under her feet, and not far ahead a gigantic tree began to topple as its roots were undermined. A thick root tore up through the ground, pulled as taut as a hawser, then snapped, flinging mud in all directions. A clot smacked stingingly into her right cheek.

Scrambling backwards, she caught hold of a vine as other roots tore out of the ground, the tree tilted and, with majestic slowness and a deafening roar, crashed into the river, sending waves in all directions. As the tree was dragged downstream by the current, the roots tore out and the ground where it had stood liquefied before Maelys's eyes. The slurry poured into the river, leaving a hole the width of a cottage.

Now a series of concentric cracks formed in the soil,

centred where the tree had been, then began to widen and the ground between them to sink. The earth moved under Maelys's feet; it was cracking out here as well. She ran the other way and caught hold of a solid vine as the river flooded into the hole and began to eat the soil away.

Scrabbling across to the most likely ambush point, she noted arrows embedded in a branch. Nish had been fired upon, but had they got him? Maelys saw no blood, though the downpour would surely have washed any away. If he'd escaped, he should be in the lower clearing by now and, with the enemy about to attack, could not afford to wait for her.

Afraid she was going to be left behind, Maelys was heading for the track when she trod on something that did not give under her weight – the hilt of Vivimord's black sabre. Nish would not have left it behind, therefore he must have been taken. Which way? The spongy ground held no tracks, but a company of soldiers would have trampled the exotic fungi and mound-mosses underfoot and she saw no sign of that. Who, then?

Closing her eyes, she took the taphloid in her right hand and turned around. It was unlikely to be a scrier; they located their victims, then waited for the soldiers to take them. That only left Klarm – and he had the tears.

FIVE

Klarm was as bruised, battered and filthy as Nish, and a trail of blood ran from his swollen nose down his chin, but he looked as though he'd just been given an unexpected birthday present.

Nish cursed himself for not keeping a better lookout, for there was nothing he could do to save himself. Klarm will take me back to Mazurhize, he thought, and put me in that stinking cell again, and I won't be able to take it. I'll go insane.

'It had to end, Nish,' Klarm said. 'It's for the best.'

Nish tensed, but Klarm pressed the knoblaggie harder into the small of his back. 'Don't try it; I can make every nerve in your body scream.'

'I never thought of you as a sadist,' Nish said, 'but I don't suppose there's any limit to what you'll do to suck up to your master.'

'I don't enjoy inflicting pain,' said Klarm, unprovoked, 'but I'm not giving away any chances either. If you force me, I'll subdue you in the quickest way possible.'

Nish turned around, slowly. Klarm's right hand had a muddy bandage wrapped around it and was seeping a thin yellow fluid, as Nish's hand had when he'd been burned by the tears. He recalled the dwarf's earlier cries, after he had used Reaper. Clearly he had not mastered it, since it had hurt him so badly.

'How did you get here so quietly? The tears, I suppose. The stinking tears.' Though Klarm was not wearing them.

'Know your enemy,' said Klarm. 'I didn't need to use them; I swung through the trees.'

'I forgot you were like an acrobat, once.'

'I *was* an acrobat, and I've kept up my skills. It's one field where dwarves are superior – we have most of the strength but only half the weight. No one else could have got to you in time.'

'What are you going to do now?'

'Follow my orders. I'm taking you back, *and* Maelys once I find her, and dispatching everyone else.'

'How you use words,' said Nish, sickened by what Klarm had become. 'You're not *dispatching* my militia, you're slaughtering good, decent people for defending their own country.'

'I'm following my orders,' said Klarm, but he looked a trifle uncomfortable.

'That excuse has served cowardly, murdering scum like you for thousands of years. Are you also *dispatching* the friends you fought beside during the war?'

'The war ended ten years ago,' said Klarm. 'Flydd and Yggur are rebels against the God-Emperor and, as I've sworn to serve him, my former friends are now my enemies.'

'My father's rule is illegitimate,' snapped Nish. 'He took power by force.'

Klarm sighed. 'Power grants its own legitimacy, as you very well know. Jal-Nish has remained God-Emperor because he has the strength to hold his empire. He's defeated every rebellion, of which there were many in the early days.'

'And you admire the way he's done that, do you?'

'I don't admire everything he's done, but I swore an oath and I cannot, will not, break it.'

'Why does everyone have to die?' said Nish.

'Because the God-Emperor ordered it, and he's the only one in a position to see how desperate our situation is.'

'You've got the tears. You can make your own decisions – unless you're afraid to!'

'No!' cried Klarm, and Nish wondered if he *was* afraid of them. 'The tears have to be studied, practised, mastered. No mancer can simply pick them up and use them. Jal-Nish held them for many years, and there is still much he doesn't know about them –'

Klarm broke off, then added, 'Santhenar is in mortal peril from Stilkeen and without unity we can't survive, so this rebellion has to be crushed. That's why I follow Jal-Nish's orders to the letter.'

'What a load of self-serving tripe,' said Nish. 'You've been supporting Father for years.'

'He first saw the danger from the void a long time ago,' said Klarm. 'And every time he looked again, the threat grew more serious.'

'Anyway, you could leave the militia here. With no food or supplies they'll almost certainly die.'

'Even Flydd and Yggur? Don't take me for a fool, Nish.'

'If my father does come back, you could say that they disappeared in the jungle.'

'When you've given your word, do you only *pretend* to keep it?' Klarm said coldly. '*My* word is my sacred bond; I will put Santhenar's interests above those of any individual's, no matter how painful it may be to me personally.'

So he did care, just a little. Was there any way to use that?

Klarm pressed the knoblaggie to Nish's chest and he felt a sharp pain there. 'Get moving.'

*

How long ago had Nish been taken? Maelys thought it could be as much as twenty minutes and, assuming that Klarm had returned to the upper clearing, they would be there by now, unless he had taken Nish away on the air-sled.

She pushed through the forest to the track, beyond where the tree had fallen. The river had risen further and other trees were quivering. She stepped onto the track and ran, praying that there were no enemy stragglers ahead.

At the upper edge of the forest she peered into the clearing and saw Klarm not far from the caduceus, hauling Nish onto the air-sled. Maelys was scuttling across the slope, taking advantage of every bit of cover – drifting mist, rotting logs and dead soldiers – when she noticed that the lowest part of the clearing was flooding up through the trees.

Tulitine had said that the river was partly dammed nearby by fallen trees, and the troops from the far ridge must have crossed by walking along the trunks. After the torrential rain of the past hour the river was rising rapidly and spreading out from either side of the dam, and it could well rise further up the clearing.

She crept from fog bank to hollow until she reached the centre. The air-sled was only a dagger throw from her and the mist was thinner here, so she went down on hands and knees in the mud, dragging the sabre. A ragged wheel of bodies encircling the caduceus marked the place where the militia had made its stand.

Klarm glanced around sharply, as if he had sensed her, then pushed Nish to the deck of the air-sled. Unsnapping the locks on a metal box, he gingerly drew out Gatherer and Reaper and hung them around his neck from the chain, the way Jal-Nish had worn them. The caduceus flared and Maelys made out, faintly, the hackle-raising song of the tears.

Her taphloid gave another of those off-centre wobbles, warmed and momentarily she saw luminous vapours streaming up from them.

Klarm began to tie Nish to the tall pole at the front of the air-sled. Next he would fly away and her chance would be lost. She had to move faster.

She wriggled upslope past a young militiaman dead from a blow that had almost cut him in half. Maelys turned her head away, fighting the urge to be sick, and went around him towards a pile of bodies. One was a woman no older than herself, pinned to the ground with a spear.

She scurried on, past dead with wounds so ghastly she would have nightmares about them for months. More terrible yet were the soldiers who were still alive. She could not bear the look in their eyes, nor the whispered pleas to be put out of their misery.

There was no blood, though. The rain had washed every drop away, and the bodies had a bleached look, as if they had been soaked in water.

As she was crawling by the caduceus, Klarm pulled Nish's last knot tight and sprang off the air-sled, frowning. Its frame was twisted, the prow buried in mud where it had crashed to the ground.

Maelys passed a tangle of bodies, all Imperial troops. That they were the enemy did not make her feel any better. She was about twenty paces from the air-sled now, and there wasn't much cover between her and it. Klarm hacked away some of the mud with a knife, clambered on and extended his right hand towards Reaper, but drew it back. Turning away, he paced in a tight circle.

'You must,' he said to himself, and touched the surface of Reaper with a quick, nervous flutter of the fingers. The air-sled shuddered and tried to lift itself out of the mud; the stern rose but the prow did not; it was stuck fast. He jumped off again, carrying a spade, and began to excavate mud from the front and sides.

Maelys tried to look like a corpse until he went aboard and tried Reaper again. The air-sled began to shake and shudder; mud flew through the air and plopped down all around but the prow would not come free.

The shuddering stopped and Klarm went down the back, rummaging in the metal box that had held the tears. She crawled forwards, a little ball of mud, never taking her eyes off him. If he got down now he must see her.

Nish was watching her. His hands were bound behind him and another rope had been pulled tightly around his chest, fixing him to the pennant pole. He inclined his head to the right, then again. Did he mean her to go around the right side?

Maelys was crawling that way when Klarm slammed the lid of the metal box and went to the right side. She hastily wriggled under the prow where he'd dug the mud away, knowing that it did not overhang enough to hide her if he came up the front. Clinging to the heavy sabre, she tried to think of a way to attack the most powerful man on Santhenar.

Nothing came to her. She could not see onto the air-sled from here, nor hear anything but the rain pounding on the metal deck, and Klarm could be anywhere. She fought the urge to crawl away and save herself. She had no idea how to free Nish, only that she must. He had been a hero of the war when she was just a little girl; he was the only one who could save the militia now.

'You're making a bad enemy, dwarf,' Nish said loudly.

Maelys did not hear any reply, but once more the air-sled began to shudder.

'What if Father never comes back?' said Nish.

It sounded as if he were trying to distract Klarm. Did that

mean he was coming to the prow? She pressed herself deeper into the mud.

'I'm his only heir,' Nish went on. 'The Imperial throne comes to me, and the first thing I'm going to do is purge my enemies.' Nish paused, then added, 'But there's still time for you.'

'Save your breath,' said Klarm from close by. 'I'm not going to break my oath.'

Reaper sang, a shriller note, and the mud heaved and began to steam. The prow of the air-sled lifted fractionally but fell back, cracking her on the top of the head.

Maelys slumped into the mud and for a few seconds she could not move. The air-sled lifted again, further this time, and she heard the suction breaking, the mud beginning to slide underneath and carry her with it. If the craft dropped now she would be crushed to death.

Fighting a splitting headache, she dug the sabre into the mud and dragged herself out as the air-sled splatted down again. Maelys fell flat in the mud, shaking.

'– and you're going to be my very first victim –' Nish cried, sounding panicky. What was the matter with him?

'Aha!' cried Klarm, and before Maelys realised that he'd seen her a fiery noose twisted around her waist, another around her ankles, and she was lifted from the mud and dropped onto the air-sled. The sabre rang on the metal deck as it slipped from her hand.

Klarm was several strides away, his fingers just above the surface of Reaper. He'd won, and how he was enjoying his triumph. Maelys tried to stand up but the nooses would not allow it.

Nish was staring at her, and when she caught his eye he gave a stiff little nod. Did he have a plan? She didn't see how he could; there was no way he could get free. The sabre was just a few ells from her hand but she could not move to take it.

As Klarm came for her with a length of rope, Nish kicked the dwarf's legs from under him. He fell hard, lost contact with the tears and Maelys's nooses vanished. She snatched at the sabre as Klarm struggled to his feet, the tears swinging on their chain. He was going for Reaper when Maelys lashed out.

The sabre struck the chain near the point where it was attached to Gatherer. The tears shrilled, sparks flew in all directions and she *saw* something rouse briefly inside her weapon, then fire ran along the blade and it sheared through the chain. Gatherer went flying over the side; Reaper hit the deck, trailing the chain, and rolled across until it was stopped by the metal rim.

Klarm collapsed, his little legs drawn up to his belly and his arms wrapped around his middle. Maelys went after Reaper and was about to flip it over the side with the sabre when Nish cried, 'No!'

Fool, she told herself; the slightest contact with Reaper could burn her hand off. She darted across to Nish and cut his bonds.

'Come on,' he said, rubbing his hands to get the circulation back.

They jumped down and she gave him his sabre as they hurried away. It was raining as hard as ever.

'I'll never forget this, Maelys,' he said, clearly moved that she had gone through so much for him. 'I couldn't take that again.'

'Take what?'

'Imprisonment in Mazurhize; and being in the thrall of my father when he comes back. As I know he will.'

Maelys did not reply. Her heart-rate was slowly returning to normal. She'd done it, and now she could hand over the unwanted responsibility.

'You remind me, over and again, who my real friends are,' he said. He looked back over his shoulder and walked faster. 'Where's the militia?'

'In the lower clearing. I sent them up the top, to the best defensive position I could see, but that was at least half an hour ago. And the enemy were close behind. I – I'm really worried.'

'Were Flydd and Yggur there?'

'Yes, and Tulitine, but they weren't much better.'

'They'll think of something,' he said. 'Flydd is the best man in the world in a difficult situation, and Yggur is almost as good.'

He was putting on a show of confidence for her sake, but she was not convinced. She looked back. Klarm was on his feet, walking awkwardly and holding his belly. He clambered off the air-sled and began to paw through the mud.

'Lucky it was Gatherer that fell over the side,' she said. 'Had it been Reaper he could have used Gatherer to find it.'

'Mmm,' he said, breaking into a run. 'Come on.'

Maelys stayed beside him for a while, but she was exhausted from labouring through the mud all this time and could not keep up.

'Go ahead,' she said, knowing she was holding him back. 'You've got to reach them before Klarm does. I'll be close behind.'

He slowed until she caught up. 'I'm not leaving you,' Nish said, his jaw knotted.

'I'll be fine, the taphloid will protect me. Two scriers looked directly at me on the way here and didn't see a thing.' Though they *had* sensed something amiss. 'Go!'

'All right. But be careful.' He kissed her on her muddy brow, the first intimate gesture she'd ever had from him, then ran down to the forest without looking back.

She plodded after him, checking over her shoulder.

larm had found Gatherer; she could see it shining from ere. He carried it carefully to the metal box, wound the hain attached to Reaper around his wrist and looked about. aelys froze, then slowly crouched, knowing he would see er if she ran.

The song of Reaper swelled to a jarring cacophony. The aduceus, which had died to a dull orange, flared white-hot gain and she felt the taphloid's insides wobble. There's too uch Art in this place, she thought, and too many uncanny evices interfering with one another. Something has to give, nd if it's my taphloid . . .

The air-sled shook violently and tore free, sending clots f mud spinning in all directions. Klarm curved it around e clearing, looking for her. Maelys lay down so her pale ce would not stand out against the mud, and prayed. It was l she could do. If he saw her, she was lost.

Klarm made another circle, closer in. Did he know she as still in the clearing? Probably – he was the most astute f men. Her only consolation, as he circled for the third me, was that every minute's delay increased Nish's hances of reaching the militia. He must be well into the rest by now.

The air-sled was only a few spans up, with the dwarf anding at the prow, his head swinging from side to side as e studied every hump and hollow, every body. He would ass close by and she did not think the taphloid could con- eal her at such short range.

She held her breath, monitoring his progress by the abra- ve notes from Reaper. Klarm was now so close that she ould sense the malevolent core of the Profane Tear. He ust see her. Should she jump up and run, or attack with er knife? No, Reaper could kill her as brutally as it had ain the red-haired archer.

A slow shudder rolled through the sodden ground, lifting

her minutely and letting her down again. Maelys ignored it, forcing herself to remain as still as the dead, but the ground heaved again, harder this time. Was it an earthquake?

Klarm let out a furious oath and the air-sled shot away, banking in a semi-circle and soaring up over the forest at the river side of the clearing, out of sight. The flood level had risen visibly there. Maelys climbed shakily to her feet, faint with relief. Why had Klarm gone *that* way? What could be more important than catching Nish?

There was no way of telling, so she ran, and was almost to the deer track at the lower edge of the clearing when two people emerged from the forest near the top of the slope. She recognised them at once, for few men were as tall as Yggur, while only Tulitine had that elegant, upright carriage. What were they doing?

Maelys was running up to intercept them when there came an ear-shattering roar from the direction Klarm had taken, and a three-span-high wall of water and torn-up trees swept across the lower side of the clearing and slammed into the forest where she had been heading. It sheared off the giant rainforest trees as if they had been weeds, then thundered downriver. The dam had given way.

The air-sled went shrieking towards the lower clearing but she knew Klarm would not reach it in time, and if Nish was still on the forest path he could not survive. The flood would tear the forest along the river to pieces then batter its way through the gorge, filling it from top to bottom.

SIX

Maelys plodded up to Yggur and Tulitine, who were star-ing at the churning floodwaters. Every step took an effort now. What was the point of going on? She didn't see how Nish could have survived, and soon Klarm would come back for her.

'Nish, Nish . . !' she gasped.

'Where is he?' said Tulitine.

'Klarm had him,' Maelys said. She reached them and stopped, rubbing a lump on the back of her head where the air-sled had struck it. 'I managed to free him, and he was running down through the forest . . .'

'How long ago?'

'About ten minutes, and I'm really afraid. The flood –'

'I'm sure he'll be all right,' said Tulitine. 'Nish would have heard it coming.'

'But it was so quick . . .' Maelys tried not to imagine what it would do to a human body; Nish's body.

'We saw Klarm fly over,' said Yggur thickly, swaying.

Tulitine put an arm around him, supporting him.

'What's happened down there?' asked Maelys.

'The Imperial forces seemed to be waiting for Klarm.'

'The flood might have swept the militia away,' said Maelys dully.

'They were fairly high up.'

'Yes, of course they were,' said Maelys, feeling a trace of hope. 'I sent them up there. Come on. We've got to check.'

'We have business here first,' said Yggur, and they headed on. 'There's something very strange about the caduceus and I've got to know what it is.'

She watched them go, bewildered. What could be more important than finding Nish? Just minutes ago he had kissed her on the brow; his beard had been soft and silky. How could he be dead? She could not come to terms with the thought, yet nature struck randomly, not caring who lived or died . . .

She had to pull herself together. 'What's the matter?' she said, running after them. 'What are you doing here?'

'Not now!' snapped Tulitine. 'Help me get him to the caduceus.'

'Why?' Neither answered, so she went around to Yggur's other side and tried to help him, but the taphloid grew so hot that it was burning her.

'Aah!' he gasped, doubling over. 'You're making it worse. Go away.'

How could she be making it worse? She followed them, angry and uncomprehending, as they lurched through the ring of bodies. The caduceus was a dull orange, and looked smaller now. Originally, it had been the height of a small tree; now it was the size of a tall mancer's staff. Its heat had baked the soil around it to the texture of earthenware. The rain had eased, but steam rose all around the caduceus.

'No further,' Yggur said to Tulitine, shaking her off.

She stepped away, her eyes on him, but unreadable.

He nearly fell, regained his balance and took a halting step towards the caduceus, holding his arms out like a blind man. 'Why are you here?' he said in a hoarse, old man's voice. A sudden breeze whipped his wet hair out behind him. 'Why did you call me back? What are you trying to tell me?'

'Calling him?' Maelys mouthed to Tulitine. 'What's he talking about?'

'I don't know,' she said quietly. 'But I believe him, and if such a powerful and alien device is calling, we'd better listen.'

'If it is, it's a trap,' Maelys muttered.

Yggur looked up raptly, as if seeing something visible only to him.

'Mother?' he cried, and fell to his knees before the caduceus, weeping.

'What's going on?' said Maelys quietly. 'He isn't . . . er?'

'Losing his wits?' Tulitine gave a dry chuckle. 'No, Yggur seems to be remembering part of his childhood. You know that his origins have always been a mystery.'

'I knew he was a great mancer during the Time of the Mirror . . .'

'Yggur was great long before that,' Tulitine said quietly. 'He was powerful in ancient times. He helped to create the Nightland and hurl Rulke into it, where he was held prisoner for a thousand years.

'But no one knows where Yggur came from, and the source of his great power is another mystery. He was one of only two mancers whose gift was not crippled by the destruction of the nodes at the end of the war, because his power had never depended on nodes or fields, as other mancers' had. It flows into him from an unknown place which not even he understands.'

Yggur reached up with both hands towards the head of the caduceus, repeated, 'Mother?' and crashed onto the baked earth.

His hair began to steam and frizzle. Maelys darted forwards to pull him away but, as she bent over him, the taphloid began to vibrate ever more wildly, slipped from her cleavage and cracked him on the head. He let out a great groan.

'. . . and burn them to nothingness,' a deep, rumbling voice sounded.

Maelys jumped, for it had seemed to come from the taphloid, but how could that be? Her father had given it to her to protect her, though the voice had not been his. In fact, she'd never heard the taphloid speak before.

Yggur's groping left hand closed around it, he quivered and his eyes snapped open.

'I know *this*.'

Maelys, alarmed, tried to pull away, but he did not let go and the chain began to cut into the back of her neck. 'It's mine. How can *you* know it?'

'By the feel of it in my hand. It is as familiar as my own dinner knife, though . . .' Yggur studied the little device in puzzlement, '. . . it feels smaller than it once did.'

'It's made of solid metal. How can it become smaller?' Maelys was alarmed now, for it was the only thing she had left from her father – from her life at Nifferlin, for that matter – and it was precious to her. 'I've had it half my life and my father had it before that.'

'But where did *he* get it?' said Yggur.

'I – I don't know. I always thought he'd made it.'

Yggur gave a scornful laugh and she flushed. 'He would not have had the skill. This taphloid, as you call it, was made by a master in ancient times. It looks like Aachim work to me.'

'But . . .' said Maelys. 'Anyway, we're wasting time. We've got to go after Flydd and Nish.'

'This matters more.'

'They could be dying.'

'Either the flood killed them or it didn't,' Yggur said harshly, 'and if it didn't, it will certainly have blocked the gorge. A few minutes more won't make any difference. Hand it over.' He jerked on the taphloid.

Maelys turned to Tulitine for help, but she said, 'Give it to him.'

Maelys drew the chain over her head and handed the taphloid to Yggur, sure that she would never get it back. It was hot and vibrating again. He stood with the taphloid held loosely in his fist, head cocked to one side, eyes unfocused.

'Maintain the watch against Stilkeen, Yggur,' said a deep, resonant voice from his fist, the same voice she'd heard a minute ago. 'Maintain it always, and all will be well. But if you fail . . .'

He gave a little stagger, and shook himself. 'And clearly I did fail, since I have no memory of ever hearing Stilkeen's name before it showed up.'

'Did the taphloid say that?' said Maelys, alarmed now.

'It did. What else do you know about it?'

'Nothing.'

'Has anyone else recognised it?' said Tulitine.

'Not that I remember.' Maelys thought back over the past months. 'Flydd didn't, and neither did Jal-Nish or Seneschal Vomix.' She shivered at the thought of that monster, the cause of all her clan's misfortunes, but thankfully he was dead. 'Vivimord didn't seem to think the taphloid was anything special; neither did Yalkara nor the Numinator.'

'How very curious,' said Tulitine.

'Then why does it feel familiar to me?' mused Yggur, looking more like his old self. 'Did I see it in the hundreds of years I wandered, witless and without my powers, after the struggle with Rulke that finally put him into the Nightland?

I must have done, and yet I have no memory of it, save for the way it feels in my hand.'

He turned to stare at the caduceus. 'I still feel as though it's calling to me, but I can't read what it's trying to say. Should I take it with me?'

'No!' cried Maelys. 'It's a trap, it's got to be; why else would Stilkeen have left it here?'

'Perhaps you're right. We'd better go back.'

Tulitine offered him her shoulder but Yggur said, 'I feel better now,' and strode off towards the forest as though he were completely reinvigorated, his long legs covering two paces to Maelys's one.

'I don't understand,' she said to Tulitine. 'How did he recover so quickly? Was it my taphloid?' She had to keep calling it her own, though Maelys was beginning to fear that she would never get it back.

'I think it must have been,' said Tulitine uneasily. She went after Yggur, but slipped in the mud and fell to her knees with a small, stifled gasp.

'What's the matter?' said Maelys, helping her up.

'A sudden pain – in my leg bones this time. The Regression Spell is coming undone.'

'You don't look any different.'

'And that's peculiar,' said Tulitine. 'Normally, when this spell fails, the outside ages faster than what lies within, but with me it seems to be the other way around. The caduceus must be interfering with the Regression Spell.' She drew a sharp breath, then pushed herself upright and took a painful step.

'Is there anything I can do?' said Maelys.

'Give me your hand.'

On reaching the forest, they found Yggur waiting at the entrance to a track high above the flood line. The rain had not resumed though the forest canopy dripped steadily

Tulitine winced with every footstep but made no complaint. As they approached the lower clearing Yggur slipped behind a tree.

'What is it?' said Maelys.

'Shh! Klarm is circling, looking for survivors.'

'Can . . . can you see any?'

He did not answer, so she went down, her stomach clenched tightly. Nish, where are you? The height of the flood had passed and the water level was falling, though there was not a soul in sight.

'Could the militia have gone through the gorge before the flood?' she said, though she already knew the answer.

'They were trapped up above the rock outcrop,' said Tulitine in an empty voice.

'That was a while ago,' said Maelys, clinging to the hope, in spite of all logic, that they had survived. 'They might have –'

Yggur shook his head.

The lower half of the clearing was a mess of mud and rock, boulders and tree trunks, while the gorge was now a torrent from wall to wall. The huge boulders that had previously choked the right-hand side could not be seen and the slender bridge had fallen.

'Where are Klarm's troops?' said Maelys.

'Swept away,' said Tulitine in her seer's voice. 'All – swept – away.'

It began to pour again. They waited until the air-sled had finished its circuits, whereupon it headed downstream above the gorge, flying low and slow.

'We'd better make sure there are no survivors,' said Yggur heavily, 'though I'm sure Klarm would have found them if there were any. Try not to leave tracks.'

They slogged across the sodden ground to the brown outcrop, behind which the militia had taken cover. The ferns had been torn off the lower face and a narrow, crescent-shaped pond had formed on the uphill side.

'The gorge must have been blocked at first,' said Yggur, 'and there was nowhere for the flood to go but up the clearing. It washed everyone away, then the blockage burst and the flood drained through the gorge, carrying the dead with it.'

Maelys forced her weary legs to the upper edge of the clearing but there was not a sign of human life. The disaster was so overwhelming that she could not think. Nish was gone, and dear old Flydd, and nothing seemed to have any meaning any more. She trudged down to Yggur and Tulitine.

'If Klarm comes back,' Tulitine was saying, 'we'll have to take him. Otherwise, with the *really wet* season coming, we'll never get out of here.'

How can we capture Klarm, Maelys thought. He's got his knoblaggie, and the tears, and all we have is a burnt-out mancer, a crippled seer, and me. She looked down the slope. 'Hey, I thought I saw someone down in that hollow.'

She skidded down to the former pond by the river, now a long, narrow lake, then wished she had not, for the falling water had revealed many corpses trapped among the piled boulders and tangled tree trunks. Dozens of bodies lay in the water, all naked and broken. The force of the water had torn off their clothes and boots before smashing them against the obstacles.

Maelys felt sick, but she had to make sure. She waded out to the nearest of the dead. 'I don't see Nish,' she said, clinging to the faintest hope.

'No,' said Tulitine, who had hobbled down behind her on Yggur's arm. 'These all look like Klarm's men, but I expect most of the bodies would have been swept through the gorge. Wait – I know that face. Isn't he the fellow who went over to the enemy?'

Maelys followed her to the figure draped backwards over a tree trunk. The long body was as broken as the others, but the man's face was unscathed, the bitter cast to his otherwise handsome face erased in death. He looked at peace, but he would never go home to Gothryme.

'It's Colm,' said Maelys, swallowing hard. 'We were friends once, and I liked him a lot – there was a time when I thought that he was the one for me . . . but I was wrong. Poor Colm. He had such an unhappy life.'

'His skin is pale; he's not from these parts,' said Tulitine.

'He came from the island of Meldorin, originally, but his family was driven away from their home in the war and they lost everything. He never got over losing his inheritance, Gothryme Manor, and then the death of his sister, Ketila, killed him inside.'

'An all-too-common story, but some of us cope better with it than others.'

'Did you say *Gothryme*?' said Yggur, staring at Maelys.

'Yes. Do you know of the place?'

'I stayed there a number of times, at the end of the Time of the Mirror, and afterwards.'

'Then you may have known Colm's ancient relatives, Karan and Llian.'

'Indeed I did,' said Yggur, and his frosty eyes grew hard. 'We became friends, at the end.'

'Colm said that they were famous once, and heroes, but they committed terrible crimes and became known as –'

'Karan Kin-Slayer and Llian the Liar!' Yggur ground out, his voice tight with rage. 'Don't say another word about them.'

Maelys jumped. What was the matter with him? Had they betrayed him in some way? Even if they had, they had died two centuries ago, so why was he still so angry?

'Colm couldn't bear that shame,' she said quietly.

'He refused to believe it.' Maelys touched Colm's brow with her fingertips, then turned away. 'There's no sign of Nish. Let's get going. I hate this place!'

The whistling note of the air-sled sounded from downstream. 'Quick, back to the forest,' said Yggur. 'Klarm is coming upriver. He has to think we're all dead – it's our only chance.'

'He's lost his army,' said Maelys as they hurried towards the shelter of the rainforest. 'How could he come after us?'

'They were just the advance guard. His main army is enormous and as soon as he can bring it across the pass he'll scour every ell of this valley, and the river downstream, and check every body. He has to make sure of us, and Nish, and you, Maelys.'

'I thought you were going to try and capture Klarm,' said Tulitine.

'In my condition, I don't see how I can. Besides, something else has just occurred to me.'

'Care to share it with us?' snapped Tulitine. The pain was getting to her.

'I will, once I understand it myself. Come on.'

They kept to the shallow water pooled along the narrow floodplain beside the riverbank until they reached the forest, where Yggur led them to the upper track, then along it. Maelys followed in silence, numb with grief. Nish and Flydd were dead, almost certainly, Colm definitely, and it seemed as though the entire militia had been wiped out. With Yggur so weak, Tulitine crippled by the failing Regression Spell, and the *really wet* season coming, how could they hope to survive?

'Where are we going?' she said as they re-entered the upper clearing.

'Back to the caduceus,' said Yggur.

Maelys stopped dead. 'Again? We've already been there twice.'

'It's still calling me.'

'Then we should run as fast as we can in the opposite direction.'

'I think it wants something.'

'I'm sure it does,' Maelys muttered, 'and it's not to our good.'

'Why do you say that?' said Yggur, stopping to give Tulitine his arm, for she was walking ever more painfully.

'Stilkeen took Jal-Nish, and threatened us,' said Maelys. 'And every time I've gone near the caduceus, my taphloid shuddered or grew warm. I'm afraid it is trying to attack it, *or me* . . .' Now that's odd, she thought, remembering that Stilkeen hadn't seemed to see her.

'Why would it want to attack *you?*' said Yggur, as though she was utterly insignificant.

Tulitine moved on and he went with her. Maelys trudged after them, so afraid that she could barely stand up.

'The more important question,' said Tulitine, gasping as she struggled across the slippery slope, 'is why Stilkeen left the caduceus here.'

They stopped at the edge of the baked ground. The caduceus had lost its previous orange heat and was now a black, rough-edged iron shaft with two small wings at the top, and the two long black serpents loosely coiled around it.

'As a threat,' said Yggur, holding the taphloid in his fist and frowning. 'You were right, Maelys. It's shuddering as though it's trying to break free. Does it do that often?'

'Only when it's near the caduceus,' said Maelys.

'A threat?' said Tulitine. 'That's not how I read it.'

'How do you read it?' said Yggur, gazing at her as though he'd just seen her true beauty for the first time.

'As an offer,' said Tulitine, frowning at him and stepping away.

'Why would Stilkeen offer us anything?'

Tulitine did not reply. She appeared to find Yggur's fixed regard uncomfortable.

'To help it get what *it* wants?' guessed Maelys. 'The chthonic fire.'

'You may be right,' Yggur mused. 'We know that Stilkeen needs chthonic fire so it can rejoin with the spirits severed from its physical self – its revenants now trapped in the shadow realm. Do you think, since it took Jal-Nish hostage and demanded chthonic fire in return, that it's incapable of finding any itself?'

'It makes sense,' said Tulitine, 'but even so, what are we supposed to *do* with the caduceus?'

'I don't know.'

'Is it still hot?'

Yggur moved the back of his right hand slowly towards the shaft until it touched. 'It's blood warm, but I can't sense anything in it. What can you see with your gift, Tulitine?'

With eyes closed, she extended a slender, blue-veined hand towards the shaft. 'I see us all holding it.'

'Here?'

'No,' she said slowly, as though it was taking time to see clearly.

'Then where are we?'

'I can't tell, though we're surrounded by swirling dust.'

'There's no dust on the Range of Ruin, or anywhere near it,' Yggur pointed out. 'I can feel my clothes rotting by the minute.'

'Then it has to be a trap,' said Maelys.

'Stilkeen is a powerful *being*!' said Yggur. 'It has no need to trap us – it could have taken us at any time.'

'Yet it seemed to be in terrible pain.'

'You're right,' he said, after a thoughtful pause. 'I noticed that too. But why would a *being* so powerful that it has roamed the universe for half an eternity be in pain?'

'I don't know,' said Tulitine, 'I also sensed an urge to hide; to insulate itself from our world.'

'Perhaps it's in pain because it's no longer whole,' said Maelys, answering Yggur's question. 'It seemed to me that our world was painful to it.'

'The caduceus *could* be a trap,' said Tulitine. 'How can we tell? No human can fathom how a *being* thinks, or why it does what it does. But I think it *is* an offer, and we've got to use it.'

'How?' said Yggur.

'By holding the caduceus, the way I envisaged us doing, and seeing what happens.'

'You saw us a long way from here. Are you thinking that it can create *portals*? That's a mighty Art, one of the greatest spells of all.'

'For human mancers,' said Tulitine. 'But for an immortal being that once roamed the eleven dimensions, making a portal from one place to another is probably the tiniest of spells, one it does without thinking.'

'A portal!' said Yggur in a breathy voice. 'Well, why not? And then what?'

'Chthonic fire must be found, or all humanity is in peril, and if *we* can't find it, no one can.'

'If we do find it, and give it to Stilkeen, it might rejoin with its severed spirits, then destroy humanity anyway,' said Yggur. 'I know that much about *beings* – insults to their dignity, or their majesty, never go unpunished.'

'We've got nothing to lose,' said Tulitine. 'Let's try it. Where can chthonic fire be found, apart from at the Numinator's tower?'

'I've no idea – I'd never heard of it until Flydd showed up with the wretched stuff. Interfering old fool. Why couldn't he have left well enough alone?'

'It was the only way to escape from the God-Emperor,'

said Maelys. 'Besides, Stilkeen has been searching for its stolen fire for thousands of years. The Numinator said so.'

'But surely, Flydd's use of the fire led Stilkeen here,' said Yggur. He looked around. 'We'll need warmer clothing, where we're going.'

They rifled the packs of the nearest enemy soldiers for their travelling cloaks, dry socks, and food.

'Take hold of the caduceus,' said Yggur.

Maelys did not want to go anywhere near it, or the Numinator, but she could not remain here. She grasped the shaft of the caduceus, below Tulitine's hand. Yggur's hand was near the top, below the mouths of the serpents.

The moment her fingers closed around the rough iron, the two entwining serpents slid off onto the baked mud. The wind shrilled in Maelys's ears, she felt a hard blow in the belly, then they vanished from the Range of Ruin and were surrounded by frigid, whirling whiteness – not dust but snow.

SEVEN

Nish was racing along the deer track, when the ground gave a long, rolling shudder. He stopped, alarmed, for he knew what it was – a landslide. After all the rain, the soil was so saturated that it was turning into mud.

His first thought was for Maelys, and he had just turned to run back when the ground gave a much stronger shudder, a huge landslide. He heard a deafening series of crashes, and then a thunderous roar. The landslide had gone into the dam, and the dam had broken.

There was no time to go back, or forwards; on this path he was close to the river and if he could not find a higher path he was going to die. Nish closed his eyes, turned his head from side to side and forced himself to trust his clear-sight. It wasn't easy to let go, but he had to. There, directly up the slope through the forest.

He hacked the vines and giant fungi aside, pushed through, and within thirty paces came onto another path he would never have known was there, heading uphill. Nish sprang onto it, turned left and ran up as though the flood was at his heels.

It was, for he could hear the water coming with a vast grinding roar as it tore forest trees out of the earth and razed everything to the ground. He was running up a steep slope now and had a terrific pain in his side, but he had to warn his militia. They wouldn't realise what was happening until the flood tore through the lower clearing, by which time it would be too late.

But what about Maelys? He stopped, gasping and trying to think. The landslide must have been upstream of the upper clearing or it would not have gone into the dam. Therefore Maelys only had to run up the clearing to be safe. She was quick-witted; she'd be all right. He prayed she would be, for there was nothing he could do for her.

He ran on, and soon burst out of the forest opposite the rock outcrop, which was a few hundred paces away. His militia had taken cover behind it, lances out. Klarm's troops were closer to him, halfway up the slope and advancing steadily. They could afford to take their time, for Nish's archers had shot their last arrows and their bows were useless.

The enemy were shouting taunts and displaying the heads of fallen militiamen and women on the points of their spears. Nish was close enough to recognise some of them. Was that Gi's head impaled on the spear of that brute of a sergeant? Not sweet, gentle Gi, whose clever strategy with the archers had saved them in the upper clearing! But it was and, remembering all the good times they had shared together, Nish clenched his fists in impotent fury. Oh, for a bow and a quiverful of arrows.

The sergeant saw him and bellowed. 'It's Cryl-Nish. After him!'

Nish took off, roaring, 'Run! Run for your very lives, that way!' and pointing towards the vine-tangled upper wall of the forest.

The militia were all staring at him, but no one moved. The roaring of the flood echoed down the valley, far louder here. The enemy troops whirled and stared at the river, which was rising rapidly, but they could not comprehend the magnitude of the horror bearing down on them.

'Run!' Nish bellowed, forcing more speed from his exhausted legs. He was above the level of the outcrop now, and some hundred paces away.

A wall of water, trees and rocks exploded down the river, smashing the trees in its path to splinters. Passing well below the lowest of the enemy, who must have thought they were safe, it slammed into the narrow slot of the gorge, damming it in an instant. The water behind it piled up and up, then flooded out in the only direction it could go, sideways into the clearing, and up the slope.

The first wave took the lower third of Klarm's troops.

'Go, you fools!' Nish screamed.

The militia could not have heard him over the cataclysmic sound of the flood, but they could see the danger now. They ran for the forest above.

The second, much higher wave took the rest of the enemy, including the sergeant with his gruesome trophy, while the third wave raced up the slope almost to the base of the outcrop. But a far larger surge was rolling down the river to crash against the dammed gorge, and anyone who did not make the forest before it bored its way up the clearing was doomed.

Nish ran as he had never run before. To his left, the militia were scrambling into the trees as fast as they could force their way through the tangled vegetation. Maybe half were inside now, with half to go. They weren't moving fast enough but there was no more he could do for them. He put his head down and drove himself upwards.

The great surge was hissing up the steep slope, carrying a few floating enemy with it. It overtopped the outcrop and kept going, only twenty paces behind him now, and slowing, but so was he, for his calf muscles felt as if they were tearing apart. He kept going and, as the water struck the backs of his knees, dived head-first through a gap in the vegetation, caught hold of a sturdy vine and wrapped it around himself.

The surge came through the trees in a series of streams, its force almost spent, then rose over his head in seconds and began to flow the other way; if he'd not held onto the vine he would have been carried with it. He swung in the water, clinging desperately as it drained away, carrying branches, leaves and all too many militiamen with it, then it was over.

There were other surges, though none as powerful, and after the third they no longer reached the trees. Nish pushed deeper into the forest, calling the survivors to him, and led them on until they were well beyond sight of the clearing. He stopped beneath a gigantic strangler fig whose host tree had completely rotted away, leaving a hollow inside the fig's ropy trunk.

'To me!' Nish panted. 'Gather everyone in.'

They pressed up to him. He scrambled onto a knotted root and had just begun a count of the survivors when he heard the air-sled shrieking across the forest lower down. 'Quiet! It's Klarm. Don't move.'

They waited, silent and still, while the air-sled circled the clearing several times.

'He's got an army on the other side of the mountain,' Nish reminded them, 'and he'll call them in as soon as he's finished here, so we've got to stay hidden until he's gone. Let him think we've all drowned. Now stand still while I take the muster.'

People were still straggling in. Flangers appeared, along with Chissmoul and her friend Allioun, one of the few freed captives from the Tower of a Thousand Steps who had not accepted Klarm's offer of sanctuary. She was thin and nervous, with large blue eyes and the pallor of the long-term prisoner. Nish had looked like that for months after his own escape from Mazurhize.

'Klarm has flown downstream,' said Flangers. 'He'll be checking in case we got through the gorge before the flood.'

'Then he'll be a while,' said Flydd, emerging from behind the fig tree.

He did not look much better than he had previously, but at least he was still alive. And so were Hoshi and the gigantic fisherman, Clech. Unfortunately Yggur was not with him, and Nish could not see Tulitine either.

He finished the count, and the muster was better than he had feared – a hundred and sixty-two survivors, counting himself. At least twenty had been lost in the forest, and rather more had been swept away by the flood. He ached for every lost man and woman; and yet, had he arrived a minute later it would have been far worse.

'Where's Yggur and Tulitine?' said Nish, frowning.

'Gone back to the other clearing,' said Clech, shifting his weight from one foot to the other.

'What for?'

'Er . . . Yggur said something to Lady Tulitine about taking another look at the caduceus; said it was calling to them.'

'*Calling?* And you let them go?' Nish cried. Just when he'd thought that things were under control!

'I said it was a bad idea but Yggur told me to mind my own damn business. Sorry, Nish.'

'It's not your bloody fault. What's the matter with Yggur? He couldn't walk an hour ago.'

'He got better, then he was whispering to Tulitine for a while.'

'Damn fools! I suppose the flood got them.'

'They had enough time to get there –' said Clech.

'Well, *I* didn't see them,' said Nish.

'Where have you been, anyway?' said Flydd.

'Klarm caught me and took me back to the air-sled. Maelys rescued me – I'll never know how she outwitted him – and we started down here. She couldn't keep up and I ran ahead . . .'

'After she'd just done her all for you?' said Flydd.

'If I hadn't, you'd all be dead!' The criticism was a bit rich, coming from Flydd, after all the times he'd lectured Nish about acting for the greater good. Even so, Nish bitterly regretted leaving her. 'I – I didn't know the dam was going to collapse.'

'She might have survived.'

'It's possible,' said Nish, though after witnessing that flood he had little hope.

'Or Klarm might have captured her,' said Flydd.

Yes, of course that's what happened, Nish thought, faint with relief. 'Did anyone get a close look at the air-sled?'

'I did,' said Flangers, 'though my eyes aren't as good as they used to be –'

'Chissmoul has pilot's eyes,' said Flydd, for she had been a thapter pilot in the war, the best and most daring of them all. 'What did you see, girl?'

Chissmoul was at least as old as Nish, and therefore no girl, but she said without rancour, 'There was no one on the air-sled except Klarm.' She let out a heavy sigh, presumably for the miracle of flight that she would never experience again.

'I'm going back to look for her,' said Nish, rubbing his eyes. 'And Yggur and Tulitine. Wait here –'

'You're not doing anything of the sort,' said Flydd. 'Now we're finally back together, we're staying together. We'll have something to eat then follow the forest around to the upper clearing and stay under cover while you check it. And then we've got to work out what the hell we can do.'

Klarm passed over the upper clearing from a great height and turned away towards the white-thorn peak. They waited for half an hour, in case he came sneaking back, then Nish and Flydd went down. It was early afternoon.

The flood had only covered the lowest third of this clearing, and most of the bodies remained where they had been cut down. The winged shaft of the caduceus was gone, and Nish assumed that Klarm had taken it, though the two iron serpents that had entwined it lay on the baked earth. There was no sign of Yggur, Tulitine or Maelys, and the rain, which was still falling, had washed out all tracks.

Nish was cursing himself for leaving her behind when he remembered their disturbing foreseeings at the Pit of Possibilities, months ago. Maelys had not appeared in any of the possible futures, and at the time she'd been afraid that it meant she was going to die. Had her life been snuffed out, like Gi's, in an instant, or had she suffered a lingering death? Or could she still be alive? He could not find any reason to think so, but he had to cling to hope.

Leaving Flydd studying the iron serpents, Nish plodded down towards the river through a sea of mud and debris. The river path had disappeared and the forest near the bank was gone apart from the shattered stumps of the largest trees. Numb with grief, he trudged back.

'What a stinking, lousy day,' he said. 'This has been one of the worst I can ever remember.' But not *the* worst. The worst day of all time was forever fixed in his memory and no other tragedy, no matter how awful, could erase it.

'It's not over yet,' said Flydd, holding the iron serpent with the forked tongue that had seemed to stare at him earlier. The older man had some colour back in his cheeks at last.

'What are you doing with that?' said Nish. Flydd's choice of *that* serpent felt a trifle ominous, given Nish's worries about him.

89

'There's power in it, and I'm sure it wasn't left here by accident.'

'No, Stilkeen left it to trap us,' said Nish.

'Perhaps, but Klarm isn't having it, nor the other one. Take it.'

'What?' said Nish.

'Take the serpent with the bared fangs.'

'Why? Even if it does have power, I can't use it.'

'We can't leave it here for some scoundrel to find. Besides, our situation can't get much worse, can it?'

'I suppose not,' Nish said grudgingly.

'In that case, it might get better. Take it.'

Nish gingerly touched the iron serpent, which was like a sinuous staff. He was afraid that it would come to life and sink those fangs into him, but nothing happened save that he *sensed* a surging heat within it.

'I felt sure it would be hot, but it's only blood warm.'

'It's hot inside. And there may be a time when you need that heat,' said Flydd.

'Not being a mancer, I'll never know how to liberate it.'

'You don't necessarily have to be a mancer to use an enchanted object. Some devices can be used by anyone, when the time is right.'

Not by me, Nish thought, but he hefted the serpent staff, which was his own height and rather heavy. It was one more thing to carry, and he was already worn out and feeling more hopeless every minute. Had they survived only to be trapped up here and starve? He followed Flydd back to the forest and the waiting militia.

'Where do we go from here?' said Flydd.

'With no food and the *really wet* season on the way there's only one thing we can do,' said Nish bitterly. 'Rot standing up, then die in this festering hell-hole.'

'I didn't go through the agony of renewal only to give

up,' Flydd said coldly. 'Come with me, Nish. Flangers, you too.'

They followed Flydd and, when they were well away from the militia, he pulled Nish close and snarled, 'What the blazes were you thinking, talking defeat in front of your troops? Their morale is already shaky and it won't take much to shatter it. They look up to you, Nish, even though you led them into this nightmare. I'd go so far as to say that they *love* you,' Flydd's lips quirked at this astonishing thought, 'and you can't let them down.'

'Sorry,' Nish muttered, ashamed of his minor breakdown. 'But it's at least a week's march down to the lowlands of Gendrigore and we'll never get there without food, even if the wet holds off.'

'There's always hope, while there's life and breath. The flood has given us a chance I never dared hope for, but only you can weld your militia into a fighting force to take advantage of it – to take one more step, then another, all the way to the God-Emperor's palace at Morrelune.'

Nish let out a mocking laugh. 'Haven't you forgotten one teensy little obstacle – Klarm's colossal army, just over the range?'

'I've forgotten nothing, and neither should you. The little country you came up here to protect is still in peril, for Klarm will follow his orders to the letter. And the father you swore to tear down could reappear at any moment. Nothing has changed, Nish, so pull your finger out and get on with it.'

Flangers had stopped a pebble's toss away and was looking everywhere but at them. Flydd beckoned him forwards. 'Sergeant, Nish is planning to take Blisterbone Pass and turn the enemy back, and he would value your thoughts.'

If Flangers was surprised at this statement, his lean face did not show it – but then, he'd known Flydd a long time. 'I was a common soldier, surr, not an officer . . .'

'You were a most *uncommon* soldier, and you've studied the art of war from the front line. You know fighting from the mud up.'

'I do that,' said Flangers, brightening, and for the first time Nish saw the handsome Flangers of old inside the gaunt and prematurely aged face. 'We have to take a pass, you say?'

'Blisterbone Pass, it's called, around the corner from the white-thorn peak, there.' Nish nodded in the direction of the mountain, which could not be seen for the trees. 'Though ... the Histories of Gendrigore say the pass has never been taken when defended. Unfortunately I haven't seen its approaches, and neither have any of my troops. All I know about it is a mud map the guide, Curr, showed me.'

'The guide who betrayed you?' said Flydd.

'Yes, so his map may not have been reliable.'

'No one has seen the pass?' mused Flydd. 'That's bad.'

'Except for Boobelar,' Nish recalled, 'but he's gone.'

'Who's Boobelar?' said Flangers.

Nish clenched his teeth at the memories. 'The captain of the little troop sent by Rigore province. He's an addled drunk who's out of his head most of the time, and he only came for the loot he could get on the battlefield. He hates me like poison.'

Boobelar had surprised Nish while he was bathing under a waterfall, knocked him face-down over a boulder and whaled his bare arse with the flat of his sword until Nish could barely walk. He still had the bruises, and he would never forget the humiliation.

'Later I beat him in a fight and had him tied up, but his men freed him and decamped in the middle of the night with most of our food. They'll be halfway back to the lowlands by now.'

'He's no help to us, then,' Flydd said. 'Show us Curr's mud map.'

The soil was just rotted leaves here, so Nish cut down a greenly luminous toadstool and carved its stem into the shape of the range and Blisterbone Pass, as he remembered it. 'The white-thorn peak is here, and the pass here, but that's all he showed of it. I'm told the approaches on either side of the pass are steep and dangerous; it's difficult to cross even when undefended. Most of the armies that have tried to invade Gendrigore have failed trying to cross the Range of Ruin.'

'And Blisterbone is the only pass?' said Flangers, squatting down to study the toadstool map.

'There's a higher and even more dangerous crossing called Liver-Leech Pass, but it hasn't been used in hundreds of years. That's where we were headed.' Nish carved it as well.

'Why?' said Flangers.

'Curr said he'd seen an advance guard of the enemy at Blisterbone, so we couldn't attack head-on. Our only hope was to try and take the pass from the other side of the range, after crossing via Liver-Leech. That's why he led us into this valley. Though now I've seen the landscape, how *could* Curr have seen the enemy at Blisterbone?'

'Clearly he was lying. And he betrayed you, so everything he said about Liver-Leech Pass may also be a lie,' said Flydd. 'We can't risk it. We'll have to attack up Blisterbone.'

'Any idea how many men Klarm has there?' said Flangers.

'No, though Tulitine said a few hundred men could hold the pass against an army, so even a handful could hold it against us.'

'Assuming they're expecting an attack,' said Flydd. 'But why would they? Klarm thinks we're dead.'

'He may think that, but he's a careful man, and since he hasn't seen our bodies he'll be wary.'

'Then our attack on the pass must come as a total surprise.'

'Are you talking about a night attack?' cried Nish. 'Up over the most dangerous country there is? You're out of your mind.'

Heads snapped up among the squatting militia. 'Keep your voice down,' growled Flydd. 'It's the only possibility. But first you've got to re-arm and resupply your troops, and there's only one way that can be done.'

'Rob the dead,' said Flangers.

EIGHT

A couple of hundred enemy soldiers had died at the hands of Nish's archers and most still lay where they had fallen. The archers replenished their quivers, the infantry abandoned their rustic weaponry for the fine spears and swords of the Imperial troops, and took their stout helms and shields, packs and boots. The packs contained dry clothing, carefully packed in oilskin, plus provisions for several days' march, and when everything useful had been gathered, the militia withdrew into the forest for the first edible meal they'd had in three or four days.

'I doubt that Klarm will be back today,' said Flydd. 'Having lost a small army already, he'll want to make sure that his main force safely reaches the pass; but when he does return, he'll see that we've robbed the bodies. Our only chance of surprising him lies in attacking the pass first; *tonight!*'

'Impossible,' said Nish, who was sitting on a crumbling log, making a rope sling so he could carry the serpent staff on his back. 'We had little sleep last night and we've been living on half-rotten food for days.'

'There's no choice. Tell everyone to turn in. We'll go in three hours.'

The militia rolled into their cloaks on the wet leaf litter and slept like the dead, but Nish dozed for a bare hour, all that his restless mind would allow him. How could he attack in the dark when he didn't know the terrain? He mentally traced possible paths from here to the pass.

'We'll never get to Blisterbone in time,' he said, thinking aloud. 'It's too far. Liver-Leech Pass is a lot closer from here; at least, that's what Curr said, but how can I trust *his* directions? Besides, the mayor in Gendrigore said that no army could cross Liver-Leech, and only the most desperate of climbers.'

'How much closer is it?' said Flydd, beside him.

Nish had not realised that he was awake. 'Liver-Leech Pass is five or six hours from here and, if we can cross it, it'd take another six hours to circle around to the far side of Blisterbone Pass. *If* the weather is good.'

'What about this side of Blisterbone?'

'It's more than a day from here.'

'How can it be that far? I thought it would be closer.'

'From here, the only direct route is straight up the valley, but only skilled climbers could get up the cliffs at the top. Or we could backtrack the way we came, assuming we can cross the river, and approach the pass via the track from Gendrigore. But that's a long, meandering route, and Klarm would probably be back by then.'

Nish heard Flydd fumbling in the gloom but did not look around, for he was trying to imagine what Klarm would be doing now. The dwarf had taken some heavy falls and a good few blows, plus he had that bad Reaper burn. Once he reached the main army Klarm would need to have his injuries attended to, consult his officers, eat and sleep. To thoroughly search both clearings and the river below the gorge would require far more men than he could carry on the air-sled, and there was no urgency now. Klarm wasn't young and neither was he superhuman, so surely he would stay with the army until they reached the pass sometime tomorrow.

Flydd was right – if they were to take the pass, and hoped to hold it, they had to attack by dawn tomorrow, so Liver-Leech was the only option.

Nish's wandering thoughts turned to his father. He had assumed that Stilkeen would have taken Jal-Nish to the void, since it had, clearly, been in pain, but how could he even guess what an ageless, immortal *being* might do?

Ting! A faint silvery glow formed beside him; Flydd was batting a small, spiky ball of light, like a floating soap bubble, from one hand to another.

'How did you do that?' said Nish.

'The mimemule has a little power back, now we're well away from the caduceus.'

And you couldn't think of anything better to do with it? Nish thought sourly, but that was unfair. After being helpless during the battle, Flydd was entitled to be pleased that he could use his Art again, even in the smallest of ways, and they were going to need it.

'What's it for?' said Nish.

'I've mimicked a spyball; the scrutators used them back in the bad old days of the lyrinx war. Of course, they were powered by the *field* back then, so they could work for months. This one won't last for more than an hour or two, the way I'm feeling.'

Nish felt a twinge of unease. 'What are you going to do with it?'

'Send it up to check the layout of Blisterbone: how many men are guarding it, how alert they are and so forth.'

'How can you be sure that Gatherer won't detect it?'

Flydd looked irritated. 'Klarm wouldn't let Gatherer out of his sight, and he won't be anywhere near the pass yet.'

'How do you know? Besides, he could have scriers there,

with wisp-watchers, and if they see it, they'll alert Klarm at once.'

'We've got to know what we're facing, and it's a small risk,' Flydd snapped, giving Nish one of his famous *How dare you challenge me – I used to be a scrutator* glares.

Nish put on an equally arrogant stare – *And I'm the son and heir of the God-Emperor.* 'It's a *huge* risk. If they know we're coming, we'll have no chance.'

'You can't attack without knowing the terrain – it's the first rule of warfare.'

'I thought the first rule was *Know your enemy.* Listen, Xervish, I'm the captain of this militia and I say we can't use it, but –'

'All right!' Flydd snarled, making a pass over the ball with his fingers. It vanished and the mimemule, a little knobbly wooden ball, stood in its place. He pocketed it and stalked away.

Nish looked after him, frowning. He did not remember the old Flydd, before renewal, acting in such a petulant way.

'Nish,' said Flangers quietly. 'It's not good for morale if you and Flydd fight.'

Many of the nearby troops were awake and whispering to one another. Nish cursed himself for not being more diplomatic, and cursed his old ally as well. Flydd had never liked to be challenged, though in the olden days he'd always put the greater good first. Since renewal, Nish had seldom seen the kindly Flydd, but plenty of the hard, ruthless scrutator of old. And after he'd arrived on the Range of Ruin, Flydd's eyes had often taken on a lustful gleam when he'd looked upon the tears. Nish wasn't entirely sure that he and Flydd were on the same side any more.

'I'm sorry. But I'm right, aren't I?'

Flangers hesitated. 'You're both right, and both wrong.' He turned away. 'I need my sleep, Nish. Surr!'

Flangers, no matter his private thoughts, was too good a soldier to get involved in a dispute between leaders. Nish lay there for a while, trying to sleep, then gave up and went to the top edge of the clearing, looking down on the field of battle, yawning and rubbing his eyes. It was heavily overcast, and night was falling. He thought he saw a light bobbing down below, but when he looked again there was nothing. The rain had stopped and the clearing was peaceful now, for the dim light laid a soft veil over all and the dead were just humps in the grass.

Two hundred of his militia had died today, and he had known the names of every one of them. He began to make a list, starting with sweet Gi, and Forzel the joker, as a kind of remembrance, but the list grew too long and he felt too heartsick. He couldn't even bear to think about Maelys.

And then, something moved on the battlefield.

'What's that?' he muttered, his hair rising. There had definitely been no one alive when they had left, but now he could see a low moving shape down there.

'Don't know, Nish,' said a young voice from not far away.

'Who's there?' Nish said sharply, reaching for his sword, before recognising the Gendrigorean accent.

'It's Huwld, the cook's boy.'

A gangly lad of eleven, with dark skin and incongruously ginger hair, he should never have been allowed to come on this horror campaign. 'Why aren't you in your bedroll, lad?'

'Couldn't sleep,' said Huwld soberly. All the cheer had gone out of him too. 'I can't stop thinking about the battle.'

'Me either. Come over here.' The boy came across and they stood together, watching the figure creep from one mound to another as the light faded.

'Do you think it's a ghost?' said Huwld in a half fearful, half awed voice.

'It's not floating or fluttering,' said Nish.

There was a long silence. 'Nor creeping nor growling. I don't think it's a beast, either.'

'No,' said Nish. 'It's human.'

Could it be one of the militia, gone down for a last look at dead friends? Anything was possible, but Nish did not think so. Or Flydd? No, he would not look so furtive. Nish felt sure that this visitor had some other purpose in mind, and he had to know what it was.

'Stay here,' he said. 'I'm going to have a look.'

Nish crept down the slope, low and slow, knowing that, despite the dimness, any sudden movement could attract attention. The figure was moving across the clearing, going from one body to another in no particular order, which was strange, and sometimes turning back on itself, but it looked unsteady on its feet.

Was it a forest-dwelling hermit, wits curdled from a life-time spent alone? Again he saw that fleeting, bobbing light, some distance from the figure. Were there more than one of them? Not hermits, then.

As he approached, Nish heard a thick, muttering voice. He could not make out the words but the fellow certainly sounded addled. He caught a whiff of strong drink and spicy, hallucinogenic nif-tree sap, and the food in his belly curdled.

It was Boobelar, the drunken, nif-addled captain who had nearly killed Nish a few days back, then fled with his men and most of the militia's food. Of course it was Boobelar, who had come to the Range of Ruin for one reason only – to plunder the dead. Nish felt the chill of fear, for Boobelar was a big, burly man, much stronger than Nish and a vicious, dirty fighter. He wished he had not seen him going about his grisly business, but now Nish knew, he had to stop him from dishonouring the fallen militiamen and women. This time, he vowed, he would put Boobelar down like the vermin he was.

He shadowed the drunkard across the wet grass, sabre out, while Boobelar rifled the bodies and dropped his booty into a sack that he dragged behind him. Now he was bent over a tangle of corpses, laughing drunkenly as he felt inside their clothing. Nish couldn't bear it any longer, and had just raised the sabre to cut him down when Huwld cried out from behind him and caught his wrist with both hands.

'No, Nish! Uncle Boobelar, look out!'

Boobelar spun around and came to his feet, long dagger in hand and a sick grin plastered across his face. Nish shook Huwld off, cursing. He'd forgotten that the boy was Boobelar's nephew and, no matter what he might think of his depraved uncle, owed him loyalty.

'Put down the knife,' said Nish. 'I've got two hundred militia within call.'

'How's your arse, runt?' sniggered Boobelar. 'I'll do more than whack it this time. I'll shove your head so far up you'll choke on it.'

Nish felt himself flushing, for Boobelar could always get to him. Now what was he supposed to do? He could hardly kill him in front of his nephew.

He circled, holding the sabre out, and Boobelar did too. Nish lunged at him, trying to knock him out with the flat of the blade, but Boobelar sprang sideways, took hold of Huwld and put the knife to his throat.

'Back off or I'll kill the boy.'

Nish lowered his blade, shocked to his heart. 'He's your nephew!'

'Always hated the brat and his slut of a mother. Drop the sword.'

Huwld gasped, and Nish had no choice. He let the sabre down in the mud and backed away, and Boobelar picked it up.

'Take the bag, brat,' said Boobelar. 'That way.' He pointed down the slope.

Huwld, his teeth chattering, took hold of the heavy bag and began to drag it away. Nish could not bear to let him go with the brute, but how could he stop him?

He was watching them head down the hill when he saw the bobbing light again. It shot up at Boobelar's face, flared to a dazzling, spiky ball, then Nish heard a double thump.

'Got the swine,' Flydd said with quiet satisfaction. 'Run up to the camp and send some men down, lad. We won't harm him.'

Huwld ran off.

When Nish could see clearly, Flydd was tying Boobelar by the fading light of his spiky globe. 'So those lights were you, wandering around the battlefield?' said Nish.

'Told you they'd be useful,' said Flydd. 'I saw him earlier, robbing the bodies, and remembered you saying Boobelar had only come for plunder. I guessed it was him and set a trap.'

'I wonder you didn't kill the bastard! I wish you had.'

'He's going to show us the way over Liver-Leech Pass,' said Flydd.

'You'd better hang onto him, then,' said Nish, taking back his sabre and resisting the urge to carve Boobelar up with it. 'He's the slimiest thug I've ever had the misfortune to encounter. He'd steal your eyeballs if you weren't looking.'

Shortly the militia had packed up camp, and they headed up the ridge in the dark.

'All right, Boobelar,' said Flydd to the stumbling, reeking soldier, who was securely tied, with a rope leading from his bound hands to the muscular militiamen behind him. 'Show us the way to Liver-Leech.'

'Stuffed if I will and you can't make me.'

Flydd reversed the staff and pressed its open serpent mouth up against the soldier's chest. Boobelar looked at it blearily but did not flinch. He met Flydd's eyes.

Flydd grinned. 'We'll see about that.' He lifted a half-full wineskin off Boobelar's back, sniffed the contents, grimaced and tossed it over the steep edge of the ridge. 'Hey!' cried Boobelar, 'that's neat brandy.'

'And now you've lost it. Throw him down on his face, lads, and search him thoroughly. Take everything.'

They did so, while Boobelar cursed them in a slurred monotone, and recovered several small packets which had been overlooked earlier. Flydd sniffed them one by one, 'Nif sap,' and began to toss them away.

'It might be an idea to keep some,' Nish said quietly. 'As a bribe, if all other means of coercion fail. Besides, I'm not sure he's ever been fully sober; he might not be able to function.'

Flydd nodded, slipped the last packet into his pocket and said, 'Which way, Boobelar, my friend?'

'Follow this ridge up until you reach the cliffs,' he snarled. 'Then jump!'

'How do you feel about being tied to a tree and abandoned without any drink or nif?' said Flydd pleasantly. 'It could take you a fortnight to die, and it'd be the worst fortnight of your miserable life.'

'You wouldn't dare!' Boobelar grated, straining at his ropes. 'I'm the captain of the Rigore militia.'

'We're not in Gendrigore now, and I just caught you robbing the honourable dead, which is a capital crime.'

'Kill me, then,' said Boobelar. 'What do I care?'

'Don't tempt me,' said Flydd, taking the last packet of dried nif sap from his pocket and holding it over the edge. 'Shall I drop it, or keep it until you take us across Liver-Leech safely?'

Boobelar cursed him into eternity, then said in a saliva-choked voice, 'How do I know you'll keep your word?'

'Because I'm unlike you in every respect.'

'All right, you bastard!'

'Which way?'

'I'll show you!'

'Tell me first, in case you have an *accident* on the way,' said Flydd nastily. 'Or get tied up.' He chuckled.

Boobelar made a gurgling sound in his throat.

'And it'd better be the right way,' Flydd added. 'If you don't give me the right directions, you don't get the nif.'

'Up there,' said Boobelar, pointing with a foot. 'Veer along the base of the cliffs to the left until you see a goat track running across the mountainside. Follow it towards the gap between a pair of small peaks shaped like clothes pegs – if you can see them.'

'*You'd* better see them.'

'Climb along the crest of a ridge, very steep on both sides, then crawl along several narrow ledges, with a hundred-span fall on the left, for half a league, and in through the gap between the peg peaks – that's Liver-Leech. Cross the pass then keep to the right-hand track behind the white-thorn peak for about four or five hours, then take the left-hand spur down to the main track across the range. You'll see Blisterbone Pass above you, not a quarter of a league away.'

'That's all the directions you have?' Flydd said quietly.

'All I can remember.'

Flydd bestowed a mirthless smile on Boobelar. 'Lead on, *Captain*.'

'I'll see you dead first,' said Boobelar.

'I doubt it.'

Nish resisted the urge to wallop Boobelar's backside with the sabre – that would be petty. 'It might be better if I lead,' he said. 'The sot might take us over the edge just for the hell of it.'

NINE

It wasn't completely dark, for the starlight was bright at this altitude, but every footstep had to be placed with care on the steep, wet rock.

'Take it slowly,' Nish said over his shoulder to Flydd. 'Test every step before you put your weight on it. The first part looks the worst.'

He adjusted the serpent staff, which was digging into the small of his back. The night was cool and the staff pleasantly warm, sometimes too warm. He could sense the roiling heat inside it, presumably the same force that had caused it to blaze white-hot earlier. How much, or how *little*, would be required to release it? And if it was a trap, what kind of a trap, and how could they avoid it?

It was not possible to think of an answer. He swallowed and looked ahead. Starlight touched the wet ledge here and there, a perilous path of broken stone no wider than his shoulders. Nish tested his first step. The rough rock sloped outwards but was not slippery. Then his foot slid sideways – well, not *dangerously* slippery. So far.

Flydd came behind him, followed by Boobelar and the three men who held his ropes, next Huwld, Flangers, Chissmoul and her nervous friend Allioun, and after that the militia, roped together in groups of eight with the strongest men in the middle. If the leader put a foot wrong and fell, Nish hoped that the others could hold him. And if they could not, only eight would be lost, not the entire militia.

Halfway across the cliff, something skidded underfoot and he smelled manure. 'Careful here; goat turds.'

He scraped it off his sole and continued, and heard part of his words repeated all the way to the rear. 'Careful turds. Careful turds.'

The trek was a nightmare of rain and wind as they crept along one precipitous ledge after another, each higher than the previous one and more exposed to the intermittent rain and the unceasing wind, which grew ever colder until Nish began to worry that they would get frostbite on their noses. After an hour a heavy overcast came up, the darkness became absolute, and every step had to be made by feel. Without Boobelar, who seemed to be navigating on instinct, they would never have found the way.

'This is madness,' Nish said after they had spent half an hour on the third ledge, during which time they had managed just two hundred shuffling paces. 'At this rate it'll take us days to reach Liver-Leech – if we get there at all. We've got to have light.'

Though the Gendrigoreans were used to climbing in wet and slippery conditions, this trek was testing their agility to the limits and there had been several nasty mishaps already. As the night wore on and people wearied, someone was bound to slip and, if the rest of the group did not brace instantly, all eight would be lost.

'Torches will be seen from a long way away,' snapped Flydd.

'In this weather?' Nish was desperately trying to remain calm and positive, even if everyone else was falling to pieces.

'There's nothing to burn, anyhow. There's no wood up here.' Flydd had turned surly again. His intestines were troubling him and whenever he reached the end of a ledge he would disappear behind a rock, though afterwards his discomfort did not appear to have been relieved.

'What if you conjured some with the mimemule?'

'At the moment you'd get more light out of a firefly.'

'You've got to do something,' said Nish, deliberately echoing Flydd's earlier words. 'Without light, we fail. What about a few of those little spiky globes you made earlier?'

'Sorry, they took more out of me than I thought.' Flydd stopped, swaying on his feet.

The word was passed back, 'Stopping, stopping,' and the exhausted militia hunched down in their cloaks.

'I can't make fire either,' he added, as if to forestall Nish.

'Not even with the serpent staff? I sometimes feel that I could light a fire with mine, if I were a mancer. Clearsight keeps showing me something hot and churning inside it.'

'I can't feel anything in mine,' said Flydd.

'Perhaps we should swap, then.'

'I don't think so,' Flydd said hastily.

'I thought creating light was an easy charm.'

'It usually is, though I've found it rather difficult since renewal.'

'Have you got the strength to *transport* some light here?' said Nish.

'From where? The whole range is in darkness.'

'Toadstools!'

'I beg your pardon,' said Flydd.

'Conjure one of those luminous toadstools out of the forest; we can cut it up and tie it to our boots.'

'You're touched in the head,' said Flydd. 'But then again, toadstools don't weigh much; I might be able to manage one.' He snorted. 'And the good thing is, if that bastard Klarm happens to be zooming by on his precious air-sled, he'll think he's gone mad.'

He wasn't the only one. When, ten minutes later, a huge, greenly luminous and embarrassingly phallic toadstool came soaring through the sky, bolt upright, three militiamen were so astonished that they nearly went over the edge.

Aimee, the tiny, bird-like woman sitting next to Clech, went into a fit of giggling which spread right through the militia. She couldn't regain her composure until Clech held her upside down by the legs, a remedy which, evidently, he had used a number of times before, since Aimee accepted it without complaint.

Everyone felt better afterwards; the laughter had cleared away the exhaustion and even helped with their grief. Nish sliced the toadstool into discs and passed them back, and everyone set to, peeling off the luminous skin and binding strips to the toes and heels of their boots. In Boobelar's case, they also tied strips around his scarred forehead so they would recognise him in the dark.

He was sobering up; he also appeared to be coming down from the nif intoxication he'd been under for weeks, and was behaving very oddly, one minute shouting and waving his arms, the next whining and wailing, or lying down and refusing to get up. Only the promise of a healthy dose of nif at the end of the trip could get him moving, and that lure was taking longer to work each time.

Light made all the difference and they headed on at a good speed, up ledges so high that patches of ice began to appear on them, and the rain turned to sandblasting grains of sleet. They trekked along a knife-blade ridge, then another at right-angles to it, heading towards the invisible peg peaks that framed the precipitous Liver-Leech Pass, until it was all Nish could do to put one glowing foot in front of another.

The immensity of the mountains contracted to the span or two he could see in front of him, the night lowered until it was a blank shroud over his head and shoulders, and time stretched out until it could only be measured by one step, then another, and another.

But with the light, and Boobelar's blasphemously snarled directions whenever they looked like going astray, they reached Liver-Leech well after midnight, a good hour later than Nish had hoped.

'We'll rest briefly on the other side,' he said, 'and then we've got to get a move on, or it'll be dawn before we're in sight of Blisterbone. Attacking in daylight would be suicidal – they'd shoot us down before we got close.'

Liver-Leech Pass was a vertical-sided ravine between the peg peaks, hundreds of spans deep but only one span wide at the bottom, and floored with slick ice. It was also hundreds of paces long and the wind howled so furiously in their faces that they had to get down and crawl.

Once they'd crossed the pass, and were sheltering out of the worst of the wind on the ledge that ran around the range to their right, Nish called a brief halt. Everyone needed food and hot drink but there was no fuel up here, so they munched on their hard rations, sipped the icy water from their half-frozen water skins and took what rest they could.

There was no cloud on this side of the range and starlight illuminated the ledge relatively well. Nish could see it curving more or less horizontally around the mountainside and knew that they were now on the other side of the white-thorn peak. It was still hours to the track that led up to Blisterbone, but by comparing his mental image of Curr's mud map with Boobelar's directions, he felt sure he was going the right way.

Boobelar ate and drank nothing; he had even stopped whining. He took off his boots to shake stones out of them, but the smell was so nauseating that everyone near him, even Huwld, cried, 'Put them on again.'

He did so, then passed his hand to his mouth, chewed, then turned a malicious, broken-toothed smile on Nish and Flydd.

'Must have had some nif in there,' said Nish as they set out again. 'I wonder what he's planning?'

'Well, we won't need him much longer,' said Flydd, miming a slash across the throat.

They hadn't been going for more than ten minutes, however, when there was a ruckus behind Nish and he turned to see Boobelar hurl himself over the side of the ledge, dragging the nearest roped man with him.

Nish scrambled back to grab the rope as the second man braced himself, but he was close to the edge and the weight pulled him over as well. The third man cried out and toppled just as Nish caught the flying rope, but had to let go or it would have taken him.

'Light, quick!' he yelled. Huwld was staring over the side in horror. 'Quick, lad,' said Nish kindly. 'Run and collect some lights.'

Huwld did so and they attached strips of glowing fungus to a rope, which took several minutes, and lowered it over. There was a narrow ledge only a span below, but it was empty. A broader ledge ran along out of sight, far below.

'There they are,' said Nish, 'down about fifteen spans, on the broad ledge. I'll go down.' He pulled the rope up and began to tie it around himself, though he had little hope that anyone would still be alive after such a fall. 'I'm sorry, Huwld,' he said, giving him a quick hug, but the boy pulled away and covered his face with his hands.

'Not you, Nish,' said Flydd, taking the rope. 'Who's a climber?'

'I am,' said Clech's bird-like friend, Aimee.

'Are you really?' said Flydd. 'Come here.'

Clech personally tied the rope around her and lowered her down. The lighted rope end moved back and forth, then she called. 'I – they're dead, Nish.'

'Are you sure?'

'Yes,' she said faintly. 'I mean, our three are dead . . .'

'What about Boobelar?' Flydd said in a strangled voice.

'The rope's been cut.' Aimee checked all around with her light, and over the side. 'He's gone.'

'I still don't understand how the bastard got away,' Nish muttered when they headed on. That disaster, and the loss of three more men, had cast a pall over the rest of the trek.

'He must have stolen a knife in the dark,' said Clech, 'cut his rope then dropped onto the narrow ledge and pulled the others over. Then got out of sight damn quick.'

'How could he steal a knife? His hands were tied behind his back.'

'I have no idea,' said Flydd.

'If he knew where to throw himself over safely,' said Nish, 'he must know the country really well. Where do you think he's gone?'

'Down to betray us to Klarm's army,' Flydd said quietly, so no one else would hear. 'And he'll know the quickest way to find it.'

'We'd better go,' said Nish. 'And pray Klarm is a long way away.'

He pressed on in the starlight, moving as fast as he could without being reckless, but it was never fast enough. What if the army was just down beyond the ridge? If Boobelar reached it before they attacked the pass, Klarm could fly the air-sled up to Blisterbone with reinforcements and warn the defenders, and their faint hope of taking the pass would be lost.

111

Four hours later, after an exhausting forced march without a break, they staggered off the final ledge onto the crest of another precipitous ridge and followed it down until it curved back towards the white-thorn mountain, where Nish saw the main path, which ran all the way to Taranta, curving around below them. They'd done it.

He pulled off the fading luminous strips and collapsed in a heap. He was looking up at Blisterbone Pass from the other side of the Range of Ruin. Now for the difficult part, he thought.

'I smell smoke,' Clech whispered. 'The guards at the pass must have a fire, the swine.'

'Swine,' Nish echoed dully, for the chill had begun to seep through his damp clothes as soon as he stopped moving. He was utterly exhausted after the all-night trek; they all were. He wanted nothing more than to lie down by a fire, wrap himself in blankets, drink half a skin of wine and drift off to sleep for a week, but he could not afford to rest either body or mind; not here. If he lost the edge, he'd never get it back.

He checked down the mountain, but saw no sign of camp fires nor moving lights, though that did not mean Klarm's army was far away. And if Boobelar had reached them already he would be leading them up the track, burning for revenge. Nish shivered and rubbed his cold hands.

'Stay low,' he said quietly to the militia. 'We're not far below the pass. Don't talk. Have something to eat and take a few minutes' rest, and then we attack.'

The timing, partly by accident, was right, for the moon was about to set and once it did there would be ten minutes of darkness before the first light of dawn. It was the best time to attack, for the sentries would be weary from their chilly night vigil. Nonetheless, Nish's stomach spasmed at the thought of what he was about to attempt. If Boobelar had already found Klarm's army, and he had warned the guards at the pass of the imminent attack, it would be a quick and bloody form of suicide.

His head was throbbing again. He adjusted the staff on his back, now grateful for its warmth, crawled to the edge of the ridge and looked across and up. The rocky mountainside was extremely steep, and mostly bare of cover. The setting moon showed parts of the track, which ran up a shallow gully, little more than a notch in the flank of the mountain, to the pass.

The only concealment was low-growing ferns and a few windswept bushes, though most had been tramped flat by Klarm's advance guard. At least, he prayed that it was the advance guard. If the whole army had gone by while they were climbing Liver-Leech, they had made the nightmare climb for nothing.

'I – I could creep up and scout the defences for you,' said a small voice to his left.

'Is that you, Huwld?' said Nish.

'Yes. Can I go? I've got to –'

'Don't be silly, lad,' said Nish, as kindly as he could. 'Run back now, this is soldiers' business.'

With a muffled choke, Huwld crept away. What was the matter with the lad? And what would happen to him if everyone was killed?

Flydd slid in beside Nish to the left; Flangers settled on the right, stifling a groan. Chissmoul was further around the curving ridgetop, looking downslope, though the lower parts of the mountain were wreathed in mist and there was little to see.

'How are your bones holding out, Sergeant?' said Nish in a low voice.

'I can feel every one of them,' said Flangers. 'It's been quite a walk.'

Nish was amazed that he had come this far, for Flangers had lost a lot of weight while he was the Numinator's prisoner and had not looked well when he'd come through the portal. But he was a professional soldier, knew nothing else, and the more that was asked of him the more he seemed to grow.

'It won't be easy to attack,' said Flydd.

A mighty understatement. In the moonlight, Blisterbone Pass formed a perfect natural fortress, with the precipice-bounded flanks of the white-thorn peak looming over it to the right and its lower but bulkier twin guarding the left, equally unclimbable. High above the track an ice-covered horn of rock protruded from the side of the white-thorn peak like the gigantic, beaky nose of an ever-watchful guardian.

The track up the rocky gully was such a steep climb that at several points they would have to go down on hands and knees, and the last hundred paces had no cover whatsoever. Could they do it in ten minutes, in darkness? They would have to.

The pass itself was a mere slot between buttresses of rock that appeared to be at least a span and a half high, and too steep to climb. The enemy could shoot from their tops but would be almost impossible to pick off from below, and once the fighting started Nish's archers could not fire at all for fear of hitting their own people.

'I don't see any lights,' said Flangers. 'Nor any firelight, either.'

'Doesn't mean they aren't keeping watch,' said Nish, taking out a packet of rations and breaking off a chunk of purloined journeybread, a dense cake-like substance made from flour, eggs, pounded nuts and dried fruit. It was dry and almost as hard as wood, but tasty and warming; just the thing to line the stomach of a hungry soldier before battle.

'They're disciplined soldiers; if they do have a fire it'll be small and well back, so it doesn't destroy their night sight.'

He squinted up at the pass, willing his clearsight to see through solid rock, but it had deserted him yet again. 'We've got to know how many guards there are. It'll be a tough battle if the garrison is twenty men; if it's two hundred, we've got no chance.'

'There's no way of finding out,' said Flydd, clutching his iron serpent like a wizard's staff, 'and dawn isn't far off. We'd better move.'

A sudden wind rustled the shrubs further down. Nish shivered and pulled his thin coat more tightly around him.

'Surr?' Chissmoul hissed.

'Yes?' Nish said distractedly.

'I can see lights, far below.'

He crept across to her vantage point. The wind was breaking up the mist and he made out three tiny points of light, widely separated; now seven lights; now dozens; hundreds. A chill that no warmth could disperse spread over his back. 'It's Klarm's army. Have they been there all the time?'

'Undoubtedly,' said Flydd. 'So if Boobelar hasn't reached their camp already, it won't take him long.'

'If he'd reached them already, we would have heard Klarm coming on the air-sled.'

'Not if he took a roundabout route. Alternatively, he could have flown up to the pass before we got here. And even if he isn't there yet, he soon will be. The army is surely less than two hours away. What do you know about their path, Nish?'

'I was told it's as hard a climb as the way we came from Gendrigore.' The wind died and the mist swept back, obscuring all lights save the initial three. 'Chissmoul, are those lights moving?'

'Yes,' she said quietly. 'They're coming this way.'

'And even if Klarm doesn't know yet,' said Flydd, 'once

either the garrison above or the army below gets wind of us, they'll signal to their comrades and we'll be trapped – between an impregnable fortress and an army so vast it'll annihilate us.'

Nish considered that prospect in silence. The moon went down and darkness settled over the mountains; the first light of dawn was but ten minutes away. 'We're going up. Pass the word. We must have *absolute* silence.'

The message was relayed back. Nish stuffed the rest of his journeybread into his pack, for his mouth was so dry he couldn't swallow. 'Clech?' he said to the huge fisherman. 'I'd like to have you with me.'

'It will be an honour, Nish.'

'I don't want you risking yourself –' began Flydd.

'My militia don't have the experience,' said Nish. 'I've got to lead them. And of all the sergeants I've ever met, I'd choose you to be my right hand, Flangers.'

'I'll be there. It'll be just like old times,' said Flangers.

'And you, Chissmoul, to my left,' Nish added, sensing that she was about to ask it. She could not bear to be parted from Flangers, though Nish suspected that this was going to be their final hour. 'More than anything I need a good pair of eyes and an unflinching heart.'

'I'm with you, Nish, to the bitter end.'

'Thank you.' They roped together for the climb, not because it was particularly dangerous, but to be sure they kept close together in the dark. 'Check your weapons and follow me.'

TEN

It would be the bitter end for him, too, most probably, but Nish wasn't going to think about that. He slipped the sabre up and down in its sheath to be sure it would come free when he needed it, tested the knife on his other hip and adjusted the serpent staff on his back.

When everyone was roped up and ready, he went hand over hand down the broken ridge rock and onto the track. The chill breeze drifted up past him, carrying that faint tang of wood smoke, though the lights could no longer be seen.

Nish didn't try to suppress his anxiety. It was right to be afraid before battle, and there was much to fear: ignominious defeat, or the price of victory if they should achieve it, and most of all, the loss of so many more friends . . .

He cancelled all such dismal thoughts and concentrated on what he could see of the track, now no more than a glimmer of reflected starlight here and there. The pass was about four hundred paces up.

He began to feel his way up the track, step by step, and knew that he was taking much too long. At this rate dawn would expose them halfway, and even in this forsaken place there was no chance of the guards being asleep at their posts. In the Imperial army, the punishment for neglecting one's duty was dire.

He stopped for a second and Clech ran into him, then caught his shoulder, steadying him. 'I can't see a thing,' Nish whispered. 'We're too slow.'

'Let me go first,' said Chissmoul and, without waiting for permission, she untied her rope and scrambled up past him. 'I can see a bit; enough.'

They retied themselves and she went ahead, though Nish did not like it. It was his responsibility to lead and, during the war, it had been second nature for him to be alert to all manner of dangers, expected and unexpected. Chissmoul was as solid as Flangers, in her own way, but he felt the loss of control keenly.

She was quick, though. The rope was tugging at his chest and he stepped forwards, trying to guess where she had put her feet on the broken rock, but before he found a secure foothold the rope had tightened again and was pulling him off-balance.

'You're too fast for me,' he said quietly.

'Go any slower and dawn will beat us.' Chissmoul was off again.

His heart was pounding and his palms felt sticky. He wiped them on his pants, stumbled when the rope jerked again and would have brought her down with him had Clech not held him up again.

Nish did not think that the scuffling sound could have been heard, for they were still three hundred paces below the pass, but sounds carried a long way across a bare mountainside. And if the enemy had scriers or wisp-watchers they would be walking into a trap.

Within minutes they had halved the distance without incident, though Nish was developing a cramp in his right calf and the bruised and blistered soles of his feet were throbbing.

'Stop! Cramp,' he whispered.

Chissmoul stopped and Nish was stretching his calf muscle when, from below, metal clacked on stone. He froze, for the sound had been loud enough to carry all the way up.

'Down!' he hissed, and lay prone on the wet rock. 'Don't move.' The order was relayed back in whispers and he heard the faintest scrape of leather scabbards on stone as everyone lay prone.

There was no sound from above, but without warning the beam of a storm lantern stabbed down the slope from the slot, then began to sweep across the path from side to side.

'Don't look directly at the lantern, surr,' said Chissmoul. 'It'll reflect off your eyes.'

Nish watched it from the corner of an eye, sweating. Had they been fifty paces further up, they would have been seen at once; even at this distance a keen-eyed sentry might spot them. The beam passed back and forth, moved down, then back and forth again. The guards were taking no chances.

'They'll come down to make sure,' he muttered.

'Maybe, maybe not,' Clech said. 'The night is full of odd sounds when you're on guard duty.'

Nish eyed the defences, which he could see clearly now in the light from the lantern. The entry to the pass was a slot-like gash through sheer rock, barely wide enough for three men to fight abreast. Attacking the defenders in the slot, up such a steep slope, would put his militia at a massive disadvantage, while the enemy could fire down at them from the rock buttresses on either side. No wonder the pass was considered impregnable.

A sharp edge of rock was digging into his breastbone but he forced himself to ignore it. The next pass of the beam would come across Chissmoul, himself and Flangers. The guards might not make them out at this distance but any scrier with a wisp-watcher surely would. And Nish had an unnerving feeling that they did have a scrier.

Holding his breath, he counted the seconds. The beam fanned across him, swept back further down, and went out.

'Stay!' he hissed.

Stay, stay, stay was repeated down the line. A minute went by in silence, then without warning the beam swept back and forth, right over them. If anyone had risen, they would have been seen.

The beam went out but he waited another minute, feeling their chances ebbing away with every tick of his internal clock. Only minutes until dawn.

'When we get near,' Nish said quietly, 'try to breathe shallowly so they don't hear us. And before you attack, don't forget to discard the ropes.'

While the word was passed back, he worked his leg muscles, hoping to prevent a last-minute cramp. After the brutal all-night march he had just enough left for one brief onslaught, and it had better succeed. He would not have the strength for a second attempt, or even a long fight.

'Go,' he whispered. 'Quick and quiet as you can.'

Chissmoul sprang to her feet as if starting a race, and Nish marvelled that she was able to. The rope pulled him forwards; he felt icy cold now, no longer afraid, and perhaps because of that his clearsight snapped on and he could see the track.

She went as fast as it was possible to go up such a steep slope, and he went with her, counting the steps and concentrating on placing his feet squarely and softly. Behind him Clech was moving easily, his long legs covering a pace and a half with every stride, his huge feet finding a steady purchase on the roughest surface.

They dropped over a lip of rock into a broad, shallow bowl. Three or four spans deep and maybe twenty across, it had not been visible from below. The sudden descent was so unexpected that Nish would have sprawled on his face had the taut rope not held him up.

At the bottom, grit squeaked underfoot, as if the rock here had been smashed by a mallet-wielding giant. He found his footing, moved carefully across to minimise the noise, and up the other, steeper side of the bowl.

Ahead the track curved left around a knob shaped like a bladder-bat, then ran up steeply for the last sixty paces. Chissmoul turned around the knob, slipped and her arms wheeled, but she found her feet and kept going.

'Rope!' whispered Nish.

They untied, dropped it to one side and headed up the steep pinch, and Nish felt a faint hope that they would make it to the slot undetected. Fifty paces to go and his throat was burning; he was short of breath, and trying to breathe shallowly and quietly made it worse.

Even so, he was making more noise than he cared to, and someone behind him was panting. Forty paces; he landed hard on a small rock and his right ankle almost turned; he just managed to save it from going over though he felt a stinging pain in the top of his left foot and another shot up his leg. Had he pulled a muscle?

He couldn't stop. Thirty paces and his leg began to throb; now a cramp was building in his right calf. He tried to adjust his stride to stave it off but that made the pain in his left leg worse.

Twenty paces, and he didn't think he could go much further. But he had to; everything depended on surprise and the strength and determination of the leaders. If they failed, the troops behind could not make up the difference. He had to keep going, no matter how much it hurt.

Ten paces. They had to burst through the narrow slot before the enemy realised they were there. If the sentries were alerted, even a handful of soldiers could hold the pass against his little force.

Far below, someone lost their footing, fell with a stifled cry, and a shield went clattering down the rocky slope, making enough noise to rouse sleeping guards. But Klarm's guards would always be at their posts.

'Left!' hissed Flangers and, like the trained soldiers they were, Chissmoul, Nish and Clech went left off the path to the span-high buttress blocking the left side of the pass. Flangers turned right.

'I'll throw you two up and over,' whispered Clech. 'Ready?'

They shrank against the rock face as a guard loomed in the gap, drawing back the shutter of a lantern.

Chissmoul touched Clech's arm to signal that she was. He caught her under the arms and tensed.

The metal shutter scraped and the beam shone down the track, revealing the next four militiamen only ten spans down. 'We're under –' the guard cried, then died with Flangers's knife in his throat.

He fell forward and down. Flangers tore the knife free and shouldered him off the path. As he did, Clech sent Chissmoul flying up onto the top of the buttress, then took Nish under the arms and, with a mighty heave, hurled him after her. Nish landed in black shadow, wrenching his foot again, but recovered and lay prone. Flangers was thrown after him, landed like a cat and caught his arm.

'It's Nish,' Nish said. 'Chissmoul is ahead.'

Behind the other buttress, a lantern was unshuttered momentarily, revealing a group of sentries coming to their feet, half a dozen or more. Good, Nish thought, squinting to protect his vision. They've just lost their night sight and we still have ours.

'We're under attack!' bellowed one of the sentries, and there were a few moments of chaos while they snatched up their weapons. 'Reinforcements, down to the eastern pass!'

In the slot, sword clanged on sword. Clech was trying to force the entrance to the pass all by himself.

'We're in and they don't know we're here,' whispered Flangers, and Nish could tell that he was smiling. The warrior was back in his element at last, and with his vast experience he was worth three ordinary soldiers. 'I'll take these guards from behind. Go up; stay in the shadows and attack the reinforcements as they come.' He crept down the upper side of the buttress.

A long way up the pass, the embers of a small fire glowed faintly, as if through the cracks of a stone fireplace. The camp would be nearby, no doubt, and presumably the other, western entrance to the pass would also be well guarded, though Nish did not know how far away it was. He and Chissmoul headed up.

Swords clashed at the slot; the leading militiamen would have reached Clech by now. Unfortunately they could only fight three abreast and, striking up such a steep slope, would be at a severe disadvantage. And if Flangers fell . . .

'We've got to stop the reinforcements,' Nish said to Chissmoul. 'I'll scout further up. Wait here to ambush any I miss.'

She drew her blade and ducked behind a rock outcrop. From below, Nish heard a grunt and a liquid gush, and prayed that the blood spilled was the enemy's. He ran on tiptoes up the pass, which broadened out towards its crest; here it was ten paces wide. It was almost pitch dark at this level but the growing light had begun to illuminate the snowy top of each peak.

The defenders guarding the western entry to the pass would be over the crest and down, but Nish did not think they would leave their posts without a direct order, in case of an enemy attack from both sides of the range at once. He passed the camp fire, but where was the camp? He could not see any tents.

With a high-pitched whistle, a skyrocket shot up from behind the slot on a column of fire and burst high above the pass in thousands of red sparks that would be visible for leagues. Nish cursed. It was an emergency signal, and Klarm's army couldn't miss it.

The red glare starkly revealed the pass and a neat curve of supply tents fifty paces away against the cliff wall of the white-thorn peak. Scuffling came from the tents – soldiers pulling on their boots; one minute could mean the difference between victory and oblivion.

Ignoring his bruised feet and throbbing leg, he raced for the tents and slashed the ropes along the outside with huge swings of his sabre, then did the same on the other side, collapsing the tents on their occupants.

In the fading light of the skyrocket he saw movement at the end of the closest tent. Nish crept down and, as the first head appeared, took a mighty swing and cut it off. Blood spurted in his face; he dashed it away with his sleeve. A soldier began scrabbling out of the third tent on hands and knees.

Running at him, Nish thrust his sabre through the man's guard and into his side while he was still off-balance. He wrenched out the blade, put his foot in the centre of the soldier's chest and drove him backwards onto the next man.

They were now coming out too quickly to attack. He ran into the darkness and limped back towards the slot, praying that his militia had won through. If it had not, it might be too late.

There was still no light down here, which was to his advantage. He could hear people moving about and talking quietly, though it was impossible to tell if they were his troops or the enemy. He felt another prickle of fear. Had he miscalculated, leaving Chissmoul and Flangers to attack from the rear? She was not trained in hand-to-hand fighting, while Flangers was just one man.

He continued, sabre bared, and just caught sight of the flash of steel, swinging in a huge arc.

'Clech, it's me!' he cried, dropping to the ground. 'What's going on?'

'The guards are dead. We've done it, Nish. The pass is ours.'

'Not yet. Their reinforcements are on the way, maybe thirty. We'll have to try and take them down as they come.'

'No, we won't,' said Clech. 'There they are. Get down.'

He pulled Nish down flat. The running enemy were silhouetted in the dim light at the crest of the pass, and Clech roared, 'Fire!'

A fusillade of arrows whistled overhead from Nish's archers, who were already through the pass, and many of the enemy reinforcements fell. A second salvo took down more, whereupon the rest turned and ran.

'*Now* we have the pass,' said Nish, feeling a quiet satisfaction that they'd won it at so little cost. But how long could they keep it?

'Hold your fire!' said Clech. 'Archers, this way.'

As he and Nish headed up to the crest, a second rocket shot up from further down the mountain behind them, bursting with an ice-blue flare that cast a cold light on the enemy dead and the snowy peaks to either side. The last of the reinforcements were bolting down towards the western gate of the pass.

'That's Klarm's answer,' said Flydd, stepping out from behind a crag and wiping his blade on one of the fallen soldiers. 'He's on his way.'

ELEVEN

The light was growing rapidly now. 'Come on!' Nish yelled. 'We're not done yet. They still hold the western gate.'

He led half a dozen archers down the winding track, pieces of the slaty rock crunching underfoot. The pass was broader here, though it narrowed again towards the western entrance, which was several hundred paces below. It was guarded by eight soldiers plus the three survivors from the tents, and a scrier with a wisp-watcher.

'I knew I'd sensed a scrier,' he said to Flydd.

'Lucky he wasn't watching the eastern side,' grunted Flydd.

'At attack from that side wasn't very likely, fortunately. What do we do with them?' said Nish, though he already knew. With a mighty army approaching, he was going to need every fighter he had, and he could not afford to waste any on guarding prisoners.

'Cut them down. That's what they were going to do to us.'

The archers fired and two of the enemy fell, but the scrier and the other soldiers scrambled over their barricade, out of sight, and by the time Nish and Flydd had reached the gate they were way down the track, out of range.

'I hope we're not going to regret allowing them to escape,' Nish said, studying the defences.

This gate of the pass was, if anything, even more difficult to attack than the other, for the track up to it followed the crest of a knife-edged ridge for the last couple of hundred paces. Only a handful of troops could walk abreast, and barely three for the last fifty paces, where the ground was extremely steep and broken.

The enemy had built a low drystone wall across the entrance, only chest high, but a major obstacle on that slope. Nish would need ten troops to man it, plus reinforcements within shouting distance. Klarm's army was approaching from the other side of the range, but with the air-sled he could drop soldiers anywhere and both entrances to the pass might need to be defended at once.

The light was growing rapidly and for once it was not raining, though it was windy and dank. Now that the action had passed, Nish was cold and hungry, and he could feel every blister and ache. He sent a detail up to ransack the enemy bodies for weapons and provisions.

'And when you've finished, dump them well down the track in Klarm's path. I've got enough sick men and women without having rotting bodies spreading disease.'

'Good idea,' said Flydd. 'His troops will have to pass their dead comrades to get to us, and that won't be good for morale.'

'They're professional soldiers. It'll take more than that to shake them.'

'They're well trained, certainly,' said Flydd. 'But the world has been at peace since Jal-Nish crushed the last opposition seven or eight years ago. Most of his soldiers would never have seen real action, and no amount of training can make up for being blooded in mortal combat, as your militia have been. Until men have experienced that, you never know which of them will fight, which will freeze *and which will run.'*

'I still remember my first battle,' said Nish, with an involuntary shiver.

The pass had been taken at little cost – five of the militia slain, three more severely wounded and unlikely to survive, plus the man who had fallen so noisily and raised the alarm. He had broken both legs and his right hip, injuries that doomed him up here.

Clech had several flesh wounds, while Chissmoul had lost most of her left ear to a skewering blow that could easily have killed her, and several others in the vanguard of the attack had minor injuries, but the rest of the militia had not seen action.

Nish sent down troops to defend the eastern and western entrances, and organised work details to begin laying drystone walls across them so the enemy could not retake the pass as readily as he had done. The captured supply tents contained a good store of weapons, provisions, and dry clothes. After ensuring that everyone was fed with the best there was to offer and plenty of it, he had them change into clean, dry uniforms, and sleep.

Huwld came to Nish several times, bearing food and drink, but he took nothing; his stomach was still clenched so tight that he did not think he could get anything down.

Satisfied that he'd taken care of his people as best he could, Nish and Flydd climbed a spur of the white-thorn peak, where they could look down over the approaches to both the eastern and western entrances. It was fully daylight now, and there was no one in sight in either direction, but with Klarm's enormous army moving this way, Nish could not relax.

'Nice day,' said Flydd laconically.

Nish eyed him warily, unsure if he had recovered from

yesterday's fit of bad temper. 'Every day we stay alive is a nice day.'

Flydd squirted brown wine from a wineskin into his mouth, gagged, swallowed and made a face. 'Yuk! Tastes as though it's been strained through a camel's saddle blanket.'

'Then why drink the filthy stuff? I can smell it from here.'

'It numbs my guts.'

'They're still troubling you, then?'

'With every breath; every step; and every thing I eat. I curse the day I took renewal, Nish, and it's getting worse, not better; some days I'd sooner be dead.'

'I'm sorry. I hadn't realised it was that bad.'

'Ah, well,' said Flydd, raising the wineskin again. 'I knew the risks. Only great mancers can work the Renewal Spell at all, and more of them die than survive it. And of those who do survive, a good few wish they hadn't.'

Nish couldn't think of any suitable response, so he sat down and looked around, and shortly Flydd perched beside him. A watery sun peeped through the rushing clouds, but exposed to the wind as they were it was chilly, though Nish was not unduly bothered by it. Having spent his early life in the frigid south, he preferred cold to the suffocating, clammy heat he'd endured since coming to Gendrigore.

Patches of snow and grainy ice, which had slid down the steep slopes of the white-thorn peak, lay in crusted heaps on those parts of the pass where the sun did not reach, though elsewhere the ground consisted of bare rock or slaty rubble.

High above to their left a ridge extended out into the enormous overhang he'd noted previously, resembling a beaky old man's nose. Its bridge and tip were covered in a thick sheet of ice, and as he stared at it Nish's dormant clear-sight flashed on for a few seconds and he saw that at the end of the nose the ice was fissured. The wind howled around the bulbous tip and through a pair of shallow caves on the lower side, like flaring nostrils.

'I hope that ice doesn't come down on us,' he said, adjusting the staff, which had grown hot again.

'It looks solid enough,' Flydd said carelessly, offering a lump of cheese and the wine. 'Though I dare say pieces fall off when the weather warms up.'

'I think this *is* warm weather, up here.' Nish gnawed on a rind of cheese but did not take the proffered wine skin. He was too tired and, with the enemy likely to attack at any time, could not afford to dull his wits. 'Well, Xervish, against the odds we did it.'

'Very satisfactory,' said Flydd, rubbing his hands together. 'I never imagined we could take the pass at all, much less that we'd capture it at so little cost.'

Nish looked down. 'We lost nine dead or doomed in the attack,' he said quietly. 'I don't call that a *little* cost.'

'When you go to war, you have to expect casualties.'

'I do, but I'll never get used to ordering my friends and comrades to their deaths.'

It was a disagreement they'd had many times over the years, and he did not have the strength to repeat it. Nish closed his eyes, but saw the blade pierce Gi's heart, then Forzel beheaded, and had to open his eyes again, for all the other deaths he was responsible for, recent and long ago, were waiting in line to torment him and undermine the small satisfaction he'd taken in the victory.

It's all right for you, his dead seemed to be saying, but what about us? And then there was Maelys. He hadn't entirely given up hope, yet how could she have survived?

'Still, I thank you,' Nish added after a long pause.

'What for?' said Flydd, tearing at a dark strip of leathery dried meat – horse or buffalo.

'For driving me to attempt the impossible. How did you know it *was* possible?'

'I didn't, but I couldn't let Klarm win; not until he's earned it, at any rate.'

'You don't believe we can beat him?'

Nish took off his boots and peeled off the filthy, slimy socks to inspect his feet, which were bruised, swollen and had blisters upon blisters.

'You should have attended to your feet,' said Flydd. 'What's the matter with you?'

'I had to take care of my troops, first.'

'The best way to take care of them is for you to be fit for action.' Flydd stared down the eastern pass, and said, 'Beat Klarm here? If we can, they'll have to make a new Great Tale about it, for it will surely be the greatest victory against the odds of all time.'

'In Gendrigore I was told that a few hundred could hold this pass against an army.'

'That's easy to say when you're fifty leagues away, and full of piss and ale.'

'Once we've walled off the two entrances,' said Nish, 'I reckon we might be able to hold it.'

'We'll make them pay dearly for every life they take, but even if we could slay ten of them for every man of ours, how can the result be in doubt? You've got a hundred and fifty bone-weary troops, if you count the cook's boy, Huwld. Klarm has, what, eight or nine thousand. He can take losses of sixty to our one, and wear us down. There comes a time when even the strongest man can no longer lift his sword, and then he falls. Or Klarm could simply starve us out – which would only take a week and a half.'

'He can't wait that long,' Nish said gloomily. 'The *really wet* season is coming and he's got to get his army down to the lowlands before it hits.'

'Anyway, he's got the air-sled,' said Flydd. 'He can spy out our defences from above, then fly over the pass and drop thirty soldiers behind us, and do it again and again. As long as he can fly, the result can't be in doubt. He may also have flappeters or other flying, flesh-formed beasts.'

Nish's morale was sliding by the second, but he could not give in; the consequences were too dire. 'We've got to think of a way to beat him,' he said dully.

A rain squall swept up the eastern side of the range towards them. Nish shivered, and could not bear to wear his filthy, bloodstained clothes for another minute. 'I'm going down.'

'Good idea. Get some rest. You're going to need it.'

'You haven't slept in days,' Nish retorted.

'I can doze on my feet. I've got a lot to think about.'

Taking the half-gnawed strip of meat from his mouth, Flydd inspected it, looked disgusted, then put it back and headed further up the ridge, swinging the stave. The serpent's green eyes caught the light and momentarily their gleam echoed Flydd's own – at those times when he'd looked at the tears.

Down at the eastern entrance, Nish found an exhausted Flangers supervising a dozen militiamen who were blocking the slot and fitting broken rock together on top of the buttresses, raising walls there so they could not be scaled. Huwld was carrying stone up, running back and forth like a little dervish. Nish eyed the work distractedly – there didn't seem much point when Klarm could fly over on the air-sled.

Chissmoul was slumped on a rock at Flangers's feet, as pale as the snow. The bandage wrapped around her head was bloodstained over her missing ear and she was shivering.

'I'll take over,' said Nish. 'Get some rest, you two, and take everyone but the pass guards with you.'

'You need rest more than I do, surr,' Flangers said stubbornly.

'It's an order, *Lieutenant* Flangers.'

Flangers turned around, staring at him disbelievingly. 'Surr?'

'No man who ever served me has deserved promotion more,' said Nish.

'But . . .'

'Get moving. You're my best and most experienced officer and I can't do without you – well fed and rested.'

'I might say as much to you, *surr*,' Flangers said quietly.

'Where are they?' said Nish that afternoon. 'Why aren't they coming?'

He had cleaned himself up, been to the healers, and slept for five restless hours. Now he was sitting on the wall above the partly blocked slot, looking down the approaches to the pass. It was afternoon yet there was still no sign of the enemy, though the wind was wailing eerily between the peaks and the superstitious Gendrigoreans were muttering about evil ghosts and mad spectres coming for them in the night.

Nish wasn't looking forward to darkness either. The weather was thoroughly miserable; already they'd had rain, sleet and snow, and the last of the wood the enemy had left here had been burned.

Several militiamen, miners back home, had dug chunks from a thin seam of oil shale in the wall of the unnamed peak, and had managed to get the waxy rock to burn, though with clouds of pungent black smoke and a yellow flame that had little heat in it. Still, any fire was better than none and it would be particularly welcome when night fell.

'They can't be far below us, can they?' said Chissmoul.

'It didn't look that way when they fired their signal rocket,' said Flydd. 'I'd say Klarm is deliberately holding back.'

'Why would he do that?'

'He's a prudent man, and he's used to controlling everything. We've shocked him twice in days –'

'Twice?' said Nish.

'He lost five hundred men in the lower clearing yesterday and he can't be sure why. Was that flood just an accident – or did we make it happen with mancery?'

'Or was a higher agency involved?' said Nish. 'Stilkeen! And are we in league with it?'

'I hadn't considered that,' Flydd said thoughtfully, stroking his serpent staff. 'Yes! If we could make him believe that . . .'

He rose, took a turn up to the crest of the pass and back, warmed his hands at the oil-shale fire, on which Huwld the cook's boy was stirring hot soup in a cauldron, and sat down again.

'I don't think he will,' Flydd added, 'but until Klarm understands what happened yesterday and how we got away, he won't move against us. Boobelar will have spilled his guts, but he's an unreliable witness and Klarm will want to see for himself. He's probably searching the clearings and the river now and checking our dead.'

'Before he attacks, he has to know if I'm here,' said Nish. 'And Maelys, and Yggur and you – his prizes and his enemies. If he knows *I'm* here, he's got to extract me alive –'

'Of course he knows you're here. The guards who got away would have told him, and so would your friend Boobelar.'

Nish yawned. 'But not Yggur or Maelys. Boobelar wouldn't have known if they were among us.'

'Klarm's other worry must be how he lost the pass. For a man who takes pride in controlling everything, this defeat would have been an even bigger shock. How did we survive the flood; how did we break his defences with so few? He's got to know before he moves. Get some more sleep, Nish.'

'There's too much to do. I've got to find a way to neu-tralise the air-sled – and his advantage in numbers.'

'You're not indispensable, no matter how much you might like to think so.'

Nish bridled, until he realised that Flydd was baiting him.

TWELVE

The afternoon passed, and most of the night, without a sign of the enemy. An hour and a half before dawn, the mist began to lift.

'They're here,' said Flangers.

Nish looked over the wall and saw a vast carpet of lights fanning out down the mountain from a few hundred paces below them. Though he had been expecting it, the sight so shocked him that he rubbed his eyes and looked again.

'It's still there,' said Flydd from his left, with a mirthless chuckle. 'I wonder what Klarm's plan is?'

'It wouldn't matter if he was the best general in the world,' said Flangers. 'There's only one way to attack, and we've got it covered.'

'We haven't got the air-sled covered,' said Flydd.

Nish glanced upwards, involuntarily, but saw nothing save the jutting, nose-shaped ridge of rock with the ice sheet on top. The cavities at the lower end were hung with icicles, like oozing nostrils.

'Those icicles are hanging above the track,' he said thoughtfully. 'Do you reckon we could shoot some off, down onto the soldiers as they come?'

'Pick the nose and flick it at the enemy, as it were. I like it,' grinned Flydd. 'Though even if you killed a dozen or two, it wouldn't make any difference.'

'It might worry the ones behind them.'

'Klarm will drive them up, no matter how scared they are. We need a better plan, Nish, a shocking, outrageous one. Your hundred and fifty simply can't hold off eight or nine thousand in hand-to-hand fighting.'

'I'm finding your pessimism a trifle irksome, Flydd,' said Nish.

'As I keep telling you, we can't win by defending this place, no matter how stoically. Our only hope is to do something wild and unpredictable.'

'Like what?'

'Attacking Klarm. I'm going after the air-sled.'

'What?' cried Nish. 'It'll be too well guarded. How would you find it, anyhow?'

'I've a feeling my serpent staff might help . . .'

'How?'

'I think it can find the tears,' said Flydd.

That unnerving gleam was back in his eye. What was he really up to? Had the tears been his goal all along? And if he got them, what would he do? Nish wasn't sure whether to hope for his success, or his failure.

'I can't get the tears, if that's what you're thinking,' Flydd said hastily. 'They're almost certainly set to attack anyone who tries to take them from their rightful owner. But I might be able to control the air-sled, if I had a good pilot . . .'

'Chissmoul? She'll never leave Flangers.'

'I think she will, for the right price. Once you've experienced the wonder of flight, it's not easy to give it up.'

Flydd and Chissmoul had only been gone an hour, temporarily and to Nish's mind poorly *cloaked* via a 'trifling mancery' Flydd had worked with the mimemule, when

137

dawn broke, another blue rocket burst high above them and the attack began – from both sides at once.

'So that's why Klarm delayed so long,' Nish said to Flangers as they ran down to the eastern pass, below which the main force was concentrated. 'He must have sent some of his troops around the mountain and over Liver-Leech, guided by Boobelar, and had to wait until they were in position.'

Flangers did not answer, for a company of the enemy's biggest and strongest troops had stormed up the track and reached the wall with only four casualties to arrow fire. Half of the troops began to form living ladders in an attempt to boost men onto the recently constructed walls on top of the buttresses. The rest attacked the guards at the slot, which was now blocked with a head-high barrier of broken slate.

The defenders fired through arrow slots in the barricades and hurled rocks down from the heights, and finally the two surviving soldiers broke and retreated, leaving their backs exposed. Neither survived.

But Klarm sent another attack, and another after that, each time using as many men as could fit on the steep and narrow track, and as soon as each attack was beaten off he ordered another squad up. After several hours, the gully track was littered with so many dead that the attackers could partially shelter behind them. Only the final fifty paces, so steep that the fallen kept rolling away, remained clear.

Everyone took their turn in the slot, hacking down from the barrier at the soldiers trying to climb it, while the archers up top fired until their fingers were raw. The lancers thrust the living ladders away at spear point and the swordsmen fought until they could no longer raise their blades, when they were replaced by fresh militiamen. Huwld was up on top of one of the drystone walls, throwing rocks, along

138

with Aimee and another small woman, plus a militiaman who had been stabbed in the thigh and could not stand up.

By mid-morning at least a thousand of the enemy had fallen, many to Gens the gnomish shoemaker's consummate knife work, in partnership with Stibble the blacksmith's skull-crushing hammer, but Nish knew it had made no difference.

He took his turn at the eastern entrance, and then the western. They were holding the enemy off, at little cost to themselves so far, but the militia were so few that any cost was prohibitive. He kept scanning the sky, expecting Klarm to attack from the air-sled or send a flight of flappeters after them.

Flappeters bothered him most of all, for the huge, flesh-formed beasts could land on top of the defenders and smash down half a dozen of them with one sweep of their tails, or tear the drystone walls apart, and either form of attack would mean the end. Flydd had been right but, try as Nish might, he could think of no clever plan to turn the tables on his enemy.

He kept praying that Flydd would turn up on the air-sled, but there had been neither sight nor sound of it. Flydd and Chissmoul's suicidal plan must have failed.

On the eastern side, where Klarm had troops to burn, the attacks continued until the track was so slippery with blood that the enemy had to spread dry fern fronds on it before they could move. Nish's casualties were mounting too, and he could not afford any of them.

'All quiet at the western entrance,' said Clech, coming up to the top of the pass to report in the afternoon. 'We haven't been attacked in three hours.'

'Why do you think that is?' said Nish, though he had a fair idea.

'I don't think they got many men over Liver-Leech Pass. That trek was hard enough for us, and we walk the mountains all the time. But flatlanders! I'll bet half of them fell over the side.' Clech hawked and spat on the rocks to the side of the path, then headed down to his post.

'So they're saving their strength for the final attack,' Nish mused, 'and it can't be far off. How many of us left, Lieutenant?'

Flangers was being rested from his duties at the eastern defences. 'Just under half – we have seventy-one still on their feet. We've lost at least fifty, killed, and the rest are too badly injured to fight. When I know all is lost I'll put them out of their misery – I'll not have Klarm taking them back for trial and torture. They're heroes, every one, and they deserve heroes' deaths.'

'My Gendrigoreans are as brave as any I've fought beside,' Nish said quietly, 'and I'll see them honoured. Can we last until sunset?'

'I don't know. Do we need to?' Flangers had the look of a man expecting a miracle from Nish, but it wasn't going to happen this time.

'I was hoping Flydd could pull something off, as he's done so often before, but . . . it doesn't look as though he and Chissmoul are coming back.'

'I always thought it was a suicide mission, yet how could I ask her to stay behind when she could fly again? I – I –' Flangers's lower lip trembled; he stiffened it. 'I couldn't hold her back, just for me.'

'And yet,' said Nish, regretting having been so negative, 'if anyone can succeed at such an outrageous attack, it's Xervish. I'm not giving up hope,' he lied, for Flangers's sake. For himself, Nish had given up hours ago. How could Flydd hope to steal the air-sled in the light of day, in the midst of that enormous army?

'Ah, Chissmoul,' said Flangers, bowing his head. 'This is the first time we've been parted since the fatal feast.'

'Fatal feast?' said Nish, who was still thinking about Flydd.

'Ten years ago, at the end of the war, when Jal-Nish turned up so unexpectedly.'

When he had ordered Irisis slain. With an effort, Nish shook off his gloom. 'I'm sure they're alive. Take heart, Flangers; we'll win through yet.'

'You're right,' said Flangers, brightening, 'Flydd is probably waiting for darkness.'

'Then we've got to hold out until he comes. I have a plan.'

'I knew you'd come up with something, surr,' said Flangers. 'What is it?'

His faith in Nish was touching; also burdensome. 'I'm going to climb up to that great nose of rock and see if I can knock some of the ice down on the enemy.'

Flangers's eyes lifted. 'How would you do that, surr?'

'I've a mind to use my serpent staff.'

Nish didn't want to say too much about that, because he wasn't sure it would work. Indeed, he didn't know why he thought it might, save that the staff felt right in his hand and, previously, Flydd had hinted that Nish might be able to use it, when the time came. Sometimes he felt as though the staff was *waiting* for him to use it, and that was worrying. Why *had* Stilkeen left it there? And if it was a trap, what would happen if he did use it?

'Still warm, is it?'

'Warm as ever.'

'It might make a difference,' Flangers said doubtfully.

'It's not much of a plan but it's the only one I've come up with. The ice is directly above the track, and if I can knock enough off it might kill fifty of the scum – even a hundred.'

'It won't stop them, though.'

'No,' said Nish, 'but if it delays them for an hour or two, it'll gain us the time we need.' Assuming Flydd was coming.

Flangers, a good soldier to the last, said, 'How long do you need?'

Nish studied the ice-covered overhang. Climbing up there would take more than an hour, and even if he succeeded in dislodging some ice onto the enemy, it would take another hour to return. There was just enough time to do it before dark, as long as nothing went wrong.

'Three hours. If we haven't succeeded by then, we never will. I'll take Clech – he's a good climber.'

'Then go. We'll give you three hours, whatever it takes.'

THIRTEEN

Clech studied the route up to the nose-shaped ridge, rubbing his bristly jaw, which was covered in black stubble like fine wire. He turned in a circle to check the sky – what could be seen of it between the towering peaks. Nish felt his stomach churn, for the clouds were growing blacker by the minute and the light was fading. It could rain at any moment and, whether it fell as water, sleet or snow, it would make the climb immeasurably more difficult.

'We can't do it by ourselves,' said Clech.

'You sure?'

'I'm a good climber, but not that good – spent too much time fishing. Besides, I'm too heavy to lead, and if I slip we both die. We need a mountaineer.'

Nish frowned. 'One man less at the defences could mean the difference between . . .'

'A quick defeat and a slow defeat?' said Clech, grinning.

Nish marvelled at the Gendrigoreans' capacity to laugh in the most desperate situations. 'Precisely. Who would you suggest?'

'Aimee,' said Clech after a long pause. 'She – she was born near the Range of Ruin, and she's the best climber I know.' He sounded wistful.

'But she's not much bigger than my thumb!' That was a gross exaggeration, but Aimee, who had gone down on the rope after Boobelar escaped, barely came up to Nish's shoulder and was as gracile as a reed.

'People are always putting her down because she's so little, Nish,' Clech said with a hint of reproach. 'It's tough for her, and she tries so hard. You've seen her climb. Aimee's light and strong, like a gecko. She can go places that lumps like me and you would never dare.' He was glowing as he enumerated her qualities. 'She's clever, too. And she doesn't have the reach to fight at the slot, so the defences aren't losing anything if she comes with us.'

'All right, if you can convince her. This is a volunteer mission, remember?'

'She'll volunteer,' said Clech. 'The thing is . . .'

'Yes?'

'Aimee feels a bit useless. She can't take her place in the front line and she's too small to be a good archer – she can't pull a full-sized bow.'

'And she sure can't cook!' Their cook had been killed down in the clearing and Nish remembered Aimee's solitary turn on cooking duty with horror. He would not have thought it possible for anyone to make their dreadful food worse, but she had done it. 'All right, go and get her.'

Clech came back with Aimee beside him, taking three skipping strides to his one. She wore her dark hair in a single plait over her left shoulder and her round brown eyes were fixed on Nish with all the seriousness of a child. Indeed, she looked about twelve, and Nish, who was in his mid-thirties, suddenly felt Flydd's age.

'How old are you, Aimee?'

'Twenty-four.' Her voice was high, childlike, and defensive; little wonder, being a mature woman yet always being looked upon as a girl. 'What do you want me to do?'

'Save us,' said Clech, looking down at her fondly.

'Don't mock me,' she snapped. 'I thought you, of all people –' She broke off, looking confused, though not as confused as Clech.

'I would never mock *you*,' he said.

Nish realised that he had often seen them together. Did they fancy each other? They would make an odd couple, though not the oddest Nish had ever seen. 'Come over here.' He led her to the other side of the pass, where there was a better view of the mountain towering above them. 'How do you rate our chances, Aimee?'

'We're all going to die,' she said without expression.

'I agree, *unless* we can come up with a clever new way to attack the enemy. We've killed well over a thousand of them today, and General Klarm must have lost at least as many again on the way here, to fevers, falls, tropical ulcers, dysentery and the like, but that still leaves thousands of men.'

'What do you want me to do?'

'See the great overhang up there, shaped like a nose?'

It projected from the mountainside for over a hundred spans, before ending in an uptilted knob where the greatest depth of ice had accumulated, many spans deep.

She looked up and sniggered. 'The Emperor's Warty Pizzle, we call it.' Aimee faltered, as if remembering that Nish was the son of the God-Emperor and, despite everything that had been done to him, might take offence at insults to his father.

He restrained a smile. 'And the huge mound of ice? If we can knock a bit of it off, down on the enemy –'

'You'll never do it,' said Aimee. 'The ice will be welded tight to the rock. It would take an earthquake to shake it loose.'

She was quick, Nish had to grant her that. 'There's a

fissure near the end. I saw it with my clearsight, earlier. If I can get to it, I might be able to send the ice *below* the fissure sliding off the Emperor's er, Pizzle.'

'How would you do that, Nish? It's really thick there.'

He swung the serpent staff off his back. It felt warmer than before; almost hot. 'Remember how this glowed white-hot after Stilkeen embedded it into the rock? Those fires still burn inside it, and once I set them free . . .' If he could. Nish prayed he wasn't taking Aimee and Clech up there for nothing.

She shivered and moved a little closer to Clech, who swallowed. Few Gendrigoreans were comfortable with mancery, and there could be no more deadly or unknowable power than Stilkeen's.

'All right,' said Aimee. 'I reckon I can get you up there. And maybe you *can* lever off some ice with your hot snake, but how do we stop the ice taking us with it?'

'I don't know,' said Nish.

'Or are you asking us to commit suicide?'

'I would never ask that of anyone. You're the climber – tell me how we can do it, and survive.'

'There are ropes and climbing irons in one of the enemy's supply tents,' said Aimee. 'There might be a way, but I won't know until I get there.'

'You mean we're going up onto the nose without knowing if there's any way down?' said Clech.

'Yes,' she said softly. 'Though a big dumb lump like you could bounce all the way down on your head without doing any damage.'

He grinned. Clech wasn't easily offended. 'You can jump after me and use my belly for a pillow.'

'It's doughy enough!' she snapped, though Clech was all muscle.

'Is that a yes?' said Nish.

'Yes,' said Aimee. 'We'll head up that cleft.' She pointed to it.

'We'd better move,' said Nish. 'Try to keep out of sight. If Klarm sees us up there, he might guess what we're up to and pull his troops back, out of danger.'

'We'd be doing some good, then,' said Aimee. 'Let's go.'

'You'll need a coat,' said Nish, for Aimee, like the rest of the militia, wore only a long-sleeved shirt, pants and boots. 'It'll be freezing up there.'

'I haven't got one. No one wears coats in Gendrigore; it's too hot.'

'And the enemy greatcoats would go around her four times,' said Clech. 'She can't climb like that.'

'Then we'd better be quick.'

'I am quick,' said Aimee, 'but I'll bet you won't be.'

They gathered ropes, climbing spikes and hammers. Nish slung the serpent staff over his back, and where its spirals pressed against him he could feel the sluggish, churning heat. The warmth would have been welcome, had it come from any other source, but how could anything left behind by Stilkeen be trusted?

Besides, he still did not know how to liberate its heat – assuming it was possible. He felt like a fraud. What would Aimee and Clech think if they knew how little hope he had? And what if his clearsight let him down again?

Though only mid-afternoon, it was almost as dark as twilight and getting darker. As Aimee reached for the first handhold, it began to rain: big, freezing drops with pellets of ice inside. Wisps of mist formed all across the mountainside and the base of the clouds had moved steadily down during the afternoon; it was not far above the top of the nose-shaped ridge now.

The mist would help to conceal them, but if the cloud base dropped much lower they'd be feeling their way in fog.

147

They might not reach the ice sheet before dark, and certainly would not get down again.

The slope here was about fifty degrees, yet Aimee was already three spans up and climbing like that gecko. Clech had been right – she was light, agile and perfectly suited to this kind of work.

'Not so fast,' Clech called, looking more bear-like than ever. He wiped his wet face on the back of his arm and followed, grunting with the effort.

Nish was only a span up the slope when there came a roar from the eastern side, and the furious clash of weapons. His heart jumped and he turned to go down, for the defences could not be seen from here.

'Flangers will handle it,' Clech said quietly.

And if he did not, there was nothing Nish could do. He had to put all other concerns aside and concentrate on his own job.

The first twenty spans were an easy climb, since the rock in the cleft was broken and provided good foot- and handholds, though above the cleft broadened and became shallower until it was just a crease in the side of the mountain. Aimee was going up rapidly, clinging with fingers and toes to handholds that Nish could not even see.

Clech was also moving steadily, but when Nish tried to climb out of the cleft his body felt heavy, his arms and legs weak, and his blistered feet shrieked. The serpent staff seemed to weigh twice as much as before, and it was hot now. I'm not up to this, he thought. I'll never get there.

But that's why Aimee and Clech were with him. 'I'm going to need a hand,' he called.

She came down to him. 'Sorry, Nish. I keep forgetting you're a *gwishin.*'

'A what?'

'It means a foreigner and a flatlander,' rumbled Clech, his

chest heaving as if he were holding back laughter. He exchanged glances with Aimee and a small light danced in her dark eyes.

Nish suspected *gwishin* also had a rude meaning, for the Gendrigoreans were fond of vulgar jokes, though if it did they would never tell him.

'I wouldn't exactly call myself a flatlander,' he said. 'My homeland is rugged enough, though it's in the far south and much colder than here. No one would ever go climbing there for fun.'

Aimee stood up on the steep slope, not even holding on. Her slender fingers were blue from cold. She rubbed them together and put them into her armpits. 'How could anyone live in such a miserable place?'

'We lived well enough,' said Nish. 'I remember sitting by the fire when I was little –'

'Yes?' said Aimee, when he did not go on.

'It doesn't matter.'

Nish hadn't thought about his childhood in years and did not want to now. He had been fond of his sister, who had died a long time ago, but he had not got on with his hard, ambitious father nor his three older brothers, also dead now, who had been just like their father. His mother had been cool and distant, and had driven her children relentlessly.

Where was she now? She had abandoned Jal-Nish after he'd been hideously maimed in a lyrinx attack thirteen years ago. Had that rejection driven him to become the power-crazed loner who had hunted down the Profane Tears, then murdered his own men so no one would realise he had them? Nish often wondered what had turned his father from a hard, calculating man to a thoroughly evil one. He also worried that, in trying to overthrow him, he might end up as bad.

'Nish?' said Aimee.

'Sorry, what did you say?'

'You'd better take these.' She had three metal spikes in her hand, each with a ring on the end.

'As soon as we start hammering spikes into the rock, they'll know we're climbing, and it won't take Klarm long to work out where we're going.'

'What can he do about it?' said Aimee.

'A lot, with the air-sled.'

'These aren't normal climbing irons,' said Clech. 'They must be specially made for the Imperial army.'

Aimee handed Nish one. 'They're split. You jam it in a crack, wind the ring on the end, and it pulls tight.'

The climbing iron was beautifully made, which came as no surprise. Nish's father had always been fascinated with machines and devices, and as God-Emperor he had the means to indulge that passion without limit. Nish turned the ring, holding the spike tightly in his other fist, and the two split pieces of metal moved outwards, forcing his fist open.

'We tested them yesterday,' said Aimee. 'They're easy to tighten, and one spike can hold twice Clech's weight when it's seated in good hard rock.' She threaded a length of rope through three spikes, knotted it and tied the other end tightly around Nish's chest.

'Put the rope over my staff,' said Nish. 'I wouldn't want to drop it.'

As she was doing so, he looked up the mountain and swallowed. Even with irons it wasn't going to be easy to climb up the bulge above them. Distantly he could hear the clang and clash of weapons at the slot. He should be down there, helping them. Nish was the most experienced fighter they had, apart from Flangers, and if he fell the defenders would be leaderless.

'The best way to help them is to get this job done,' said Clech.

Again Nish wrenched his thoughts back to the here and the now. Aimee, who was moving steadily up, called, 'There's a good crack here.'

Climbing was awkward with the serpent staff tied to his back, but Nish heaved himself up to the crack and pushed in the first of his irons. When he turned the ring, the split spike pulled so tightly against the sides of the crack that no heave could budge it. There must be mancery in the spike, or the most brilliant craftsmanship, he thought, ruefully remembering his days as a barely competent prentice artificer.

Nish had used climbing irons before, the kind that one hammered in, usually whacking one's fingers in the process, and these were a luxury. He inserted his three in a vertical line, stood on the middle spike and stretched down to twist out the lower one, but could not quite reach. He'd put the spikes in too far apart.

Unslinging the serpent staff, he went to poke the point of its tail through the ring, but as he touched it the ring rotated, pulling the split spike together, and it fell out of the crack to hang from his rope. Another marvel.

He went up quickly after that, and within minutes had joined Aimee and Clech at the top of the bulge, where a nodular protrusion was wide enough to sit on, assuming one had no fear of heights. Nish wasn't terrified of heights but he had a healthy respect for them, so he pushed in a spike first and tightened the rope around his chest.

The cloud base was just above their heads now, an undulating layer of white cutting off all sight of mountains and sky. 'I'm not looking forward to going up through that,' said Nish. 'How are we going to find the way?'

'But you studied the side of the mountain from the pass,' said Aimee. 'Surely you remember where to go?'

'I'm not good at that kind of thing.'

She looked at him pityingly. 'Lucky you've got us.'

'I give thanks for my good fortune every minute,' he said drily.

'From here we head up to the right,' she said, 'around the curve of the mountain towards the bridge of the nose. If the wind comes up and blows the clouds away, anyone looking up will see us, so we'd better be quick.'

'Rope together now,' said Clech.

They did so. Aimee scrambled up through the cloud base and they followed into a clammy white-out where Nish could barely see the rock he was clinging to. The slope wasn't as steep here, and there were more handholds, but every surface was wet and it was very cold. He had not been really cold for a long time – before he'd come to Gendrigore, certainly, six weeks ago.

The wind had dropped and it was only drizzling now, though it was darker than ever and another downpour could not be far off. Nish tried to move faster, but it proved impossible in the miserable conditions.

There was no sound save their heavy breathing, the click of metal spikes on stone and, muffled through the fog, intermittent sounds of fighting below at the slot. The rope running up from his chest faded into whiteness within a span; he could see nothing save the moss- and lichen-covered rock.

There was no other sign of life, no sounds from above, and after a while his mind began to play tricks on him. Was he heading up the slope, or down it? His eyes told him down, even though the strain on his legs proved he was going up, and now he began to doubt that there was anyone else on the other end of the rope.

What if he reached the top and Jal-Nish was waiting there, luring him to Stilkeen? The idea was absurd, but it would not go away, for there was no end to his father's cunning and he loved to set people up, allowing them to think

152

they'd won, just for the pleasure of bringing them down and crushing them utterly.

He had sacrificed an army once so that Nish would think he'd had a great victory, then mocked him for believing it. The revelation had been shattering; only now was Nish recovering his self-confidence.

'Clech?' he said softly.

'Is something wrong?' Clech replied.

'No, I just wanted to be sure you were there.'

'Where else would he be?' came Aimee's high, scornful voice.

'This mountain is an uncanny place,' muttered Clech. 'I feel it too.'

They headed across an icy patch where Nish never felt secure, despite the spikes. The mist was thinner here, Clech a lumbering shadow a couple of spans ahead. Nish only saw Aimee fleetingly but he could hear her teeth chattering, and once she must have dropped a spike for he heard the metal ring off rock, and her muffled curses.

'I'm level with the Emperor's Warty Pizzle,' she called shortly, shivering in her thin clothing. 'What now?'

Nish climbed up to her. A few spans to his right the rock swelled into a broad, out-jutting ridge crusted with smooth ice – the bridge of the nose. Nothing could be seen beyond that, though he knew that the nose broadened further down before a knob of black rock at the tip, which acted as a dam for the ice. Somewhere, way down there, was the flaw or fissure he'd seen with clearsight, but unless it returned there was no way of telling where that flaw was.

'Down to the end. I'll know the spot when I get to it.' He hoped. 'I'd better go first.'

He edged across, only now appreciating what he was trying to do. The bridge of the nose was about twenty spans

153

across and ran down steeply. The ice sheet was thin here but he'd seen from below that it grew ever thicker towards the tip.

Clech anchored the rope to a spike, tested it and nodded. Nish moved down onto the ice, which felt rough beneath his boots though it looked smooth further down, where the wind swept across the top of the ridge. Aimee stopped at the edge of the ice sheet and waited.

He continued slowly, choosing each step with care. 'I can't see any cracks. We'll have to hammer spikes directly into the ice.'

'They'd want to go awful deep,' said Aimee, and for the first time he could hear tension in her voice. 'Solid rock is one thing, but trusting our lives to brittle ice is quite another.'

'They'll hear us hammering,' said Clech. 'Can we scramble along the side of the nose?'

Nish's throat tightened at the thought. This side was almost sheer and the dark granular stone was partly covered by overhanging ice like the roof of a thatched cottage, with down-thrusting icicles as long as javelins. 'That would take forever, and I'm already worried about the time. We'll have to risk the bridge of the nose.'

He headed down the ice. The first few steps were secure enough, where the surface was corrugated, but beyond that point the ice was glassy where it had partly melted and refrozen, and there were no crevices in it. Taking a hammer from his pack, Nish bent to tap a spike into the ice and his feet went from under him.

He landed on his back, banging his head painfully, then slid over the edge, and there was nothing he could do about it. He tried to jam the spike into the ice but he was moving too fast.

'Brace!' cried Clech, but Aimee did not have time; Nish's

weight pulled her off the ridge and they fell together, separated by a span and a half of rope.

The rope pulled tight around Nish's chest and he stopped with a jerk that snapped his head backwards. Above him, Aimee cried out as his weight tightened the rope around her chest. If Clech lost his footing his massive weight could rip the climbing iron out of its crack.

He grunted, and Nish saw him being pulled forwards, but Clech bent his knees to absorb the shock and slowly stood up. 'I've got you. Don't struggle or swing on the rope; it's slippery underfoot.'

Nish revolved on the end, the rope so tight around his chest that he could hardly breathe, and one of the hot curves of the serpent staff was gouging into the middle of his back. His head swam; he closed his eyes until it passed and, when he opened them again, Clech was pulling himself backwards until his boots were on firm rock. He heaved on the rope and Aimee gasped.

'What's the matter?' he cried, peering anxiously at her.

'Think I've broken a rib,' she said in a high voice. 'Don't jerk the rope like that.'

'Sorry.' He began to draw in the rope smoothly, hand over hand, watching her all the while.

Nish could see the strain on her face, the spasms that wracked her with every movement, no matter how careful Clech was, and it could not be otherwise with Nish's weight pulling the rope crushingly tight around her little frame. If the broken rib punctured a lung she would die.

He shook off the morbid thoughts. There was nothing he could do to ease her pain save to keep as still as possible.

'Hurry it up, you big oaf,' said Aimee, her voice cracking. 'Slow is nearly as bad as fast.'

Clech pulled her up, tied her to a spike and she lay on her back while he recovered Nish, then unfastened her chest rope. Nish undid his own; his ribs were aching and he could feel a groove around his sides where the rope had cut into him.

Aimee pulled up her shirt. Clech flushed and looked away. 'Don't know nothin' about healing,' he mumbled.

Nish crawled across. 'I've seen plenty of broken ribs on the battlefield.'

Her ribcage wasn't much bigger than a large turkey's. One rib, low down under her left breast, was clearly broken, and the surrounding flesh was bruised and swollen, though he did not think there was any internal damage – so far. He managed to bend the broken end of the rib out a little. She clenched her teeth, and tears formed in her eyes, but she did not cry out. Nish knew he would have.

'Is that the only broken rib, Aimee?'

'How would I know?' she snapped.

'I'll have to check . . .'

Her cheeks went a ruddy colour, then she pulled her shirt up above her little breasts. 'Get on with it.'

He traced the ribs along, one by one, and she winced several times, though she made no sound.

'Nothing else broken,' said Nish, binding her chest with strips of cloth torn from the tail of his shirt, to immobilise the rib as much as possible, 'though you're going to be sore –'

Aimee whipped her shirt down again. 'We came to do a job, so let's get on with it.'

FOURTEEN

'We can't risk the ice again,' said Clech. 'And the rock on this side looks solid all the way along. I don't see anywhere we can put in a spike.'

'Then we'd better go to the other side,' said Nish. Having come this far, he was determined to find a way.

Another round of sword blows echoed up from the slot – or were they coming from the western side of the pass? He could not tell, but if the militia were being attacked in force from the western side as well, it must surely signal the final onslaught.

They roped together, though this time Clech fashioned rope harnesses which would distribute the strain more evenly if they fell. Nish did not want to contemplate that. They would not be so lucky a second time.

'I'm not sure about this crutch rope,' he said. Whichever way he moved it, it lay across a sensitive part of him. 'If I fall, it's really going to hurt.'

Aimee smirked, which in the circumstances he had to ignore.

'This time *I'll* go first,' she said pointedly. 'You're not a good enough climber to go along the side of the nose. Stay here until we get back.'

'I can't,' Nish said tersely, for his chest hurt more every minute, and he wondered if he might not also have broken a rib. 'You don't know where the flaw in the ice is –'

'You said it was near the end of the nose.'

'That's a big area. Besides, you don't know how to shift the ice.'

'How are *you* going to shift it?' said Clech.

'With the serpent staff.' He hoped. It had grown hot when he'd first seen the fissure in that flash of clearsight.

Aimee gave an audible gulp. Clech's eyes flicked nervously away.

'All right. Follow me,' she said. 'Clech, don't move until Nish is spiked down, and whatever you do, don't fall. We'd never haul your great mass of blubber up again; we'd have to cut you loose.'

The joke fell flat, for they all knew it to be true. Her eyes glistened, then she turned away abruptly and began to move along the outer curve of the nose, just before it dropped away almost sheer. The ice sheet formed a thick curved cap over the top and overhung the sides, ending in a ragged fringe of icicles, many as thick around as Nish's thigh.

'If we climb in underneath the ice we might find it easier,' said Aimee.

Nish doubted it, but he wasn't the mountaineer, so he nodded stiffly.

'Fix on tight,' she added. 'I'll swing in.'

He fixed a spike in a crack, checked it twice and said, 'Go.'

Aimee lowered herself over the edge, between a pair of icicles, and began to swing back and forth, a spike ready in her right hand. The rope tightened on Nish's harness, digging into his chest and groin. He could hardly bear to watch as she moved in and out between the icicles, and could not see how she would get a grip on the steep rock behind them, halfway down the side of the nose.

The rope tightened and she didn't come out.

'Aimee?' he called, his voice cracking. If she fell, he would not know until her weight came onto his line.

After a long pause she said, 'Fixed it good and tight. Come down.'

He glanced up at Clech, who nodded. 'Ready.'

Nish looked over the edge, not liking the thought of hanging over that terrible fall again, with just a rope between himself and oblivion, especially since it could all be for nothing. What if he got to the flaw in the ice and could not unleash the fire in the serpent staff?

What if clearsight failed him again? He unclenched his jaw, which he'd clenched so tightly that his back teeth were aching, and began to go down.

Shortly he was hanging on the line, looking in underneath the ice. Aimee was standing up on a narrow ledge, holding the rope for him.

'Swing in between the icicles,' she called.

He swung his legs back and forth, though it did not move him inwards measurably. He swung harder, to no effect. 'Sorry, I'm just not a mountaineer.'

'I'll have to pull you in,' sighed Aimee, rolling her eyes.

She gave a great heave on the line just as Nish swung forwards, legs wide, and he tilted over and slammed, groin first, into an icicle the width of a flagpole.

'Aaahhh!' he roared, then cut off the involuntary cry, praying that it had not been heard. Tears welled in his eyes; he doubled up as the pain rang right through him, and began to revolve on the rope.

'Sorry,' said Aimee, turning him the other way until the rope untwisted, then pulling him between the icicles, under the lip and onto the ledge.

Nish lay there with his knees drawn up, for the pain was so bad that he could not move. By the time it began to diminish, Clech was down and onto the ledge without incident.

'We'll leave that spike in place,' said Aimee, 'so we can get out again.' She looked down at Nish, evidently deciding that he was all right and it was time to get her own back. A mischievous light danced in her round eyes. 'Do you want me to check, in case you've broken something?'

Clech chuckled.

Why was a blow to the male groin so damned amusing? 'No thanks,' Nish said curtly. 'Can we get on?'

'It looks like an easy climb from here down to the knob of the Emperor's Pizzle,' said Aimee, still grinning. 'We can follow this ledge most of the way, then step down onto a lower ledge for the last bit.'

The ledge sloped outwards, was icy and at no point was more than Nish's foot's length across, yet, compared to what they had done already, it would be an easy path. He could just make out the lower ledge in the drifting mist, but not where it led to.

With the marvellous split spikes securely embedded in the rock he felt relatively safe negotiating the upper ledge and then the lower one, until it petered out at the side of the knob. Here the mass of ice overhung so thickly that, even when Aimee swung well out from the ledge on her rope, she could not see the side.

'It's worse than I'd thought,' she said, swinging back. 'I don't know how we're supposed to get up on top from here. Where was the flaw in the ice sheet, Nish?'

'It can't have been far from here . . .' *I hope.* 'Keep looking. I'll try my clearsight again.'

'While you do, we'll go under and check the other side.'

Clech and Aimee spiked on and made their way under

the tip of the nose out of sight, leaving Nish alone on the ledge. He checked that his spikes were tight and his rope secure, and closed his eyes the better to use clearsight.

It didn't come but he was not unduly concerned – he often had to fight to get anything out of it. He'd always supposed that was due to his clearsight being created by his father's Profane Tears – and they would not want to help him unless he was in the most dire peril.

It was miserable here, for the overhanging ice seemed to be radiating cold down on him, while the icicles reminded him unpleasantly of the bars of his stinking cell in Mazurhize prison, where he'd spent ten agonising years, aching with grief for Irisis, fighting his father, and failing every time. The wind had picked up and began to shake the transparent tips of the icicles, fetching brittle notes out of them.

He strained until his heart pounded and he felt it skip a couple of beats, but the cursed clearsight told him nothing. A shriek echoed up from the slot, someone dying in agony. How many of his militia were left, out of the five hundred who had set out from Gendrigore in such high spirits a few weeks ago? Fifty? Forty? Thirty? At this rate they'll all be dead by sunset, Nish thought. I gambled with their lives and lost.

The wind was hissing between the icicles now, generating a mournful humming like a hymn for the dead. The mist whipped around him, then thinned until he could see, as though through a strip of gauze, the enemy advancing steadily up the gully towards the eastern entrance. The line appeared to extend down for half a league, and they were moving with a deadly purpose. Had the pass fallen?

He could not tell, for a patch of mist clung to the slot. He strained to see through it, heart hammering, then it blew away and he made out his proud, exhausted defenders, standing in an arc behind the blocked entrance, ready to reinforce the men holding it when they fell, or became so exhausted that they could no longer wield a sword. Tears stung his eyes. He tried to count the defenders but could not complete the tally, for they kept moving. Certainly less than fifty, though.

And the enemy? Nish could tell, without counting, that there were three or four hundred on the upper track, while the blur of red uniforms extending down the gully and spreading across the lower mountainside to their encampment must contain thousands of men.

They did not matter, though. The hundreds on the upper track were sufficient to finish the job, and even if he could wipe a few dozen out with some falling ice, it would amount to no more than a punch in the nose for Klarm. The end was no longer in doubt.

I don't suppose it ever was, Nish thought wearily. Did I ever *really* hope to defend the pass and hold the enemy back? Only around the camp fire on the first few days, when the wine was flowing and the Gendrigoreans were treating the affair as a great adventure, a walk in the mountains and then a triumphant return, unscathed.

They had never expected to see the enemy, much less fight them, for the Range of Ruin had, one way or another, beaten every army to invade their little nation in the past thousand years. Nish had hoped and prayed that it would defeat his father's army, too, though deep down he'd known that it would not. Jal-Nish was too powerful, and too careful. He could not bear to lose, so he made sure he thought of everything that could go wrong before he set out.

Everything except Stilkeen!

Distantly Nish made out the gentle tapping of Aimee inserting her spikes into ice. Nish could tell it was her, because she did it delicately, while Clech drove his spikes

162

home with a single forceful blow. It didn't sound as though they would be back in a hurry and now, studying the arrangement of forces below, Nish knew the end was not far away. If he was to bloody Klarm's nose in a last futile act of defiance, he had to act at once.

Taking the serpent staff off his back and gripping it below the head, he held it up. Again he sensed that fiery heat churning within it. His head throbbed twice and the eyes of the serpent appeared to blink, though when he looked again they were solid iron like the rest of it.

But the ice wasn't. The light brightened a little and he saw that, some distance beyond the end of the ledge, the overarching dome of ice had a flaw in it. It was visible as a faint blue line curving across the base. Was that the fissure he'd seen from below, with clearsight? He could not tell from here; he had to get closer.

'Clech!' he yelled. 'Aimee, I think I've found it.'

No reply. He called again, but did not expect an answer, for they must be on the other side of the nose by now and his voice would not be heard over the wind.

There wasn't time to go after them – the slot could be taken in minutes and, once it had been, the pass was lost and their efforts up here would be wasted.

The serpent staff was even hotter now, almost burning him. Was it trying to tell him something? It had to be and, acting on intuition, Nish poked the ice at the end of the ledge with the tail. *Sssss.* The ice liquefied, revealing that the ledge continued on.

Anxious about the time, he unfastened his rope, left it hanging from the spike and stepped out, his boots taking a comforting grip on the rough surface. He prodded ahead and again, with a faint hiss, the ice turned to water, revealing the ledge beneath.

Nish wasn't consciously doing anything with the Art – he

had no gift for it – so it had to be the staff. To test it he reached behind him and prodded a wart of ice sticking out from the side. Nothing happened, yet whenever he touched the ice ahead it liquefied.

How did the staff know where he needed to go? Was it still linked to the caduceus, or to Stilkeen? Surely it must be. Because he was doing what Stilkeen wanted?

Afraid that he was, Nish grounded the staff for a moment, then continued, knowing that he had no choice. The ice grew ever thicker above him, the curved flaw brighter, but how was he to dislodge the ice from beneath and survive? Or was he meant to die in the attempt?

He looked back but there was no sign of Clech or Aimee. He prodded the rock ahead; this time nothing happened. Had he used up the power of the staff already? Surely not – it belonged to an immortal *being*.

He reached towards the curving flaw in the ice and it melted and flowed before he had touched it. The staff was definitely leading him, but where? How could it know, anyway? And then he had a really unpleasant thought. What if Stilkeen could see out of the serpent's eyes?

He shuddered and almost threw the staff away, thinking that he held a *live* iron snake. Or did its master maintain a presence within it? He started to turn the head of the staff towards him, then stopped hastily. If Stilkeen was looking out through those eyes, Nish definitely did not want to look into them.

With no other choice, he followed the path which the staff was melting, up through the base of the ice just before that curving fissure. Now, with each probe of the serpent's tail, the ice above him turned to water and gushed down on his head and shoulders.

Nish had to keep wiping his face before the water refroze. Shaking from the cold, he dragged himself up the slick-walled meltwater cavity by digging a spike into the ice. His clothes crackled with every movement and shed tiles of ice below him. His boots filled with water but Nish dared not stop to empty them. There wasn't time.

He squelched up and up, feeling the water turning to a churned-up mush in his boots; he had to stamp harder to keep the blood circulating. He had climbed several spans up into the ice sheet, following a path coiled like a corkscrew, and with every step it grew darker.

What would happen if he reached the flaw – indeed, in such gloom, how would he know he had? What if he broke through it? If the ice at the tip of the nose began to slide, with him inside, there would be no way out. Stilkeen's revenge?

And yet, one quick death was much the same as another and there was no point dwelling on it. He continued corkscrewing up and shortly realised that it was lighter above him than below – he must be near the top of the ice sheet. Quick, now! Nish thrust up the tip of the staff as hard as he could and, with a hiss like water spilled on a hotplate, broke through.

He scrambled up onto the top of the ice and found that the rising knob at the end of the great nose was not far below him, like the wall of a dam holding back the monumental mass of ice.

He scuttled down the slippery surface, over a narrow, deep crevasse a couple of spans from the end of the ice sheet, and thence onto the solid, secure rock of the knob. Behind him, the crevasse in the ice went down for spans; it had to be the flaw he'd seen from below.

But would the staff unbind the ice below the crevasse and make it fall? He crawled to the tip of the knob and peered over, careful not to make a silhouette against the sky.

His militia still held the slot, but bands of the enemy were hauling up scaling ladders made from slender tree trunks, which they must have carried for leagues, since there were no trees within sight. Nish could not imagine how the enemy would stand their ladders against the barricades on the steep ground on either side of the slot, but with enough men they could hold them in place by hand. Why didn't the militia shoot them?

None of Nish's archers were firing; they must have used all their arrows. Gloom settled over him – the pass must fall within minutes. Aimee and Clech weren't visible from the left side or the right, nor did they answer his calls. He presumed they were still on the other side of the nose, looking for a way up.

After emptying out his boots and wringing the water from his socks, he tried to decide what to do. He could not wait, for hundreds of the enemy had massed far below him in the broad, shallow bowl where he had almost fallen in the assault on the slot. The instant the scaling ladders were up, they would rush the slot and burst through by sheer weight of numbers.

'Clech, Aimee!' he called, as loudly as he dared. Still there was no reply.

Nish paced back and forth on the centre of the knob. If he freed the ice at the end and they happened to be climbing it, they would die. But if he waited much longer, the pass, the battle and the war would be lost.

Besides, the ice could take a while to get going, and in the unlikely event that Clech and Aimee were on the small wedge at the end, they should have time to scramble back to safer ground. At least, he hoped so.

He had to act now. He went back to the crevasse, which ran across the ice for three or four spans. Ice must fall every summer, he thought, although that was still some months

166

off. Yes, that must be how the bowl had formed below him, the successive impacts of thousands of years of ice smashing the surface to dust and grit.

'Here goes,' Nish muttered, and raised the staff.

Again the serpent's eyes glittered, but this time a pearly drop appeared at the tip of each fang. He shook the drops off before they landed on his wrist and they fell into the crevasse.

He checked the fangs, which thankfully were clear of any more venom, and was lowering the tail of the staff into the crevasse, hoping it was the right thing to do, when he made out an echoing, satisfied *ssss*. The ice let out a mournful groan, and the whole ridge shuddered.

'Nish?' came Aimee's voice from way below him, echoing hollowly up the hole he'd melted in the ice.

'Up on the centre of the knob,' he said in a low but carrying tone.

'What have you done?' She sounded afraid.

'Nothing yet, but I'm about to. Are you spiked on?'

The ice gave a deeper groan.

'No, we're coming up your tunnel.'

Nish had a sudden vision of coming disaster, and nearly choked. 'Go back to the ledge and spike on, *quick!* Keep your heads down and hang on tight.'

He heard her speaking to Clech, then their scrambling footsteps. Was she going down or coming up? Either way he could do nothing to help her for, with a *crack, crack, crack*, the crevasse lengthened to left and right, breaking the tight weld of ice to rock, then widening and deepening until he could see down three spans, five, now all the way down.

Way down there, something as pearly as snake venom shimmered, *ssss*. With a deeper groan, the last ice-weld tore and the wedge of ice below the crevasse cracked in the middle and began to slide to left and right.

'Aimee?' Nish shouted over the noise. 'Run!'

There was no reply. She would not have heard him over the grinding and crackling. The whole out-jutting nose seemed to be shaking now, its knobbly tip shuddering so hard than he fell to his knees. Icicles were falling from the fringes of the ice sheet. He scrambled down towards the steeply sloping tip of the nose, heedless of the danger, and looked to left and right, but Aimee and Clech were still concealed by overhanging ice.

The troops gathered in the bowl were staring up – he could make out the ovals of their upturned faces. Could they see him? There was no point in concealment now – indeed, they should know that the coming ice fall was no accident, but the deliberate action of their enemy. And so should his militia, who needed all the help they could get.

Finding a secure place to stand on the tip of the quivering knob, he stood up straight and waved his arms. The enemy troops cried out, and pointed. Someone aimed a crossbow up at him, but Nish gave him the finger; being an expert with that weapon, he knew that he was out of range.

A chunk of ice the size of a mammoth separated from the left-hand side, below the crevasse, and fell. He watched it dwindling in size as it hurtled down, and the soldiers frantically scrambling to get out of the way.

It was too late for the dozen directly underneath, for the ice slammed into the ground, smashing to fragments which knocked down every surviving soldier in the bowl and many on the track above. The shattered ice turned red.

The rest of the soldiers got up again and stumbled for the sides of the bowl, but a horn sounded and, like the disciplined troops they were, they pulled together into a line. At the slot the fighting had stopped, for the impact had brought down the scaling ladders and broken rungs off two of them. The attackers drew back some fifty paces, out of rock-throwing range, to repair their ladders, but that would not take long.

More ice fell from the left, and then the right, the last of the mass below the crevasse. Nish looked over and cursed. The twin impacts had knocked the soldiers lined up around the bowl off their feet again, but few seemed to have been harmed this time. After all the effort it had taken to get up here, he'd hope for a bit more damage.

The horn sounded and officers shouted orders. The ladders had been repaired, the attackers were advancing towards the barricades again, and the soldiers in the bowl were about to move up for the final onslaught.

Suddenly the ice sheet went *creak-crack* as if it had been twisted in two hands; crisscross cracks appeared on its upper surface, and Nish felt a sudden and terrible foreboding.

It had never occurred to him that the whole vast ice sheet might fall, and if it did, he would almost certainly be thrown off the knob. The ice groaned and hundreds of icicles, each longer than a man, broke away. Most shattered harmlessly on the rocky slopes, but one or two soldiers collapsed in red, silent messes.

Another few chunks of ice fell into the bowl, missing the soldiers crossing it, though the impacts knocked one or two down. They soon got up and appeared to be unharmed.

'It's safe now,' Nish heard an officer bellow. 'A thousand pieces of gold to the squad that takes the pass. Go!'

The scaling ladders were being carried up and the leading attackers were approaching the slot. Nish eyed the ice, which was still groaning, still creaking. The crisscross cracks over the top had widened a little, but the ice sheet had not moved at all. It must be still frozen tightly to the bridge of the nose.

Nish clambered off the knob, down several spans, then

169

up the steep end of the main ice sheet, where it had been split by the crevasse. At the top he prodded the ice, hoping to dislodge some more, but nothing happened. Why not? Why had the staff showed him the way, and assisted his passage through the ice sheet, then stopped helping him?

A great mancer might have been able to free the ice, but he could not, for he did not know how to use the power locked within the serpent staff.

Unless he was being too timid. Perhaps that was the answer – Stilkeen certainly wasn't timid. Raising the staff high, Nish speared the tail-tip of the iron serpent down, the way Stilkeen had buried his caduceus deep in rock.

'Ice, shatter!' he roared.

Cracks radiated out from the tip of the staff, met the crisscross cracks on the surface and kept going, and without warning the ice dropped beneath his feet. What do I do now, he thought, sure he was going to be carried away with the ice. The surface was too slippery to run up so, ripping the staff out, he scrambled back down the steep face, then up onto the wildly shaking rock knob.

He only just made it as, with a deafening roar and crackle, the ice sheet broke apart and began to slide over the sides of the nose. A monstrous ice-fall poured down towards the bowl and the track above it, where it shattered to fragments on impact and swept down the slope.

More ice followed it, and more, until it was all gone and the great nose of rock jerked upwards from the release of weight. Nish, thrown onto his belly, clung on desperately as the end of the nose quaked up and down.

He crawled to the edge, hanging on as the rock continued to twitch, and looked over. The multiple impacts had shaken the track so powerfully that not a single enemy was left standing. Many went hurtling over the sides of the gully, or rolling and thumping down towards the bowl, where he lost sight of them under a roiling cloud of smashed ice.

Below the bowl, the ice poured down the steep, narrow gully until it appeared to form a glacier, save that the shattered ice was hurtling down with the speed of an avalanche. It overwhelmed the climbing soldiers as though they were ants and carried them down with it, all the way to the red-uniformed blur of the army encampment on the mountainside far below.

The avalanche could not last, Nish knew. It must spread out and lose force before it reached them. The army must have thought so too, for the soldiers in the camp were not moving.

Now they began to run; red masses surged to left and right, but the roaring avalanche wall was travelling twenty times as fast. It carved through the camp, white through red, sweeping it away out of Nish's sight, and the following clouds of ice dust covered all.

When it had settled, there was no sign of the army. It hadn't been Jal-Nish's entire army, Nish felt sure, but certainly a good part of it. A few enemy survivors still clung to the slope above the bowl, which was now a glittering oval of pulverised ice, but Nish did not think they would attack.

Utterly demoralised and leaderless, they began making their shaky way down. There would be no attack tonight, but tomorrow, in all likelihood, the survivors below would pull back together and the onslaught would resume with even greater fury. Klarm would make them pay for this monstrous humiliation.

The roar of the avalanche faded. Nish rubbed his ringing ears and headed back up the knob to look for Aimee and Clech.

'Help!'

The thin, feeble cry came just on the edge of hearing.

Aimee! He looked over the edge, back along the left-hand side of the nose. From spikes embedded there a rope ran down, as taut as a wire cable.

From the rope, another five or six spans down, hung Clech. Aimee dangled below him from the harness secured around his enormous chest. And from where Nish stood, he did not see any way of saving them.

Fifteen

Why hadn't he waited one extra minute? But there was no profit in that train of thought. The deed had been done.

Nish slung the staff onto his back, scrambled down and followed the ledges across to the spikes from which Clech's rope was suspended. They were tight; there was no danger of them pulling out, but that wasn't the problem.

'I'm sorry,' he yelled. 'The ice was already moving, and . . . and the enemy were storming the slot. I couldn't wait any longer or –'

'You don't have to explain,' said Clech. 'You've always looked after us as best you could.' He looked down at Aimee, slowly revolving on the line below him. 'How is your . . . er, chest?'

'Painful!' she snapped, then, softly, 'I think I've broken another rib.'

'Can you climb up the rope to me?'

'Don't think so. Every time I move, I get a sharp pain here.' She indicated her right side, midway down. 'The broken rib is sticking into something.'

Her lung, Nish thought. 'What are *you* like at climbing

ropes, Clech? I don't think I'm strong enough to pull you both up.'

'I'm hopeless,' said Clech. 'And the rope is wet.' He clenched his fists around the rope, high up, strained, and managed to raise himself a third of a span, but could not maintain his grip and slid down again.

'Aaahh!' cried Aimee.

Now Nish was really worried, for it had been the tiniest of jolts. If the rib was sticking into her lung, any jerk could puncture it. 'I'll have to let down my rope and lift you separately.' Though even if he could get Aimee onto the ledge, how was she going to climb down to the pass with broken ribs?

'Where's your rope, Nish?' said Clech.

'I left it attached when I went up the tunnel in the ice . . .' The rope was gone, and so were his spikes, torn out of the rock by the ice fall. 'No matter. I'll just have to lift you both.'

Clech and Aimee exchanged glances. 'It can't be done,' Clech said quietly. 'Get going, Nish. You've got to save yourself.'

'I'm not leaving you.'

He moved across to their spikes, found a secure place to stand on the narrow ledge, then, taking hold of the rope, heaved with all his strength. Nothing happened save that the wet rope scorched across his palms as it slipped. He had not raised Clech the width of a hand, and he knew he never would. The load was far too heavy.

'You're at least half the weight of a buffalo,' he muttered.

'Sorry,' said Clech.

Though he knew it was hopeless, Nish could not give in that easily. He heaved until he could feel his face going purple and coloured spots floated before his eyes, and he kept on heaving until the pain in his scarred left hand was unbearable.

174

'Keep doing that and you'll burst your bowels,' said Aimee. 'Nish, you can't save us. Pull me up, Clech – gently, you great lug!'

Clech pulled her up until her chest was level with his. 'Are you all right?'

'I'm cold. Hold me.'

The wind had risen again and was whistling through the few remaining icicle stumps. Clech tied off her rope so she would not slip down, and wrapped his arms around her. She winced, then snuggled against his chest.

Nish clenched and unclenched his aching fingers, waiting for the pain to diminish so he could try again. He closed his eyes as he ran through his artificer's training of twenty years ago. There had to be a way to lift them. Could he run the rope through the rings of several spikes, so as to make a crude pulley? Not without unfastening the rope first.

If only Flydd had succeeded in stealing the air-sled, he could have carried them all to safety. For that matter, with the air-sled they could have flown up here and done the job in minutes.

Nish had not heard its characteristic whine since they had left the clearing, which was curious. If he were in Klarm's position he would have personally directed the attack from high above the pass, or even dropped troops at the crest with it, to attack the defenders from behind. Could the air-sled be damaged? It would explain why Klarm had waited so long to attack.

There was another possibility, though not one Nish wanted to dwell upon – that Flydd *had* stolen the air-sled, but had fled on it with the tears, leaving everyone here to their fate.

Nish had always known Flydd to be ruthless, though the old scrutator he'd fought beside during the war would never have stolen the tears and abandoned his friends. Nish wasn't

175

so sure about the renewed Flydd, who looked different, acted differently and was certainly different inside. Did that reflect what Yalkara had done to him during renewal? Had she changed him fundamentally?

He took hold of the rope for one last attempt. Clech and Aimee had their faces close together and she was whispering to him. He glanced up at Nish, then nodded. Nish heaved until he felt a sharp pain in his lower belly and knew he was on the verge of tearing something. Again he failed. He wasn't nearly strong enough.

'I'm going down for help. I won't be long –' he began, but broke off, realising how stupid that sounded.

'You can't,' said Aimee. 'You'd never have climbed up here without us, and you won't get down by yourself without a rope.'

That hadn't occurred to Nish. 'Then I'll call for help.'

'They won't hear you over the wind; besides, they'd never get up here and down again before dark.'

Taking a deep breath, he roared, 'Flangers, hoy!' until his throat hurt, but none of the people in the pass looked up. The guards were watching the mist-shrouded track, while everyone else lay in attitudes of exhaustion. There was no way of telling what the survivors of Klarm's army were up to, for the lower slopes were completely obscured again.

'There's nothing you can do,' said Clech. 'It's over, my friend.' He looked down at Aimee and gently kissed her brow.

She kissed him back, then looked up. 'But you can still save yourself, Nish.' She nodded to Clech and passed him her knife.

Clech reached up above the point where her rope was fixed to his, and drew the blade across and back.

'No!' cried Nish in horror. This couldn't be happening. 'There's got to be a way.'

The rope parted and Clech fell with Aimee wrapped tenderly in his arms, into the mist. Nish blocked his ears so he wouldn't hear the impact.

He never knew how he made it down again, for he could only think about Clech and Aimee making the ultimate sacrifice for him, and how little he deserved it. Now he *had* to win. He had to find a way to do the impossible and beat Klarm; their sacrifice could *not* be for nothing.

He raised the severed rope, extracted the spikes and went across the ridge then down the wet rock towards the pass as they had come up, spike by spike, ell by ell, barely thinking about what he was doing. It was a dangerous climb for a lone man in the drifting mist but Nish felt no fear of falling, even in the most dangerous pinches. He took no unnecessary risks but did not waste any time, either. Klarm could not give in, any more than Nish could; the attack might be renewed at any time.

If he were Klarm, Nish would have done so at once, while his troops were still numb from the catastrophe. Give them the night to think about the avalanche, the loss of so many comrades, and the unexpected and humiliating defeat, and they could break, even mutiny. Immediate peril was the best cure for that malaise – to drive them so hard that they had no time to think about anything except their own survival.

It was almost dusk by the time he jumped down to the floor of the pass. His knees were shaky and almost collapsed under him, but after a minute to steady them he went on.

Everyone not on guard was asleep in their tents, save for Huwld, who was asleep by the sputtering, reeking, oil-shale fire, looking as though he'd collapsed from exhaustion. And not surprisingly, since he never seemed to stop working.

There was no one to clap Nish on the back and congratulate him, for which he was thankful. The mission *had* been a brilliant success, but two friends had died because he hadn't been careful enough, and that was all that mattered just now.

He scooped out a warming mug of soup and drank it in a gulp, without tasting a thing. He was also responsible for the deaths of thousands of the enemy. War was war, he mused as he limped down to the eastern defences. One did what one must, as honourably as possible, but there were so many deaths chalked up on his slate that he could not have counted them, and all had been human beings with much the same hopes and fears, dreams and nightmares, as himself.

Flangers was dozing behind the high wall, wrapped in a purloined military greatcoat, but he must have recognised Nish's tread for he said, 'Well done, surr,' before opening his eyes.

He stood up, wearily, and shook Nish's hand. 'We had fifty fighters left, last time I counted. They're grinding us down but we're not beaten yet.'

'I lost Clech and Aimee,' said Nish, and sat beside him, shoulders hunched, to tell the tale. 'I mucked it up, old friend. I should have been more careful.'

'We're not perfect, Nish,' Flangers said at the end. 'We can only do our best. I've also sent men and women to their deaths today, when a better plan might have saved them. And once, long ago, I followed orders and killed people I had sworn to protect,' he added quietly.

Nish knew that tale, but did not speak.

Flangers knew that Nish knew the story, but must have felt a need to unburden himself before the end, for he went on, 'Thirteen years ago I followed orders and shot down the scrutators' air-floater, sending everyone on it save Klarm to their deaths. That broken oath still haunts me.'

Though Nish had not been there, he was well aware of the facts. 'Your superior gave you a legitimate order, and she was acting for Flydd, when he was still commander-in-chief.'

'But the scrutators had authority over Flydd.'

'In the course of a battle, that's debatable.'

'That may be so,' said Flangers, 'but I caused the deaths of some of our leaders, and there is no escaping it.'

Certainly not for Flangers, who was the most honourable of men. For Nish himself, and knowing how bad most of the scrutators had been, his conscience would have accommodated the conflict long ago.

'There was a time, afterwards, when you seemed to have a death-wish,' Nish said carefully.

'I felt that the only honourable course for a dishonoured soldier was to atone with my life, and I fought recklessly in dozens of battles, never caring whether I lived or died. Indeed, I wanted to die, but each time my life was spared. Is there a reason why I lived, when so many more deserving lost their precious lives?'

'I don't know,' said Nish. 'When I ponder the big questions, I either find too many answers, or none. But perhaps you were spared so you could lead the defence of Blisterbone yesterday and today and, hopefully, tomorrow.'

'Perhaps,' said Flangers with a brief, wintry smile. 'It has done me good, this fight that can never be won. I no longer want to die; I feel as though I *have* atoned, in my soldierly way.'

'Your conscience must be a damned hard taskmaster if it's taken you thirteen years. If only my father were as honourable –'

'Let's not talk about him just now.' Flangers sighed and settled down in his greatcoat. 'I expect I will be killed now, since I've found a reason to love life again.'

And not just life. Where were Flydd and Chissmoul, anyway? Having no way of finding out, Nish pulled his coat around his ears, settled his back against the rock and closed his eyes.

'What's that?' one of the guards hissed, then, 'Lieutenant Flangers!'

Flangers was awake and up before Nish's sluggish mind could register what was happening. He staggered to his feet but his knees gave way and he fell onto the sharp-edged slate rubble. Every muscle in his body was aching, every bone. It was dark, the wind had dropped and he could feel the damp mist drifting around him.

'What is it?' he said quietly, climbing up onto the right-hand wall.

'Mifly heard rock crack on rock, down the track,' said Flangers.

'Could they be ready to attack again so quickly?'

'It's been five hours since the avalanche.'

'Really?' Nish felt as though he'd slept for ten minutes. He peered over. 'I don't see any lights.'

'This fog is thicker than mud. Besides, the enemy might have a way of seeing in the dark, just as you do with clear-sight.'

'If they can see in the dark, it's a lot better than my clear-sight,' Nish muttered.

'It showed you the flaw in the ice.' Flangers told the guards to be ready, not that they needed orders. 'Runner, stand by to wake our reinforcements when I say so.'

Huwld was standing by. 'I could run up to the tents now, surr.' Though the Gendrigoreans called Nish by name, they always deferred to Flangers.

'Let them sleep. They need it.'

Clack. 'There it is again,' said Flangers. 'And not far down.

180

The enemy must be sneaking up, hoping to catch us asleep. As if *my* men would ever sleep on duty.'

Nish smiled thinly. Almost any man might sleep on duty, if sufficiently exhausted. He had even done it himself, once or twice. But not Flangers, evidently. 'Duty can be the breaking of a man, if it's too onerous.'

'And the making of another,' said Flangers. 'I've often found it to be a crutch when my courage was faltering.' He moved to the edge of the wall, which here, founded on top of a rock buttress, was a good three spans above the slope.

'They're close,' he said to the defenders. 'And remember that they need not be men – the enemy has all kinds of beasts, both savage native ones and fell creatures flesh-formed to suit Jal-Nish's vicious purposes. We must be prepared for anything. Are the torches ready?'

'They're ready,' a woman said, from the darkness below. 'Shall I light them?'

'Yes, and hold them high so we can see our attackers. But don't expose yourselves to enemy fire.'

Light flared behind the wall and Nish caught a pleasantly pungent whiff of burning pine resin. Resin-coated torches, bound to spears, were carried up onto the left and right walls, and raised high. Nish and Flangers crouched down and peered through arrow slits in the outer wall. The flaring light reflected off the drifting mist, and Nish caught only occasional glimpses of the track.

'I saw something moving, about fifty paces down,' whispered a guard. 'It's huge, but low to the ground. Want me to put a spear into it, lieutenant?'

'Let's see what it is first,' said Flangers. 'When dealing with beasts, you should always know what they are before you attack.'

'It's hard to see through this cursed mist,' said another. 'Looks like a bear, creeping on its belly.'

'Bears can take too much punishment, and they climb too well,' muttered Flangers. 'If Klarm has a squad of bears, they'll snatch this pass in no time.'

'Raise the torches a bit,' said Nish, standing up to look over the outer wall, heedless of the risk of being taken by an arrow. He could just make out a low, bear-like shape, mounded in the middle, humping along the ground.

'That's no bear. It's a man,' he muttered. 'Hold your fire! It's a wounded man.'

'We should finish him off,' said the guard on the left. 'That's what they'd do to us.'

'Don't fire!' bellowed Nish, feeling the hairs rising on the backs of his hands, for he had just had an outrageous thought. He scrambled down the steps at the back of the barrier, ignoring the pain in his legs, and ran around to the slot. 'Out of the way. Let me through.'

He pushed between the guards, scrambled over the rock wall blocking the lower half of the slot, and moved down, slowly now. Could it possibly be him? Tears sprang to his eyes and he could barely swallow for the lump in his throat. Yes, he'd know that enormous shaggy mop anywhere.

'It's Clech! Get a stretcher.'

Clech was forcing himself up the steep slope on his back, using just his mighty arms. His legs trailed below him and each movement raised him only a couple of ells. A little mound rested on his belly, on its side. Aimee's body. And then it moved! She moved, and groaned.

Nish felt the hair rise on the top of his head. He swallowed painfully. It was impossible, but she was alive! They both were, but they were in bad shape.

'Clech?' said Nish, as two men came scrambling down, bearing a stretcher made from tent canvas bound to a pair of spears. 'What happened?'

'Bloody fool broke both legs,' said Aimee in the barest

whisper. 'I told him to land on his big fat head, but he took no notice.'

'Had to hold you like a baby,' Clech croaked. 'Had to look after those little sparrow ribs of yours.'

'Sparrow ribs!' she whispered in outrage.

They continued bickering as they were loaded on the stretcher, still locked in each other's arms, and Nish called another two men down to lift the weight.

'I thought you were dead,' said Nish. 'How did you survive?'

'We expected to die,' said Aimee quietly. 'But the bowl was full of wet ice, smashed into powder, and we went down a span or two before it broke our fall. We nearly suffocated getting free.'

'Why didn't you call for help once you were out?' said Flangers.

'Silly lunkhead slipped and knocked his head on a rock. Took him ages to come to, and I didn't have the breath to yell.'

'I'm not surprised, with broken ribs,' said Flangers. 'Still, the healers know how to deal with those. Let's get you into shelter, in case the enemy are about.'

Nish embraced them both, not bothering to hide his tears, and left them to the healers. Their survival was a little beacon of hope in the darkness that had surrounded Santhenar for so long, and the best possible ending to such a desperate day.

Sixteen

'Surr,' Flangers shook Nish by the shoulder. 'Wake up.'

He felt as though he had been submerged in treacle. His body clung to sleep; his exhausted mind yearned for it and had to be prised awake.

'Is something wrong?' he said groggily.

'They're attacking again, from both sides, and they mean to finish us off.'

Nish sat up, rubbing his eyes, and glanced out through the tent entrance, into darkness. 'What time is it?'

'Just before dawn. The enemy troops are throwing themselves at the defences. I – I've never seen anything like it; they're taking suicidal risks. Klarm must have upped the reward, made it so high that they'll do anything to get it. Things are getting a bit desperate.'

Nish snapped awake, for Flangers never exaggerated and if he was worried, it must be really bad. Nish pulled on his boots and crawled out, the sabre's sheath dragging on the ground, for he'd been too exhausted to take it off. He brought the serpent staff as well, though he had no idea if it could be used for offensive purposes.

Outside, the sky had cleared and the stars were visible.

He hadn't often seen them in Gendrigore. 'Where do you need me, Lieutenant?'

'The western pass. There are a lot of torches down the track; the enemy could have five hundred men down there.'

'Has Klarm marched more reinforcements across Liver-Leech?'

'I assume so.'

'Then they must have left before the avalanche.'

'No doubt of it.'

Nish rubbed his bristly jawline. 'In that case, they may not know that a good part of his army has been destroyed.'

'Klarm's scriers would know, surely?'

'I'm not sure they can talk to him from a distance, up here,' Nish said. 'When Klarm attacked us in the clearing the other day, he kept flying back and forth as if he didn't know what was going on.'

'He may not be as expert with the tears as Jal-Nish,' Flangers speculated.

'And maybe his wisp-watchers and the like can't talk to the tears in this rugged country. Therefore, if the air-sled isn't working . . .' or Flydd has nicked off with it, Nish thought blackly, 'Klarm will be as much in the dark as we are.'

'That must mean this attack was planned yesterday, before the avalanche. And he had to go ahead with it, because he had no way of telling the force he sent over Liver-Leech about the avalanche.'

Nish felt a brief flare of hope. 'Yes. How big is the attacking force in the east?'

'At least a hundred that I could see through the mist. Though I dare say there are massive reinforcements further down.'

The hope died. 'Undoubtedly.'

'Still, while we live, anything is possible,' said Flangers, rather cheerily for a man facing imminent death. But then, he would die with a clear conscience. He'd atoned for the crime he'd been ordered to commit by a long-dead superior, and had never failed in his duty since. No man could have done more.

'If you think the main attack is going to be on the west, should we move the healers' tent?'

'Why?'

'To protect the injured. If the enemy break through, they'll put them to the sword.'

'They won't go after the helpless while there are armed militiamen to deal with. I'll go down to the eastern pass.'

'I suppose you're right. I'll take command of the west,' said Nish, not feeling the least bit cheery. They'd done so much, come so far, wrought miracle after miracle, yet it was never enough; it never seemed to gain them more than a day.

'What's the matter with the weather?' Nish grumbled when they were taking a brief respite from the fighting, hours later. 'It hasn't rained in half a day, and I'd swear I've never seen that glowing orb in the sky before.'

Bright sunshine had always been a rarity in rainy Gendrigore, but a cloudless day was almost unprecedented. The sun was beating down into the pass, shining on their backs, and Nish was a sweltering, sweat-sodden mess. He moved into a small patch of shade and put his back against the cool rock wall.

'It means the *really wet* season is almost upon us,' said Hoshi quietly.

'Is that so?'

'The sun comes out, the skies clear for a day, sometimes even a week, then the winds change and it rains like you've never seen it rain before.'

186

'I've seen it before,' said Nish. 'It rained like that the other day, just before the flood that washed the enemy away.'

'Only for an hour. In the *really wet* season it can pour like that for weeks at a time.'

'Our plan was to hold back the enemy until the *really wet* season was on the way,' said Nish. 'Then, with every creek flooded, there would be no way for them to get into Gendrigore.'

'And we've succeeded,' said Hoshi gloomily, for he was still grieving for Gi and nothing could cheer him up. 'They'll never get in now – or out!'

'Or out?' said Nish.

'Every river, creek and gully on both sides of the Range of Ruin is in flood, and impassable, in the *really wet* season. The rest of Klarm's army will be trapped here and they'll starve to death. Even if they've killed us all, you will have done what you set out to do.'

'Klarm must know that the *really wet* season is close, so why has he kept going?' Nish said to himself. 'Because he's in so deep he can't pull out. He's going to lose an army but he can still win the prize – *me.*'

'It won't do him any good,' said Hoshi. 'He'll die like all the others.'

'Not Klarm,' said Nish. 'He's far too cunning.' He heard someone running, calling his name. 'Who's that?'

'It's Huwld,' said Hoshi, rising wearily.

Nish rose as well, knowing that he was needed before the messenger boy spoke.

'They're coming again,' the boy gasped as he lurched up the hill. 'We need reinforcements bad.'

Nish got up, weary in body and mind, and staggered back to take his place at the western gate of Blisterbone. Huwld went with him, red-faced and silent. He'd been a lively little joker once, but all the humour had gone out of him as well, and how could it be otherwise after the bloodshed he'd witnessed in the past days?

At least two hundred troops had massed below, waiting their turn to scramble up the narrow and precipitous path and attack the defenders at the gate. After making a forced march through the night over Liver-Leech Pass, Klarm's troops were almost out on their feet, yet they had the numbers, and they were after a mighty prize.

For every man who fell, ten ran to take his place; they were practically fighting each other to get to the front, and their chance at a reward that would make them as rich as princes.

A good three hundred now lay dead below the western entrance to the pass, but the enemy could afford those casualties more easily than Nish could the seven men and one woman he'd lost here. All his troops were exhausted, and the end was very close now, for the enemy must soon force the entrance.

Could he and the survivors run across to the eastern side and join with Flangers's forces? Without a rearguard they were likely to be cut down from behind, but if they made it they might counterattack the attackers at the eastern slot and break through – assuming there were only a few of them, which was unlikely.

There are too many ifs, he thought despairingly, so tired that he could barely think straight. He just wanted to lie down, close his eyes and see an end to it. What was the point in fighting on when the result was no longer in doubt? They had done their best; they had saved Gendrigore and could do no more; there were simply too many of the enemy.

But Nish remembered the duty he owed to his dead, and all the friends he'd lost, and especially Maelys. She would not give in; she never did, and neither could he after all they'd been through; not when the cost of surrender was an ignominious death for all his friends. Far better to die an heroic death in battle; at least their tale would live on to inspire other rebels.

The enemy were moving up the slope, slowly and purposefully, and their leaders had just come up against the defenders at the entrance when there was an outcry from the crest of the pass, an almighty crash, and shortly he heard the staggering footsteps of exhausted men. Nish whirled and headed up the slope, fearing the worst.

'They've broken through,' a haggard militiaman gasped, the first of three to top the rise. He was drenched in blood, though he did not appear to be injured badly.

Nish ran towards them. They still bore their weapons, so it wasn't a rout. 'Are you the only survivors?'

The bloody man shook his head. 'There are others. Our lieutenant had a surprise rigged up for them. When –' He bent over, gasping, caught his breath and said, 'When he knew they were going to break through the slot, Flangers brought the right-hand wall down on them; buried at least ten of the devils.'

'Then how did they get in . . .?'

'Collapse made a ramp over the defences. A dozen men can cross it at a time now, and we can't defend it. The next wave of the enemy are just below the bowl. In a couple of minutes they'll be through.'

Nish looked around. 'Hide behind the healers' tent and keep watch over our wounded, but don't show yourself unless the enemy go for them.'

He continued to the top of the pass, where he encountered Flangers and the last thirteen of the militia from the eastern side, ten men and three women.

'I knew collapsing the wall was a risk,' Flangers said, 'but they were about to break through. This way, it's gained us a few more minutes.'

'Not enough,' said Nish.

'While we're alive, anything can happen. How are things here?'

'I don't see how we can keep them out this time.'

'Then let's put our backs together and make a last stand.'

They plodded down to the western entrance and, during the first respite, took their places behind the rock wall. Flangers still carried the heavy Whelm jag-sword, Nish his sabre.

He would have preferred a proper two-edged blade in this situation, but the sabre did suit his hand and, though it had belonged to an enemy, he felt lucky when he carried it. Sometimes it seemed to know better where to strike than he did, which wasn't the blessing that it seemed.

'How come you kept the jag-sword?' said Nish.

'It only ever takes one blow to bring the enemy down,' said Flangers.

A pair of soldiers were scrambling up the steep slope, short lances out. They looked young enough to be Nish's sons, and alike enough to be brothers, or even twins, but Nish and Flangers had worked out a defence for every kind of attack long ago, and they did not hesitate.

The two soldiers began to scrabble up the steep rubble wall. Partly shielded behind it, Flangers stepped left, dropped down and swung the jag-sword in an almost horizontal circle, striking the lance underneath and driving the point up.

The blade of the jag-sword skidded along the underside of the lance, tearing through the young man's knuckles, and when he flinched Flangers cut him down with a single spearing blow to the upper chest. It wasn't pretty, but it was quick; he was dead when he hit the ground.

Nish waited until the last second. Exhausted from charging all that way uphill, his opponent stumbled, and Nish turned side-on to evade the point of the lance and thrust his sabre out. The soldier could not stop in time, drove himself onto the point and his momentum did the rest. Nish, quite gently, pushed him off the blade. The body rolled down the slope to join the hundreds already lying there.

And so it went on. Some soldiers died easily, others hard, and some fought all the way to Nish's throat before he finally finished them, but they all fell in the end, being at such a disadvantage.

The bodies continued to accumulate until they formed a low barrier; about twenty of the enemy took shelter behind it to catch their breath. Nish's men had exhausted their arrows long ago, else they would have cut the enemy down before they came close. They hurled rocks and the enemy's spears back at them once they came within range, but to little effect.

Now all twenty sprang out at once, and only two had fallen by the time they reached the defences. Four turned side-on on the narrow path so as to attack together up the rubble wall, though that left their stroke play rather cramped. Nish and Flangers finished their two, but the defenders to either side of them fell.

Two more enemy took the place of the fallen two and Flangers's opponent, a huge, brawny sergeant, snapped the blade of the jag-sword with a mighty sweep of his broadsword.

Flangers hurled the hilt at the sergeant, striking him so hard on the forehead that he stumbled, dazed, but the others came on and no one had come forward to fill the breaches on either side of Nish and Flangers. Then a small, carrot-topped figure slid in beside Nish, waving a sword that was far too big.

'Huwld!' Nish cried. 'Get out of here.'

'I have to make up –'

The sergeant shot up like a striking snake, lunging and trying to spit the boy like a suckling pig. Nish swung his sabre sideways, knowing that he couldn't parry that fierce blow in time, but the sabre seemed to leap in his hands, dragging him with it, and slammed into the sergeant's sword not far from the tip.

Huwld screamed, and Nish was sure he'd been mortally wounded. He heaved the sabre sideways, slamming the back of the blade into the sergeant's forehead with colossal force, and he fell away. But more of the enemy were coming up fast, and he knew the gate was lost.

'Fall back!' he cried, fighting two soldiers at once with the sabre.

Flangers snatched up the sergeant's broadsword and retreated down the uphill side of the wall, dragging Huwld with him. The other two militiamen were dead; Nish left them where they lay.

'Same plan as at the eastern pass,' Flangers grunted as they backed through the narrow gap behind the barrier.

'What?' said Nish, defending furiously. Within the gate, with its rock walls towering to either side, only two could come at him at the same time, but they were driving him backwards.

Flangers dropped Huwld, who groaned. Taking hold of a dangling length of rope embedded in the wall, he heaved, and the cunningly constructed wall collapsed from the top, filling the gap and burying the two soldiers Nish had been fighting, plus another two behind them.

'A little trick I thought up in my idle years as the Numinator's prisoner,' Flangers said with a wry smile.

It had saved them, though, as with the collapse of the eastern defences, it had formed a rubble ramp over which seven or eight soldiers could storm the gap at once, ruining an almost perfect defensive position.

Nish bent over Huwld, who sat up, weeping with pain. 'My finger.'

'There's no time to look at it.' Nish threw him over his shoulder.

As they moved up the slope to meet the survivors from the eastern side, Nish did a quick count – twenty-five of the militia were still on their feet, counting the three he'd sent to guard the wounded.

Another fifteen wounded were still alive, including Aimee and Clech, plus two healers, lanky Dulya and plump, palely pretty Scandey. The third healer, Ghosh, had been killed while Nish was up at the ice sheet. Forty-two still alive of the three hundred and sixty he'd had down in the clearing, but there was no way out now.

They formed a semi-circle with their backs to the cliffed flank of the white-thorn peak, and waited. The enemy were coming over the western wall and gathering inside. The advantage was all theirs now and they could afford to wait until they had the numbers. There were at least seventy of them.

The attackers from the eastern pass appeared at the top of the hill, just a handful at first, then more until another thirty stood there. They stopped, watching, waiting.

'Where's the rest of the army?' said Nish. 'Why is Klarm holding back?'

'He doesn't need any more,' said Flangers. 'A hundred of them versus twenty-five of us.' He hefted the broadsword. 'And yet, I've fought against worse odds.'

'So have I,' said Nish, 'but not out in the open like this.' He turned to Huwld. 'Give me a look at you, lad.'

Huwld held up his left hand, which was covered in blood, and his index finger was gone; the sergeant's sword blow had severed it and badly cut the next finger and thumb. 'It's my punishment,' he said limply. 'It's all my fault.'

'Don't be silly,' said Nish, putting his arm around the boy's narrow shoulders. 'You were doing your best; it could have happened to anyone.'

'It is my fault. *It is!* I gave the knife to Uncle Boobelar. Why didn't he cut himself free and jump? Why did he have to drag those three men over with him?'

Because he's scum, Nish thought, but he could not say it. The boy felt guilty enough as it was. No wonder he'd been working himself to exhaustion, day and night, trying to make up for it.

'We all make mistakes, Huwld,' he said gently. 'I should know. I've made more than most.'

'Not as bad as this,' said Huwld.

'Even worse,' said Nish. 'Hush now; go back to the ranks, lad.'

A little man had appeared beside the troops at the top of the pass. He said a few words to them and headed slowly down. It was General Klarm, here for the victory.

He stopped ten paces away, nodding stiffly to Nish and Flangers. He wasn't carrying the tears, Nish noticed.

'What a waltz it's been, these past days,' said Klarm.

Nish bowed ironically. 'I don't suppose you get many.'

'Many what?'

'Dances. Being what you are.'

It was a low blow, sneering at any man's physical attributes, and Nish had suffered as much as anyone for his lack of stature and unhandsome features, but it had been a terrible day of an awful week and he had to do something to wipe the smile off the face of his enemy.

Too late he remembered Flydd telling him, way back in the days of the lyrinx war, that the dwarf was a great favourite of the ladies – not just for his equipment, which had the stature he lacked and more, but for the inventive ways he wielded it.

Klarm laughed in his face. 'Weakest yet, Nish. I've been insulted by masters, and you'll get no rise out of me that way. I've got to hand it to you,' he went on in that rich, melodious voice, 'I never would have thought it possible, but you've beaten me over and again. Another few hours and well . . . you didn't get them, did you? What a tale this struggle would make for the Histories, if I could permit it to be told. But it never will be.'

'What do you mean, another few hours?' said Nish. 'You've still got half an army down below – *haven't you*?'

'If only it were so,' said Klarm. 'If you could have held out an hour longer, you might have had the victory you so desperately crave – *and* the Great Tale to go with it.'

Nish could not speak. How could it be so? Klarm had to be lying, or making a monstrous joke, just to grind them down even further.

'And if you had won,' Klarm went on after a studied pause, 'and I'd survived, I would have been the first to salute you, for I know a brave man when I see him, and a born leader. I would have honoured you, but you broke too soon and the victory is mine –' He smiled, then dropped the bombshell. 'Though these are the only men I have left.'

'Out of ten thousand?' Nish cried. He couldn't help himself.

'I lost half of that number to dysentery, fevers, ulcers, flesh-eating worms, broken legs, arms and heads, and all the other hazards of this aptly named Range of Ruin, before my advance guard even reached the pass. Five hundred fell in the clearings on the first day of battle, or were swept away by the flood, and well over a thousand died at the two passes before . . .'

'My avalanche took most of the survivors,' said Nish wonderingly. 'And all but a hundred of them have been killed today.'

We went so close, he thought, fighting to contain his anguish while knowing it was written large across his face. If we'd known how few the enemy were after the avalanche, surely we would have found that little bit extra in courage or cunning to hold them off.

A well-placed rockslide, even a higher defensive wall might have done it. But I gave up hope of winning; instead, as Flydd pointed out, I took refuge in stolid defence which could never bring us victory. If only I'd known, he thought bitterly.

'How come you didn't use flappeters against us? That's what I would have done.'

'Almost all of them were wiped out when the sky-palace came down on Mistmurk Mountain; and the bladder-bats too. Plus the pens of other flesh-formed creatures Jal-Nish had aboard, just in case . . .'

Klarm's handsome face twisted in disgust. Evidently he did not approve of such creatures.

'So the avalanche was your doing, Nish,' he went on. 'I thought I saw your hand in it. Who else could have the clear-sight to see the flaw in the ice up there, and the imagination to find a way to release it. Tell me, how did you unbind the ice?'

There was no harm in telling him now. Nish lifted the serpent staff over his head. 'With this. Are you going to take it from me?'

Klarm's eyes crossed and he took an involuntary step backwards, but hastily came forwards again. 'Why do you think I left the caduceus behind?'

'You were too scared? Or wouldn't the tears like the competition?'

Klarm smiled thinly. 'I don't think they would, since you mention it. I didn't go near it because it's a trap I didn't plan on falling into. Stilkeen left it in the clearing for a reason, and not for our good.'

'It helped me when I needed help, and has done nothing to hinder me at other times.'

'And what does that tell you?'

'Nothing, so far.'

'It means that Stilkeen wants you to tear down your father. But if you should ever do so, unlikely as that seems, beware of its price. You can bet your personal equipment that there will be one, and it will be unimaginable.'

Nish knew he was right. He'd always been uncomfortable with the caduceus; it had to be more than it seemed. 'What are you going to do now?' He felt sure he knew, since Klarm was a man of his word.

'Exactly what I promised when you rejected my offer after Stilkeen took my God-Emperor. You and Maelys will become my prisoners, and everyone else will be put to the sword. Where is she?'

'I haven't seen her since the flood, three days ago.'

Klarm paled. He had not expected that. 'Are you sure?'

'Search the camp,' Nish said. 'After she freed me, I ran ahead to get to my militia, and she was following. Clearsight told me to strike up through the forest, and it saved me from the flood, but only just. If Maelys was on the river path she could not have survived.'

He met Klarm's eyes, so the dwarf could read the truth and the grief in them, then bent his head. Nish regretted her loss more than anything, even his failure to correctly read the enemy's numbers. Why hadn't he waited one extra minute for her? In all his life he'd had no better and more loyal friend.

Nish reeled at the thought, for it was one he'd never had before. He had never compared anyone to his beloved Irisis, not on equal terms. She had been friend, comrade, lover and life partner – Irisis had been everything to him, and he to her. And yet, though Maelys had been neither his friend nor his lover, and in the early days he had often treated her badly, she had remained steadfast.

He analysed the heretical thought, but found it genuine. Maelys *had* been as good and loyal a friend to him as Irisis, which meant that he must finally be coming to terms with her loss. He would never forget her, and a corner of him would always grieve for her, but Irisis was gone forever and he had to live again. Unfortunately, that realisation had come too late.

'I'm sorry,' said Klarm with genuine regret. 'Maelys was a fine woman, one of the best I've ever met.' He bowed his own head for a minute, then said, 'Are you going to surrender?'

'No,' said Nish.

'I'm sorry about that, too.' Klarm nodded formally and headed back to the top of the pass with that rolling dwarf's gait, as if he had lived his life on the deck of a ship.

Nish returned to the militia, debating whether to tell them what Klarm had said, but decided he had to. In the last hour of their lives he owed them absolute honesty.

He met their eyes, one by one. 'This is the end, my friends, and no better friends has any man had. You've done everything I've asked of you and much, much more, and I love you every one.'

He went down the line, embracing each of them, and the wounded and the healers too, before going back to the front. 'We've done miracle after miracle in defence of Gendrigore, and Klarm has just revealed that these are all the men he has left.'

The militia turned left, then right, staring at the hundred enemy, incapable of believing that they were the only survivors of such a vast army.

'He began with ten thousand,' Nish went on, 'and is now reduced to these hundred fighting men. We set out with five hundred, sent a third back with illness, and now have twenty-five able-bodied. Had we known – had *I* known his numbers were so few – we might have beaten him. No, I say we would have sent him scurrying home with his tail between his stumpy little legs. We *would* have beaten him.'

The militia cheered, laughed, cried and embraced one another.

'But it was not to be, and now it's over.' He bowed and they cheered again, then he turned and saw Klarm giving the signal to his troops above and below. They drew their swords and advanced, slowly and steadily, as if they were expecting one final trick – part of the mountain to fall down on them, perhaps, or a pit to open up beneath their boots.

But Nish had nothing left. He swallowed. They would take him first, and there was nothing he could do about it . . . unless the serpent staff could save him. He raised it in his right hand but it felt cold now, heavy and inert, and he could sense nothing at its core. Why had it helped him before, only to abandon him now? Or had it not been helping him at all, only *Stilkeen*?

The enemy were less than fifty paces away, and advancing with wary, remorseless tread, when Nish made out a faint, familiar hissing whistle. His heart jumped, for it had to be the air-sled. But Klarm showed no reaction; he did not even look around, and the faint hope died. One of Klarm's subordinates must be flying the craft.

The air-sled came shrieking up the slope towards the western gate of Blisterbone, lifted and passed high over their heads, then shot towards the cloud-wreathed tip of the white-thorn peak. After banking at the last second, it came shooting down in a series of exuberant spirals that it had certainly never performed when Klarm or Jal-Nish had flown it, and Nish's skin rose in goose pimples, for he *knew* it wasn't any of Klarm's men at the controls.

He'd only ever met one pilot who flew with such extravagant, exuberant daring. Chissmoul had to be at the helm. The air-sled rocketed over Klarm's head, buffeting his hair, skidded sideways though the air, slowly rotating horizontally on its axis as it did, then settled like a feather in front of Nish and his militia.

'How does she do it?' Nish said, laughing for sheer joy. The craft was far more battered and bent than before, and covered in dried, flaking mud, and it looked as though it had crashed several times since he'd last seen it.

Chissmoul, still wearing the bloodstained bandage around her head, sprang off, her eyes searching the militia. Then, spotting Flangers, she ran and hurled herself into his arms so forcibly that he went over backwards and the troops behind him had to hold him up.

The militia laughed and cheered and wept to a man. It was a second wonderful moment in the grimmest of days. Nish turned back to Flydd, who had remained aboard.

'Where the bloody hell have you been?' he said, though inside he was exultant. Of course Flydd hadn't betrayed them, and with the air-sled, and his mancery, they might get out of this yet. 'You were supposed to be back yesterday.'

'I had to take a little detour and was delayed longer than I expected,' Flydd said blandly. 'Pile on. We don't have much time.'

'Lieutenant?' Nish called to Flangers. 'Bring your troops to the air-sled without delay.'

'Don't move!' rapped Klarm in an amplified voice. 'I've got your wounded, and the healers.' He gestured to the left, and half a dozen of his troops rose from behind the healer's tent, where they had disarmed Nish's three guards. 'Surrender or they die.'

Flydd glanced at Nish and some message flashed in his eyes. Was he telling him to abandon the prisoners and run while they had the chance? Nish gave a tiny, imperceptible shake of the head. He wasn't leaving anyone behind.

Flydd sighed. 'I didn't think you would. Too bad, though.' He glanced up at Klarm, then down the slope towards the troops moving up from the western gate.

Klarm came towards them and Nish made out the faintest humming – the song of the tears. The dwarf had them around his neck, just as Jal-Nish had worn them. Was he planning to use them on the militia, or would he leave that pleasure to his exhausted but blood-lusting troops?

'Lay down the serpent staff, Xervish,' said Klarm. 'And step right off my air-sled.'

PART TWO

THE QUEST FOR FIRE

Seventeen

The whirling blast of snow settled and Maelys could see again. The portal had taken her, Yggur and Tulitine from the Range of Ruin to the low, windswept shore of a treeless land whose further reaches were lost in the distance. Granite boulders littered the shore; wiry shrubs and spindly clumps of grass struggled for life between them. Though the ice that had once covered the bleak landscape was gone, she knew where she was.

Ahead lay a vast, sullen sea, grey as slate and covered in ice, except near the shore where the slanting rays of a red sun, hanging above the horizon, reflected off still water.

'When we came here last time, we were trying to find the antithesis to the tears,' said Maelys.

'What do you mean, *antithesis*?' said Tulitine, shivering violently despite her purloined army cloak.

'The one single object or power or force that can break the power of the Profane Tears and bring down the God-Emperor.'

'How do you know there is one?'

'I learned about it at the Pit of Possibilities. It's one of the reasons why Flydd agreed to take renewal. He thought the

Numinator would know about the antithesis, but she said that she did not. I don't suppose you do?'

'No,' said Tulitine. 'This must be –'

'The Island of Noom,' said Yggur, taking off his own cloak and wrapping it around her as well. 'But the ice is gone and even the Kara Agel, the Frozen Sea, is thawing. The distilled chthonic fire that the Numinator blasted out in all directions as we fled her tower is eating the ice away.'

'And even now must be spreading across the steppes,' said Tulitine softly. 'What if it never stops?'

Yggur shrugged. 'The meltwater may freeze again; Noom is a cold, miserable place. But if it does not, and the icecaps and glaciers melt, the ocean must rise and flood the land. Chthonic fire caused the volcanic death of the world of Aachan, it's said. Will rising seas be the ruin of ours?'

Maelys shivered and stamped her feet, for she had discarded her furs when she ended up on the Range of Ruin, and under the cloak her clothes were still damp. 'We came here for chthonic fire. Let's get on with it before we freeze to death.' She peered around. 'I don't see the tower.'

'It was blown to pieces as we fled,' said Yggur.

'Everything looks different with the ice gone. How are we going to find the place?'

'The ancient stone arch should still be standing. If we head up to the top of that ridge we might see it.'

Only days ago, Noom had been covered in snow and ice, but there was water everywhere now, trickling around each boulder in a braided network of icy rills. They trekked up the slope, and soon Maelys's feet were so cold that she could barely feel her toes.

'I don't suppose you could do something about warm clothes or dry boots?' she said.

'How, exactly?' said Yggur, scowling.

'With your Art of mancery.'

'You have an exaggerated notion of what can be done with the Art.'

'Maybe that's because no one will tell me about my own gift!' she snapped.

'I beg your pardon,' he said, looking down his nose at her.

'Sorry,' she said hastily, shocked that she had spoken so rudely to such a great and powerful man, for Maelys had been brought up to be polite and demure, and to show respect for her betters. 'But Flydd –'

'Just because Flydd conjured furs out of nothing with the mimemule, substantially aided by whatever talent Yalkara imprinted in him during renewal, it doesn't mean I can do the same. Besides . . .' Yggur looked away, a muscle in his cheek twitching.

'What is it?' said Tulitine, whose face was pinched and the tip of her nose red. Despite two cloaks, she was still shivering fitfully. 'Yggur, are you in pain?'

'Nothing compared to yours,' he said, putting an arm around her and drawing her to him. 'I'm afraid . . .'

'What is it? What's wrong?'

'I'm afraid that my Art is failing,' he said quietly, 'and it's everything to me.'

Maelys felt for him, for Yggur was as old as the ages, and to lose such a gift, after wielding it all that time, must be like going blind. Suddenly ashamed of her ill-temper, she said, 'I'm really sorry.'

'Why is your Art failing?' said Tulitine. 'Can it be the caduceus?'

'I don't know,' said Yggur. He looked away, his brow furrowed. 'The Numinator drained all my power for seven years, and then Reaper blocked me from using my Art, save right next to the caduceus. Perhaps I've lost more than my body could bear.'

'But you made the portal,' said Maelys.

'No, the *caduceus* made the portal. I only visualised where I wanted it to go.' He strode off, his long legs covering twice the distance of her steps.

From the top of the ridge the view was vaguely familiar, though the distant, rounded ranges appeared much the same in every direction. 'I don't know if we're close to the tower, or on the other side of the Island of Noom,' Maelys said, her thick black hair fluttering in the icy wind.

Tulitine, who was still struggling up the slope, seemed to be in greater pain than before. Maelys went back and gave her an arm.

'I've never been to Noom,' Tulitine said faintly as they reached the top. 'As you know, the Numinator is my grand-mother, but she wanted nothing to do with me.' She shook her head as if, even after all this time, she could not come to terms with that.

'From what I know of her, you've had a lucky escape!' Maelys muttered.

'I dare say, but still it hurts.'

'I think we're close,' said Yggur, marching down the other side.

Maelys scurried after him, up the following ridge, and shortly she made out the old stone arch – at least, part of it – at the top. The right-hand pillar and half of the arch had collapsed, though the rest still stood. She went through the arch and looked down on the valley below.

The Tower of a Thousand Steps had been set on an icy island in the middle of a lake, protected from intruders by constantly shifting patterns of water and berg, but the lake had been reduced to a narrow ring of shallow water and mud around a mound of broken rock and debris. The ice was gone, and there was no sign that the tower had ever existed.

'I can't see any chthonic fire,' said Maelys, crouching

beside the pillar where there was shelter from the wind. She'd hoped to gain a little warmth from the stone, which faced the sun, but its feeble light had not warmed the pillar at all.

'There may still be some, deep in the foundations,' said Yggur. 'But how are we to reach them?'

'If you think I'm wading through that water –'

'Be quiet. I'm trying to think.'

'What about?' she said automatically. 'Sorry.'

'I'm sorting through my memories of the tower. The foundations came out past the edges of the lake, below ground, and there might be a way in.'

'Won't it be flooded?' said Maelys.

'The lake is practically gone. The collapse must have cracked the ground below the tower, and the water has drained away.'

They went down and began to circumnavigate the ring of shallow water and half-frozen mud, which was littered with broken furniture and timbers, and many, many bodies, the fruits of the Numinator's dreadful and ultimately failed breeding program. The exposed parts of many of the bodies had been eaten by scavengers, down to the bones, though the corpses further out in the mud and shallow water were still whole. Even in this climate, the smell was gaggingly offensive.

Maelys was stumbling along, so cold that she began to fear that her blood would freeze, when the ground ahead of her rose in irregularly-shaped slabs, like a layer of frozen earth that had been forced up from below until it shattered.

'That's odd,' she muttered. 'Yggur, what do you think this is?'

He peered underneath the slabs. 'I can see a hollow in there; no, a hole. Something has broken the frozen ground from below.'

He walked around the slabs, frowning. 'I think I see what's happened. The explosion blew the top of the ice tower to bits but the rest remained intact until it hit the ground, and part of the frozen foundations must have been forced up through the earth here, as the buried roots of a tree break through the soil when it falls. There might still be some white fire deep down. Maelys –'

'I'm not going down there,' said Maelys, who'd had her fill of underground passages within Mistmurk Mountain.

Yggur tried to raise a slab but it proved too heavy. 'You're a little thing. Squeeze under here, would you, and see how deep that hole goes.'

'*You're a little thing!* That's just what Flydd and Nish said when they sent me down that chimney infested with swamp creepers!' she muttered. 'Why is it always me?'

'It isn't always you,' said Tulitine. 'We've all got strengths and weaknesses, and we each have to do what is required with them.'

Maelys felt like a small child being lectured by a stern teacher, but Tulitine certainly couldn't go in. 'All right,' she said quietly, trying to conceal her unease. 'Can you *at least* make me a light, Yggur?'

It sounded like a criticism, though she had not intended it to be, and her mortification deepened when, after several minutes of straining, Yggur had not produced a glimmer of light. He turned away, shoulders slumped.

After an uncomfortable interval, Tulitine reached into an inside pocket and drew out a small object like a miniature dumbbell, which she tapped three times on the end. It began to shine brightly.

'What's that?' said Maelys.

'A seer's light – also called a twinklestone. It won't hurt you.'

Nonetheless, Maelys flinched as the twinklestone was

laid on the centre of her palm. It looked searingly hot, yet had the cool, damp feeling of a pair of soap bubbles, and weighed little more. She blew on it and it wobbled but did not blow away; it was stuck to her skin, though she lifted it off easily enough.

'It doesn't twinkle and it's not stone, so why is it called a twinklestone?'

'I've no idea,' said Tulitine. 'You can stick it to your forehead if you need to use your hands, but make sure your skin is dry.'

'Why?'

'If it touches anything wet, it sticks so tightly you'll have to tear the skin to get it off. You can also pull it apart, if you need two lights for a while. If you need more light, carefully stretch the twinklestone and it will expand and shine more brightly.'

'What if I just want a little light?'

'Squeeze it in your fist and it'll go back to this size, or even smaller.'

'Thanks. All right; what if I find some chthonic fire? How do I bring it back?'

'In this.' Yggur held out a midnight black circle, about the diameter of his hand and fingers.

'And this is . . .?' said Maelys, drawing away. The circle made her scalp crawl, for it was far blacker than black, she could not tell what it was made from and, looked at side-on, it disappeared completely.

'It's a dimensionless box,' said Yggur, who was holding it by the very edge. 'I stole it from the Numinator. If you find any fire, push the dimensionless box onto it and the fire will be sucked inside and preserved.'

'How do you get it out again?'

'You turn the dimensionless box inside out and eject the fire into a suitable container.'

'Er,' said Maelys, 'is the box dangerous?'

'Extremely,' said Yggur cheerfully.

His sudden good humour seemed a trifle macabre. 'What if it accidentally sucks *me* inside?'

'It won't unless you're foolish enough to press it flat against you. If you do, you will be drawn inside and will become a singularity within the dimensionless box.'

'And then what?' said Maelys, afraid to go near it.

'Nothing,' said Yggur.

'What do you mean, *nothing*?'

'You would cease to exist. When the box was turned inside out again, there would be nothing recognisable left of you. No living thing can survive the dimensionless box – and few things that aren't living.'

It got worse and worse. 'Then how do I carry it safely?' she cried.

'Just screw it up and stuff it into your pocket, and it's harmless,' he said, as if that were obvious. 'The box only works when it's perfectly flat.'

'What if it unfolds?'

He sighed. 'If you put it in a small pocket it won't be able to.'

Maelys took the dimensionless box, which was eerily weightless, gingerly screwed it up and stuffed it into her shirt pocket, buttoning down the flap to be sure it was safe. She would sooner have carried a live scorpion there.

'Off you go,' said Yggur.

She pressed the twinklestone against her brow and it stuck – it felt slightly itchy – then she tested the slab in case it was loose. When it did not move she wriggled in under it. The light from the twinklestone had a bluish tinge which made her surroundings appear even bleaker and colder.

The space underneath was broad but low and she had to flatten her bosom against the icy ground to get through;

even so, her prominent bottom scraped painfully on the underside of the slab. To her right the cavity continued towards a wedge-shaped patch of darkness.

'What do you see?' said Yggur.

'I think it does go down, though I don't see how you're going to get through. I can barely fit.'

'Keep going.'

She squirmed to the wedge-shaped darkness, which turned out to be a hole, leading down. Maelys put her head over the edge. 'It's like a shaft. It goes down further than I can see, and it's pretty steep.'

'Can you climb down, and more importantly, back up?'

'You could if you could get in,' said Maelys, persisting with the fiction that she was just having a look around up top, and he was going to do the dirty work. 'The sides are like frozen, fractured soil –'

'Broken permafrost,' said Yggur. 'Let's hope it goes all the way down. Keep going, as far as you can.'

'It . . . it doesn't look very safe.'

'Keep a close eye on the sides and you'll be all right – the permafrost won't fall in. If you come to running water or thawed ground, don't go any further or you could set off a collapse. Ready?'

'I was also thinking of other kinds of dangers,' said Maelys in a tiny voice. 'What if the Numinator buried some of her experiments down below?'

'It'll be all right,' Yggur muttered.

'I'm scared.'

'It's no picnic up here in the freezing wind, and we're in more danger than you are, should any of those re-animated corpses still be around.' His voice faded; he must have turned away. 'Keep a weather eye on the water, Tulitine. They could be lurking under the surface, waiting for us to turn our backs.'

Maelys wished he hadn't spoken. She had not seen the bodies that Zofloc, the Whelm sorcerer, had reanimated with darts full of distilled chthonic fire, but she had heard all about them.

Shuddering, she plucked the twinklestone from her forehead, attached it to the middle finger of her right hand and reached down. The shaft was a good span wide and sloped down steeply, though it was climbable as long as she did not encounter any smooth ice.

She put her feet in, began to go down backwards, then her feet slipped on an icy patch and she caught frantically at the top edge while she scrabbled for a solid footing. The icy patch proved to be small, and below it was solid permafrost again, but she checked carefully with the twinklestone before she continued. It would be easy to fall, and if she did, she would go all the way.

'I'm halfway down,' she called a few minutes later, after she'd descended some twenty spans. 'I can see the bottom.'

Her voice echoed oddly, and shortly came a reply so garbled and echoing that she could not make out a word. Had Yggur and Tulitine heard what she had said, or merely the sound of her voice? Again she hesitated; if she got into trouble further down there would be little point calling for help. Not that they could get in to save her, anyhow.

It reminded her of other unpleasant expeditions she'd made below ground, though thankfully this place appeared free of life; animal or vegetable.

She continued to the bottom of the shaft, over piles of broken rock and permafrost into a tunnel that was several spans across and equally high; it extended in both directions further than the light reached.

Ahead of her, the walls and floor were as smooth as polished stone. She must be inside the former ice foundations of the fallen tower. Maelys assumed that the ice had been consumed by chthonic fire and the meltwater had seeped away.

Sticking the twinklestone to her forehead, she proceeded slowly in its bleak light, checking each wall for traces of white fire. She found none, though the floor contained scattered pools of water, now freezing again. Evidently, after consuming all the ice, the fire had gone out. Every so often, narrower tunnels ran off to her left, presumably the remains of cross-foundations. She passed them by.

Further on, the tunnel turned left, then continued. She was trudging along it when a distorted, unidentifiable roar echoed down. Maelys pressed herself against the wall, her heart fluttering. It might have been Yggur shouting, but she dared not reply in case it was someone – or something – else. Such as the reanimated corpses of those poor people on whom the Numinator had done her dreadful breeding experiments.

On she went, around another left-hand corner, and after that two more, which meant that this tunnel formed a square many hundreds of paces on each side. She could see, distantly, the fractured shaft she had climbed down; she was heading back to her starting point.

Not far away, another of those narrow tunnels ran off to her left and she stood at its entrance, uncertainly. She had seen no solid ice so far, and not a trace of white fire. Was there any point going that way?

Maelys thought it unlikely, but since she had come this far there was no point leaving the job half done. She dragged her weary body sideways down the narrow conduit, eventually emerging in a huge open space, three spans high and further across than the light of the twinklestone could reach. She struggled to work out what it had been, for she was not good at imagining shapes in her head.

She guessed that it had once contained the solid ice foundations supporting the inner tower, the smaller one that

Flydd and poor Colm had climbed after they had rescued Yggur, Flangers, Chissmoul and the other prisoners. Maelys had been in the Nightland at the time but she had heard all about it. In the Nightland, lying with Emberr . . . it had been the most romantic time of her life; and then the most tragic.

So much had happened since that she had not even begun to grieve for him. Wiping her eyes, with an effort she put him out of her mind; she could not afford to be distracted now.

Cracks ran across the ceiling here and there, and along them delicate icicles had formed. How long could the roof hold? After studying the icicles, which were unbroken, she decided that it was probably safe to go further.

Halfway to the centre she stopped, squinting into the gloom. Could that faint, writhing worm of light up ahead be chthonic fire? Her heart thumped.

In the middle of the open space, a ragged column of ice the width of a small cottage extended from floor to ceiling, like the well-gnawed core of an enormous apple. A ragged line of fire lit one of the edges facing her. There wasn't much fire, though, and if she tried to collect it, it might go out. She needed as much as she could find.

Maelys continued around to the left and, on the far side of the ice core, she discovered a brightly glowing patch of white fire near the floor.

She squatted down to study it. The fire made a faint crackling sound as it consumed the ice, and it was strong and vigorous. As she was psyching herself up to collect it with the perilous dimensionless box, something scraped behind her and Maelys whirled.

A tall and unusually gaunt man stood in the shadows, dressed in a black loincloth and wearing a crown of iron barbs, and his glittering, lidless eyes were fixed on her.

'I knew one of you would return for the fire,' said the Whelm sorcerer, Zofloc.

EIGHTEEN

'The air-sled isn't yours,' Flydd said imperturbably to the dwarf. 'You're only minding it for the master whose filthy boots you lick clean every night.'

Klarm scowled. 'Drop the staff, Flydd, or feel all the power of Reaper.' His hand hovered above its roiling surface.

Nish looked from Klarm to Flydd, back to Klarm, and gnawed his lip. Even at the height of Flydd's powers, a long time ago now, he had never been a match for the tears.

'*All* the power?' scoffed Flydd. 'Come now, Klarm. Jal-Nish would have given you as little of Reaper's power as he could get away with. He was always terrified of rivals.'

'Do you seriously believe that he would leave his empire unprotected?'

'Not if he'd known Stilkeen was coming. But he didn't.'

'He has long known of a threat from the void – he just didn't know what it was.'

'My point stands,' said Flydd, though with less confidence than before. 'Besides, we both know that it took Jal-Nish years to master the tears – you can't have done it in a few days.'

'I've served him loyally for many years,' said Klarm. 'I've had plenty of time to learn all about them. Are you prepared to risk it?'

Flydd did not reply; he must have been having second thoughts. Nish would have done the same, for he still bore the scars from the touch of Reaper, and still felt the pain. But Flydd had to go on; he was their only hope now and he had to call Klarm's bluff – if it *was* a bluff. How much of the tears' power *had* Jal-Nish allowed the dwarf to use?

'Xervish?' Nish said. 'When Father first tempted me, on the day my ten-year sentence was up, he boasted about his mastery of the tears. Then he said, *I've made sure no one can use them but me.*'

'Did he now? How very interesting, Klarm.'

'He was lying. He taught me more than enough,' said Klarm. 'Drop the staff.'

'I don't think I will.' Flydd rotated the serpent staff until its forked tongue pointed at the dwarf. 'I suspect I'm going to call your bluff.'

'You can't possibly know how to use that thing,' said Klarm ringingly, though now *his* confidence sounded forced.

'Care to risk it?'

Klarm's hand twitched as though he was going to attack, and Nish tensed.

But he withdrew his hand, which was still bandaged from where it had been burned days ago, and said, 'I don't care to reveal my powers at this stage – you never know *what* might be watching.' Turning, Klarm said in an amplified voice, 'Take Nish and do not harm him. Cut the others down.'

'I wouldn't, if I were you,' said Flydd, grinning broadly. 'You like to believe that you think of everything, General Klarm, but you've seriously underestimated me.'

'What are you talking about?' said Klarm, gesturing to his troops to stop.

'You assumed, as did certain others,' Flydd was looking sideways at Nish now, and the grin had faded, 'that I was only out for what I could get. That I had abandoned my friends and fled on the air-sled to save my miserable skin.'

Nish swallowed, but said nothing. Words meant little and Flydd was exceptionally good with them. Deeds were what counted now.

'I admit it,' said Klarm. 'You're a strange man, Xervish, and you've grown far stranger since you took renewal. I watched you with Gatherer after you stole the air-sled, and you fled straight as an arrow for Gendrigore until I lost you behind the mountains.

'What brought you back – a crisis of conscience? No – I don't believe you have one. You came back for the tears. I've seen the way you've looked at them ever since Jal-Nish brought them to the Range of Ruin. You *burn* for them; you've got to have them, whatever the cost.'

Flydd gave a scornful laugh. 'I put on that expression every time you looked in my direction, to gull you. And it worked.'

Klarm did not look convinced, and neither was Nish, for he remembered Flydd's lustful stare from the battle in the clearing. He had seen it in his eyes whenever the tears had been mentioned, even when Klarm had been out of sight. So where *had* Flydd been all this time, and what had he done? And, most importantly, why *had* he come back? It had to be for the tears. How could he so betray them?

'But Xervish,' said Klarm, 'you forget that we were scrutators together in the olden days, and that I once interrogated you. We had special ways of sorting truth from deceit and if any scrutator was more skilled at it than you, it was I. I *know* you're hiding something.'

'Indeed I am,' said Flydd blandly, 'and if you care to climb a few spans up the mountainside you'll discover what it is.'

'I'm not going to fall for that one,' said Klarm.

'Then send one of your men – the least and most useless of them.'

Klarm stared at Flydd, who met his eyes evenly, shrugged and gestured to the man nearest to him. 'Climb up the mountainside, trooper, and tell me what you see.'

The soldier began to scramble up the steep slope. It was hard going, and it took several minutes to reach a height of ten spans. Everyone watched him in silence.

What was Flydd getting at? Nish wondered. If it was a trick, it would soon be uncovered.

The soldier turned, found a sound footing, looked down over the defences at the western gate, then started. 'Soldiers, surr! An enemy army.'

Nish's feet almost lifted off the ground in relief. Of course Flydd hadn't betrayed them.

'What?' cried Klarm, scrambling up to see for himself. 'Whose army; how many? And how close?'

'They're not in uniform,' said the soldier. 'They're dressed like farmers, though they're well armed and moving fast. They'll be coming over the western gate in a minute or two.'

Klarm reached the soldier and followed his gaze. 'Farmers!' he cried, staring at Flydd. 'Where the blazes did they come from?'

Flydd laughed. 'I got the idea from something Nish said, not long after we arrived in the clearing from the Numinator's tower. You know Boobelar, of course, the drunken captain of the so-called militia from Rigore province.'

'I've spoken with him,' said Klarm, his lips thinning. 'He would betray his own grandmother.'

'He put a knife to his nephew's throat.' Flydd's smile faded. 'Weeks ago, Boobelar told Nish that the militia from Gendri province weren't coming, but I know the reputation of the stolid folk from Gendri – the flatlanders, as everyone calls them, somewhat ironically, since there is no flat land in Gendrigore. They don't make promises they can't keep, and therefore Boobelar had to be lying.'

'The Gendri militia never turned up at the rendezvous in Wily's Clearing,' said Nish.

'And you didn't wonder why, knowing the honest folk of Gendrigore as you did?' said Flydd. 'No, you were already pressed for time and could not wait. But the answer seemed obvious to me. The militia hadn't come because Boobelar had given them false directions – he wanted the battlefield plunder for himself – and they were still lost in the mountains when you left Wily's Clearing for the Range of Ruin.'

'So you went looking for them.'

'And found them, not far away,' said Flydd, barely able to contain his glee. 'I set them on the right path and told them to come on at all speed, for their countrymen were in peril and desperately needed aid. And here they are, five hundred and sixty-two men and women of Gendri, all fit and strong, well-supplied with the rations that failed to reach you at Wily's Clearing, Nish, and thirsting to defend their land and their people. Plus another forty-six of your own militia, from the lot you left behind with dysentery, now recovered. Well, Klarm? I think they have the measure of your exhausted hundred.'

A horn blasted, and the first of the Gendri militia topped the ramp over the western gap. Big, brawny farmers they might be, but their spears made a neat line against the sky and they were marching in step, singing as they came.

'Whoever leads them, they're well-trained,' said Nish, signing to his troops, who raised their swords and let out a full-throated cheer of defiance.

Klarm's hand slipped towards Reaper.

'I'm calling your bluff,' said Flydd, pointing the serpent staff at the dwarf again, 'and your troops don't have time to do their dirty work. You've lost, Klarm. The Histories will tell of this battle as the Deliverer's first victory, and the empire's greatest defeat. I might even take a shot at writing

221

the Great Tale myself, once I retire.' He grinned mockingly. 'I'll accept your surrender now.'

The quicksilver surface of Reaper began to churn and bubble, and in a flash of clearsight Nish saw something hot and black and eager below the surface. The hovering hand froze and he caught his breath. If Klarm did know how to draw upon the dreadful power of Reaper, and dared to take Flydd on, he could turn defeat into victory in a moment.

Flydd's fist tightened on the serpent staff, which was limned with a baleful green luminosity.

Klarm swallowed, went to lower his swollen, bandaged hand onto Reaper, but at the last second snatched it away, struggling to control his terror. How interesting, thought Nish. He's used Gatherer many times, and Reaper once or twice, but he's still afraid of it.

It had burned him when he'd destroyed the red-haired archer's arm in the clearing, and perhaps at other times, which would explain why he had not attacked the pass directly, using Reaper's power to shatter the defences and destroy the militia. But Klarm, for all his courage in other ways, was too afraid of the uncanny tears.

'Be damned!' Klarm raised his voice. 'Piper, sound the retreat.'

A soldier raised a horn and let out several abrasive blasts.

'Surr,' said a deathly-white sergeant, 'where would you have us retreat to?'

'Back over the pass,' said Klarm. 'Head down the Range of Ruin, all the way to the barracks in Taranta, Sergeant. I thank you for your loyal service, and I pray that you make it.'

'Surr?' The sergeant's voice quavered. 'Are you not coming with us?'

'I must take a path that no mortal man may follow,' said Klarm. 'At least, no one who does not hold the Profane Tears.

222

Even with them, I may not survive it, but I have to try. I must find a way to fight Stilkeen. Farewell.'

The sergeant saluted and turned away, and his one hundred tattered and broken men followed him up and over the crest of Blisterbone, out of sight.

'They'll never get there,' said Flydd. 'The *really wet* season will hit any day now.'

'I'm afraid you're right,' said Klarm regretfully, 'but I could not take them on the path I'm forced to follow.'

'Into the shadow realm?' said Flydd.

'Yes. Aren't you going to stop me?'

'How could I? You've got the tears – why won't you use them?'

Again Klarm's hand moved towards Reaper; again drew back. 'The cursed tears,' he said heavily, like one old friend confiding in another. 'I only took them out of duty, though I never thought the burden of carrying them would grow so heavy.'

'It would not be as heavy if the burden was shared,' said Flydd slyly.

'With you?'

'Why not? You know what a monster Jal-Nish is, and he's gone, probably never to return, so why do you still serve him? Why continue to do his evil work?'

'He is a monster,' said Klarm. 'I see it now he's gone –'

'Because the deceptions he worked upon you with Gatherer have faded,' Flydd suggested. 'I never thought you, of all people, would be so easily taken in.'

Klarm ignored that. 'But there is also good in Jal-Nish. He loves Santhenar, and he saw long ago that it was under threat.'

He tried to tell me many times, Nish remembered, but I refused to listen. I thought he was trying to manipulate me again. *You have no idea of the vicious creatures that lurk in the eternal void between the worlds, desperate to get out,* Jal-Nish had said at the beginning, *but I do. I've seen them with the tears, and every one of them hungers for the prize: the jewel of worlds that is Santhenar.* And he had been right.

'The God-Emperor is determined to protect our world,' Klarm went on, 'and he's the only one who can. That's why I cannot break my word to him. Loyalty matters to me and I will not turn my coat; I also know that no one else can protect Santhenar from Stilkeen.'

'We can,' said Flydd, 'once we bring the empire down and wield the tears.'

'How long would the world be racked by civil war before you succeeded – *if* you did? Months? Years? I can't take the risk, Flydd. Besides, as you pointed out, it takes great strength of purpose to master the tears, and much practice. Jal-Nish spent thirteen years learning their powers and perils; you could hardly do it in less.'

'I believe I could,' said Flydd. 'All modesty aside, I was a better mancer than he was. Far better.'

'Maybe so, but it does not mean you can pick up the tears and wield them in our defence. I'm sorry, Xervish, I cannot yield. I swore to my God-Emperor and I will not give them up, not even to you. Farewell . . . and don't think too badly of me. I may have done bad things, but I did them for good reasons. We were the best of friends once, weren't we?' There was the slightest pleading note in his voice.

Flydd wasn't going to give him any satisfaction. 'Were we?' he said coldly. 'I often reckon up my true friends and give thanks for their steadfastness, but I never see you on that list.'

Klarm shivered, bowed stiffly from the waist, then cupped his left hand above the surface of Reaper. He turned away, growing ever more transparent, walked into the solid rock of the white-thorn peak and disappeared.

NINETEEN

'That was interesting,' said Flydd as the Gendri militia came streaming up the track, and Nish's survivors stumbled down to greet them.

'I'm not sure that I take your meaning,' said Nish distractedly.

'Klarm is afraid to use Reaper, and that astonishes me, for he's the bravest man I've ever met.'

'Physical bravery is one thing; courage in the face of such unknown and uncanny Arts is quite another,' Nish said, with feeling.

'I quite agree, but Klarm is a mancer of both power and subtlety, and long experience. As a scrutator he created hundreds of devices for mancery, and I never knew anyone with a more subtle understanding of those Arts. Why should he be afraid of the tears?'

'Because he does not understand the particular Art behind them?'

'There must be more to it than that,' said Flydd. 'I wonder . . . can he fear that the tears have been shaped by the warped mind of their master, and now have a malicious life of their own?'

'If he's so afraid, we should also be wary of them,' Nish said pointedly.

Flydd shrugged and turned to stare at the mountain into which Klarm had disappeared. Was he planning to follow him, even into the shadow realm? Flydd had once proposed to take that dreadful path himself, thinking it was the only way to escape from Jal-Nish's cordon around Mistmurk Mountain, but Yalkara had intervened and he had ended up in the Nightland instead.

Thunder rumbled in the distance. Nish forced his thoughts back to the present, his quest to overthrow his father and, most urgently, how they were going to get off the Range of Ruin before the *really wet* season broke and trapped them for its five-month duration.

'How many people can the air-sled carry?' he said.

'Chissmoul?' Flydd called. 'Leave off groping Nish's lieutenant and come here.'

She came across, not in the least abashed. 'Surr?'

Flydd repeated Nish's question.

She frowned and touched the bandage over her missing ear. 'If we sling safety ropes around the edges we might pack everyone on. Why do you ask?'

'I presume you don't want to walk all the way to the centre of the empire. Besides, the Gendri militia can't carry our wounded down,' Flydd said to Nish. Another crack of thunder sounded, louder this time. 'The *really wet* season is going to break any day now. You'd better send them back at once.'

'I don't think any force on Santhenar could shift them just now,' said Nish, choking up as he watched the Gendrigorean troops embracing one another like long-lost friends. 'It's been a long time since my militia have had anything to celebrate. We've got to give them time to greet old comrades, begin to grieve for all they've lost, and celebrate their victory.'

Flydd seemed slightly irritated, but finally nodded. 'It's been a long time for us all. You'd better join them; you'll appear proud and standoffish if you hold back.' But then he smiled and extended his hand. 'Magnificently fought, Nish. No one else could have done what you've achieved here today. I'm sorry we took so long to get back, and left you no word.'

'What did take you so long?' Nish asked as they walked down to where his militia lay sprawled in the sunlight while the Gendri men were setting out the best food they had. A line of stretcher-bearers was carrying the wounded, attended by the two healers, down to join them.

'I'll tell you some day, when we've got the time. Suffice it to say that Klarm had the air-sled well guarded, and it took all our ingenuity plus a good slice of luck to get to it then, modestly, a stroke of sheerest genius for us to steal it from under his nose.

'He retaliated with Gatherer, of course, and if it had not been for Chissmoul's brilliance, the air-sled would have fallen from a great height, which would have been the end of us. I could not take that risk again, so we went to ground some distance away along the Range of Ruin, and there was no way to contact you.'

'How did you take control of the air-sled?'

'I tried using the serpent staff and, to my surprise, it worked – eventually.'

'So did mine,' said Nish, 'though *why* it worked bothers me.'

'Indeed,' Flydd said perceptively. 'The caduceus wasn't left behind as a warning – Stilkeen left it so we would use its separate parts to get ourselves out of trouble. It's moving us around like pieces in a board game, and I don't know why. But we can worry about that later.'

'I worry about it all the time,' said Nish, then forced it from his mind and headed down for the feast.

*

The thunder was growing ever louder and even the slightly tipsy Gendrigoreans were beginning to look anxious.

'We'd better go,' said their captain, Glemm, a thickset farmer from the south of Gendri province with shiny black skin and eyes the same colour, and an incongruous tonsure of white hair around a bald patch as shiny as a polished army boot. 'We've got crops to harvest. We can't be trapped on the range for the *really wet* season.'

'Could you survive if you were trapped?' said Nish. 'I thought that was a death sentence.'

'It would be for *gwishin* like the enemy. And even for you, Nish, resourceful as you are. But we know the mountains; when we have the time we can find food anywhere, plus the herbs we need to keep the ulcers and fevers at bay. It would not be easy to feed us for that long but we would survive . . . at least, those of us who are unharmed . . .'

Nish had anticipated that. 'We'll take the injured with us, on the air-sled.'

'Back to their homes?' said Glemm.

Nish hesitated, and Flydd interposed at once. 'Unfortunately not. The air-sled has been giving us a lot of trouble and I'm not sure how long we can keep it flying. The mancery that powers it –'

Glemm shuddered and flicked his hand over his left shoulder, a sign to ward off evil. Those nearby emulated his gesture and a murmur of unease spread like a wave through the sprawled militia.

'You don't need to worry about that,' said Flydd. 'But I can't take the risk of going to Gendrigore in case the air-sled fails and strands us there. Your war may be over but ours is just beginning, and we've got to go south to the heart of the empire with all speed. As soon as the news gets out that Stilkeen has taken the God-Emperor –'

Glemm repeated his gesture, three times.

'– every rebel on Santhenar will be out for what they can get, and between them they'll tear the empire apart, unless . . .'

Flydd rose to his feet and addressed them all. 'Unless the Deliverer makes himself known throughout the empire at once, and stands ready to fulfil the promise he made at the end of the war. Nish must tell the world that his father has been taken by a *being* from beyond, and immediately claim the Imperial throne. If the news about Jal-Nish gets out first, it will be too late.'

Nish stirred but did not contradict Flydd, since that could only make things worse. However he was not planning to claim the throne, and as soon as they were in private he intended to remind Flydd of that vow.

'Nish may claim the throne,' said Glemm, 'but not everyone will support him.'

'Many will stay loyal to Jal-Nish,' Flydd agreed. 'At least, until they can be sure he's never coming back. And others will try to seize power for themselves. Unless we act fast, there will be civil war.'

'Where are we going, Xervish?' said Nish.

'As far down the east coast as the air-sled will take us.'

'It would be faster to fly across the corner of the Sea of Perion,' said Nish, mentally tracing the route, 'then from the mountains of the Wahn Barre and all the way south-east to Father's palace, Morrelune, near Fadd.'

'Aye,' said Flydd, 'if we trusted the air-sled to take us that far. But the craft has already given us trouble and we can't afford to be marooned in empty lands if it should fail. We'll head south to Taranta, which isn't far as the air-sled flies, and make the initial announcement.

'From there we'll fly east to Crandor, the wealthiest nation on Santhenar, and also the most independent and rebellious. Its capital, Roros, is a great and proud city where people will remember your promise, Nish, and many will welcome you. From Roros we'll hop from city to city down the coast, spreading the news and showing your face everywhere. Then, should the air-sled fail us, we'll be able to take a fast ship south.'

He paused, then looked over the militia. 'Of course, the Deliverer – Nish – can't go alone . . .'

No one spoke for a long time, then Aimee rose painfully to her feet, holding her ribs. 'We've followed our captain all this way and we're not going to abandon him now. I'm with you, Nish, and so is this great lump.'

She put her hand on Clech's woolly head, which was level with her waist though he was sitting down. 'Though what use he'll be, since he's stupidly broken both his legs . . .'

'Thank you,' said Flydd, pointedly shaking the tiny hand and the huge one. 'Roros has healers whose spells can work marvels upon broken bones, and they'll have you on your feet in weeks.' He surveyed the seated militia, frowning.

'What's the matter with you lot?' cried Aimee. 'Stand up for the man you believe in. Up, *up*!'

One by one, the twenty-five able-bodied men and women of his militia rose and came forwards to stand beside him, looking abashed. 'We're with you, surr,' Hoshi said quietly. 'All the way.'

'Thank you,' said Nish, deeply touched despite Aimee's coercion. 'Though it's a bit late to start calling me "surr" now.'

'Sorry, Nish,' grinned Hoshi.

Nish caught sight of a small, carrot-topped figure among the militia, one hand heavily bandaged, and his smile faded. 'Huwld, you can't come with us.'

'I must,' cried the boy. 'I set Uncle free, and he brought the enemy here. It's my fault that most of the militia are dead. I've got to make up for it.'

'What's this?' said Glemm, frowning. 'How could the boy –?'

230

Nish explained, briefly.

'Ah, yes,' said Glemm. 'We know about Boobelar.'

'How?' said Nish.

'We caught him below the entrance to the pass, robbing the dead.' Glemm spat on the ground. 'The brute tried to escape –'

'What happened to Uncle Boobelar?' whispered Huwld.

'In war, lad, there can only be one punishment for such behaviour – we would have put him down . . .'

'But?' said Nish, praying that Boobelar hadn't got away again.

'He tried to escape over the side of the ridge, but with the weight of all his loot he lost his footing and fell. He's dead.'

'And I have to make up for what Uncle did,' said Huwld. 'I've got to go to war with Nish.'

'No, Huwld,' said Nish. 'If I'd known you were with us, I would have sent you back at Wily's Clearing. Besides, you've done as much as any of my soldiers could do, and you've lost a finger to prove it.'

'I have to pay,' wept the boy.

How could it be so hard to tell a child what to do? Nish was beginning to despair when Flangers came forwards.

'Huwld, we've fought together at the defences these past days, and your work has saved many lives. I understand how you feel – and you know I do, for we talked about my own troubles one night – but you've done enough, soldier.'

'Please, Lieutenant –' said Huwld.

'No, lad,' said Flangers. 'You're going home. And that's an order from your commanding officer. You do know what the penalty for disobeying orders is, in war?'

'Yes,' said Huwld quietly, 'but I would never disobey *your* orders.' He forced a smile, and saluted. 'Surr!'

'Thank you,' Nish said softly to Flangers after the boy had turned away. 'I was afraid I would never convince him.'

'He's a good lad, with as stout a heart as any kid I've come across. But too young to take such burdens upon himself. Far too young.'

'Perhaps it's a lesson to us all,' Nish said pointedly, 'to not blame ourselves for things we've paid for long ago.'

'You may be right, *surr*,' said Flangers.

A mass of cloud swirled up and over the tops of the mountains, blotting out the sun, and a chilly wind tumbled down the slopes into their faces. 'Not long now till the *really wet* season begins,' said Glemm, rising. 'Not long at all.'

The remaining food was hastily packed away; the Gendri militia replenished their supplies from the enemy's stores, and Nish's troops scoured the battlefield to refill their quivers and replace their notched swords and battered shields. A network of ropes was strung across the rear half of the air-sled for the troops to hang onto – a wise precaution with Chissmoul at the helm.

Nish limped up to the top of the pass, in case the survivors of Klarm's army were planning a suicidal counter-attack, but they were already out of sight. He took one last look at the rubble-filled slot where so many of his troops had died, and the scoured slope down which his avalanche had passed, then turned back, shaking his head at the futility of war.

By the time he reached the air-sled the fifteen injured were being carried on, bound to their stretchers, which were tied fore and aft to the safety ropes. After making their farewells, his militia crammed on.

Chissmoul sat at the front beneath the empty pennant pole, in a seat made of wood and canvas fixed to the deck. Flydd stood beside her, clutching the pole in one hand and his serpent staff in the other, and Nish took his place on the other side.

'Take it gently,' said Flydd as Chissmoul slipped her

fingers in between the wires and crystals of the air-sled's controller. 'We've got fragile passengers now, remember?'

'I know,' she said mildly.

'Ready?'

'Yes.'

A flurry of cold rain swept up the pass. Lightning flashed; there was a shattering crash of thunder and a deluge fell upon them. The Gendri militia pulled their oilskin hoods over their heads, waved and turned down towards the western gap, and the long march home.

'Farewell,' Nish said quietly, knowing that he was unlikely to return to Gendrigore, or to see any of them again.

Flydd banged the tip of the serpent staff into a socket beside the pennant pole. Chissmoul wiggled her fingers within the wires; an inner crystal shafted out a single beam of blue light, as if to mark the way forwards; the air-sled lifted, revolved on its axis and headed up and over the pass, then south for the city of Taranta.

'The first phase of the war is over,' said Flydd. 'Now the real battle begins.'

TWENTY

'I'm glad it is you, Maelys Nifferlin,' said Zofloc, 'since your coming led to the destruction of my master's tower and the death of her hopes. Had I been informed in time, I would have prevented it, *permanently*. In the aftermath I must exact a suitable punishment – as a lesson to all who threaten my master's plans.'

The sorcerer's black and glittering eyes were locked on her, and Maelys remembered someone talking about him previously. Unlike the other Whelm, who had no interest in any but their own kind, Zofloc took a keen interest in normal humans . . . but not a healthy one.

'W-what are you going to do to me?' Her voice went hoarse. Why, why hadn't she answered when Yggur had called earlier?

'I'm going to kill you with slow sorcery, then wrap your broken body in a treated shroud to make a perfect print of your torments. And wherever I go I will exhibit your death shroud, to demonstrate that our master must never be trifled with. Come.' He crooked a bony finger at her.

'Er, no,' said Maelys, edging sideways along the fire-licked ice. 'It's awfully decent of you but I'm finished here now.'

How could she combat a sorcerer? What were the Whelm's weaknesses, anyway? Flydd had talked about the topic once, but what had he said?

They had a terror, born of their long and tragic Histories, of being cast out by their master. The Whelm were born to serve and without a master they were tormented, purposeless creatures. Unfortunately, Maelys did not see how she could use that fear.

The only other option was to run for her life. Whelm were slow and awkward and, if she could get away, she might beat Zofloc to the base of the steep shaft, but it would be exhausting to climb. Whelm were also tireless and relentless, and if she slipped he would have her.

Once she reached the shaft she could scream for help, and Tulitine and Yggur would probably hear her, but that was no help if they could not find a way in.

She backed around the fire-eaten pillar. Zofloc followed, unperturbed; clearly he wasn't worried about her escaping. She moved faster, realised that she could no longer see him, and whirled.

'Aaaahhh!'

He had gone the other way and was right in front of her, reaching out with those repulsive spatulate fingers. One more step and they would have slid around her throat . . . or lower. She did not like the look in his eyes, nor what she imagined his *interest* in humans was.

Spinning on one foot, Maelys bolted, but slipped on a frozen puddle and went skating forwards, her arms wheeling. Unable to regain her balance, she fell and skidded across the ice on her palms and knees, trying to scrabble away.

Zofloc stalked after her, his jerky Whelm stride covering the distance deceptively quickly, and caught her by the ankle before she could get up. She kicked furiously but had no hope of freeing herself; he stood head and shoulders above her and was immensely strong.

Yanking her backwards, he lifted her by the ankle and raised his arm until her head dangled several handspans off the floor. Her loose trouser legs slid down to her knees, exposing her chalk-white calves. Blood was trickling from her left knee.

Holding her well away, Zofloc inspected her neat ankles and slim calves. Maelys knew that she looked very different from the Whelm women, who were generally tall and lean, with grey skin, thick, prominent bones and large feet and hands. They certainly didn't have her well-endowed thighs or broad hips – their bodies were long and brick-shaped, with practically no waist. No bosom either, she realised as her shirt slid down towards her bust.

He was so strong! His arm wasn't even quivering from her weight. She tried to kick him with her free foot but he caught her other ankle and locked fingers and thumb around it.

Now he was staring at her bosom, squinting against the light from the twinklestone, and she remembered another weakness of the Whelm. Being creatures of the cloudy south and the deep forests, strong light was painful to them.

Raising her hands as if to cover her chest, she yanked the twinklestone off her forehead and stretched it as far as it would go. Instantly its dumbbell shape swelled to the size of a pair of oranges and the light flared so brightly that it hurt her eyes.

Zofloc cried out incoherently and dropped her on her head. Fortunately she did not fall far, though it took a few seconds to recover from the impact.

She found her feet and backed away, holding the twinklestone high and watching him carefully. The sorcerer wasn't pretending; he was holding his callused grey hands in front of his streaming eyes, clearly in pain. Knowing it was the only chance she was going to get, she fled back the way she had come.

As she was squeezing through the narrow passage, she heard his wooden sandals clapping against the floor. He was after her, and this time he would be more careful. Maelys reached the end of the passage, where it opened into the broad outer tunnel, and looked back.

She could no longer hear his footsteps, and when she shone the twinklestone down the passage, it was empty. However, many such narrow passages ran out from the centre; he must have taken another of them and he would know how she'd entered the underground labyrinth. If he reached the steep shaft before she did, she would be trapped.

And perhaps he knew a quicker way there. Her breath was rasping in her throat, her stomach churning sickeningly. She turned right into the broad tunnel and ran, only to realise that she'd gone the wrong way. Maelys had never had a good sense of direction; she should have turned left, not right.

She ran back, panting so loudly that Zofloc must hear her, and surely he would be nearly there by now. As she pounded along, she held the dazzling twinklestone out in front of her, for it was the only advantage she had.

But not much of an advantage, she thought ruefully. If he cornered her, he could advance with eyes closed and arms spread from one side of the tunnel to the other, and catch her by feel.

Ahead she made out the steeply sloping shaft; her light was winking off the broken permafrost. Maelys glanced over her shoulder but there was no one behind her, and there were no side tunnels between her and the shaft. She was going to make it after all.

Then Zofloc stood up suddenly; he'd been waiting a few spans from the junction with the shaft, and he was laughing. She thrust out the twinklestone but, as she'd predicted, he closed his eyes and spread his arms, low down so she could not get by.

Putting on a burst of speed, she sprang as high as she could, her left foot just grazing his right arm, and landed at chest height on the slope of the shaft. Pain shrieked through her knees and her palms, and the light went out. Where was the twinklestone? She must have dropped the wretched thing and there was not a second to look for it. As she dragged herself up the broken permafrost into the darkness, Zofloc's sandals sounded below her and he made a muffled crowing noise.

She was scrambling higher when a pinpoint of light reflected back at her from an icy facet. You silly fool, Maelys thought, you landed on the twinklestone and crushed it down to a mote; that's what happened to the light. It was still stuck to her finger but she didn't have time to stretch it to brightness, because the sorcerer was only a span below. And, she remembered, Whelm could see in near darkness.

She scrambled up the slope, tearing the soft skin of her palms on the iron-hard permafrost and praying that the speck-sized twinklestone would not stick to it and be lost.

With a snorting grunt, Zofloc lunged. She threw herself upwards but his flat fingertips caught the heel of her left boot, tightened, and jerked. She tried to kick him, but he was holding her too tightly.

Maelys attempted to shake him loose though that did not work either, and her foot began to slip out of her boot. If it was the only way to get free she would gladly lose it. She wiggled her small foot back and forth, it came out and she pulled herself up another half a span.

Her filthy sock kept catching on the broken surface so

she threw it in Zofloc's face and kept going, up and up, though after she had climbed five spans or so Maelys realised that she could not hear him. Was he close? Or had he gone another way to cut her off?

She stood up, swaying on the steep surface, and stretched the twinklestone until it reached its original size and cast bright light up and down the shaft. Maelys checked below her, yelped and nearly fell into the sorcerer's arms, for he was only a span away. He had discarded his wooden sandals and was creeping up like a four-legged insect, his broad, flat fingers and toes clinging securely to the iciest surfaces.

Stretching the twinklestone to its fullest extent, Maelys thrust it down at him. Pain wrenched his grim features out of shape and he swayed backwards so far that it seemed impossible he could cling on, but he crouched, turned his head away and began to move up again.

She would never escape him on hands and knees; she wasn't quick enough. Maelys stood and tried to run up the slope, but it was too steep; her legs did not have the strength, nor her feet the grip.

Whacking the twinklestone against her forehead, she used her fingers to pull herself up. The glow was so brilliant that she had to squint to see, but there was no time to reduce it.

She gained a span; he closed the gap in a scrabbling lunge. She forced herself up further; again he nearly caught her. Twice she turned and pointed the twinklestone at him without warning, and twice he evaded the light just in time.

Maelys was exhausted now, her strength failing rapidly, and she wasn't yet halfway. She would never make it to the top. Might as well get frostbite in both feet as in one, she thought, then wrenched her other boot off and hurled it at Zofloc's head.

At this range she could hardly miss and, with his eyes

screwed shut, he did not see it. The boot heel slammed into his nose with a satisfying crunch, and he swayed backwards. His feet slipped and for one glorious moment she thought he was going to fall all the way, but he caught a firm handhold a few spans below her and hung on.

She'd gained a respite, though only a temporary one. 'Yggur, Tulitine!' she screamed. 'Help, help!'

The distorted echoes chased themselves up and down the permafrost shaft, slowly dying away, and she thought she heard a reply, though she could not make out any words. Yggur and Tulitine certainly weren't nearby; they must not have found a way in.

Now Zofloc was coming again, every breath making a repulsive nasal gurgling. Blood was flooding from his nose; he licked it away with a long grey tongue. If anything, he was moving faster than before. She'd hurt him and clearly he planned to brutalise her, before . . . before he made that shroud from her battered and broken body.

'Help!' she cried plaintively.

He looked up, eyes carefully averted, and smiled. They both knew it would soon be over. Only one thing could save her now: the dimensionless box, and if she unfolded it and held it edge-on, he could not see it.

Maelys unbuttoned her pocket, carefully caught the scrunched-up box by its edge, as Yggur had held it, and drew it out. While she'd been thinking about the attack, Zofloc had climbed another span. Now he was crouching not far below, his lower face smeared with blood.

She backed up a step, then another, but one of his long strides closed the gap again. Maelys held the twinklestone out before her, like a weapon. He glanced at her, sideways, then hastily away. His eyes were watering but as long as he kept them averted from the light he could still see.

As she tried to move up another step, her foot slipped on

240

an icy patch. She steadied herself, moved a little sideways and tried again. Again she slipped.

The sorcerer rose from a crouch to his full height, and she tensed. One leaping lunge and he would have her. She prepared to whip the dimensionless box around and slam it into him.

They faced each other for a minute or two, perfectly still. Her heart was thundering now; why didn't he move? She wanted him to attack first, for she was afraid to.

He crouched suddenly, as if to spring, but shot upright again and feinted with his left hand, swinging it at her middle. Maelys went at him with the dimensionless box, not realising until too late that his stroke was a feint and he hadn't leapt at all; his body was well out of reach.

As she began to overbalance, she swung desperately at him. He reached out to grab her wrist; she twisted at the last second and the flattened dimensionless box slapped against the side of his right hand.

Air shrieked into the box; Zofloc let out a harsh cry of dismay, followed by words of sorcery, and batted at his right hand with the left. A bright light flashed in the darkness and the dimensionless box went flying. She felt it whine past her ear, something cool splattered against her face, and she lost sight of it.

The sorcerer was gasping and shaking his right hand, which was red-raw and dripping blood. All the skin was gone, down to his wrist, and some of the flesh – it had been drawn into the box and disintegrated in an instant. She found a firm footing and backed up carefully, feeling sick at what the box had done. And where was it?

She glanced behind her, knowing that it had fallen not far up. If she stepped on it, it would do the same to her and she had no sorcery to protect herself. Maelys could not see the black circle anywhere, and dared not swing the twinklestone that way to look for it in case Zofloc went for her.

'Maelys?' came Yggur's voice, and her heart leapt, though from the timbre of the echoes he was a long way up.

'Down here,' she shouted. 'Zofloc's here!' Maelys turned instinctively, hoping for a glimpse of Yggur, even a reflection from his eyes, but nothing moved in the darkness.

She heard the sorcerer's scrabbling leap, his gurgling gasp, and before she could move he was flying at her, arms and legs spread. He landed on top of her, eyes closed, and crushed her against the slope.

Laying a knee across her hips, he pressed her against the broken permafrost. He forced her arms behind her back, pinned them there with his other knee across her chest and, when the light was hidden behind her, opened his eyes.

She humped her back; Zofloc's arm flailed, his skinless hand bumped against the side of the shaft and he bared his teeth in silent agony. He was so strong and stoic: had it happened to her, Maelys would have screamed until her throat bled.

'What are you going to do to me?' she said faintly, for with his weight on her chest it was hard to draw breath.

'A very particular kind of sorcery, Maelys Nifferlin, known only to us Whelm and developed for one single purpose – to savagely punish our master's enemies.'

There was a ferocious, bloodthirsty gleam in his eyes. She'd hurt him and he was going to do far worse to her.

'Why?' she squeaked. She had to keep him talking, though she did not think he would allow Yggur to get close. What could Yggur do, anyway? His powers were fading – he could not combat a sorcerer as strong and determined as Zofloc. 'Why do you hate us so?'

'I don't hate you; your kind are nothing to me. Had you

not thwarted my master, I would not have turned my head as you went by.'

Maelys could not hear any sound from above; Yggur was not coming to help her. She had to save herself. Zofloc took his weight off her chest and bent to lift her, and Maelys's right hand, which still held the twinklestone, slipped free.

While it was still concealed behind her back she separated the twinklestone into two between her fingers and thumb, stuck one to the tip of her middle finger and the other to her index finger, and loosely curled her hand to hide the lights. She did not think her feeble plan could work, but it was her only hope now.

He caught her shirt-front with his good hand, but as he heaved her upright, Maelys whipped her right hand out and the lights shone brilliantly. Had he closed his eyes she would have failed, and died, but instead he turned his head to the left to escape the brightness and she thrust her index and middle fingers at his eyes. The twinklestones stuck to his moist eyeballs; he let out a roar; his grip relaxed and she scrabbled away.

He tried to tear the twinklestones off but they would not come. His tear-flooded eyes had gone red, and when he pulled on the twinklestones his eyeballs came halfway out of their sockets, which was one of the more unpleasant sights Maelys had seen lately. She felt sick at what she had done, for nothing but a knife could remove the shining stones now.

Zofloc began to flail about, making a dreadful squealing as he tried to rid himself of the burning rays, but could not close his eyes. He slipped, snatched frantically at the permafrost with his skinless hand, failed to get a grip and fell all the way down. Maelys heard a hollow crack that she did not want to consider too carefully, then lay back on the slope, gasping.

'Maelys?' said Yggur distantly.

'Here,' she whispered.

'Where are you?'

'Further down,' she called. 'Be careful – the dimensionless box is up there, somewhere.'

A faint yellow gleam appeared above, and directly she saw him, his long features made grotesque by the uplight limning his fingers – not a twinklestone but another kind of sorcerous glow altogether.

'I thought you couldn't use the Art?' said Maelys.

'When the need was great enough, I found a wisp of it.'

'More than a wisp, to move all that broken rock and get in.'

'That wasn't mancery,' Yggur said, 'that was honest muscle.'

A few spans above her Yggur bent, picked up the crumpled dimensionless box, squeezed it in his fist and thrust it into a pocket. Going to his haunches beside her, he inspected her scratched knees and palms, her blood-spattered face. 'Are you . . .?'

'I'm all right,' said Maelys, clinging to him. His big hands were also scratched and torn. 'I fell a few times. Zofloc didn't harm me . . . but he was going to.'

'Where is he now? Did he run when he heard my voice?'

'You've got a high opinion of yourself,' she muttered, looking up at his stern and craggy face.

'I dare say I have,' said Yggur, smiling. 'You get like that when you've lived as long as I have, and had your way for most of it. Well?'

'I think he's dead. I twinklestoned his eyeballs.'

'Did you now?' he exclaimed admiringly. 'Well done – there could be no better way to disable a Whelm, had you known it.'

'He fell all the way down and – it sounded like the impact made rather a mess. I'm sorry about that.'

'Why are you sorry?' said Yggur. 'He was going to kill you; you're entitled to defend yourself, in whatever way you can.'

'I'm sorry because I'm not going back down. If you want the white fire, you'll have to go past Zofloc's body to get it.'

'You found some?' he said eagerly.

'Yes, on a central foundation pillar of ice. It would have been under the inner tower. You go down –'

'I'll find it.'

'And bring my boots when you come,' she called after him, hugging her aching feet. 'I'm freezing.'

TWENTY-ONE

Chissmoul flew them south-east to Taranta, a ramshackle old city occupying the narrow isthmus that had once joined the northern tip of the continent of Lauralin to the great island of Faranda. To the north stood the tropical ocean surrounding the peninsula of Gendrigore, while on the south, Taranta's peasant quarter had once looked over the mighty cliffs onto the unrelenting aridity of the Dry Sea.

However the Dry Sea had been flooded at the end of the lyrinx war and its level, still rising slowly, now lay less than fifty spans below the top of the cliffs, which had begun to crumble, carrying parts of the peasant quarter with them. The people rebuilt their hovels a few paces away and went on with their lives as though crumbling cliffs were an every-day matter.

That afternoon, not long before sunset, as the air-sled completed the relatively short flight from Blisterbone Pass, and Chissmoul was circling high above the city, Flydd stood up to address them.

'We'll have to be careful now. Taranta is a conservative place and the God-Emperor's biggest garrison in the north is based here – fifteen thousand men, though many of them would have been in the army you've just wiped out. The dead will have many friends in Taranta, and it's one of the most loyal outposts of the empire, so they won't be thrilled to hear our news. But we can't afford any delay – Klarm could turn up anywhere, at any time, and we've got to get our story out first. The first version of a story is the one that most people will believe. How are we going to play it, Nish?'

He had been thinking about that question for the whole trip, but Nish hadn't come up with a decent plan and did not think he was likely to; their opposition was too overwhelming.

'Call a secret meeting with the city elders, the Imperial seneschal, the governor and the commander of the garrison,' he said. 'Tell them the bad news and beat a hasty retreat towards Roros.'

Flydd frowned, looked back at the militia, as if for inspiration, and shook his head. 'That won't do at all.'

'Why not?'

'If we run, we'll look scared and they'll think we've got something to hide. We must appear strong, measured and in control. Besides, the Deliverer is the heir to the Imperial throne; he can't slink away, no matter how much he might want to.'

Flydd favoured Nish with a sour stare. 'And if we were to run, they could accuse us of any villainy imaginable. They could make us out to be worse monsters than your father – and they will.'

'Surr?' said Flangers tentatively, as if he had no right to express an opinion in such weighty matters.

'Yes?' said Flydd, pacing in a circle around the serpent staff, which was embedded in its socket at the prow.

His outstretched fingers trailed across it as he walked; he had hardly let go of it since they'd left the pass. What did his mancery see in it, Nish wondered, and how did he plan to use it?

'They don't know *we've* got the air-sled,' said Flangers. 'And no one knows that Stilkeen has snatched the God-Emperor, so everyone will assume that he's flying this craft. If you hover high above the square, where you can't be identified, and give your orders, the city's leaders will obey without question.'

'Very good,' said Flydd. 'I knew there was a reason why we rescued you from the Numinator.'

Chissmoul, whose hands were embedded between the wires of the controller, scowled and jumped up, glaring at Flydd. The air-sled lurched and dropped sharply; she corrected automatically and it resumed its steady circling.

Flangers chuckled and touched her on the shoulder. 'Take no notice,' he said *sotto voce*. 'The old fellow doesn't mean to be insulting; it's just his way, as surely you remember of old.'

'After all you've done!' Chissmoul gritted, slamming down into her pilot's chair.

'Go on, Flangers,' said Flydd, unfazed.

'What if you were to order a general assembly in the main square – not just the city elders, but also the landowners, lawyers, merchants and traders, and everyone else of note, and the common people as well. Wait – what if you held it in that great square over there in the peasant quarter?' Flangers indicated the ramshackle suburb by the cliffs.

'That would get the city elders and the governor offside.'

'They'll be offside anyway, since they're hand-picked by the God-Emperor, but with thousands of people in the square they'll never suppress your story. People will start spreading it tonight, by skeet, to the four quarters of the world.'

Flydd stared at him in astonishment. 'You show an amazing grasp of political manoeuvrings for a humble sergeant, Flangers . . . even one recently raised to lieutenant for heroism above the call of duty,' he added hastily as Chissmoul directed another blistering glare at him.

'I didn't make him lieutenant because of his courage under fire,' said Nish, wishing he'd thought of Flangers's idea. 'I did it because of his mastery of battle tactics and his brilliant leadership.'

'Whatever you say,' said Flydd, eyeing Flangers curiously. 'How come this talent didn't manifest itself during the war? You might have made general by the end of it.'

'I never wanted to be a general,' Flangers said quietly. 'Sergeant was always good enough for me. But since you ask, for the seven years we were held prisoner in the Numinator's tower, Yggur and I spent our free time talking about the nature of power and the art of command. You can learn a lot in seven years, if you've a mind to, and I want to make Santhenar a better place.'

'Very good,' said Flydd, losing interest. 'Nish, what do you think of the lieutenant's plan?'

'I wish I'd thought of it.'

'Chissmoul,' said Flydd, 'head to the *main* city square and hover, fifty spans up so they can't see me, while I make the announcement.'

She turned towards a large paved square, actually pent-agonal in outline, in the wealthy part of the city. An ornate marble building of several storeys, fronted with columns, extended along a third of its northern edge. A series of domes soared from the centre of the structure, framed with pairs of tall, slender towers on each corner.

'That's the governor's palace,' said Flydd.

'You know Taranta, then?' said Nish.

'Of course; I've been here several times. It was the wealthiest city in the tropics once, but it fell on hard times when the Sea of Perion dried up, thousands of years ago. The enormous mansion on the far side of the square belongs to Jal-Nish's seneschal – the governor's rival in Taranta.'

As they went lower, Nish saw that the columns of the

palace were grimy and the stone was pitted, while the once magnificent paintwork above the portico was faded and flaking.

'Hover here,' said Flydd as they approached the governor's palace. 'Now, how did Klarm work that amplifying spell to throw his voice so far?'

He thought for a moment, touched his throat while holding the serpent staff, then stood on the prow of the air-sled and spoke in a rolling, sonorous voice that echoed across the square and back. Nish knew it as Flydd's scrutator's voice, the one he'd once used to persuade, to charm, and to get his way, and he had been a master of that Art.

'Folk of Taranta, I call upon you one and all, from the highest to the lowest, in the name of the God-Emperor.'

People appeared at windows and doorways. Shopkeepers looked up from the market booths clustered at the far side of the square. Dignitaries and officials came running down the steps of the palace, and burst out of the front door of the seneschal's mansion.

'Folk of Taranta,' Flydd repeated, 'in the name of the God-Emperor Jal-Nish Hlar, I bring urgent news of the war. You are required to assemble in the old square in the peasant quarter one hour after sundown, to hear the news.'

'The peasant quarter!' cried a large, florid man wearing extravagant robes of black and crimson, as though Flydd had insulted him personally.

Flydd ignored him, and the air-sled drifted over Taranta for the next hour while he repeated the announcement over every public square and local market.

'Enough,' he said. 'Let's get on with it. Chissmoul, to the peasant quarter.'

Its old square was also surrounded by manors, mansions and great public buildings, once magnificent but now fallen into sad decay. The vast square had been hastily lit by a thousand lanterns, large and small, their oily fumes drifting in dark grey clouds across the assembly.

The place was packed to overflowing and abuzz with excitement, for the God-Emperor of all Santhenar was not given to public proclamations and indeed, may not ever have visited Taranta before. And if he had, Nish thought, Father certainly would not have deigned to address the common folk.

As he looked over the side, he noted dozens of patches of colour in different parts of the square, each marking the individual racial or ethnic attire of a group of the myriad peoples who dwelt in Taranta, from the scarlets and browns of the desert dwellers who went veiled against the sand-storms on the high plateaux of Faranda, to the striking mustard-yellow gowns of the former Dry Sea salt-gleaners, now driven into poverty-stricken exile by the flooding of that vast abyss, to the sapphire blue blouses and emerald kilts of the whelk gatherers of the city foreshores, and many others he had no knowledge of.

The city governor sat in a gilded throne on a platform in the centre of the square, and the God-Emperor's seneschal – the florid fellow who wore the black and crimson robes – on another throne of equal magnificence, the two men glaring at each other, forever kept as rivals, yet forever subordinate to the whim of the God-Emperor, who had held the reins of power tightly and delegated only when he had to.

And even then, the empire kept a careful lookout. Nish saw that, at the four quarters of the square, tower-mounted wisp-watchers were whirring back and forth, their watch unceasing, their vision all-seeing, reporting everything of moment to Gatherer – assuming Gatherer was in a place where it could receive such messages, of course.

Nish wondered, briefly, where Klarm was now, if he were still alive. What would happen to the tears if he were not?

A brightly clad contingent of military officers occupied the table to the right of the seneschal, the beribboned commander of the military garrison at their head.

Other dignitaries and city elders had their own tables nearby, but the greatest of all, a board ten spans long and three wide, and so polished that Nish could make out the reflection of the air-sled in it, had been laid out well-spaced from any other, as befitted the God-Emperor of the civilised world. His table and magnificent throne were empty, of course.

'How did they do all this in an hour?' Nish marvelled.

'They're expecting to see the God-Emperor,' said Flydd. 'And he does not tolerate failure, or personal indignity, in large ways or small.'

'Do you think this is a good idea?'

'What?'

'Allowing them to believe that Father is aboard the air-sled? They'll be angry when they discover they've been tricked.'

'I dare say,' said Flydd, 'but if we had revealed ourselves in advance it would have given our enemies time to prepare an attack. This way, they'll be as surprised as anyone.'

'They may already be suspicious.'

'Why would they be? When your God-Emperor has been all-powerful for a decade, and has crushed all opposition, his defeat is unthinkable until it actually happens. Quiet now – it's time.' He nodded to Chissmoul. 'Hover twenty spans above the God-Emperor's table.'

'You're not proposing to go down, are you, surr?' Chissmoul said anxiously, her previous outrage forgotten.

'Certainly not,' said Flydd. 'But be ready for a hasty get-away in case they don't appreciate what I've got to say. Tell your militia to stay down, Nish,' he warned. 'I wouldn't want to lose anyone overboard.'

Nish gestured to his troops, who were peering over the sides in a yokelish and undignified fashion. Chissmoul hovered over the God-Emperor's table. Flydd renewed his voice-amplifying spell and went to the bow, hanging on to the serpent staff with his left hand.

The wisp-watchers and loop-listeners swung around to point at him and so, Nish noted, did various smaller devices on the tops of other buildings, each operated by a black-robed scrier. Already they would be trying to identify Flydd, though they were unlikely to succeed, since few people alive had seen his renewed self.

We'll never get away with it, Nish thought. The eyes and spies of the God-Emperor never sleep. And Father might be gone, but the command structure he put in place is intact and will crush any insurgency as brutally as he would.

'Seneschal, Governor, Commander, city elders, and people of Taranta,' Flydd boomed. 'I bring you the gravest tidings.'

He paused while a stir rustled from one end of the gathering to the other.

'That's not the God-Emperor,' someone cried.

'Who is it?' yelled another.

The dignitaries rose to their feet, staring at the air-sled. The Imperial seneschal was gesturing to a red-robed chief scrier, while the commander of the garrison was speaking urgently to his officers.

'You'd better tell them, quick,' said Nish.

Flydd moved closer to the edge, raised his voice, and put a little of his rhetorical Art into it.

'My name is Xervish Flydd.' He paused as a louder murmur ran through the crowd. 'Many of you will know of me, for I was a scrutator and commander-in-chief at the end of the lyrinx war.'

The buzz of talk, quickly silenced, indicated that he was

remembered, though not necessarily favourably by all. Flydd had taken hard decisions at that time, and Nish knew he had made many enemies.

'My face is different,' Flydd went on, 'because, hunted near to death by the God-Emperor, I had no choice but to use a great spell, which few mancers have survived, to *renew* my failing body. But inside I am the same Xervish Flydd who fought and routed the enemy lyrinx, then negotiated an honourable peace . . . when all others wanted nothing but eternal war.'

'That's not how I remember it,' Nish hissed. 'The peace wasn't your idea –'

'Shut up,' Flydd said in his own voice. 'There's a purpose behind my every word.'

'There had better be.'

Flydd raised his free hand and used the amplified voice again. 'You are wondering why I am in command of the God-Emperor's own air-sled, and calling this conclave in his name. I bear grave tidings to the people of Taranta, indeed, to all Santhenar. The *gravest* tidings of all.'

He paused for a minute to let that sink in, and continued. 'As you know, several weeks ago the God-Emperor's proud army, ten thousand of his finest troops, set out from Taranta to cross the Range of Ruin by the high pass called Blister-bone. They marched to punish the little land of Gendrigore for sheltering the God-Emperor's only surviving son, Cryl-Nish Hlar, and the army was commanded by the dwarf, General Klarm.

'The advance guard crossed the pass, and so did the God-Emperor, riding on this very air-sled, and there he met his son. Nish commanded a pathetic little militia of Gendrigorean farmers and hunters armed with mattocks and cudgels – just three hundred and fifty men, *and women.*'

There came a stir from the rear of the air-sled, and Nish

could understand why. What was Flydd up to, denigrating his militia in this way?

'Yes,' Flydd went on, 'Gendrigore has fallen so low that it even sent *women* into the front line of battle.'

The militia began to mutter among themselves.

'Nish, shut them up before they ruin everything,' Flydd said from the corner of his mouth.

Nish ran back. 'Flydd knows what he's doing,' he said quietly. 'Please give him the chance.'

'He speaks with the forked tongue of his iron serpent,' Clech growled, sitting up on his stretcher, but he gestured to the militia and they fell silent.

'But before Jal-Nish could do battle with his son's little ragtag militia,' said Flydd, 'something happened that no one on Santhenar, not even the all-seeing God-Emperor, could have foreseen. A mighty *being* from the void, an immortal creature called Stilkeen, materialised out of nothingness, seized him in its claws and took him hostage.'

The crowd gasped, cried out, stared at one another, then everyone began shouting at once. The governor stood up, held up his hand and the clamour ceased.

'I don't believe you,' he said with an anxious glance at the chief scrier and the seneschal, as if he would be held personally responsible for Flydd's heretical statement. 'The God-Emperor has never been defeated; and he never will be.'

'Be assured that he has been taken,' said Flydd, 'overcome in an instant, despite his mighty Profane Tears. And Stilkeen will only return him in exchange for a treasure beyond price – chthonic fire – stolen from it thousands of years ago.'

'Your tale grows more outlandish by the minute,' shouted the governor. 'What is chthonic fire, and who stole it?'

'It is the dreadful force of binding, *and unbinding*, that caused the volcanic death of Aachan. You remember, I'm sure, that fifty thousand Aachim fled to Santhenar in a fleet of constructs thirteen years ago, because their world was being destroyed before their eyes. Chthonic fire did that. And now, if we are not very careful, it will wreak the same havoc on Santhenar.'

There was a long pause. Flydd's losing them, Nish thought. He's made it too complicated, and he's taking too long to get to the point.

'*Who* stole the fire?' bellowed the God-Emperor's seneschal, not to be outdone by his rival. He whispered to a runner beside him and the man ran off, elbowing his way through the crowd.

'The Charon, Yalkara, but that no longer matters,' said Flydd hastily, evidently sensing that the situation was slipping from his grasp. 'Since Stilkeen holds the God-Emperor hostage, there is no choice but to find this chthonic fire.'

'What has this to do with you, an outlaw with a price on your head?' said the governor. 'And before that you were a lying scrutator, so why should we listen to anything you say?'

Flydd lowered his voice until the crowd had to stand on tiptoes and cup their hands around their ears to hear him. 'I'll tell you why –'

'You have no authority,' snapped the governor. 'The God-Emperor's deputy is General Klarm and we take our orders from him alone – or in his absence, someone who bears his signed and sealed authority. Should Klarm require us to find this chthonic fire, we will act on his word instantly, but as for you – begone!'

Flydd stood at the prow, holding the serpent staff, a faint smile creasing his broad features. 'Are you finished?'

'Nothing more needs be asked, *or said.*'

'You haven't asked about the God-Emperor's army.'

The governor said, as if by rote, 'The God-Emperor's

forces are as numberless as the stars in the sky, and in ten years they have never been defeated. They will crush Gendrigore like a cockroach on a dinner plate and carry its rebellious inhabitants into everlasting slavery.'

'Ah!' said Flydd, and paused meaningfully. 'But –'

'What?' cried the governor.

Flydd just stood there, looking down his nose and smiling.

'What do you know?' cried the seneschal.

After another agonisingly long pause, Flydd said, 'Over the past few days, there has been an almighty battle on the Range of Ruin.'

'And our glorious army annihilated the upstart Gendrigoreans,' said the seneschal.

'Alas,' said Flydd, 'it did not. Several days ago, Nish's little militia, in a surprise attack, seized the impregnable pass of Blisterbone.'

The seneschal swayed and grasped at the nearest object, a water carafe, for support, but it shattered in his hand. He looked down stupidly at his bloody palm. 'But so small a number could never hold it – not even Blisterbone – against ten thousand.'

'They held it,' said Flydd.

'It isn't possible.'

'They held it,' Flydd repeated, and now his voice boomed out in triumph across the vast square. 'With courage and guile, and sheer bloody determination to save their country, whatever it took, Nish's Gendrigoreans held off Jal-Nish's army again and again. They fought their enemy to a stand-still and, at midday today, when the remnants of the God-Emperor's once proud army finally retreated from the pass, only a broken and beaten hundred survived.'

'No!' cried the governor. 'This cannot be!'

The Imperial seneschal swayed on his feet. The

commander of the garrison drew his brightly uniformed officers into a huddle. Several people screamed, a hundred wailed, and then, as the catastrophe sank in, a dreadful lamentation ebbed and flowed across the square.

'It was the greatest defeat in the history of the God-Emperor,' Flydd went on inexorably when the clamour had died down. 'Of ten thousand men, only one hundred survived, plus the dwarf, Klarm. While of the militia –'

He gestured behind him and Nish waved his troops to their feet. Chissmoul tilted the air-sled and slowly circled the square so everyone could see the heroes. 'Here they are. Forty-two, counting the injured,' Flydd concluded. 'People of Taranta, you stand in the presence of giants.'

'Where are our hundred?' said the beribboned commander of the garrison. 'We cannot take your word for this.'

The seneschal caught his arm and whispered in his ear. The commander nodded. Another runner was sent.

Before he had disappeared, however, the short, red-robed chief scrier came striding across the square, two attendants before him knocking everyone out of his path with their knobble sticks, two behind hauling a head-high device on a wheeled cart. It looked like a combination of a loop-listener and a snoop-sniffer, and Nish felt a worm of ice crawl up his backbone. What had the scrier discovered?

'Your hundred are marching down the track from Blisterbone,' said Flydd hastily. 'They are the bravest of men and I salute them,' he snapped upright, performing the action, 'but the *really wet* season is about to break and without aid they cannot survive.'

'Why does this matter?' hissed Nish. 'Get on with it.'

'It matters,' Flydd replied quietly, 'because they corroborate our story. They have to be heard.'

'We cannot lose an entire army to so few,' said the commander, who was white-faced and haggard. Under the

God-Emperor's reign, he would bear part of the responsibility for the shattering defeat. 'We would become a laughing stock. There would be uprisings; civil war.'

'I could not countenance that either,' said Flydd. 'You must find a way to rescue them.'

The scrier slithered in behind the seneschal and began whispering to him.

'How can that be done?' said the commander.

'Nothing can save them while they remain in the treacherous high peaks of the Range of Ruin. No flying craft, save an air-sled, could negotiate the furious updraughts there. But should the survivors reach the lower parts of the range, you could ferry them out on an air-dreadnought.'

'There are no air-dreadnoughts,' said the commander, 'but we might muster an obsolete air-floater or two.'

'Then do so without delay,' Flydd said with lowered voice. 'Morale must be maintained at all costs.'

'And General Klarm?' said the governor. 'What of our mighty dwarf?'

'He lives,' said Flydd.

'After such a defeat he should have been the first to fall on his sword,' grated the commander.

'And I'm sure he would have,' Flydd said smoothly, 'save that he has a greater responsibility, one I'm sure you have not forgotten. In the God-Emperor's absence General Klarm wields the Profane Tears and is responsible for the maintenance of the realm. And though I am now and ever will be Klarm's most bitter enemy, I will not demean him in your eyes, for he has an even more vital task to perform.'

'Indeed?' said the commander coldly.

'Klarm has gone into the deadly shadow realm, all alone, in a desperate attempt to uncover the one weakness that will enable us to drive Stilkeen off – *or bring it down.*'

The commander blanched. 'I cannot ask about that place; I must take you at your word. Are you done?'

'Not quite.' Flydd gestured behind him to Nish, to come forwards.

Nish did so, waiting out of sight from below. He could see why Flydd had left him until last, but Nish had an uncomfortable feeling his appearance was going to come too late.

'With Jal-Nish gone, perhaps never to return,' said Flydd, 'and his anointed deputy lost in the shadow realm, Santhenar is leaderless for the first time in a thousand years.'

'There are many men capable of stepping into the breach,' said the commander. 'I, myself –'

Flydd let out a scornful bray of laughter and the commander broke off. 'Quite so. But there are others.'

Nish noticed that the chief scrier had moved behind the seneschal and was focussing his device on the air-sled again. The seneschal sat bolt upright, staring at Flydd, and the governor was at his side, though Nish felt that they were no longer listening. Flydd had tried to do too much, too soon, to an audience full of closed minds.

'I don't like the look of that scrier,' Flangers said from behind Nish. 'Chissmoul –'

'Don't teach me my job,' she hissed. The tension was affecting them all.

'None among you have the legitimacy or moral authority to take command,' said Flydd. 'If you tried, there would be civil war. The empire would be defenceless and Stilkeen would destroy our beautiful Santhenar . . .'

'But?' said the commander.

'One man can save us,' Flydd boomed, and everyone in the vast square snapped to attention. 'The genius who led his tiny, untrained militia to a shattering victory over the greatest army on Santhenar. The man who swore to bring down the God-Emperor ten years ago and usher in a more peaceful world. The soldier who, despite a decade in the grimmest pit of Mazurhize Prison, refused to go back on his solemn oath.

'People of Taranta,' Flydd said, ignoring the dignitaries to sweep his gaze back and forth across the ordinary folk of the city, 'you know who I am talking about – Jal-Nish's only surviving son, Nish. Nish was a hero of the lyrinx wars and an architect of the peace that ended them. Nish is the one man on Santhenar who can step into his father's boots and lead us through this terrible peril – and here he is.'

Nish came to the prow beside Flydd, rehearsing what he was going to say.

'Damned if I'll take this!' cried the seneschal, pushing himself to his feet. A big, burly man with a sagging belly and a jutting, pugnacious jaw, he was seething. 'My scriers can sort truth from falsehood in an instant, and they have read Flydd's words – if that man *is* Xervish Flydd, which I doubt.'

He flung out his right arm. 'That villain has stolen the God-Emperor's air-sled, and now he's trying to steal an empire, and I won't allow it. Flydd is a condemned rebel; his speech was a dunghill of deceit. There *is* no Stilkeen! There is no such thing as chthonic fire! Our glorious army has not been defeated – *and never will be.'*

He gestured behind him and, on cue, his followers cheered.

'We will *never* be defeated,' he repeated, more loudly. Now cheerleaders throughout the crowd began to cheer, and it spread in waves across the square until everyone was brandishing their fists and praising the God-Emperor's eternal reign.

Though not all with equal enthusiasm, Nish noted. Many people were mouthing the words and waving their fists, while their faces remained carefully expressionless. It gave him a little hope.

'Bring them down!' snapped the seneschal.

Squads of soldiers appeared at the corners of the square and, on the top of the building opposite the largest mansion, soldiers scrambled onto a huge pair of javelards – devices like giant crossbows that fired spears large enough to take down charging elephants.

TWENTY-TWO

'Chissmoul?' Flydd rapped, but the air-sled was already moving.

'Hang on tight, everyone!' Nish said, springing backwards to grasp the pennant pole.

With a bound, Flydd was beside him, taking hold of his staff. The air-sled shot up so quickly that Nish's battle-weary legs could not support him, and he landed bruisingly hard on his knees on the metal deck.

A heavy spear whistled through the space they had just left, travelling so quickly that it outran the metallic twang of the javelard's steel cable. It soared across the square and smashed into the portico of the mansion, sending out clouds of dust and a scything spray of rubble.

'Get out of here, Pilot!' said Flydd.

A pair of spears bracketed the air-sled to left and right.

'They're damn fine shooters,' said Nish, who had fired many a javelard in the war and knew how difficult it was to bring them to bear on a rapidly moving target.

He glanced over his shoulder. Flangers was clinging to the back of Chissmoul's seat, the militia hanging onto their safety ropes. There was nothing anyone could do; their survival was up to Chissmoul now.

Her eyes were alive with the fierce and terrible joy that he had last seen when she had been a thapter pilot during the war, the best of them all. If anyone could save them, she could.

The air-sled zigzagged left, shot up, then dropped sharply at the prow before banking and curving away in the direction of the Sea of Perion. A javelard spear came out of nowhere to clang off the iron top of the pennant pole in a shower of sparks, and Nish jumped. That had been too close.

'How can any shooter be that quick and accurate?' said Flydd.

'I don't know,' Nish muttered. 'I was accounted a good shooter in my day, but I couldn't have done what they're doing.'

'Where did that last spear come from?' Chissmoul cried, side-slipping to the left.

'The alley running down to the sea cliffs,' said Flangers, who possessed the rare gift of being able to take in the action on a whole battlefield within seconds.

'I need a spotter,' she said. 'Tell me where they are and when they're firing. I can't fly and locate their attacks at the same time.'

'Get out of the square,' said Flydd. 'They're bringing up reinforcements.'

'I'm trying, but they've got too many javelards as it is –' Chissmoul broke off, working her fingers furiously inside the controller. The air-sled dropped sharply then went into a whirling pancake turn.

Nish tasted field rations in the back of his throat, while three militiamen lost their footing and were flung halfway over the side by the force of the turn. They cried out involuntarily as their fingers were torn from the safety ropes, and were only saved when the air-sled shot the other way, slamming them into their fellows, then streaked off. He heard retching.

'Tie onto the ropes,' he yelled.

'We can't take much more of this,' said Flydd. 'They're too good, and if we can't get out of the square soon, we never will.'

As the air-sled zoomed back the other way, a flight of three spears whistled over their heads.

'How can their shooters be so uncannily accurate?' Flangers said.

'You're right. It *is* uncanny,' said Nish.

He squinted at the nearest javelard. Could that be a little wisp-watcher mounted on the side? Yes, it was, and it was operated by a scrier; Nish could see his black robes flapping in the wind.

The other javelards also had wisp-watchers and scriers, and why should he be surprised? His father had ever been one for new devices of war or mancery, all inventive, some extraordinary, and many bizarre. Most had failed to perform in battle, for one reason or another, but occasionally Jal-Nish had won an unexpected victory with a weapon no one had seen before.

'The scriers are using their wisp-watchers to tell the javelard operators where to shoot, but even so, they're too accurate – it's as if they know which way Chissmoul will go the instant she changes direction.'

'It does seem like that,' said Flydd, clinging to the pole as she hurled the craft backwards.

'How *could* they know?' mused Nish. 'I don't understand it.'

'I have no idea.'

They were penned in the square, unable to fly away or climb out of range. More spears arrowed in at them and Chissmoul was flinging the air-sled about ever more wildly in her desperate attempts to avoid being hit.

As the craft banked side-on, Nish's gaze swept across the square, which was emptying rapidly. Crowds of people were bolting down every street and alley, while the dignitaries had already taken refuge in the crumbling mansions or were huddling behind overturned tables.

The buildings surrounding the square had been hit by dozens of heavy spears, and a line of debris through the centre of the market stalls showed where a ricocheting spear, two spans long, the weight of a small flagpole and spinning like a top, had shattered the booths and flung their occupants out in bloody ruin.

More dead lay in random heaps across the paved square, victims of other stray spears, while a mound at the entrance to an alley was evidence of a stampede gone wrong, the smallest and weakest trampled to death in the rush to escape.

'The seneschal doesn't care how many innocent people die,' said Nish, 'as long as he brings us down.'

'That's the kind of world your father has created.'

'And the scrutators trained him,' Nish snapped.

'They trained me too,' said Flydd mildly. 'Good can come out of ill, and the reverse.'

Nish did not reply, for he still maintained some small reservations about Flydd's own character.

'Damn you,' Chissmoul was muttering as she tossed the air-sled this way and that. 'Damn you, damn you, damn –'

She had just put it nose-up when there came an almighty crash, the craft jumped in the air and the hardened point and steel shaft of a heavy spear burst up through the deck beside the pennant pole, tearing the metal around its mounting socket. The pole was knocked out and toppled towards Chissmoul, who was too busy to protect herself.

Flangers threw himself sideways and tried to take the

blow on his shoulder, but he was too far off-balance to stop the heavy pole. It drove him down, struck Chissmoul on the right arm and knocked her sideways off her chair.

She managed to hang onto her controller but lost control of the air-sled, which tilted over and plunged towards the centre of the square at frightening speed. Chissmoul shook her arm, crying, 'It's gone numb. Can't feel a thing.'

'Use the controller,' cried Flydd, staring at the rapidly approaching paving.

She kept shaking her right arm uselessly. The fingers of her left hand were moving inside the wires but it was not enough to take back control.

Nish sprang over Flangers, who was still lying on the deck with the pole across his back, caught Chissmoul's right hand and thrust it into the wires. The air-sled dipped momentarily, then continued its plunge.

'I can't *see*,' she cried.

'I can,' said Nish, for his clearsight was suddenly there, as it sometimes was in an emergency. He could not work the controller – he would never have that gift – but he could tell where Chissmoul's fingers were supposed to be because five of the spaces between the wires were outlined with faint white light. Pulling her right hand out, he reinserted her fingers one by one into the outlined spaces and rubbed her elbow. As the numbness faded, the fingers of her right hand began to move.

But they were very close to the ground now. Too close.

'Look out!' Flydd cried, covering his head with his arms.

Nish did too, for he was sure that they were going to smash into the pavement. Chissmoul shouldered him out of the way and the air-sled's dive began to ease, though not quickly enough to stop them hitting at high speed.

They were about to when the spear shaft embedded in the keel screeched across the paving stones, pushing the prow up slightly and creating a trailing wake of sparks before it broke off.

The keel hit hard, making a colossal bang and another flurry of sparks, bounced, and Chissmoul gained a measure of control. The prow slammed into the God-Emperor's throne and table, demolishing them. Wooden shards and splinters went everywhere. She curved around and shot along the front of one of the mansions, between the columns and the front wall, and zoomed up again.

Nish lifted the pole off Flangers, who wasn't injured, laid it on the deck and tied it down.

'Well done,' said Flydd in a shaky voice. 'But they're bringing up more javelards,' he added quietly to Nish, 'and if we can't get out of the square, sooner or later they're going to score a direct hit on our pilot.'

'No one could aim a javelard so accurately as to bring Chissmoul down with a single spear. Not even the scriers could train a javelard that accurately on a rapidly moving target.'

'A lucky shot kills you just as dead as a well-aimed one –' Flydd's head whipped around. 'What the blazes is that?'

Something blurred and unidentifiable was coming at them with frightening speed, making an unnerving humming whistle. Nish had heard that sound once before, but where?

'Down!' he roared. 'Flat on the deck,' and dropped prone as the sound grew ever louder.

The missile hissed just overhead, *splat-whack*. Warm, sticky fluid was flung in all directions, and then it was gone.

'The scum are using chain-shot,' Nish said, coming to hands and knees and shuddering at how close it had been. It could have killed them all. He wiped spatters of blood off his face. 'I never thought my father would sink so low.'

'Lengths of heavy chain, fired from a special javelard with

268

colossal force,' said Flydd, glancing towards the bloody mess down the back. Most of the militia had got down in time, but two had not. 'It spins through the air and can scythe every man off the deck of a ship in a single pass. It simply smashes them to pieces.'

Chissmoul, back in her seat, hurled the air-sled one way and then another. At the rear, bloody-faced and bloody-handed militiamen were pushing the ragged remnants of their two comrades off the back. Someone was weeping; Aimee was swearing, the same word over and over.

Twenty-three able-bodied militiamen left, Nish thought, and how long have they got? 'With chain-shot, you don't have to be accurate. What are we going to do?'

'Get out of the square, Pilot,' said Flydd.

'I can't,' said Chissmoul.

'Then climb above their firing range.'

'I can't.'

'Wait a minute,' said Nish. 'Their other wisp-watchers and loop-listeners are linked to Gatherer, so presumably the ones on the javelards are as well.'

'Almost certainly,' said Flydd.

'And both Klarm and Father used Gatherer to direct and control the air-sled when they had it . . .'

'That was my understanding.'

'But what was Gatherer actually controlling?'

'I'm not with you.'

'What makes the air-sled go?' said Nish.

'A device the God-Emperor had built for the purpose, though I haven't got the faintest idea what it is, and I'm not sure Chissmoul does, either. Wait a minute – are you saying that Gatherer could *still* be linked to the air-sled?'

'If it is, and it's *also* linked to the wisp-watchers, it would explain how the scriers know which way she's going to turn. As soon as her controller signals to the device that makes the air-sled go, Gatherer knows it, and it tells the scrier.'

'How does one sever a link to Gatherer?' mused Flydd.

Another length of chain-shot came howling towards them but this time Chissmoul was ready and evaded it easily.

'I don't know – wait!' said Nish. 'Maelys did it once.'

'Really?' breathed Flydd. 'How?'

'It was just after she rescued me from Mazurhize. I was in bad shape; I don't remember it well, but we were on the flappeter, Rurr-shyve –'

'I remember Rurr-shyve,' Flydd said. 'We escaped from the inn at Plogg on the beast a few weeks ago –'

'So I've heard.' Nish managed a grin.

'Until the wretched thing went into a mating ritual with a male flappeter in mid-air.'

'I gather it wasn't the only mating ritual that night.' Nish laughed aloud.

'It had been a very long time,' Flydd muttered. 'Can we get back to your point, *before we die?*'

Nish's smile faded. 'Seneschal Vomix was trying to take control of Rurr-shyve via its flesh-formed speck-speaker, but Maelys was so afraid that she hacked the speck-speaker off, and the link to Vomix was lost instantly.'

'There must be a similar device inside the air-sled, between the deck and the keel, linked to Gatherer. Unfortunately, without a way of cutting solid metal, there's no way to open it.'

'You'd better think of one –'

'Down flat, *now*!' roared Flangers.

The militia hit the deck. This time the missile consisted of two heavy chains linked by an iron bar, spinning like a propeller and making a *whoomph-whoomph* sound as it came. Everyone was prone save Chissmoul, who remained slumped in the canvas chair, unmoving, her face strained.

The air-sled dropped suddenly; the chain-shot shrilled over her head, and she sat up and wiped the sweat off her brow.

'When I say *down*,' snapped Flydd, 'I mean everyone. If you die, we all die and the war is lost – maybe the world.'

'Sorry, surr,' said Chissmoul. She looked exhausted, and her movements were slower now. 'I – I went blank for a moment. The scriers must be getting to me.'

'Then we'd better find the mechanism, fast. Where do you think it would be, Pilot?'

'What?' said Chissmoul dully.

'The mechanism that makes the air-sled go.'

'Oh, that! Below deck, directly behind me. But there's no way to get into the deck.'

'Maybe there is,' said Nish thoughtfully, picking up his serpent staff. 'This served me well up on the ridge . . . when it wanted me to succeed with the avalanche.'

'But it failed you at other times,' said Flydd, who had heard Nish's tale on the way to Taranta.

'When it was going to help me it felt hot and heavy, as if it was churning with power. At other times it just felt warm, but empty.'

'How does it feel now?'

'As though something is boiling inside it.' Nish weighed it in his hand.

'Then get on with it,' said Flydd.

As Nish hefted the staff, Chissmoul flung the air-sled around violently then dropped it about five spans, and he went sliding towards the side. Flangers caught him by the collar and Nish was bracing himself when there came a shattering boom from overhead, where they had been mere seconds ago, and an umbrella of fire formed from a thousand blazing fragments exploding outwards and falling all around them. Dark smoke drifted in the air, shaping a sickle whose curve surrounded them on three sides.

'What uncanny Art is he using now?' cried Flangers.

The militia were cowering on the rear deck, sick with terror.

'No Art,' said Flydd. 'That looked like something the scrutators' alchymists came up with many years ago – an exploding powder set off by a fuse, inside a brittle shell filled with tar. The tar is ignited by the explosion and sticks to everything it touches; you can't get it off.'

'That's horrible,' said Nish, who was rapidly revising his earlier thoughts about one swift means of death being much the same as another. He watched the falling fire until it hit the ground and formed a blazing ring in the centre of the square.

'It was one of many weapons considered during the lyrinx war,' said Flydd. 'I dare say that's where your father got the idea, but it was deemed too barbaric by the scrutators. Even Chief Scrutator Ghorr – may he lie rotting in the most infested depths of the shadow realm – said no. Are you going to stand there all day?'

Nish aimed the base of his serpent staff at the deck behind Chissmoul's chair.

'I suggest you do it to one side,' said Flydd with a wry smile. 'It wouldn't do to destroy the mechanism that keeps us in the air.'

Nish slammed the tip of the staff against the deck and, the moment it struck, knew it was going to go through. The staff hissed like a red-hot poker pushed into a chunk of ice, the metal deck around it took on an orange glow, then droplets of molten metal were flung out in a corona, burning pits in his military boots.

He shook the droplets off and pressed harder on the staff. More droplets were flung out then it dropped sharply. He was through.

'Drag the staff around in a circle,' said Flydd.

Nish pushed the staff tip sideways and, though neither the Art nor the power that was cutting the thick metal could possibly be coming from him, it was hard, draining work. Before he'd completed a semicircle his knees began to wobble and he felt vacant in the head, as if he'd gone days without food. He clenched his jaw and forced the staff the rest of the way to complete the cut.

The fuming circle of deck fell inside and he pushed it away with the tip of the staff, which felt lighter now, cooler, and as lifeless as any ordinary length of metal. Going down on his knees, he peered inside and saw a complicated, knee-high structure below and behind Chissmoul's chair, where she'd said it would be.

'Can you see anything that looks like a speck-speaker?' said Flydd.

'No. You'd better go in. You know all about such things.'

'I've never seen one before. I spent nine years trapped at the top of Mistmurk Mountain, remember?'

And I spent ten years in prison, damn you! Nish thought. He was shaking with exhaustion, and as he lowered himself into the hole Chissmoul wrenched the air-sled sideways to avoid another flight of spears, flinging him against the hot metal. A fierce pain shot across his back at kidney height; he smelt burning cloth and the whiff of charred skin.

It was not a serious injury, though it was damnably painful. Doing his best to ignore it, Nish slipped into the shallow space between the deck and the keel and crawled across to the shadowy mechanism.

'Down flat!' yelled Flangers.

People thumped to the deck all around and he heard the *whoomph-whoomph* of more chain-shot; the craft wiggled left and right, then shot away in a steep climbing turn. He held on until it levelled out, his skin crawling. It was bad enough being under fire on the deck; being trapped down here in the dark, unable to see what was going on outside, made it so much worse.

It did not take long to find the little device he was looking for. It was mounted on top of the air-sled's mechanism and resembled the speck-speaker Maelys had cut from Rurr-shyve, save that it was made of metal and glass. A brain-shaped protrusion was topped by a luminous yellow noose filled with little dark specks.

The air-sled changed course abruptly and momentarily the specks glittered like cold fire, then dulled. Chissmoul changed course again; again they glittered. It had to be the device that was linked to Gatherer.

But what if it also relayed Chissmoul's movements to the mechanism? If it did, and he destroyed it, the air-sled would fall from a great height.

'Get a move on,' growled Flydd.

'I'm afraid of doing the wrong thing and killing us all.'

'If you don't do it now, we'll all be dead anyway.'

Nish had left the staff on the deck, but the thick circle of metal lay nearby, and it had cooled just enough to pick up. He slammed the circle into the speck-speaker's stalk. The device flicked back and forth at great speed, showering dark and bright specks everywhere, but the moment it went still they reappeared in the noose.

He tried again, and this time the stalk snapped. The little noose shattered and the sparks went out.

Chissmoul let out a shriek of agony.

TWENTY-THREE

'I thought you said Zofloc was dead?' said Yggur, after climbing back to the surface with a dimensionless box of chthonic fire, and Maelys's boots.

'I thought he was.' Maelys was huddled against Tulitine in the meagre shelter of the uptilted slabs above the shaft, shivering violently. 'He must have fallen twenty spans, and when he hit it sounded like . . . like a melon bursting. It was horrible. Did he attack you?'

He shook his head. 'The body was gone. All I saw were some unpleasant white smears where he dragged himself away – or something else did.'

'*White* smears?' said Maelys.

'Do I have to spell it out? Spilled brains, girl! Zofloc cracked his head open.'

'Then he could hardly have dragged himself away,' said Tulitine, blowing into her cupped hands. 'And whatever did, I don't want to meet it.'

'I should never have sent you down there alone,' said Yggur.

'Well, we've got the fire,' said Maelys. 'You'd better take us to Stilkeen.'

'I don't think it's quite that easy,' said Yggur.

'It never is!' she muttered. 'What's the matter now?'

'I'm worried that this chthonic fire might not be any good.'

'Why wouldn't it be?'

'Fire changes when it's used, and the stuff Flydd took to the Tower of a Thousand Steps didn't seem powerful enough. We touched it, if you remember, and it didn't harm us. You even had some on your skin when you went to the Nightland –' He broke off.

Maelys stiffened. She had been trying not to think about Emberr's death, which had been caused by contact with chthonic fire, and her unwitting role in it. Getting up, she stumbled away from the jumbled slabs and the mud with its half-eaten bodies, so distracted that she gave no thought to them.

After reaching the Tower of a Thousand Steps with Flydd and Colm, she had discovered that the Numinator was planning to enter the Nightland through a fire portal. Desperate to save Emberr, Maelys had followed her but had ended up with a residue of the fire on her skin.

It had done her no harm, and was gradually dying, but when she and Emberr had made love in his cottage, the last of the fire had transferred to him, and because he had been born in the Nightland, it had been inimical to him. Instead of saving him, Maelys had caused his death.

In an even more dreadful irony, the Numinator had not been hunting Emberr anyway. Suspecting that he had Charon blood, she had merely planned to test his fertility, in the hope that he might be used to fulfil her two centuries' long plan – to create a superior human species as an eternal memorial to her dead Charon lover, Rulke.

Too late, the Numinator discovered that Emberr was Yalkara's only surviving child, fathered by Rulke in the Nightland and left there because it was the only place where Emberr would be safe from Stilkeen's vengeance. Now, if

Maelys should be pregnant by him, both Yalkara and the Numinator were determined to take the child, and Maelys was equally determined that they should not have it.

And, she realised, Emberr's body still lay where he had died, and it wasn't right. It was her responsibility, surely, to send him on his final journey with respect and all due rites. How could she properly grieve for him when she had not taken care of his final needs, though the thought of returning to the cottage where she had been so happy, knowing she had caused his death, was almost unbearable.

She headed back to Yggur and Tulitine, sick at heart. 'What about the fire I took to the Nightland?'

'It too might have changed for the better – or the worse – but I don't have the strength to go there now, and neither does Tulitine.'

'What other fire is there?'

'There's the distilled fire that Zofloc made,' said Yggur. 'It was certainly stronger, but it's hard to imagine Whelm sorcery making it better.'

He glanced at Tulitine, whose lips were blue. 'I'd better get you somewhere warm, while I still have the strength.'

'Flydd found the original chthonic fire below Mistmurk Mountain,' said Maelys. 'It's good and warm there.'

Yggur made a portal to Mistmurk Mountain, a thousand-span-high, cloverleaf-shaped plateau rising out of tropical rainforest. The portal opened in the steamy forest near the base of Mistmurk, where, for as far as they could see, the ground was littered with broken rock, shiny white pieces of sky-palace, and the gnawed bones and fire-scorched armour of the God-Emperor's personal Imperial Guard.

Maelys shuddered. Bodies, everywhere we've been. Will there ever be an end to it?

'What's happened here?' said Tulitine.

Yggur glanced up at the peak. 'Jal-Nish's sky-palace fell onto the plateau from a great height, smashing to pieces, and everyone on board it must have been killed.'

It had also gouged a canyon a hundred spans deep across the formerly cloverleaf-shaped plateau, and now two small flat-topped peaks, one on either side of the rubble-filled chasm, were all that remained of that rain-drenched place. A waterfall discharged from the end of the canyon, cascading halfway down the cliffs before the spray was carried up again by the unceasing updraughts.

'Those poor men,' said Maelys, for the image of the sky-palace falling would be forever embedded in her memory.

'They weren't nice fellows,' said Yggur, who was shaky on his feet now. 'And it would have been quick.'

'I suppose so. Are you feeling all right?'

'I'll just sit down for a minute. Portals take a lot out of me.'

'I thought the caduceus was doing all the work?'

'It is, but each time I make one, I get such aftersickness that it's as though I'd worked the spell unaided.'

He sat down on the spreading roots of a large tree. Maelys walked back and forth, luxuriating in the tropical heat until the chill of Noom was only a memory.

'Do you know where to look for chthonic fire?' she said after they had set up camp and eaten, and Yggur was feeling better.

'As Flydd told the story,' said Yggur, 'it was deep below the peak, so we've got to find a way in, and down.'

The following morning, they began the long search for a way to get inside the mountain, which had once been riddled with tunnels and chambers. Tulitine went with them, but scrambling up the steep ravines was so painful for her that Yggur told her to go back to the camp. Tulitine hated anyone telling her what to do, but to Maelys's surprise she complied without a murmur.

After more than a week of searching the overgrown lower

parts of the peak, Maelys and Yggur found a fern-choked crevice that led inside. They went into the moist darkness for a few hundred spans. Even here, the walls of the cavern were cracked from the impact of the sky-palace, and there were piles of rubble all over the place, but the way down appeared to be open.

'It looks *fairly* solid,' said Maelys, holding up a blazing torch which was burning all too rapidly, and wishing she still had her twinklestone. 'And it goes down.'

'Very good,' said Yggur. 'Off you go, then.'

Her stomach clenched. 'You want *me* to go? Again? Down there?'

'No, I want you to go back to the camp and take care of Tulitine. Her bones seem to be shrinking more every day, and I'm really worried about her.'

Maelys was too. Though Tulitine was a master of the healing Arts, she could do nothing for herself. She did not understand what was happening to her, or why the Regression Spell was reverting this way, but she knew it was going to get worse.

'You can't go alone,' Maelys said feebly. 'Not after what I went through at Noom. There could be anything down below.'

'It's because of what you went through at Noom that I'm sending you back, though I don't expect to have any trouble here, apart from the odd falling rock. Go on, I don't want to leave Tulitine alone any longer than I can help it.'

Maelys turned back and Yggur headed down into the riven depths, to search for the remains of the casket in which Yalkara had originally stored the stolen white fire, the fire that Flydd had liberated, and which was now spreading out in all directions from the Island of Noom. What if it did consume all the ice in the frozen south? *Would* the seas rise and flood the world?

*

'I found some,' Yggur said wearily when he finally returned, days later. He sat down by the camp fire in the warm rain, tossing a second dimensionless box from hand to hand. 'We've done all we can. Now the only thing we have to do is find Stilkeen.'

'And survive,' muttered Maelys, 'after we give it the fire.'

Tulitine barely looked up. She was huddled under a waterproof military cloak Maelys had found among the scattered bones and broken armour, holding her hands out to the flames and looking thoroughly miserable.

Though it was a sweltering tropical night, and Maelys was sweating in just pants and shirt, Tulitine's hands and feet were cold. She was always cold now, and Maelys was afraid that her heart was going, as well as her bones. She studied the healer across the fire.

Normally, when the spell reverted, it aged the user quickly and terribly, but Tulitine had not aged at all. She was as beautiful as ever, yet more fragile than she had ever been as an old but lusty woman. Her skin had thinned to translucency, allowing the pink of her flesh and the blue of her veins to show through. Her joints were stiffening, her flesh wasting, and her bones seemed to shrink a little each day.

Though she was in constant pain, and could not hide it, she made not a whisper of complaint, which Maelys found hardest of all to endure. Yggur felt sure the Regression Spell was being affected by the caduceus, but they could do nothing about that, either. They had to keep it; it was their only way to get back to civilisation. Their only way to find Stilkeen.

'And then?' said Tulitine, haltingly.

'I'm sorry?' said Yggur, frowning, for minutes had passed since he had spoken.

'After you've given Stilkeen the fire, what then?'

'We get rid of the caduceus. I'm sure it has a lot to do with your troubles. And there are healers –'

'No healer can do anything for this affliction, and I knew it before I embarked upon the Regression Spell.' Tulitine forced a smile. 'Besides, you're not getting rid of me that easily.'

'I don't want to get rid of you . . . but I do care about you.'

'Do you?' Tulitine raised an elegantly sculpted eyebrow. 'What a sorry affliction that must be.'

'You know I do,' Yggur said, restraining his irritation, 'and I'll thank you not to mock me for showing my true feelings. It's not an easy thing for me and I don't do it lightly.'

Maelys had noticed how gentle he'd been with Tulitine lately. He was quite unlike the stern, cool and dominating Yggur she had seen previously.

After some time Tulitine said, contritely, 'I do know that you care, Yggur, and if it wasn't for the gnawing pain in my bones I'd show you how much I care about you.' Her roguish smile flickered on and off.

Maelys felt her blush rising, for even as an old woman Tulitine had never been short of young and vigorous lovers, and she'd made no secret about what she wanted from them.

'Out of regard for you I would not ask for that,' Yggur said hastily.

'And out of regard for you I long to give it, but it cannot be.'

'Then let's not talk about it.'

'Where are we going next?'

'I don't know,' said Yggur. 'I'm worried that the caduceus is bait – and these easy portals a trap.'

'How else can one look upon a device that takes us where we want to go so conveniently?' said Tulitine.

'Do you mean that the caduceus is telling Stilkeen where

we're going and what we're doing?' said Maelys, looking over her shoulder instinctively.

'I believe so.'

'Then there's no point putting it off,' said Maelys. 'Let's take the fire to it.'

'Unfortunately I don't know where Stilkeen is,' said Yggur.

Lightning flashed, reflecting off a white-helmeted skull lying among the leaves, and Maelys jumped. Another flash lit up the camp, followed by a dull rumble of thunder, and this time the caduceus, which Yggur had embedded in the soil beside the fire, shook slightly.

Tulitine let out an uncharacteristic mewling cry and the back of Maelys's neck prickled. Yggur half rose to his feet but settled down again.

'What was that?' said Maelys.

'Just thunder,' said Yggur, wiping sweat off his brow. 'Maybe a storm will cool things down.'

'Thunder would hardly shake the ground.'

'Perhaps it's another cave collapsing inside the mountain,' he said irritably. 'I'm tired, Maelys. I've hardly slept in three days and I don't care.'

The caduceus shook again, more vigorously. Yggur stood up, looked around, but sat down and closed his eyes again.

The ground shook once more but this time the head of the caduceus revolved in a circle, leaving a blue trail behind, like a smoke ring. It drifted up and swelled to become a transparent blue sphere that hung in the air, touched redly here and there by the firelight, and an image appeared on the surface: a broad, flattened head with flaring bony plates like a winged helmet, a split nose and yellow eyes covered in nictitating membranes.

'I am Stilkeen,' it said, its voice low and soft, like thunder heard from a great distance. Wisps of red flame dripped from its nostrils; it snapped at them with needle-sharp teeth. 'I have roamed the eleven dimensions of space and time for an eternity and a half. I cannot die, and nothing –'

Lightning flashed; the image dissolved in jags and the voice was lost in an irritating crackling buzz.

'– without fire and spirit, I am diminished and in pain . . . and when I hurt, I *hunger* to make worlds pay –'

Another flash, and more crackling.

'. . . who brings Stilkeen the *true, uncorrupted* chthonic fire will be rewarded beyond their dreams . . . keeps true fire from Stilkeen will suffer . . . agonies . . . endlessly prolonged. Bring the fire to Morrelune within fifteen days, or . . .' Another long interruption. '. . . from the void . . . engulf . . . your civilisation.'

The blue sphere vanished, and Stilkeen with it.

'*True, uncorrupted* chthonic fire,' said Yggur. 'What can that mean?'

'I suppose it means that the fire we've found is no good,' said Tulitine. 'It must have been corrupted, as you thought.'

'How could Stilkeen know it's no good?' said Maelys, her heart sinking even further. Had all they'd done since leaving the Range of Ruin been for nothing?

'If it *is* linked to the caduceus, and I'm sure it is, Stilkeen must be able to tell that our chthonic fire isn't pure. I think it's getting impatient.'

'Then why doesn't it get the wretched stuff for itself?'

'Presumably it can't.'

'Fifteen days!' said Maelys. 'And we haven't got the faintest idea where to look for *pure* fire – or how it gets corrupted.'

'It explains why the caduceus has been so cooperative,' said Tulitine. 'Stilkeen definitely left it there to help us.'

'As long as we use it for the right purpose,' said Yggur drily. 'I doubt it would bless us if we went hunting treasure.'

'Do you think the message only came to us?' said Maelys.

'How would that profit Stilkeen?' he said. 'I'm sure many people saw it.'

'What do you think *rewarded beyond their dreams* means?'

'We're dealing with a subtle *being* here,' said Tulitine, 'and it could be offering a demon's bargain. *Rewarded beyond your dreams* might be a threat.'

'It might, but the greedy will only see treasure, and by tomorrow every fortune hunter on Santhenar will be after the true fire. We can only pray that none of them find it.'

'It reinforces the urgency of our quest,' said Yggur. He looked at Maelys. 'And since we don't know where else chthonic fire might be found, we'll have to go to the Nightland.'

They prepared to leave at first light. The time of day never varied in the Nightland but dawn seemed the best time to be going.

The caduceus grew hot and heavy when Yggur announced the destination, and trembled as if its interior was in churning motion, though for a good few minutes they remained in the rainforest. The caduceus seemed to be struggling to pierce the barrier that had cut the Nightland off from the world and the void for so long.

Finally the barrier parted like a pair of curtains, they were drawn through and Maelys found herself on that flat and featureless black plane again.

Tulitine was rubbing her hands together. The Nightland felt colder than before – so cold that the chill went straight up through the soles of Maelys's boots. Cold as my dead lover, she thought, and her eyes stung.

'Which way?' said Yggur, peering into the darkness.

'I don't know,' said Maelys, almost choking. She wished they were a thousand leagues away. She could not bear to think about Emberr lying here, dead, and she did not want to talk to anyone about him, nor for anyone else to see his body – in whatever state it was in by now.

'But . . . surely – you've been here twice . . .'

'And I have no idea where Emberr's cottage is.'

'How did you find it in the beginning?' said Tulitine gently.

'When I came here with Flydd and Colm . . . Emberr scented me while I slept. He called me, mind to mind, and gave me directions.' Maelys smiled at the memories.

'And the second time?'

'After I followed the Numinator through the fire portal, I called Emberr with my mind. I didn't expect it to work but he must have been waiting for me, and he told me where to go. His cottage was under an enchantment and no one could find it unless he willed it; he said it was made that way.'

'By Yalkara, to protect him, I suppose,' said Tulitine.

'But the Numinator found the cottage,' said Yggur.

'That was my fault,' said Maelys. 'After Emberr and I . . . lay together, I got up. He was still sleeping . . .' She rubbed eyes that were already red. 'At least, I thought he was asleep. I went to the front door and looked out, but the Numinator was nearby, searching, and as soon as I opened the door it broke the enchantment. She saw me and I couldn't keep her out.'

'Why do you blame yourself for that?' said Tulitine. 'She didn't harm Emberr.'

'At home, every time something went wrong it was my fault. What if we can't find the cottage?'

'The caduceus has a powerful link to white fire,' said Yggur. 'If there's any here, we'll find it.'

He made a fist, held it upright, laid the caduceus across it and spun it gently, three times, but each time it came to rest pointing in a different direction. 'Not a very good start,' he said ruefully.

'Why did Stilkeen want to revenge itself on Emberr, anyhow?' said Maelys. 'Yalkara committed the crime.'

'Perhaps it thought that destroying her child, the sole surviving Charon male, was a better revenge,' said Yggur. 'Let's get on.'

They found no sign of Emberr's cottage on the first day and had no idea where to look next; since this part of the Nightland was so featureless, there was no way of telling where they were going or where they had been. They camped for the night and made a frugal meal on the supplies they had brought with them. Afterwards the Nightland provided them with black blankets, in the same way that it had provided food and bedding on Maelys's first visit, and she lay down to rest.

Yggur helped Tulitine off with her boots, tucked her in, folded his own blankets and put them under her head for a pillow.

'What about you?' said Tulitine, sighing as the weight came off her troubled bones.

'I wasn't planning on sleeping yet.'

She lay there, eyes on him as he moved back and forth. With the point of the caduceus he prised out a length of the black floor, a firm, yet plastic substance unlike any material Maelys had ever seen, and fashioned it into a simple stand which curved over at the top. Drawing a black thread down from the end, he tied it around the centre of the caduceus and moved it back and forth until it was suspended horizontally.

'Is it a direction finder?' said Maelys.

'I hope so.'

He spun the caduceus gently, and it came to rest pointing past Tulitine. Maelys sat up and peered that way, but Yggur spun the caduceus again and it pointed in a different direction, and different again the third time.

'I hate this place,' said Yggur, adjusting the caduceus and thread, 'which is ironic since I had a hand in creating it, well over a thousand years ago. But it's greatly changed, and in ways that I cannot fathom.'

'All things change,' said Tulitine.

'And things fashioned with the Art change in unpredictable ways. The more they're used, or the more powerful the mancers who use them, the more radically they can be transformed. It's one of the first principles of mancery, and why the same spell never works exactly the same way twice.'

'My taphloid seems to change all the time,' said Maelys. 'Whenever I think I understand it, it does something to surprise me.'

'Ah yes, your taphloid,' said Yggur, staring so fixedly at the chain running down between her breasts that Maelys felt uncomfortable and hugged herself protectively. 'Where did it come from – and why did it feel so familiar in my hand, when I've no memory of having seen it before?'

'There's a long gap in your life,' said Tulitine. 'When you . . .'

'Wandered witless?' said Yggur. 'I don't mind you saying it.'

'Can you teach me the Art?' said Maelys, who had been lost in her own thoughts. 'Father had my talent suppressed to protect me. Though . . . I know I'm really old to be starting on mancery . . .'

'*Really* old?' said Yggur, smiling. 'How old are you?'

She flushed. Was he laughing at her? 'I'm nineteen.'

He idly spun the caduceus, which came to rest pointing over her shoulder. 'It's true – unless one begins mancery at an early age it can never be truly mastered, just as one who learns a new language after childhood will always speak it with an accent. It may already be too late for you.'

He frowned at a sudden realisation. 'I must have learned my own Art from the earliest age; I cannot remember a time without it.' He spun the caduceus again; again it pointed over Maelys's shoulder.

'Will you teach me, when all this is done?'

Yggur twisted the tip of the caduceus in the opposite direction. 'I expect I would be an indifferent teacher –'

The caduceus shuddered, tore out of his grasp and pointed over Maelys's shoulder again.

'That's definitely a sign,' Tulitine said. 'I suppose I've got to get out of bed.'

'I'm afraid so,' said Yggur.

Maelys stared in the direction the caduceus was pointing, and swallowed. It had to be pointing to the cottage; to Emberr's abandoned body.

They walked through the black, featureless wastes of the Nightland for the best part of an hour, at which time she made out a small square shape in the distance.

'There it is!' said Maelys, and took off.

'Wait,' said Yggur.

Tulitine murmured, 'Maelys, it may not –'

The happiest hours of Maelys's life had been spent there, followed by the darkest, and whatever lay ahead of her she could not hold back now. She ran until she had a stitch in her side and each breath was tearing at her throat.

The cottage had been a pretty little wooden place with warm light streaming through its windows to illuminate gardens full of flowers at the front, a paved path and a rustic timber fence. At the rear there had been a vegetable patch, fruit trees and a small forest fading into the darkness.

But no more. 'What's happened?' she panted, coming to a stop outside the crumbling gate. 'I was here only a couple of weeks ago. How can it be so changed?'

'Time passes differently in the Nightland,' said Yggur, who had run after her. 'Sometimes fast, at other times with interminable slowness. It was designed that way so as to punish its solitary prisoner.'

'Emberr's cottage had been so warm and lovely. Now look at it.'

The garden was dead, the fruit trees leafless, while the light leaking from the broken, sagging windows was a dingy grey. There was a hole in the roof, and the garden and path were littered with fallen, rotting shingles.

There came a low, distant thud. The floor of the Nightland quivered gently, and in the woods behind the cottage something fell with a cracking sound, like a long-dead branch breaking. It's all dead, she thought. Everything's falling to pieces.

She pushed on the gate but it did not move, for the hinges had rusted; the timber broke under the pressure of her fingers. It was powdery and crumbling, eaten away by dry rot.

Maelys picked her way along the path, afraid of what she would find inside, but even if Emberr was rotting flesh or mouldering bones she could not stop now. She swallowed, tightened her jaw and continued.

'Wait,' called Tulitine, who was still some distance away, and her voice sounded more strained than before. Every step, even on the smooth floor of the Nightland, troubled her. 'We'll come with you.'

'I'd prefer to see Emberr alone,' said Maelys over her shoulder. 'No matter what state he's in. I caused his death; the least I can do is take care of the – the body.'

'As you told the story,' said Yggur, 'Emberr saw traces of white fire on your skin and knew what it was likely to do to him, but lay with you anyway. He was born in the Nightland; he had spent more than two hundred years here and could never leave; maybe he'd had enough.'

Maelys could not listen; Emberr was dead and that was all that mattered. What use was reasoned argument, or excuses? Going up the steps, feeling the rotten wood giving underfoot, she pushed on the sagging door.

It swung open, scraping across the floor, and she looked down the hall. The wall and floor timbers were decayed now and everything was covered in fine black dust. She did not recall seeing dust in the Nightland previously.

She crept down the hall into the small room with the rugs on the floor. The rugs by the fireplace where . . . There was a lump in her throat; she swallowed but still found it hard to breathe. As she went in, she saw the cushion Emberr had given her to sit on, and beside it the platter of food, now just shrivelled and unidentifiable shreds.

And there was the kilt he had taken off before they lay together on the rug. It was still indented with the shape of his long, muscular body. But the body was gone.

TWENTY-FOUR

Nish scrambled out from under the deck of the air-sled. 'What's the matter? What have I done?'

The air-sled was lurching and wobbling across the sky, for Chissmoul was flying it with her eyes closed and her face was screwed up.

'It burns,' she gasped. 'It feels like the backs of my eyes are burning. Aah! Aaaaah! Flangers, put your hands over my eyes. Press hard, then tell me which way to go.'

He did so and she zigged and zagged, banked and climbed, completely blind. His head was swinging this way and that, keeping watch on the javelards coming from the front and sides, and calling out instructions to go fast or slow, climb or descend, turn east or south or west or north.

Flydd, facing the other way, was also calling out directions, and Nish marvelled that Chissmoul could follow them both at the same time. Even with her eyes blocked, she always knew which direction the air-sled was heading, and never hesitated.

The javelards were firing as fast and furiously as before, but suddenly their spears and chain-shot were no longer coming close.

'It's working,' Nish said dully, hanging onto the back of

the seat with both hands, for he was so drained from using the staff that he could barely stand up. 'Gatherer has lost the link.'

'I'm all right now,' Chissmoul said. 'It's coming back.'

Flangers took his hands away and she opened one eye, winced, and then the other. After checking that the missiles were missing by wide margins, she wiped her brow on her sleeve and began to climb out of range, up into the night sky where they could no longer be seen. Shortly she headed away, across the city and out over the Sea of Perion.

No one spoke for ten or fifteen minutes; everyone save the pilot lay on the deck, exhausted. Nish stared up at the sky, thinking about the encounter. We couldn't even sway the leaders of one provincial city, he thought. How can we hope to seize the empire? It's hopeless, even more hopeless than the battle for the pass. At least there I knew how to fight my enemy. I have no idea how to deal with these people.

But he had fought his crippling self-doubt before, and knew how to recognise it now. Nish had vowed never to give in to it again, and he would not. He was going to fight on; he would find a way to combat these foes and until then, for the sake of morale, he had to appear calm and in control.

He lay there for a good while, slowly coming to terms with these fears, and when he felt that he had overcome them for the moment, and the lights of Taranta had disappeared, he took a number of deep breaths and sat up.

'I have to say, Xervish,' he said mildly, 'that wasn't one of your greatest speeches.'

'Should have known better than to try it here,' Flydd said ruefully. 'I'm sure it would have worked a treat in Roros, or wicked old Thurkad that is no more, but what can you expect from these inbred, back-country rubes?'

'Not everyone was against you,' said Flangers. 'I saw some groups looking very attentive.'

'But the seneschal has sowed doubt in everyone's minds, which is a pity. Wherever we go, the God-Emperor's loyal servants will have heard their lies, and they'll be expecting us.'

'Now they know the God-Emperor is missing,' said Flangers, 'they might swing their allegiance to Nish.'

'A few might, but could he trust them? It would be different if we could prove that Jal-Nish was dead, but a man who turns his coat when his master needs him most is likely to do it again. We don't want such a man, or such an army, at our backs.'

'How long will it take to reach Roros?' said Flangers. 'The militia are tired and hungry and desperate for sleep, and their bladders must be bursting – I know mine is.'

'Days,' said Chissmoul, who had flown all over Lauralin during the war. 'It's two hundred leagues away. I can't go much further today, surr; I get aftersickness too, you know.'

'I know. We'll fly over the range and hide for the night,' said Flydd, 'but first I've a mind to show Taranta the sting in our tail, if you can manage it.'

'I don't think that's a good idea,' said Nish.

'We have to. They nearly destroyed us, but we can't allow them to think we've fled in panic. We've got to strike back and leave with our heads high.'

'How?' said Nish, uneasy at the thought of returning to a place they had been lucky to escape from.

'You'll see,' said Flydd mysteriously. 'They go to bed early here. Chissmoul, head back towards Taranta, high and slow, so we make no sound.'

She did so, which took the best part of half an hour.

'Now,' he added, 'circle over the peasant quarter. Stay high.'

It was nearly nine in the evening and the square where they had been attacked now lay in darkness. The night was cloudy, the city dark and still.

Flydd was looking towards the main city square, half a league away. 'The governor's palace and the seneschal's mansion are still lit,' he said thoughtfully.

'They've got a lot to talk about,' said Nish.

'Go down slow and quiet, Chissmoul, and make for the alley where they had the stampede.'

'You're not going to do something terrible with those bodies, I hope?' Nish said suspiciously. The old Flydd would never have demeaned the dead, but Nish could not always predict how the renewed man would react.

'Certainly not!' said Flydd in high dudgeon. 'What do you take me for? I've something far better in mind.'

Nish was scarcely relieved. What was the old scoundrel up to?

'Careful now,' Flydd whispered, as Chissmoul crept the air-sled down. 'There's bound to be a few sentries about. Go low over the rooftops; I wouldn't want any wisp-watchers to pick us up. Head along the alley to the building there, with the flat roof. See it?'

'Isn't that where one of the javelards was sited?' said Flangers.

'It is,' said Flydd.

'The one that fired the chain-shot and exploding tar balls?'

'Precisely,' said Flydd. 'We're going to teach the seneschal a lesson. Quiet now.'

The air-sled nosed silently across the tightly packed rooftops until, ahead, Nish made out the top of the javelard, still pointed towards the square. 'It'll be guarded,' he whispered.

'Of course,' said Flydd. 'The God-Emperor won't let any rebels arm themselves at his expense. I need a few volunteers.'

Every able-bodied man and woman put up their hands.

'I'll take Flangers, and you and you,' said Flydd, going down the back and selecting militiamen in the near-darkness. 'Chissmoul, set down on this roof.'

She did so, and momentarily the roof timbers groaned under the weight of the air-sled. 'What about me?' said Nish.

'I thought you were worn out?' said Flydd.

'I am, but if there's a chance to tweak the enemy's nose, I'm taking it.'

'Thought you might,' Flydd said complacently.

How easily Flydd had manipulated him. Having checked his sabre, Nish followed across one flat roof, then another. The javelard loomed ahead and he made out a shadow pacing back and forth. A single guard was rarely effective; there were bound to be two, or even more.

'No need to kill the guards, unless they're trying to kill you,' said Flydd. 'Knock them out and tie them.'

They were climbing across onto the roof, trying to make no noise, when there came a low, harsh cry. 'Who's there?'

'Scrier!' hissed Flydd. 'Cut him down before he gives the alarm.'

The scrier turned and ran, his gown billowing, towards a wisp-watcher mounted on the side of the javelard. If he reached it, every scrier in Taranta would soon know.

Nish sprinted after him. He could have tracked the scrier in the dark by the sulphurous pungency of his breath, a side-effect of the herbs they chewed to enhance their vision, but he was too far ahead. Nish sent his sabre spinning through the air. The flat side of the blade struck the scrier in the back and drove him to his knees, but he rose and scrambled up towards his wisp-watcher.

Nish launched himself through the air and tried to drag the scrier off the javelard. He wriggled free, jumped into his seat, touched something in the darkness and a little speck-speaker slowly came to light. He was leaning towards it when Nish threw himself at the scrier's back, driving him against the wooden frame. Ribs cracked but he twisted like a snake in Nish's arms, bringing a knee up for the groin.

Nish blocked it with his own knee but the blow to his kneecap was so excruciating that he dropped his guard. The scrier's left hand flashed into his coat, emerging with a knife whose blade might have been made from ice, save that it shone with the same bile-green light as the rat-neck noose of a loop-listener.

The knife flashed for his throat, but stopped with the point pricking through the skin under Nish's chin. 'The son of the God-Emperor!' the scrier said hoarsely, then grinned in triumph. 'You're mine, and all the reward – *umph*!'

Nish had kneed him in the groin and, when the scrier doubled over, brought a fist up from ankle level in an upper-cut that slammed him into the side of the javelard. The knife went flying, the scrier's head struck a beam, and he col-lapsed.

All was quiet now save for Nish's heavy breathing. 'Xervish?' he said softly.

'We've finished them. You?'

'The same; I don't think he got a warning off, though he did recognise me. Let's get what we came for and go.'

Flydd made a double hooting sound; the air-sled appeared and hovered beside the javelard. They loaded on one round of the double chain-shot plus a number of the large spherical objects that Nish deduced were the exploding tar balls.

'What are you going to do with them?' whispered Chissmoul.

'Let me guess,' said Nish. 'He's planning to attack the gov-ernor's palace.'

'I would, were he the man who really gave the orders in Taranta,' said Flydd. 'We're after the seneschal's mansion.'

'Better pray that my scrier didn't get a warning off, or our welcome might be warmer than you expect.'

'If you'd done your job properly we wouldn't have a problem,' Flydd said equably. 'Shut up and give me a hand with these.'

They laid the heavy, clanking chains out across the deck, then tied two of the exploding tar balls to each end and the last two to the bar in the middle. 'How do you set them off?' said Nish.

'Fuses. I've got them in my pocket. I won't put them in until the last minute, because the least spark can set them off – and then we'll all be sent to oblivion, coated in burning tar.'

'No, thanks,' said Nish. 'Are you sure this is worth it? The seneschal's guards will be on alert.'

'He called us liars. If we run now, it will be seen as proof that we are.'

'The commander will soon discover that Taranta's army has been destroyed and we were telling the truth.'

'Seneschals are professional manipulators, Nish.'

'Like scrutators?' said Nish, smiling.

Flydd ignored that. 'He'll give a dozen plausible reasons why the army was lost – fever, flood, avalanche – and none will have anything to do with us. Besides, if we don't strike back it will prove that we're gutless, and no one would trust cowards with the leadership of the empire and the defence of the realm. We made – I made – a bad start, and we've got no choice but to put it right.'

'What can this little attack do?'

'It's symbolic. It's a public act of defiance. The seneschal might cover up the annihilation of an army in the wilderness, but he can't conceal our attack in a public square in front of thousands of witnesses, many of them rich and powerful people. If we succeed, everyone will know we thumbed our nose at the God-Emperor's seneschal and got away with it, and that's worth as much as the defeat of an army. More!'

'All right,' said Nish, 'though I don't see how we *are* going to get away with it.'

'We can't fly around the mansion without being seen,' Flydd mused. 'We'll have to con the area on foot first, and find out the best way to attack.'

'No!' said Nish.

'I beg your pardon?' Flydd said coldly.

'I said no. If we get into trouble, there'll be no way of getting out of it.'

Flydd's eyes glittered and his jaw was tight. He did not like being challenged, but Nish wasn't going to give in, and finally Flydd turned away. 'Flangers, what do you say?'

'Nish is right; getting off the air-sled is too risky. If we're caught, we lose everything. What if we fly in at top speed, chuck our tar balls through the nearest windows, then scarper?'

'Chissmoul?' said Flydd. 'Have you got the strength for it?'

She was slumped on her chair, head on her arms. 'As long as it doesn't take too long, but it's not going to work.'

'Why not?'

'You won't be able to throw those heavy chains as far as I can spit.'

Flydd cursed. Evidently he hadn't thought of that practicality, and neither had Nish.

'It's a stupid idea,' came Aimee's high little voice from the rear. 'We should be doing something really outrageous – surr,' she added unconvincingly.

'I'm happy to listen to any *sensible* suggestion you've got to make,' Flydd said with an underlying air of menace.

'Mount the javelard on the air-sled, then stand off the

298

front of the mansion, out in the square where everyone can see, and fire your black balls and chain through the front door.'

Flydd stalked down the rear and Nish was afraid that he was going to explode. Clech was looking anxious, until Flydd shook Aimee's little hand.

'It's beautiful,' he hooted. 'How better to humiliate the seneschal than by attacking his mansion with his own weaponry?'

'The javelard is too big and heavy,' said Chissmoul. 'The air-sled will never lift it.'

'Load it on,' said Flydd. 'There's only one way to find out.'

It required the strength of every able-bodied man and woman straining at the ropes to raise the javelard and inch it onto the air-sled, and they would never have managed it had it not been for Nish's long-neglected skills as a prentice artificer. It took ages, and they had to stop every time Aimee, the lookout, alerted them that a patrol was moving along the street below them.

'This is taking too long,' said Nish, sweating in the hot night. 'What time do they change the guards?'

'How would I know?' said Flydd. He thought for a moment. 'Every eight hours, as a rule, so probably at midnight.'

'It can't be far off midnight now.'

'Then you'd better work harder.'

'Any sign that the guards are changing, Aimee?' Nish whispered.

'I'll tell you if I see them.'

Finally they had the enormous javelard loaded dead-centre and roped down. Its base was almost as long as the air-sled and half as wide, and the top was a span and a half high, while the horizontal, crossbow-like mechanism stuck out over either side.

Flydd began to fit the fuses to the tar balls, and six troopers lifted them carefully, along with the linked chains, into the leather firing bucket of the javelard. Once everyone had piled on, Chissmoul took the controller.

'Someone's coming,' hissed Aimee.

'Do we wait or go?' said Nish.

'Go,' said Flydd. 'We don't want to get in a fight now.'

'I'll try to take her up to knee height,' Chissmoul said anxiously.

The air-sled shuddered violently, and Nish thought it wasn't going to lift at all, but eventually it rose in a series of jerks. Through the hole cut in the deck he could hear the mechanism rattling.

'Hoy!' someone called from the street. 'What's going on up there?'

'Get going,' said Flydd, 'before the bloody thing shakes itself to pieces.' He cursed under his breath. 'At this rate, they'll hear us coming half a league away.'

'Keep still, everyone,' said Chissmoul. 'She's so top-heavy, she could roll over at any time.'

After offering this comforting thought, she lifted the air-sled at a shallow angle and it began to shudder across the rooftops. Nish made out several faces staring up at them, trying to work out what was happening in the dim light, then they were lost to sight.

'I'd love to see them explain this to their superior officers,' said Nish.

'We haven't succeeded yet,' said Flydd. 'You're our only experienced javelard operator, Nish. Get it ready.'

'Can I climb onto it, Chissmoul?' said Nish.

'As long as you don't make any sudden movements,' she said in a strained tone.

He checked the javelard by feel, making sure that nothing had slipped out of alignment during loading. The air-sled was shaking more wildly than before, and he was drenched with sweat. One misstep could cause the craft to roll, dumping everyone off, and the javelard would tear free and come down on top of them. How the seneschal would crow then.

Somehow, Chissmoul's genius kept them in the air, even while he climbed up and began to wind the huge cranks that tensioned the steel firing cable. When they were fully wound, he pushed in the safety rods so the javelard would not go off if jolted.

'It's ready.'

They were approaching the seneschal's mansion from the rear. Most of the lights around the square had been extinguished, though lanterns still burned in front of the governor's palace and the mansion.

'There's a barracks right at the back, and after that a walled garden,' said Aimee, who was still keeping watch. She was seated on Chissmoul's right, looking out from below the javelard's firing bucket. 'Then another high wall, with a lawn between it and the rear of the mansion. Windows run across the rear but it'll be difficult to get near them with all those trees.'

'Left side, or right?' said Chissmoul, who sounded exhausted.

'The trees are close by on either side. We'll have to attack at the front.'

'I *want* to attack the front,' said Flydd. 'That's where the staterooms and audience chambers will be. It'll be a much more public show, and a bigger insult. Go over the roof, Pilot.'

The air-sled drifted over the high roof, jerking and lurching, and out to the centre of the square, where it hovered in the darkness some distance above the paving stones.

The square was well-lit in front of both palace and mansion by street lamps reflected downwards, and the mansion

301

had a pair of gigantic front doors, broad enough to admit the air-sled, though they were closed. There were bay windows to left and right, equally grand, and Nish could see shadows moving behind the filmy curtains to the left. Though the stateroom on the right appeared larger, it was dimly lit and did not appear to be occupied.

'There's no one about at this time of night,' said Flydd, sounding vexed.

'The patrolling guards will see us as soon as we move down into the light,' said Flangers.

'I'm not doing this for *their* amusement! Stay at this height, Pilot,' whispered Flydd. 'I'm making a slight change to the plan.'

'What are you going to do now?' said Nish, alarmed.

Flydd untied one of the canvas-wrapped tar balls and hefted it in his arms. 'I'm waking everyone up; we've got to have an audience. Have you picked your target, Nish?'

What was he up to? 'Er, yes,' said Nish. 'I'm going to aim at the front doors and smash them down.'

'If they're iron-reinforced, they might not break,' said Flydd. 'If our attack isn't spectacular, we've failed.'

'What if I fire through the right-hand bay window into the stateroom?'

'Sounds good. Get ready.' Taking a flint striker from his pocket, Flydd snapped it at the fuse of his tar ball, which caught at once, burning with a fizzing sound and the smell of sulphur. He studied the speed of burning, counted to five under his breath, then tossed the tar ball over the side into the centre of the vast square.

The fuse sparked once or twice as the tar ball hit the paving stones and rolled, but that was all.

'Damnation,' said Flydd. 'Has it gone out, or not?'

'Fuses are perilous things, in my experience,' said Flangers. 'Sometimes they burn fast, sometimes slow. And sometimes you think they've gone out, when they haven't. Even if you wait five minutes, or ten, it could go off in your face.'

'That's what I'm afraid of,' said Flydd, 'but I'll have to go down and relight it.'

'You could throw another tar ball,' said Aimee.

'We can't afford to waste them. If the attack is a fizzer, all Taranta will be laughing – but at us. Take us over it, Chissmoul.'

Chissmoul, now so exhausted that Aimee was holding her steady, wobbled the air-sled over the tar ball, about six spans up.

Flydd tied knots at intervals in a line, fixed it to the side, shinned down and snapped the flint striker at the fuse.

'Hey, you!' a man bellowed from the darkness. 'What do you think you're doing?'

It was a guard on the far side of the square. The air-sled hung above the level of the lanterns and would be just a huge shadow to him, but Flydd was clearly visible.

'Get a move on!' Nish muttered.

Footsteps sounded, running across the square.

'Put your hands above your head or we'll shoot,' the first guard shouted.

TWENTY-FIVE

Flydd kept snapping the flint striker and finally the fuse began to spark. A crossbow bolt whined above his head, another glanced off the paving a little to his left. He leapt for the rope and was up to the third knot when the spark faded again.

'Blast and botheration!' Flydd cried. 'What's the matter with the damn fuse?'

'Probably damp,' said Flangers.

'You can't go down again,' Nish hissed. 'The guards are too close.'

Flydd ignored him, and was sliding down when the spark reappeared.

'It's still burning,' Nish called. 'Get up here, quick!'

The air-sled lurched. Was Chissmoul losing control? Nish could not imagine how she had held the air-sled up this long. This is going to be a disaster, he thought. Even if we survive, we'll be a laughing stock. *I'll* be a laughing stock, and I'd sooner die. He meant it, too, for his reputation meant more to him than his life. And it'll destroy any chance of bringing the God-Emperor down. No, we've got to succeed, no matter what it takes.

More bolts shot past Flydd and one plucked at the fabric of his trousers, near the knee.

'That was a bit too close,' said Flangers. 'He's not climbing fast enough.' He grabbed the rope and began heaving Flydd up. Nish went to him and took part of the load, counting the seconds and praying that the tar ball would not go off, *yet*.

Flydd came over the side, gasping like a stranded carp. 'If the bloody thing doesn't –'

There was a colossal boom, the air-sled lurched wildly and hundreds of lumps of burning tar splattered against its metal underside, while the rest formed a technicolour fountain spraying up into the air all around them.

One of the guards began to scream and tear at his tunic, which was ablaze with tar in three places. Another man dragged him away.

The lumps of fallen tar now formed a broad, blazing ring in the centre of the square, issuing clouds of black smoke. On the other side, the doors of the governor's palace were flung wide and there was a roar of, 'Guards! Guards!'

Lights were being lit all around the square; people rushed out of front doors and peered through windows. A squad of guards came pounding up the side of the palace, but stopped at its closed front gates and stared.

Nish could hear someone shouting at them. More roaring came from the rear of the seneschal's mansion, presumably from the barracks. Time was rapidly running out.

'Get to your post, Nish,' cried Flydd, 'and take aim. Pilot, get to the front of the mansion then bring her down into the light.'

The air-sled wobbled towards the mansion.

'You haven't lit the damned fuses,' Nish snapped as he scrambled up into the shooter's seat and turned the aiming wheels. The air-sled lurched again. Chissmoul seemed to take an eternity to steady it, and Nish knew she could not last much longer.

Flydd swore, ran for the leather bucket, held the fuses of the five tar balls together and lit them all at once. 'Ten,' he called.

The bay window of the mansion was fixed in Nish's sights when the vast double doors were flung wide and half a dozen people ran out onto the porch, then stopped, staring. The air-sled must have been a hellish sight, hanging in the air in front of the mansion with the huge javelard fixed on them at point-blank range, for its keel was peppered with chunks of blazing tar, their tongues of flame licking up above the four sides, and all was wreathed in choking black smoke.

'Nine,' said Flydd.

'Guards!' screeched the seneschal.

His guards came boiling around the side of the mansion, then stopped.

'Seven!' said Flydd.

Nish swung the javelard until it pointed at the doorway, and the people there scattered. The seneschal's face collapsed as the sights fixed on him. Nish was happy to terrorise him but people weren't his target, no matter how depraved.

'Five,' said Flydd.

'Take them down!' cried the seneschal.

The air-sled lurched left, then right. Hold it, Chissmoul, Nish prayed, adjusting the sights, and it steadied.

'Three!'

The guards whipped their crossbows up to their shoulders and aimed at Nish, who was only partly shielded from that angle, but he did not flinch. He had a job to do.

He aimed the javelard over the seneschal's head and down the vast hall where, halfway along, he saw the base of a magnificent staircase. From this distance he could hit it with his eyes closed.

306

'Fire!'

No time to regret the architectural magnificence he was about to wantonly destroy – Nish fired.

The chain-shot whirled out to its fullest extent and slammed into the front of the mansion, splintering the open doors and sending chips of stone in all directions. Several of the guards were knocked down and the rest were lost behind clouds of blinding dust and flying splinters.

Recoil forced the javelard backwards until its ropes creaked – Nish had not thought of that. The prow of the air-sled shot up, the rear tilted down, and for an awful moment he thought it was going to overturn in the air and land on top of them, splattering everyone like cockroaches. As he sprang from his seat several crossbow bolts spanged off the metal prow. Had he succeeded? He could not tell; he'd lost sight of the target.

He was scrambling up to the top of the javelard frame so he could see, when the stern of the air-sled slammed into the paving stones and the impact broke the force of the recoil. Nish's teeth snapped together and he tasted blood from a bitten tongue.

The right-hand chain had destroyed the bay windows on that side and disappeared inside. The left-hand chain had demolished the left bay window, and all the tar balls had broken free. The central tar ball had gone hurtling down the hall, to explode against the base of the staircase, flinging burning tar across the open central area of the mansion and setting fire to everything it touched.

The tar balls that had gone through the demolished bays also went off, and in an instant the curtains were ablaze and black smoke began to gush out of the windows. Nothing could save the mansion now.

The people at the front ran for their lives, the seneschal's sagging belly flopping up and down. More people were swarming out of the servants' quarters at the rear, though they were not in danger.

However, everyone on the air-sled was in peril, for the impact with the paving had snapped several of the over-strained ropes holding the javelard, allowing it to slide to the right and unbalancing the air-sled.

'Get to the left,' Chissmoul screamed as she fought to keep the lurching, swaying craft aloft. There was no time to land and right the javelard, for the guards from the palace were running across the square, weapons at the ready.

Nish's militia surged to the left, tilting the craft in that direction, but now the front of the javelard swung that way, for more of its ropes had broken. Nish, still perched up top, wasn't game to move in case he made things worse.

'Hoy!' cried Flangers. 'You and you, over there. And you three, put your shoulders against the javelard, and your backs into it.' He directed everyone like a conductor until the weight was balanced and the air-sled had steadied, as much as Chissmoul could manage it.

'Take her up, Pilot,' said Flydd. 'Nish, what the blazes are you doing up there? Come down.'

Nish slid down off the javelard, watching the running soldiers, who were within firing range.

'Down, everyone,' said Flangers, and they ducked.

A flight of crossbow bolts thudded into the uprights of the javelard.

'We've done what we came to do,' said Nish. 'Let's get going before Chissmoul collapses.'

'After our lap of honour,' said Flydd. 'You can manage *that*, can't you, Pilot.'

Chissmoul nodded, too exhausted to speak.

'You're out of your mind, Flydd!' said Nish.

'This is the icing on the cake of your credibility, *Deliverer*,' said Flydd. 'Pilot, take your craft all the way around the edge of the square. Militia, brace yourselves against the javelard and when it slips, ease it back into position.'

'That's not going to be easy to do,' said Nish as they climbed, 'the way it's sliding around.'

'Then bang some wedges under it!' snapped Flydd. 'Do I have to think of everything.'

Nish wedged the javelard as best he could.

'Make it quick, then. If they bring up another javelard, we're carrion.' He searched the rooftops and alleyways in case the enemy was already doing so, but outside the lighted square it was too dark to tell.

Chissmoul lifted the shaking, quaking air-sled to a height of fifty spans, where there was little danger from a crossbow strike, and coaxed the faltering craft around the square. Despite the wedges, the javelard moved on the metal deck with every change of direction.

'Put your backs to it,' said Flangers, tapping the wedges in again.

A dozen times Nish thought the javelard was going to slide all the way and scrape them off the deck, but each time the combined efforts of the militiamen and women held it – just. They could not do it much longer, though; everyone was close to collapse.

The square was thronged with people now, thousands of them staring silently at the absurd sight of the air-sled wobbling through the sky bearing a javelard that seemed bigger than it was.

'The governor and the seneschal won't explain away this defeat so easily,' Flydd crowed.

'We haven't got away yet,' Nish said sourly, though inside he was exultant. Flydd was a bloody annoying old bastard, but he'd got more out of them than Nish could ever have imagined, and if they could succeed . . .

'Half the city is witnessing their humiliation, and within days the furthest reaches of the empire will know about it. Just one more thing, Chissmoul, if you can manage it, and then we go. Fly over the mansion, if you please.'

Smoke and flame were gushing from the windows of the ground floor, but as yet the upper floors were unscathed. Over the highest point of the mansion Flydd shouted, above the roar of the flames, 'Now to dump the rubbish. Ready, Chissmoul?'

'Ready,' she said dully.

'Everyone on the right, come around to the left and hang onto the safety ropes. Flangers, cut the safety ropes on the right, knock the wedges out from under the javelard and join us. Pilot, you'll have to balance the weight –'

'Don't tell me how to do my job!' she snarled.

The air-sled quivered as more weight came on the left, and canted that way. Chissmoul levelled it, though it took an effort. Her cheeks, in the fading light from the tar-splattered sides, were streaked with sooty sweat.

Nish's eyes were still roving around the square, and now he caught tell-tale movements in the distance. 'Hurry up. They're bringing a javelard down the street to the north . . . and I think I can see others further back.'

Flydd looked at Chissmoul questioningly. She nodded. 'I'm ready.'

'Militiamen,' said Flydd, 'heave the javelard towards the side. The instant it starts to slide, grab your safety ropes and hang on tight.'

They heaved, and Nish did too, until he thought his heart was going to burst, but the javelard would not budge. 'It must be caught on something.'

Surely the enemy javelard would be in a position to fire by now. Feeling a target centred on his back, he grabbed the fallen pennant pole, jammed it under the side and levered.

The javelard lifted slightly, cleared a ragged edge of the hole he'd cut in the floor, and began to move.

'It's away!' said Flydd. 'Hang on tight.'

The javelard kept sliding, faster and faster, and went over the edge. The air-sled tilted so sharply that Nish did not think Chissmoul could save it, but yet again she managed to bring it upright. The enemy javelard must have fired, for a metal spear shrieked off the tilted stern, but Nish did not have the energy to look around.

The javelard plummeted onto the middle of the mansion roof, smashing the slates and snapping the timbers, and battered its way down through floor after floor until the crashing ceased and it came to rest, out of sight.

Flydd peered through the shattered hole. 'There's no sign of fire here yet, but it can't take long. Let's go – no, wait.' He studied the hole again and a mischievous light sparked in his dark eyes. 'I can see the pantries. One final insult. Nish, you'll want to be in on this.'

'No, I won't,' said Nish. 'All I want is to lie down and sleep for a month.'

'You'll sleep a lot better after we come back in triumph. Flangers, tie a rope harness around Nish, and another around me. Fasten a net on the end of a third rope, then lower us down.'

'You've got to be joking,' said Nish. 'We've done enough, Flydd. Why risk it all for nothing?'

'This is going to be beautiful,' chortled Flydd. 'The seneschal's humiliation will be complete – he'll never recover from it.'

'It's insane; I'm not going down there. The roof could fall in at any moment.' Besides, a dozen javelards could be aimed at them by now.

'Of course you are. Come on.'

Flydd could not be quelled; he seemed intoxicated by the

drama and the danger, and shortly they were lowered over the side into the roof hole. As they went down, Nish looked up at the air-sled, which was shuddering worse than before, sure that this was the stupidest of the many stupid things he had done. 'Where are we going, anyway?'

'To the seneschal's private pantries.'

'Pantries?' Nish was too tired to think straight.

'We're going to rob him of the delicacies he keeps for the God-Emperor, in the unlikely event that *he* would deign to visit such a backwater as Taranta.'

'I like a good feed as well as the next man,' said Nish sourly, 'but I don't see why we're risking our lives for it.'

'Because this is the final, glorious insult, the one that will have the whole of Santhenar talking about us,' said Flydd, 'and, reckless though it may be, I can't resist.'

'But the mansion is on fire. There isn't time.'

Flydd looked down again. 'There's no sign of fire near the pantries.'

'I've seen whole cities burn, and so have you. There can be no trace of fire one minute, and the next the place is an inferno.'

Flydd did not bother to reply.

'Keep low,' Nish yelled up. 'Watch out for javelards.'

Flangers, who had a crossbow in hand, waved him away.

The first pantry had been demolished by the javelard, but the next was unscathed. Nish was looking along the shelves when Flydd jabbed him in the ribs and gestured down. The hole, which continued through into a dark cellar full of stacked barrels, had a powerful aroma of freshly spilled wine.

They went down. Flydd conjured light from the tips of his fingers and scampered – there was no other word for it – along to a barred and locked compound at the end of the cellar, which was marked with the sign of the God-Emperor. Pulling a small, stubby rod from his pocket, he pressed its end to the lock, which exploded in a spray of metal cinders, and wrenched the door open.

'Heave that barrel over your shoulder,' he said, pointing at the third one from the end.

Nish did so. Flydd lifted a large flagon from a shelf and turned away. 'That'll do. Pity the rest has to burn.'

They put several flagons and barrels in the man-sized net and scrambled up to the pantries, which were thick with smoke now. Nish could hear the roar of fire, and a series of crashes, followed by a louder roaring. 'The front of the mansion must be coming down, Flydd. It'll drive the fire towards us.'

'Grab anything that takes your fancy, and make it snappy.'

Nish tossed cheeses, hams, sausages, smoked fish and other delicacies into the net at random; Flydd came running down the shelves with an armload. His pockets were bulging, and each time he moved, they chimed.

'What have you got in your pockets?' said Nish.

'The seneschal's finest goblets.'

'Now I know you've lost your wits.'

'You can't drink fine wine out of a metal cup.'

'After the past week, I'd drink it from my military boots.'

There was another, louder crash, and burning air blasted in under the outer pantry door. 'Time to go,' said Flydd.

Nish wasn't about to argue. After making sure his harness was secure, he tugged three times on his rope, the agreed signal, and it was pulled up in a series of jerks. Below them, the door fell with a crash and fire coiled up, *whoomph*, reaching almost to their toes before it died away. *Whoomph-whoomph*; this time he had to beat out smouldering threads on the ragged ends of his pants.

'It's coming higher each time, as though it's fed by a bellows.'

'And every collapse feeds it.'

The ropes were pulled up more quickly, but not before the third *whoomph* sent flames up to Nish's waist, and he felt his nasal hairs singeing. The next blast would come up past them and set fire to the rope, if not themselves.

Suddenly he was jerked up as though a giant had taken hold of the line, and out through the broken timbers. The fire roared and flames leapt up through the hole, higher than the roof, as they were dragged over the side onto the air-sled along with their precious cargo. Clech's stretcher had been brought to the ropes and it was his mighty strength that had saved them.

'One good turn must be repaid by another,' he said. 'And a drop of the wine in that barrel, if you can spare it.'

'Is that all, Flydd?' said Nish. 'Can we go now, or have you got an even more reckless finale in mind?'

'Only to take a bow to our audience,' said Flydd, smiling. 'And give them a present.'

'The javelard –' Nish began.

'I brought down the operator,' said Flangers, waving the crossbow. 'And the other javelards aren't quite in position yet.'

'To the centre of the square,' said Flydd, taking some of the wines and delicacies out of the net and stacking them on the deck.

Chissmoul took them there, and everyone lined up along the side of the air-sled and bowed to the throngs gathered at the east, the south, the north and the western sides of the square.

'The Deliverer sends compliments to the good people of Taranta,' boomed Flydd, 'and begs you to celebrate his victory with the finest food and drink the seneschal has to offer, from the private stores kept for the God-Emperor.' The net was carefully lowered to the centre of the square, and its ropes cut. 'And now the Deliverer takes his leave, for he must now seize control of the empire, and fight Stilkeen.'

At the last bow, the gathering gave them a ragged cheer and surged towards the net.

Flydd said, 'We're done,' and Chissmoul turned away, out over the silent city, heading east.

'You old bastard,' said Nish, and shook his hand. 'I would never have thought of that, much less attempted it, yet you've pulled it off.'

'And the rest is up to you, *Deliverer.*'

TWENTY-SIX

On the journey to Roros they planned to keep to un-inhabited places, camping in uplands or on hilltops where there was not so much as a cottage in sight, though Flydd was not afraid of the people of this land. Even the most desperate troublemakers would have kept well clear of the scarred and battle-hardened militia.

'It's best if we disappear for a while,' he said to Nish the following night, when they were sitting around the camp fire after everyone else had gone to their bedrolls. 'We've created a sensation, and if nothing more is seen of us for a while, the rumours will spread more strongly than if we popped into every town. Let the authorities worry about what we're going to do next, and the people wonder, and our strength and cunning will grow with each telling.'

'Sounds good to me,' said Nish limply, for he was so worn out that he'd had trouble sleeping, day or night.

'Besides, we've been pushed beyond endurance since Jal-Nish attacked Mistmurk Mountain six weeks ago, and we deserve a holiday. And now, old friend, the payoff.'

Flydd levered the bung out of one of his flagons, sniffed deeply, then poured a healthy red-gold measure of liqueur into a pair of the etched glass goblets he'd lifted from the pantry. Handing one to Nish, he said, 'Now tell me this doesn't taste better than it would from a mouldy wineskin.'

Nish twirled his goblet, admiring the way the light twinkled off the delicately etched surfaces, as fine as silver filigree. 'There's no comparison, but I still wouldn't risk burning to death for the privilege.'

He took a tentative sniff and the bouquet rushed up his nose, burning deliciously, enchantingly. He sipped and it was even better. Tears formed in his eyes; it reminded him of older, happier times and he felt an urge to reminisce.

'It's a good while since we were on the road together, Xervish. Do you remember the last time we shared a cup of wine?'

'I do, though the memory is a trifle hazy.'

Nish snorted.

'And not because of the quantity *I* drank, though I recall *you* found it hard to stand up afterwards.' Flydd chuckled. 'It was on the little bench outside my amber-wood cabin on Mistmurk Mountain, after you came out of the swamp to break my lonely nine-year exile.'

'That was a good day,' said Nish dreamily.

'It was a very good day.' Flydd took another sip. 'As it happens, my recollections of the time immediately before renewal are hazy, though my older memories are as clear as this goblet. Do you remember when we drank together before that?'

Nish's smile faded. 'I'll never forget a minute of that terrible day. It was ten and a half years ago in Ashmode, on the shores of the Dry Sea, which was, even then, starting to fill. We were having a victory banquet – at least, the best that could be managed with the rations we had. The war had been won and we'd made an honourable peace with the lyrinx, who had turned out to be rather like us, *inside*, despite their fierce outer appearance.'

'Very like,' said Flydd. 'We all want the same things, when you get down to it.'

'After a hundred and fifty years the war was finally over, and I think we all felt numb. We couldn't believe that we were going to have peace at last. We were sitting around a long table in the town square, drinking that dreadful wine and talking about our futures.'

'Our futures.' Flydd raised his glass as if toasting the man he'd been back then, or the memory of him.

'As I remember it, you were planning to write the true Histories of the war, and after that you were talking about a cottage and a little garden. We found that highly amusing,' Nish snorted.

'It might seem so, if you were in your cups,' Flydd sniffed.

'The great Scrutator Flydd, one of the heroes of the war, living in a cottage and growing *flowers*? We couldn't come to terms with that, either.'

'You always did lack for vision,' Flydd said with a touch of the asperity of old. 'When times change, a man must change with them and, *if you recall*, all of us who had fought so hard during the war were overthrown at the end of it, by generals greedy for power.'

'They didn't hold it long,' said Nish quietly. 'We talked about our hopes and dreams for the future that day. Did any of us achieve them?'

'I don't know,' said Flydd. 'Though I did write my Histories, in the lonely years at the top of Mistmurk, and I think they were the finest of all my works.'

'What works? I didn't know you had any.'

'I've always kept my own personal Histories. And up on Mistmurk Mountain I wrote the tale of the times in five journals. I kept them under my bed, in an amber-wood box for luck, and in my exile I often imagined the sensation they would cause when I finally brought them forth, because I didn't hold back. Unsuspected traitors would have been revealed, and several great names ruined. Alas, no one has read them but me, nor ever will. Mistmurk was smashed to bits by the fall of Jal-Nish's sky-palace, and my journals would have been destroyed.'

'I dare say,' said Nish, distracted by that memory, though it was hazy due to his being in Vivimord's thrall at the time.

The embers settled with a flurry of sparks. Flydd tossed more wood on, for their camp was at a high altitude and the night was chilly. 'Thinking back to the banquet, I distinctly remember Irisis telling us about *her* dreams and hopes. She had never expected to survive the war –'

Nish choked and Flydd gripped him by the shoulder. 'Drink up lad, and remember. It does no good to block out the past, no matter how terrible it is. It's far better to relive it, when you're ready, and keep doing so until its horrors no longer have any power over you.'

Nish said nothing. He couldn't speak. He did not want to remember, but neither was he willing to try and forget.

Flydd dropped his hand and continued. 'When Irisis did survive the war after all, she planned to follow her lifelong dream and become a master jeweller. And to wed her man, of course.'

Nish buried his head in his hands and Flydd went on, 'Though she never did. Ah, that was one of the very worst days of my long life – no, it was *the* worst. But Nish, as I recall the banquet that day, you never talked about your dreams, nor what you wanted for the future.'

'No, I didn't.'

'Why not?'

'I'm not sure. Perhaps I had a premonition of what was to come; perhaps I was afraid to jinx the future. If only I'd known,' he said bitterly.

'Or maybe you were just struck dumb, that so beautiful,

brave and brilliant a woman as Irisis should want an ugly little coot like you,' Flydd chuckled.

Nish managed a feeble smile. 'I wouldn't have put it quite so plainly, but yes, I'm sure there was an element of that in it.'

'Though now I think on it,' said Flydd, 'I'm not sure Irisis entirely believed what she was saying about that lifelong dream.'

Nish's head shot up. 'I don't follow you.'

'I never told you this before, because she only talked about it when she'd had more wine than was good for her, and swore me to secrecy afterwards, though after all this time I think you're entitled to be told. I don't know where she got the idea, but Irisis had come to believe that she had a destiny – one that could only be fulfilled after her death.'

Nish reeled. 'I hope you're not saying that she wanted to die? That she had a death wish?'

'Don't be absurd, of course she didn't. She wanted to live as much as any of us, and she had more to live for than most.'

'Then what *are* you saying?'

'That she believed her death was going to change the future.'

'It has,' said Nish. 'If she hadn't died, if we'd escaped that day, I would never have sworn to overthrow Father. And I wouldn't have spent ten years in Mazurhize.'

'That's not what she meant. Irisis felt that, despite all she had to live for, her destiny required her to die . . . yet that would not be the end of it.'

'I don't understand,' said Nish.

'Neither do I, though I've thought about it many times. I'm sure that's why she never expected to survive the war. You must have heard her say so.'

'Many times,' said Nish, feeling tears forming in his eyes,

320

'until I begged her not to mention it again. Let's not talk about this any more, Xervish; I haven't the heart for it.' He knocked back the rest of his goblet and surreptitiously wiped his eyes. 'And stop hogging the liqueur, you greedy old bugger.'

'I've taken renewal; I'm no longer considered old,' Flydd said in superior tones, and poured Nish a trifling measure.

'Fill it up, damn you. I'm going to get so roaringly drunk that I won't remember a thing.'

Flydd gave him a little more. 'I don't think that will help, really I don't.'

'When I want your advice I'll ask for it. You used to be an old soak, anyway, you hypocrite – a veritable piss-bucket.'

'And still am, when I can get drink of quality,' Flydd retorted, 'since I need to numb my renewed internal organs. I have no problem with you getting drunk, not that it ever helps. But not yet.'

'Why not?' Nish said surlily.

'We have to talk about your campaign, and I can't do that on an air-sled with forty other people listening. It's got to be now.'

'We should involve Flangers at least. And Chissmoul.'

'Later, once you and I have worked out what to do and how to do it.'

'Don't you trust them?'

'It's not a matter of trust. The more people know your secrets, the sooner the enemy will get to hear of them.'

Nish knew he was right; he was just arguing for the sake of it, and, even though he'd slept on the air-sled for most of that day's shuddering flight, he was exhausted in mind and body. 'Very well. Let's talk so I can go to bed.'

Flydd glanced at the sleeping militia, who were some distance away, and lowered his voice. 'There are several ways you could begin the overthrow of the empire. You might set up a government-in-exile in a friendly city, say, Roros, and gradually extend your power.'

'I could.' Nish leaned backwards. The stars made a vast pinwheel against the black velvet of the night sky, as bright as he had ever seen them, though many of the constellations were different from those of the southern skies under which he had spent most of his life. 'But I would soon be besieged from all sides and no longer in control of my own destiny. That's no way to bring down an empire.'

'To *take* an empire,' said Flydd pointedly. 'Bring it down and you create a power vacuum, which all the scum on Santhenar will scramble to fill. But I agree, so let's put that plan aside.'

'I'm minded to foster a series of small rebellions as I march up the coast, speaking to as many gatherings as I can and gathering arms and men, then take cities as I go and head for the centre of Father's empire.'

'The way Vivimord, when he was known as Monkshart, planned to make you into the Deliverer?'

'Well, yes,' said Nish. 'Do I gather that you don't think much of the idea?'

'It's the strategy your father would expect you to follow.'

'Oh!'

'Therefore, even in his absence, and Klarm's, there will be plans to combat such a campaign. The art of war lies in being unpredictable, Nish, and that's how you've gained all your successes so far, both on the Range of Ruin and in Taranta. But if the God-Emperor's seneschals and generals guess what you're going to do, and how you'll do it, his mighty war machine will be waiting to crush you as soon as you appear.'

'He doesn't know where I'm going to appear,' Nish said mulishly.

'He has wisp-watchers and loop-listeners in each town

and village. Each town has scriers and spies, and informers are everywhere. Once you start making speeches and raising an army, Gatherer will know within hours.'

'But Klarm has Gatherer, and he's in the shadow realm.'

'He could have returned by now. He could even be in Morrelune. Even if he isn't, since watchers and scriers can communicate via Gatherer, Klarm may be able to give them orders the same way.'

'He couldn't communicate with his troops on the other side of the Range of Ruin,' said Nish, 'which means that the reach of Gatherer is limited.'

'It's better to overestimate the power of the tears than underestimate them.'

'I quite agree, though last time Father didn't take me seriously. He *let me win* my first battle, near Guffeons, even though it cost him an army.' The bitterness rose up Nish's throat like vomit. 'And he did it just so he could later have the pleasure of telling me so – to undermine me and rob me of the satisfaction of my victory against the odds. He's done it to me all my life, ever since I was a little kid.'

'He might have been lying,' said Flydd.

'What?' Nish realised that he was slurring his words a little. He put the goblet down and concentrated.

'What if that victory *was* yours, and your father was lying because he couldn't bear to admit the truth – that you had beaten him?'

It would have been a blinding revelation if it could possibly have been true. 'But I've never beaten him,' Nish said dully.

'You did on the Range of Ruin. Besides, it's Klarm we've got to deal with and he doesn't play games. If you threaten the empire he'll crush you. He's got to, and quickly, so he can turn his attention to Stilkeen.'

'Klarm didn't do so well at Blisterbone,' said Nish.

'Because he had been ordered to take you alive if at all

possible, and that constrained him severely. But any direct threat to the empire has to override that order, and if he can't take you, he'll have you killed, anonymously. What could be easier than an assassin's arrow when you're exhorting the masses to rise and join you? Or a poisoned cup; or a knife in the back from the crowd? If Klarm decides that you must be killed for the good of the empire, no amount of vigilance can stop him.'

'If your purpose is to frustrate me and undermine every plan I put forward,' Nish said irritably, 'you're succeeding. What would you do?'

'I don't know. I just wanted to get you thinking. Once we reach Roros, we've got to have a solid plan and be ready to put it into instant action.'

'When you've thought of one, please let me know.' Nish drained his goblet and set it upside down beside the cooking ware.

'I'm going to bed.'

'What's the matter with it now?' said Nish as the air-sled began to shake violently.

'How would I know?' snapped Chissmoul. 'I'm a pilot, not a mechanician. I'll have to go down again.'

It was their third morning since the attack on Taranta and the air-sled had been giving trouble from the moment they'd boarded it. She had landed the craft twice already, and crawled through the hole to fiddle with the mechanism inside, but it hadn't made any difference.

'Is it far to Roros?' said Flangers carefully, for she had been touchy ever since leaving Taranta.

They were flying along the western side of the mountains of Crandor, over desert lands where there was little chance of being seen, but not even Flydd was familiar with these parts and they did not have a map.

'I haven't got a clue!' She banked the air-sled, scanning the range for a suitable landing place.

'It doesn't look very promising,' said Nish to Flydd.

'The country or our journey?'

'Either. I'd hate to be marooned here.'

'It would certainly spoil your plans,' Flydd said laconically as the air-sled stuttered towards a rock-littered river bed, which was as dry as every other river they had seen in the past day.

Below them an upland desert stretched in every direction as far as Nish could see, a hilly, eroded land whose stony ground was scattered with withered grey shrubs. Being in the rain shadow of the great mountains of Crandor it did not rain here from one year to the next and, as far as Nish could tell, the recent flooding of the Sea of Perion had made no difference to the climate.

In summer it would bake, yet now, at the beginning of spring, the nights were decidedly chilly, and it would take hours to gather enough spindly bushes for a decent fire.

Chissmoul guided the craft to a skidding landing on the sand between the rocks, but it kept sliding and thumped up onto a rounded boulder before screeching to a stop, canted to the left. Several of the injured slid forwards on their stretchers and ended up jammed together behind Chissmoul's seat.

'Can I help you with anything?' Flangers said, polite as ever.

'Go away!' snarled Chissmoul.

He bit his lip, turned aside and jumped onto the sand. The militia carried the stretchers off and lay down in the sun. They seemed to have an infinite appetite for sleep and Nish could not blame them.

'Let's go for a walk,' said Flydd. 'You too, Flangers.'

They strolled down the river bed, the grey sand squeaking underfoot.

'What's the matter with her?' said Flangers. 'I'd have thought Chissmoul would be happy, since she's flying again, but she's more cranky every day.'

'She loves flying; it's her life and her joy,' said Flydd. 'But she's afraid the air-sled will break down at any minute and that will be the end of flight for her, forever.'

'I dare say you're right,' Flangers said morosely. 'There's nothing we can do about it, then.'

'And maybe she feels that she's letting us down,' said Nish. 'She knows how urgent it is that we get to Roros, and if the air-sled fails she might blame herself.'

'That's ridiculous,' said Flangers. 'It was having problems even when Klarm was using it.'

'But she's the pilot. She can't *not* feel responsible if her craft lets us down.'

Twenty-seven

Maelys could not stop shaking; even on the ice-covered surface of the Frozen Sea she had never felt so cold.

'He's gone,' she said when Yggur appeared, followed by Tulitine. 'Yalkara has taken Emberr's body and I'll never see him again. Never get the chance to say farewell.'

'I'm sorry,' said Tulitine, folding Maelys in her arms. 'Let it out.'

'I can't. It's not finished and now it never will be, and all because of her, the evil cow. She stole the fire and caused all this trouble. I hate her!'

There was a long pause, after which Tulitine said gently, 'Yalkara is his mother, and Emberr was her only surviving child. She also had the right.'

Maelys wept.

Yggur searched the cottage, the garden and the black forest behind it, and came back. 'There's no white fire here, not a trace. We've come all this way for nothing.'

'But the caduceus pointed here,' said Tulitine. 'Why would it do that unless the fire was here at the time?'

Yggur squatted down and inspected the indented carpet. 'The fibres are slowly springing up. I'd say the body was taken not long before Maelys came in.'

'You mean Yalkara is still here somewhere?'

Yggur shook his head. 'That thud as we arrived must have been her leaving the Nightland. She realised Maelys was coming and took the body away.'

'Where to?' cried Maelys.

'Two centuries ago she went back to the void with the surviving Charon and their dead. She would have taken her son's body –'

'You've got to take me there,' said Maelys desperately, clutching at Yggur's arm. 'I have to –'

'I'm sorry, Maelys,' he said gently. 'It's quite impossible. I can't take you to the void, and even if I could, how would you find him? It's infinite. Besides, none of us could survive there for a single minute.'

Maelys subsided to the floor, blindly stroking the depression in the carpet, which was all she had left of him, and even that was disappearing by the second. Soon there would be nothing.

'As you said, the days can pass swiftly in the Nightland, especially when you don't want them to,' said Tulitine. 'St-ilkeen gave us fifteen days to find the true fire, and our time is rapidly running out. Where to now?'

'I don't know where else to look,' said Yggur.

'Someone must know. We just have to ask the right people.'

'I don't even know where to begin.'

'Then I'd start where all such searches would have begun in the olden days,' said Tulitine. 'The Great Library.'

'I'm not sure anything is left of it,' said Yggur. 'Wasn't it sacked by the lyrinx at the end of the war?'

'So some people say,' said Tulitine, 'though I don't know if it's true.'

'And if anything of value remained, Jal-Nish would have carried it off when he proclaimed himself God-Emperor.'

328

'I don't think so. If you recall, when he met Yalkara on the Range of Ruin he had never heard of Stilkeen, *or* chthonic fire.'

'Then we'd better get going,' said Yggur. 'Each portal hurts me more than the last, and I'd hate to fail with the one taking us out of the Nightland.'

'It would be ironic indeed,' said Tulitine, 'if you ended up a prisoner in the prison you helped to create.'

Maelys knew, because Yggur had told her, that the Great Library was situated in Zile, a once great city on the River Zur near the north-western tip of vast Meldorin Island, west of the Sea of Thurkad.

But Zile had fallen into decay long before the war – when the Sea of Perion became the Dry Sea the climate had changed and the fertile floodplains of the Zur had dried out and blown away, leaving a desert crisscrossed by the salt-crusted ancient irrigation canals. The people of Zile were long gone, save for a few hardy folk who, Yggur had said, lived in the abandoned city like lizards dwelling in the cast-off shoe of a giant.

'Yet the Great Library, one of the wonders of the ancient world, still survives,' he added as the portal deposited them on its roof many hours later. He breathed deeply of the dry evening air, as if tasting its differences to all the other places they had been. 'I had not thought it would.'

'The librarians once claimed that it held the entirety of Santhenar's Histories,' said Tulitine, walking painfully across to the edge. Yggur went after her and put his arm around her, and she clung to him gratefully.

Maelys wandered along the side of the enormous rect-angular roof, pleased to have something unfamiliar to distract her from her cycling miseries. The Library, a simple, classi-cal building built from red marble, had many storeys, but all the lower levels lay below the drifting sand and the dunes were almost up to the roof in places. How long until they came over the top and covered it completely? How long until its magnificence was erased from human memory, as her own home had been destroyed?

She paced back and forth, immersed in her melancholy thoughts, for she loved books and could still remember that nightmare night, as a child, when Vomix had ordered the library of Nifferlin Manor burned.

Maelys took a deep breath, forced both Emberr and the past behind her, and tried to concentrate on the reason they were here. If they couldn't find true fire before the fifteen days were up, Stilkeen had said the world would be destroyed from the void.

And she believed it, for everyone knew that the void extended forever and was full of beasts of all kinds, each endlessly evolving in a desperate attempt to compete with their savage, intelligent predators. The Histories told that the most vital desire of every intelligent species there was to escape into the physical universe and find a world of its own. Every species yearned for that, and there were few worlds better than Santhenar.

Yggur had calculated that six days had passed since Stilkeen's proclamation; only nine to go. Time was rapidly running out and, even if they found the true fire, how could they be sure that Stilkeen would keep its word?

'Maelys?' Yggur called out, sounding pleased about something.

He and Tulitine were leaning on the rail, looking towards the city of Zile, and Maelys saw many magnificent public buildings, all with colonnades and arches, along broad avenues lined with palms and spreading trees.

'How come there's no sand in the city?' she said.

'That's a very good question,' said Yggur, gazing beyond

Zile to where the River Zur formed a green, fertile ribbon meandering into the distance.

'I thought you knew your Histories,' said Tulitine, who was more cheerful than she'd been in weeks. 'There was a prediction made of old, *Not until the Sea of Perion once more thunders against the jewelled shores of Katazza Mountain will Zile rise again.* And now that the Dry Sea has become the Sea of Perion again, and is nearly full, the climate of Zile *is* changing back. The people must have started to return years ago, to have scoured the city so clean of sand. See the pennants flying from that building on the hill?'

'But they haven't come as far as the Library,' said Maelys. 'How do we get in?'

'There's a roof door down the far end,' said Yggur, pointing. 'I've been here many times, though not in the past decade, of course.'

They had just turned that way when a silver head appeared, climbing a set of steps that Maelys had not noticed. It was an old woman, small and thin, with a long, rather pinched face and thick spectacles perched on her bony nose. She wore a shapeless gown that went down to her sandals, and carried a black bamboo cane with a curved handle. Leaning on it at the top of the steps, she squinted at them, then let out a delighted cry.

'Yggur!'

'Lilis,' he beamed, striding towards her with his arms out.

'Lilis became the Librarian here after the great Nadiril finally died, two centuries ago,' Yggur explained after the introductions had been made and Lilis was leading the way down the steps. Despite her age, and the cane, she went down quickly and was steady on her feet.

'Do you have Aachim blood, Lilis,' asked Maelys politely, 'to have lived so long?'

'No,' said Lilis. Her voice was high but strong, not a

quavery old woman's voice at all. 'The position of Librarian here requires a mastery of the Art and comes with one benefit, long life, for when a document must be found we rely almost entirely on the memories of our librarians, and there is only so much anyone can read in a normal lifetime. I assume you have come here to consult us?'

'I was not sure that the Library had survived,' said Yggur. 'I've been out of the way for the past seven years –'

'Held in thrall to the Numinator,' said Lilis.

'How did you know that?'

'The Library has many sources; it is our business to know such things.'

'Not even the God-Emperor knew of the Numinator,' said Maelys.

Lilis paused on a landing. The steps continued down out of sight. 'Ah, the God-Emperor. He also consults us at times.'

'Really?' said Maelys. 'I'd have thought he'd just take what he wanted.'

Lilis gave a delicate little cough. 'Zile does not lie within the empire. Surely you knew that?'

'According to the God-Emperor,' said Tulitine, 'the empire covers all the known world, save the island of Faranda where the Aachim dwell.'

'Sometimes the God-Emperor exaggerates,' Lilis said diplomatically. 'In any case, the particular skills of my librarians could not be duplicated with less than a hundred years of training, nor are they readily coerced. He's not a fool; it's far easier for him to pay our fees.'

'But he's a monster,' said Maelys. 'How can you –?'

'The charter of the Great Library requires that we provide information to all, impartially, as long as they can pay the fee, and it can be high. Even with the few librarians I have left, the cost of maintaining the Library is prodigious.'

'What if someone poor needs information?'

'The fee may be waived for the genuinely indigent,' said Lilis coolly. 'I was a street waif when I was a child; I can always tell the genuine supplicants from the cheats. But enough chitchat. You've come about chthonic fire, of course. You want to know where to find it.'

'How did you know that?' cried Maelys, then saw that Yggur was grinning.

'When you're selling information,' said Lilis, who was also smiling, 'you must always appear to know more than your customers. That's one of the first principles my master, old Nadiril, taught me when I came to the Library as a waif, just ten years old. Stilkeen's message came here as well, but if it hadn't, my sources would have soon told me about it. You're the first to arrive but you won't be the last, and I'll tell everyone the same thing.'

'Then I would advise you to take strong precautions for your security,' said Yggur. 'The worst men and women in the world will be after Stilkeen's pure fire, and some of them would think nothing of closing your mouth forever – or even burning the Library – to make sure no one else can learn what you have told them.'

Lilis looked shocked, though she recovered quickly. 'Thank you for the warning,' she said gravely. 'The Library, despite its appearance, is not unprotected, but I will take extra precautions.'

'You should consider sealing it so no one can enter from outside.'

'You forget yourself, old friend,' Lilis snapped. 'The bedrock on which the Great Library was founded, almost three thousand years ago, was the unfettered exchange of information with all comers.'

Yggur bowed. 'I'm sorry for the presumption. But come now, Lilis, you would not hand over a depraved or obscene volume to a child, and neither would you give a deadly

333

secret to a lunatic. Limits must often be placed on what information you provide.'

'That is so, of course,' said Lilis, more calmly. 'The past cannot be allowed to bind the present.'

Maelys expected to be ushered into a vast room crammed with books and scrolls, but Lilis led the way down a broad corridor, turned off it into a narrower one, down the steps to a narrower yet, and stopped outside a plain door, which she opened.

The room she entered was small and spare, containing but a high bench the length of one wall, covered in manuscripts, a stool, a small hard pallet in a corner and a few shelves, one of which was empty.

'This was Nadiril's room, and after I succeeded him I took it for mine. I like it. There's no clutter and no distractions.'

She indicated the pallet and they sat down on it. Tulitine lay back, letting out a small sigh as she took the weight off her aching bones. Lilis perched bird-like on the stool.

'Since I knew the question would soon be asked, I made sure I knew the answer,' she said. 'Firstly, our catalogues contain nothing about chthonic fire – it is never mentioned. Of course, the catalogues are sadly out of date, but since chthonic fire would have been brought to Santhenar a long time ago, that does not matter. Neither do any of my junior librarians – some older than I am – recall the term, and nor do I. I certainly never heard Nadiril mention it.'

She wrinkled her brow, then went on.

'Yalkara must know, and I have re-read all we have here about her, though I did not find anything. The Charon were ever secretive and she most of all – Yalkara may not have told anyone else about this white fire, though it is difficult to imagine that the other Charon, at least the most important of them, would not have known.

334

'The other places to look would, of course, be the strong-holds of the only three Charon to came to Santhenar.'

'Kandor's fortress of Katazza,' said Yggur, 'Yalkara's abandoned tower at Havissard, near the ruined Aachim city of Tar Gaarn, and Carcharon, in the mountains above Gothryme, which Rulke made his own for a while.'

'Quite,' said Lilis. 'If the information you seek does not lie there, and I suspect it does not, then either it does not exist, or it is hidden where no one living, save Yalkara herself, knows where it can be found.'

'Even with a portal to take us there,' said Yggur, 'to search any one of those places would require more time than we have.'

'I agree,' said Lilis. 'It might be more productive to ask those who hated the Charon, and have every reason to tell you their secrets.'

'I've heard nothing about the Aachim since I was taken by the Numinator,' said Yggur. 'Are they –?'

'As I mentioned, the God-Emperor's realm does not extend over them, though there was a degree of . . . border adjusting, shall we say, after he seized power. There are Aachim at Stassor, their principal city, and of course the great island of Faranda is their domain. And Clan Elienor, where Karan's Aachim ancestor came from –'

'Karan Kin-Slayer?' said Maelys, who had always been curious about her.

'I knew *Karan*,' Lilis said deliberately, and her eyes glinted. 'I met her as a child; I really liked her, and Llian.'

Yggur had also grown angry when their names had been mentioned, Maelys recalled. Had Karan and Llian betrayed Lilis too? Even if she had, Maelys felt for her, for Karan had been pursued relentlessly by Maigraith, just as Maelys had been.

'What was she like?'

'She was small; a little taller than you, I'd say, but her hair was the most brilliant red – the colour of a smoky sunset. She was clever, and good at most things; she did not suffer fools gladly.'

'And she was a sensitive,' said Yggur. 'She felt things far more deeply than normal people.'

'As I was saying,' Lilis added, 'at the end of the war Clan Elienor went to Shazmak.'

'Do you know if Malien is still alive?' said Yggur. 'Of all our allies from the olden days, she's the one I most want to see.'

'Did you know her back in the Time of the Mirror?' said Maelys. She knew that the Aachim were a long-lived species, unlike *old humans*.

'I did. There aren't many of us left from that era now.'

'I saw Malien some years ago,' said Lilis. 'She dwelt in Shazmak at the time, though I believe she has since returned to Stassor. Malien was looking rather old – a fate that comes to us all, even librarians.' Lilis smiled. 'My time is almost up, and I can't say I'll be sorry to go. Two hundred years is long enough, even for a Librarian.'

'What will you do when you retire?' Maelys said curiously.

'Perhaps I'll go on the road and seek my fortune.' At Maelys's astonished look, Lilis laughed aloud. 'I look back on my adventuring days, an orphan child in the company of the mighty, with a certain nostalgia. The Library never changes, and few people come to consult us in these troubled times. Sometimes the days can be a trifle dull.'

She studied each of them in turn. 'I haven't been much help, have I?'

'You've told us everything you know,' said Yggur.

'But you're disappointed I can't tell you more.'

'I confess it.'

336

'What is your second question?'

'Does the Library mention any way to attack a *being*?'

'Anticipating that question, I've done some reading already,' said Lilis. 'I haven't uncovered anything so far and, even if the answer is in our archives, it could take months to find. But . . .'

'Yes?' said Yggur.

'It would depend very much on the nature of the *being*. I wouldn't look to attack one with some mighty power or force, like the Profane Tears. I would ask myself what the true nature of the *being* is, and where, given that nature, its weakness lies. Once you know that, it may be a simple matter to attack it. I will consider the subject further after you've gone. And your third question?'

'I don't have another question,' said Yggur.

'You surprise me,' said Lilis.

'May I ask one?' said Maelys.

'On Yggur's account?'

'I, er, don't have any money –'

'On my account,' said Yggur brusquely.

'You may ask,' said Lilis.

'What will happen if someone finds the true fire and gives it to Stilkeen?' said Maelys. 'Will Stilkeen accept it and go away?'

'The future is out of my realm, child,' said Lilis. 'That is a question better put to Tulitine; she is the seer among us.'

Tulitine sat up, painfully. 'Not even the greatest seer can read the future that clearly. However, judging by Stilkeen's demeanour in the two times I've seen it, I doubt that it will go away.'

'Perhaps your question, Maelys, should have focussed on what I know of *beings*,' said Lilis. 'The answer is, not much, though they are never humble, and Stilkeen has suffered terribly from what Yalkara did to it. Did she steal its binding fire out of malice, I wonder, or come upon it by accident and take it, thinking it was a treasure beyond price, only to discover that there was no way of using it safely?'

'I understand that chthonic fire gave the Charon their way out of the void,' said Yggur. 'It has a unique ability to dissolve the walls that separate the eleven dimensions of space and time.'

'But once she stole the fire,' Lilis went on, 'Yalkara must have discovered that there was no way to return it. Whatever she did with it would leave a trail leading straight back to her. Furthermore, immortal *beings* have a powerful sense of their own importance and cannot suffer an injury meekly.'

'You have confirmed my own thoughts on the matter,' said Yggur. 'Stilkeen will want to make humanity pay for the monstrous sacrilege done to its sacred person by Yalkara and, by extension, all humanity. It won't let us go unharmed, even if we give it the true fire.'

'What is your final question?' said Lilis.

'I have no other,' said Yggur, frowning as if trying to locate an elusive memory.

'Are you sure?'

'There's nothing else that comes to mind.'

'I have another. Do you know anything about taphloids?' said Maelys, clutching at it through her shirt.

'There was only ever one device of that name, to my knowledge,' said Lilis.

'Was it this one?' Maelys pulled the chain over her head and handed the taphloid to Lilis.

She studied it carefully. 'Yes, this is it. I never thought I'd see it again, but such things have a way of returning to the place they came from.' She was looking at Yggur, head to one side. 'The Library obtained it four hundred years ago, from a private collection Nadiril had acquired.'

'Who sold it?' said Yggur.

'That does not matter,' said Lilis. 'If the seller does not want their name revealed, we do not reveal it.'

'Even after four hundred years!' cried Yggur.

'Even so. Our confidentiality is absolute and enduring. In any case, the owner did not know where the taphloid had come from originally; it had been sold and resold many times, for it is a beautiful thing. Neither did anyone know what it was for.'

'It protects me by concealing my aura,' said Maelys. 'And I was told that it contained information that would be vital, later on.'

'It contained a series of lessons,' said Lilis. 'Nadiril learned that much, but not even his vast Arts and experience could recover them, though he did discover that the taphloid had first been sold in the Clysm. That was a series of terrible wars between the three Charon who dwelt on Santhenar, and the Aachim,' she explained to Maelys, though Maelys, who had been taught the Histories by her father, already knew it.

'Santhenar was devastated by those wars and it took hundreds of years to recover from them,' Lilis continued. 'And apparently the original owner of the taphloid was left destitute and sold it. That was all Nadiril could discover. It was just another inexplicable curio from the past, and there are many of them in the Library.'

'Then how did Father end up with it?' said Maelys.

'That's another story, though it comes from the most recent era. The Library was not greatly troubled by the lyrinx during the great war, for they had a reverence for the Histories, and for knowledge generally. They seldom came near the Library, save for information.'

'Do you mean to say that you even provided information to the enemy?' growled Yggur.

'Indeed,' said Lilis, unperturbed, 'though they were not *my* enemy, since the Great Library has from its beginnings, under an ancient charter, always been an independent entity. I found the lyrinx to be entirely courteous, well-mannered and prompt in paying their accounts, unlike some *old humans* I could name. But won't,' she added hastily.

'In fact, I found them to be rather more human than many humans I've dealt with. Over the hundred and fifty years of the war the protection was only broken three times, each time by lyrinx who were outcast from their communities. They gave us no great trouble, though the last time, twenty years ago, three broke through our defences and stole a number of valuable items, including this taphloid.

'I tried to get it back, but in war things become lost and sometimes no one knows what happened to them. I can only assume that your father must have taken it from a dead lyrinx on a battlefield and, having a strong gift for the Art, he recognised its potential. Even recognised that it contained lessons.'

Lilis pressed the taphloid against her forehead and closed her eyes.

'With my Librarian's Art I can read an intention in the device, one I don't believe was here when I last held the taphloid, a long time ago. Wait a moment; I'll have to search my memories of that time. So many years, so many memories,' she mused. 'An old Librarian's mind is like the Library itself – rather dusty, a trifle battered and decayed, some memories mislaid, others put on the wrong shelves, and yet others gone forever. But I'm sure I can find this one. Ah!'

She lowered the taphloid to the bench.

'Yes, I have it. Maelys, your father must have recognised that it was a teaching and shielding device, and attempted to put a number of lessons into it, to teach you about your gift for the Art when you were old enough; and when it was safe to do so.'

'I knew it,' said Maelys. 'Ever since I was told that I had a gift, I've been trying to find someone who could teach me to use it, and yet my teacher was hanging from my neck the whole time. Can you unlock the lessons for me?'

'No,' said Lilis, and Maelys's face fell.

Lilis took up the taphloid and again pressed it to her forehead. 'I can read that your father worked hard at your lessons. It must have taken him many months, and he *thought* he had put them into the taphloid correctly, keyed in such a way that no one could ever recover them save you. He would have done so for your protection since, under the God-Emperor's rule, it is illegal for private citizens to possess enchanted objects.'

'Then what went wrong?' said Yggur. 'I assume something *has* gone wrong.'

'The original lessons must have been put into the taphloid by a master, probably the one who made it, so they could only be read by the person for whom they were intended. Unfortunately, Maelys, two such sets of instructions could not occupy the same place and, I believe, your father's lessons corrupted the earlier ones. In the Library we are adept at recovering information from the most fragmentary of sources, but I can tell at a touch that *I* can't get anything out of your taphloid. I'm sorry.'

'A voice spoke from the taphloid, twice,' Maelys remembered, 'when Yggur first approached the caduceus with it, before we left the Range of Ruin.'

'*Twice?*' said Yggur.

'Yes. Surely you remember?'

'I remember it telling me to keep watch, but that's all.' Yggur was looking at Maelys as if she were mad.

'The first time it spoke was before that,' said Maelys.

'Just before you fell down against the caduceus and we had to drag you away. Your hair was smoking.'

He put his hand to the top of his head, feeling the frizzy patch there. 'I believe you, though I don't remember that either.'

'I heard it too,' said Tulitine. 'It was the same voice, a deep, reverberating man's voice, speaking in an accent I did not recognise. It said, '. . . *and burn them to nothingness.*'

'. . . *and burn them to nothingness*?' repeated Yggur, frowning. 'That could mean anything.'

'Quite so,' said Lilis. 'The taphloid is one of the more enigmatic devices I've had to deal with. Now if you're quite finished . . .'

They took the hint.

Twenty-eight

The air-sled made its stuttering way east towards the mighty mountains of Crandor, and when they were winding their way up the valleys and over the lowest passes, Flydd said, 'We're not far from Roros now – only fifty leagues in a direct line, I'd guess. Do you think you can get us that far, Chissmoul?'

'I'll do my best, surr.'

Her best lasted a day and a half, until the following evening, though her stops to tinker with the mechanism became more frequent, until she was spending half an hour on the ground for every hour in the air. They had made it over the mountains and across the rainforest on the eastern side, almost to Roros, keeping away from cleared land and any evidence of habitation, so there would be no warning of their coming.

On a hot, steamy tropical evening, the air-sled was creeping along the coast half a league offshore, so as not to be seen, for Crandor was a fertile and heavily populated land. They were flying so low that waves were thumping against the keel, when an unpleasant sound of metal grinding against metal came from the mechanism and it began to rattle and shake violently.

Chissmoul hastily turned towards the distant shore. 'I was afraid that was going to happen,' she said to Flydd. 'It's finished this time, surr.'

'Can you get us to land?'

'I'll try.'

'Hardly any of my militia can swim,' said Nish. 'And the wounded will certainly drown if we come down in deep water. Get everyone ready, Lieutenant.'

While Flangers organised the troops, Nish made sure that the stretcher lashings were unfastened and slung the serpent staff loosely over his back so he could drop it if he got into trouble. The food and drink were packed on the far right corner of the air-sled though, unless they made it to solid ground, it would have to be abandoned.

It became increasingly evident that they would not reach the shore, for the air-sled dropped lower and began to crash into the waves, dashing salty spray in their faces, and none of Chissmoul's increasingly frantic movements with her controller were making any difference.

'What if you set down on the water and give the mechanism another tweak?' said Flydd.

'Can't!' she wailed, in despair now that her precious craft was failing. 'Something's broken and I've no way of fixing it. Besides, she won't float with that whacking great spear hole through the bottom.'

'What if we plugged it with something?'

'Would you crawl inside the deck in the dark,' said Chissmoul, 'and try to find a spear hole by feel, when the craft could sink and carry you with it?'

Nish's heart sank, for he knew what was going to happen next.

'If we don't,' said Flydd, 'everyone who can't swim will die.'

'I'll have a go,' said Flangers.

'Can you swim, Lieutenant?'

'Not much more than a dog paddle.'

'Stay here,' said Nish, 'and get the troops off the instant we reach shore. I'll go – I've been inside the deck already.'

The air-sled, moving slowly now, crashed through another swell. The coast was a dark shadow not far ahead, but waves were bursting on a steep and rocky shore. 'I can't lift her at all,' said Chissmoul dismally.

'As long as you can keep going forwards,' said Flydd, 'we'll be all right.'

'We can't land there – we'd be smashed to pieces on the rocks.'

'I think there's a little cove further south. Head that way and beach the air-sled on the sand.'

'If I can get her that far,' said Chissmoul grimly.

'What are you going to plug the hole with, Nish?' said Flangers. 'It'll need to be jammed in tight or the water will force it straight out again.'

'I don't know.'

Flangers hacked a length off the pennant pole with his broadsword. 'This is about the same width as a javelard spear.' He rummaged among the gear purloined from the army at Blisterbone Pass and brought out a hammer.

Nish took them. 'I'd better take a knife in case I have to whittle it down to size. How far are we from shore?'

He could not tell from here, for it was a cloudy night and the dark rocks were almost indistinguishable from the sea and the sky.

'Couple of hundred spans,' said Aimee from behind. 'But the cove is three times that.'

It might as well be a hundred leagues, Nish thought. The air-sled isn't going to make it.

'Wish me luck,' he said, taking off his sabre and staff and handing them to Flangers. He crawled down the hole into the deck.

'Good luck,' they said, with feeling.

The floor was already awash, though at least the water was warm, which was a novelty in Nish's experience. Inside it was totally dark and he crouched there for a few moments, getting his bearings. The mechanism must be a few paces ahead of him. Yes, he could hear its grinding. The spear hole would be diagonally some four spans to his right, near the prow, since it had come through under the pennant pole.

He crawled that way, holding the wooden plug in his right hand, the knife and hammer thrust through his belt. The water was deeper at the front and came up to his elbows. People were moving around on the deck above his head; below him the hull was thumped regularly by the swell. The air was hot, the humidity stifling, and in the darkness Nish felt the first stirrings of claustrophobia. He fought them down and continued until his head struck the inside of the prow.

He could not find any hole in the keel, though the water definitely seemed to be rising. The hole should be directly below the pennant pole socket, he reasoned, and he must be able to see that as a slightly lighter circle.

He crawled back and forth, feeling the floor with the palms of his hands, but could not feel or see a thing. He must have crawled too far to the right. Nish turned around and, distantly, could just make out the pale circle of his entry hole. He oriented himself again and headed for the point where the socket should be.

The sound of the mechanism stopped abruptly and the air-sled thumped onto the water. Chissmoul cursed, loudly and volubly, and shortly it lifted again, with a series of wrenching shudders.

'How are you getting on down there?' said Flydd, his head down the hole. 'Nearly done?'

'I can't find the bloody spear hole.'

'It's below the pole socket,' Flydd said tersely.

'I can't find that either.'

'Really?'

'It's darker than a lyrinx's appendix down here.'

'But you must be able to see –'

Flydd broke off and Nish heard him striding across the deck, then the scrape of wood on metal, and he came back.

'Some fool put a crate on top of it. That better?'

When he looked the other way, Nish could see the pale dot of the socket. 'Thanks. How far are we from shore?'

'A good way. Clech has been taking soundings and the water is still eleven spans deep, so get a move on.'

'I'm not down here for my health!' Nish said irritably.

The spear hole wasn't directly beneath the socket when he got to it, for the spear had come through the floor at a shallow angle and struck the base of the pole slantwise, however after feeling around in increasing circles for another minute he tore his palm open on the ragged metal edge of the hole in the keel.

Nish cursed, then felt the hole carefully. It seemed smaller than his plug, and even after he'd tapped all the ragged edges down flat it still would not fit.

He was settling back on his haunches to whittle the plug to size when the mechanism stopped again, the air-sled dropped sharply and water gushed through the spear hole, right into his face. He fell backwards, struck his head, and knife and plug went flying.

As he was feeling for them Flydd called again, rather more sharply, 'Are you done now? We seem to be taking in a lot of water.'

'The cursed plug is too big,' Nish snapped. 'I've got to cut it to size. Tell Chissmoul to fly prow-down so some of the water can run out.'

'I don't think she can.'

'It's important.'

'So is your job, and if it takes much longer there won't be any point.'

Nish restrained the urge to insert the plug into Flydd, sideways, and felt for his knife. The air-sled lifted even more reluctantly than before and some water dribbled out.

He whittled the end of the plug, which was extremely hard wood, and tried it again, but it was still too big. Outside he could hear crashing waves; they must have drifted closer to the rocks, and with such big seas there would be little chance of anyone getting off onto the steep shore. He tried the plug and this time it just fitted.

He tapped it in. The plug felt tight, but the air-sled dropped again, hit the water and the pressure blew it out, whacking him in the mouth. He rubbed his bruised lips and replaced the plug.

'Nearly done?' said Flydd. 'We're awfully low in the water.'

'Impact keeps pushing it out. Chissmoul has to stay up longer.'

'Flying this heap is hard enough without lifting all that extra water.'

However the air-sled did lift, went prow down, and the water began to gurgle out the spear hole.

'Where are we now?' Nish yelled.

'Nearing the entrance to the cove, but the water is still deep. If we go down I can swim to shore . . . but I don't think anyone else could.'

'Well, I certainly can't from here!'

Nish jammed in the plug and hammered it down until his arm was aching. He could feel the air-sled moving now.

'Done it!' he yelled. 'I'm coming out.'

'We're in the cove,' Flydd said. 'I don't think we can get as far as the beach but there's a little rock platform to our right; Chissmoul is going to try and beach the air-sled on it.'

'Gather your packs and weapons,' ordered Flangers, 'and get ready to jump. Stretcher-bearers, stand by.'

Nish crawled through the elbow-deep water towards the hole. The mechanism raced, rattled, raced again. The air-sled seemed to accelerate then the prow struck the rocks and slid across them. Nish heard the plug shear off, not that it mattered now. They were on the platform, safe.

'Stretchers off first,' Flangers bellowed.

Heavy feet ran across the deck.

'Look out for that following wave,' cried Clech. 'Hang on!'

Nish was at the hole when the wave crashed over the rock platform, lifting the air-sled and turning it around. The surge began to carry it back towards the water and he lost his bearings momentarily. Before he could grab the rim, the prow of the air-sled must have gone over the edge, for it dropped sharply, he was carried down with the water and slammed against the inside of the prow.

He clawed his way up for air, aware that seawater was spurting in through the spear hole again and there was nothing he could do about it. The plug and hammer could be anywhere.

'Get off!' Flydd was roaring.

'Hoy!' yelled Flangers. 'Grab that stretcher before it floats away. Carry them up the slope away from the surge.'

Nish heard people shouting, yelling and screaming; he could see the hole above him but the air-sled had caught on a projection at the edge of the rock platform and was still suspended, prow down, so steeply that he could not climb the wet metal.

At this angle the water was up to his shoulders and would soon rise above his head. He tried again, slipped and went under, and salty water went up his nose and down his windpipe.

He splashed up again, spitting out water and gasping

for breath. Could he squeeze up along the side of the craft, where the hull tapered?

'Where's Nish?' came Aimee's high voice.

'I thought he was out,' said Flydd. 'Has anyone seen him?'

'I'm in here,' he croaked, though he did not think he could be heard over the crash of the waves and the grinding of the keel against the rocks.

There was nothing to hang onto along the side, no way to pull himself up. He had swallowed so much seawater that he felt ill, and was seized by a deadly fear that he was going to drown.

'Here!' he screeched, banging on the underside of the deck with his knuckles.

'He's still inside,' said Aimee. 'Get him out before it sinks. Chissmoul, do something.'

'Can't! Wave tore – controller – away,' she said dully. 'We're finished.'

'Be buggered!' snapped Flydd. 'Flangers, can we get to the hole? He must be trapped down in the prow.'

'I'll try and drop a rope down to him,' said Flangers. 'Nish, can you hear me?'

'Yes! Hurry up.'

'I won't be long. Stay calm. We'll get you out.'

'Big wave!' sang out Clech. 'Move away from the edge.'

The wave hit the air-sled, metal ground on stone underneath Nish and the craft moved further onto the rock platform; the angle of its tilt shrank fractionally, though not enough for him to climb out. He was waiting for it to drop further, thinking he was safe, when the surge went the other way, carried the air-sled with it over the edge, and it dropped like a boulder.

On the way down it tilted again, the water carrying him the other way in a great surge and slamming him against the inside of the stern. The air-sled kept falling, hit the bottom stern-first, rolled over and thumped down on its deck.

Nish lay there with the water over his head, battered black and blue; even his teeth hurt. Stay calm, he told himself as he rolled over and sat up. Just swim to the hole, out and up. But first he had to find the hole in the deck, and there was not a skerrick of light down here.

He took a deep breath, steadied himself, and could hear the precious air gurgling out through the spear hole. How long would it last? He could not guess, but at least that told him where the prow was – behind him. Nish swam the other way, sweeping his hands out from side to side, and shortly came up against the mechanism. The exit hole had to be to his left and it didn't take long to find it. He felt through the hole and touched the seabed!

It was completely blocked by hard sand. In his dazed state he had not taken in that the air-sled was upside down. Panic exploded; he was trapped and, as soon as the last of the air was gone, he was going to drown.

Nish fought for self-control and tried to think, but in the darkness and the strange environment his thoughts were unusually sluggish. The air-sled was already half full of water so he didn't have long. He took another breath and probed through the hole. Could he dig enough sand away to get out?

That would depend on what the seabed was. If it was all flat sand he was doomed, for he'd never move enough to reach any of the sides and get out from underneath. But if the deck was partly resting on rocks there could be a gap at one side or one end.

He wouldn't know until he tried. Nish began to claw away the sand with his hooked fingers but it proved slow work, since the sand to either side kept slumping into the hollow. He needed a better, faster digging tool.

Crawling through the water to the broken mechanism, he kicked it with the heel of one boot until it fell apart. After sorting through the pieces, he settled on a clamshell-shaped metal cover. He could dig five times as fast with it.

He attacked the sand, lifting it inside the hull and dropping it to the side so not a grain would fall back in. The sides of the hole kept slumping, but in a few minutes he had excavated a hollow down to the length of his arm, and rather wider than the exit hole. Putting his head and shoulders down, he felt around.

Solid sand lay to his left, but ahead and on the right he felt a depression in the seabed, though there was no way of telling how far it went. He pulled himself down to his hips and felt again. The way ahead was blocked but the depression continued to the right. He was almost out of air, so Nish went backwards into the air-sled and squatted there, catching his breath.

The water level was much higher now, up to his neck, and the air was still gurgling out as rapidly as before. It would be gone in a few minutes. And what if he went through and there was no way out, or he became stuck?

Nish could feel the panic rising again, his claustrophobia returning. It was much harder to fight this time, for the thought of being trapped and waiting to drown made him want to shriek and batter his fists against the deck. He took another breath, and another, now having to tilt his head back to do so.

All right, he thought, here goes. Don't do anything in haste – that will only make the panic worse. Taking the deepest breath he could draw, he grabbed his scoop and went through the hole and out along the seabed depression under the deck, concentrating on moving quickly but steadily. He wove to the right, trying to slip through the water like an eel.

Beside him he felt rock; ahead the depression continued. He swam along it confidently but it ended, *everywhere*, and panic exploded in his mind. The urge to scream and thrash was almost irresistible, but he knew that would be the end of him.

He went backwards, found that the seabed depression continued further to his right, on the other side of the rock the deck was resting on, and moved that way. His chest felt tight now, and he was a little short of breath, but he had to keep going. Left, left, right, then straight ahead, and he felt sure he had to be near the edge.

He touched the deck overhead to check, and encountered the ridge along its side. Only half a span to go, but now the way was blocked by a curving ridge of sand that must have been thrown up when the side of the air-sled hit the bottom.

He attacked it steadily, carving the face away and sliding the sand to his left. His chest was heaving now; he had only a few seconds' worth of air. Nish kept on steadily, knowing it was his only option, and broke through. Carving another layer away to be sure he could get out, he let the scoop fall.

The passage proved a tight squeeze, and the pressure on his chest made the urge to breathe desperate, but he forced himself to keep going and felt his legs come free. He had to breathe; *had to*; and there wasn't time to swim to the surface, but if he could just reach the stream of air issuing from the spear hole . . .

Nish breathed out as he dragged himself across the hull, seeing red flashes before his eyes, and clamped his mouth over the ragged hole, heedless of the sharp metal edges cutting his lips.

He drank down the warm air, gasping it and feeling it bringing life back to his numb limbs. In, out, in, out, he breathed, then looked up to the surface. He couldn't see anything. It might be two spans up, or twenty.

However deep it is, he thought, I'm going to make it. *Nothing* can stop me now. He swam up slowly, trickling air out of his nostrils, and in under a minute his head broke the surface.

'Hoy!' he yelled to the people standing on the platform. 'Where's that bloody rope you were going to send down?'

Flangers tossed it to him and they hauled him out, and he embraced them one by one, even Flydd. The militia gave him a quiet but heartfelt cheer.

'Back from the dead,' said Aimee, 'and we're going to follow you all the way to victory.'

TWENTY-NINE

'I know Roros well,' said Flydd after they'd collected their packs and weapons, plus what little food they'd saved, and climbed the first hill. Higher hills blocked their view to north and south, and inland.

'The coast forms a series of rocky ridges and little coves here,' he went on, 'rising up to steep, barren hills, and there's an abandoned watch-tower on the highest. That'll be it there, see, where the cliffs rise straight up from the sea. A league beyond it, across the river, is Roros.'

'Not tonight,' groaned Nish, whose every bone and joint ached. 'I feel as though I've been set upon and beaten.' He stumbled and nearly fell.

Flydd put an arm around him. 'We can't get there tonight, and they wouldn't let us in the gates if we did. Besides, after our brilliant performance in Taranta we're not going to turn up looking like drowned rats. We'll sleep in the watch-tower, if you can make it that far.'

'Has someone got my gear?' Nish mumbled, feeling close to collapse.

'I'm carrying your pack,' said Flangers, 'and the staff, but I lost your sabre. Sorry.'

Nish could not have cared less. 'It was Vivimord's, anyway.'

'It was a beautiful blade,' said Flydd, 'though designed for dark purposes. I'm glad it's gone. I always had an uneasy feeling about it.'

'It did everything I asked of it,' said Nish. 'And sometimes, when I was fighting with it, it seemed to go to the target of its own accord.'

'A handy thing in a melee – unless it starts choosing its own targets.'

Nish squirmed away from that thought. 'I was always in control of it.' Except for the time he'd saved Huwld's life, he realised.

'I dare say. Anyway, it's not the right weapon for the Deliverer . . . or whatever you plan to call yourself.'

'Vivimord gave me that title. I won't be using it again.'

'What are you going to call yourself, in this campaign to bring down the God-Emperor?'

'Nish,' said Nish. 'I've been Nish to my friends half my life. It's a fine, ordinary name and suits me perfectly.'

'Emperor Nish,' said Flydd sourly. 'It doesn't have an imperial ring to it.'

'Since I don't plan to be emperor, it doesn't matter!'

'Quite!' snapped Flydd. 'As for the blade, I'll get you a better one in Roros. They make fine weapons here.'

'I wouldn't mind my serpent staff. I'm not sure I can stay on my feet without a prop.'

Flangers handed it to him and they made their slow way to the watch-tower. Flangers eased the plank door open, checked that its three levels were unoccupied by man or beast, and they went inside and barred the door. Nish had no idea what they did after that. He staggered up the stairs to the open lookout platform at the top, where the warm air was so humid and soupy that the only bedding needed was a coat for a pillow, and collapsed.

*

When he woke late the following morning, the hot sun was burning his bruised face and Flydd was gone.

'He went to Roros at dawn, in disguise,' said Clech as Nish stumbled down the steps. The fisherman was sitting on the floor with his splinted legs stretched out in front of him, before a small blaze burning in an open fireplace. 'Hungry?'

Nish could have gnawed off his right arm. 'What have we got?'

'Fried ham and seagull eggs.'

The last remnants of the purloined Taranta ham sat on the stone floor beside him, below a sling bulging with little eggs hanging from a rusty hook. Clech sliced ham as neatly as if he were filleting a fish and tossed it into a pan. Scooping out a handful of seagull eggs he crushed them in his fist and strained the eggs from the shell through his grubby fingers into the pan.

'Did Flydd say when he'd be back?' said Nish, sitting down. He was so sore that every movement took an effort.

'Nope.'

After breakfast he went outside and tried to work out a plan to attack the empire, but Nish could not see how he was going to raise an army without being captured or assassinated. He had to have an army; but he could not raise one; but he had to have one. The dismal thoughts went back and forth, without hope of resolution.

He was sitting in the shade of the tower, looking over the cliffs at the sea and wistfully remembering those placid and mostly carefree times on the clifftops of Gendrigore, when Flydd rode up the track from the south on a large black horse. Nish remained where he was, fanning himself with a banana leaf. The midday heat of Crandor was almost unbearable and at the clifftops there was a slightly cooler breeze.

'Any luck?' he called as Flydd was tethering the horse to a bush.

'Ah, there you are. Luck with what?'

'Whoever you went to Roros to see. How do you know people there, anyhow?'

'That's a silly question, Nish, after all the time you've known me. The scrutators had to know the most important, influential, clever and talented people in the world, in every field, and when we went out in the world we didn't carry written records. We were taught to remember everything.'

'I thought you lost most of your old memories in renewal?'

'It turns out they weren't lost at all – I'd just forgotten how to find them – and they're slowly coming back. Ten years ago I knew a thousand names and faces in Roros, and on the way here I've remembered half of them. Of course, many have died, and some are in the God-Emperor's work camps and prisons, but it's surprising how many are still around. I met half a dozen this morning – contacts who make it their business to know what's going on – and they've given me much to think about.'

He looked Nish up and down. 'You look like a rat-gnawed corpse.'

'Thanks! I don't feel too hot, actually.' Nish flapped his banana leaf and wiped the sweat off his throbbing brow.

'You've got fresh purple bruises over last week's yellow ones, and your head is like a melon.'

'Enough compliments – I can't afford for it to swell any further,' Nish said drily. 'I'm going to lie down in the shade. I'm not designed for this climate.'

'Good idea. Get some more sleep. We're going out tonight and we won't be back till late.'

'Going where?'

'I'll tell you when we're nearly there.'

*

It was after ten when they left, and everyone was asleep apart from Flangers and the guards. Flydd mounted the horse and helped Nish up in front of him, onto the horn of a saddle as hard as stone, then flicked the reins and the horse began to pick its way down the gritty track.

'Shouldn't we be disguised in some way?' said Nish after a while.

'What for?'

'Wisp-watchers.'

'Already taken care of.'

Flydd did not say how. He wasn't in a talkative mood and neither was Nish, who endured the jolts in pain-filled silence. They turned onto a paved highway and followed it over a river on a bridge of many arches, before taking a muddy cart road that led towards the shore.

There were fields on the left, freshly harvested, and an infestation of shanties and shacks to the right, like a series of boils growing out from the high wall of the city.

Turning in at a minor gate in the wall, Flydd said in Nish's ear, 'The guards have been bribed. Pull your hood down and keep out of the light. Say nothing.'

He rapped on the gate with the butt of his knife. The gate was opened and a pair of watchmen, one thin as a bean, the other a stocky wrestling type, stared at him.

'Who comes?' said the wrestler.

Flydd said something incomprehensible and held out what appeared to be a signed and sealed safe conduct, on vellum. The wrestler took it and held it close, squinting at it in the lantern light. Flydd tapped his serpent staff on the cobbles, whereupon one of the wrestler's eyes rolled to the left, the other to the right. He swayed and passed the vellum up to the beanpole.

He did not even look at it before saying in a shrill voice, 'That seems to be in order,' and handing it back.

Something slipped from Flydd's hand to the beanpole's in the exchange, he waved them through and the gate banged behind them. They rode up a muddy road between houses that leaned out above them on either side, before following a winding path through a hundred unmarked alleys and mean streets until Nish marvelled that Flydd could find his way at all. Eventually he turned up a winding thoroughfare to a series of mansions on a flat-topped hill standing above the coast.

'This should be the place,' said Flydd as they approached a large house of several storeys built of grey stone, surrounded by a high wall with spikes along the top.

He scanned the street before approaching the high iron gates. A uniformed guard shone a lantern on his face, and Nish's. He nodded, swung the gate open, locked it behind them, and held the reins of the horse.

Flydd sprang down. Nish tried to follow and fell off, for one leg had gone numb from sitting on the horn of the saddle. Flydd helped him up. Another guard led the horse away and Flydd set off down a paved path with flower beds on either side. Nish stumbled after him, aching in bone and sinew, and his entire backside feeling bruised.

'We've come to see Yulla Zaeff,' said Flydd quietly.

'Zaeff?' said Nish. 'I know the name, though I can't remember where I've heard it before.'

'At the end of the war she was the governor of Crandor, the wealthiest nation on Santhenar.' Flydd lowered his voice. 'She's a greedy, conniving woman who made herself rich beyond your dreams –'

'You'd be surprised at how modest my dreams are these days.'

'Unfortunately!' Flydd said pointedly. 'Yulla was once so wealthy and influential that even Jal-Nish, when he became God-Emperor, did not care to bring her down, though he dismissed her as governor and installed his own puppet. I knew her well, once, and she was a great help to us in the lyrinx war –'

'I remember now,' said Nish. 'You gave her the first spare thapter, even though you knew she would use it to enrich herself immeasurably.'

'Yulla was worth it. Despite the qualities I've mentioned, she was the best of governors. She loved her country, defended it stoutly, and made sure that even the meanest of her citizens shared in its wealth. And she kept her promises.'

'You sound as though you admire her.'

'I disliked her thoroughly, and she me, yet we worked well together when we had to.'

'But surely she no longer has to, so why would she help us?'

'Because your father has long since stripped her of the monopolies that made her rich, and taxed most of her wealth away, and she wants it back. Besides, Yulla is a patriot. She can't bear to see her beloved Crandor suffering under the tyrant's yoke, and its wealth stolen to prop up the God-Emperor's corrupt and brutal realm. I think she'll help us, for a price. Indeed, she's the best person in Roros to do so. Yulla is no longer powerful, but she has the ear of almost every important person in this land, and they will listen. Hush now.'

The front door opened silently the moment they reached it, and Nish felt his heart miss a beat, for the woman who stood in the hall was so striking that she took his breath away.

She was his height, and slender, yet nicely curved in all the right places, with skin the colour of melted chocolate and a perfect oval face. Her hair was woven into a single braid, and her smile lifted the corners of her mouth enchantingly. The people of Crandor often filed their teeth to points, which Nish loathed, but her teeth were small, white and perfectly even.

She held out her hand to Flydd, and her voice was low and melodious.

'You are Xervish Flydd? I studied the artists' images of you, which were done before your renewal of course, but even now there is a likeness about your eyes . . .' As Flydd gripped her hand she studied him, head to one side. 'Yes, I'm sure you are Xervish Flydd. My name is Persia bel Soon.' She pronounced it Purr-*see*-arr. 'I presently serve Yulla Zaeff in several capacities, but more of that later.'

He seemed a little reluctant to release her hand, and Nish could understand why.

She was turning to Nish when Flydd said, 'Bel Soon? That is a name from the Histories, and also mentioned in a Great Tale, is it not?'

'Indeed,' said Persia, still smiling, though not so welcomingly.

'So many Histories, so many names,' said Flydd. 'And my memories haven't all come back, but . . . was it the twenty-third – the *Tale of the Mirror*?'

'The tale that you scrutators had banned, denounced as a lie, and rewritten?' she said in a chilly voice.

'*I* did not denounce it,' said Flydd, slightly taken aback.

'Our family name is mentioned in that tale, which,' said Persia, 'according to our Histories, was written by my grandmother of many generations back. Her name was Tallia bel Soon. And *every word* of the Great Tale was true.'

'Tallia, of course. She served the great mancer, Mendark, for a time, and most honourably I understand, until her indenture was completed.'

'As with her, so with me,' said Persia. 'But I am discourteous.' She turned back to Nish. 'You are Cryl-Nish Hlar, known as Nish. There is no difficulty recognising you from

362

your portraits, despite the bruises. I have a salve that will ease them, if they are troubling you.'

'Very much so,' said Nish, imagining her applying salve in all kinds of places. He pushed the distracting thoughts away.

She extended her hand, which was cool and strong. He winced as she squeezed his bruised fingers and she let go at once.

'Would you come this way.'

She led them down a broad hall with family portraits to either side, all of broad-faced, unattractive people. Her gown was clinging and Nish found his eyes irresistibly drawn to her prominent, swaying bottom. He swallowed and looked aside, telling himself that he was here on a mission of vital importance and could not afford to be distracted, but distracted he remained.

After climbing several stairs, Persia opened a door, stepped through into a large though dimly lit room with curtained windows on three sides, and announced, 'The renewed ex-scrutator, Xervish Flydd, and the son of the God-Emperor, Cryl-Nish Hlar, to see you, Lady Yulla.'

The windowless inner wall contained shelves extending from floor to ceiling, each divided into many small compartments which appeared to contain rocks and minerals. There was a small table and a high-backed chair by the right-hand window, another long, low table further down, with soft chairs around it, and a high-backed wing chair down the far end.

The chair by the right-hand window creaked and a large, fleshy woman rose and turned to face them. She had triple chins, small grey eyes set in flesh bloated from over-indulgence, and her sagging skin had an oily sheen. In her left hand she held a piece of rock crystal, which she was examining through a large hand lens. She looked up, her gaze passed over them indifferently, then she turned away and resumed her study of the crystal.

How rude, Nish thought, disliking her on sight. She cares more about that stupid crystal than she does about us.

'Would you take your places here,' said Persia, leading them to the soft armchairs around the low table.

Nish sank into the cushions of his chair with a grateful sigh and Flydd sat beside him.

'Have you dined?' she said.

Nish was about to say, 'Not since lunchtime,' when Flydd said, 'Yes, thank you.'

Persia's lovely eyes searched his face. 'Lady Yulla will be with you directly.' She went out and closed the door.

Nish looked around. On the far side of the room a man with unkempt grey hair and a bald patch was slumped in the wing chair as if asleep. He was facing away from them and Nish could not see his features, though a lamp on a stand behind him shone on a large piece of paper on his lap.

A bookcase held a number of ledgers, plus a matching series of thick volumes with gold leaf on the spines. They might have been a complete set of the Great Tales, or Yulla's own family Histories. Shelves held vases, pieces of statuary and other small items of exquisite artistry.

Suddenly aware that Yulla was sitting in the large chair across the table from him, Nish swung around. For a big woman she moved quickly, and silently.

Nish rose to his feet, and extended his hand. 'Good evening, Lady Yulla, I'm Nish.'

Her eyes met his but she did not extend her hand and he sat down, discomfited. Persia returned bearing a tray, a decanter, and glasses. She took a chair halfway across the room and sat side-on to them, looking towards the old man in the corner, though Nish could tell that she was aware of everything they did, and ready to defend her mistress in an instant should the need arise.

Yulla still held the hand lens; the piece of rock crystal stood on the table in front of her. It was a beautiful specimen, an array of dozens of crystals all intergrown, all perfect, and Nish briefly wondered if she were a geomancer.

Geomancy had been one of the most powerful of the Secret Arts, in the olden days, but the destruction of the nodes had taken a greater toll of it than any of the other Arts, and to the best of his knowledge geomancy no longer existed.

'Flydd,' she said. Her voice had a hoarse, rasping quality, as if she had eaten too much, drunk too much, and smoked more herbs than she should have. 'Renewal has done you no favours – I preferred you the way you were last time we met.'

'A gaunt old man who looked as though the spare flesh had been gouged off his much-broken bones.'

'He was a better man than you are. But I am wasting time. What do you want?'

The implication was that they were wasting her time.

'You will have heard our news already, I think.'

'Of the abduction of our *beloved* God-Emperor by a *being* called Stilkeen; the defeat of Jal-Nish's army in the mountains by a meagre force of farmers and hunters led by Nish; and an insolent attack on the seneschal's mansion in Taranta by a band of renegades using the God-Emperor's personal air-sled? The tales came to me by skeet two days ago, but are they true?'

Yulla's small eyes were fixed intently on him and Nish suddenly saw the clever, determined woman within the saggy folds of flesh. She smiled thinly; her teeth were filed to points in the old Crandorian way, which, he recalled, had rather gone out of fashion since the war ended.

'I can't answer for the details of what you were told,' said Flydd, 'though your précis is correct in every particular. Is there any news of General Klarm?'

'No. I heard that he walked into the rock of the mountain and disappeared.'

'Nish and I both saw it. He used the Profane Tears to enter the shadow realm, the place where spirits dwell, *and hunt*. I am one of the few people who know what that place is like, and if I were forced to go there I would not rate my chances of survival highly.'

Unease shivered her plump cheeks and triple chins. 'Yet Klarm is a man of the utmost resourcefulness – and he has the tears.'

'He does –'

'Though I felt he was afraid to use them,' said Nish.

Flydd gave him a blank stare, but Nish sensed that he was annoyed; had he not wanted that piece of information revealed?

'That *is* interesting,' said Yulla. 'Go on.'

Nish glanced at Flydd, who looked away. Now Nish had to continue and he sensed that, having been such a powerful governor, Yulla would read any evasion or omission instantly. 'Klarm doesn't want power badly enough.'

'He did not get where he is today, with all his physical handicaps, without a deep yearning for power and what it brings and buys,' she said frostily, as though Nish's assumption was offensive to her.

Nish refused to be cowed. He too had taken on the mighty in his time, and beaten some of them.

'But he doesn't want to become God-Emperor. Klarm is a magnificent deputy, but he lacks the vital, selfish drive to risk everything for his own ambition. That's why he holds back with the tears – he doesn't want what they offer badly enough to risk destruction. That's how I read him, anyhow.'

'If you're right, it indicates a weakness that can be used against him when he returns; assuming he does.'

Yulla heaved her bulk to her feet and twitched the curtains together more tightly – from behind she had the shape of a rectangle distorted by the effects of gravity – then turned back to Flydd. 'What do you want from me, and what can you do for me?'

'I want to use this opportunity to take Nish to the throne.'

'Not as God-Emperor!' said Nish.

Again Flydd favoured him with that blank look, but Nish felt he was saying, *Keep your bloody mouth shut and let me do the talking.* Nish wasn't going to have that; he wasn't going to be Flydd's puppet as he had once been Vivimord's.

'You don't want absolute power either?' said Yulla in astonishment. 'Or wealth beyond any man's dreams? Or the most beautiful women in the world for your bed?'

Nish thought of Persia walking ahead of him down the hall, and swallowed.

'I am not immune to such desires, but at the end of the war I swore an oath to tear down the tyrant and restore peace and justice to Santhenar, and the common wealth to all.' He met her eyes. 'Would you do business with a man who did not keep his word?'

'If our word cannot be relied upon,' she said sententiously, 'nothing can.'

'We've got to strike fast,' said Flydd, smiling now. 'Jal-Nish's seneschals are watching for us, and as soon as Nish starts giving his public addresses, and appealing for volunteers to join his army, the enemy will strike with a force we cannot match. Not even the God-Emperor's only son is safe if he threatens the throne.'

Nish wondered why Flydd was talking about that plan when he had already derided it in private.

'And you want something from me?' said Yulla.

'A small measure of coin, protection for ourselves and the militia we brought with us, plus the contacts to recruit a small army, swiftly and secretly.'

How could they recruit an army secretly? It was, by definition, impossible. And so is overthrowing the empire, he thought gloomily. Father has thought of everything.

'Is that all?' said Yulla.

'We also require ships to convey the army swiftly to Fadd, so we can strike at the heart of the empire – Jal-Nish's palace of Morrelune.'

'Coin I can provide,' said Yulla. 'I am no longer wealthy, but the type of campaign you propose – small and fast – is within my capacity. Ships also. I only have two in Roros at the moment, but trusted allies could supply the rest. My protection is yours, of course, while you remain in Roros. The army is another matter. What did you have in mind?'

She was looking at Nish again.

'As – as Flydd said, I plan to show myself publicly, announce my intention to overthrow my father and call for volunteers. I –'

'No, no and no,' she cried. 'There can be no appearances, no public announcements, no recruitment of volunteers.'

'But –' began Nish.

'Surely I don't need to explain it to *him*?' said Yulla.

'He would not hear it from me,' said Flydd.

'Show yourself publicly and the seneschal of Roros will move against you with overwhelming force – he's already planned his attack for the moment you appear. Merely saying that you plan to overthrow the God-Emperor is sedition and you will be shot on sight by anonymous assassins.'

'The seneschal wouldn't dare,' said Nish weakly.

'He would not have while your father was around, but your announcement in Taranta changed everything,' said Yulla. 'Clearly, Jal-Nish is no longer the all-powerful God-

Emperor he once was. The sharks can taste blood in the water, and they're already circling. Besides, if you call for volunteers, half of those who come forward will be in the pay of the empire, and after taking you, they'll come for me.'

'Then what can I do?' cried Nish. Realising that he sounded like a petulant child, and that Persia was taking in everything he said and judging him on it, he went on more calmly. 'I must have an army, but how am I to raise one?'

'*You* can't, but *I* could put a small corps together,' said Yulla. 'I have several hundred men on my wage rolls, all former soldiers from Crandor's army during the war. Men rejected for Jal-Nish's forces because of their loyalty to me.'

'And you've kept them on all this time?' said Nish, looking at her through new eyes.

'Any leader who demands loyalty of her troops must show the same loyalty to them, in good times and in bad. And I have influential friends who also have their own private corps. We could muster an army of two thousand, given a little time.'

'I can't take the empire with such a small force,' Nish said quietly.

'Didn't you just defeat ten thousand men with a few hundred?'

'With a great deal of aid from the Range of Ruin, and from nature.'

'If you want my aid you'll find a way, because two thousand is all I can bring you, and even if I had more, there would not be the ships to carry them south. Well?'

'If that is an offer,' said Flydd, 'we'll take it.'

Two thousand men, Nish thought, shaking his head. How can I attack the might of the empire with so few?

'Not so fast,' said Yulla. 'What are you offering me?'

'The governorship of Crandor.'

'I would expect no less. What else?' She leaned forward greedily, her jowls quivering.

'Restoration of the monopolies the God-Emperor took from you, plus restitution for the unfair taxes imposed on you to destroy your wealth.'

'Agreed,' said Yulla at once. 'With compound interest, of course.'

'Come now,' said Flydd evenly, but in the tone that signified he was not going to negotiate. 'I'm not going to bankrupt the empire for you.'

'My losses have been very high. And this campaign will cost me a fortune.'

'You've reduced your outlays enormously since you lost the governorship, so you're not nearly as badly off as you maintain.'

'I'll have to call in a host of favours; and reward those who aid me.'

'With what I've offered, you can easily afford it.' Flydd folded his arms.

She picked up the hand lens, studied her crystal cluster for a minute or two, then said, 'I'll concede the point. Go on.'

'A seat on the God-Emp–' Flydd glanced at Nish, saw his scowl and amended, 'on the advisory council set up in the event of Nish's victory.'

'A *permanent* seat.'

'Agreed,' said Flydd, then added, 'as long as you remain of sound mind and body, and are capable of occupying that seat and doing your duty.'

After hesitating fractionally, Yulla agreed. 'However, all such offers are contingent on your success, which is far from guaranteed. What can you offer me now?'

'*Now?*' said Flydd, frowning.

'If the plot is discovered, I lose everything and so does my family. I must have a down-payment.'

'I've been on the run since the war, Yulla. My resources arc meagre.'

'I wasn't thinking of coin. I'll accept the God-Emperor's air-sled.'

'That piece of junk!' cried Nish.

'There's no flying craft like it in the empire. And with such a vehicle . . .'

'I gave you a thapter once,' mused Flydd. He looked at her sideways. 'It was a mighty gift.'

'And I repaid you twice over in aid. Besides, I only had it for a few months, for it failed when the nodes were destroyed.'

'As did every thapter and construct; my gift was made in good faith, and given in good order.'

Yulla frowned, turned her crystals over and studied them from the other side, holding them as if they were the most precious of nature's blooms. 'I will accept the air-sled as your down-payment. An adviser tells me that it has . . . potential.'

'Oh?' said Flydd sharply, but she did not elaborate, and he added, 'Very well. But if you can get it going again, I may need to call upon it to prosecute the war.'

'I agree that you may *ask* for it. Where did you hide it?'

'It's lying at the bottom of Cockle Cove, near the abandoned watch-tower. I should warn you, it was failing in flight, a problem with the mechanism . . .'

She'll reject the offer, Nish thought gloomily, and we'll have to start again.

'Nothing that my adviser can't fix, I'm sure.' Yulla raised her voice a little. 'Mel, would you come here for a minute?'

The old man laid down his paper and rose from the chair, only it wasn't a man. It was a short, plump woman of nearly sixty years, with thin grey hair and a small bald patch. She was dressed in patched, shabby and rather grubby shirt and trousers, but as soon as she turned those keen eyes on him, Nish knew her, though he had not seen her for thirteen years. And so did Flydd.

'Mechanician M'lainte,' they exclaimed together.

'Just M'lainte,' she said, smiling broadly as she shook Flydd's hand, then Nish's. 'The old titles were thrown out with the rubbish of the war, and good riddance.'

M'lainte had been a genius with any kind of mechanical device, especially those powered by the Art, and she had designed and built the first air-floater from a rude sketch Nish had given to Flydd. Nish had subsequently flown it, and drifted in it, halfway across Lauralin, but M'lainte had remained in the south and he had never seen her again.

'You can talk about old times later,' said Yulla. 'M'lainte, can you repair the air-sled's mechanism? Since it's the only craft of its kind in existence, it is beyond price.'

'I imagine so,' said M'lainte. 'I believe I understand how it works, and even if some of the parts are broken, they can be replaced. If you can make available a suitable vessel I'll raise it tomorrow night – assuming the seas are calm.'

Yulla nodded and turned back to Flydd. 'Then I'll accept it as down-payment. Are we agreed?'

'Agreed,' said Flydd.

Nish echoed him, feeling as though he'd been railroaded, though he could not see what else he could have done.

'Persia?' said Yulla. 'Would you come over so we can seal the agreement?'

Persia carried the tray across and poured a lime-coloured liquor into three glasses until they were full to the brim. 'Each of you will drink one third of your liquor and pass your glass to your right. When the glasses have returned to their original holders, empty, the agreement is sealed – and cannot be broken without the consent of all parties.'

She handed drinks to Yulla, Flydd and Nish.

They raised their glasses and sipped. The liquor was thick and sweet, with the aromatic flavour of lime zest, and very strong. After taking a third, Nish passed it to the right, to Yulla, accepted Flydd's glass in turn, and shortly the agreement had been sealed.

'It's done,' he said, feeling the burden that had weighed him down lifting just a little. There was a long way to go, and they would probably fail, but at least they had a plan.

THIRTY

Afterwards Persia led them downstairs into a reception room at the rear of the mansion overlooking the sea. 'If you would wait here,' she said, 'I'll make the necessary arrangements.'

'What arrangements?' Nish said, but she had already gone.

They sat down. The windows had many small panes and through them he could see all the way to the horizon. The sky was clear and the crescent moon touched the crests of the waves with red and silver. It was a beautiful sight, yet he could not enjoy it. How could he take on the empire with two thousand men?

Nish was not looking forward to the long voyage south, either. The sea was not his element and, on the one time he had sailed, the ship had been wrecked in a storm and most of the people aboard had drowned. He and Flydd had been marooned on a miserably cold island for weeks, living on worms and grubs, and, though it had been many years ago, he could still remember the taste of them, going down and coming up.

'I gather you're not entirely happy with this strategy,' said Flydd.

'I feel as though it's been forced on me, and that you've negotiated all my choices away.'

'If you had a better plan, you should have mentioned it earlier.'

'Everything is moving too fast. I like to think things through.'

'There isn't time. No matter how careful we were on the way from Taranta, the air-sled could have been seen, and if the seneschal of Roros should guess we're here, he'll bring in so many wisp-watchers and scriers that not even Yulla will be able to hide us.'

Nish shivered, his hopes dwindling. 'Did you have to agree to all her outrageous demands? Reparation *and* restitution? She's robbing us blind.'

'Of course she is, but I don't have time to look for a better ally, and if I did, I doubt I could find one. Yulla has many qualities and we can't do without her.'

'But a seat on the council! Why concede that?'

'She would not have agreed without it. Wealth can be lost far more quickly than it was gained, and it's hard to hold onto it without power. A position on the advisory council guarantees Yulla that power. Besides, she was an excellent governor of Crandor and she will be invaluable on any such council.'

'You might have asked me first.' It sounded petulant, though Nish had not intended it that way.

'Is that what this is all about?' snapped Flydd. 'You don't even know her, Nish. As scrutator I negotiated with Yulla, and dozens like her, for more than a decade. I can read her; I know what she'll accept and what she won't. I gave her nothing we could not afford, and no more than the minimum she would accept to help us.'

'Even so,' said Nish, 'you could have told me this on the way.'

'I didn't know she was alive until I got here.'

'But you had this plan in mind, or one like it. You're manipulating me, Flydd, the way Vivimord did, *and my father*. You don't feel like my old friend any more, and you haven't since taking renewal. You're acting like an arrogant scrutator, moving around lifeless pieces on a game board.'

Flydd opened his mouth to speak, evidently thought better of it and stalked to the furthest window, his chest rising and falling.

Nish watched his rigid back for a while, then sighed and leaned back in his seat. Flydd *was* using him, of course he was, but did he have any choice? Nish's irritation began to fade as he realised that Flydd was right and that this plan was the only one with any hope of success.

Even so, he missed their comradeship of old, which had largely vanished on renewal, and perhaps that was what this was all about. Nish felt alone now, so desperately alone and helpless.

He closed his eyes. He was always tired these days, and he ached all over. You're not a young man any more, he told himself. You're approaching middle age, you've done too much and you can't keep it up. But he had to; there was still so far to go.

Persia came in. 'Nish, if you would come this way, I'll show you to your room.'

'I beg your pardon?' said Flydd, swinging around.

'Nish will be staying here until we're ready to sail. Since he was a hero of the war and is the God-Emperor's son, everyone knows his face, and Yulla can't allow him to be recognised.'

'But my gear,' said Nish, 'the militia –'

'M'lainte's crew will collect your gear, and the militia, when she raises the air-sled tomorrow night. If you need anything else, it will be provided.'

'What if I have to go outside?'

'If it's absolutely necessary I will accompany you, and you will be disguised. From now on I will be your bodyguard –'

'You!' Nish exclaimed, for she was neither tall nor muscular but, indeed, exceedingly feminine.

She raised a perfectly sculpted eyebrow. 'I have been Yulla's bodyguard for almost seven years, and I assure you I'm very good at it.'

'As was Tallia bel Soon,' said Flydd thoughtfully. 'According to the Great Tale, she was a master of armed and unarmed combat.'

'It's in the family,' said Persia.

'Then I'll leave Nish in your safe hands. I'll just have a word with my former mechanician before I go, if I may. It's late and there's much to be done tomorrow.'

'I'll show you to M'lainte's quarters. Nish, I won't be a minute.' Persia led Flydd away.

Nish sat down and stared moodily out the window, feeling less in control than ever. He was practically a prisoner here, and what if Yulla turned out to be a traitor? Flydd had said that she kept her promises, but a lot could change in ten years. Klarm had also been a reliable man who kept his word . . .

Technically Klarm had not broken his word, Nish conceded, since he did not change sides until long after the war had been won and the world lost to the God-Emperor. And if Yulla was a secret ally of the empire's –

'You seem troubled, Nish,' said Persia from behind.

She was also a master of moving silently. 'I hadn't expected to be kept here,' he said coolly.

'Yulla is sorry about that.'

I'll bet! Persia might be sorry but Nish was damned sure Yulla wasn't. She did not appear to be troubled by normal human emotions, save greed.

'Why does she have all those rocks and crystals upstairs?' said Nish. 'Is she a geomancer?'

'Not at all,' said Persia. 'She collects beautiful things, wherever she can, and perfect minerals satisfy her most of all. She also appreciates their solidity and permanence . . . in a world that is transient and unreliable.' She gave him a measuring glance, as if assessing his own reliability. 'But you must be hungry by now.'

'I'm starving.'

'Come with me. You will want to bathe. I'll bring a tray to your room afterwards.'

He rubbed his hair, which was stiff with salt. 'That would be splendid. I itch all over.'

The bathing chamber had both hot and cold running water, an unheard of luxury, and Nish lay in the huge tub until the warm water had eased the worst of his aches and bruises. He donned the robe laid out for him and found her waiting outside the door with his tray.

His room was on the other side of the house and had a view up the rugged coast, which made a series of jagged outlines against the palely silvered sea. Nish noticed that the windows, unlike those in the upstairs room, did not open.

'Am I a prisoner, Persia?' he said, careful to pronounce her name correctly.

'No, you're being held here for your protection.'

If anyone else had said that he would have called them a liar, but Persia's face seemed incapable of concealing deception or falsehood. He wasn't blinded by her beauty – Nish had known many beautiful liars – but over the years he had learned to read faces, and he seldom misjudged people.

She turned down the bed and Nish sat in a chair by the window, picking at the food on the tray. He was starving but his stomach was so knotted and his throat so tight that he had to force each morsel down.

'Is there anything you would like to ask me before bed?' she said, delicately concealing a yawn behind her hand. 'It's nearly two in the morning.'

He shook his head and stood up, yawning as well. She was turning away when his robe slid off one shoulder, revealing his battered and bruised chest and side. Her eyes widened.

'You look as though someone tried to batter you to death.'

'That's one way of putting it,' said Nish.

'What happened?'

'Surely you've heard our tale by now?'

'Just an outline. I've been away and only returned this evening.'

'You're tired. It can wait until the morning.'

'Not if you're carrying injuries that could affect the campaign. Take your robe off and lie on the bed.'

In other circumstances Nish might have lusted after Persia, and he didn't want to reveal himself to her in his present condition. 'I'll visit a healer in the morning.'

'Now!' she said mildly. 'I'm stronger than I look, Nish.'

He certainly wasn't going to suffer the indignity of her stripping the robe from him, so he did as she asked.

Though her gaze was entirely cool and professional, Nish felt self-conscious and embarrassed. She rolled him over, exclaiming at the fading bruises and sword-edge scars on his buttocks, and touching the ancient crisscross scars on his back.

'There's hardly an unmarked spot on you,' she said. 'I would not have thought any man could have suffered such punishment and lived.' She didn't look so professional now; there was a soft look in her eyes, as if she felt for him.

'You should have seen Flydd's body before he took renewal. Compared to him I've got skin like a baby.'

379

'Stop trying to change the subject,' she said with a lilting laugh. 'How did these scars on your back come about?'

He had long since lost his embarrassment about that punishment. 'I was flogged at the manufactory where I worked as a prentice clanker artificer. But don't feel sorry for me; I was a callow, obnoxious fool, out for what I could get, and deserved every stroke.'

'I'm sure you were quite a rogue,' she said, smiling as though she did not believe a word of it, and her hand lingered on his shoulder.

Persia was thorough, he had to grant her that. She questioned him about every scar and every bruise, and felt his bones and skull all over, after he told her about being flung about inside the falling air-sled.

She peered into his eyes, and frowned. Her breath smelled like tangerines. 'Were you knocked unconscious at any stage?'

'No. If I had been, I probably would have drowned.'

'Have you ever been unconscious?'

'Quite a few times. I can't remember all the battles I've fought in. Is something the matter?'

'I'll tell you if there is.' She studied his scarred left hand. 'What happened here?'

'An encounter with Reaper.' He told her about it.

'It's a wonder you're not dead a dozen times. We'll have to take better care of you if you're to fulfil your destiny.'

'And restore Yulla's fortune,' he said without thinking.

Persia went still, all the warmth went out of her eyes, then she said stiffly, 'You came begging her favour and asking her to collaborate in a sedition that could cost everyone here, *and* our families, their lives. She did not approach you.'

She went out and pulled the door closed.

Nish got into bed, his cheeks flaming. Why hadn't he

thought before he'd opened his mouth? Had he damaged the campaign? Surely not. The agreement had been made and could not be broken. But even so, he needed Yulla's regard, and he wanted Persia's even more. For a moment there she'd seemed to care about him.

Putting her out of mind, he lay in the dark, listening to the waves breaking on the shore below and going over the day's events, trying to think of another way to attack the empire, but he could not come up with one.

What of the campaign Yulla had proposed? Suppose she did raise an army of two thousand, and they took the long sea voyage down to Fadd, a perilous journey of some four hundred leagues along a coast notorious for its sudden storms, uncharted reefs and treacherous currents.

It would take a week if the weather was fair and the winds favourable, two or three times that if not, and should the weather turn bad they would have to wait it out in the nearest port, running a grave risk of being discovered. How could the departure of a fleet of ships be kept secret anyhow?

Even supposing they reached Fadd, its garrison held at least five thousand troops and if he did slip past them, and march his little army up into the mountains without being attacked, the army guarding Morrelune and the grim prison of Mazurhize must be even larger. How could he evade the first army, and beat the second? Nish had no idea, and little hope.

A frustrating week had gone by, which Nish had mostly spent staring out the window or pacing back and forth. Though his room was large, beautifully decorated and had a glorious view, he felt as though he was in gaol, and that raised hideous memories of the ten years he had spent in Mazurhize.

M'lainte had successfully raised the air-sled and taken the militia on board the salvage vessel, but it had sailed to a secret location and he had not set eyes on them. He only saw Persia when she brought his meals, and Yulla not at all. As far as he knew, no progress had been made on finding enough ships, or assembling his army.

Without either company or news, Nish grew more anxious every day. Was the empire's net drawing ever tighter around them? Even if the air-sled had not been seen heading to Roros, it was one of the most likely places to begin a rebellion, and its Imperial seneschal would have his scriers on high alert.

'I've got to go outside,' he said when Flydd finally appeared.

'What for?' grunted Flydd, who seemed more preoccupied than usual.

'I feel like a prisoner.' Nish paced the track he'd worn in the carpet.

'Here?' Flydd exclaimed.

'I nearly went mad in Mazurhize,' Nish said quietly. 'I'm a trifle sensitive about gaol.'

'You'd better speak to Persia,' said Flydd. 'I've got to go away for a while.'

'What for?'

'Private business.'

'What about?'

Flydd scowled in the scrutatorly way Nish knew all too well, and turned towards the door. He constantly queried others about their affairs, but did not like to be asked about his own. It refreshed Nish's anxiety about what Flydd was really up to.

'How are your insides, Xervish?'

'Worse,' grunted Flydd over his shoulder. 'I'm not sure how much more I can take. Oh, I brought you this.' He turned back, unbuckling a finely tooled sword belt and sheath, and handed them to Nish.

Nish drew the sword, a light, double-edged blade so keen that he could have shaved with it, and so finely polished that it reflected his face. The metal had a reddish cast, the hilt was subtly engraved, and the weapon was perfectly balanced.

'Thanks,' said Nish. 'It's a beautiful sword, but not a showy one. I appreciate that.'

'You're a plain, down-to-earth sort of a fellow,' said Flydd, looking pleased for once. 'I didn't think you'd want anything flashy.'

He went out, leaving Nish to wonder if he'd just been complimented, or insulted.

When Persia brought his lunch, he asked to go outside.

'Into Roros?' she said, frowning.

He explained about nearly going insane in Mazurhize, and how, ever since, he could not bear to be held against his will.

Again he saw that soft, caring look in her eyes. 'I understand perfectly. I'll speak to Yulla at once.'

When she returned, Persia said, 'You'll have to be disguised, though I'm not sure what disguise would be best. Could you pass for a dark-skinned native of Crandor, I wonder?'

'That depends on how good the disguise is.'

'Illusion is best if you only want to fool the common folk, but unless it's a powerful one the wisp-watchers will see straight through it.'

'Don't powerful illusions have their own problems?' said Nish.

'They do. The seneschal has sensitives capable of detecting such forms of the Art.'

'What about shape-changing?'

'That's mighty mancery, way beyond my minor powers. Besides, the shape-changing spells are cousin to the Regression and Renewal Spells, and you already know how deadly they can be.'

'Poor Tulitine,' he said, wondering if she could still be alive.

'I think we'll go for a physical disguise,' said Persia. 'When done well it can even fool a scrier close by. Should I make you into a native of Crandor or a foreigner?' she said thoughtfully. 'A foreigner would be easier and there are plenty of them in Roros, but if word gets out about you every foreigner will be taken in, and you'll be uncovered. I'll make you into a local.'

'I don't look much like a local,' said Nish. 'My skin is too pale and I'm the wrong build.'

'There are stocky Crandoreans, such as the silver miners of Twissel. Exposure to all that silver turns their brown skin a hideous silver-blue, and everyone despises them, so it's a good disguise. And the rest – beard, frizzy wig, grime under the fingernails, silver-black teeth – is easy. It'll be fun making you up,' she said, smiling for the first time in a week, and he saw the lovely, warm Persia again.

'More fun than looking at myself in the mirror after you've finished with me, I dare say.'

'What do you care? You want people to avoid you.'

'I don't know why,' said Nish, 'but I've always cared about my appearance, such as it is. You couldn't understand that, being so beautiful.'

She started, then knitted her brows. 'Beauty has benefits but also many drawbacks. It attracts all the pests and parasites in the world, and when you do well, some people imply that you achieved it, er . . . horizontally. I often wish I could walk through a crowd and have nobody notice my passing. Speaking of which, this is the way miners walk, and you'll

384

have to learn it. The seams they mine aren't thick enough for them to stand up.'

She demonstrated a bent-backed shuffle, which Nish did his best to imitate.

'Not like that,' she said, smiling again. Putting her hands on his shoulders, she bent his back a little more and tilted his face sideways. Again her hands lingered, before she said briskly, 'Try that.'

Several hours later, Nish looked in her full-length mirror and saw a man so grotesquely ugly that he would not have spoken to him in the street, and there was no question that he was unrecognisable.

'You're an artist of rare skill, Persia.'

'Thank you,' she said. 'It's been fun. I – I haven't had a lot of fun, lately.'

'I've enjoyed watching you do it.'

She was an oasis of calm and perfection in a world that, lately, had mostly shown him its ugly side, and he wanted to see more of her.

They headed down a long underground passage. 'This comes out in a mean little alley which isn't watched,' said Persia. 'But when we get there, I'll go out first, to make sure. When I walk past the exit, follow me, but don't say anything or meet my eyes.'

'Why not?'

'My dress tells everyone that I'm high caste, rich and beautiful, while you're a filthy silver miner, one of the lowest castes of all. I would not acknowledge your existence, and you wouldn't go near me in case I ordered you flogged.'

'Thanks,' Nish muttered. 'Do you often have people flogged?'

She laughed. 'Not as often as some of them deserve.'

'So, did you choose this disguise to trim me down to size?'

The smile faded. 'Why would I do that?' she said quietly.

'You're the son of the God-Emperor and a hero of the wars. High caste though I may be, I could never aspire to move in *your* world.'

Her silky cheeks had taken on the faintest ruddy tinge, and Nish felt mortified, and humbled. 'I'm sorry, I really am. It's just that . . . I don't see myself as the son of the God-Emperor. I never have.'

'Really? What do you see yourself as, deep down?'

He would not have said it to anyone else, but Persia's manner invited confidences, and he knew she would not use his against him.

'The boy who was always trying to please a harsh father and an indifferent mother . . . yet, no matter how hard he tried, it was never good enough.'

'Ah, Nish, I'm sorry. If only we could see ourselves as we really are, and not through the distorted prism of the expectations of others.' She stopped, looked into his heavily made-up eyes, then moved on. 'But you're still a hero among heroes. Still far more elevated than I.'

'I suppose I am,' Nish said absently. 'A hero, I mean,' he added hastily in case she took offence. 'Well, of course I am, and everyone sees me differently because of it, but I don't puff out my chest and recount my mighty deeds before breakfast. I've only done what I had to do, but I had the good fortune to survive when so many other people, many braver than me, did not.'

'Then we're not so different after all.' They were approaching the alley. 'Outside, I won't acknowledge you in any way, but I'll always be close by and, in case of trouble, you must do exactly as I indicate. If we're separated, come back here, press this hollow and someone will come for you.' She indicated an oval depression in the rough stone wall.

Persia went out and shortly she walked past the exit. Nish

followed, using the bent-backed miner's shuffle she had taught him, and keeping his eyes lowered. Despite these handicaps, he felt his spirits lift the moment he was outside, in the great city.

She led him through the alleys to an enormous square filled with hundreds of market stalls, all with colourful signs, streaming pennants, peddlers crying out their wares and thousands of people sampling them. Roros was also famous for its food and he could smell a dozen different kinds of cuisine, not to mention the hanging bundles of spices, the dried fish and meats, the blossoms and perfumes and enchanting stacks of pastries.

This would be a good place for spies to meet, he thought. Two wisp-watchers loomed over the square but they could only see part of it, and it would be easy to exchange secrets privately among the teeming shoppers.

Nish had no interest in anything being sold here. All he wanted from the outing was a respite from feeling like a prisoner, and to see the great city of Roros and assess its people through his own eyes. He did not get the chance to do either.

He was wandering between the stalls when a coruscating light burst from the huge wisp-watcher mounted at the far end of the square, dazzling him. He threw his arm over his eyes, but felt the burning rays of an equally brilliant beam issuing from the wisp-watcher behind him.

It's Father, he thought, and acid burned a track up his throat. He's got free; he's back and this disguise hasn't fooled him. He's pinned me like a beetle to a board.

Nish began to back away, but the beam remained on him and he bumped into the front of a booth clustered with boots, bags and belts. He could smell hot leather.

Where could he go? Nowhere; he could barely see while the wisp-watchers had him, and they wouldn't let go.

Then, incredibly, the broad beams from both wisp-watchers slipped off him. He rubbed his eyes. The beams were moving upwards until they faced each other. What was going on? They must be signalling to Gatherer, who would alert the local seneschal.

Nish was about to slip under the booth when a ground-shaking rumble issued from a pair of huge loop-listeners he had not noticed. Booths toppled and objects smashed on the ground.

The two beams combined, brightened, and a tower-high figure of light formed in the air between them, the same figure that had appeared so shockingly in the little valley below the white-thorn peak and seized Nish's father. It was *Stilkeen*, or, rather, the image of it.

The hair stirred on the top of Nish's head; even the skin on the soles of his feet was crawling. Persia cast him a wide-eyed glance but Nish, remembering that he was a silver miner of Twissel and therefore low-caste vermin, looked away.

Stilkeen had a broad head, flattened at the top; bony plates flared out from the sides and swept back like a multi-winged helmet. The small yellow eyes were covered in clear membranes that swept slowly across and back; its nose was split at the bottom, revealing two clusters of nostrils, and its gaping, thick-lipped mouth held hundreds of needle-shaped teeth. Its long clawed fingers were webbed, as were its broad flat feet, while a frilled membrane flared out from the backs of its long arms all the way across its shoulders.

'I am Stilkeen,' the figure made of light rumbled. Wisps of red flame dripped from its nostrils; it snapped at them. 'I have roamed the eleven dimensions of space and time for an eternity and a half. I cannot die, and nothing you may do can harm a *being* such as me, but I can *ruin* you and your world. Oh yes!'

THIRTY-ONE

A woman began screaming hysterically. Beside Nish, a man collapsed in apoplexy. The leather seller had retreated under his counter and Nish could hear his teeth chattering. From the corner of his eye Nish noted Persia edging towards him.

Stilkeen went on. 'Long ago a mortal, Yalkara, stole that which was most precious to me, the *rancicolludire* or white-ice-fire – you call it chthonic fire – which for all of my existence had bound my physical and spirit aspects together. Without fire and spirit, I am diminished and in pain . . . and when I hurt, I *hunger* to make worlds pay.'

Nish felt his own silver-black teeth chatter. He clenched his jaw.

'Because of this crime,' Stilkeen went on, 'one of your Three Worlds, the world of Aachan, has been destroyed by volcanic fire, and Santhenar stands in peril. Corrupted chthonic fire has been spilled in the south and now consumes the ice across that vast wasteland. Should the great ice cap at the southern pole melt, Santhenar will drown. Only I can stop it, but why should I?'

The figure of Stilkeen paused, and its eyes seemed to look directly at Nish, then it went on.

'Your God-Emperor failed me and has paid the price –'

People cried out, and Nish missed the next few words. What did Stilkeen mean, *and has paid the price*? What had it done to his father?

'– who brings Stilkeen the true, uncorrupted chthonic fire will be rewarded beyond their dreams. Who keeps true fire from Stilkeen will suffer such agonies as no human has ever felt, endlessly prolonged. Bring the fire to Morrelune within *fifteen* days, or I will release the most savage creatures from the void into Santhenar, all human life will be erased – and the waters will engulf the ruins of your civilisation.'

Something struck Nish as odd about Stilkeen's words but, with another booth-shaking rumble, the beams went out. For a few seconds there was a shocked silence, then chaos erupted. The woman began screaming hysterically again; a man bellowed in fear; a thousand other throats joined them and the crowd stampeded towards the exits from the square.

Persia appeared beside him, her eyes wide and staring. Grabbing his arm, she hissed, 'We've got to get back, *right now*.'

He pulled away, saying from the corner of his mouth, 'I'm a low-caste miner from Twissel and the wisp-watchers could be watching right now.'

'Not after *that*!' However, she let go and stepped away. 'Now!'

He ran with the crowd until he felt sure that no one could have followed him, but when he entered the alley and looked back, Persia was close behind. They went up the secret passage in silence, Nish trying to think through the implications of Stilkeen's ultimatum.

No one could now be in any doubt that the God-Emperor was missing, yet in Klarm's continued absence with the tears, no legitimate deputy had stepped forward to take his place. The empire was in desperate peril, and with no one in charge, there was a real danger that when Santhenar most needed unity it would be plunged into civil war.

'We saw it too,' said Flydd when they met in Yulla's rooms at the top of the mansion that evening.

'The message issued from every wisp-watcher, loop-listener and speck-speaker in Roros,' said Yulla, 'and probably in the whole empire. That tells you how all-encompassing Stilkeen's power is.'

'Its power is great,' said Flydd, 'yet not nearly as great in our material world as it would be on the ethereal planes, since, I'm told, many of its powers cannot be used here. Stilkeen is severely constrained in what it can do on Santhenar, and that's our best hope. Surely that's why it has ordered us to search for the true fire – because it can't do so itself.'

'But did it speak the truth when it said we could not harm it?' said Persia.

'That depends what you mean by harm. It would take a mighty weapon, or a very particular one, to kill an immortal *being* or do it serious damage, but that doesn't mean it can't be hurt. Since being severed from its spirit aspects, Stilkeen's mere presence in the physical world causes it pain and therefore, if we should encounter it, our best defence would be to cause it so much pain that it has to retreat.'

'A *being* might be able to endure a lot of pain,' said Nish absently.

'Or it might be so used to having whatever it desired that *any* pain would be unbearable.'

'It's a risky plan,' said Yulla, 'but I don't see any alternative. I'll consult the librarians; let's find out what will cause a *being* greater pain. However, that can't save us. We've got to have a weapon that can threaten a *being's* very existence.'

'Little has been written about *beings*,' Flydd said mildly. 'They've seldom been encountered in the Three Worlds or the void and, when they have been, it has commonly proven fatal to the observer.'

'Nonetheless, if humanity is to survive, we need that weapon.'

'What about the tears?' said Persia.

'I don't think the answer lies in sheer power,' said Flydd. 'Nish, are you listening?'

'Sorry,' said Nish. 'I've just worked it out.'

Yulla raised a grey eyebrow.

'I've been thinking through what was so odd about the proclamation. When we first met Stilkeen and it took Father hostage, it demanded chthonic fire in return. But this time it demanded the *true, uncorrupted* chthonic fire. Has the ordinary chthonic fire been corrupted?'

'That is the nature of such things,' said Flydd. 'Once taken from their natural place, and especially when carried via portals between worlds, as the fire Yalkara stole was, uncanny objects or forces often become corrupt.'

'Then this changes everything,' said Nish. 'There's no point heading for Morrelune now. We don't have any pure, uncorrupted fire.'

'It changes nothing,' said Yulla coldly. 'Morrelune is still the heart of the empire, and that's where Stilkeen is. And you heard what it said about Jal-Nish. *Your God-Emperor failed me and has paid the price.*'

Nish froze. 'Was Stilkeen saying that Father is dead?'

'That's how I would interpret it,' said Flydd.

'As would I,' said Yulla. 'And every rogue in the empire will soon be on the way to Morrelune to try to seize it.'

Nish couldn't take it in. His all-powerful father *dead*?

'Nish, you've got to get to Morrelune first,' said Flydd. 'We must have a steady hand at the centre, and a leader who *isn't* there for what he can get. One that the common folk can believe in, and the wealthy and influential rely on. One who has a legitimate claim to the throne –'

'I will not become my father,' Nish said coldly, for he knew how corrupting absolute power could be, and in the past he had often longed for it. It was so very tempting and he could not afford to give in to that temptation. 'I've made that clear many times.'

'What if some upstart steps forward,' said Yulla, 'saying he's the bastard son of Jal-Nish and claiming the throne by right? If there is no true heir, many will see his claim as legitimate, and the only way to stop him is for you, your father's acknowledged heir, to claim the throne.'

She was right, of course, and Nish was starting to feel trapped. At every turn, circumstances were forcing him to take a course he'd sworn to avoid.

'You've got to continue with the plan,' said Flydd, breathing heavily. 'You've got to get to Morrelune.'

'Within fifteen days,' said Yulla, who alone among them seemed calm and in control. She thought for half a minute. 'All right, this is the plan. You'll have to allow eleven days to sail to Fadd then march up into the mountains to Morrelune. Adding a slim contingency of two days for all the things that can go wrong makes thirteen days. Therefore, you've got to sail within forty-eight hours.'

It was another insight into the woman who, greedy though she was, had been such an accomplished governor. She had the gift of instantly summing up each new threat and calmly responding.

Nish wished he had her presence of mind. In fifteen days, a hundred things could go wrong, any one of which could prevent him from reaching Morrelune in time. He fought to control his panic, to appear as calm as she was, though the situation already seemed beyond control.

'That schedule allows no time to get the fleet away in secret,' said Flydd. 'And our departure must be secret, for every power in the empire will be after Nish now.'

Yulla steepled her pudgy fingers and rested her chin on them. 'I have it. Nish has to show himself in Roros, tomorrow morning, then fly away on the air-sled.'

'How is that going to help?' cried Nish.

'The moment you appear, then disappear,' said Yulla, 'the seneschal of Roros will know you're up to something, and he'll send his army after you, plus most of the scriers and wisp-watchers in Roros.'

'How can you be sure?'

'He has to. If the seneschal takes you, he has removed the biggest obstacle to his seizing the throne; but if he loses you, and you take the throne, you'll get rid of him at once.'

Yulla turned a black crystal over in her hands, then went on. 'I've been moving my corps out of Roros in small numbers over the last week. Once the seneschal's army and scriers have gone after you, Nish, the fleet will slip out of port, load your army in the isolated cove of Kralt, south of here, and sail for Fadd at all speed.'

She looked around, smiling like a crouching toad.

'How do *we* get to Fadd?' said Nish. 'On the air-sled?'

Yulla's smile vanished. 'I have other uses for it. M'lainte will take you to the fleet and bring the air-sled back.'

'I don't understand why I have to show myself,' said Nish warily. 'There's got to be a good reason, otherwise the seneschal will be suspicious.'

'He'll be sure you're after chthonic fire, so you can claim the empire.'

'I don't understand,' said Nish. 'Why would he think I'm after the fire?'

'Because you're going to attack an ancient monastery not far from Roros.'

'A monastery!'

'It's called the House of the Celestial Flame, and it's built over a vent that has been burning for thousands of years.'

Flydd stared at Yulla. 'And you think the pure chthonic fire could be hidden there?'

'I wouldn't know,' said Yulla, 'though I know that a good place to hide something is where everyone can see it. Once the seneschal thinks you're after the fire, Nish, he'll be determined to take you, and it's all that matters.'

'So you want me to steal some of the monks' sacred fire, *tomorrow*?' said Nish.

'Yes. Then run for the mountains on my air-sled. M'lainte has repaired it but she'll pretend that its mechanism is failing. The seneschal is bound to take most of his army, and his scriers, since he can't afford to give you the slightest chance to escape. Once you've led him well away from Roros, M'lainte will double back to the coast at night and you'll go aboard ship for Fadd.'

'And the seneschal will follow us.'

'He won't be able to,' said Yulla. 'He won't have any ships.'

'I like it,' said Flydd.

Nish did not. Events were moving too quickly for him. 'How can I plan an attack on a place I've never seen, in so little time? If something goes wrong we could be trapped.'

'If it's planned properly,' said Yulla, 'nothing will go wrong.'

Statements like that only made him feel worse. 'If this diversion is necessary, why can't it be done by someone else?'

'The seneschal won't lead his army out of Roros after anyone else, and he's got to go or I won't be able to get the fleet away. You have to do it, Nish, and it has to be tomorrow.'

'The House of the Celestial Flame?' said Flydd thoughtfully. 'I can't say I've heard of it.'

'For three thousand years its monks have worshipped at the sacred vent, and they're a wealthy, secretive order with powerful friends. When Nish's father declared himself God-Emperor, most other monasteries were dissolved and their wealth was appropriated, but the Order of the Celestial Flame went untouched.'

'Where is the monastery?' said Nish.

'In a valley a few leagues west of Roros, a place of great natural beauty,' said Persia. 'Its walls are granite cliffs hundreds of spans high, threaded with waterfalls; the floor of the valley is lush with sweet grass and a hundred kinds of wildflowers. There are geysers, mud baths and mineral springs, and the animals that dwell there are so tame that they can be fed from the hand, for the monks of the Celestial Flame eat neither flesh, fish nor fowl.' She sounded wistful.

'Tomorrow,' Nish said dazedly.

'Yes,' said Yulla. 'You'll leave here in the early hours, rendezvous with M'lainte and your militia and depart on the air-sled at dawn, so you can be seen, and reach the valley an hour later. The great city wisp-watchers will note your path, but it'll take the seneschal's fastest riders all morning to get to the monastery.'

'It doesn't leave a lot of time to deal with the monks and find the white fire – *if it's there*,' said Flydd. 'If you want everyone to believe Nish is after the true fire, he's got to do a convincing job.'

'It's all the time we have,' said Persia. 'We can't leave before dawn, because Nish has to be seen leaving Roros.'

'How many monks are there?' asked Nish.

'About sixty, though many are old and some infirm. At least half the number are young and will doubtless put up a fight; you'll have to subdue them without harming them.'

Nish's heart sank even further; it would be like fighting with his hands tied. 'What's the layout?'

'The monastery is set halfway up a broad valley with rivers to either side,' said Persia. 'It's a single building shaped like a wheel, one storey high, easy to attack and impossible to defend. The order has no enemies.'

It does now, Nish thought.

'And the Celestial Flame is where?' asked Flydd.

'There's a temple at the centre of the wheel, built over a subterranean vent. Its vapours have burned continuously since the monastery was established.'

Flydd raised an eyebrow. 'The parallels with Mistmurk Mountain, where I first found the chthonic flame, are unmistakable.'

'But they may be coincidental,' said Yulla. 'Flames fed by natural vapours occur at several places in Crandor.'

'Has anyone built temples over them, and protected them for thousands of years?'

'Not to my knowledge.'

'Then the true fire could well be hidden at the monastery and, since no one had heard about chthonic fire until I found it at Mistmurk, it would be perfectly safe there. Even if the place was ransacked, fire would attract no attention.' Flydd paced the room. 'Surely it can't be that easy?'

'If it *is* there,' said Nish, 'we can't let the God-Emperor's seneschal get hold of any.'

'You'll have to search the place thoroughly, steal any white fire you find, and put out the sacred flame.'

The monks are going to love that, Nish said to himself. 'Who is the seneschal, anyway?'

Yulla looked at Persia, who was staring straight ahead, her hands clenched. 'Persia!' Yulla said sharply.

Persia drew a shuddering breath. 'He –' Her voice went shrill, but she controlled it with an effort and said, 'He comes from the south and has an evil reputation. His name is Vomix.'

Nish felt the acid burning his throat again, for Vomix had destroyed Maelys's home, Nifferlin Manor, and eliminated most of Clan Nifferlin, all because of a thoughtless remark she had made as a child, when the seneschal had passed her on the road. And what did Persia know of him?

'That settles it,' said Nish, thinking about the relentless way the seneschal had hunted him and Maelys after the escape from Mazurhize. 'He's a brute and no depravity is beyond him. If I get the chance to strangle the bastard with my bare hands, I will.'

'Under the terms of our agreement,' said Yulla icily, 'you will take no unnecessary risks.'

'I don't recall that being mentioned before,' snapped Nish.

'It must have slipped my mind,' she said blandly. 'You will carry out the diversion, take the fire, fly away on the air-sled and hide until dark. Later that night M'lainte will fly you, your militia and Persia to the fleet, and Persia will carry the flame to Morrelune, in case it is the pure, uncorrupted fire.'

'I hadn't realised she was coming with us.'

'I have to protect my investment,' said Yulla with another toad-like smile.

So Persia wasn't only here to protect him, but also to spy on him and report back to Yulla. Nish ground his teeth together. He was fed up with being manipulated, first by his father, and Vivimord, then Flydd and now Yulla.

'We still have one unsolved problem,' said Flydd.

'What's that?' said Nish.

'To save Santhenar, we've got to find *pure* fire, but if it isn't at the monastery we don't know where to look for it.'

'That must be your task, Flydd,' said Yulla, 'and it may be that you're the only one who can do it.'

'It may be that no one can do it,' said Flydd.

They were supposed to be leaving Yulla's mansion in the early hours, but Persia woke Nish before midnight. 'It's time to go.'

He checked the stars through the window and saw that he'd been asleep for no more than an hour. 'Is something wrong?'

She was looking down at him, and Nish thought he saw a momentary sadness in her dark eyes.

She hesitated before saying firmly, 'Yulla thought it best that we leave early.'

He got ready, yawning and feeling more than usually dull-witted. Persia led him on foot to an empty warehouse by the harbour, where the militia were camped, still asleep. He found a spare blanket, lay down and slept at once.

Not long before dawn, Chissmoul and M'lainte landed the rebuilt air-sled on the warehouse roof, which sloped towards the sea and was not visible from Roros. The craft now boasted an ornate cabin over the stern half, framed in brass and black iron. Small windows all around were made from thin, flexible sheets of clear mica, and there were also angled arrow slits. Rows of benches inside would seat the militia during flight, while double doors at the front would keep out wind and weather.

'The walls and roof are of bimblewood,' said M'lainte, 'a timber so light that a beam of it can be picked up by a child, yet so strong that it will keep out a crossbow bolt fired from close range. But not a javelard spear, unfortunately.'

'I hope it won't come to that,' said Nish.

'Best to be prepared for every contingency,' said M'lainte, rubbing her stubby, oil-stained fingers through her thin hair and smearing black oil across the bald patch.

'Like keeping the wretched thing in the air!'

'You won't have that problem again; I've rebuilt the flight mechanism. Considering it was the personal air-sled of the God-Emperor, it was remarkably ill-made. It'll be much more reliable now, and twice as fast.' Her old eyes gleamed at the thought.

'Everyone must stay inside during fast flight,' M'lainte went on as the militia assembled, 'otherwise they'll be in danger of going over the side with every change of course.'

'What about Chissmoul?' said Nish. Her canvas seat had been replaced by an extravagant, sleigh-like bench, wide enough for two, made of iron and red cedar. A pair of belts were looped through the rear slats.

'I've got to be able to see.' Chissmoul wore leathers; a pair of insect-spattered goggles were pushed high on her fore-head.

She took her seat, M'lainte sat beside her and Flangers led the militia inside. Nish was glad to be back with them after the past frustrating week. The injured had been left behind, save for Clech who, after allowing a risky experimental bone-healing spell to be used on him, so as to heal his thigh bones quickly, was hobbling about on crutches, and Aimee, whose healing ribs were bound so tightly she had trouble bending over.

Dawn streaked pink rays across the sky. Chissmoul looked questioningly at Nish, who was standing with Persia on the roof. In the blushing light she looked more beautiful than ever.

'A few more minutes,' she said. 'Nish has to be seen.'

He went through his mental list again, fretting that he had

forgotten something vital. In daylight, the attack seemed fool-hardy, even reckless.

'Where's Xervish?' he said abruptly.

'Gone,' said Persia, who was looking out to sea. A pleas-antly cool breeze ruffled a few dark hairs that had escaped her braid.

'I thought he was coming with us.'

'He was never coming with us,' she said quietly, not meeting his eyes.

'And no one thought to tell me? Wait a minute! That's why we left early, isn't it? So you could separate us.'

'It wasn't of my doing,' said Persia, again colouring deli-cately. 'Yulla thought it was best.'

'Really?' snapped Nish, still furious about the way he'd been manipulated by everyone. 'Why does Yulla want to separate us?'

'I can't say.'

'Can't, or won't?'

'I can't betray my mistress's confidences or plans, any more than you would betray Flydd's.'

'Right!' he snapped. 'Thanks for reminding me that you can't be trusted.'

It was as though he'd slapped her across the face. 'I can always be trusted,' she whispered. 'My word is everything to me.'

'You're not here to protect me at all, are you? You're here to control me – you and that cow, Yulla. Well, I'm not taking it.'

All the softness went out of her eyes, and all the warmth. Persia did not say a word, but walked away across the gently sloping roof, her jerky steps betraying her agitation. He went after her, caught her by the arm and she swung around.

'*Where's Flydd?*' he said furiously.

'He made a portal with his serpent staff and went through to search for the true fire.'

'A portal! I didn't know he could make portals with it. Why didn't he tell me?'

She did not reply.

If Flydd had that ability, why hadn't he used it earlier? They might have come directly here from Taranta, or the Range of Ruin for that matter. And if Flydd had known all along – if he could have saved them at the Range of Ruin but had chosen not to do so – it must prove that he was up to no good.

What about Yulla? Was she planning to betray them both, or did she hope to seize the chthonic fire if Flydd came back with it? She was a master strategist who manipulated people without even thinking about it . . . and Persia was her willing acolyte. He scowled at her but she was hunched over, her shoulders shaking.

The light was growing rapidly now. 'Time to go,' Nish said curtly, and climbed aboard. As Chissmoul lifted off, he sat down with his back pressed up against the rear of the sleigh-shaped seat and held on to the base of the frame.

'It's not safe there,' said Persia. 'You must go inside.'

'I couldn't give a damn whether it's safe or not,' he gritted, so furious that he could not contain himself. 'Go into the pen, where you belong.'

A spasm passed across her face but Persia did not move. As his bodyguard, she must remain by his side. She stood behind Chissmoul, holding onto the back of the bench, rocking back and forth on the balls of her feet.

She stared blindly ahead as the air-sled shot across the city, her eyes watering in the wind. It passed low and fast over the square where they had heard the announcement yesterday, and both wisp-watchers swung to follow their path, as did the heads of the people already swarming there in the cool of the morning.

No question but that we've been seen, Nish thought. This gamble had better work.

'Where to?' said Chissmoul.

'Fly west, straight as an arrow and at all possible speed, for the Monastery of the Celestial Flame. Let no one who sees us be in any doubt about our destination, nor the urgency of our quest.'

THIRTY-TWO

From the Great Library, Yggur, Tulitine and Maelys went to Zile and equipped themselves for their coming journey, then travelled by portal to the Aachim city of Stassor, which lay hidden within the glacier-woven mountains several hundred leagues south of Roros.

Maelys stepped out of the portal onto flat ice. She faced a series of snowy peaks across a broad valley, and an icy wind was blowing. They had obtained mountain clothing in Zile, but even with her furs pulled tightly around her it was miserably cold, and the thin air at this altitude was hard to breathe.

'Each portal takes more out of me than the one before,' said Yggur, swaying on his feet and pressing his forearm across his belly.

Maelys steadied him. 'I thought the caduceus was doing the work?'

'It is, yet I feel as drained as if I had drawn power for the mighty portal spell from within myself, and that's strange.'

'Is your aftersickness getting worse?'

He doubled up, groaning, and Maelys thought he was going to vomit, but at length he straightened. 'You could say that. Enough of my troubles; turn around, look up and see the majesty of Stassor.'

The three of them turned together, and Tulitine said, with a dry little cough, 'Now that sight is worth any amount of pain.'

Maelys looked up, and up. Stassor was more astonishing than she could have imagined, for it was set on a mountain-top that had been planed off save for four upthrusting peaks framing the bottom corners of a vast white cube, the city itself.

They were standing outside one of its lower corners and its walls reflected the surrounding peaks; from a distance Stassor must have blended into the snowy mountainscape. On closer inspection, the walls shimmered like oil on water, while colours and patterns within a deeper layer were like the play of colours in precious opal.

'This way,' said Yggur, walking to his left along the plat-form, which appeared to be made of compressed ice and extended all along the base of the city.

They proceeded to the middle of the wall, where the lower part of the cube's face was marked with a grid. As they approached, a dark line divided the grid vertically into two halves, then each grid square separated and rotated, reveal-ing that they were the front faces of an array of cubes. The glassy cubes drifted upwards and inwards, creating an open-ing through which gushed a current of warm air.

Inside the opening stood a woman, rather taller than Maelys, with several lingering touches of flame in her thick, silvery hair. Her eyes were grey-green and her cheeks lined, though she had an air of wisdom about her, of having lived long and seen much, that Maelys had not encountered pre-viously.

'Hello,' she said, when neither Yggur nor Tulitine spoke. 'My name is Maelys, but you would never have heard of me. Are you Malien, by any chance?'

'I am,' said Malien, extending her hand. Despite her age,

her grip was almost as firm as Yggur's and her extraordinarily long fingers wrapped right around the back of Maelys's hand. 'And I know of you.'

'H-how could you?' said Maelys.

'Stassor isn't at the end of the world. We hear the news regularly, via skeet. How is my old friend, Nish?'

The pit of Maelys's stomach dropped sharply. 'He – he fell on the Range of Ruin. And Flydd. At least – we're afraid they were swept away by a flood . . .' With those intense grey-green eyes on her, Maelys couldn't think straight.

'And you sighted their bodies?' Malien said sharply.

Maelys saw in her mind's eye the smashed and battered corpses in the lower clearing, and felt ill all over again. 'No; we couldn't get through the gorge. But I'm sure . . . how could they –?'

'I won't count Nish among the fallen until I have good evidence that he is. I've known him too long for that. And as for Flydd –' Malien looked past Maelys towards Yggur and Tulitine. 'But I am discourteous, and if my fellow Aachim were here they would justly rebuke me.'

'Hello, my lady,' she said to Tulitine. 'I am Malien, Matah of the Aachim. The title is an honorary one,' she explained, 'but being Matah frees me from the oppressive rituals and obligations of my people.'

'Tulitine is my chosen name,' she said, shivering despite the mild breeze flowing from within, 'yet if I were to tell you that my true name is Liel and my father was Illiel –'

'I saw Illiel within days of his birth, and held him in my arms, though not his twin brother. Illiel was a fine scholar, as indeed was his mother –' Malien broke off.

'The Numinator and I are estranged,' said Tulitine bleakly.

'The *Numinator*?' Malien turned to Yggur. 'No! Yggur, you knew Maigraith. Tell me it is not so.'

'It is so,' he said heavily. 'I saw her just weeks ago, at the Tower of a Thousand Steps. For nearly two hundred years Maigraith has been the Numinator, and I fear that her obsession has driven her insane. If we might go in – Tulitine is unwell.'

'Come, come,' said Malien, shaking her head. 'I'm sorry. Lady, take my hand.'

'I can manage, thank you,' said Tulitine.

The moment they passed through the entrance, the cubular door reassembled itself; Malien led them into a reception area to the right and sat them down. From there they could see, through the glass walls, the majestic eastern and southern mountains.

'I'm sorry for keeping you waiting on the doorstep, Yggur,' Malien said. 'The old grow forgetful and neglect their manners.'

'Since I am far older than you,' said Yggur, shaking her hand with both of his, 'am I to take that as a reference to my own sad decline?'

'Not today. Have you come far? Are you hungry?'

'Starving. We've come across the known world in space, but only a blink in time. We have been at the Great Library. Lilis sends her best wishes and hopes to see you when she retires.'

'Dear Lilis,' said Malien. 'I still think of her as that little waif I met back in the Time of the Mirror.'

'Do you really?' said Yggur. 'I can't say that I do.'

'I'll bring food and drink, if you will excuse me.'

'You have no people here at all?' Yggur looked surprised.

'They've all gone to Faranda for another of their interminable conclaves. We Aachim, or, rather, *they*, can debate a vital matter for years without ever coming to a decision,' she said to Maelys, and went out.

After they had dined, and admired the beauties of the sunset, Malien said, 'But the Matah is not like her fellow Aachim. To business! You have come about Stilkeen's proclamation.'

'You saw it here, too?'

'I believe the whole world did so.'

'We also came to ask if you know anything about chthonic fire, for Lilis did not,' said Yggur.

'Nor I,' said Malien. 'Not a whisper, though some of my kin might.'

He told her about going to Noom and Mistmurk Mountain, and showed her the two fire samples in the dimensionless boxes.

Malien stared at the fire and said solemnly, 'Yalkara kept that secret very well hidden, and little wonder. I cannot but see the grim irony in her crime, and its outcome. As a mother who has also lost her children, I feel for her.'

She glanced at the window, which, now darkness had fallen, reflected the room, and added savagely, 'But as an Aachim whose world was stolen and whose ancestors were reduced to slavery, whose beloved Aachan was destroyed because of the chthonic fire she stole and carelessly set free, I wish her all the misery in the Three Worlds – and may Stilkeen consume her after she sees the failure of all her hopes!'

Maelys gasped and shrank back in her seat, clutching at her taphloid.

'I have shocked you,' said Malien, the fierceness fading. 'But why should we not be bitter? We did nothing to offend the Charon before they stole our world, and after thousands of years of slavery and suffering at their hands, to hear that Yalkara's criminal folly destroyed Aachan is more than I can bear.' She turned to Maelys. 'I know something of your life; you too have been stripped of all you held dear because of the greed or malice of another. You must understand.'

'I would not have when I left home, but half a year has changed me immeasurably.' The taphloid was hot now, and vibrating gently against her chest; Maelys opened her hands to look at it.

'Where did you get that?' hissed Malien, rising to her feet.

'My father gave it to me,' said Malien, closing her hands around it protectively.

'I'm sorry, I did not mean to frighten you. May I see it?'

Maelys did not want to let go of it, but she could hardly refuse.

Malien studied it carefully, opening and closing its compartment, running her fingers over its smoothly curved surface and holding it against her ear. Finally she laid it down on the table between them.

'Did you know it was of Charon make?' she said frostily.

'C-Charon? No!'

'Then how did you come by it?'

Maelys explained, and added, 'How can you tell a Charon made it?'

'I have the gift of knowing,' Malien said, but did not elaborate. 'And I also know where it came from. It was made by Kandor, the least of the three Charon who dwelt on Santhenar.'

'Kandor!' Yggur cried, pushing himself to his feet.

'Is something the matter?'

'I recognised the taphloid the moment I held it in my hand – yet I would swear I've never seen it before.'

'When you held it in your hand?' said Malien in a curious voice.

Yggur told her what he'd heard and felt that day in the clearing below the Range of Ruin, when he'd taken the taphloid towards the caduceus. 'And yet, when I looked down at it, I was surprised to discover how small it was. I thought it was made by an Aachim.'

'No, I'm sure Kandor built it, though I cannot say what for.'

'It's surprising Yalkara did not recognise it,' said Yggur.

'She would have known it was Charon made but, after all this time, perhaps it was of no interest to her.'

'Could any of your people tell me about it?'

'I expect so, but you'll have to take it to Faranda. My Stassor kin are there at the moment, at the city of Blemph, in the mountains behind Nys.'

'Then let us go to Blemph,' said Yggur. 'We can ask your kin about chthonic fire at the same time.' Getting up wearily, he raised the caduceus.

'You'll have to use that outside,' said Malien. 'My people would not want you to employ an unknown Art in their principal city. Besides, I'm not sure it would work, given all the protections bound around this place.'

They returned to the platform of compressed ice, which lay outside the protections. Malien showed Yggur where Blemph lay on a map, and described the city to him, and they took hold of the caduceus.

No portal opened, and there was no sensation of movement at all, though Yggur groaned and slipped to his knees. 'It's not working, though it hurts as much as if I had made a portal. Malien . . .?'

'Perhaps the caduceus doesn't want to take me,' she said, releasing it and stepping back towards the cubular door.

Yggur tried again, but the result was the same: no portal formed, yet it was as painful and draining as if one had carried them across the world.

'It's not going to take us to Blemph,' said Maelys.

'No,' said Yggur. 'Let's make a try for Havissard, Yalkara's stronghold that she abandoned long ago.'

The caduceus would not take them to Havissard either, and after the final failure Yggur was on his knees.

'Each attempt is more painful,' he wheezed. 'I can feel the life draining out of me.'

They helped him inside and put him to bed; any further attempts would have to wait until the morning.

Maelys went to her own bunk, which was rather cold, since the Aachim did not heat their sleeping chambers. Six days had passed since Stilkeen's proclamation, and all they had to show for their efforts were the two dimensionless boxes of white fire which Yggur felt sure had been corrupted. Time was running out.

'What about trying Katazza, in the once-dry sea?' said Tulitine in the morning, after they had gone to check on Yggur and found him to be deep in a coma-like sleep. 'Since Kandor lived there, there could be some clue . . .'

'Katazza collapsed long ago. It's just a pile of rubble.'

'Rulke's tower of Carcharon?'

'Even more unlikely,' said Malien, 'for I searched it after his death. And I can't think of anywhere else that pure chthonic fire might exist on Santhenar.'

'Then we've failed,' said Maelys. 'We've lost.'

'Hold on,' said Tulitine. 'You said, "On Santhenar". What about Aachan?'

'My home world is a boiling, sulphurous hell,' said Malien stiffly.

'How do you know?'

'The Aachim who fled here told me so, after they came through their portal to my secret refuge inside Mount Tirthrax.'

'But that was, what, *thirteen* years ago? The eruptions could have stopped. And time passes differently in the Three Worlds, so more years may have passed on Aachan. Surely it's worth having a look.'

Malien's eyes gleamed. 'We can certainly look – if Yggur is up to it.'

Maelys visited Yggur later that day. He had finally woken, though his breathing had a clotted rasp and his eyes were yellow-tinged. Tulitine was asleep in a large chair beside him, one transparent hand dangling over the side.

'Good afternoon,' Maelys said brightly. 'Are you feeling better?'

'I wish I could say I was,' said Yggur, 'but I won't be going anywhere today.' He closed his eyes.

When she went out she found Malien standing outside the cubular entrance, watching the shifting colours wash across the snowfields and glaciers.

Malien turned and her old eyes shone with captured sunset. 'I love this time of day.'

'It's a beautiful sight,' Maelys agreed.

'I never tire of it,' said Malien.

Maelys pulled her furs around her. 'It's a little too cold for my liking, though.'

'How is Yggur?'

'He looks worse than yesterday.'

'I was afraid he might,' said Malien. 'I've known him for more than two centuries, and he's scarcely aged in that time, but now he looks worn and withered; eaten away from within.'

'Is it the caduceus?'

'I think so. How long has this been going on?'

'Several weeks – since we arrived at the Range of Ruin and Stilkeen appeared. From the moment Yggur tried to use his Art near the caduceus, he said that it was feeding on him. But I'm worried that his troubles go back much further.'

'What do you mean?' said Malien curiously.

'Seven years ago the Numinator put silver shackles on his

wrists to stop him from using his power, and they drew it from him constantly to maintain her tower and her dreadful work.'

Maelys rubbed her arms and backed closer to the cubular door, where it wasn't quite so cold. Its smaller cubes split and stirred; she could see them moving from the corner of an eye. Her teeth chattered.

'And you're afraid that, after being drained over and over, Yggur has nothing left?' Malien came over to Maelys.

Maelys nodded stiffly, intimidated by Malien, whom she knew from the pages of the Histories and from a Great Tale. 'If he can't make another portal, what are we going to do?'

'Let's see how we go. He has a strong constitution. He may be better in an hour or two.'

The day passed but Yggur grew worse and by dinner time he was too weak to sit up. Maelys could not imagine how the strong man who had heaved those enormous blocks of frozen ground aside just weeks ago had fallen so low.

'I don't know what's happening to me,' he said after they had come to visit him for the third time, late that night. Tulitine had been sitting at his bedside all afternoon but was now in bed with him, trying to warm him up. 'I'm cold and there's no strength in my legs. No strength anywhere.'

'Maelys said it was like aftersickness,' said Malien.

'I don't recall ever having aftersickness this bad. I've scarcely used mancery since we left the Range of Ruin, but I'm as exhausted as if I've been doing it non-stop.'

'Get some rest. We'll try again tomorrow.'

After they were out of earshot, Malien said, 'I'm going to take a look at the caduceus later on. You can help me.'

'Are you a mancer too?' said Maelys.

'You might say that,' Malien replied drily.

By the frozen light of a ringed moon, Maelys carried the caduceus out onto the ice platform and stood by while

Malien attempted to make a portal. Nothing happened; she might as well have been holding an iron bar.

'Clearly, Stilkeen doesn't want us to use it,' said Maelys.

Malien gave Yggur various Aachim medicines but the following day he was no better, nor the five days after that, and only on the succeeding morning – the fourteenth day after Stilkeen's proclamation – could he find the strength to get out of bed.

'You're not ready,' said Tulitine, wincing as she took his weight on her fragile bones.

'And if our positions were reversed?' he said wryly.

'I'd tell you to mind your own damn business,' she chuckled, 'but it has to be done, and I'd do it too, no matter how much it hurt.' She added, more soberly, 'We're out of time, my friend, but we don't have to try for Aachan. We could go straight to Morrelune with the fire we have.'

'Of course we must go to Aachan,' said Yggur, 'and right away, before I fall down. Pure chthonic fire is our only bargaining chip; we have to have it.'

'Bargaining chip?' said Maelys. 'I don't understand.'

'In the frozen south, corrupted fire is consuming the ice and spreading ever faster, as fire does when it has plenty of fuel. If the great southern icecap melts, Santhenar will drown, and we may not have long to stop it. Indeed, we have no way of stopping it, but I'm sure Stilkeen can; and it might be convinced to do so in exchange for pure fire.'

From what she had seen of Stilkeen, Maelys thought that was doubtful, but she did not say so.

'I would not have this world lost,' said Malien, 'as my own has been.'

'What if Aachan is still uninhabitable?' said Maelys. 'We might end up in the middle of a volcano or something.'

'I'll hold the portal until we're sure it's safe,' said Yggur.

'What if it isn't?'

'We'll come straight back –'

'Assuming we can,' she muttered.

'And while we're there,' said Yggur, steadfastly ignoring Maelys, 'keep your eyes open for a weapon – anything at all – that we might be able to use against Stilkeen. Is everything ready?'

'It's ready,' said Malien. She wiped her eyes. 'Beloved Aachan, you cannot imagine what this means to me. This way.'

THIRTY-THREE

The air-sled had just passed over the outskirts of Roros, and Persia's eyes were already red and watering from the wind. Being both watcher and bodyguard, she had to stay close to Nish wherever he was. He was already regretting the way he had spoken to her, but he felt so manipulated that he could not bring himself to apologise.

'Hey!' said Chissmoul. 'That looks like a small army below us.'

Nish peered over the side and saw a long column of horsemen riding west at a fast pace. 'Surely that can't be Vomix's force already?'

'It is,' said Persia stiffly. 'We passed over the barracks a few minutes ago. They're heading for the monastery and the rest of the army won't be far behind.'

He looked back and saw what was, unmistakably, a walled army barracks and parade ground. A considerable army – some thousands of men – was forming into ranks and the leaders were marching out the gates. Vomix was taking no chances.

'How can he have reacted so quickly?' Nish said.

He knew how long it took to mobilise an army, for he'd done it many times, and for Vomix to get his cavalry armed and on the road this quickly, surely meant he had been forewarned. Could there be a spy in their midst – *or a traitor*? He glanced back at Persia, who was still staring over the side. Nish could not believe it of her, though almost anyone could be bought if the price was high enough – or coerced if they would not betray willingly. But if not her, who?

'Vomix has had them on full alert for days,' said M'lainte. 'This could get a little awkward.'

'But those riders are *ahead* of us. They must have known where we were going.'

'Not necessarily,' said M'lainte. 'Once the scriers in the market square told him our direction, Vomix would have plotted it on a map and seen that we were flying directly for the monastery.'

'How far away is it?' he said, not at all mollified. Betrayal still seemed the most likely explanation.

'A few leagues in a direct line.' M'lainte did not consult her map. 'Five at most, the way Vomix must go.'

'Then his cavalry will be there in under three hours.' It was far too soon. 'After we reach the monastery, we'll have less than two hours to subdue a host of furious monks and search the place from top to bottom. It's not enough time; not nearly. Can you go faster, Chissmoul?'

'Not without tearing the cabin off.'

Within an hour the air-sled had reached the valley, which proved to be as beautiful as it had been described. The monastery was set on the flat crest of a gentle hill between two small rivers. There were cultivated fields to the left, separated by low hedges, while open pasture lay to the right, streaked with outcroppings of grey rock.

Trees shaded the northern and western sides of the monastery but were not big enough to conceal their approach. There were no walls, ditches, palisades or defensive structures of any kind – it looked undefended and was certainly undefendable.

417

'Go up a bit,' he said to Chissmoul. 'I need to get a better picture of the place.'

The air-sled lifted, and shortly he was looking down on the monastery as if it were a plan drawing. For the first time Nish understood the perfection and symbolism of its design: a perfect wheel with the temple at its hub, joining sky and earth, sacred and profane, celestial and *chthonic*.

The monastery is like a sign, or a pointer, he thought in a blinding flash of realisation. It's got to be. Is it intended as a sign to the *being* whose chthonic fire was stolen? Is that who the monks really worship – Stilkeen? How could he find out?

'They're coming fast,' called Flangers.

Nish looked back east, and in the distance saw a cloud of dust made by Vomix's racing cavalry. His stomach spasmed. 'They're making incredible time over such rough country.'

'We haven't got much more than an hour,' said Flangers. 'Not the way they're riding.'

There was no time to find out about the monks and who they worshipped; all he could do was snatch some white fire in the special container Flydd had left with Persia, and run. But if it *was* the true fire, and he felt sure now that it must be, what a victory it would be. With it, suddenly anything seemed possible. Nish's mind was racing as he ran through his strategy.

'Chissmoul, land next to the temple – we don't have time to search the other buildings – then go up and hover so the monks can't attack you, and keep watch for Vomix. Persia and I will go inside, along with four militiamen. Flangers, you'll seal the entrances to the temple so we can search it without being attacked by the monks. Keep me informed, and call us out if there's a danger you can't handle.'

'Surr!' said Flangers.

'Don't take any risks. We have to get away the moment

Vomix's cavalry comes into view. We're not here to fight him, and we certainly don't want to hurt any of the monks.'

'What if they attack us?'

'Everyone has staves and cord. Knock the monks down if you must, knock them out if there's no alternative, and tie them up. Ready?'

'Yes,' Flangers said, looking dubious.

'It might be useful if I came with you,' said M'lainte.

'Er,' said Nish.

He liked M'lainte, and was awed by her utter mastery of the artificer's trade at which he, despite all that hard work in his youth, had never been more than mediocre. He did not want to offend her, but she was old and slow, and would be a liability if they got into trouble.

'If chthonic fire *is* hidden in the temple,' M'lainte said, 'I rather think I can find it.'

'Is that so?' said Nish. 'How?'

'My gift allows me to see beneath the surface of physical things, and I've trained it to a high order. I can spot traps, hidden drawers, false walls and most other hiding places merely by looking.'

'What about objects concealed by the Art?'

'It depends on which Art has been used to hide them, and how powerful the adept was who used it.'

'All right,' he said. 'If the true fire is here, we've got to have it. But if I say so, you'll go at once . . . won't you?' Nish's cheeks grew hot; he felt like a prentice giving orders to his master.

'Of course,' said M'lainte, amused. 'A force can only have one leader and I would not have it otherwise.'

'All right, Chissmoul,' said Nish. 'Go in fast.'

She zoomed in over the left-hand river and across the fields. Several monks, hoeing weeds, looked up with mouths agape as the baroque craft hummed overhead.

It lifted over the circular roof of the monastery and headed for the temple at the centre, which had been built on exposed grey rock and was surrounded by short green grass. Constructed in a style that had not been used for thousands of years, it was circular, with columns around the circumference, and roofed over by a large stone dome with a broad round vent at the top.

'That's the main entrance,' said Persia, pointing to an opening between the columns.

'Set down there,' said Nish.

Chissmoul landed the air-sled on the grass. Nish and Persia leapt off, then Hoshi the apprentice potter, Beyl the short, dark woodsman, his ear-of-corn earring swinging, followed by thin and nervous Allioun, and finally stocky Zana, her dark hair cropped short like a soldier's, all carrying their staves. They all wore blades but had been cautioned not to use them on the monks. M'lainte began to clamber down and Nish's heart sank, for she wasn't as mobile as he had thought.

'How dare you!' a heavily-built monk shouted from the veranda of the monastery. His black, spade-shaped beard had a white patch below his lip and it quivered with every furious word. 'Take your abominable contraption and go, profaners of the Celestial Flame!'

He brandished a staff at them, and other monks appeared behind him, while more were running from the other side of the circle.

Nish cursed. This was going to be even harder than he'd thought. 'Come on!' He ran for the temple.

It was cooler under the circular colonnade, beyond which he saw a line of thicker columns – no, they were arranged in a square, and inside that was a triangular array. The only other visible structure was a steep, narrow stone ramp, broken by several landings, that curved around the inside of the dome to the circular vent at the top, where there was a platform and an altar, presumably for observing the celestial flame, or the heavens, or both.

'A triangle within a square within a circle,' puffed M'lainte. 'The symbol of the celestial realm. And for symmetry, I'd expect to find the symbol reversed inside. I don't think we'll find anything out here but we'd better make sure.'

They hastened in between the columns. M'lainte turned right and began a circuit of the temple walls, with Hoshi and Beyl behind them on the left, and Allioun and Zana to the right, like a trailing pair of wings.

At the end of the circuit, M'lainte shook her head. 'Nothing.'

'What about the ramp and altar?' said Nish.

She looked up. 'Unlikely. The celestial realm would be linked to the chthonian, so the fire, if it is here, would be kept below us.'

From outside, Nish made out the clash of staff on staff, the outraged bellowing of the monks, and cries of 'Sacrilege!' and 'Blasphemer!' He put them out of mind. Flangers would deal with them.

Inside the triangular array of columns the floor stepped down in a series of white stone benches like a triangular amphitheatre, and the stone had been polished until it shone. The lowest, central point contained a square hole rather bigger than the width of Nish's shoulders. He assumed that the flame worshipped by the monks issued up through it, though no flame was visible from here. A spicy smell of incense hung in the air.

'There's nowhere else to search,' said M'lainte, heading for the nearest bench. 'We'll have to look down there – oh!'

Three lean and wiry monks in white robes sat on the benches near the bottom, their shaven heads bowed, while another lay prostrate beside the square hole and a fifth, a withered old man, swung a censer back and forth, emitting blue puffs of smoke which formed swirling patterns above the hole.

Nish cursed under his breath; if merely entering this place was sacrilegious, what he was about to do was so much worse. But he had no choice.

'We have come for the chthonic flame, also called white-ice-fire, stolen by Yalkara from the shapeshifting *being*, Stilkeen, in ancient times. What do you know about it?'

The withered old monk turned slowly and the censer slipped from his hand, fell to the step and came open, spilling burning incense across the white marble. He looked up, clenching blue-veined fists, and spoke slowly, coldly.

'This place is forbidden to all but the monks of the Celestial Flame. You have polluted our temple and debauched the sacred ceremony. Now all must be cleansed and purified before we may worship here again. Get out!'

The other monks rose, save for the prostrate one. The old monk nudged him with a gnarled toe. 'Rise, brother; your penance is wasted and must be begun anew, but first the temple has to be cleansed, and that will take from one full moon to the next.'

The prostrate monk rose, pulling his robes together. He was only a youth, but big and muscular with callused hands. He bowed to the old monk, hands humbly clasped together, then glanced sideways at Nish and his eyes blazed with a terrible fury. He did not look humble now. A violent rage burned in him and he wasn't going to be easy to deal with.

'I'm sorry, venerable monk, and brothers,' said Nish. Though he was not a believer, he did not wish to offend anyone who was. 'We do not come to harm you, but we must have the chthonic fire.'

'I have no idea what you're talking about,' said the old monk. 'We worship the *celestial* flame, and it is blue. There is no white fire here, and never has been.'

Nish cursed inwardly, for he did not think the monk was lying. Could everyone have been so wrong about this place? Were all the resemblances to Mistmurk no more than coincidence? No, he had to be sure.

'It could be locked away in a small flask or casket. It may have been hidden for thousands of years. Think!'

'You – are – mad,' the old monk enunciated clearly. 'Fire can't be locked away; it must be fed with fuel and air, or else it goes out.'

'Chthonic fire is different,' said Nish desperately. It had to be here, and he had to have it.

'For three thousand years we have studied the nature of flame. Fire must be fed. There – are – no – exceptions!' The old monk turned away. 'Brothers, throw them out.'

Nish glanced at Persia, who gave him a blank look. M'lainte mimed, 'You have no choice.'

Nish gestured to his militia. 'Move them out of the way.'

The four advanced, holding out their staves. The old monk gathered up his robes and lurched up the benches, swinging bony fists. The other brothers followed his lead.

Hoshi pushed the old monk aside with his stave but he stumbled and fell, cracking his head on a bench. A thin line of blood ebbed from his forehead and he lay there, dazed.

'I didn't want this,' said Nish quietly.

'Yet it was inevitable,' said M'lainte, 'since we are two opposing forces, neither of which can give in. Time is running out. Let's get it done.' She lumbered down the benches.

Nish moved around the other side of the triangle, leaving his troops to deal with the monks. He had no idea what he was looking for; he was just keeping an eye out for anything that did not fit.

At the bottom he peered into the square hole. A slight warmth issued from it, and down an inner, circular shaft he made out a flame flickering some distance below but, as the monk had said, it was blue. Blue! His heart sank. No, he refused to believe it. Chthonic fire was infinitely precious; it would be hidden to elude the most determined searchers.

He felt all the joins in the floor stone and peered down the hole, singeing his eyelashes, but saw no evidence of concealed rooms or lower levels. Persia and M'lainte completed their inspections.

'Anything?' Nish said, feeling the prize sliding through his fingers.

Persia shook her head. 'My meagre Arts tell me nothing.' She headed up.

'Mine tell me a lot,' said M'lainte, 'but nothing to our advantage. The temple is just what it seems and there's no white fire here. We were sent on a wild goose chase.'

It had always been a long shot, but Nish had talked himself into believing otherwise. Nonetheless, the disappointment was so crushing that he tasted bile in the back of his throat. 'Or have we been betrayed to Vomix?' he muttered.

He would not have thought Persia could have heard him from so far away, but her head shot around and her fists were clenched. 'How dare you! What are you implying?'

'Nothing,' he said hastily, wishing he could have taken the words back. 'I never said it was Yulla.' Too late; he'd made it worse by mentioning her name. Far worse.

'Yulla would *never* have anything to do with him.'

That's easy for you to say, he thought.

On the temple floor above, his militia were still struggling with the monks, who were proving difficult to subdue. The big, angry youth was wresting with Hoshi, the two of them swaying backwards and forwards not far from the top bench. Hoshi tried to whack the youth with his staff but was

424

kneed in the groin, then as Nish watched helplessly the staff was wrenched from Hoshi's grip and slammed into the side of his head. His eyes rolled back and he collapsed, unconscious.

'Blaspheming dog of an infidel,' the youth cried fervently. 'How dare you defile our temple?' Swinging the staff through the air so swiftly that it hummed, he sent it spinning into the backs of Allioun and Zana, knocking them down, then, picking up Hoshi by collar and crutch, with an effort the youth raised him above his head.

'No!' cried Nish, running up the benches. 'Put him –'

With an almighty heave, the youth hurled Hoshi over Nish's head and down towards the centre of the triangle, where he struck the lowest bench headfirst. His neck bent back, there was an audible snap and he slid off the bench, down through the square hole. Hoshi, Nish's first friend in Gendrigore, was dead.

The old monk tottered to his feet, blood running down his cheek. 'Brother,' he whispered, 'what have you done?'

The youth stood there, chest heaving and big hands hanging by his side. 'They defiled the temple, Father.'

'We could have cleansed it. But now . . .' The old monk scrambled down the benches, squinted into the square hole through which Hoshi had fallen, then fell back and let out a cry of anguish. 'Brother, my brother, this stain can not be erased. The very stones of the temple must now be taken down and replaced – all of them. And you – your time among us has ended – you must go.'

'Go?' breathed the youth. 'But the Celestial Flame is my guiding light. Without it I am homeless, wretched, broken . . .'

'As is that man broken, and you slew him *in our temple*! You cast him down *onto the sacred flame*. You have extinguished the flame, *which has never gone out*. Go, my son, and never approach this place again.'

He went to the youth, tore his robes from him and cast them on the floor.

The other monks were staring at the loincloth-clad youth in horror. Allioun rose and heaved Zana up. She was swaying on her feet, moaning, for the spinning staff had struck her hard in the back, near the kidneys.

The youth was making an incoherent grunting sound but his eyes were flaming now, his rage running out of control. He stooped, came up with the staff and swung around, ignoring Beyl, who was struggling with two of the brothers further off. The youth's gaze fixed on M'lainte and he started down.

He must think she's the leader, Nish realised. The attack had been a disaster from the start, it was getting worse, and it had all been for nothing. Holding his own staff across his body, two-handed, Nish moved to protect her.

Persia stepped into his path. 'Leave the youth to me, Nish.'

'He killed Hoshi,' said Nish in a low voice and, remembering the fun-loving young man he'd first met on the sea cliffs, a red mist obscured his own vision. First Gi, then Forzel, now Hoshi. Of his four Gendrigorean lieutenants, only Clech survived, but crippled, and Hoshi had to be avenged. 'I can't –'

'Stand aside!' Her free hand gripped his wrist, crushing it.

'Leave him, Nish,' said M'lainte. 'It'll do no good and we're out of time.'

Foam flecked the corners of the youth's mouth. He was moving slowly and warily, swinging the heavy staff from left to right, then right to left, making it difficult to approach him.

'Get going, Nish; you too, M'lainte,' said Persia, 'You've got a job to do, and so have I.'

Never on the battlefield had Nish taken shelter behind a fellow soldier, especially not a woman, and as he went behind Persia his cheeks burned with shame. She held her staff lightly in the two-handed grip and moved up and down on the balls of her feet as she waited.

She might be skilled in armed and unarmed combat but the youth was much bigger, fit and muscular from heavy work on the monastery's farms, and had the uphill advantage. Springing down three benches, he swung the staff at her head. The blow was so furious that it was difficult to parry, and Persia did not try. Angling her own staff up, she deflected the blow above her head, then swung down and into the right side of his body.

He let go of his weapon, took the blow with a grunt and, swift as a striking snake, caught her staff in his right hand. She tried to heave it away before he gained a firm grip but he was too quick. The youth yanked on the staff, pulling her towards him, and she came forwards a half-step before realising that she did not have the strength to tear it from his grasp.

Persia allowed him to draw her in, used her momentum to propel herself at him before he could raise the staff, and drove her head into his midriff. The youth went backwards, winded, and in an instant she had spun him around, twisted his arm up behind his back and forced him face-down onto the benches, her knee into the middle of his back. Nish's admiration for Persia grew; he had never seen anything like it.

'Bind him!' she rasped.

Nish bound the youth's hands behind his back with a length of cord. Up above, Allioun and Beyl were tying two of the monks, but the other had fled, and so had the old monk.

Sick at heart, Nish ran up to the floor of the temple and looked out through the columns.

'How long do we have left before Vomix gets here?' he said as he reached the square of columns. 'I've lost track of

427

time.'

'No more than twenty minutes, I'd say,' said M'lainte, puffing along behind him.

Outside, the militia had formed a semi-circle around the temple entrance and were defending themselves against at least forty enraged monks, who were attacking with staves, clubs and reaping hooks without heed for their own lives. They were led by the burly monk with the black beard, and very effectively: two militiamen lay on the ground, while many others bore bloody wounds. Nish counted eleven monks down.

'What a fiasco,' he muttered. 'We'll never subdue them; they're too handy with their weapons, even the old fellows.'

'They're trained to defend their temple,' said Persia.

'Call Chissmoul,' said M'lainte. 'I've a feeling Vomix is closer than we think.'

'She would have warned us,' said Nish. Nonetheless, he ran out into the open, looking up. The air-sled was still circling the top of the temple. He waved; Chissmoul banked and curved down. 'See anything yet?'

'No,' she yelled over the wind.

'Go higher!'

She turned in climbing spirals, far above the temple, and came zooming down again. 'The leaders are crossing the river, about fifty of them. They'll be here in minutes.'

THIRTY-FOUR

'Come on!' yelled Nish to his militia. 'We can't fight Vomix; we've got to go *now*.'

'Surr, look out.'

Another dozen monks burst from a door on the other side of the great wheel of the monastery, a hundred paces away, waving lengths of timber, kitchen cleavers, and axes. Clearly there were far more monks here than he'd been told. Panic flared; Nish fought it down as he tried to think.

'Do you want me to land?' yelled Chissmoul.

'Yes. No, *wait*!' Nish scanned the green battlefield, looking for Flangers. There he was, holding a bloody shoulder. 'Lieutenant!' Nish ran to him.

'They're putting up stronger resistance than I'd expected,' said Flangers.

The monks were advancing from either side. 'Can we hold them off long enough to get everyone onto the air-sled?'

'There's too many of them. Unless we use our swords . . .'

'No! No killing.'

'They're happy to cut us down, surr,' Flangers said quietly.

'I know. Hoshi was killed inside,' said Nish. 'But I'm not going to start my campaign by slaughtering innocent monks.'

He turned to M'lainte, who had come to the front of the militia. 'Can we get out through the roof?'

'You want Chissmoul to land on the top of the dome?' She considered. 'It'll be tricky getting the wounded up through the hole – it's a couple of spans above the platform – but I'll find a way.'

'Then do it. Flangers, organise the retreat,' rapped Nish. 'Chissmoul?' He pointed to the top of the dome. She repeated the gesture, questioningly, and he yelled, 'Yes!'

The air-sled curved that way, but they'd lost a lot of time and the monks were close now.

'We'll never hold them off long enough to get the injured aboard,' said Persia.

'Unless I can scare them,' said Nish. 'Get going, Flangers!'

Edging through the semi-circle of the militia, Nish drew the serpent staff from his back and brandished it at the monks. They stopped, watching it warily. They recognised power when they saw it.

'Stand back,' he said, pointing the open serpent mouth at them.

The monks swayed away. From the corner of his eye Nish watched the militia backing towards the temple entrance, the ones at the rear carrying the wounded, the men at the front making a barrier with their staves. He backed after them, Persia moving in step with him.

'Flangers, send everyone up the ramp. You, Persia and I will form a rearguard.'

Over the groans of the wounded and the clash of weapons, Nish made out the drumming of hooves. Vomix was close.

The monks must have thought Nish had called for re-inforcements, for they attacked in a mass. Three of them ran at him and Persia, swinging clubs and reaping hooks, while more surged past on either side, going for the militia. Nish and Persia defended as best they could as they backed between the columns into the temple.

'This way,' called M'lainte breathlessly from inside. 'Get the wounded up first.'

Two monks came at Nish, the black-bearded, thickset leader bearing a spiky cudgel made from the root of a tree, the other a reaping sickle on a long handle. Nish parried the sickle blow; the curved blade rang as it struck the serpent staff and was torn out of the monk's hands. Nish kicked his feet out from under him then went for the neck of the black-bearded monk who had the raised cudgel. The monk took the blow on his shoulder, twisted around and swung the cudgel with enough force to dash Nish's brains out.

He could not get out of the way in time, and Nish was sure he was going to die when Persia, who was to his left, dived and knocked him aside. The cudgel swept down and again he heard the sickening sound of bones snapping.

She gasped and tried to rise, but could not. Nish scrambled to his feet as the monk raised the cudgel to strike her dead. His face was a bloody, engorged purple, there was blood on the white patch in his black beard and he had a murderous look in his eye.

Nish sprang over Persia, putting himself between her and the monk as he began his ferocious downswing. There was no time for niceties now; if Nish had misjudged the moment, both he and Persia would die. Aiming the staff like a javelin, he thrust it at the monk with all his strength, and the tip of the serpent's iron tail went through his chest to the heart.

As he fell dead, the other monk backed away, eyes like twin eggs. 'He killed the abbot! Murderer! Blasphemer! Despoiler of all that is sacred!'

Nish threw the cudgel at him, but it missed and the monk ran out into the middle of the lawn, roaring, 'Murderer!'

The other monks gathered around him, staring at the abbot's body, now pinned to the ground by the staff, which had taken on a blood-red glow.

'There was no help for it,' said Flangers. He helped Persia up.

Nish wrenched the staff out and brandished it at them, and they backed away. It was hot and heavy again, churning inside, as if the blood sacrifice had woken it. He didn't like the way it felt, not at all, but he couldn't leave it now. He looked around; the militia were out of sight, inside the temple.

As he retreated, holding the staff up threateningly, the drumming of hooves grew ever louder. The seneschal's troops were just outside the monastery now, and the monks were staring at the entrance in dismay.

Nish turned to Persia, whose left forearm hung at an odd angle and was swelling visibly. 'Thank you. You saved my life.'

She was staring at him as if she'd just had a revelation. 'I simply did my duty, but you risked your life to save mine.' She shook her head. 'My arm is badly broken. I've let Yulla down.'

'Don't be ridiculous.'

'You don't understand. My indenture –'

He cut her off, for the huddle of monks was breaking up. 'They're going to attack again. Go up the ramp.'

'I can't!' cried Persia; her chocolate skin had gone a muddy grey. 'Yulla ordered me to guard you.'

'I'm in charge of this disaster. Carry her up, Lieutenant.'

Heaving Persia over his shoulder, Flangers went into the temple. Her troubled eyes were on Nish all the way, but she did not struggle. She appeared to be in too much pain.

There was no time to wonder about the nature of her indenture to Yulla. He dismissed them both from his mind

432

and concentrated on keeping the monks at bay. The saturnine woodsman, Beyl, fell in beside him, and two others, one left, the other right.

'We can do this, Nish,' said Beyl encouragingly. 'We'll beat 'em the way we beat the enemy up at Blisterbone.'

Nish hadn't realised he'd looked so downcast. 'We must.'

The monks were almost onto them when the leading riders burst through the entrance of the monastery and stopped on the green lawn. The monks froze, then turned to face the new threat.

Nish slipped behind a column, gestured to his rearguard to go up, and peered out. The horsemen leaned forwards over their saddle horns and raised their swords. The warhorses pawed at the lawn.

The monks must have seen their doom approaching, for their rustic weapons would be useless against armed and armoured troops, but not one of them turned and ran. They were brave men.

The officer at the head swept his blade down and the horses leapt forwards. Uprooted grass flew up from their hooves as they raced across the turf, and at their head, directing his mount with touches of his knees, was the man Nish despised most in all the empire – Seneschal Vomix.

He had never been a handsome man, but since Maelys had tricked him into taking hold of her taphloid, months ago, Vomix was grotesque. His nose was a flattened blob, while his face looked as if it had been torn off, ripped into three pieces and nailed back on. Half his teeth were gone and his right arm, severed at the wrist, now ended in a triangular, three-bladed spike. In his left hand he held up an enormous scimitar, the light winking off its polished, curved blade.

'Go up!' Nish hissed to his lurking men, and they went, reluctantly.

Nish waited, knowing there would be a crowd at the top of the ramp. He had to see what Vomix was up to, and what he knew. If there *was* treachery afoot, he might reveal something that would give away the traitor's name.

Half the monks had lined up in the middle of the lawn; the rest moved to block the entrance to the temple. More riders raced through, until they must have numbered fifty. Vomix wheeled to come alongside a monk who was holding up his skirts as he ran, and plunged his spike into the man's back so hard that it came out his chest. The monk's hands opened, he tripped on his skirt and fell flat on his face. The spike slid free and Vomix held it up, dripping red.

The old monk who had been at the flame earlier tottered out, brandishing a walking cane. 'This monastery and temple are forbidden to all but the monks of the Celestial Flame,' he said in a reedy voice. 'You pollute our retreat with your vile swords and wicked ways. Begone!'

The seneschal trotted across to the monk, lifted him by the bunched robes and said, 'Where is the white chthonic fire?'

'There is no such fire here, and never has been. We are worshippers of the Celestial Flame, which has . . . had never gone out since we built our temple three thousand years ago.'

'Liar!' said Vomix, swatting him across the face with the side of his bloody spike.

'Our flame is not white,' said the monk feebly, 'and it has never been called chthonic. Indeed, it is the very opposite, for within it we read the movements of the heavenly bodies, and from them tell the future.'

'I'll bet you didn't predict this future,' leered Vomix.

'As it happens,' the old monk said with dignity, 'your coming was foretold two thousand years ago. Had we known *when* you were to appear, we would have been prepared.'

'We're going to take this place apart, and then *you*, until we find it.'

The monk did not shrink away. 'You are not the first to threaten us, but our founder's foretelling states that the Monastery of the Celestial Flame will survive until the end of the Third Empire and that –'

'The empire is finished, you old fool,' sneered Vomix. 'Did you not see Stilkeen's proclamation on the wisp-watcher yesterday?'

'There are no wisp-watchers here,' said the old monk, looking uncertain now.

'And that is a capital offence!'

'We have an exemption signed by the God-Emperor –'

'Who has been deposed by Stilkeen, a shapeshifting *being* from the void. The empire is at an end.' Vomix tossed the old monk to the ground. 'Take him inside and roast him over his precious Celestial Flame until he reveals the location of the white fire. Then roast him some more.'

'You know what to do,' he said to the twenty riders on his left, and they began the killing. Vomix glanced up at the top of the dome, smiled a savage smile and said to the thirty riders to his right, 'The air-sled is almost empty; we have Nish and his militia trapped inside the temple. Once he is dead, the first man to reach Morrelune will take the throne – as long as he has the pure fire.

'Kill them, monks and militia all!' he roared. 'Let not a single witness live. If Nish has the white fire, bring it to me. If he does not, we're going to take the temple and monastery apart, stone by stone, until we find it.'

Nish slipped inside. Could he make Vomix believe that he did have the true fire? The dead abbot lay to his left; through the columns he saw the cast-out youth running for the far side of the monastery, his hands still bound. He wouldn't last long.

He ran in, through the triangle of columns and down the benches to the square hole. The youth's white robes lay on the stone beside it.

'Nish?' called Beyl from halfway up the ramp.

'Go up. I won't be a minute.'

The riders were outside, revelling in the slaying, and fear tightened Nish's chest. He was not afraid of dying, but he was terrified of Vomix, a depraved brute who loved to torment and brutalise.

When he'd served Jal-Nish, Vomix had dared not harm his son. But now, with the God-Emperor gone and Klarm missing, there was no law save the might of men like the seneschal and, after being humiliated by Maelys and Nish, Vomix would feast on vengeance.

Was there a way to fool the brute? Nish picked up the fallen censer and emptied the smouldering incense down the hole. Bundling up the chain, he coiled it inside the lower half of the censer, twisted the top half on and tore the back out of the youth's white robes. He wrapped the censer in the cloth, tied a knot so it could not fall out and slung it over his shoulder.

A thin haze of smoke issued from the square hole, scented with incense. The Celestial Flame might have been defiled, but it had not been entirely extinguished. He checked again; still blue, and no use to him.

Nish crept up the benches to the top of the triangle and peered over. There was no one in sight though he could hear the clack of shod hooves on the smooth paving stones. They must have finished the last of the monks and were riding into the temple.

The narrow ramp up into the dome was about fifty paces away. Nish was about to run for it when Vomix rode through the columns and saw him. He bolted, the bundled censer bouncing on his back, knowing he'd left it too late; the

436

warhorse would cover the distance to the ramp in a few strides.

Vomix stared at the bundle over Nish's shoulder, cried, 'He's got the white fire! He's mine!' and spurred his warhorse, but as it sprang forwards, its rear hooves slipped on the polished stone and it went down.

With a furious oath, Vomix leapt off and pounded after Nish. For such a big man he was very fast. Nish made the ramp with just paces to spare and leapt up it.

Vomix swung the scimitar at his back, trying to cut the bundle free, and barely missed. Nish scrambled up another few paces, but slipped and landed hard on hands and knees. Vomix came after him, lunged, and the three-bladed spike passed between Nish's arm and his ribs.

He kicked backwards, driving his heel into Vomix's knee, then went on hands and knees up the ramp to the first landing, where he turned and swung the serpent staff at Vomix's head. The seneschal's eyes widened.

'Where did you get that?' said Vomix. 'You're no mage.'

'It's part of Stilkeen's caduccus, and it has powers you'll never dream of.'

'Not in your hands,' snarled Vomix.

'How do you think my little militia beat ten thousand of Father's finest?' Nish sneered.

Vomix hesitated, then lunged again, but Nish was ready and thumped him in the side of the head, slamming him into the temple wall. Vomix arrested his fall by dragging the tip of the scimitar down the stone in a shower of sparks and lunged again, this time stabbing with the spike.

It speared into the fleshy part of Nish's left thigh and struck the bone with an excruciating flare of pain. Nish swung the staff in reflex, slamming it into Vomix's shoulder and driving him down several paces before he could stop himself. Blood pulsed from Nish's thigh as he hobbled backwards up the ramp. If the spike had cut an artery he would collapse from loss of blood before he could get to the dome.

His trousers were soaked and blood was flowing down the inside of his leg, though he did not think it was coming out fast enough for him to bleed to death. It was hideously painful though, and he was starting to feel faint from shock. He pressed the heel of his hand hard against the wound and kept going.

Far below, two soldiers had dragged the old monk down to the square hole above the flame. Another pair of soldiers were rolling a barrel between them, directed by a robed scrier.

The old monk was stripped, stretched over the square hole and held down, and the oily contents of the barrel poured in. Yellow flames gushed up and he began to writhe, but did not cry out.

'Tell us where the white fire can be found,' said the scrier, 'and we may let you go.'

'Liar,' said the monk. 'You're going to burn me alive and it will do you no good, for I can tell you nothing.'

Vomix chuckled. 'Roast him some more.'

Nish turned away, feeling sick, and limped up, wincing with every step. He could now see the edge of the air-sled through the circular hole in the dome, and his militia were scrambling up knotted ropes, watched by Flangers. M'lainte stood on the platform surrounding the altar, binding a splint around Persia's broken arm, and she was staring down at Vomix as though she was about to throw up.

Beyl and two other militiamen were not far above Nish, waiting.

'Go up,' he gasped. They could not help him, since the ramp was only wide enough for one, and they carried neither bows nor spears.

Vomix leapt up and struck at Nish again, but he slammed his staff into the seneschal's arm, below the spike, and Vomix reeled backwards, shaking his wrist.

'Fall down and break your stinking neck,' Nish cried, but Vomix recovered and struck with both spike and scimitar at once.

Nish wove out of the way of the scimitar but could not avoid the spike, which speared into his thigh an ell or two above the first wound. Now, when he moved, his foot squelched, for his boot was filling up with blood.

Nish's leg would barely support him, but he dragged himself up another pace or two. His head was spinning and he felt like throwing up, but he fought the shock for his very life. He had to finish Vomix somehow; Nish knew he couldn't get away unless he did.

Vomix was watching the blood pulsing from the twin holes in Nish's thigh, grinning viciously. He had his victim where he wanted him and was in no hurry to end the fun. Nish stood upright then swayed, pretending that he was near collapse, hoping to lure Vomix into coming too far forwards.

Vomix bared his few remaining teeth. 'You won't get me that easily.'

Nish backed up another pace, and another, widening the distance between them, then deliberately fell backwards onto the ramp, crying out in pain. It wasn't feigned; his leg was giving him agony.

Vomix came after him, raising the spike to stab for the belly. With his last reserve of strength, Nish flicked the heavy serpent's head up into Vomix's groin.

It hurt him, though not as much as Nish had hoped, and unfortunately Vomix fell forwards, crushing him against the ramp. Knowing that he'd made a fatal miscalculation, Nish attacked with his knees and fists and, when the seneschal

439

went for his throat, head-butted him on the bridge of his broken nose.

The blow must have been excruciating but the brute seemed almost immune to pain. His eyes were red with rage, his breath so foul that Nish gagged, and snotty blood gushed from his nostrils. Vomix took hold of Nish's head and began to bang it on the stone ramp. He tried to poke his finger in the seneschal's eye but he pulled back sharply and, with the strength of desperation, Nish slammed the heel of his left hand up against the seneschal's larynx.

Vomix let go, his hands clutched at the air and he began to gasp and wheeze. Nish brought up his knees and forced Vomix off, hoping that he would choke. He slid a few spans down the ramp but after several laboured gasps he gained a breath.

'Take him,' Vomix gasped to the soldiers who were coming up behind.

Nish turned and went up in a hopping stagger, trailing blood down the ramp and knowing that he'd never outrun the soldiers.

Thirty-five

Nish scrambled up and up the curving ramp, his breath tearing at his throat and his thigh burning, knowing that he wasn't going to make it. He reached a short landing and his blood-drenched leg collapsed under him; he could go no further.

The enemy soldiers had climbed over Vomix and were coming on quickly. Flangers was running down from the platform but he could not haul Nish up and fight at the same time. They were going to take him, though he wasn't going to give Vomix the satisfaction of winning.

'Flangers!' he gasped, struggling to his knees. 'I've got the white fire. Catch!'

Flangers stopped, and Nish tossed up the bundle of cloth with the censer inside, but his thigh twanged agonisingly and the throw went wide. For an awful moment he thought it was going to fall to the floor of the temple and burst open, revealing his meagre deception, but Flangers stretched out, caught the trailing end of cloth and reeled it in.

He passed the bundle up to Persia, who handed it to Beyl, and he threw it up to M'lainte. She dropped a large two-handled amphora to him, which he threw to Flangers, who caught it one-handed, nearly overbalanced under its weight and said quietly, 'Duck!'

Nish did so, wondering what marvel of the mechanical Art M'lainte had constructed. The amphora soared over his head, smashed at the feet of the leading soldiers on the ramp and oil went everywhere. No marvel at all; it was full of oil.

The leading soldier skidded backwards onto the upraised sword of the man behind him, arms wheeling. Blood gushed; he fell and slid down on the spreading oil, bringing the other two down with him. The lowest soldier clawed at the oil-covered stone but could not get a grip and went head-first over the edge of the ramp. The man above fell as well, and the injured man followed them.

'Let's get you away,' said Flangers.

Despite his bloody shoulder, he took Nish under the arms and dragged him up the ramp, which flared at the top, where it met the platform below the circular hole in the dome.

As they reached it, reinforcements came running up, but stopped below the oily patch, which was too long to leap, and the first man began to edge his way up, clinging by his fingernails to the stone of the temple wall. It was slow work, yet he and the other soldiers would reach the platform before the short line of militiamen could be lifted to safety and Nish, Persia and Flangers could take their turn.

Through the hole Nish could see his troops lined up along the side of the air-sled, peering down anxiously, while M'lainte sat with her plump legs dangling over the edge, calmly knotting ropes to make a net. Whatever the situation, she seemed unflappable.

Persia eased past Flangers and Nish, holding her splinted arm at an angle, and went to the edge of the platform, facing the line of climbing soldiers. The leading man let out a snort of derision.

'Seneschal,' he said over his shoulder.

Vomix limped up to the oiled stone, his red eyes flitted across the three on the platform, and his belly shook with silent laughter.

'Wait until the world hears this,' he said venomously. 'The great Deliverer, the son of the God-Emperor and Hope of the World, slaughters a monastery full of peace-loving monks, then hides behind a pretty woman with a broken arm because he's too gutless to face justice.'

Was this whole raid a set-up, its aim to destroy Nish's reputation in the eyes of the people? And if it was, was Yulla in on it? Well, Nish wasn't giving up, and if he had to die here, he was going to die on his feet.

'They'll believe me before they'll believe scum like you,' Nish said. 'Vomix by name, and by nature.'

'You won't be talking to anyone, Nish,' said Vomix. 'You'll be dead and dismembered, and your body parts nailed to the gates of the city.'

'I'll live to piss on your corpse.' Never had a boast sounded so hollow.

'Take him, lads. No need to be gentle, but save the woman for me. I never finished –'

Persia choked back an involuntary cry and Vomix roared with laughter.

'Go up, Persia,' Nish said out of the corner of his mouth. 'I know what the bastard is like and –'

'So do I,' she whispered, and he turned to stare at her. He had not seen Persia lose control before, but now her face had frozen and there was something dark and hollow in her eyes, as if she had personal knowledge of the seneschal's depravity. 'I cannot break my word to Yulla.'

And Nish could not leave her to defend him from Vomix; not like this. 'Let me go, Flangers.'

Flangers continued to hold him. 'Surr, your wits are addled. You can't fight.'

'I'm your commanding officer,' Nish hissed, 'and I've given you an order.'

Flangers let go and Nish tried to stand upright, but his thigh would not move. He would have fallen and made a fool of himself had the lieutenant not held him up by the back of his shirt. Nish looked over his shoulder; there were still three militiamen to be lifted to the air-sled.

'We've got to hold the enemy off for another minute or two. Where's my sword?' He groped at his scabbard.

Flangers pressed the hilt into his hand, though Nish struggled to raise the light blade. He took it in both hands, as he'd done during his lessons in swordplay as a sixteen-year-old boy, propped himself up with it, and felt a little stronger.

'Come back to me,' he said to Persia, since he could not move to join her.

All the blood seemed to have withdrawn from beneath her brown skin, leaving her a sickly grey colour. 'I have my orders.'

'In warfare, mine take precedence. For the sake of the empire you may stand beside me, but not before me.'

She moved backwards, taking her place to his left and sliding a long, slender sword from her sheath. It had an ornate hilt of metal basketwork that protected her hand, though the blade had no edges, just a pointed tip that could only be used for thrusting.

'What's *that*?' he muttered.

'It's a rapier.'

Nish had encountered many weapons in his career but he had never seen a sword like it. The point could kill if it found its target, though without an edged blade she would be at a tremendous disadvantage.

The soldiers grinned and nudged one another, mocking the ridiculous, girly weapon.

'Take them,' yelled Vomix.

The first two soldiers were scarred veterans, the third a young man with a shock of yellow hair and a shiny weapon that might never have been blooded. It soon would be. Nish raised his sword, now so weak that it shook in his hands, thinking himself a proud fool. And yet, the whole empire believed him to be their Deliverer, and expected him to fulfil his oath, so he could do no less.

Another step and the soldiers would be within lunging distance. His pulse was pounding in his ears. His opponent tensed, about to strike. Nish lifted his sword and prepared to defend, knowing he would be too slow, and afraid that if he moved either foot his thigh would collapse under him.

Beside him, Persia went into a crouch and her opponent's eyes narrowed. He was lifting his blade when she lunged, the rapier flashing out too fast to see, then whipping back.

What was she up to? It wasn't until a red spot appeared in the centre of the soldier's chest that anyone realised she had thrust the point through his heart.

As he toppled backwards she lunged again, this time at Nish's man, the rapier sliding between the ribs before he saw it move. The youth, dismayed to find himself alone, hacked at Flangers with the shiny sword but Flangers knocked it out of the way, cut him down and thrust his body onto the next three, sending two over the side and the third skidding down the ramp on his back. The soldiers below managed to avoid him but he knocked Vomix's feet from under him.

'Not laughing now, seneschal?' sneered Nish.

'Get them!' roared the seneschal as he came painfully to his feet. 'Cut them to shreds. A thousand pieces of gold for Nish's balls.'

He threw his coat down on the oily patch, crossed it and began to lurch up.

'We're done!' yelled M'lainte, hurling her completed rope net down onto the other end of the platform. 'Come on!'

445

'Go!' said Flangers. 'I'll hold the top of the ramp. Lend me your rapier, Persia.'

She slapped it into his hand and he tossed her his weapon.

Nish hobbled backwards, with her assistance, and fell into the net. Persia scrambled in, militiamen pulled on the ropes on its four corners and it lifted them as if they were in a basket. The next soldier came rushing up the ramp, swinging his broadsword in a roundhouse sweep at Flangers's middle, a blow difficult to evade and impossible to parry with a rapier.

Flangers did not try; he swayed backwards, the blow coming so close that the sword tip cut through his shirt, then lunged. The rapier was so light that no ordinary sword could match it for speed, and when perfectly aimed it slid into living flesh like butter.

The soldier toppled down the ramp and Flangers turned to the net, but its base was already shoulder-high and rising fast, and there was no way to get into it. He sheathed the rapier, ran and threw his right arm through the meshes as the remaining soldiers rushed the platform.

We left it too late, Nish thought. They'll never lift us in time.

'Go!' bellowed M'lainte to Chissmoul.

The air-sled shot up, jerking the net after it, with Flangers dangling underneath. The wound on his gashed left shoulder had broken open and was bleeding again. The leading soldier dodged by him and took a hack at the net, trying to spill Nish out. Flangers kicked him in the head, drew his legs up out of reach and then they were over the altar, the net swinging wildly, directly towards the underside of the dome. Nish held his breath, sure they were going to be pulped against it.

As they were about to hit, Clech yanked sideways on his

rope, centred the net and they shot up through the hole, but Nish and Persia were thrown to the bottom of the net and she screamed as she landed on her broken arm.

In the impact, Flangers lost his grip and his hooked arm began to pull through the meshes. Nish caught his wrist and Persia groped for his other hand as he was sliding free.

'Can you hang onto the net with your left hand?'

'Sorry,' said Flangers. 'Can barely raise it. My shoulder –'

'Careful!' Persia yelled at the air-sled. 'One more jerk like that and we won't be able to hold him.'

Nish heard M'lainte speaking to Chissmoul, after which the air-sled steadied and moved slowly away from the temple, above the green lawn now littered with the bodies of the monks of the Celestial Flame.

Nish strengthened his grip on Flangers's right arm; Persia took his hand with her good hand. Her broken arm must have been excruciating, for there were tears in her dark eyes. Blood began to run from Flangers's left shoulder down his arm and off his fingers.

'Hang onto him,' called M'lainte. 'Not long now.'

'It better not be,' gasped Nish. 'We can't hold him much longer.'

A troop of soldiers outside the temple saw them, then scrambled onto their mounts to follow the slowly moving air-sled. Several javelins whistled up, passing not far below Flangers. Vomix came lurching out of the entrance, saw them and roared a series of orders. Soldiers ran from everywhere.

'Tell Chissmoul to go faster,' Flangers said.

'If she does, you'll fall.'

'I'm not afraid of dying.'

Nish tightened his hold, but he was weak from loss of blood and his grip was failing. 'I'll never win the war without my most trusted lieutenant – and dearest comrade-in-arms.'

'Thank you, surr,' said Flangers, deeply moved.

'You'll have to set down,' yelled Persia.

They began to pass over the great wheel of the monastery, heading in the direction of the rainforest and the mountains, but too low and too slowly.

'There's more soldiers outside,' called Aimee. 'We can't set down.'

'We can't hold him!' cried Persia.

Their drifting flight continued, not far ahead of the enemy riders. Some carried bows and began to ready them, and once they came within range they would pick people off the air-sled with ease.

'You must let me go, surr,' said Flangers.

'No!' Nish ground out.

'One man can't jeopardise your chances of taking the empire.'

Seized by the fear that Flangers would let go, to save them, Nish cried, 'Hang on, Lieutenant, and that's an order.'

'Surr,' said Flangers.

The net could not be hauled over the side for fear that he would be shaken free. Nish didn't know what to do. His consciousness was slowly fogging over and, once he lost his grip, he did not think Persia would be able to hold Flangers.

'Stay with us, Nish,' she said. 'Just another minute.'

'What's the point?' he said weakly. 'We can't set down or they'll have us.'

'Stay with us.'

He clenched his teeth and held on, and then little Aimee was lowered down on a rope behind Flangers. She swiftly tied another line around his middle, he was hauled up and the net heaved aboard, and it was over.

The air-sled shot away, the militia jeering at Vomix and casting aspersions, undoubtedly true, on his parentage. He bellowed out a volley of oaths, then his voice was lost in the whistle of air around the cabin as they accelerated away.

Nish was laid on his back on the deck, biting down on his wadded-up sleeve as the healers cut his trouser leg off and began to clean the spike wounds. Now that he had nothing to distract him, the pain doubled and redoubled until he could scarcely think of anything else.

'Fly due west,' he ground out, 'towards the mountains. Make – make sure they see us. After nightfall, head for Kralt.'

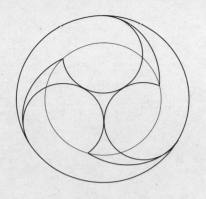

PART THREE

THE FINAL BATTLE

THIRTY-SIX

'Where's the fleet?' said Flangers as the air-sled slowly circled the cove at Kralt a few hours before dawn the following day. It was a clear, hot night and the whole bay could be seen in the light of the waning moon, but there were no ships at anchor, nor any troops visible. 'Are you sure this is the right place?'

Nish, who was wrapped in a blanket behind the pilot's bench, shivering one minute and burning the next, peered listlessly over the side. The healers had done their best for his two thigh wounds but they were still a mass of pain and the bone throbbed mercilessly.

'Quite sure,' said M'lainte, who held the map, though she did not bother to check it. 'Chissmoul, circle around low and slow, in case it's a trap.'

Chissmoul moved her fingers inside her controller but the air-sled continued on its course. She swore, shook it and the craft turned, though sluggishly.

'Is something the matter?' M'lainte said sharply.

'The stupid controller is acting up again.'

'I'll take a look at it in a minute.' M'lainte squatted down, her plump knees popping, and rummaged in a wooden crate.

Chissmoul circled over the scrub behind the sand but when there were no suspicious signs she set down on the middle of the beach, close to the water.

'Stay at your posts in case of an ambush . . .' said M'lainte, who had taken command as if she were born to it, 'though our soldiers and ships have gone.'

'Gone?' said Nish dully. 'Without us?'

'There are tracks in the sand at the far corner of the beach. Yulla's men must have crossed there, heading for that flat rock sticking out over the water. It's the best place to embark, quicker than carrying everything through the surf.'

'Why didn't they wait?' said Nish, trying to get up. He rose halfway but could go no further; the pain was too bad.

'How would I know?' said M'lainte mildly. 'Let's see what we can find. Guards, keep a sharp lookout. Lie down, Nish. You're not looking too good.'

He fell down, cracking his head on the deck. Persia, who was ever solicitous of his welfare, put a folded coat under his head and spooned more potion into him.

Flangers and Clech took a troop and quartered the area behind the beach, searching the scrub with lanterns. Nish huddled under his blanket, watching the lights, which kept going in and out of focus. One minute the hot blood was roaring in his ears, the next he felt that he would never be warm again.

'There might be a perfectly good reason why the fleet has gone,' Persia said to Aimee and Clech, though from the tone of her voice she was trying to convince herself.

'I can think of several perfectly *bad* reasons,' Aimee said darkly.

Nish closed his eyes and drifted into a daze where time passed slowly, then quickly, then seemed to stand still . . .

*

'Wake up, surr.' Flangers was shaking him.

Nish surfaced slowly, having no idea where he was or what he was doing here, though he remembered a dream where he had been watched by black-robed scriers. He had always been afraid of them and the dream-fear still touched him. His hot, tight thigh throbbed with every heartbeat, and he was incredibly thirsty.

'Leg hurts.'

'Bugger your leg,' M'lainte said. 'Pull yourself together; we're in trouble.'

He opened his eyes. He was still on the deck of the air-sled and the sky was starting to lighten. 'What kind of trouble?'

'Chissmoul's controller isn't working.'

'Are you saying the air-sled won't go?'

'It's like last time,' said Chissmoul. 'It'll go forwards, but not up.'

'Thought you fixed it, M'lainte?' Talking made Nish's head ache.

'This is a different problem,' said M'lainte. 'The air-sled's controller was so badly made I'm surprised it works at all.'

'It's taken a lot of punishment,' said Chissmoul defensively, as though criticism of any part of the craft was a criticism of her.

'Weren't you making a better one?' said Nish.

'I haven't had a chance to test it,' said M'lainte.

He pushed himself upright, which felt like climbing a mountain. She had something in her lap and her stubby fingers were working on it in the semi-dark.

'Drink,' he croaked.

'You've got a fever,' said Persia exhaustedly. 'You can't have strong drink.'

Her broken arm must be causing her a lot of pain and yet she had watched over him all night. Nish bitterly regretted the way he had spoken to her yesterday.

'Give the sod a drink,' said M'lainte, 'and bring me one as well – a big one. I'm going to need liquid inspiration to get this thing working.'

Persia turned away stiffly.

'I only wanted a drink of water,' said Nish.

M'lainte chuckled. 'Don't spoil my fun; you should have seen her face. Your prim and proper bodyguard doesn't approve of strong drink.'

'Don't tease her,' said Nish. 'She saved my life.'

'And you saved hers, so you're even. Ah, Clech, what's that you've got?'

The giant was hopping across the deck on a pair of crutches, swinging a familiar, stolen flagon in one enormous hand. Aimee trailed in his wake.

'Where did you get that?' said Nish, remembering the enchanting liqueur, though it was the last thing he wanted now.

'Divers found it on the bottom when they were putting the lifting ropes around the air-sled,' said Clech. 'Had to confiscate it, of course.'

'How come you didn't give it back to Flydd?'

'Reckon the old coot has had enough to last a lifetime.' Clech pulled the bung out.

'What's the matter with you lot?' Aimee snatched the flagon from his hand and put it behind her back. 'You're not getting any 'till we're safe on board ship.'

'Does the prohibition include me?' said M'lainte fiercely. She wasn't a tall woman but she towered over Aimee.

'Yes, it does!' hissed Aimee. 'And I don't care how proud or important you are.'

They faced each other like a plump old turkey and a furious bantam hen, and finally M'lainte grinned. 'Then I'd better get the controller going.'

She sat down and continued working on the device in her

lap. Suddenly the air-sled's mechanism produced a low, humming note, followed by a higher one, before dying away.

'Did you find anything out there?' said Nish. His mind felt a little clearer now.

'A lot of footprints, and the wheel marks of supply wagons,' said M'lainte. 'In the dark it's hard to tell what's happened, but a group of soldiers definitely boarded ship. The overhanging rock is worn where they marched across it, though . . .'

'What?' said Nish.

'It wasn't an army of two thousand; nothing like it.'

'Maybe Yulla couldn't raise a whole army,' said Nish.

'She did,' said M'lainte. 'I've seen it.'

'Then where is it? And where's the fleet?'

The light grew; it wasn't far off dawn and his foreboding deepened. Had this been a set-up from the beginning? Thinking that Persia was out of earshot, he said quietly, 'Do you think Yulla . . .?'

'She's rock-solid, Nish,' said M'lainte. 'Which leaves only one alternative –'

There was a long silence. 'That . . . that we've been betrayed by one of her allies,' said Persia from behind him. 'The army must have been captured. Maybe the fleet never came, only one or two of Yulla's ships.'

A spasm lanced through Nish's thigh to the bone. Could this be the end, before the real campaign had even begun?

'They want you, so they must be out there somewhere,' said Flangers, peering into the darkness. 'Why haven't they attacked?'

Nish was fever-hot again; his leg began to throb unbearably and it took an effort to follow the simplest train of thought.

'If I were the enemy,' said Flangers, 'I'd wait until – Nish, what is it?'

He had gone from feverish to freezing in an instant, and the grogginess was blasted away by a rolling wave of clear-sight. 'Soldiers, and scriers, on the southern headland. Where is everyone?'

'Sleeping,' said M'lainte, 'or cooling down in the cove.'

Nish pulled himself up onto the pilot's bench. A dozen militiamen and women were swimming, finally relaxing after the brutal day and sleepless night. 'Call them back! Chissmoul, get it ready.'

As everyone ran to their posts, dawn broke and the shrubbery stirred on the headland.

'Ambush!' yelled Clech to the people in the water. 'Into the cabin. Everyone!'

A force of several hundred troops rose above the scrubby bushes and began to storm down the slope. Their archers would soon be within firing range.

Nish cursed. 'They'll kill everyone in the water.'

The air-sled jerked forwards, stopped and began to shudder as if it was caught on a sticky surface. 'What's the matter with it now?' wailed Chissmoul.

'Their scriers must be interfering with your controller,' said M'lainte.

A flight of arrows pocked the surface around the swimmers, one missile skipping across the water like a stone.

Chissmoul stood up, shaking the mechanism over her head, and the air-sled broke free and shot towards the cove. Unable to rise, it skidded sideways, sending out an enormous curving plume of spray that temporarily obscured all the swimmers. Naked men and women churned towards the air-sled and were dragged over the side, but not all of them made it.

An arrow, fired from the rocks at the far end of the beach, struck Chissmoul's pale, nervous friend Allioun in the forehead as she was climbing aboard. She fell back with the arrow sticking straight up; her blood darkened the water.

Chissmoul gasped and tried to dive in, but Flangers held her.

'There's nothing you can do, love,' he said gently. 'She died instantly.'

'I'm sick of this,' she whispered, tears streaming down her cheeks. The wire and crystal controller dangled from her right hand, forgotten. 'I can't take any more.'

The last of the militia were dragged over the side. Persia and Flangers carried Nish into the cabin as more arrows fell around them, zinging off the metal deck and embedding themselves in the bimblewood walls. The attackers were halfway down the headland already.

'Give me the controller,' said M'lainte.

'You're not taking that from me as well,' Chissmoul said in a deadly voice. 'Get out of my way.'

'Chissmoul –' began Flangers, reaching for her.

She slapped his arm aside. 'Get down and stay down – you too, Mechanician.'

'I'll be beside you all the way,' said M'lainte. 'Try this.'

She handed Chissmoul the object she had been working on, which was red and the shape of a watermelon cut in half across the middle, with a single knobbed lever rising from its rounded top.

'Stick the bottom to the deck and hold the lever. It controls everything – forwards and back, left and right, up and down – and the further you move it, the faster it goes.'

'What about stopping?' said Chissmoul.

'Er, I haven't done that yet,' said M'lainte.

'Then you'd better hang on!'

Nish clung to a bench, shivering, as Chissmoul jerked the lever towards her.

'That's backwards,' cried M'lainte as the air-sled shot

backwards, bouncing off the water and curving around towards the headland.

'There's no shelter for us if I go forwards,' said Chissmoul grimly.

The air-sled bounced across the water, went blazing up the gentle slope of the beach and turned south along it, Chissmoul wobbling the stern to left and right so she could see past the cabin. She turned sharply up the headland, crushing the bushes in their path and barely missing boulders to either side.

Nish, who was peering through one of the mica windows, could not imagine how she was steering the ungainly craft so accurately. The metal keel hit a bump, shot upwards, and not far ahead he made out the attackers, a dark, running mass in the dim light. Arrows thudded into the bimblewood; he ducked, instinctively, and his thigh screamed at him.

An arrow smashed into the mica pane, tearing it from its timbers and sending it *flub-flubbing* past his ear across the cabin. The stern wobbled left, right, left so fast that his head spun, accelerated up the slope and he heard sickening thuds as it drove through the soldiers, scattering men to left and right and crushing dozens beneath its keel.

Thumpitty thump thump, thump thump. The keel careered off a small boulder, tilting the air-sled sharply to the right, and for a dreadful second he thought they were going to slam into the ground at high speed.

Chissmoul managed to right it but it tilted the other way, hurtled over the steep side of the headland and down towards the cove, leaning one way and then the other, and flattening out only to bounce off the water so hard that Nish's teeth snapped together. He collapsed on the floor.

As the air-sled shot high into the air and straightened, Chissmoul managed to head it through the entrance of the cove and out to sea, but then the craft turned and kept turning until it was heading landwards again, racing directly for the cliffed headland.

'Up!' M'lainte yelled. 'Pull it up.'

'It won't go up,' said Chissmoul, her voice tight with fear. 'I can't control it.'

The cliff loomed ever closer. Nish rolled over and could see her struggling with the lever. M'lainte grabbed the controller, heaving the lever this way and that while muttering what sounded, to Nish, like a Spell of Breaking, and suddenly the scrier's command of the controller snapped.

From up on the clifftop, a man screamed. M'lainte wrenched at the knob and the air-sled rocketed up, up and over the top of the cliff, so close that the keel brushed against the heath growing there. Arrows bounced off the thick metal as they soared away, out of range, and finally out of sight of the enemy.

Nish lay on the floor until his breathing had returned to normal and the pain in his leg had subsided to a dull throb. They'd got away, but what was he supposed to do without a fleet or an army?

As they climbed, the sun tipped the eastern horizon and shortly the lookout called, 'A sail, due south.'

Chissmoul, who had snatched back the controller, turned the craft in that direction.

'Sail, or *sails*?' called Nish.

'I can only see one so far, and it's not a fishing boat; it's a ship.'

'One of Yulla's?'

'It's too far away to tell,' said M'lainte. 'If her captain was alert, he might have escaped as the trap was sprung, with the troops he'd taken on board. Go closer, Chissmoul.'

Nish crawled around until he found his serpent staff then, using it as a crutch, limped to the side and scanned the seas. From this height Roros was a smoky smear to the north.

A number of sails could be seen on the water near the city, though most appeared to be fishing boats or little coastal traders. There was no sign of a fleet.

'Yulla said the fleet would be at least twenty ships,' he said to Persia, who had come up beside him. 'We'd need at least that number to carry two thousand men, plus all their gear and provisions, but there's no sign of *any* ships save the one to our south. And the weather has been perfect for sailing . . .'

'Yes, it has,' Persia said uneasily.

'Did you actually *see* Yulla's fleet, M'lainte?'

'She only had two ships in Crandor,' said M'lainte. 'She arranged to borrow the rest from Pensittor.'

'Who's he?'

'An old friend from the time when she was governor. He was her lieutenant in the old days, but he bought the spice monopoly after the God-Emperor deposed her, and is now very rich. Pensittor has fleets of ships; he trades all the way up and down the east coast, and west as far as Taranta.'

'And I dare say he's dependent on the favour of the God-Emperor to keep his monopoly,' said Nish. 'So what has he to gain if Father is overthrown?'

'He's been good to Yulla,' said Persia severely. 'After your father took her governorship away, he taxed her until she was bankrupt. Pensittor loaned Yulla enough to get started again, and he's a man of his word.'

Nish looked questioningly at M'lainte. 'I've met him several times,' she said, 'and he seemed an honest fellow to me – for a merchant, I mean. Though I did wonder where he got the coin to buy the spice monopoly. His family weren't wealthy.'

'What are you thinking?' said Nish.

'That his offer to lend ships to Yulla was genuine, *when it was made*, but Stilkeen's proclamation changed everything.

Before that, Nish, you stood a good chance of taking the empire, since everyone knows your claim is legitimate. However, after the proclamation you lost the advantage, because the local warlords could reach Morrelune long before you could and, as the empire collapsed into civil war, you would be just one of a dozen rivals for the throne. Vomix is another, one of the strongest. He was Seneschal of Fadd province for many years and he's still more influential there than the seneschal who replaced him.'

Persia was clinging to the rope rail, shaking her head. 'I can't believe it. Pensittor is a man of honour –'

'What if Vomix had a threatening word in his ear?' said Nish, following M'lainte's train of thought, 'telling him that there was little to be gained by supporting Yulla or me, but much to be lost. If Vomix can get his army to Morrelune quickly, he can take it, but he'll need a lot of ships. He must have demanded that Pensittor betray Yulla and lend him the ships, in exchange for more monopolies when Vomix becomes God-Emperor. What choice would Pensittor have? If he refused, and Vomix became God-Emperor, Pensittor would lose everything.'

'An honest man would have spat in Vomix's face,' said M'lainte. 'But a prudent merchant with flexible morals would see where his best interests lay.'

'So Nish was right. Yulla has been betrayed,' said Persia bleakly, 'and everyone who aided her is in peril. And our families too, *what's left of them*, if Vomix succeeds.' She stared blindly over the side for a moment before going on. 'His troops must be embarking on Pensittor's fleet now, preparing to set sail for the south at all speed.'

Nish swayed on his serpent staff as they drew closer to the ship, trying to put as little weight on his injured thigh as possible.

'Even if this vessel is Yulla's, what's the point of going on?

I can't attack the might of the empire with a handful of troops.'

'You certainly can't if you're not at Morrelune in thirteen days,' said M'lainte. 'And you must go there, for that's where the fate of Santhenar will be decided. It's also where Flydd will come, whether he finds the true fire or not.'

'I've got nothing left,' said Nish, grinding his teeth with every bump and lurch of the air-sled. 'I can't do it.'

'Nish, we had no hope from the beginning,' Flangers said. 'We never expected to take Blisterbone, nor hold it against Klarm's army, but we did. And we bloodied Vomix's nose back there, and made him look like a fool. I say we go on, because we can't go back and we can't give in. The moment we put a foot on the path to Morrelune, we had no choice but to follow it all the way to victory – or oblivion!'

It was a long speech for Flangers, who was taciturn by nature.

'And you'll feel better once your leg has healed,' said M'lainte. 'Snap out of it, Nish. Everything relies on you.'

If M'lainte had meant to be encouraging, she failed dismally, but Nish reminded himself of all those who had died so that he could stand here today, and knew he could not let them down. 'All right. Head for the ship.'

They were gliding down when Persia said quietly, 'M'lainte, Pensittor's ships are faster than Yulla's.'

'And the scriers back there saw which way we headed,' said M'lainte. 'Therefore, Vomix will send his fastest ships after this one.'

'We'd better fly directly to Morrelune,' said Nish.

'I have to return the air-sled to Yulla. It may be all she has left,' said M'lainte.

'She'll be in Vomix's cells by now.' Nish did not want to give up the air-sled; it was the only advantage he had. 'If she's –'

'Alive at all,' Persia said bleakly.

'Yulla is a wily old dog,' said M'lainte, 'if I can use so vulgar an expression. All her life she's been alert for treachery –'

'Not alert enough,' snapped Nish, for the pain was getting worse. 'She didn't see this betrayal coming.'

'Maybe she did, but had no way of getting word to us. Anyway, I said I'd bring the air-sled back and that's what I'm going to do.'

'You'll lose it, and your life,' Nish said bitterly.

'I too am a wily old hound,' smiled M'lainte, 'and I don't think my time is up yet.' She looked over the side. 'It's definitely Yulla's ship. Take us down.'

THIRTY-SEVEN

On the ice platform outside the cubular door of the city of Stassor, the four of them took hold of the caduceus. Maelys's pale hand was lowest, since she was much smaller than the others; next was Malien's weatherworn and long-fingered hand, then a gap to Tulitine's slender fingers, her flesh pink and blue, sluggish blood clearly visible through transparent skin, and another gap to Yggur's big dark hand.

'I'm not sure how to get to Aachan,' he said shakily, for he was far from fully recovered. 'Making a portal to a place you know is hard enough, but travelling between worlds is far more perilous than jumping within them, and I've never been to Aachan.'

'You have seen it clearly, though,' said Malien.

'I have?' said Yggur, frowning.

'It was at the end of the Time of the Mirror, when Maigraith took Rulke's body and his construct to Aachan, where Yalkara and the other surviving Charon had gathered. They were about to go back to the void –'

'I wish they had,' gritted Maelys, 'and taken Maigraith and Yalkara with them.'

'As I was saying,' said Malien pointedly, 'the Charon were preparing to return to the void when my people attacked.

466

They were about to kill Maigraith when Yggur did something that had never been done before, and saved her life.'

'I loved her, once,' said Yggur, 'long before she became the Numinator.' His mouth twisted. 'But she would not have me. She cast me aside.'

'That day you did something that should have been impossible, and no mancer has ever understood how you *could* do it. You fired a bolt of force across the Way between the Worlds to destroy the construct. And to do that, you had to see Aachan clearly.'

'You're right,' said Yggur in amazement. 'I did! Though I cannot remember *how* I did it.'

'I'm not surprised. It nearly killed you.'

'I remember the pain – awful, tearing pain, as if my inner organs were being torn apart. So! I *have* felt worse than I do now, and yet I recovered. I can do this.' He straightened his bowed back. 'Ready, Maelys?'

'What?' She had lifted her hand from the caduceus. 'Sorry.' She took a firm grip, expecting a painful passage . . . if the portal worked at all.

It went so dark that Maelys could not see their hands. She was weightless – she no longer felt the heavy pull of gravity on her breasts, nor the accompanying tension that was always present in her shoulder muscles. Air whispered around her ears and she floated for some seconds, her weight slowly coming back, though not as heavily as previously, before she settled on something hard.

When her sight returned, the light was dim and ruddy, the air cool and humid; it smelled powerfully of sulphur and tingled in her nostrils. Their four hands appeared, placed as they had been before, with Yggur's big chest blocking her view. Looking to one side, she made out a dismal black plain, beyond which shard-like mountains marked a jagged horizon.

A small red sun hung a third of the way up the sky, haloed by yellow bands, its meagre light struggling to penetrate the thick air.

Yggur staggered, his fingers slipped and he clung to the caduceus for support, pulling it backwards. Maelys and Tulitine, who were on the opposite side, struggled to hold it; Tulitine stifled a cry of pain.

'Yggur,' Malien said sharply, 'if you can't stand up, sit down.'

After finding his balance with an effort, he wiped cold sweat off his brow. 'It doesn't hurt as much as the last portal; I think I can manage it.' He looked around. 'We're here.'

'Aachan, beloved Aachan.' Malien took a deep, shuddery breath and walked away so light-footedly that she appeared to be bouncing.

'It's more comfortable here,' said Tulitine. 'My bones hardly ache at all.'

'I too feel a little stronger,' said Yggur.

As Maelys's eyes adjusted to the light, she saw that the plain was a congealed lava flow, its surface dark, ropy and twisted. The rock was cold beneath her feet, and puddles of water lay here and there, while further on, yellow vapour drifted up from crevices.

A stone's throw to her right a number of large structures, half buried in the lava, looked like reflective metal bubbles. Some were singles, others grouped in clusters, and several were encircled by platforms like planetary rings.

'Are they houses?' Maelys wondered, for she had never seen any buildings remotely like them.

'They were, before the lava flowed,' said Yggur. 'The Aachim are brilliant architects, builders and artists, and everything they make is beautiful, but different, for they cannot bear to build to the same design twice.'

468

She sniffed the air which, though pungent, seemed perfectly breathable. 'Do you think the ones who came to our world at the end of the lyrinx war lied about Aachan being destroyed?'

He shook his head. 'The Aachim love their world with a depth and a passion we cannot understand, because the Charon took it from them and held it for thousands of years. When they fled through their portal to Santhenar, maybe thirteen years ago, this world was almost uninhabitable.'

Malien came back, breathing deeply in the chill air, and her cheeks were moist.

'I was born on Santhenar,' she said as softly as a sigh, 'as were my parents and grandparents, yet the longing for Aachan is etched into our very bones. Every Aachim dreams of making pilgrimage to our home world, though I never thought I would.'

'Why not?' said Maelys.

'Crossing from one world to another has rarely been possible, and it would not be possible now, I suspect, had Stilkeen not allowed it.' Malien rotated in a circle, studying the sawtooth horizon, her chest heaving and her grey-green eyes shining. 'After Yggur destroyed the construct two centuries ago, and the Way between the Worlds was lost, I thought we were destined to be forever exiles. Even then,' she mused, as if looking back at that distant time, 'the volcanoes were erupting out of control.'

'Are they finished now?'

'There's no way of knowing. This country is high up and may have been spared the worst, but much of Aachan's low-lying land was flooded hundreds of spans deep in lava. It must have been a desperate time.'

'It's a grim-looking world,' said Maelys without thinking.

'It must seem so to you, but we love it more than our lives.' Malien looked around wistfully. 'I wonder if anyone could have survived? In the catacombs life may have struggled on during the worst of the eruptions. For a while, at least . . .'

'We came for chthonic fire,' said Tulitine gently, as if reluctant to bring Malien back to reality, 'and we don't have long to find it. Where might *it* have survived?'

'Possibly in association with molten lava, if chthonic fire caused the eruptions,' said Malien.

'If it is, it'll be deuced hard to get to,' said Yggur.

'The caduceus might know where to look for it,' said Tulitine.

'If it's that easy,' said Maelys, 'why doesn't Stilkeen find the fire itself?'

'It can't,' said Yggur. 'When chthonic fire bound Stilkeen's physical and spirit aspects together it could roam the universe at will, but once severed from those spirit aspects – the revenants now trapped in the shadow realm – the physical worlds became excruciatingly painful for it. You saw, in that brief appearance before Stilkeen snatched Jal-Nish, how much it was suffering. To search our world, or this one, would be impossible.'

'That has to be why it left the caduceus for us,' added Tulitine. 'That's why it's manipulating us, and why Stilkeen made its proclamation to the whole world – so someone, somewhere, might do what it could not.'

'What if you gave the caduceus its head?' said Maelys.

'Yes, that's the answer! Create a portal, Yggur, but instead of thinking of the destination, think about what you want to find there. Can you make another?'

'I should be able to. The aftersickness isn't as bad here – at least, *so far*. Put your hands on the shaft.'

They did so, and were whirled away to the top of a range of volcanic hills whose tops were as jagged as broken glass, where the brittle lava had shattered leaving a series of steep littlc pcaks. Thc ground fcll away on all sidcs into shccr ravines, and in the base of one, far below, Maelys saw a broad river of red-hot lava. On its surface, at the centre, several bright worms of white fire writhed.

'There it is,' she said, thinking that it seemed a little too easy.

'We can't climb down there,' said Yggur. 'The rock would cut our hands and boots to pieces, and the merest slip would be fatal.'

'Can't you make a portal to the fire?' said Maelys.

'Onto molten lava?' Yggur studied the flow, frowning and shaking his head. 'The white fire is right in the middle and we can't get to it. I'll try again.'

This time they ended up on a dark, undulating plateau with a great canyon snaking across it, and brooks and rills tumbling over its sheer sides. There were patches of wiry grey scrub on the plateau, swathes of tough blue grass and flat clumps of blue-black luminous flowers like six-petalled daisies.

They walked to the edge of the canyon, the blue grass springy beneath their boots, and looked over. The sun was almost on the horizon here, the canyon lay in shadow and its bottom was dizzyingly far below.

More luminous plants sprouted from the canyon walls; some were like toadstools, others resembled the growths on fallen logs, and they came in an extraordinary variety of shapes and colours.

'I don't see any white fire,' said Maelys, her confidence fading.

'Keep looking,' said Yggur tiredly. 'I'm sure the caduceus didn't bring us here for nothing.'

'What's that?' said Tulitine, leaning over the rim of the canyon. 'It's glowing.'

Maelys went down on her hands and knees. 'Just sap,

471

trickling out of the stalk of one of those luminous toadstools. Besides, it's yellow.'

'Luminous plants and fungi are common here,' said Malien. 'In olden times, the roots of that black daisy were used by seers to follow the paths of the future, not that it did them any good.' She laughed mirthlessly. 'We Aachim have never had trouble seeing into our futures – only in deciding on any course of action.'

She crouched beside Maelys and looked down. 'The juice of those toadstools gives a good light for reading or fine work,' she went on. 'Unfortunately it only lasts a few hours.'

Maelys reached down with her knife and scraped off some juice. 'It might come in handy after sunset.'

'We'd better keep looking,' said Malien. 'Tomorrow is the fifteenth day. It'll be dark here soon, but if you take us west, we'll still be in daylight –'

Yggur was shaking his head. 'I can't do any more today, or I'll have nothing left to get us home. Where would be the best place to camp?'

'In the canyon, on a ledge or in a cave, if we can find one. Predators roam the high plains at night and they're very quick.'

'Would a fire keep them away?' said Maelys, scanning the darkening plateau.

'It would help. I'll see if I can find some dead bushes. Look for a camp site.'

Not far below the canyon's rim they found a narrow ledge running down to a broader one, and at its back the wall had a deep indentation, which, if not quite a cave, could be defended – at least from small predators.

The light faded, and here and there along the canyon wall trickles of toadstool sap began to glow like necklaces of pale yellow jewels. Malien appeared, dragging a couple of dead wire-bushes, and made a small fire. After dinner, Yggur, who was silent and exhausted, lay in his blankets at the back of the indentation and Tulitine joined him.

Malien sighed. 'Aachan, Aachan.'

This world was mentioned in a number of the dark stories Maelys had been told as a little girl, but it was an alien place to her; she could never be at home here. She shivered and tried to think of a cheerful tale, but her thoughts kept going back to the Tale of the Mirror, and the two people whose story it had been.

'Did you know them well?' she said absently.

'Know whom?' said Malien.

'Sorry. I was thinking about the Time of the Mirror, and Karan Kin-Slayer and Llian –'

'Don't call them that!' snapped Malien. 'Yes, I knew them both very well. And I don't want to talk about them.'

'Sorry,' Maelys muttered. Yggur and Lilis had reacted in much the same way when the two names had been mentioned. The betrayal must have been a dreadful one, yet, the more Maelys heard about Karan, the more she wanted to know about her.

They sat in silence for a long time. In the distance, some native creature let out a whistling shriek.

Maelys jumped, thinking that it had met a violent end. 'What was *that*?'

'Perhaps a flightsinger,' said Malien. 'A small night bird, calling to its mate.'

'Oh.'

From above, there came a long, vibrating howl that echoed off the canyon walls. 'And *that*?'

'A gruvellor, I'd say – a predator like a wolverine, only larger and faster.'

Maelys put her back against the wall and took hold of the handle of her knife. 'How large? How fast?'

'Enough to take down a human by itself, should one carelessly wander into its territory – and should the bigger predators allow it.'

She swallowed. 'Are we in its territory?'

'Of course. If it hasn't already scented us, it soon will.'

'And then?'

Malien shrugged. She was standing near the edge, staring down the canyon. Maelys remained behind the fire, as far away from the brink as possible, for the sheer drop unnerved her and it would be easy to go over in the darkness.

Malien said abruptly, 'I'm going for a walk. I'll be back for my watch.'

'But, you can't go up there . . .' Maelys didn't want to be left alone – at least, effectively alone.

'I know how to deal with them, Maelys. Here in the land of my ancestors, my Art is powerful. In any case, I require little sleep, and I can't bear to waste the few hours I will ever have on Aachan,' she said wistfully. 'I would brave *any* predator for a little more time here.'

Moved by Malien's passion for her world, Maelys said impulsively, 'I'll take your watch. Stay out all night if you like.'

'Thank you. That's most generous – I know how afraid you are. I'll be back before dawn.'

Maelys wouldn't have gone up onto the plateau in the dark for anything. 'What if something happens and you don't come back?'

'Then you must leave without me.'

'We can't do that!' Maelys whispered.

'Why not? I'm near the end of my days, and my life can be set at naught compared to the fate of a world.' Malien headed away along the ledge and was lost to the darkness.

The gruvellor howled again, closer, and another

answered it in a lower register. Were they calling each other to attack Malien, or to creep down the ledge?

The fire died down to a few dull coals and would soon go out, since there was no more wood. Maelys kept an anxious watch along the ledge to left and right, not that she would be able to see an approaching predator now.

She unsheathed her knife and held it up. The luminous juice gave out a steady yellow glow, enough to have read a book by, but, thinking that it was more likely to attract the predators than deter them, she put it away and continued her lonely vigil.

In the morning they would only have one chance to find the true fire, for if it failed there would be no time to try again. Had they come here for nothing? She felt sure they had. And what would happen when they went back empty-handed?

The night sounds continued for hours, before dying away. Did it signify that the gruvellor were gone, or were they creeping closer? Or eating Malien? Every second seemed to take an eternity and Maelys desperately wanted to wake Yggur and Tulitine, but restrained herself. They needed the rest more than she needed company.

When the stars told her it was midnight she went across to wake Yggur, but Tulitine said, 'Leave him, I'll take the watch. He needs his sleep if he's to get us home.'

Maelys clutched her blankets and furs around her like a defensive wall and prepared to wait out the night, but soon fell asleep and did not wake until Malien returned at sunrise, her cheeks flushed from the cold air. She looked serene.

'Thank you,' she said. 'All night I have been communing with the land of my ancestors. If only my bones could rest here after I die, I could pass away in peace.'

Maelys shivered at the morbid thought. She wouldn't

want *her* bones to lie in such a gloomy and forlorn place. 'Did you see any predators?'

'A number, including a hunting pack of gruvellor. They were following your scent, so I had to lead them away.'

'How did you manage that? Weren't you terrified?'

'There was a tense moment or two,' said Malien drily. 'But this is my world, and I knew it would be worse for you.'

After breakfast they trudged up onto the plateau to make a final attempt to find the pure fire. The small sun had risen some time ago but it was only a hand's breadth up on its low arc across the sky, and its light was dim.

They took hold of the caduceus while Yggur concentrated on finding a new source of chthonic fire.

'That's odd,' he said after several minutes had passed and nothing had happened. 'It isn't even attempting to make a portal. Am I too weak, do you think?'

'Who can fathom the workings of such an enigmatic device?' said Malien. 'Or the one who left it for us. Try again.'

After three attempts, Yggur's knees were trembling and there were globules of sweat on his forehead, but the caduceus hadn't budged. He slumped to the black, ropy rock, wiping his brow.

Despite his previous illness, it had never occurred to Maelys that Yggur could fail; he had been too great and powerful a figure for too long, and in the past he had overcome every obstacle. Now, contemplating the thought of remaining on this alien world until she died, *or was eaten*, she felt her pulse race and her jaw clench. To never see Santhenar again, or her family, to fail and allow Stilkeen to destroy the world – it could not be borne. There had to be a way out of here, but it was beyond her understanding.

She sprang up and began to walk in circles around the others, so fast that she was panting.

'What's happened to your sheath?' Tulitine said sharply.

Maelys looked down at it. The leather had gone black and crumbly at the bottom. She drew her knife.

'That's odd,' she said, studying the glowing marks on its tip. 'Didn't you say that the luminous juice only lasted a few hours?'

'I did,' said Malien.

'I collected this yesterday and it's as bright as it was then.' A shiver made its way across the backs of Maelys's hands. 'Though it's not yellow any more; it's *pure white*; and flickering like . . .'

Everyone rose, and Tulitine was reaching out with a fingertip when Yggur cried, 'Don't touch it! *Pure* chthonic fire could eat through human flesh as easily as it's consumed the leather.'

Tulitine took the knife, held it up, and the faintest flame flickered on the tip. 'It's white fire, all right, but is this enough?'

'It might be corrupted already,' said Yggur. 'Better collect it afresh.'

Maelys collected all the glowing juice she could get from the toadstool, directly into Yggur's third and last dimensionless box, then wiped her knife carefully on the ground and threw away the crumbling sheath. They sat down to wait and, after a couple of hours, the yellow luminescence disappeared and the pure white fire it had been masking flickered to life. Yggur folded over the dimensionless box.

'Is that why the caduceus wouldn't take us anywhere?' said Maelys. 'Because the white fire was right here?'

'I hope so.'

'We were also going to look for a weapon against Stilkeen. If we went back to those abandoned buildings we saw earlier, or to an Aachim city, do you think we might find some Aachim device we could use to attack Stilkeen?'

'We can't delay any longer,' said Malien. 'Today is the last day.'

'Let's see if we can get to Morrelune,' said Yggur.

'Where the jackals will be gathering,' said Tulitine, 'to rob anyone who approaches with the true fire.'

'We'd better take precautions,' said Yggur. 'Maelys, you know Morrelune. Think of a safe place for us to appear.'

'I don't know the area well,' said Maelys. 'I've only seen it once.'

'Do your best. What's our destination?'

She thought for a moment. 'A gully in the range above the palace, not far off the path up to Nifferlin, my home – before Jal-Nish ordered it torn down.' Maelys bit her lip, understanding how Malien had felt last night, and must be feeling now. 'I led Nish that way after we got him out of Mazurhize.'

'Take my hand. Concentrate on where you're taking us, and keep it carefully in mind until we arrive, *or we never will*. Everyone else, blank your minds, just in case.'

Maelys closed her eyes and held her breath. Now their survival, and the hope of the world, did depend on her and how well she could imagine their destination. She prayed that she was up to it.

THIRTY-EIGHT

It was late on the eleventh day since Stilkeen's proclamation and Nish, hobbling onto the quay at the little fishing port of Tungst, was worn thin from throwing up.

Yulla's ship had carried a mere hundred of her troops, the only ones to escape the ambush and, with no option but to continue, Nish and his militia had gone aboard. As M'lainte turned the air-sled north towards Roros, the ship's captain had fled south for Fadd as fast as his craft could go, looking over his shoulder all the way.

On the fifth day a trio of Vomix's fast cutters had appeared far astern and steadily ran them down. Yulla's captain had put on all the sail his creaking craft could carry in the stormy weather but the cutters had continued to gain by the hour, and on the following morning they were almost within bowshot.

The strengthening storm had become a gale and it had raged for almost a week. Nish had been thankful at first, since it was near impossible for the enemy to find them in such conditions, but as the weather worsened Yulla's round-bottomed tub had rolled her guts out.

The soldiers and Nish's militia had thrown up in the cramped holds until the bilges were awash and the ship reeked of vomit from the bowsprit to the anchor lockers. They could not go up on deck – the one soldier foolish enough to try had been swept over the side and never seen again. Of the militia, only Clech the fisherman had been spared seasickness, but Aimee had made up for it, heaving so violently that she had cracked one of her healing ribs, for which he mocked her gently but mercilessly.

Finally, this afternoon, racing with the wind on bare masts, the battered craft had ridden out the storm, but Nish hadn't dared sail into Fadd. It had been close to midnight when the captain had docked at Tungst, two leagues north, where he had scraped the soldiers and militia onto the dock like muck from the bottom of a shoe.

'I'll never take on such filthy landlubbers again,' he muttered, while the holds were hosed down and the polluted bilges pumped out into the harbour.

Nish thanked him and looked around the deserted quay, which was dimly illuminated by a single lantern hanging from a post a pebble-cast away. He made out the lights of a tavern further around the small bay, but that was all. The fishing village was hidden in a sheltered fold in the hills, the captain had told him, though at this time of night not a single light glimmered there.

At the other end of the quay a wisp-watcher hung from its pole, smashed. Even this close to the heart of the empire, rebellion was everywhere now that the God-Emperor had disappeared.

The hills, Nish knew, ran up to a steep coastal range, at the top of which Morrelune lay on a long, narrow plain skirting a higher chain of mountains. The palace was two hard days' climb from here and he wasn't looking forward to the journey, assuming they could get away undiscovered.

Clech was pacing back and forth along the shore, limping just a little. With the aid of the healing spells his broken bones had knitted quickly, though he was not yet back to full strength.

The soldiers and the militia were huddled at the end of the dock, wanting nothing more than to lie down on ground that was not rocking and sleep a full circuit of the clock. No one yearned for it more than Nish, but he had to know what was going on.

'Flangers?' he said quietly.

Flangers looked as ill as any of them, but he rose at once. 'Surr?'

'Lead everyone out into the countryside, bed them down in the first patch of cover you come to, and don't let anyone out of your sight. I'm going to the tavern; I'll be back in an hour or two.'

'You'll have to go in disguise,' said Persia, Nish's silent shadow, who had only left his side on board ship when one of them had been throwing up.

She was always polite, and never failed to do her duty, but they had not regained the friendship that had begun when she was making him up as a silver miner. Nish felt sure that he had mortally offended her by suggesting that Yulla might have betrayed them. It seemed an enormous over-reaction to what had been an imprudent, yet wholly reasonable, inference on his part, but it did not seem as though Persia was ever going to forgive him.

He should have known better, but it was too late now. Sighing for what might have been, he concentrated on what she had said.

'A disguise? Is that really necessary at this hour?' He was so unkempt, bearded and haggard that no one would have recognised him from the portrait made by his father ten years ago.

'We can't take any chances. It won't take long.'

'All right.'

'That'll do,' she said shortly, studying his made-up face in the dim light. 'Let's go.'

'I'm going alone,' said Nish. 'As Yulla's bodyguard, your face is too well known.'

'I'll disguise myself.'

'There isn't time, and you'll be a liability – especially if Vomix has spies here.'

She shivered. 'Yes, of course.'

It was well after midnight when he limped into the waterside tavern, desperate for news. Nish gagged as he entered, for the place reeked of bad food, sour ale and other unpleasant things, and had his stomach not been emptied out long ago, he would have disgraced himself in front of everyone. That would certainly attract unwelcome attention, he thought wryly, noting that the drinkers were eyeing him. He looked as disreputable as any of them; his clothes were filthy and his coat still smelt faintly of the vomit that had permeated the whole ship.

After buying a large drink he had no intention of touching, he sat in a corner with his hat shading his eyes until the attention of the customers returned to more interesting matters.

Despite the hour, the tavern was packed. Everyone was talking about the great armies racing each other up the God-Emperor's Highway from Fadd to Morrelune, and what they would do once they got there. Nish made a mental note of the names of their leaders, though only the last meant anything to him.

'My money is on Seneschal Vomix,' said a squat, bald sailor with skin like a crumpled leather handbag. 'He's the mean-est bastard in the world.' He glanced hastily over his shoulder as he spoke. 'This Stilkeen beast won't know what hit it.'

'He's a right one, Vomix,' said an equally leathery old

woman who was smoking tea leaves in a clay pipe. She tamped them down with a tarry finger and drew an appreciative lungful.

'Vomix can't get there in time,' said the bartender, picking his nose and wiping it on the apron he was drying tankards with. 'Hackel's army will be halfway to Morrelune by now.'

'Vomix's advance guard landed at Fadd this morning,' said the bald sailor, 'and he's already got the support of the army there. He was Seneschal in Fadd for years, remember? He'll be God-Emperor within the week.'

'And make our lives a misery again,' said the old woman. 'But the Deliverer is coming to save us,' she muttered, emitting clouds of blue tea smoke. 'He gave his word, ten years ago.'

Nish stiffened, then tried to relax. She wasn't looking at him, and there was no reason why anyone should associate him with the Deliverer. He looked like a drunken bum, and stank like one, too.

'The Deliverer can't beat Vomix without an army,' said the bartender, shooting an anxious glance towards the far corner, where a thin man sat hunched over his drink as if it was the only thing in the world to him, though he hadn't touched it since Nish had entered. Spy, or scrier, Nish knew, looking away and drawing back into the shadows. Realising that his own untouched drink was a giveaway, he took a mouthful of the sour, unpleasant brew, swallowed, and almost brought it up again.

'Nish had a mighty victory on the Range of Ruin,' said the old woman. 'He'll come.'

'I heard that Vomix killed him up north,' said the bald sailor.

'Gruin Plebb said Nish was strung up in the torture chambers, begging for his life,' said a plump, red-faced young man.

'Gruin Plebb is a famous liar,' said the old woman, 'and so

deep in Vomix's pocket he'd need a ladder to get out. I don't believe his lies for a second. And even if Nish *is* a prisoner, he'll soon get free.'

'No one escapes from Vomix,' said the bartender, speaking as if by rote.

'Nish got away from Mazurhize,' said the old woman. 'He'll come to our rescue, mark my words.'

This pronouncement was so comprehensively laughed down that Nish suspected the opposition was organised. Vomix could not allow him to develop a personal following; his spies and followers would ensure any such buds were trimmed early.

No one was betting on Stilkeen to emerge the victor, he noted. It was universally mocked as a crude but savage beast, though to his own ears the drink-fuelled revelry had an end-of-the-world hysteria about it.

He heard no word of Flydd, which suggested that he had failed in his quest. If he had returned, Nish felt sure Flydd would have made himself known, so as to give hope to his allies. Unless he was really after the tears, or had plans to steal the throne for himself . . .

No! Nish had been friends with Flydd for many years, and he'd always been solid and reliable. Besides, Nish knew that one of the God-Emperor's most important weapons was undermining the opposition by sowing suspicion and dissension, and he wasn't having it. Self-doubt had crippled him in the months following his escape from prison and it had taken all his will to overcome it. He wasn't going down that path again, either.

He had learned enough. He took another pull at the vile drink, grimaced and quietly went out. Though he was desperate for sleep he had to get his army going at once. The wisp-watcher might have been destroyed, but the eyes of the enemy were everywhere.

An hour later he was leading his sick and unhappy troops across the fields towards a minor path that ran into the hills. As they moved up a small wooded slope he caught sight of Yulla's ship, weighing anchor.

'Good riddance,' he muttered. 'From now on, wherever I've got to go, I'm going on my own flat feet.'

He had put Flangers in command of Yulla's soldiers and told him to allow them no respite, knowing that Vomix's spies were bound to hear about the little army by morning, and in the light of day they would soon discover which path it had taken. It was a race to get to Morrelune first; every moment counted now.

'You can't drive them any harder, Nish,' said Flangers that evening, when they had been going with barely a rest for sixteen hours. 'My men are on the brink of mutiny and your militia aren't much better.'

Nish rubbed his burning thigh. The healers had worked miracles on his wounds during the long voyage but the brutal march felt as though it had torn the muscle deep down. He had driven himself this far through sheer, grinding determination though it would not carry him much further.

'I know, Lieutenant, but what else can I do? We're all that stands between Stilkeen, the void, and the end of human life on Santhenar. If Vomix catches us, he'll cut us all down, and a lot more will be lost than our brief lives.'

'Then we'd better leave the path and make it harder for them to find us, but we still have to rest.'

'If we leave the path, we'll get lost,' said Nish.

'As long as we put our backs to the sea and keep climbing we can't go too far astray,' said Persia. 'And when we top this range, we'll see the long plain of Morrelune; we can hardly miss it.'

They trudged across broken country for another exhausting hour and, several ridges away, out of sight from the path, camped for the night. Nish slept restlessly, knowing that the opposition was too vast and too powerful. He'd had one miracle victory already in this campaign; he could not hope to repeat it in open battle.

They climbed through equally rough ridgelands for two more days and, around midnight on the fourteenth day, finally reached a broad area of level ground, partly obscured by low-lying mist.

Nish drew everyone back down into the shelter of the trees, by a trickling stream, and lit a stub of candle so he could check the map. Persia sat beside him, kneading her calf muscles with her good hand. Her broken arm was healing but it was still weak. The last day's march had been as hard as the first and everyone was footsore and bone-weary.

'This has to be the plain of Morrelune,' Nish said to Flangers and Clech. 'Tell your men we'll have a break for twenty minutes, and they'd better fill their water skins.'

When they returned, he went on, 'The plain forms a crescent of flat land separating the coastal range we've just climbed from the ridges running up to the high mountains. Maelys's home, Nifferlin, was up there.'

Memories stirred, of the terrible time after her little sister had broken him out of Mazurhize, and Maelys had shepherded him up into the mountains. Nish had been ill and delirious, and yet he had a vague memory of her carrying him at some stage, which was incredible. Afterwards he had treated her shabbily, and he had not properly made amends. Too late now. He forced the distracting thoughts away.

'The plain is about four leagues long,' said Persia, 'but only a league wide at its broadest point, and we're at the northern tip. Morrelune must be a couple of leagues to our left.'

The four of them studied the map. 'We'll have to go carefully now,' said Flangers. 'The other armies will be camped within striking distance of Morrelune, and . . .'

'My head will be a great prize to any of their commanders,' said Nish. 'I know.'

'I don't suppose there's a chance they'll fight each other?' said Clech, who was shivering. To Nish it was a mild spring night, but not for someone who came from hot, steamy Gendrigore.

Nish shrugged; the question was unanswerable.

'We'll skirt the northern end of the plain and continue up on this track,' he said, tracing it across the map with a fingertip. 'It runs into the mountain path about a league west of Morrelune. We'll sneak down it until we see the palace, then take cover and wait. The enemy armies won't have camped up there –'

'Why not?' said Clech, thumping his massive thighs, which had wasted while his broken legs were healing.

'There's no water. The armies will camp below the plain where there are springs aplenty. Let's move out.'

They skirted the end of the plain, marched up along the path for some hours and, a little before dawn on the fifteenth day, he crested a rise, with a silent Persia beside him, looked down and saw the lights of his father's palace below them.

Nish stopped, breathing heavily. The last time he'd seen Morrelune, dragged there by his father's guards, it had been framed by the rearing mountains immediately behind it, and it had looked airy, delicate and stunningly beautiful. A crescent-shaped lake, called the Sacred Lake, curved around its northern side, and from there both the palace and the framing mountains were reflected.

Sets of broad steps rose on all four sides to a wide promenade surrounding the palace, which was built from white and golden stone. It consisted of nine levels, tapering upwards, each being like an open temple supported on many columns arranged in interlinked circles.

There were no walls, not even in the highest level where Jal-Nish had dwelt, which was roofed over with a sky-piercing spire covered in lapis lazuli. The God-Emperor had no need of walls, for no one would have dared to spy on him, and with the tears he could even control the weather around his palace.

But not any more. He was gone and Morrelune had been transformed; it was ablaze with light like a glowing jewel, but it was now Stilkeen's, and Nish turned away hastily.

He could not make Mazurhize out from here, since it lay another half a league across the plain. Mazurhize, the grimmest prison in the empire, was surrounded by a vast expanse of paving, though all he could see were the mist-haloed lamps around the four gigantic, tower-mounted wisp-watchers that scanned the paving with relentless, microscopic precision.

It was the converse of Morrelune in every respect – it too had nine levels, but they tapered downwards, for the prison lay entirely underground and was massive, dark and claustrophobic. The ninth level, the dankest, most putrid and festering of them all, contained only a single cell and it had been reserved for the God-Emperor's son. That was where Nish had served out his ten-year sentence.

At the memories, his chest tightened and he fought to control the frantic impulse to run, *anywhere*.

'Nish?' said Persia. 'Are you all right?'

'Just remembering my prison days,' he said lightly.

She laid a hand on his shoulder and the panic eased, but it wasn't going to go away. As long as there was an empire, and he was an outlaw, the threat remained.

In Nish's eyes Morrelune was equally tainted, for when

his ten years were up he had been taken to his father's court and tempted beyond endurance. He had almost broken; he had gone so very close, but in the end the proof demanded by Jal-Nish as the price of fealty had been too high.

He had repudiated his father, who had then, to punish Nish, shown him the perfectly preserved body of his beloved Irisis, in a crystal coffin. She had looked exactly as she had the moment before she'd been slain, ten years before. Irisis might still have been alive, save for the thread-like seam where her head had been rejoined to her body.

Subsequently, Jal-Nish had claimed that he could bring her back from the dead, exactly as she had been before death, and Nish had been half-mad with longing, but he had fought it and rejected his father once more. He would never again be tempted; yet neither could he entirely free himself from the desperate yearning to have her back.

The sound of brass sliding against brass shook him from his reverie – Persia was surveying the eastern side of the plateau through a fieldscope.

'I can see lights in three places, Nish – army camps.' She pointed them out.

'There were supposed to be five armies,' Nish fretted. 'Where are the others?'

'If they're further down the ridges, we wouldn't see them from here.'

Nor if they're up here somewhere, hunting me, he thought. 'Take a look at Morrelune. It doesn't seem quite right.'

She trained the fieldscope on the palace and let out a yelp of dismay.

'What is it?' he whispered. 'Have you recognised someone? *Father*?' No, not at this distance, surely.

'The palace still has the *shape* of Morrelune, but –'

'You've been here before?'

'I accompanied Yulla, three years ago,' said Persia, 'when

she came to plead for the return of her monopolies. The God-Emperor turned her away, of course. See for yourself.'

She handed him the fieldscope. He looked through it, adjusted the focus, and stared. The palace was *ablaze* – every floor, column, stair and spire flickered with yellow and orange fire – yet there was no smoke, nor any evident damage. Morrelune was burning, but not being burnt.

'It's as if the very stone has been replaced by fire,' he said breathlessly. He moved the fieldscope back and forth but the air around Morrelune had a mirage-like shimmer and he could not make out any finer details, nor any trace of the great enemy. 'Why would it do that?'

'You said Stilkeen was in great pain when you first met it,' said Persia.

'I'm not sure what you're getting at.'

'If it's in such pain in our world, it makes sense that it would rebuild Morrelune so as to minimise its suffering. And being a creature of fire and shadow, it has remade Morrelune in that guise. Let's see . . .'

Persia took a number of crystalline plates from a bag, pushed one into a slot in front of the eyepiece and looked through the fieldscope. Shaking her head, she replaced the first plate with another, and another, then swallowed and lowered the fieldscope, staring blankly.

'You'd better take a look.' She passed it to him.

Nish looked; his heart skipped several beats and began to thump erratically. The fire palace was clearer now, but that wasn't what had bothered her. Between Morrelune and the distant mountains, a translucent barrier could now be seen rising up from the land to the sky like a monstrous wall, and blurred shadows were moving behind it.

'Is that what I think it is?'

'I think so,' said Persia. 'The barrier that protects San-thenar from the void, made visible.'

'Stilkeen threatened us with the void. It told us to bring the fire to Morrelune within fifteen days, or after that time, it would empty the void into the Three Worlds and all human life will be erased.'

'Was that a threat?' said Persia quietly, 'or was it a promise? I think ... Stilkeen has been hurt badly ... and its sacred person has been insulted and profaned ...'

Nish followed her train of thought to its unpleasant conclusion. 'And if it doesn't just blame Yalkara, if Stilkeen thinks all of us are complicit –'

'It may decide to punish us by opening the void into Santhenar, even if it gets the pure fire.'

It would be the end of the world – at least, for humanity. His stomach burned as if it was brimming with acid, for this was a problem he could not solve with arms; it was beyond any of them. It had to be the end.

'What can I do,' he said, 'with five armies waiting for me to appear, plus Stilkeen, *and* the most savage creatures in the void waiting to be released? And all I have to oppose them is a company of worn-out soldiers.'

Persia did not reply, though the look on her face told him that she had no more hope than he did. They trudged back to the wooded fold where the rest of his force was hidden but, as they reached it, there came a crash from the other side of the ridge above them, then the sound of rubble sliding down a slope, and silence.

'What was *that*?' said Clech, rising to his feet, gigantic sword in hand. He was out of his element in the chilly, barren south, and did not like it.

'Has Stilkeen opened the void already?' whispered Persia.

'It can't have,' Nish said unconvincingly. 'It's too soon; it hasn't got what it wants.'

'We can't predict what a *being* will do,' said Persia.

491

THIRTY-NINE

The journey from Aachan back to Santhenar seemed to
take forever, and all the while the caduceus shook
beneath their hands as if buffeted by a gale, though not a
hair on Maelys's head was disturbed. She could see nothing,
yet she had an uncomfortable feeling that something was
watching her – the back of her neck burned as if a searing
gaze had focussed on it. Yggur began to pant, and once
Tulitine cried out in pain. Malien was silent save for several
stifled sighs, presumably for the world she would never see
again.

What if we're too late? Maelys kept thinking. Time passes
differently in the Three Worlds, as in the Nightland; days
could have gone by while we were on Aachan. If the dead-
line had already passed, Stilkeen might have emptied the
void into Santhenar already.

Yggur groaned and the caduceus tilted right over. Malien
said sharply, 'You can't give up now. If we stop in between,
we could end up anywhere. *Or nowhere.*'

'Can't hold it,' he slurred. 'It's sucking me dry.'

'Tulitine?' Malien said urgently.

The caduceus shook wildly, as if trying to throw them off.
'I can barely hang on,' said Tulitine.

'What's the matter with it?' cried Maelys.

'Stilkeen must know that we've found the pure fire,' said Malien, 'since the caduceus led us to it. And here, within the portal, we're close to its ethereal realm. If Stilkeen can maroon us here, it might be able to take the fire from us, instead of suffering on Santhenar while it waits for us to bring the fire to it – and perhaps it's afraid we won't. Fight it, Yggur. If Stilkeen was strong here, it would have snatched the fire at once.'

'Nothing left . . .' whispered Yggur.

'Maelys, hang onto him.'

Maelys pulled herself up the furiously vibrating caduceus until she caught Yggur's hands.

'Don't let go,' he slurred. 'Might fall out of portal.'

'What if I do?'

'You'll go nowhere – *forever*.'

She took a tighter grip and the taphloid swung against Yggur's wrist.

'What's that?' he said sharply.

'My taphloid.'

'Give it to me. Quick!'

She handed it over reluctantly, wondering what the connection was between Yggur and the taphloid, and why he had recognised it back on the Range of Ruin, yet had no memory of ever seeing it.

Yggur let out a great sigh, Maelys felt him relax and the caduceus stopped shaking. The feeling of eyes on the back of her neck disappeared, as did all sensation of movement. Did it hide Yggur, the way it did herself? It must. Unfortunately, they seemed no closer to Morrelune than before.

Light grew in the distance, spreading around a horizon, and Maelys saw that they were suspended just above a flat surface faintly marked with a grid of squares. Not completely flat – it was dimpled below the caduceus and again below the taphloid, now held in Yggur's outstretched right hand.

A distorting wave passed through him as if he were a figure made of jelly, then he was his normal self again. '*Maintain the watch against Stilkeen, Yggur,*' he said in the voice an adult might use to a young child.

'What did you say?' hissed Malien.

He blinked twice and shook his head as if to clear it. 'The words just came to me, as they did before we left the Range of Ruin. Didn't I tell you about that?'

'You said a voice told you to keep watch; you didn't say "against Stilkeen". And that wasn't *your* voice. It sounded like a father speaking to his son – but what father would have known about Stilkeen in the distant age when you were a boy?'

'I don't know,' said Yggur hoarsely, as if afraid of the answer. 'According to Lilis, not even Nadiril the Librarian could find any early reference to Stilkeen. Who could have known it but Yalkara . . .?'

'Or another Charon, close to her,' said Malien.

He started. 'But only two Charon men ever came to Santhenar, and of them, Rulke was ever my enemy. What are you saying? Do you mean . . .? Could *Kandor* be my father?'

'That's it!' cried Malien. 'Kandor and Yalkara were close in ancient times, and if anyone would have known about the stolen fire it would have been him. He might have warned her about it, but Yalkara was ever proud and headstrong.

'What if they fell out over chthonic fire?' she mused. 'Kandor would have known that a *being's* patience is infinite, and that eventually it must discover who had stolen the fire. He could not force Yalkara to give it back, for she was far more powerful than he was. Neither could he hope to stop Stilkeen when it came, but Kandor had recently had a son by an *old human* woman, and he must have known that the boy possessed a brilliant gift for mancery. With the proper lessons his son – you, Yggur – might be able to protect the world from Stilkeen.'

'So that's why the taphloid felt so much smaller,' sighed Yggur. 'When I first held it, I was a small boy.'

'I see it now,' said Malien. 'Kandor made the taphloid and hid your lessons in it in case something happened to him. It was designed to protect and instruct you, and only you, once you were old enough.

'But soon afterwards he was killed in the Clysm, and it was such a bitter war that your mother must have been afraid to tell anyone, even you, who your father was. Left destitute, and not knowing the taphloid's importance, she sold it to survive, and eventually it ended up at the Great Library.'

'It also explains why my Arts are so enigmatic,' said Yggur, sounding stronger now. 'Because the Charon came from outside the Three Worlds.' His face cleared suddenly and he said, 'Now I know that my duty was to maintain the watch against Stilkeen, I'm going to fulfil my destiny.'

'You don't have to,' said Malien. 'The past cannot command the future.'

'I *want* to do it. It's the only way I can bond with the father I never knew.' He passed the taphloid back to Maelys. 'Do you still have our destination in mind, Maelys?'

She focussed on the memories. 'Yes.'

'Then hang on tight – we're going all the way this time.'

The caduceus began to shudder but Yggur forced it to stillness and the gridded plane faded away. Wind whistled about Maelys's ears, Tulitine let out a soft cry, then they emerged from darkness into a chilly morning, landing heavily on a flat rock perched on a steep slope. As the rock began to move, they leapt off and it slid down the hill, a little landslide following in its wake, to crash into a patch of scrub further down.

'Where are we?' said Malien, rubbing a bleeding knee.

Maelys looked up at the mountains in the distance, and they were *her* mountains; she knew every one of those peaks. 'Not far above Morrelune.'

'And we've just told anyone within a quarter of a league where to find us,' said Tulitine.

'But are we in time?' said Malien.

It reminded Maelys about her visions in the Pit of Possibilities, months ago. She had appeared in none of the possible futures she and Nish had seen there. Was she destined to die soon, *today*?

'Where's Morrelune?' said Yggur.

Maelys pointed away from the mountains. 'We'll see it from the top of that ridge.'

And Mazurhize, where Jal-Nish had held her mother, Lyma, her aunts Haga and Bugi, and her little sister, Fyllis. Could they still be alive after all these months? Maelys had last seen them in the image Jal-Nish had shown her at the top of Mistmurk Mountain, a long time ago now, and they had looked starved, listless and beaten. She could not bear to think of what they had gone through.

'Someone's coming,' said Yggur urgently. 'We'd better hide.'

She had tried to hide on these barren slopes with Nish, last autumn. The only cover nearby was a scatter of spindly bushes and an occasional depression or boulder. Further up stood a patch of woodland, and there was scrub in the gully, though neither would conceal them from a determined search.

As they were heading for the woodland, a huge soldier limped over the rise directly ahead, followed by a dark, beautiful woman and, partly concealed behind her, a smaller man.

The big soldier looked vaguely familiar, though Maelys had never seen the woman before. She was turning to run when the smaller man moved out from behind the woman and her heart leapt. Could that shaggy, haggard wretch be Nish, *alive*?

'Nish!' she cried, and pelted up the slope. 'Nish, we saw the flood; we were sure you were dead.'

The trio froze, staring, then Nish came on a step. 'Maelys?'

She crossed the distance in seconds, past the grinning giant and the beautiful woman, and threw herself into his arms so hard that she almost knocked him off his feet.

He clung to her, smiling in bemusement. 'And we were afraid *you* had drowned. Is that Yggur and Tulitine?'

'Yes,' said Maelys, hopping up and down, still holding him, before realising that Nish might not share her feelings – the feelings she had not realised she'd had for him – and that the woman with him might be more than a friend. She disengaged herself and stepped back at once, confused and embarrassed.

He was staring at her as if she were a long-lost treasure. 'You can't know how much I've cursed myself for running on ahead that day. How did you escape the flood?'

'I was high up, with Yggur and Tulitine. When we went back to look for you, everyone was gone. I was so afraid. Where's Xervish? He's not . . .?'

Nish was looking over her shoulder. 'Malien?' He ran to her and Yggur, leaving Maelys even more confused.

They crossed to the other side of the ridge, where Nish's small force lay hidden in a patch of scrub that extended the length of the gully. Persia had quietly left the old friends together, and Nish led Maelys, Yggur, Tulitine and Malien back to the camp, where they breakfasted on field rations and Malien's strange but delicious Aachim food, before settling down to briefly tell their tales.

Maelys's eyes never left Nish's face while he told the story of the battles at the Range of Ruin, and all that had happened since. Surely she can't be that pleased to see me, he thought, after the way I treated her. But it was so good to have her back, unharmed, and as strong, brave and beautiful as ever. Maelys had always bolstered his faltering heart and he felt all the stronger for her being here. There might be a faint hope after all.

'So you found the pure fire,' he said when everyone had finished. 'I don't know how you did it –'

'And *we* can't imagine how you beat that mighty army at Blisterbone,' said Yggur drily, 'so we're even. What's the plan?'

'We're waiting to see which army moves first,' said Nish.

'If I were a rebel, and had chthonic fire,' said Malien, 'I'd let someone else go first.'

'What if they were rewarded *beyond their wildest dreams*?' said Tulitine.

'I'd be working out how I could take the reward away from them. Or, if they suffered an unpleasant fate at Stilkeen's hands, I'd quietly withdraw.'

'How many armies are down there?' said Maelys.

'Five, we believe,' said Nish, 'including Vomix's.'

Maelys moved closer to Nish. 'I thought he died on Mistmurk Mountain!'

'The man we saw there wasn't Vomix; it was Vivimord transfigured to take his place. Vomix is alive; I fought the bastard a couple of weeks ago, and unfortunately failed to kill him, though he very nearly killed me.'

She clutched at his arm.

'The others include the present seneschal of Fadd, Lidgeon,' Nish went on, ticking them off on his fingers. 'He leads a force only half the size of Vomix's, I've heard, but he's a cunning devil. There's also a private army that sailed north from Tiksi, led by Hackel. The Jackal, they call him. A pleasant fellow to your face, but don't let him get behind you.'

'Who else?' said Yggur, lying down and putting his head in Tulitine's lap. She stroked his brow.

Nish did not reply for a moment; he was too surprised. He had not seen his old ally with a woman before, and Tulitine of all people. Clearly, much had changed in the four weeks since they had been separated.

'General Nosby, the commander of the Imperial Guard at Morrelune. It's fanatically loyal to the God-Emperor and if Father does comes back, or his appointed deputy, Klarm, every man of the Guard would give their lives for him. I don't know what they'll do if Father really is dead.'

'Would they transfer their loyalty to you, Nish?' said Maelys.

'An excellent question,' said Yggur, 'to which we don't have an answer.'

'I've heard rumour of one other army,' said Nish, 'but I don't know anything about it.'

By this time the sun was riding up a clear, brassy sky; it was going to be a hot day and Maelys was wilting. 'I'm really tired. If nothing is going to happen for a while . . .'

'Good idea,' said Nish, yawning. 'We marched half of last night and I'm not planning to move before mid-afternoon unless I have to. The lookouts will warn us if anything happens.' He rose. 'There's a nice, shady napping spot further up.'

He was looking at Maelys, and she accompanied him up the slope, though the others remained where they were.

'You didn't mention Xervish, after Roros,' she said. 'Where's he gone?'

'There's so much to tell,' said Nish, putting a companionable arm across her shoulders. 'He went looking for chthonic fire two weeks ago and I haven't heard anything since. I – I didn't want to mention it in front of everyone, but I'm worried about what he's up to.'

'I don't understand.'

They settled down in the coolest patch of shade and Nish went though his concerns about Flydd: his odd behaviour, frequent disappearances, his apparent obsession with the tears, and, most damning of all, that he had not made a portal with the serpent staff until he left Roros. 'Renewal changed him, and not for the better. I'm worried that he's after the tears – and not to destroy them.'

'No!' Maelys said flatly. 'He *has* been different ever since renewal, though that's to be expected – especially since Yalkara interfered with it. But deep down he's the same old Flydd –'

'How would you know?' he said quietly.

'I – I believe in him.'

'But Maelys, when he took renewal, you'd only known him for a day. Flydd and I fought together and travelled together for years during the war, and he's definitely different now; he's harder and meaner, and it bothers me.'

'Let's wait and see what happens when he returns.'

'If he does,' Nish said darkly.

Maelys frowned, clearly uncomfortable with the topic. She was the most loyal of friends and had never stopped believing in him, even when Nish could not believe in himself. It was one of her defining qualities and he could hardly fault her for it.

'Is there any news about Klarm and the tears?' she said hastily.

'Not since he went into the shadow realm, but if he turns

up the tears could change everything.' He paused. 'Tulitine isn't looking well.'

'The Regression Spell isn't reverting the way she expected. She hasn't aged, outwardly at least, but the pain in her bones grows ever worse.'

'And she only used that spell on herself to save me,' said Nish, shaking his head at a generosity of spirit which, for all his courage on the battlefield, felt beyond him. 'Yggur looks worn out, too.'

'His Art is almost gone, and I'm sure it has to do with the caduceus.' Impulsively, Maelys took his hands, but realised what she had done and hastily dropped them. 'How are you, Nish? You look exhausted.'

'I am. What a bunch of crocks we are,' said Nish, leaning back against a tree and staring at her until the blood rushed to her cheeks. 'We're all knackered, battered, broken, or decayed, except you. You're more beautiful than ever, Maelys –'

'I – I – Don't talk nonsense. The aunts always told me how little and plain and mousy I was.' She looked away.

'Plain? Mousy!' Nish snorted. 'What nonsense. How can you believe anything they say?'

'They're all I have left.'

And that was his father's fault. He changed the subject hastily. 'Have you learned anything about *your* gift?'

'No, and I never will; I'm too old to begin with the Art, and the lessons Father put into the taphloid for me are lost forever. But then, I didn't know I had a gift until a few months ago, so I haven't really lost anything.'

The tone of her voice said otherwise.

FORTY

In the early afternoon, Maelys was sitting on the coarse grass with Nish, watching Tulitine, whose head was bowed. She was using her seer's skills, aided by a decoction Malien had given her, made from a root of the black-petalled Aachan daisy, to search for Klarm. Nish felt that the dwarf and the tears were his only hope now – and a very slim hope at that.

'I have him!' she said suddenly.

Maelys leaned forwards but Nish put a warning hand on her arm and she sat back again.

'Catacombs,' said Tulitine. 'Very deep, dark; deadly. The dwarf staggers; his arms and chest run with blood; but he will not set down the tears. He is gone.'

Her head sagged to her breast and she slept, her breathing light and fluttering, for ten minutes, before rousing drowsily.

'I know no more,' she said as Nish opened his mouth. 'Klarm is in the depths of some catacombs, and the time is now, though I can't tell if he's close by or a hundred leagues away.'

'So he escaped the shadow realm and he still has the tears,' said Maelys. 'Your enemies would pay a fortune to know that.' She got up.

'Let's hope their seers aren't as clear-sighted,' said Nish.

They went with Tulitine to the edge of the copse and watched her make her painful way down the gully.

Maelys said, 'Even if Klarm does turn up, he won't help us, will he?'

'If you were trying to save the world, would you ally with the *weakest* army here?' said Nish, scanning their surroundings and running his fingers through his thinning hair. 'Why isn't anyone moving? Anything would be better than this interminable waiting.'

'It won't be long now. Are you all right? You look terrible.'

'My guts are burning like acid and I want to throw up. I've done everything I could do, Maelys; I've driven myself to the limits of what mind and body can take, and I'm afraid it's not going to be enough. I can't bear to think that Santhenar might end here, *today*, because of something I've done wrong – or failed to do.'

'You can't take that burden on yourself,' she said softly. 'Stilkeen is an immortal *being* – it's bigger than all of us.'

'Someone has to. And what if it *is* the end? How can beautiful Santhenar be destroyed because of something Yalkara did thousands of years ago? I can't come to terms with that.'

'Surely . . .' she began.

'That's what it's come down to, Maelys. It's not right, but Stilkeen has roamed the universe for half of eternity. It must have seen a million worlds, so why would it care about ours? If it gets the pure fire back, it could crush Santhenar the way you or I might swat a fly.'

Shivers ran up and down her back. 'There isn't much hope, is there?'

'Between Vomix and the other armies on the one hand, Stilkeen on the other, and the threat of annihilation from the void, I don't see how there can be. And what if it deliberately drew everyone here so it could destroy all its opponents at once?'

'Why would it do that?' said Maelys.

'I've no idea. We're dealing with a superior *being*. How can we possibly out-think it?'

'We can't. Yggur lost most of his Art just when we needed it most, Tulitine can barely walk, you look like you fell out of your own coffin, and I . . . we need help desperately, Nish.'

'We're not going to get it. We're on our own.'

Psshhhhfffit! With a whispering sigh and a puff of fog that vanished as swiftly as it had appeared, a glassy, bubble-shaped portal opened further up the slope and a small, skinny, horribly scarred and incredibly ugly man stepped out. A very familiar figure that Maelys had never expected to see again – no, *could not possibly* see again.

'Xervish!' she cried, for the man looked exactly like the Xervish Flydd of old, *before* he'd taken renewal. She began to run towards him, but stopped. This had to be an illusion or chimaera created by one of their enemies.

'Wait!' said Nish, who had his sword in hand, 'Who are you? Stay back, Maelys, it could be Yalkara. She once pos-sessed Flydd, remember? Stop right where you are,' he shouted.

'It's me, you bloody moron,' the original Flydd's harsh and acerbic voice was unmistakable. 'Is there another man on Santhenar who could wear this body with pride?'

Maelys, incongruously, giggled. It was Flydd, of course it was, and suddenly the despair lifted. With Flydd at their side, anything was possible, even taking on a *being*.

'Certainly not me,' said Nish, sheathing his sword and looking as though he'd just been relieved of an unbearable burden. 'If I was that ugly I'd sew myself into a warthog's skin and count myself fortunate.'

'Why you obnoxious little sod,' cried Flydd. 'It took me

fifty-six years to look this way, plus the services of the Council of Scrutators' ten best torturers. You're almost as hideous and you can't be thirty-five.'

He came down the hill, swinging the serpent staff with the forked tongue, and Nish ran and embraced him. Flydd returned the hug, though only briefly, then pushed him off. 'Let's not get carried away. I haven't missed you *that* much.'

Flydd embraced Maelys heartily and long, and she knew he was delighted to see her; she also knew that he had a fondness for beautiful young women and, despite his appearance, had no trouble getting them . . . at least, while he had been a scrutator. Before –

Remembering what she'd seen when he had been naked and going through renewal – or rather, what he had lacked – she bit her lip and stepped away.

'Why did you go back to the old Flydd, surr?' she said timidly.

'My renewed body didn't fit properly, and it was giving me all manner of trouble, to say nothing of changing me in ways I didn't like. You must have noticed.'

'No,' said Maelys hastily, 'not at all.'

'Liar,' he said cheerfully. 'Moreover, the ladies weren't nearly as satisfied by the renewed, middle-aged me as they had been by the scrawny old man I'd been fifteen years earlier –'

'Funny that,' said Nish.

Maelys was looking in every direction but at Flydd, her cheeks hot.

'– and since the serpent staff allowed me to make portals,' Flydd went on, giving Nish a keen glance, 'and do one or two other things –'

'You took renewal again,' said Nish.

'I certainly did not; do I look that stupid?'

'Well, since you ask . . .' grinned Nish.

Flydd swiped at his head. Nish ducked.

'I thought I'd try *reverting* the renewal,' said Flydd, 'and to my surprise the staff assisted me.'

'Wasn't that a terrible risk?' said Maelys, remembering the agony he had gone through during renewal. Flydd had barely survived it.

'It was, but I was in such pain I didn't much care whether I lived or died, as long as the pain stopped. The *reversion* wasn't fun either, and it certainly wasn't pretty, but it worked. And most importantly, I got rid of the woman in red,' he muttered. 'There's no one in my mind now except me.'

'But you didn't revert to the er, *old* Flydd you were just before renewal,' said Maelys tactfully.

'You put it so nicely, my dear. He was on his last legs, no use to man or beast, so I allowed the Reversion Spell to run a bit longer than it should have. I wasn't greedy, mind. I didn't want to go back to my youth – I merely returned to fifty-six.'

'You were older than that when we first met, weren't you?' said Nish.

'A year or two,' said Flydd, who seemed very pleased with himself.

'And, er, therefore you would, must have –'

'Yes, I've got back the *equipment* that the Chief Scrutator's torturers cut from me that day on the platform suspended above the rooftops of Fiz Gorgo,' he snapped, 'if it's any of your damned business. And I'm planning to put it to vigorous use once we've cleaned up the little mess down below.'

'I don't want to know about your sordid private life,' said Nish hastily.

'And neither does sweet little Maelys, I'm sure,' said Flydd. 'Look, she's blushing again. I've never met anyone else who colours so easily nor, now that I think about it, so prettily. You could do a lot worse, Nish.'

Nish frowned, looking anywhere but at Maelys, who turned away hastily, her cheeks flaming now.

'What are you talking about?' they both said at the same time.

Flydd gave them a superior smile. 'I'm right; you'll see. Let's go down and you can brief me on what everyone has been up to.'

'I'd like to know what *you've* been up to.'

'There isn't time to tell it twice. Have you got anything to eat? I'd forgotten how hungry this old body gets.'

After gratifying expressions of astonishment at Flydd's reversion from everyone except Malien, who had known the old Flydd well but not met the renewed version, they briefly told him their tales. Maelys noticed that Persia kept staring at Flydd, a wistful yearning in her dark eyes. What was it about the old scoundrel?

'Just as well you brought back chthonic fire,' he said, munching on curled-up shavings of spiced, preserved meat from Malien's stores. It was as black as char, as hard as a lump of wood and so spicy that it lifted the roof off Maelys's mouth, but Flydd ate it with equanimity. 'I didn't find any.'

'Too busy looking after yourself?' said Yggur. 'Having a holiday at our expense?'

The old rivalry between them was as strong as ever, only this time Yggur was at the disadvantage and he did not like it.

'I wouldn't call it a holiday, exactly.' Flydd directed a sympathetic glance at Yggur though, judging by his scowl, he did not appreciate that either. 'I figured I could leave the fire to you. After all, you had a head start.'

'How did you know we were still alive?' said Yggur.

'Several times, when I was using the staff, I picked up

fleeting images of far-off places, such as the Tower of a Thousand Steps and Mistmurk Mountain.'

'Where have you been, anyhow?'

'When I left Roros I made a portal to Blemph, in Faranda, and consulted the greatest Aachim mancers there. They concluded that the serpent staves were linked to the caduceus, and to each other, which should have been obvious, had I thought about it. I then knew you three were alive, and from your destinations you must have been searching for chthonic fire, which freed me to do other things.'

'We tried to go to Blemph from Stassor,' said Maelys, staring at his scarred, familiar face. She'd only known it for a day, yet it seemed more right than the renewed Flydd she'd known for months. He was his old, irascible but kindly self again; the mean streak was no longer evident. 'But the caduceus wouldn't take us there.'

'If I was there at the time, it could not open another portal to the same place.'

'About that . . .' began Nish.

'What?' said Flydd.

'How come you didn't make a portal at the Range of Ruin, or afterwards? You could have saved –'

'Don't you trust me, Nish?' Flydd said mildly.

'Of course I do.'

'Then you shouldn't need to ask. You know that making portals is the greatest and most difficult Art of all.'

'What sort of an answer is that?'

'They're moving,' called Clech from the lookout.

Maelys, Nish, Flydd and Yggur went to the top of the next ridge, and the others followed. Morrelune was below them and to the right, looking much as it had months ago, for in the brilliant sunlight the fire palace Stilkeen had made of it could not be seen clearly.

Maelys squinted at the paved roof of Mazurhize, between the four wisp-watchers, wondering if her family could still be alive, but the blank stones told her nothing.

'Here they come,' said Persia.

On the seaward side of Mazurhize, a large army was moving up the ridge onto the plain and assembling in front of Morrelune. 'Who is it?' said Flydd.

Persia focussed her brass fieldscope. 'It's flying Vomix's standard.'

'His personal standard?' said Flydd. 'Or his banner as the God-Emperor's seneschal for Roros?'

'His personal standard – a spiked fist on a sea of red.'

Persia passed back the fieldscope and Flydd checked the edges of the plain. Maelys waited impatiently, and finally he said, 'The other forces are also coming out. It's going to be a battle of five armies.'

'Plus our mighty force,' said Nish ironically. 'Don't forget us, Flydd.'

Flydd pushed the brass tubes together and handed the fieldscope back to Persia. 'We'd better join them.'

'They'll cut us down!'

'The son of the God-Emperor has to be there,' said Flydd, who seemed unfazed by the overwhelming numbers of the enemy. 'This is your hour, Nish. It's time to stake your claim.'

'I've told you a hundred times, I will not become my father.'

'There's no need to get excited. You promised to over-throw him ten years ago, you've repeated that promise over and again, and you can't retreat now. What kind of message would that send your long-suffering people – that the thugs of the empire had the courage to face Stilkeen for what they could get out of it, but you were too afraid to defend those who put their faith in you?'

Maelys felt for Nish; Flydd had deftly manipulated him into doing what he wanted. And yet, ever since she had helped Nish escape from Mazurhize they had been fighting to reach this point, so why was he hanging back? It wasn't fear of dying, she knew – at least, not for himself.

Nish met her eyes. 'If you get a chance, run for it,' he said quietly. 'We're doomed, but –'

'What do you take me for?' she hissed. 'I'll be standing beside you until the end, whatever it may be . . . and we're going to win!'

The ever-present worries about her family rose again but, Maelys realised, Mazurhize was probably the safest place for them right now.

Feeling a little stronger for Maelys's faith in him, Nish collected his pack and made sure his weapons were in good order. The women and men of his militia shook his hand as he went down the line, and Yulla's troops, mostly veterans of the lyrinx war who were older than he was, clapped him on the back. He swallowed hard and did his best to look confident of victory, though he did not think he was fooling anyone.

As they prepared to march out, Persia fell in behind him, hand on the hilt of her rapier. He looked around, her dark eyes met his, and he had to make amends before it was too late.

'I'm really sorry,' he said.

'Why, Nish?' she said politely.

'For the things I said in Roros, and the way I treated you. I know it was unforgivable –'

She gave him one of those warm, lovely, yet slightly sad smiles; he hadn't seen one in ages. 'I forgave you long ago.'

'But –'

'Sometimes you have an awkward way with words, Nish, but your deeds are clear as crystal.'

He frowned. 'What do you mean?'

'Even after I'd helped Yulla to manipulate you, you risked your life for me at the monastery, and that was too much.'

'Too much?'

'It raised you too far above me. The gap was unbreachable.'

Nish didn't have a clue what she was talking about. 'But . . . you've been so cool to me. I was sure you were still furious.'

'I had to stay cool. I – I cared – *care* too much for you, and it's now clear that it can never be.'

'I don't understand,' he said.

'Perhaps it's just as well.'

He could see the ache in her eyes now. For *him*? 'What will you do afterwards . . .?'

'If we survive?'

'Yes.'

'My seven-year indenture to Yulla ends here, one way or the other, and if I survive, I must make my own way in the world.' She glanced down, gnawing her lip. 'I'm really afraid of that. Yulla has looked after me ever since I . . . came to her, but who will take care of me once I leave? The world can be a cruel place when you're by yourself.'

It was a side of the strong, competent Persia that he had not seen before, an unexpected fragility, and again he wondered what had happened to her when she was young. 'If *I* survive, you must come –'

'That is kind of you, but no.'

'Well, thank you for being my bodyguard,' he said after a pause, 'though I don't think your skills can save me this time.'

The sadness was back in her eyes. 'No, I don't think they can. We'd better go down.'

At the head of the troop, Clech was fiddling with a long lance. He raised it high and a yellow banner fluttered from its end, with a single silver star in the middle.

'Sewed it myself,' grinned Clech. 'What's an army without a standard to fight under?'

'Thank you,' said Nish. 'Lead on.'

Clech, who was hardly limping at all now, led the tiny force down the ridge, onto the plain and along it towards Morrelune, heading for a large space between Vomix's huge army and the sizeable one of the mercenary adventurer, Hackel. Two smaller armies stood further away, one led by Seneschal Lidgeon from Fadd, and another that no one could identify, while the fifth force, the Imperial Guard of some eight hundred men commanded by General Nosby, stood closest to Morrelune.

'This is suicide, Flydd,' said Nish.

'Keep going,' said Flydd, unperturbed. 'I'll think you'll find Vomix is more worried than you are.'

'He couldn't be!'

From this close, even in bright sunlight, Morrelune's nine levels, its broad encircling steps and towering columns, and the heaven-piercing spire on top, were wreathed in Stilkeen's orange and yellow fire. One edge of the Sacred Lake could just be seen behind it, and the mountains beyond that.

As his little force wheeled and moved between the mighty ones, there came a chorus of catcalls and jeers from Vomix's army.

'Ignore them,' Nish said over his shoulder. 'They don't know what *we* know.'

Thankfully, no one asked him to explain, since there was nothing behind his brave words.

Vomix trotted his horse to the fore, glaring at Nish across

a hundred spans of paved plain, and then at Maelys, to his left. Nish felt a tremble beginning in his right knee, and had to clench his injured thigh until it burned, to stiffen his leg.

'I'll *have* you, when I'm done with him,' said Vomix to Maelys, and his grotesquely scarred face broke into a sickening leer. 'And you,' he said to Persia.

Maelys choked down on her instinctive cry, swayed, but managed to stand firm. Nish was glad she had; if she had broken, he did not think he could have defied the brute. Persia stiffened but said nothing.

Vomix raised the arm tipped with the triangular spike, which was stained with old brown blood – monks' blood, presumably. A trumpet blasted; his army performed a right turn, all six thousand men at once, and the front three rows lowered their lances. The army moved slowly forwards, and the front line began curving around from either end to encircle Nish's force.

They'll cut us down, he thought, then seize the fire and offer it to Stilkeen. We've lost before we begin.

'Hold your nerve,' Flydd said quietly.

'If you've got any kind of a plan, now would be a good time to reveal it,' said Yggur.

'I was waiting to see what Stilkeen would do,' said Flydd, 'but all right.'

He moved back into the open space behind Nish's troops, lifted his serpent staff above his head, then slammed it down so hard that it cracked a paving stone.

'Flydd,' Nish gasped. 'What are you doing?'

It was a direct challenge, not just to Vomix and the other generals, but to Stilkeen itself, and he turned towards the fire palace, expecting the *being* to fly forth in world-shattering wrath.

It did not. However, with a rumble and a roar, with flashes of lightning at the points of the compass and a rolling heave of the ground beneath them, an enormous portal formed behind Flydd, a shimmering circle a good ten spans in diameter. It was mist-grey in the centre but crackling with static electricity around its periphery.

Vomix's horse reared up onto its back legs, pawing at the air and whinnying shrilly, and he struggled to control it. His army stopped abruptly, staring at the uncanny sight in wonder and unease. The empire had been taught that all mancery was controlled by the God-Emperor or his appointed servants, yet Flydd had just worked the mightiest Art of all – portal making. What would he do next?

'Cut them down, you swine!' Vomix roared.

The front line of his army did not move.

'What's Flydd up to?' said Yggur.

'I haven't the faintest idea,' said Nish.

And then, from within the portal, he heard the rhythmic tread of a host of marching soldiers, and shortly a ten-wide rank of tall, dark-haired men came forth. They had faint crests over the tops of their heads and exceptionally long fingers that wrapped all the way around the hilts of their swords. Their leader was young and burly, dark of skin and eye, and carried a blade that must have been a span long.

'When the empire is held in thrall by scoundrels,' said Flydd in an amplified voice that echoed back from the surrounding ranges, 'one must look outside for aid. And so I have.'

'Why, you old villain,' cried Nish. 'Why didn't you tell us what you'd been up to?'

'There wouldn't have been any surprise,' said Tulitine. 'Nor any theatre – and at moments like these, theatre matters more than might.'

Flydd boomed. 'One thousand Aachim from Faranda, led by Lord Garthor.'

'Take Nish!' Vomix bellowed.

Flydd saluted him ironically. 'Your army is too gutless.'

And so they proved to be, for Vomix's army still hesitated and the opportunity to crush Nish's force was lost. Half of the thousand Aachim had come forth already, formidable fighting men in armour that would repel most sword blows, and even longbow arrows.

When the last had emerged, the portal sphinctered shut, reopened and more Aachim marched out in a swirl of fog, led by a compact man with flame-red hair.

'The Aachim of Clan Elienor, numbering four hundred, from Shazmak,' Flydd announced gleefully. 'Under the command of Yrael.'

Malien let out a glad cry, for Clan Elienor was her clan. As she ran to Yrael, the sun caught her age-faded hair and, momentarily, it flamed the same colour as his.

'Karan's hair was just that colour,' said Yggur in a husky voice. 'It so reminds me of her . . .'

'Elienor are a brave and noble clan,' said Nish, 'And I remember Yrael well. With his people at my side, I can hope again.'

Vomix met Flydd's eyes across a hundred spans of paving. Flydd sketched him an exaggerated bow, withdrew the serpent staff from the cracked paving and deliberately turned his back.

'Take him down!' cried Vomix to his archers, enraged by the implication that he posed no threat at all.

Before they could do so, the Aachim formed into their deadly flying wedge formation, pointed directly at Vomix's position, and he stuttered, 'H-hold your fire!'

Every eye in every army was now on Flydd as he sauntered to his right and created a second portal, as large as the first but egg-shaped and green. Who would come forth this time?

The marching footsteps were heavier, slower, and less

515

rhythmical, but nothing could be seen within, for this portal was full of billowing steam which gushed out like a geyser. As it parted, Nish caught a glimpse of a beautiful, forested world, and when he smelled its sweet, spicy air, his heart leapt.

'Five hundred lyrinx, from the world of Tallallame,' Flydd announced.

Hundreds of soldiers cried out; the entire mass of Vomix's army swayed backwards; further off, the smaller army that no one could identify turned and began to creep away.

'Boo!' roared Flydd, his voice echoing off the mountains, and the retreating army bolted.

'Hold firm!' bellowed Vomix. 'Any man who moves will be shot.'

'Violence is the only hold you have over them,' said Flydd. 'It won't be enough this time, Seneschal.'

'And you would begin the lyrinx war all over again,' cried Vomix. 'Truly, the God-Emperor was right to condemn you as a traitor.'

'Jal-Nish only did one thing in the war,' Flydd said coldly. 'He ran like the cur he is, abandoning his loyal army to annihilation.' He turned away. 'Come forth, people of Tallallame, in friendship!'

And out they came, a seven-wide rank of huge winged humanoids as tall as bears, with red or green crests running across the top of their enormous heads and chameleon colours shimmering across their armoured outer skin. Their mouths were great with teeth, their hands were clawed, and their folded wings were leathery.

'Stand firm!' Vomix ordered his quailing men. 'Five hundred lyrinx are nothing to us.'

'They'll tear Santhenar apart,' cried a soldier at the front.

'It took us a hundred and fifty years to beat them last time,' said another.

'Lyrinx!' It roared through the ranks of troops like a tidal wave. 'They eat their victims. Run!'

'Stand your ground!' bellowed Vomix.

It was no use. Panic had set in and, though most of his soldiers did hold their positions, many hundreds broke, fled across the plain and disappeared into the scrub. None of Nish's troops moved, and he was tempted to give Vomix a derisory finger, but restrained himself.

Once all the lyrinx had marched out, they took position beside the Aachim. At their head was a wingless male, smaller than most, and Nish felt his spirits lift at the sight of him, and his consort who prowled back and forth beside him. Though she had glorious, shimmering wings, she lacked the thick, armoured outer skin of the other lyrinx – hers was fine and transparent, revealing the almost human underlying skin. The male's eyes, and hers, searched the plain, he saw Nish and they hurried across.

'Well met, old friend,' said the male, extending a monstrous hand, the claws politely retracted.

'Ryll,' said Nish, so moved that he felt tears sting his eyes, for they had been enemies all through the lyrinx war, only to become friends by the manner of its ending. He shook Ryll's hand gingerly for, even when the lyrinx held back, his grip was crushingly strong.

'And Liett! I never expected to see either of you again, but thank you, thank you.' Nish shook hands with Liett, then, without thinking, embraced her.

The lyrinx army let out a rumbling growl, all as one, at his boldness, and Nish stepped back hastily. What had he been thinking?

Liett cuffed him across the chest, knocking him off his feet, but picked him up at once and dusted him down, grinning so broadly that she could have swallowed his head.

'It is very good to see you,' she said, then lowered her voice.

'Don't ever do that again, for Ryll is a jealous husband and I cannot answer for his fury, should he see an *old human* fondling me in such an intimate manner. Aren't you, Ryll?'

'Beg pardon?' said Ryll, pretending not to hear.

'A jealous husband,' roared Liett, flashing out her beautiful wings in a fierce display.

'Oh, insanely jealous,' grinned Ryll, shaking Nish's hand again with both of his own. 'When we've cleaned up this rabble, what say you and I slip away for a jar or two?'

'Nothing could give me greater pleasure,' said Nish wholeheartedly then, glancing sideways at Liett, 'Er, assuming you *can* get away.'

'Five hundred lyrinx,' Flydd repeated, louder than before. 'And as fighters, one lyrinx is worth two ordinary soldiers.'

'Four!' snapped Liett.

Ryll bowed to Flydd and said in a booming voice, 'We have answered your call, to show our gratitude for the way we were treated by you and Nish in the past, and to demonstrate our cousinship with all the human species of Santhenar – now and in the future.'

The portal closed, but Flydd was not finished yet. He now created a smaller one between the Aachim and lyrinx.

'Who on earth can this be?' said Maelys softly.

'I can't imagine,' said Nish.

The new portal was only half the size of the others, and the air eddying from it felt bitterly cold and carried whirling flakes of snow that swiftly melted in the warm air. From within, all he could hear was the faint rustle of cloth on cloth, and a melodic jingling.

A golden-skinned man appeared, no taller than Nish but reed-slender. A woman marched beside him, only Maelys's height, though she was slim of hip and narrow of chest.

'I am Galgilliel,' said the man.

'And I am Lainor,' said the woman. 'Our three hundred

and fifty fighting men and women are here to represent the sole survivors of the Faellem species. We remained behind in our southern forests two centuries ago when Faelamor led the rest of our kind back to Tallallame, and to self-immolation when they discovered what her folly had done to our beautiful world.' She came across to Ryll, who was twice her height and ten times her bulk, and extended her hand. 'You are the custodians of Tallallame now, and I am sure no one could take better care of it.'

'We're slowly exterminating the void vermin that infested the world at that time,' said Ryll, 'though the task will take many generations.'

'Do you ever see any trace of our ancestral selves?' said Lainor. 'The Faellem who regressed to barbarism long ago? Or have they vanished as well?'

'They are shy and easily frightened,' said Ryll, 'but we see them from time to time.'

'We would so love to see Tallallame again,' she said wistfully. 'Might we – one day –?'

'Perhaps,' said Ryll firmly. 'But not yet.'

The portal appeared to close but reopened at once, now rimed with ice. It had gone a frosty blue inside and Nish made out the clatter of wooden-soled sandals.

'The sorcerer Zofloc . . . *reanimated*, and eighty Whelm,' Flydd announced.

'You old devil!' cried Yggur admiringly. 'You have been busy.'

'But Zofloc was dead,' whispered Maelys, remembering the way her skin had crept at his touch. 'Yggur, you said his fall killed him.'

'Flydd did say *reanimated*,' said Yggur.

'The way the dead in the Tower of a Thousand Steps were brought back to life?' asked Maelys, shuddering. 'By shooting them with needles of distilled fire?'

'Let's wait and see, shall we?' said Yggur.

The clatter grew louder and out lurched Zofloc, who looked almost as horrible as Maelys's other nemesis, dead Phrune. The sorcerer's grey skin, the colour of lead, was touched with writhing worms of off-white fire; his scarlet, protruding eyeballs sparkled from the twinklestones still stuck to them, while jagged pieces of bone stuck out in a crest from the back of his evacuated skull.

'I expect he carried a needle of his distilled fire,' said Yggur, 'and plunged it into himself as he lay dying.'

A good distance behind Zofloc, and looking at him askance, came a disorderly throng of Whelm clad in loincloths or ragged robes. The men carried jag-swords and the women long stilettos, but they had a forlorn, hangdog air about them.

'I thought the Whelm were a proud people,' said Nish, who had not encountered them before.

'They are when they have a master,' said Yggur. 'Whelm are born to serve and without a master they are miserable creatures. The Numinator must have cast them off.'

The portal closed, but reopened almost at once, and out of it stepped a woman of Nish's age and height, at least seven months pregnant, and an older man who had only one hand. Nish recognised the older man at once, but the woman was so changed that he stared at her for a full minute before he knew who she was, for her long dark hair was streaked with white, and she was rather plumper than when he had known her.

'Tiaan?' said Nish.

She also looked at him without recognition, then smiled and came across.

'No one has heard anything about you for ten years,' said Nish, embracing her awkwardly, since her bump got in the way. 'We were afraid that Father had ordered you killed.'

520

'I'm sure he would have,' said Tiaan, a dimple flashing in her cheek, 'had I not foolishly destroyed all the nodes, thus delivering the gift of Santhenar to him. He hunted us down, Father and me – you remember Merryl?'

'Very well,' said Nish, smiling and shaking hands. He'd always liked Tiaan's father.

'Jal-Nish threw us in prison down south, near our old manufactory,' Tiaan went on, 'along with my mother, poor old Marnie. But six months later we were set free and I was given work as an artisan. Marnie and Father got back together, but . . .'

'She was a terrible wife,' said Merryl, 'as you told me she would be.'

'Marnie ran away within the month,' said Tiaan, 'but I have a good man now, and two children, and Merryl.'

'You look happy,' said Nish, pleased for her. 'In all the time I knew you, you never seemed happy.'

'I wasn't. I was always searching for something, but until I found Father at the victory feast, I did not know what it was.'

'Yet you, alone of all of us who sat down to the feast that day ten years ago, were the one to find happiness. How oddly things turn out. What are you doing here?'

'So pregnant, you mean?' said Tiaan. 'I destroyed the nodes and made it possible for your father to become God-Emperor, and I've never stopped regretting that stupidity. Even if I cannot undo it, I had to be here.'

'What about your children?'

'If I don't come back? I pray that I will, but if the worst happens Marnie will look after them – it's what she does best. I had to help make up for the ill I've done, Nish. You do understand, don't you?'

'Of course,' he said. 'Better than anyone, and I'm very glad to have you with me.'

FORTY-ONE

How had Flydd done so much, so quickly, Maelys wondered. But then, who better to pull such an unlikely alliance together, since he'd spent the last years of the war doing just that. It was another reason for *reverting* to the old Flydd that people knew and trusted. No matter how persuasive the renewed man might have been, he'd looked, and had been, too different.

Stilkeen had not emerged from the palace but, within thirty minutes, the military arrangements outside had been transformed. Vomix and Seneschal Lidgeon had amalgamated their reduced forces, putting Vomix in command of an army no less powerful than he'd had before.

Hackel had lost few men, since his mercenaries had come to plunder the wealth of the God-Emperor, and their greed for loot outweighed their unease. Nosby's fiercely loyal Imperial Guard had stood firm to the man.

Nish's allies now numbered two and a half thousand, a powerful force, but still greatly outnumbered. Maelys stood behind him, covertly watching these famous names from the pages of the Histories. They might have been enemies once, but all seemed to be old friends now, and she felt quite intimidated by them.

'V-Vomix has raised a blue truce flag,' called Persia. 'He wants to parley.'

'Don't go near him, Nish,' said Maelys. 'He means to kill you.'

'Hackel and Nosby are also raising parley flags,' said Persia.

'The real enemy is still inside the palace,' said Nish. 'I have to go, but I won't be taking the pure fire, so killing me will do Vomix no good.'

'It'll rid the empire of the one legitimate heir,' said Maelys.

Nish glanced at the sun, which hung not far above the mountains to the west. 'It's getting late, and we've got to take the fire to Stilkeen before it comes after us. I'm going to the parley.'

'Not alone,' said Persia.

'How many is Vomix bringing?'

She looked through her fieldscope. 'Just himself, a standard bearer and a witness.'

'Then I must do the same.'

'But –'

'Ranking my allies behind me would mean that I lacked confidence in myself,' said Nish. 'I will march behind my standard bearer, Clech, with one old friend as witness. Maelys, will you stand beside me?'

'Me?' she squeaked. Vomix had suffered excruciating agony because of her, and she knew he wanted to make her suffer equally.

'I need you.'

Maelys could not imagine why, but since he had asked, how could she refuse? She took a deep breath. 'Then I will come.'

Clech led them out, and she felt very small and conspicuous in the vast paved space between the armies. On her left,

Vomix's flapping standard sounded like a whip being cracked; to her right, Hackel's pennant showed a black jackal on a blue background. The officer in the white uniform was General Nosby, behind the flag of the Imperial Guard. Renowned for his loyalty to the God-Emperor, Nosby, at least, was unlikely to be after Nish's blood.

They came together. Nosby was a tall, bluff man with white hair and pouched eyes. He had lost a lot of weight recently and did not look as though he'd slept in a week, which was understandable. If Vomix took over, he would slaughter everyone loyal to the former God-Emperor, including Nosby and his entire family.

Hackel the Jackal was lean, wiry, and tremendously hairy. His yellow-brown eyes burned with a hunter's intensity, he had a snout of a nose and his underslung jaw was studded with canine teeth. When he moved, it was with an alert, eager step, as though he were straining at the leash, longing to run down his prey. On his left hip was a short sword with tendrils of white fumes drifting up from its scabbard; a small leather bag the size of a wine skin swung from his right hip.

Seneschal Vomix strode up, brandishing his spike-ended right arm, and Maelys stared at him in horror. He had never been a handsome man but, after the touch of her taphloid had inverted his aura months ago, his face resembled a painting that had been ripped into pieces and rudely pasted back together.

'We meet again, Cryl-Nish,' he said, bowing ironically, but his eyes were on her, and they said, *You'll pay for what you did to me.* He extended his left hand.

'Don't bother,' said Nish. 'What do you want?'

Vomix's eyes glittered and he dropped his hand. 'The fifteenth day is nearly up. Do you have the pure fire?'

'Do you?' said Nish, looking at Vomix, and then Hackel, and Nosby.

'I don't know what chthonic fire is,' said Nosby wearily. 'I am here to defend my liege lord's realm, as I swore to do.'

'Then it's between us three,' said Vomix. 'Shall we draw lots to be the first to approach Stilkeen? Or do you claim that right, Cryl-Nish, as the son of the God-Emperor?'

Maelys could read Nish's hesitation. Stilkeen was an enigma; could its word be relied upon, or was it also planning revenge? And how would it react if the chthonic fire they gave it was not pure enough?

If its offer was genuine, the first person to bring it the true fire would be rewarded beyond his dreams, though, with Vomix and Hackel waiting outside, he might not enjoy it long.

Yet if Stilkeen had revenge in mind, it might be better to allow Vomix or Hackel to go first. It was unlikely that they had found true fire, and if they had not, let its wrath fall upon them. However, if they *had* found true fire, the game was lost.

'I do not claim that right,' said Nish at last.

His brow shone with sweat; he was afraid he'd made the wrong decision. Maelys noted that both Vomix and Hackel were smiling. They had also read him.

'Then it will be lots,' said Vomix, drawing some tally sticks from a pocket.

'Put them away,' said Hackel. 'I enjoy a wager, but I won't have anyone tilting the odds against me.'

Vomix pocketed the tally sticks. 'Do you have a better alternative?'

Hackel considered the standard bearers and witnesses. 'You have the only guileless face among us,' he said to Maelys. 'Draw a large circle on the ground.'

With her knife, Maelys described a wobbly circle on the paving stones.

'Pick up three pieces of gravel, the same size, and mark them with a V, N and H.'

'I'll make my own mark,' said Vomix.

'The devil you will,' said Hackel. 'No one touches them but the girl.'

Maelys scouted around until she found three suitable pieces of gravel, inscribed the letters on them and held them out so Nish, Vomix and Hackel could inspect them.

'We'll walk away,' said Hackel. 'You, girl, are to stand in the circle, shake the gravel in your hand and hurl it upwards. The piece of gravel that falls closest to the centre of the circle indicates the first to confront Stilkeen, and the furthest piece, last.'

'What if she cheats?' Vomix said sourly.

'How can she?' said Hackel.

A layer of grey cloud passed across the setting sun, and in the sudden gloom the fire palace flared and flickered. Maelys did not want to go near it. Was she going to meet the death the Pit of Possibilities had predicted, in Morrelune?

She hurled the gravel straight up and moved out of the way. One piece fell inside the circle, a second near the rim, and the third, further off.

'An unambiguous result,' said Hackel. 'Pick up the stones, one at a time.'

Hackel, Nish and Vomix approached. The outer stone was marked H.

'Oh, well,' Hackel said philosophically.

The second stone had a V on it. And the third, an N.

'So Cryl-Nish approaches Stilkeen first,' said Vomix. 'And I've a feeling the reward is not going to be to his liking. We will assemble outside Morrelune in ten minutes, then go in together.'

*

Nish led his allies forwards: Yggur, Tulitine and Flydd, Maelys, Malien and Persia, Garthor representing the Aachim, Ryll and Liett the lyrinx, Galgilliel the Faellem, and Zofloc the Whelm.

Nosby was waiting below the broad steps of Morrelune with two uniformed officers. Vomix came marching up from the left with six men, and Hackel from the right with his four. They stopped, eyeing each other warily.

Maelys tried to conceal herself behind Yggur, though she knew Vomix could see her. Surely that unpleasantly thick and rancid smell emanating from him, like the fumes from a cauldron of congealed blood, indicated that there was something desperately sick inside him.

'Shall we go in?' said Hackel with a toothy gambler's smile.

He's no more to be trusted than Vomix, Maelys thought.

They formed into four separate ranks and prepared to march into Morrelune together. As they reached the first step a current of warm air rushed past them, the structural flames stood out more brightly, and Maelys heard a distant roaring, like the inward breath of a furnace.

'Do you think it's wise to carry the caduceus and the serpent staffs into Morrelune?' said Malien in a low voice.

'Good point,' said Flydd. 'Give them here.'

He fitted the two serpent staffs around the caduceus, as it had been when Stilkeen first appeared and, with a flash of red fire, they welded themselves back in place. He raised the complete caduceus, struggling with its weight, climbed the steps and slammed the tip into the marble paving stone directly before the open doorway of Morrelune.

Thunder rolled, cracks zigzagged out from the riven stone, and Maelys shuddered. How would Stilkeen meet this challenge?

'Be very careful now,' Yggur said in a low voice. 'Close to Stilkeen, our Arts may not work properly – or at all.'

Flames leaped up from the palace, higher than ever, but they gave forth neither heat nor any smell of burning. They weren't eating the stone away, they were a replacement for it, and they appeared to burn without ever consuming anything. Maelys did not want to go near the place.

The hum rose again and a white barrier appeared behind Morrelune, like the one Nish had mentioned seeing earlier, through Persia's fieldscope. It slanted up from the ground to the sky until it blocked out the mountains completely, then its dazzling whiteness slowly faded to translucency and moving shadows appeared behind it – the blurred shapes of beasts and monstrosities.

'There's thousands of them,' Maelys whispered, pressing her hand against her fluttering heart.

'Millions and billions uncounted,' said Yggur. 'We're seeing the barrier that protects our world from the void, made visible. Stilkeen threatened to empty the void into Santhenar if we failed to give it the true fire. And if it does –'

In the unseen distance, something made a low, purring yet mechanical hum.

'Do you think that could be Klarm?' said Nish, looking around.

'There's no reason to suppose it is,' said Flydd. 'Nor that he'd help us.'

Maelys covertly studied the other three leaders, trying to guess what they would do. Vomix was nervously licking his ruined lips; Hackel's broad and unwavering smile might have been stretched out with hooks, while Nosby's cheeks were bloodless and he was struggling to control a twitch near his left eye.

'We'd better go in,' said Flydd casually. If he was anxious about meeting Stilkeen, his gaunt, ugly face did not show it.

'You first,' muttered Vomix.

He was afraid, which did not make Maelys feel any better.

Flydd returned Vomix's earlier bow, mockingly, and headed for the entrance of the palace. Maelys followed, keeping so close to Nish that her shoulder touched his upper arm. The flaming walls, floor and ceiling burned bright but cold and she felt no more than a tickle as she moved into the fire – it was not of this world, barely here. Had Stilkeen shifted the dimensions slightly to make it so? Her mind whirled at the thought; other dimensions were, like Yggur's dimensionless boxes, beyond her imagining.

Beneath the fire, the original stone floor appeared solid, though when she stepped on it her foot came down with a thud; it was slightly lower than it seemed. Stepping carefully, she crept along the grand entrance hall.

Every so often, as if from the corner of her eye, she caught another glimpse of the translucent barrier and the shadows moving in the void behind it. How much would it take to release that alien horde into Santhenar, and if they got in, could humanity survive? The lyrinx war had begun after a mere handful of lyrinx escaped from the void, and it had lasted a hundred and fifty years.

Ahead now, at the heart of the palace, stood Jal-Nish's majestic audience chamber, a vast oval space a hundred spans by sixty, with its ceiling soaring fifteen spans above them. Sweeping curves of slender golden columns marked the edges of the chamber, the flames coiling in impenetrable walls between them. All was monumental, eerie and beautiful. This was a room suited to a God-Emperor, or to a *being*.

'There it is,' breathed Nish as something moved at the far end of the chamber where his father's throne had once stood.

Stilkeen hung suspended in webs of fire and shadow,

which had the lazy swirl of flames seen through the door of a furnace. Yalkara had said that it could take any aspect imaginable, but it wore much the same guise as when it had abducted Jal-Nish – the broad, winged skull, the membrane-covered yellow eyes and the massively muscled body. Maelys wondered why it still looked the same. Could it be trapped in this one form? Might that be a weakness they could use against it?

'Why the fire webs?' said Tulitine.

'In its severed state, the physical worlds cause it great pain –' said Yggur.

'And me,' she said wryly.

'– which gets worse the longer it spends here,' Yggur continued. 'But by *shifting* the palace slightly, to keep our physical world at a distance, and remaking the building in flame, Stilkeen can remain here relatively pain-free. You'd better give me the taphloid,' he said quietly to Maelys.

'Why?' She didn't want to give it up. It was the only protection she had.

'When you're wearing it, Stilkeen won't be able to see you.'

Maelys eyed the great creature hanging in its webs. Its eyes seemed to be looking directly at her. 'I don't want it to see me.'

'It has to. Give it here.'

She handed the taphloid over and Yggur moved aside so that Nish and Maelys were at the head of the procession.

Stilkeen stirred as they approached, raised its needle-toothed head, and its voice had the thundering reverberation of air being pumped into a furnace.

'Who brings the *uncorrupted* chthonic fire will be rewarded beyond their dreams. Who keeps true fire from Stilkeen will suffer such agonies as no human has ever felt. Have you brought the fire?'

When Nish didn't move or speak, Flydd nudged him in the middle of the back. Nish squared his broad shoulders and stepped forwards, putting on a show of confidence he could not be feeling. He bowed to Stilkeen, though not in subservience; rather, as one equal to another. Maelys was amazed that he could do so; she was so afraid that she would have fallen on her face.

'Lord Stilkeen,' said Nish sonorously, 'we have brought you fire from three sources, as pure and white as we could find, and preserved as best we could. We cannot tell if it is the fire you seek.'

'Bring it to me,' said Stilkeen, and Maelys thought she saw a trace of eagerness in its small yellow eyes as the nictitating membranes swept back and forth across them, protecting them from contact with even the air of the real world.

Yggur handed three flat black circles, the dimensionless boxes, to Maelys. Each had a different marking on the outside, to show where the contents had been found.

'Why are you giving them to me?' she squawked.

'You're the best person to do it,' he said quietly. 'Stilkeen won't see you as a threat, since –'

'I can't use my gift! What if it doesn't like what's in the boxes?'

'I don't know what it will do, Maelys, but rest assured, it'll happen to us as well.'

That was not comforting.

'Give them to me,' said Nish, whose knuckles were white on the hilt of his blade. 'It's my job. I don't want Maelys –'

'Yggur's right, Nish,' Flydd said quietly. 'She's the best chance we've got.'

Maelys felt better for knowing that Nish was worried about her, though only a little. She took a small step, then another. How was one supposed to address a *being*, anyhow? Would it be insulted if she got it wrong, or wouldn't it care?

531

'Oh Great Stilkeen, Roamer of the Celestial Realms –' she began.

'Give – me – white – fire,' said Stilkeen, reaching out. The webs of fire and shadow must have been sticky, for they made zipping sounds as its movements separated them.

And despite the protection of the webs, it was in pain. Maelys could sense its torment, as she had the first time she'd seen it. 'I hope these can ease your suffering.' She bowed low.

Stilkeen regarded her silently, then reached out with one enormous hand.

'Th-this fire came from the Tower of a Thousand Steps,' said Maelys. 'I found it deep in the icy foundations.' She handed Stilkeen the first dimensionless box.

Stilkeen plunged one hand in through the blackness – clearly it had no fear of being enveloped by the box – and plucked out a fistful of white fire, which it tossed into the air and swallowed. Throwing the dimensionless box to one side, it said, 'Not pure enough.'

She handed it the second box. 'This fire was clinging to the shattered casket Yalkara hid long ago, deep below Mistmurk Mountain.'

Stilkeen put its thick lips to the box and sucked out the fire. 'Purer, but not pure.'

Her skin crawled. This was their last chance, and if it failed, then what? She gave it the third box. 'This fire I found on the ruined world of Aachan, where it had been taken up by toadstools growing in a canyon.'

Stilkeen hooked a nail into the nonexistent edge of the dimensionless box and peeled it apart into two identical black circles. Fire flickered between them but it was no longer white – it had gone a raw, bleeding red. After studying it carefully, Stilkeen put one black circle over the other until they fused into one, sealing in the fire, then crushed the dimensionless box in its fist until it vanished.

'Your passage from Aachan corrupted the white fire and rendered it useless. Is that all?'

Dread was now an icy waterfall down Maelys's back. 'There is more on Aachan. You can easily –'

'Stilkeen cannot go to Aachan; and fire cannot be brought from Aachan without becoming corrupted.' It looked her up and down, incuriously. 'As you tried honestly, you will not be consumed immediately. You may yet serve.'

FORTY-TWO

Nish swallowed the lump in his throat as Maelys shuffled away from Stilkeen. He had been so afraid for her that he could hardly breathe. When she reached him he took her upper arm and drew her gently backwards, and the rest of his company moved with them. Yggur slid the taphloid into her hand and the *being's* gaze slipped off her onto Nish, then to Hackel and Vomix.

'Well?' it said.

Hackel glanced at Vomix, who did not speak.

'I too have found white fire,' said Hackel, putting his hand into the bag slung on his belt. 'I took it from the topmost chamber of Yalkara's abandoned fortress, Havissard, many years ago. I did not know what it was, and I have always kept it in the sapphire case in which I found it. If it was pure then, it should be pure still.'

Stilkeen's yellow eyes narrowed to points. 'In *Havissard*?'

'Just so.'

'Bring me the case.'

Surreptitiously, Hackel signed behind him to his men. What was he up to?

From his bag, he withdrew a rectangular blue case, like a jewel box, and slunk towards Stilkeen like the jackal that was his namesake. Nish edged backwards until he felt Flydd's hand touch his shoulder.

'Don't move a hair,' whispered Flydd.

Hackel's boots appeared to skim the flame floor without touching the solid stone beneath. He went to his knees before Stilkeen, bowing so low that it seemed insolent, and raising the case above his head. As Stilkeen reached for it, Hackel's thumb slid across a projection in its base.

The lid of the case flipped up and something exploded out of it, unzipping and expanding at colossal speed – a light-touched net that unfolded in the air, soaring up and over Stilkeen to envelop him, and every winking shard of light reflecting from it marked a little tri-pronged barb. The instant it touched, Stilkeen shrieked and began to writhe in agony.

Hackel's men stormed the webs of fire and he whipped out a fuming sword that was similarly light-touched. He was leaping up to thrust it into the *being's* throat when Stilkeen dashed the net aside. Red welts were rising all over its hand and arm where the barbs had touched it, the points concentrating the pain of contact with the physical world. Had the net enveloped the *being* completely, it might have been rendered helpless by the pain.

Its left arm lengthened; its hand expanded enormously and shot towards Hackel, catching him immovably around the chest. His fuming sword fell, repelling the flames in a circle as it struck the floor. Stilkeen's right hand became a hammer that went up, then slammed down onto the first soldier as if driving a nail, smashing him into a smear on the floor. It whacked another five times, finishing the others, before pulling back into a normal hand.

The room was silent now. As a demonstration of power, it had been terrifyingly convincing.

Hackel tried to smile. 'It was worth the gamble.'

'Was – it?' Stilkeen said in a staccato voice, as if every word hurt now. It closed its enormous fist as if squeezing a lemon, and when no more red sludge could be squeezed out of Hackel it tossed the crushed bone-bag aside.

Nish avoided looking at the mess. Their fate hung on Stilkeen's slightest whim, and no one knew what might set the *being* off.

'Does – anyone – else – have – fire?' said Stilkeen, rubbing the welts and twitching.

Vomix's men were backing away. Where was he? In the confusion, he had slipped out, abandoning them. 'You – red-haired – man. Does – your – master – have – fire?'

'No,' whispered the red-haired officer. 'Seneschal Vomix . . .' He licked dry, flaking lips. 'He planned to steal it from Nish.'

Stilkeen transformed an arm into a scythe and cut the officer and his men down before they could move.

'Anyone – fire?' repeated Stilkeen. Its eyes narrowed; it was looking behind Nish.

Outside, something hummed over the paved plain, then back the way it had come. It can only be Klarm, Nish thought. In our most desperate hour, he comes. But the hum faded and disappeared.

'Master!' cried a harsh, dead voice. 'My new master.'

The reanimated Zofloc was lurching forwards, carrying a small round glass flask whose contents were bubbling.

'What – have – you – there?' said Stilkeen.

'White fire, Master, purified of all baseness and corruption. I distilled it myself.'

'You – presume! How – could – you – know – what – was – corrupt?' Stilkeen's mouth opened and closed; little flames shivered up and down its throat. It shook its blistered arm, making a faint moaning sound.

'Try it, Master.'

Stilkeen swirled the flask, tasted some distilled fire on a finger and spat it against a column. Pink flame belched up. Stilkeen dropped the flask on the floor, put a huge foot on it and smashed it. With the other foot, it did the same to the sorcerer, sending squirts of Zofloc in several directions. One splattered the lower third of General Nosby's white uniform.

Its feet returned to their normal size; Stilkeen swung back into its webs and hung there, shivering and wincing. Its small eyes turned to General Nosby. 'And – you?'

'I command the God-Emperor's Imperial Guard, Your Highness,' said Nosby, looking sick. 'I am here to protect my God-Emperor.'

Stilkeen closed one claw upon another and an image of Jal-Nish was painted on the air before them. His father's naked body was the mottled blue-green colour of a month-old corpse, and it had been strung up, unmasked and upside-down, from the ceiling of the ninth level of Morrclune. The seeping mouth was clustered with flies, as were the ruined nose, empty eye socket and the hideous scars made by a lyrinx's claws. Even with the tears, he had never been able to heal himself, and Nish couldn't bear to look.

'Poor Father. He must have suffered terribly.'

'So have my family, and thousands of others,' said Maelys coolly. 'Your father made his own choices, while they suffered simply because he ordered it.'

'Even so,' said Nish. 'He was my father.'

'That – *thing* – call – himself – God-Emperor?' said Stilkeen.

'He was to me,' Nosby said, clearly shaken to see his master's great power and presence reduced to nothing.

'No – God-Emperor,' said Stilkeen. 'Just – pitiful, mortal – man.'

The image faded and its eyes moved back and forth over

the survivors. Nish wished he'd run while he had the chance. Stilkeen pulled at a length of the flame-and-shadow web, bound it around its blistered hand and arm, and pressed it down until it could barely be seen. Its pain appeared to ease.

'You have no more fire to offer?' said Stilkeen, speaking smoothly again.

'We searched everywhere,' said Nish. 'There *was* no pure fire.'

'Yet it exists, not far away,' said Stilkeen. 'It will be preserved in a vessel made of corundite, the only substance that can maintain it uncorrupted. I know the pure fire exists; I can *feel* it, but corundite does not permit me to locate it.' Its eyes narrowed, the needle teeth slid seamlessly together. 'After the creatures from the void have exacted retribution, they will find it for me.'

Stilkeen raised a hand and the flame ceiling thinned until Nish could see the translucent barrier behind the palace, like an endless, sky-high wall. It appeared more transparent than before, while the shapes clustering on the other side were clearer and more menacing. Stilkeen was going to open the void and no one could stop it.

Then, as they waited for their doom, the humming Nish had heard earlier rose to a howl and an extraordinary contraption hurtled in through the flame-wreathed entrance of Morrelune.

It had the deep keel and curving sides of a sea-going galleon, save that they were made of brass interleaved with black metal intricately decorated with silver. Its bow was high and pointed, with flaring metal shields extending along the sides of the deck in place of rails, while several white hooplike structures rose above the deck like covered wagons. An inscription in flowing writing on the bow read, *Three Reckless Old Ladies*.

'Reckless old ladies?' said Nish, bemused.

A small javelard, set in a rectangular, box-like wooden frame, was mounted behind the bow shields, and on a platform at the stern stood a catapult on a swivelling mount.

The sky-galleon flashed by, skidded sideways across the centre of the audience chamber, buffeting the flames all around, and a jowly old woman with jiggling chins – Yulla, no less! – fired the contents of the catapult point-blank at Stilkeen.

Nish couldn't tell what she had fired, but Stilkeen let out a shriek of agony, shrank to a quarter of its former size and wrapped the webs of flame and shadow tightly about itself, shaking wildly and squealing.

The sky-galleon curved around towards everyone, dropped sharply and its keel screeched across the solid floor beneath the flame.

'Get in!' yelled a little old lady, her eyes huge with excitement in her lined face. She trotted along the deck, hurling rope ladders over the side.

'Lilis!' said Maelys in astonishment, and ran for the nearest ladder. 'What are you doing here?'

'I've retired from the Great Library to go adventuring,' Lilis said, pulling on Maelys's arm as she reached the top. 'Quick!'

Nish scrambled up and the others followed. M'lainte, as unkempt as ever, stood in the wheelhouse holding a protruding knob where the wheel of a ship would normally have been mounted. It rather resembled the controller she had made for the air-sled after the attack on the monastery. 'Ready?'

'Ready, set, go!' shouted Lilis, as if she were ten again, and leapt up and down, clapping her hands. 'Beautiful shot, Yulla. Fire again.'

The sky-galleon took off with a jerk that threw everyone

against the wheelhouse, and began to circle the audience chamber. Yulla emptied a bag of sand into the catapult bucket, hauled her bloated body into the seat, aimed and fired again.

This time the sand went wide, save for a scatter which struck the webs covering Stilkeen's lower parts. It shrieked in agony, shot upwards like an unbound spring and the clinging webs peeled apart, the fire webs dangling below it, the webs of shadow sticking to the floor and wall. Stilkeen propelled itself through an opening in the ceiling and the fire webs were jerked up after it, out of sight.

'Never has any face been so welcome, M'lainte,' cried Nish, shaking her hand.

'I told you Yulla needed the air-sled,' said M'lainte, beaming all over her old face. 'I made the sky-galleon from it. Er, you can let go now.'

He released her hand. Maelys was looking at the three old women in bemusement.

'Maelys, meet Yulla and M'lainte,' said Nish. 'Back in Roros, Yulla was planning to look for a weapon against Stilkeen – but *sand*?'

'If it was in such pain from simply being in our world,' said Yulla, 'we reasoned that contact with any physical object must be so much worse.'

'So we hit it with hard, gritty sand dug from the River Zur beside the Great Library,' said Lilis, 'a million sharp grains at once. The pain was so bad that it had to run.'

'We'd better do the same,' said Flydd. 'Stilkeen was about to open the void.'

'I believe this is yours,' said M'lainte, handing Nish Vivimord's sabre. 'I found it when I raised the air-sled.'

'Thanks,' said Nish absently, putting it down on the side, for his own sword was much more to his liking.

The craft spun on its axis, hurtled down the broad hall,

and outside. The sun had set and the surroundings of the palace were now lit by hundreds of concealed lanterns.

Nish, looking back, saw something hanging from the ceiling of the open ninth level, directly below the spire. He touched M'lainte's arm.

'I think that's Father's body. We'd better check.'

She curved the craft back towards the highest level, and inside. As they approached, Nish could smell the rotting body and he had to turn away. No matter his father's crimes, and they were legion, he could not bear to see him like that.

'Is it definitely Father?'

'It's him,' said Flydd sombrely.

'And he's dead?' said Nish. 'It's not some spell or cunning illusion?'

'No illusion can exist this close to Stilkeen,' said Malien. 'The body looks as though it's been dead for weeks.'

'The God-Emperor is dead,' said Flydd, then took a deep breath. 'Long –'

'Don't say it!' gritted Nish, knowing that Flydd was about to say, *Long live the God-Emperor*. 'Don't you dare put that on me. M'lainte, get out of here.'

Flydd's mouth snapped closed. M'lainte headed outside, set down and they climbed over the sides of the sky-galleon onto the elevated, four-sided promenade surrounding Morrelune. Between the palace and the range, the endless barrier wall of the void cut through ground and sky, half a league away.

Yggur cleared his throat. 'Your armies await your command, Nish.'

'Command?' said Nish, still thinking about the death of his father. 'Yes, right.' He had to focus. Once Stilkeen tore open the void, the attack could come from anywhere – or everywhere.

'Pull yourself together!' said Flydd, thumping him hard

on the shoulder. 'This is the moment we've been fighting for ever since you escaped from Mazurhize.'

Nish studied the featureless barrier. 'How can we defend ourselves against what's up there? Any kind of creature imaginable could come out.'

'Without the aid of our enemies, we can't.'

'Vomix will be a threat as long as he lives,' said Nish, 'and Hackel's army is hungry for loot. They won't help me.'

'They will while their own survival is at stake,' said Flydd, 'and I'm going to do my best to ensure that any attack falls on them first. Talk to Nosby; he'll be looking to the son of the God-Emperor for leadership. Tell him that you're committed to the survival of the empire, and to recovering your father's body – you can say that much without compromising your precious principles, surely?'

And you never give up, Nish thought irritably. 'I'll have to get to Hackel's mercenaries before Vomix does, or they'll blame me for what happened inside.'

'Flydd can take care of that,' said Yggur. 'Get moving, Nish. I'll make a truce with Vomix – for what it's worth.' He headed one way, and Flydd the other, then both stopped, staring.

A needle beam of white light went angling up from the top of the palace towards the barrier wall and touched it, hundreds of spans above the plain. Vapour wisped out and the needle of light moved across the barrier, cutting through it in a semicircle, then began to shake and abruptly went out.

'I don't like the look of that,' M'lainte muttered.

Someone handed Nish a fieldglass and he focussed it on the ragged semicircle. Shadows behind the barrier converged on the curved cut and forced it outwards to form a horizontal flap, a platform about twenty spans long and equally wide. A broad path ran up to the opening from the void side, and a gaggle of creatures, some familiar to Nish from the Histories, others bizarre, appeared there, jostling and snapping at each other.

A large crocodilian beast broke free and scuttled across the flap or platform, but plummeted off the edge to the paved plain far below, killing itself instantly.

'The void doesn't have gravity as we know it,' said Ryll, from behind Nish, 'and it can take a while to get used to. Let's hope a few more go the same way . . .'

A host of winged lizards forced their way through, unfurled long wings and glided down to attack Vomix's army, which was nearest to the opening. A snake with fins wriggled under the platform and disappeared. Other beasts, many and various in shape and size, climbed down, clinging to the Santhenar side of the barrier with claws, hooks or barbs.

The flow through the opening from the void stopped suddenly; creatures small and large darted to left and right. Drums thudded like mallets thumping into wooden blocks. Nish slid the tubes of the fieldscope back and forth, trying to focus on the blurred shapes beyond the opening.

An upright, bear-shaped creature appeared in the opening. It was a span and a half high, as big as a large lyrinx, though its thick, streamlined body had grey skin as smooth as a seal's. A pair of long teeth protruded from its upper jaw like the tusks of a walrus, only larger. Its body was long, its legs short and, even from this distance, its eyes were bright and intelligent. A bandolier slung from its left shoulder to its right hip had various objects thrust through it, and it carried a trident in its right hand. It pounded its left fist against its belly, making the drumming sound, *thumpa-thump-thump*, *thumpa-thump-thump*.

'What's that?' Nish said hollowly.

'Atatusk,' said Ryll. 'I hope it's the only one.'

Nish had a feeling it wouldn't be. 'Are they bad?' he said, looking up at Ryll. Though he was a small lyrinx, he stood head and chest above Nish.

'Put it this way,' said Ryll, bright colours shivering across the armoured skin of his chest; Nish hoped he wasn't regretting coming to the aid of Santhenar, 'when we dwelt in the void, atatusk ate us for breakfast.'

The atatusk approached the edge of the platform, drew an object like a bamboo fieldscope from its bandolier and surveyed the scene. While thus occupied, one of the winged lizards tried to creep by, belly to the ground. Without looking, the atatusk backhanded it across the side of the head; it went tumbling down, hit the paving and did not move.

The *thumpa-thump-thump* grew louder, and the front line of a marching rank of atatusk appeared, six wide. Nish could not see how far back it extended.

The first atatusk put two flat, flipper-like hands around his mouth and said in an enormously amplified, barking voice, 'I, Lemno Gorgandyre, lay claim to this world for the atatusk nation.' Over his shoulder, he added, 'Find the white fire for Stilkeen, then stamp on all those squirming grubs.'

Gorgandyre seemed to be looking directly at Nish now, and a creeping terror washed over him. Once these creatures gained a foothold on Santhenar, it would be impossible to get rid of them.

'We've got to keep them out,' he said, knowing that he had no way of doing so.

'Too late,' said Ryll.

Gorgandyre lifted a coil of rope from his back, snapped the hook on its end over the edge of the platform and threw himself off, sliding down the rope so fast that smoke rose from his grey palms. He reached the plain, spat green gobs into his hands, then grounded the butt of his trident and waited as the rest of his troop followed, thirty in all. Another troop of atatusk appeared at the opening.

'We'll never defeat them,' said Ryll, colours flashing all over his armoured skin. 'It's hopeless.'

'We've got thousands of men,' said Nish. 'And your five hundred lyrinx.'

'And the atatusk in the void are numberless. I'll go back to my own.' Ryll bounded away.

A messenger came running from the Imperial Guard, carrying signal flags on a pole. 'General Nosby's compliments, surr, and he stands ready to follow your orders.'

'Signal him to stand by,' said Nish as more runners converged on him. Hackel's officers also offered their support, however Vomix demanded that Nish abandon any claim to the throne and swear allegiance to him.

Nish did not bother to reply, for Gorgandyre's platoon of atatusk were converging on the seneschal's forces and he would soon be fighting for his life. As another platoon of atatusk started to slide down, Nish began to formulate a battle plan. Standing on the top steps of the promenade, where he could see most of the nearby plain, he weighed up his troops, taking account of their capabilities and weaknesses, and began to issue orders. The signallers sent them to his detachments and they wheeled to face the enemy.

He checked his sword, then mentally noted where Flydd, Persia and Yggur stood, Tulitine and Malien, Ryll and Liett, and all his other allies. The sky-galleon shot by, Lilis at the javelard, Yulla seated on her catapult, then hurtled off to the attack. Everyone could be accounted for except Maelys. Where was she? She'd been here only a few minutes ago.

Then the fighting swept towards him and there was no time to look for her.

FORTY-THREE

Maelys was pacing along the side steps of the promenade surrounding Morrelune, which were not
fire-touched, thankfully, but good, solid stone. Stilkeen had
said that the pure fire was not far away, hidden in a corundite vessel, but what was corundite? No one knew, not even
Lilis, who was on the deck of the sky-galleon, at the base of
the steps.

'It sounds like a mineral,' the librarian said. 'Why don't
you ask Yulla?'

'Why would she know?' said Maelys, who knew nothing
about Yulla save that she had once been the governor of
Crandor.

'She has the best mineral collection in the world. Yulla?'

'Corundite is a very hard and heavy mineral,' said Yulla,
who was readying the sky-galleon for take-off, 'like ruby or
sapphire, but it can be any colour.'

'Thanks,' Maelys said absently. So she had to find a vessel
made from a hard, heavy mineral that could be any colour.
It was no help at all.

The sky-galleon lifted and shot away. Maelys had just
passed in front of the entrance to the palace when Stilkeen
slid down its webs into the audience chamber, gathered

546

spilled chthonic fire from the floor and, shaking with pain, formed it into a tight beam which it directed upwards to cut a semicircle through the void barrier. Its webs slipped, it let out a shriek and the beam cut off; Stilkeen wrapped the fire webs tightly around itself once more and disappeared upwards.

The flap cut into the barrier was forced down to form a horizontal platform, and through the opening Maelys saw a broad path leading into the void, with dozens of strange and savage creatures clustered on it.

She watched in horror as the alien beasts poured forth and came down to the plain. The Histories told many stories about the creatures that inhabited the void, and all were desperate to escape from its unrelenting brutality.

What was she to do? She had no skill at arms and could not fight them; the least of those creatures would kill her in an instant. But there had to be *something* she could do to help.

If Stilkeen tried again it might make so many openings that the defenders would be overwhelmed, but after the ruthless way it had dispatched Hackel and Zofloc she did not want to go anywhere near it. And yet, while she wore the taphloid it did not appear to see her . . . and it *was* crippled by pain, which evened the odds a little.

Dare she try to stop it? Maelys crept back and forth, peering between the columns into the palace. She looked around to ask someone for advice, but the promenade was deserted and suddenly there was fighting all across the plain.

The longer she hesitated, the more people were going to die and the greater the risk that Stilkeen would breach the barrier again. She had to act now. Alone and without a plan of attack, she headed into the fire palace.

Maelys darted from column to column along the hall towards the audience chamber. Her palms were sweating;

one minute her heart was racing, the next she could barely feel it beating. If Stilkeen *could* take on any aspect, it might be hiding there now. And even if the taphloid concealed her from its sight, it might hear or smell her.

The shadow webs still hung at the rear of the audience chamber, though they appeared to be empty. As she crept closer, sand grated underfoot, the sharp sand that had driven Stilkeen away, but where had it gone?

The hair rose on the back of her neck. Someone was watching her, *but not with their eyes.* Maelys loosened her knife in its sheath, slowly turning around.

'Who's there?' she said hoarsely, trying to control her terror, for the taphloid only hid her from Stilkeen. What if it was Vomix behind her? Her throat went so dry that it was hard to get the words out. 'W-what do you want?'

'Help!' called a deep voice from somewhere below her. A voice she recognised.

It was Klarm and, for as long as she'd known him, he had been her enemy, but if Stilkeen was everyone's enemy, maybe Klarm was on her side now. 'Where are you?'

'Caught in one of the God-Emperor's stinking traps! Come down the stairs to your left.'

He sounded in great pain, and Maelys did not think it was feigned, so she obeyed. These stairs were also wreathed in the pale fire that burned constantly yet gave off no heat. She could feel its radiance on her face and hands, like firelight, and it tickled where it touched bare skin.

The lower level was a large open space framed by curved arrays of columns much like the rest of Morrelune. She looked right and left. The flames were less visible here and behind them she saw silken tapestries on the walls, a plain but elegant silk carpet on the marble floor, but no Klarm. Was it an ambush? She felt for her knife.

'Up here,' he said softly. 'Don't laugh.'

The dwarf hung upside down from the ceiling, several spans above her. His left boot had been caught in a wire noose that must have whipped up after he'd stepped in it, and it had drawn so tightly around his ankle that he could not free himself.

Klarm's lips were drawn back from his teeth and sweat dripped from his brow. His right hand was wrapped in a filthy, frayed bandage, possibly the same one as he'd worn when she'd freed Nish from the air-sled on the Range of Ruin weeks ago.

'Why would I laugh?' said Maelys. 'I take no pleasure from others' pain.'

Klarm was scratched and bruised, his clothes were torn as if by large claws, and his face was a congested purple. 'Snared in a trap of my own design,' he muttered. 'I'll never live this down.' He caught her eye. 'Will you help me?'

Maelys could not forget that he had once been a devious scrutator. And he *had* condemned her at the Range of Ruin. 'You've got the tears; free yourself.'

'I dropped them; besides, this noose is a *livewire*. Once you're caught in it, it keeps tightening and there's no way to stop it, even via mancery – unless the God-Emperor wills it.'

And he's dead, thought Maelys. Hurrah!

The tears lay on the floor some distance away, while Klarm's sword and knoblaggie were directly beneath him; they must have fallen from their sheaths when he was jerked upside down. Her heart began to pound. If she could get the tears to Flydd, they might turn the tide of the battle.

She crept across and stood looking down at their roiling quicksilver surfaces, sick with fear. The song of the tears was just the faintest drone, but she had seen what their kiss could do. She reached for the chain, then drew back as Klarm spoke.

'I wouldn't,' he said softly. 'Few people – indeed, few

mancers – can wield the tears, and you certainly are not one of them.'

'I wasn't thinking of using them.'

'Even to pick them up by the chain is taking a mortal risk. If Reaper came at you, how would you protect yourself?'

'C-came at me?' She remembered Nish's agony after he'd touched Reaper, and how terribly it had burned his hand. She knew the scars still troubled him.

'Oh, yes,' said Klarm. 'Reaper *hates*, Maelys, and Reaper longs to devour. It's been shaped that way by its master, and even a mancer of my power must be ever on his guard against it. Are you going to help me, or not?'

She stepped away hastily and studied the livewire, a fine, coppery binding cutting through the boot into his ankle. 'How am I supposed to get you down? Do you want your knoblaggie?'

'The livewire can't be undone, even by mancery,' he reminded her. 'Throw me my sword.'

She picked it up, wondering how she was going to toss it that high without hitting him. She hacked a piece from the silk carpet, wrapped it around the blade and gave a small heave to gauge the weight.

'Careful. It's fiercely sharp,' said Klarm.

She wrapped the carpet around again, tied it on with some loose threads, aimed and threw. The sword flew to Klarm's left but he gave a convulsive sideways jerk and his outstretched hand caught the hilt. He swung upside down again, grimacing at the pain in his ankle, allowed the carpet sheath to fall and bared the blade.

Only then did Maelys realise what he was going to do. 'No!' she whispered. 'There's got to be a better way.'

'I designed the trap, Maelys. There's no other way out of it. Step aside.'

Klarm's jaw tightened, then he twisted his body and

swung the sword before Maelys could look away. It crunched straight through boot and bone above his ankle and he fell, still holding the sword, tumbled over in mid-air and landed on his one foot. The livewire tightened on the severed ankle, squeezing it out of the noose, then his foot fell to the floor beside him. It was no bigger than one of her own small feet.

The stump was pouring blood and if it wasn't stopped he might bleed to death. Maelys was wondering if she could bind the wound with strips of carpet when Klarm dropped the sword, hopped across to the tears and pressed the severed end of his leg against Reaper.

'No!' she yelled, feeling faint at the thought of such a terrible remedy.

There came a ghastly sizzling and Klarm let out a single, choked-off shriek. Smoke fumed up all around him; she smelt burned meat and charred bone; Maelys felt a shocking pain in her middle, as if Gatherer were radiating Klarm's agony in all directions, but it faded and he lay gasping on the floor.

She ran across. His eyes were tightly closed but tears were leaking out of them.

'What can I do?' she said, taking his hand. 'Tell me what to do.' He was no longer her enemy, just a little man in agony.

'Get my knoblaggie,' he said through clenched teeth. 'And a length of wood or metal.'

The tapestries were suspended from metal rods. She tore one down, wrenched the rod out and gave it to him. Using the power of the knoblaggie, he bent the rod double and fused its ends to form a blob, flattened on the base, which he bound to his lower leg to form a crude foot. The gruesomely cauterised wound began to drip a straw-coloured fluid.

'Help me up,' he gritted.

She did so.

'Where's Jal-Nish?' As he took an awkward step, pain shivered across his handsome face.

'He's dead.'

'Dead! Are you sure?'

'We all saw his rotting body, and he looked as though he'd been dead for weeks. It wasn't pleasant.'

'Where was he?'

'In the top level of the palace.'

'I swore an oath to him, and I've come all this way,' Klarm said. 'I'll see him laid to rest. You'd better get out of the palace; it isn't safe.' He turned aside.

'Wait!' said Maelys. 'Stilkeen has cut a hole in the void and they're coming through.'

He froze, turned painfully. '*What's* coming through?'

'Beasts I have no name for – savage, terrible creatures. It offered Santhenar to them; it told them to get rid of humanity and find the white fire.'

Klarm stumped back, caught her arm and pulled her down to his level. 'And who's to hold them off?' he said hoarsely. 'I've had no news since I left Blisterbone and went into the shadow realm, and in there I can't even tell how time is passing.'

'You left Blisterbone nearly four weeks ago.' She told him about the armies gathered outside, and Nish's allies.

'Extraordinary,' said Klarm, stumping away past his amputated foot, and back. 'I hadn't thought any of you would survive.'

'And Vomix has an army as well. Maybe six thousand men.'

'Seneschal Vomix? What's he doing here?'

'Trying to take the empire for himself.'

'Like hell!' Klarm thought for a moment. 'You'd better come with me.'

'I'm looking for a way to attack Stilkeen.'

'I've been trying to think of one ever since I left Blisterbone Pass –'

There came a barking bellowing from outside, as though a great beast was raging into battle. Weapons clashed and a thin, squealing scream echoed down the steps, but was cut off. Someone had just been slain.

'My friends are dying out there and I can't fight beside them,' said Maelys. 'But I've got to do something.'

'You helped me.' Dispassionately, Klarm studied the crusted, seeping mess on the end of his leg. 'And I'll do what I can for you. I can only think of one man who might know Stilkeen's weakness. Unfortunately . . .' He looked her up and down as if weighing her resolve.

'I'll do anything,' said Maelys.

'Unfortunately, he's been dead for two hundred years. But if you truly are brave enough to do *anything*, that need not stop you.'

Her toes curled. 'What do you mean? You don't mean . . .'

'The one man who might know is Old Nadiril, the greatest librarian of all. I saw him in the shadow realm as I came though, but I don't see how you could possibly survive in that place, Maelys, doughty though you are.'

Neither did she. She definitely did not want to go there, but she had to do something.

'My taphloid conceals me from Stilkeen, and also hides my aura,' said Maelys. She hastily explained about Kandor's protection, and Yggur. 'Kandor made the taphloid to give Yggur a warning when Stilkeen drew near; and to help conceal him.'

Klarm rubbed his beard, thinking. 'The taphloid must suppress its wearer's aura on *all* the planes, and it might conceal you from Stilkeen's revenants, too, but it won't hide you from the normal spirits in that place. Your old friends

Vivimord and Phrune are among them – Phrune asked after you the moment I entered the shadow realm.' His face twisted in disgust.

The thought of meeting Phrune again made Maelys physically ill, but she could not back out now. 'What choice do I have?'

'No more and no less than I do,' he said quietly. 'We are each prisoners of our given word, yet our oaths may also serve us, in dark times. Take this.'

With his fingertips Klarm tapped a beat on the knoblaggie, which was like three brass balls fused together, and handed it to her.

The knoblaggie felt as heavy as solid brass. 'How will you defend yourself?' she said, amazed that he would offer her something so precious to him.

'I have the tears,' Klarm reminded her. With exquisite care, he picked them up and put them around his neck; their song rose and fell.

Maelys stepped away hastily. 'How do I use the knoblaggie? *Can* I use it, without any Art?'

'Yes, I've *allowed* you to. If you're in danger, you must will a physical shield around yourself, matching the concealment the taphloid gives you. It may save your life – *once.*'

'What if I get attacked a second time?'

Klarm closed his eyes, smoothed his hand over the surface of Gatherer, not quite touching it, and turned his head from side to side. 'There's a blade lying on the floor above here. Get it.'

She did not move. 'What good can it do in the shadow realm?'

'You never know,' said Klarm. 'If you escape, leave my knoblaggie here – I'll need it afterwards.'

She did not ask what he meant, but ran up the stairs. The blade turned out to be the sabre M'lainte had returned to

Nish – Vivimord's sabre – which he'd left on the side of the sky-galleon. It must have fallen off. The sabre was way too long for her, but better than nothing, so she took it and went back to Klarm.

He started when he recognised it. 'I've a fancy Vivimord would be glad to see that.'

'Why?' said Maelys.

'It's been enchanted for a special purpose, but don't reveal it unless you have to. It might be worth something to you down there.'

She wrapped the sabre in the length of silk carpet and tied it firmly in place. 'How do I get into the shadow realm? Is it far from here?'

Klarm slid his hand above the surface of Gatherer again and a pit appeared in the floor between them.

'The shadow realm lies everywhere, Maelys, and touches all places equally. Jump in.'

She did not move; she wasn't ready. 'I thought it would be harder than that. When Flydd was trying to get into the shadow realm, once –'

'Normally it's very hard to get in,' said Klarm. 'But with Stilkeen so near to us, the barriers between the dimensions have thinned.'

She looked down, but couldn't see anything save vague flittings and scurryings in the darkness. She was sick of darkness and flame; Maelys wished she was outside, and that the sun was still shining. But there was no point to wishing; the job had to be done.

'Thank you,' she said, and jumped. 'Waaaaiiit!' she called as she was falling. 'How will I recognise Nadiril, among millions of spirits? And how do I get out again?'

There was no answer. The pit had already closed over.

She drifted down, almost weightless, though she could still feel the heaviness of the knoblaggie and the warmth of the taphloid between her breasts, vibrating ever so slightly. The carpet-wrapped sabre was tucked under her left arm.

Mist wreathed across the space she was falling through, and the air sparkled here and there. Rays of light streaked above and below her, illuminating rods of sky like a searchlight shining through rain. Another ray went right through her as though she had a glass belly.

A transparent woman in a green gown shot by, head forward, arms clasped behind her, gliding through empty air like a skater across a frozen pond. A pair of children whirled and danced the other way, as excited as puppies chasing a leaf.

Maelys was smiling after them when she sensed something behind her, turned and came face to face with a chubby, malevolent spirit whose pale skin shone as if painted with oil. His head was shaven, apart from a gleaming queue, and his cheeks were so plump that his eyes were mere slits. However his ears had been cut off and the tip of his nose was split, revealing its revolting insides.

'Phrune!' she gasped, backing away through the air and groping for the knoblaggie. She did not go for her taphloid, since it'd had no effect on Phrune's reanimated body after he had died.

'One of me,' he said in a treacly voice. 'But the other four Phrune spirits aren't far away, as distances run in the shadow realm. We've been watching the entrances for you, little Maelys. Vivimord said you'd join us before too long.'

There was no sign of the injuries Phrune had suffered when she'd stuffed her taphloid into his open mouth, apart from his swollen, torn and blistered lips. Nor, thankfully, of the intestines that had been hanging out for most of the time that dead Phrune had hunted her.

'Where's Vivimord?' she asked, looking over her shoulder.

Her voice sounded higher in the shadow realm, almost shrill. The other Phrunes were not in sight, though she could see spirits everywhere now; the levels below her were thick with them, all flitting and fluttering as only the disembodied could.

'Around,' said Phrune vaguely. 'Don't you worry about him. I'm going to look after you.'

If she used the knoblaggie, it would probably shield her from this Phrune, but would there be anything left for the other four? No, Klarm had said it would only work once, and she hadn't yet gained what she came for.

'I need to talk to Vivimord. It's urgent.'

Phrune let out one of those incongruous giggles that had always set her teeth on edge. 'My master is a busy man.'

'Here?' she cried. 'How can he be?'

'Vivimord wants out,' Phrune said sourly, 'and he knows there must be a way.' His red lips snapped shut as if he'd said more than his master would have liked. 'I won't be bothering him, Maelys. As if I'd do *you* any favours.'

He drifted towards her, and from the corners of her eyes Maelys saw that the other four Phrunes were also converging on her. She gripped the knoblaggie hard; she didn't know if spirits could be harmed in the shadow realm, but live people could – Flydd had talked about the dangers during their attempts to escape from Mistmurk Mountain. And if *he* had been afraid, there was much to be afraid of.

'Vivimord?' she shouted. 'Where are you? The Phrunes won't let me talk to you.'

The Phrunes clapped their hands over their ears, grimacing. When Phrune had been alive, she remembered, shrill sounds had hurt his ears, and her voice was much higher here than in the real world . . .

'I'll scream,' said Maelys, taking a deep breath and leaning towards him. 'Right in your ears!'

'Oh, very well!' the first Phrune snapped. 'It'll be nearly as much fun watching the master deal with you.'

Could Phrune be trusted? Certainly not. Was he planning an ambush? Undoubtedly, if he thought he could get away with it, so she had to be on her guard. She followed after his flitting spirit forms, finding it hard to keep up; the five Phrunes had to keep stopping for her. Eventually they spiralled through a cloud and emerged above an amphitheatre where Vivimord stood on the stage addressing an audience.

He was a very tall spirit with long black hair, black eyes and a thin, hooked nose, and every eye was drawn to him, for he was a charismatic zealot who could sway multitudes with his oratory.

At sight of the flying Phrunes, Vivimord's hard mouth curved down in annoyance, until they all pointed at Maelys. He nodded, concluded his address, bowed to his audience and drifted up towards her, showing his teeth.

'I hoped to see you here before too long,' he said, 'though I did not expect the added pleasure that you would still be alive.'

'I need your help,' said Maelys.

'The only assistance you'll be getting from me will be to join us permanently.' Vivimord's hand slipped to the knife on his belt.

'Wait!' said Maelys desperately. 'Do you know what's going on at Morrelune?'

He drew the knife and tested it by cutting his thumb off. The spirit matter hardly bled at all, and when he stuck it back onto the stump, his thumb wiggled just as naturally as his fingers. 'A little. I can't see clearly into the material planes yet.'

'Stilkeen has opened the void and, if it can't soon be closed, it will be the end of the world. You once said how much you loved Santhenar, so what matters most to you – revenge on me, or the world's fate?'

'I care less about it now than I did while I was alive,' Vivimord said. 'But you're right; I do love my world and would not see it harmed – especially as I still hope to return to it. What do you want from me, Maelys, and why should I help you?'

'I've got to find Nadiril the Librarian.'

'What for?'

She looked over her shoulder, instinctively, then lowered her voice. 'Because I'm told that he may know Stilkeen's weakness. We don't believe it will go away quietly, even if it does get the pure chthonic fire it needs to bind its physical and spirit aspects together. We're looking for a way to drive it away, or even kill it.'

His dark eyes weighed her; he thrust the point of his knife into his tenebrous thigh again and again, until an ecto-plasmic fluid spurted out. He caught it in a chalice and swallowed it again.

'I don't think a *being* can be killed,' said Vivimord. 'But Nadiril knows more than I do. Come this way.'

He took hold of her arm with fingers that had a tight, chilly clasp, like a frozen tourniquet. This time they did not float or fly, but appeared to skip in and out of existence. Maelys felt as though they were covering great distances, if distance had any meaning in the shadow realm.

Vivimord stopped suddenly, dropped into a multi-coloured layer of mist then through it into a space shaped like an enormous stone box, where a tremendously ancient spirit sat perched on a stool rather like the one Lilis had used in the Great Library, perusing a scroll.

He resembled a dying stork, Maelys thought, for he was long-limbed and had a thin and sharply arching nose. His limbs were no more than bone and sinew though his skin wasn't saggy, but rather was stretched tightly across the angular cheek- and jaw-bones. His skull was a high, bald dome, the skin there blotchy and flaking. A few wisps of white hair clung to the sides of his head and his eyes were clouded as if blind – and yet he had been reading. Did he read via the Art?

The old man looked up at Maelys and smiled. 'Hello, a beautiful, *live* young woman.' His voice was faint and whispery. 'Have you come to visit me? Goody.'

'Hello,' said Maelys. 'You must be Nadiril. I'm Maelys. I was at the Great Library recently, consulting Lilis.'

Nadiril smiled fondly. 'My little protégée, and the finest librarian I ever taught. How is she?'

'Very well. She has recently retired.' Maelys told him the tale, briefly, and how Lilis, Yulla and M'lainte had turned up just in time with the sky-galleon.

'*Three Reckless Old Ladies?*' Nadiril said delightedly. 'Capital, capital! One should always retire before it's time; I went on far too long. But live people don't risk the shadow realm for idle conversation. You've come to consult me about some weighty matter.'

Maelys explained their situation and what she was looking for.

The clouded eyes never left her face and she gained the impression that he could see her clearly. 'So old Yggur is still going, two centuries after my death?' said Nadiril. 'Who would have thought it? And Kandor was his father? Why did that never occur to me?

'Ah yes, your question,' he added as Maelys stirred. 'Time is pressing and you're rightly impatient with an old man's meandering mind.'

'Er . . .' said Maelys. He seemed such a nice old fellow and she did not want to trouble him.

'Get on with it,' snapped Vivimord. 'She has a date.' He tested the knife blade on his other thumb.

Nadiril ignored him. 'I could not have answered your

560

question before I came to the shadow realm, Maelys, but since I've been here I've kept my eyes and ears open . . . in a manner of speaking.' He laughed wispily. 'Stilkeen's revenants are silly, heedless creatures, all pleasure and no prudence. They give no thought to the future; it's no wonder Stilkeen keeps them here.'

'I didn't know they were *kept* here,' said Vivimord, suddenly attentive.

'Of course they are,' said Nadiril. 'In Stilkeen's proper state it is almost invulnerable, because it can shift quickly to other aspects and planes where few if any enemies can follow.

'And besides, being a *being*,' he smiled at the little word-play, 'it can't be killed save by another higher power. However, severed from its revenants as it is now, it has a weakness. It is almost invulnerable to the most powerful mortals, but its revenants are only safe in the shadow realm, or when they are united with Stilkeen by chthonic fire. If they leave this realm, *unbound*, there is one single way that they can be harmed – indeed, destroyed completely.'

'How?' said Maelys, finding it hard to breathe. This was the answer everyone had been searching for. Dare she try to destroy even *part* of a *being*?

'Unfortunately, I haven't learned that,' said Nadiril with a wry smile.

'But . . . have you got any idea?'

'I'm afraid not. You'll have to work it out yourself.' His clouded eyes closed, his head nodded, and he appeared to doze for a few seconds, before opening his eyes again.

'However, out in the real world, their senses fail them; the revenants are blind and they can barely hear, so you may be able to trick them. And if you should succeed, and they *are* destroyed, I believe that Stilkeen would be so hurt by their destruction that it would not be seen again in the physical worlds for a goodly fraction of eternity.'

FORTY-FOUR

'We've got to do something or the atatusk are going to run right over the top of us,' Nish said to Ryll when they met during a temporary lull in the fighting, twenty minutes later.

'We've done well to hold them back,' said Ryll, whose chest and right arm were covered in atatusk blood of a brilliant chromium green. 'They're the mightiest foe we ever encountered in the void, but they're not as comfortable on this heavy world. We're tiring them.'

'Not quickly enough.'

The atatusk were brilliant, instinctive fighters who seemed to anticipate every stroke of their opponents, and they could take even more punishment than the armoured lyrinx, for the blubbery layer under their grey skin could not only absorb mighty blows, but was self-healing. At least five hundred men lay dead already, most from Vomix's army fortunately, plus many lyrinx, and the atatusk were coming out of the void faster than they were being killed.

Ryll began cleaning the claws of his right hand with the point of a yellow atatusk tusk. It was as long as Nish's forearm and greenly bloody on the thick end, where it had been torn from the jaw.

The lyrinx were as civilised as *old humans*, Nish mused, but sometimes it was hard to keep that in mind. 'Do you know what I hate most about the atatusk?'

Ryll raised a scaly eyebrow.

'It's their contempt for us *old humans*,' said Nish. 'They *do* think of us as grubs, just vermin to be stamped on. They assume that we're feeble, cowardly creatures who will run away.'

Ryll made a peculiar coughing bark behind his hand, then turned aside hastily.

'What's the matter?' said Nish. 'You – you're laughing at me!'

'You used to think of *us* as vermin,' said Ryll, still smiling.

Lyrinx smiles showed hundreds of teeth and took a lot of getting used to, for their mouths were big enough to bite off a human head. However Nish had known Ryll a long time and, even after ten years, had not forgotten how to read his relatively immobile features. Ryll was vastly amused.

'Sorry,' said Nish. 'We were ignorant in the olden days. We hadn't seen the humanity inside you.'

'That's all right,' said Ryll. 'We *also* thought of you as pink squirming grubs with useless teeth and no claws.' He laughed thunderously.

Nish thumped him in the chest, which was like punching the trunk of a tree. Ryll retracted his long, wickedly sharp talons, then extended them again towards Nish's cheek. It was a fiercely friendly gesture, but these very claws had once laid open his father's face in terrible wounds that had never healed, and Nish's smile faded.

'We can't beat them, can we?' he said, surveying the battlefield again.

'Not unless you can stop them coming out of the void.' Ryll nodded up towards the opening. 'There could be millions of atatusk up there; probably are.'

Millions! A few hundred had come through so far and they were wreaking ruin upon the surrounding armies. 'Maybe we should have a go at sealing the opening,' Nish said, expecting Ryll to laugh the idea down.

'Maybe we should,' Ryll replied, 'though I wouldn't want to send my fliers up there.' Jagged colours flickered chameleon-like across his chest and throat, signifying his unease. 'The atatusk have always had our measure in the air.'

'But they don't fly,' said Nish. *Do they?*'

'No, they can't fly, yet they have a way of bringing us down. On heavy worlds like Santhenar, most of our fliers have to use mancery to stay aloft –'

'I remember,' said Nish. Ryll, born without wings, had been considered a misfit, though he had risen above that prejudice to lead the lyrinx nation. 'How do they do it?'

'We don't know. Atatusk aren't even great mancers.'

'Flydd might know, but I don't see him anywhere.' He looked around and saw the sky-galleon hovering not far away. 'I'll ask M'lainte –'

'Isn't she a trifle . . . er, venerable?' said Ryll.

'You mean old?' said Nish as they strode towards the sky-galleon, which had settled on the plain while Lilis scurried around, collecting fallen spears for reuse.

The fighting had swept across this area half an hour ago and the paving was strewn with bodies – here an atatusk, practically cut in half, surrounded by a halo of human bodies, there a slight, golden-skinned Faellem man without a mark on him; further on were three dead Aachim, all with red hair, and another atatusk, this one on its back with five spears sticking up from its round grey torso.

'But Ryll,' Nish added, 'during the war, old lyrinx were proud to die in the line of battle, protecting their young.'

Ryll gave another little cough as he skirted the dead,

heaved one of the spears out and carried it with him, still dripping.

'Old lyrinx remain strong and vigorous until their end, my friend, while your kind grow fat and feeble twenty years before you die. Truly, *old humans* are decadent, helpless creatures. How you climbed to the top of this world remains a mystery to me.'

The lyrinx was teasing him again but Nish didn't mind. It was a welcome distraction.

'We used our brains, not our brawn,' Nish said pointedly. 'M'lainte,' he called up to the old woman, who was sitting on the bow of the sky-galleon, sketching a device on the skirt of her grubby gown, 'we need your advice.'

The fighting was moving in their direction, a squad of atatusk charging through a company of Vomix's fleeing troops as if they were field mice, flinging bodies to right and left.

'You'd better come up.' She tossed a rope ladder over.

When they reached the deck, M'lainte lifted the sky-galleon out of spear range.

'We can't beat the atatusk unless we can stop them coming through,' said Nish.

M'lainte rubbed her fingers vigorously through her thin hair, leaving it sticking up in all directions, and raised her eyes to the semicircular opening in the void barrier. 'I don't see how you can stop them.'

'If we can't,' said Ryll, 'Santhenar cannot survive.'

M'lainte studied the opening. 'Even supposing the enemy could be kept back, can it be sealed? That would depend on the nature of the barrier.' She raised her voice. 'Lilis?'

Lilis emerged from the cabin, spectacles perched on her thin nose, studying a book as she walked, but she did not resemble a librarian now, nor a little old lady. She was dressed in a yellow blouse and red velvet knee britches held up by a broad black belt, with long black knee boots folded over at the top. Her hair was covered by a cap, and a scarlet bandanna with white spots was loosely knotted around her neck.

'You're looking most piratical today, my dear,' said M'lainte, who wore the same ill-fitting and grubby clothes as ever – indeed, they might have been the same clothes she'd been wearing when Nish had first met her, more than thirteen years ago.

He thought the librarian looked more like a messenger boy than a pirate. Lilis might have passed for a boy, being so small and slight, had it not been for her lined face and hands, and the silver hair peeking out from under her cap.

'I feel a hundred years younger,' cried Lilis. She glanced over the side, looking down at the bloody battlefield and said, more soberly, 'And even if I am to die today, I would not go back.'

'We're thinking about attempting to seal the opening,' said M'lainte. 'What do you know about such matters?'

'A hole in the barrier is a violation of the natural order of the universe,' said Lilis.

'The natural order?' said Nish.

'So the philosopher Melochtes wrote, two thousand years ago. He spent a lifetime meditating on the nature of the Forbidding.'

'Do you remember everything in the Library?' said Nish.

'Of course not,' said Lilis, smiling at the thought, and held up the book. 'But after Stilkeen made its public threat I read everything we had pertaining to the void, including this book, and I discovered that, in nature, each thing has its own order and its own pattern. The barrier between the worlds and the void forms a smooth surface which resists puncture and, if a breach is made, the barrier yearns to repair itself.'

Below them, the sounds of battle grew louder and more violent, and Nish hurried to the side. Six atatusk with heavy spears were attacking a company of some thirty Imperial Guard armed with spears and scythe-shaped blades. The Imperial Guard were holding firm; they were the best fighters here, and surely that number could separate the enemy, surround them and finish them off. And if they couldn't . . .

'Then why hasn't the barrier repaired itself?' said M'lainte, but answered her own question. 'Because it can't while atatusk are continually passing through it.'

'Melochtes wrote that a sizeable hole might take days to heal,' said Lilis.

'I wonder that Stilkeen didn't make a gigantic opening,' said Nish, 'so more atatusk could come through at once.'

'When it was cutting the hole, its light beam stopped suddenly,' said Ryll.

'It would have been a corrupted form of chthonic fire,' M'lainte surmised, 'the stuff Stilkeen took from one of the dimensionless boxes, perhaps. Nothing else could cut such a barrier, but it must have been painful to use.'

'Even if you can seal the opening,' said Yulla through the open cabin door, 'Stilkeen might make another.'

Nish turned to face her. She was sitting at a small table, studying a yellow crystal with her hand lens, and did not look up. 'How would you seal it?' she added.

'Push the platform back up into place and hold it there until the barrier seals itself,' said Nish.

'Easy to say, not so easy to do,' said Lilis. 'According to Melochtes, the barrier is neither matter nor force, but rather, something than can be matter at one time and force at another. You might find it hard to take hold of.'

'The atatusk stood on the platform,' said Nish, 'and they're a lot heavier than we are.'

'They come from the void. The platform could be solid to them yet intangible to us.'

'Great!' said Nish. 'We've got to raise a platform we can't feel, and even if we somehow get it into place, the atatusk, who *can* touch it, will simply push it down again.'

Everyone looked at M'lainte, who was an undoubted mechanical genius. 'What's the one thing around here that's not of this world?' she said distractedly.

'No idea.' Nish hated questions like that.

'The web Stilkeen left behind in the audience chamber?' said Lilis.

'Precisely,' said M'lainte. 'The sticky web, partly made of shadow, with which it protects itself from contact with our physical world. I've a feeling some web might do nicely.'

'How do we handle a web made of shadow?' said Nish.

'You collect it in a dimensionless box, of course,' she said, as though that would be obvious even to an idiot.

'And then what?' Nish had no idea what M'lainte had in mind.

She did not reply. Her eyes were closed and she was deep in thought.

'What if you nudged the platform closed with the bow of the sky-galleon?' said Lilis, 'and held it closed while the opening sealed itself?'

'The barrier force would tear the sky-galleon apart,' said M'lainte. Her eyes snapped open and she began to draw on her skirt again.

'I've got it!' she said directly. 'Nish, you'll have to stick shadow web all along the edge of the opening, then tie ropes to the web and heave the platform up. Once you've done that, you'll climb the wall of the barrier and smear chthonic fire on the edges of the opening, until they dissolve, stick together and reseal.'

It sounded like a complicated plan, even if they weren't under attack, and if anything went wrong it would fail, but Nish had to concede that M'lainte was a genius for thinking of it. 'How do we get out if the opening is sealed?'

'Leave a small section of the platform unstuck, then come through and hang from your ropes. We'll be waiting to pick you up.'

There came a series of triumphant barking roars from below. Nish ran for the side but Ryll beat him to it. 'They're all dead!' he said sombrely.

Who? Nish thought, suddenly afraid that it would be Flydd, Yggur, Maelys and all the others. He leaned over; the thirty Imperial Guardsmen had fallen, but only three atatusk; the other three were dancing on the blood-drenched corpses, waving heads and other body parts in the air.

'The Imperial Guard were our very best,' he said dazedly. 'At this rate, we'll be lucky to survive to lunchtime.'

'Then we'd better get moving,' said M'lainte, beside him. 'Call Chissmoul to fly the sky-galleon, and a squad of troops to defend the opening while you seal it.'

'They'll never hold the atatusk back,' said Nish, dismayed by what he had just seen. It was hopeless.

'I'll fetch some of my best fighters,' said Ryll. '*We* can fight them hand to hand, but you little humans haven't got a hope.' He thumped Nish on the back. 'You'll have to stay well behind. Bring your most powerful crossbows, and long spears with a crosspiece on the shaft, otherwise the atatusk will keep coming for you – even with a spear right through them. Cheer up, Nish. We're not beaten yet.'

Nish, trying to think of a way to attack the creatures, forced a smile. 'I'll take the small javelard as well, if the platform will hold it. Let's see them fight with a heavy spear through the heart!' he said savagely. 'Atatusk do have hearts, don't they?'

'Yes, but they're high up, behind the armoured bulge below their throats.'

M'lainte flew into Morrelune to gather shadow webs, the discarded dimensionless boxes and any spilled chthonic fire she could find, while Nish assembled his team: six Gendrigorean lancers and six crossbowmen to enter the void and help the lyrinx hold back the atatusk while he, Aimee and Clech closed the opening and sealed it.

He wanted Flangers but that would have left his remaining troops leaderless. Nish passed the word around for Chissmoul to come quickly.

M'lainte returned, and shortly Ryll appeared with a dozen lyrinx, plus Liett, her eyes flashing. Clearly their relationship was as stormy as ever.

'If you think I'm going to let you do this on your own,' she raged, buffeting Ryll about the face with her beautiful wings while he grinned sheepishly, making no attempt to defend himself, 'you're a sadder fool than I thought.' She rounded on Nish. 'You know how useless he is. Why do you encourage him?'

'All right,' said Nish, who had been expecting this. 'You can come too.'

'Of course I'm coming –' Liett went for Ryll again. 'You scurvy, lying . . .' Evidently searching for the worst insult she could come up with, she settled for '. . . miserable *human* of a lyrinx.'

She battered him to the ground with her wings until he rolled onto his face, laughing and crying, 'Enough!'

'You said Nish would forbid me to come,' said Liett, her crest flushed a brilliant, throbbing green.

'How could I stop you?' said Nish, who remembered her character very well. 'Besides, you're the best lyrinx flier as ever was, and I could use . . . what's the matter?'

Liett was shaking her head. 'In the old days we used the

field to fly on Santhenar, but the nodes are gone, and the *field* with them, and without the Art we're too heavy to lift off the ground.'

'How come Ryll didn't tell me that earlier –?' Nish broke off, realising his blunder, but Ryll had walked away.

'It wouldn't have occurred to him,' Liett said quietly, 'since he has no wings.'

'Besides, the nodes were destroyed after the lyrinx went to Tallallame,' Nish went on. 'He didn't know.'

'None of us did, until we tried to fly here.'

Nish paced back and forth. 'What about in the void?'

'We have little weight there. We can fly, but it's perilous to do so near atatusk.'

'So we'll also be nearly weightless in the void,' said Nish. Would that be a benefit or a handicap? Probably the latter, until they got used to it.

'If you were foolish enough to enter it,' said Liett.

Liett studied him, head angled to one side, and he imagined that she was seeing him as a pink, squirming grub. He turned away.

'Where's your pilot?' said M'lainte when the human and lyrinx troops had come aboard and all their gear had been loaded. The small javelard, which, as well as firing spears could also be fitted with a leather catapult bucket, had been unbolted from its mount and was roped down so it could be deployed quickly.

'I called for Chissmoul but she must be too far away.' Or dead, Nish thought gloomily.

M'lainte frowned. 'That's awkward.'

'Why?'

'I've got a lot to do before you can close the opening, and I can't fly this craft at the same time. Can you call her again?'

'If she'd heard, she would have come. Flying is her life.'

M'lainte tapped the toe of her boot on the deck. 'And we have no other pilot . . .'

'Wait! I'm sure Tiaan could do it,' said Nish. 'She was the very first to fly a thapter during the war; in fact, she and Malien worked out *how* to make thapters fly.'

They circumnavigated Morrelune and found Tiaan around the far side, with Merryl; both came aboard at once.

'Can you fly this craft?' said M'lainte, looking anxious for once. 'I know it's been a long time, and the sky-galleon is very different to a thapter . . .'

Tiaan settled onto the pilot's seat, clearly glad to take the weight off her feet. 'After the war, I swore I would never use such devices again. But now I have children to protect, I see that was a foolish oath. If you would give me a couple of minutes.'

Nish and M'lainte walked away to the rail and she leaned on it, looking across the plain. 'How did you end up with Yulla?' Nish asked.

'I was sent to her during the war,' said M'lainte reflectively, 'to look after the thapter Flydd had given her, and afterwards I stayed; Yulla always had something interesting for me to do. And when she took on Persia –'

'I've often wondered how she came to be indentured.'

'It's an all too common story under your father's reign. A powerful, greedy man wanted Clan bel Soon's land and manor, so he sent in a squad of thugs, cut the family down and took everything for himself. Persia was the only one to escape, and the only witness. He hunted her, caught her, and, well, you can imagine the rest. Eight years later, she still hasn't recovered from it.'

'It's a wonder he let her live.'

'He didn't plan to.'

'So how did she end up with Yulla?'

'Yulla knew Persia's parents, so she sent me to rescue her.'

'You!' Nish exclaimed. 'Sorry, I didn't mean –'

'It's quite all right,' M'lainte said equably. 'The job required *brain*, not brawn, plus the use of certain devices hidden since the end of the war. And we did it.'

'And then Persia indentured herself to Yulla for seven years, in repayment,' said Nish.

'Yes,' said M'lainte. 'And for her own safety, of course.'

It explained why Persia would not hear a bad word about Yulla; and also why she so craved the security of a powerful protector.

'What happened to the man who did all this to her?'

'He's out there now.' M'lainte nodded towards the battle-field.

'Vomix!'

'None other.'

'Poor Persia,' Nish said, remembering her terror when she'd seen the seneschal at the monastery. 'She's had to face him again and again.'

'Nothing is gained by hiding from our fears. Ah, Tiaan is ready.'

She was moving the lever back and forth. The sky-galleon shuddered forwards, then back, and Tiaan nodded. 'Whenever you're ready.'

Up at the opening, another squad of atatusk were sliding down their ropes. Nish waited until the platform was empty then said to Tiaan, 'Go, quickly!'

As the sky-galleon raced upwards, sweat prickled in his armpits. His force was pitifully small but it was all the craft could carry, and they would not have long to get everything set up on the platform. If the next squad of atatusk was close enough to charge them, everyone would be swept over the sides.

'Do they have any weaknesses?' said Nish.

'Well . . .' Ryll scratched his armoured backside, his claws making a sound like wood being sawn. 'They don't like each other; they fight in clan groups but they never form armies.'

'They won't need an army. A few dozen of them could finish us off.'

'And their eyesight is poor. They probably can't tell one human from another.'

'I recall *you* saying that we all looked the same.'

'I only said that to be insulting – when we were enemies,' Ryll added hastily. 'But their sense of smell is acute, and they pick up movement quickly with it. Strong smells trouble them, though I wouldn't exactly call that a weakness.'

'If you'd told me earlier I wouldn't have bathed.'

'I wasn't aware that you had.'

Nish swatted at him; Ryll ducked, grinning toothily.

'What kind of smells trouble them?' said Yulla curiously, emerging from the cabin, crystal in hand.

'Pungent ones,' said Ryll. 'I can't think of any other weaknesses. When you're fighting hand-to-hand, they're hard to kill unless you can get in low and close, then strike straight up under the ribs into the heart.'

'If I'm that close, I'm a dead man,' said Nish.

'That's generally the problem,' the lyrinx said drily.

'Better put a rope around the first to jump,' called Lilis as they approached the opening.

'Why?' said Nish, beckoning Aimee and Clech.

'The platform might not be very solid.'

'What do we do if it isn't?'

'Leave that to me,' said M'lainte, popping her head out of the cabin where she was working. 'Ready? The sky-galleon can't go too close to the barrier.'

Clech and Aimee roped up and the craft curved past the platform, fifty spans out. Nish looked through the opening and blanched. If that moving shadow in the far distance was a horde of atatusk, the attack was doomed before it began.

'That's bad,' said Clech.

'They're a good way back,' said Ryll. 'We *might* manage to close it before they get here.'

Now the sky-galleon's flight mechanism began to stutter, and as they approached the barrier it grew worse.

'You'd better go,' said Tiaan. 'I can't keep it here much longer.'

Clech and Aimee sprang over the side onto the platform – and plunged straight through it, trailing their ropes. It might be solid for the void-dwelling atatusk, but it was no firmer than air to humans. Ryll hauled Clech up; Nish did the same for Aimee.

'I was afraid of that,' said M'lainte, hurrying back into the cabin.

Nish made out pouring and stirring sounds, and she returned carrying a wooden bucket full of an oily liquid with pink fire flickering on it, plus a mop.

As Clech hauled himself over the side, M'lainte said, 'Here.' She immersed the mop in the bucket and handed it to him.

'What am I supposed to do with it?' said Clech.

Aimee hooted with laughter. 'Swab the platform, you lubber.'

'The liquid is distilled fire – the corrupted stuff that Zofloc brought – but I've safely diluted it,' said M'lainte. 'Mop the top of the platform and it should turn solid enough to stand on. Then swab across to the opening.'

Tiaan held the stuttering craft in place while Clech mopped a patch on the end of the platform, then prodded it. It did not yield. He jumped down, rather recklessly in Nish's opinion, and began to swab furiously, accompanied by good-natured jeers from his fellow militiamen.

When he'd done half the platform, the troops started over the side. Ryll's crew heaved the small javelard down, plus the ropes and all their other gear, and began to drag it through the opening onto the track leading into the void.

Nish was waiting his turn when M'lainte reappeared and handed him a stoppered flask with a thong tied around its neck.

'What's that for?'

'It's *undiluted* distilled fire, and unlike any other kinds of chthonic fire you may have encountered, it's deadly. One drop will burn right through the barrier, and through you as well, if you get any on you. Once you've heaved the platform into place, rub the merest smear of fire around the edges and it'll seal the opening.'

'How do you know?' said Nish.

'Because that's what it does. When you've finished, Tiaan will come back and pick everyone up.'

Nish thought *everyone* was a trifle over-optimistic, but he nodded and tied the thong to his belt.

M'lainte handed him a dimensionless box. 'This contains your shadow web.'

Nish took the box carefully, knowing how dangerous it was. 'How do I get the web out?'

'Shake the box. And you'll need this to handle the webs.' Holding a black glove by a dangling string, she dropped it into the box. 'Careful – I made it from a dimensionless box. Don't touch the outside of the glove while you're putting it on.'

'What would happen if I did?'

'I can't say, exactly, but Hackel's death would be pleasant by comparison.'

His hair standing on end, Nish crumpled up the dimensionless box and pocketed it.

'You . . . you might find this comes in handy if the atatusk are getting too close,' said Yulla, offering him a beautiful, fist-sized pink crystal, partly translucent and rather heavy.

'What is it?'

'It's the largest crystal of realgar ever found, the prize of my collection. If you burn it, it will give off choking fumes of arsenic – which smells of garlic – and sulphur, both very pungent. Use it wisely.' She turned away abruptly.

'Thank you,' said Nish, conscious that the gift meant far more to her than any of her other treasures.

He clambered down onto the platform, which felt solid beneath his feet, though slightly rubbery, and the sky-galleon sideslipped away.

Before he reached the opening he could feel the chill from beyond. Inside, the granular track, wide enough for a dozen men – or half that many lyrinx – to stand abreast, extended into the limitless void. His defenders had already gone through and were advancing in bounding strides that took them a span into the air, exclaiming at the floating sensation. There was nothing to either side of the track, nor above nor below it – literally nothing except greyness which deepened to black in the distance.

Ahead the track extended straight and true as far as he could see and, moving along it in their separate clan troops, came the atatusk horde. The closest troop was only a few hundred spans away.

'Into position,' said Nish.

The archers aimed their weapons and the lyrinx formed an armoured barrier beside them. At the rear the lancers waited.

'You'd better get on with it,' said Ryll, bouncing several spans into the air so as to see further. 'We can't hold them long.'

Nish ran out to the platform, shook the sticky shadow web from its dimensionless box and gingerly slipped his hand into the black glove without touching the outside, which was more difficult than it had seemed.

Using the glove, he pressed a strip of shadow web across the edge of the platform, waited for it to set and yanked hard to make sure it was secure. The web pulled away. He turned it over and tried the other side, with the same result. The plan wasn't going to work; the web wasn't sticky enough to lift the solidified platform.

So how were they to close the opening?

FORTY-FIVE

'I'll send you back now, Maelys,' said Nadiril, rubbing his bald and blotchy skull with his fingertips, 'for time is precious. Vivimord, you're the best orator I've ever known. You must convince the revenants that it's safe for them to leave the shadow realm and go to Stilkeen.'

The librarian's clouded eyes settled on the carpet-wrapped parcel on her lap, as if he knew what was inside.

Maelys stirred reluctantly. She felt safe here but, once she left Nadiril, she would be surrounded by enemies, including Vivimord, who hadn't yet said that he would help. For all she knew, he was still set on revenge.

'That won't be easy,' said Vivimord. 'Stilkeen has impressed upon its revenants that they must remain in the shadow realm until it lets them out, on peril of their lives. They may be foolish, thoughtless creatures, but they won't disobey it.'

Nadiril turned those all-seeing blind eyes on him. 'Yet should the revenants come to believe that Stilkeen had opened the gate and was calling them, and if *you* convinced them that it was safe to leave, I don't think anyone would be able to stop them. They yearn to rejoin with it just as much as it does with them. That longing is a constant ache, a burning need that affects them both, when they are severed.'

'I might be able to sway them,' said Vivimord. 'But what would be the point? I can't let them out of the shadow realm.'

'Can't they go out the way I came in?' said Maelys.

'The dead may take many paths into the shadow realm,' said Nadiril, again looking down at her lap, 'but they have only one way out, and that gate has not been opened in the two hundred years I've spent here. No one has the key and, assuming such a key is ever found, the gate only lets one spirit out per opening.'

'Does that mean only one revenant?'

'The revenants may all leave at once, since they are effectively one spirit – but no other.'

'What about me?' said Maelys, squeezing the heavy knoblaggie in her pocket.

'Live humans can pass through any entrance,' said Vivimord. He paused, then added menacingly, 'as long as they have the means to open it. *And they stay alive long enough.*'

Would the knoblaggie open the gate for her? Klarm hadn't said anything about that. Had he used the knoblaggie to escape – or the tears?

'Didn't you say, not long after you reached the shadow realm, that your Black Arts had fashioned a key?' said Nadiril.

'I did,' said Vivimord. 'Though unfortunately, when I died at the Maelstrom of Justice and Retribution, I did not have the key with me. Besides, it was *my* way back to life.'

'Then should you ever regain it, you will face a difficult choice. Which do you love more – beautiful Santhenar, or your own freedom?'

Maelys looked from one to the other, frowning, for Nadiril

was talking as though Vivimord did have the key, or soon would.

'You can't possibly understand, you dried-up old fool,' said Vivimord in a low voice.

'Can't I?' said Nadiril mildly.

'Your librarian's span was far more than the allotted life of any man, and by its end you must have been glad to die. My life was brutally cut short.'

'As you cut short the lives of many others,' Nadiril pointed out. 'Few people are ever *glad* to go and I was not – my research was at a most fascinating stage when I died. Besides, what use is your freedom if you return to a world that has been destroyed – *when you could have saved it?*'

Vivimord did not reply, though Maelys could see his lungs swelling and contracting through his chest, as though his spirit, which could have no need for air, was breathing heavily.

'You must abandon those dreams, my friend,' Nadiril added, 'for the dead may not return to life. But when we spirits are given a chance to ease the burden of the living, we must seize it, to atone for the wrongs we did during our own lives. Maelys, it's time. Give it to him.'

'What?' said Maelys, shifting on her seat.

The sabre, of course. Klarm had said that Vivimord might be glad to see it, because it was enchanted. What for? To cut his way out of the shadow realm? Yes, that must be it. Vivimord had talked about his delvings into the mancery of death a long time ago. *I know Black Arts that can make a corpse scream in agony*, he'd said to her after she had killed Phrune.

She turned towards Vivimord, praying that he would not use those Arts on her, and allowed the carpet to fall away, exposing the sabre.

Vivimord stared at it in wonder. 'My fashioned key! Where did you get it?'

'Klarm thought you might need it.'

'I enchanted it long ago, so as to open the gate of the shadow realm,' said Vivimord. 'Though I did not expect to be using it from the other side of death.' He reached out for the sabre. 'It's mine, and I can take it. I don't owe you a thing in return.'

'My Arts can break the key, *permanently*,' said Nadiril coldly. 'I'd advise you to act honourably to her, Vivimord.'

'Very well,' scowled Vivimord, taking the sabre. 'But I'm not sure it will –'

A ghastly rising and falling wail fluttered the clouds above them, followed by another, and another.

'What's that?' whispered Maelys, rising to her toes.

She could not see anything amiss, but now it felt grey and cold in the shadow realm, and she remembered how afraid Flydd had been of coming here. Once outside the small oasis of Nadiril's influence, how could she hope to survive? She hugged her goosepimpled arms to her chest, afraid that there was no way out for her.

'From time to time the revenants must feed,' said Nadiril, 'and they consume the life forces of the slowest and weakest spirits, the ones easiest to catch. Even in the shadow realm the hunt goes on. One day it will be my turn.'

'No!' she cried. 'Can't anyone stop them?'

'As I explained,' Nadiril said gently, 'they're quite invulnerable here.'

The screams continued until dozens of souls must have been consumed, then, in a flash, Vivimord was gone. Maelys waited, uneasily, and directly he returned.

'There is news from outside,' he said grimly. 'The void has had a great victory; an army has fallen and the other cannot last. That's why the revenants are feeding; they know they'll soon be freed.'

'What's happened to Nish?' Maelys cried, unable to bear the thought of losing him as well. After such a disastrous defeat, many of her friends might be dead; perhaps all of them. 'I've got to get back.'

'We're not quite ready yet,' said Nadiril, glancing at Vivimord, who looked away.

Panic almost overwhelmed her but she fought it down and forced herself to stay calm. If the revenants came this way, she would use the knoblaggie. And if they attacked a second time, then what?

'Stilkeen must have ordered the revenants to feed and fatten their spirits,' said Vivimord. 'It must believe that it will soon have the pure fire.'

'And, alas, the more souls they consume now, the stronger will be the bonding when they and Stilkeen are rejoined,' said Nadiril.

'How many can they consume before they're full?' Maelys croaked, for her throat had gone so dry that she could barely speak.

Vivimord laughed scornfully.

'You can't get full on spirits,' said Nadiril. 'The revenants could consume all of us . . . but that's not my big worry.'

Ice touched her veins. 'What is?'

'That they might scent *you*. A spirit housed in a living body is far tastier than we disembodied ones . . . and more fattening, too.' He rose like a creaky old crane, knees cracking and elbows flailing. 'We'd better convey Maelys to the gate, now you've the means to open it,' he said to Vivimord. 'It'll take a good while to get there.'

'I thought the shadow realm touched all places equally?' said Maelys.

'It does, but the gate is some distance away. Vivimord, gather a shell of spirits around us so we can hide Maelys from them.'

Vivimord gave him a black look, and Maelys was afraid that he was going to refuse, for in life he had been a mighty and commanding man while Nadiril, for all his wisdom and knowledge, had been just a librarian.

'Go!' said Nadiril, and his wispy voice shivered with power.

Vivimord shot off without looking back.

'I was never *just* a librarian,' said Nadiril, as though he had read her thoughts. 'I was a member of the Great Council of Santhenar for two centuries, and I would certainly have had that twerp's measure when I was alive.'

'Thank you,' said Maelys. 'But I thought the taphloid would hide me from the revenants.'

'It would, in the physical world, but not here, and I pray that we can protect you. Ah, here they come.'

A flock of spirits soared towards them like birds in flight, their garments fluttering. There were children and crones, toothless old men, pregnant young women and every other age, size and shape of humanity. They whirled into a cylinder around Maelys, took hold of her and lifted her towards the clouds above.

Glancing over her shoulder, Maelys made out something red but blurry winding in her direction like a python gliding across a carpet. More screams issued forth; the spirits tightened their grip and flew faster.

Another flock of spirits appeared on the left, coming to her protection, but a second sinuous red shadow curved around them, this time like a tiger circling a herd of deer. The spirits flocked one way, then another, like frightened birds. A red shadow darted, snapped; a straggling spirit wailed as it was gulped and devoured.

So it went on, as they fled across the shadow realm for

what seemed like hours. There were seven revenants, and they took down the spirits in the second flock one by one, then the flock Vivimord recruited after that, until the last spirit had been taken and no others dared approach. Soon they would come after Maelys.

'They're gaining; we must go faster,' said Nadiril to her spirit shield.

'We can't carry her any faster,' said a strong, heavy-bodied spirit, in an exhausted voice. 'She's alive. She has weight and we have none.'

'We must all try a little harder,' said Nadiril, taking Maelys's arm in his fleshless hand.

'The revenants are coming,' said a spirit youth who could not have been older than thirteen when he died. He looked like the little brother Maelys had often wished for. 'Why should we be consumed to save *her*?'

'Because it's the right thing to do,' Nadiril said gently.

'I'm scared,' said the boy.

'So am I,' said Nadiril. 'Come in beside me, lad. We'll get there yet.' Nadiril moved up ahead, taking the boy with him.

Now the five Phrunes came slithering in between the spirits of her flock, rubbing their chubby hands together and leaving snail trails of ectoplasm behind them. 'We promised revenge,' leered the first of them, 'and we're going to have you.'

Maelys clutched the knoblaggie. Was now the time to use it? No, for that would surely cost her protection as well, and the gate was not yet in sight.

The Phrunes approached, leering, and her stomach churned with revulsion; in life he had been a sadistic killer and death had not improved him. The plump fingers were almost touching her when Vivimord appeared from above. 'Phrunes, begone!'

'But, Master, you promised!' they wept.

'Things have changed, and now she's mine. I have no further need of you.'

'Master!' snivelled the Phrunes. 'I gave my life for you.'

'And I thank you for it, but I am going where no spirit can follow. Leave us.'

The Phrunes wailed and shot out like sparks from a firework, without looking where they were going. The circling revenants snapped as one, gagged, swallowed and the Phrunes were gone.

But the revenants weren't satisfied, and they were moving in – they must have scented her. They looked larger, stronger, more solid now, and they began to dart at the tail end of her protecting flock, picking them off one by one. Maelys was afraid that her spirits would abandon her, but Nadiril kept encouraging them and, though they were terrified, none fled or tried to save themselves.

A revenant shot by in a long red blur streaked with black. Dark spots at the front seemed less than eyes; it had a swaying tail like a running crocodile, limbs that dissolved and reformed, and a round, fleshy maw that appeared better suited to suction than to biting. Maelys did not find that comforting.

'They're shapeshifters,' said Nadiril, who was still holding her arm, 'as is Stilkeen itself, and before being severed they could take on any aspect they wanted, though in the shadow realm they always look much the same – rather reptilian. For half an eternity they had whatever they wanted and they believe it is their right. That's the arrogance of absolute power, the arrogance of the *being* – look out!'

Two revenants shot in, one from either side, nosing the spirits out of the way and going for Maelys like red rockets. Just as they were about to strike, she willed a solid shield around her with the knoblaggie.

It formed around Vivimord and Nadiril as well, and the

revenants slammed into it and recoiled, snarling and snapping at their tails. Unfortunately the remaining spirits, sent tumbling through the air, were hurled aside by the shield and gulped down one after another. The boy who had been so frightened was attacked last of all, his wet eyes staring desperately at them.

'Nadiril, help me!' he cried.

'I'm sorry, lad, I can't reach you.' Nadiril, trapped inside the shield, could only watch as the boy was taken.

Tears sprang to Maelys's own eyes. He had died so young; and now his spirit was gone too, forever. It didn't seem fair.

As they continued, the knoblaggie's shield slowly faded. There were only two spirits with her now: Nadiril and Vivimord, and Nadiril was thinning visibly.

A revenant bored in at him, expecting another easy victim. Nadiril raised his hand, a stubby wand was outlined there, and the revenant was blasted away. It rolled over and over, snapping at its tail, before sinking out of sight.

'Get on with it, Vivimord,' said Nadiril faintly. 'I've used half my ectoplasmic essence and I didn't have much to start with.'

The revenant came slinking back up and the others joined it. Vivimord stopped in mid-air and called out to them, though Maelys only caught the first part of his oration.

'Revenants, Stilkeen has the white fire at last; that's why it told you to fatten up. And now it is calling you to rejoin with it, to come together as one. Just think how wonderful your reunion is going to be, after thousands of years of *severance*. It will soon be safe to leave the shadow realm and I, Vivimord, or Life-in-Death, am the one person who can cleave the shadow realm to the real world to let you out . . .'

His voice faded as she passed out of hearing, but shortly the revenants reappeared. Had Vivimord's oratory failed, or had he offered *her* to them?

They came spiralling in from the rear, seven attacking at once, and Maelys put on a desperate spurt, thinking she was gone. Again Nadiril drove them off with his wand, but not far this time, and it was clear he could not do it a third time.

Vivimord renewed his siren song, more compellingly than before, and the revenants dropped back. Maelys could see the great gate now, not far ahead, but before she reached it the revenants came streaking for her like a seven-headed trident, and Nadiril was struggling to keep up.

'Sorry, Maelys,' he said, trying to smile. 'There's nothing left of me.' He was much more transparent than before; barely there, for the power he'd used had been drawn from his spirit and could not be replenished. 'And I had so much to mull over,' he added huskily. 'A whole lifetime of reading to digest. Ah, well; all things must pass. All lives, and all deaths.'

Her heart went out to the ancient, gentle spirit. 'We can still make it.'

She took his arm and clutched the useless knoblaggie to her chest with her other hand, wishing it was the weapon that could destroy the revenants out in the real world. If she got the chance, she would not hesitate.

'Make it,' he echoed.

As they raced for the gate, Vivimord flew alongside the revenants, and his oratory would have charmed a snail out of its shell. Unfortunately, with such a sweet, fleshly victim so near, they would not be distracted.

The seven of them dived for her, lunged together, but Nadiril's long, bony arm hooked around Maelys's waist and from the last of his essence he drew the strength to hurl her at the barred gate, so hard that she felt sure she was going to break her neck. She was trying to protect her face with her arms when light stabbed from the old librarian's wand and the gate opened just wide enough to let her through.

The revenants turned on him, snapped, and Nadiril was gone. The gate slammed closed, the shadow realm faded and she went skidding across one of the floors of Morrelune on her backside.

Maelys came to a halt and sat up, rubbing her bruised bottom. Old Nadiril, that great librarian and dear old man, was gone forever, his spirit *consumed*. How was she going to tell Lilis?

She got up, shaking. A great and noble spirit had been lost, and for what? She still did not know how to stop Stilkeen.

'Who else must be destroyed?' she raged. 'How many more are we going to lose?'

And she had rewarded one of the most sickening scoundrels in all Santhenar. She had given Vivimord the means to come back from death, which surely he was going to take.

She was trudging towards a stair when she slipped on a sticky patch of floor and saw Klarm's boot and severed foot. She had returned to the level below the audience chamber. She set the knoblaggie down beside it and looked around for him, trying to think.

The creatures from the void have had a great victory, Vivimord had said. *An army has fallen and the other cannot last.* But which army had fallen – Nish's? She climbed the steps, stumbled across the sand-strewn, bloodstained audience chamber and out a side entrance to the promenade, to look down over a scene of chaos.

Smoke drifted across the paved plain, and in the garish, fume-yellowed glow from the lanterns of Morrelune and Mazurhize she saw bodies everywhere in gory, unidentifiable heaps.

Around to her left, not far from the edge of the Sacred Lake, a company of the white-armoured Imperial Guard was fighting a horde of beasts like long-tailed bears – no, not beasts, for they carried forged weapons and knew how to use them. Further off, a phalanx of lyrinx was in furious melee with several winged serpents, and other struggles were visible fleetingly through the smoke.

A monstrous creature rose from the fumes, standing on its back legs and beating its chest with a pumpkin-sized fist, making a sound like a huge drum. It was at least two spans high, and in its other hand it held two Imperial Guardsmen. Raising them to its mouth it bit their heads off, spat their plumed helmets high into the air and beat its breast again.

Now it began to lay into a squad of Vomix's soldiers with the bodies, battering the troops out of the way with great sweeps of its arms. It turned, caught sight of Maelys on the steps, dropped the headless bodies and headed in her direction.

For a few seconds, she couldn't move. Had it seen her? Even if she ran, she could not hope to get away, for it could take six strides to her one.

The sky-galleon came rocketing around a corner of the palace, piloted by Tiaan. It banked sharply and M'lainte, who was seated at the javelard, fired three spears at once into the chest of the beast. They disappeared, it slapped its chest as if it had been bitten by a fly, and kept coming.

Maelys forced her paralysed legs into action and was backing away when a river of brown blood fountained from the beast's mouth and it crashed to the paving stones at the foot of the steps, shattering several of them.

'Thanks,' she said, raising an unsteady hand, but the sky-galleon had already zoomed away.

The smoke was getting thicker; she could hardly see anything now, and apart from M'lainte and Tiaan she hadn't recognised anyone. Her friends might all be dead.

Even if they were, she had to fight on. Stilkeen had to be

beaten and the world saved; there must be a way. Nadiril had said that there was one single way to beat Stilkeen, and it involved the revenants. Maelys turned, puzzling over that, and ran straight into Yalkara.

'So,' Yalkara said, holding her so tightly that there was no chance for escape.

Maelys had not seen her since her arrival at the Range of Ruin, weeks ago. 'What do you want with me?' she whispered, looking up at the much taller woman. 'Oh! What's happened to you?'

The right side of Yalkara's face was black and blue, a ragged scar marred her once-perfect left cheek, and her nose had recently been broken. Her clothing was tattered but, more tellingly, she no longer wore the aura of ageless self-assurance that had so characterised her previously. Yalkara looked defeated.

'I have been fighting the Numinator ever since Stilkeen came to the Range of Ruin,' she said breathlessly, and her voice had the hoarseness of old age now. 'And she has beaten me. My own granddaughter has brought me down. Yet I still have one hope.'

Placing her battered hands on Maelys's belly, Yalkara pressed gently, eyes closed, as if reading what lay within. Her fingers were hot and had a slight tremor. What was she reading?

Yalkara froze, the tremor stopped and the heat drained from her fingers, replaced by a prickly chill.

Maelys jerked away, more afraid than ever. 'What are you doing to me?'

Yalkara was trembling again, her whole arm this time, and she could not stop it. She rubbed her fingers, which were blue, while her knuckles were red and swollen like the joints of an arthritic old woman. 'I would never harm you, nor the child you carry.'

'What?' said Maelys dazedly. 'Are you saying that I *am* pregnant?'

'Yes.'

'Definitely?'

'Yes, of course. Haven't you been feeling ill in the mornings?'

Maelys was stunned. Pregnant? She had hardly thought about the possibility since the Range of Ruin. She had not wanted to think about it, and when there had been no signs, not even sore breasts, she had decided that she could not be pregnant.

'No . . . but it hasn't yet been a month since Emberr and I . . . What's the matter? Is there something wrong with the baby?' Her voice rose; she was shaking too.

'You carry a perfect, *old human* baby,' said Yalkara. 'And all my endeavours have come to naught. I will never see Emberr's child, for soon I will be dead.'

Being pregnant changed everything. 'Then my baby will be all alone,' said Maelys, for she felt sure that the rest of her family were dead.

'I'm sorry. My life is running out, but before I go, reparation must be made.'

'You can start by telling us where you hid the pure fire.'

'The Numinator and I saw Stilkeen's proclamation during one of our battles,' said Yalkara absently. 'But she does not know where any pure fire lies, and neither do I.'

'How can you not know?' said Flydd, staggering out of the smoke with Yggur. They were supporting each other, and both were blood-spattered, smoke-stained and bleeding from many small wounds. The rivalry was gone; for the first time they seemed like old friends, and Maelys smiled to see it.

'You stole the fire and hid it,' Flydd snapped. 'You alone had custody of it until you brought it to Santhenar.'

Yalkara did not reply. Maelys ran and threw her arms

592

around Flydd, then Yggur, heedless of the blood. 'How goes the battle? I heard, in the shadow realm –'

Flydd's eyes nearly started out of their sockets. 'What the blazes were you doing in there?' he bellowed, wrenching Maelys from Yggur's grasp and shaking her furiously. 'Who let you in? And how did you ever get out?'

'If you'll stop shaking me, I'll tell you. Is – is Nish all right? I heard that an army had fallen and another was on its knees.'

'The Imperial Guard has fallen,' said Flydd. 'Nosby is dead, and two-thirds of his men – they took the brunt of the attack and died valiantly.'

'And Vomix's army is on its knees, more than a thousand dead already –'

Yggur broke off as Tulitine hobbled out of the smoke. She had a long cut across her brow and two rents down her left shoulder, almost to the elbow, and yet, astonishingly, she looked better than she had hours ago. Yggur helped her up to the top step, where they sat down together.

'You should not be fighting,' said Maelys, going to her knees beside Tulitine. She had to keep busy; had to distract herself from the thought of being pregnant, not to mention her worries about Nish. 'Let me bind –'

'The wounds are clean and I can barely feel the pain,' said Tulitine. 'Indeed, it's a welcome distraction from my aching bones.'

'What about Vomix?' said Maelys. As long as he lived she could not feel safe.

'He disappeared not long after the atatusk first attacked,' said Flydd.

'Dead?' she said hopefully.

'Alas, no. He took his best thousand men and said that he was trying to outflank the enemy, but he hasn't been seen since.'

'Has he run?'

'Not Vomix. He'll be in hiding, waiting for us to fall so he can claim the spoils,' said Flydd, and spat down over the steps. 'But not if I can help it.'

'Where's Nish?' Maelys caught Flydd by the arm. 'What's happened to him?'

'We don't know where he is,' he said wearily. 'He and Ryll made some absurd plan to try and close the opening into the void, but . . .'

Maelys looked up, but the barrier could barely be seen through the smoke and the opening was not visible. 'I've got to find him.'

'Not in all this mess,' said Flydd. 'And you have questions to answer. What the blazes were you doing in the shadow realm?'

'Looking for a way to attack a *being*. Klarm let me in –'

'Where is the little runt?' growled Flydd. 'With his help, and the tears –'

'I don't know . . .' Too many thoughts were crowding through Maelys's mind; she could not tease them apart. 'He sent me there to find old Nadiril, and *his* spirit told me . . .' Her voice faded as she thought about that dear old man, giving up all he had left to save her, '. . . before the revenants got him. Nadiril gave his spirit to get me out.'

'What did he *tell* you?' said Flydd.

'That the revenants can only be attacked when they're outside the shadow realm. Vivimord is trying to convince them that it's safe to come out –'

'How is he going to release them?'

'I gave him his enchanted sabre. It's the key to opening the gate.'

'You gave Vivimord the means to return from death?' Flydd said dazedly.

Maelys crossed her fingers behind her back. 'I had to take the risk.' And she prayed that it worked.

'It's a big risk. What if he comes back and leaves the revenants there?'

'Then I've failed,' said Maelys. 'But if they *do* come out, and we can attack them before they rejoin with Stilkeen, they can be annihilated and Stilkeen will be crippled for half an eternity . . . at least, that's what Nadiril said.'

'How *do* we attack revenants?' said Flydd.

'Unfortunately Nadiril didn't know that . . .'

'So either we face a resurgent Vivimord back from death,' said Flydd, pacing, 'if he betrays his word, or if he keeps it, the revenants will come forth to rejoin with Stilkeen. Once that happens it will no longer be crippled; it will be a thousand times as powerful, and bent on revenge.'

Through the thickening smoke, the sounds of battle rose and fell. 'It's got to find the true fire first,' said Maelys.

'I feel I should know how,' said Yggur, who had his arm around Tulitine.

'How to find the true fire?' said Maelys.

'No – the way to destroy the revenants. The answer feels . . . just out of reach.'

Maelys started, for she'd had a sudden flash of memory – the rain, the caduceus steaming on the hillside – but it eluded her too.

Flydd stalked across to Yalkara, who was slumped on the promenade some distance away. 'I don't believe that you know nothing about the pure fire. Charon *never* give up.'

'The other Charon gave up at the end of the Time of the Mirror,' said Yalkara. 'They went back to the void, and to extinction, if you recall.'

'And you returned, so it's hardly extinction.'

'It is now. I've burned out my Art fighting the Numinator, I'll not get it back, and I'm ready to die. I can't help you – I have no idea where the pure fire is to be found.'

Flydd was watching her carefully, and finally he nodded.

'You speak the truth. Very well; before you go, would you answer one question for me?'

'If I may,' Yalkara said indifferently. She looked old now and seemed to be fading by the minute.

'When I found Rulke's virtual construct in the Nightland, it was *live*; therefore it had been used after Rulke died – after the Nightland collapsed and was rebuilt. Did you use the construct?'

'Of course not,' said Yalkara. 'When I left Emberr there, I departed via the gate through which I had entered, and could not return.'

'What about Emberr?'

'He could never leave the Nightland; not even with a virtual construct.'

'How curious,' said Flydd. 'Now, to the pure fire. Stilkeen said it wasn't far away. Was any lost, when you first had it?'

'Not when I *first* had it,' said Yalkara. 'I guarded it with the utmost care.'

'But later? After you brought it to Santhenar?'

'I thought some might have been taken, once, but who can be sure? Fire grows, and fire dies down. You can't measure it in a bucket.'

'When was this?'

'At the end of the Clysm, not long before Kandor died –'

'Ahhhh!' said Yggur.

FORTY-SIX

Nish absently slapped his leg with the flat of his sword, trying to work out a way to seal the opening, assuming they survived long enough to try, which was looking increasingly doubtful.

The human and lyrinx guards were arrayed in a semi-circle inside the opening, on the track that extended into the chilly void. There was nothing to either side of the track – literally *nothing* – though further away separate bands of atatusk were moving along it like beads on a wire until they blurred into the distance.

'There's thousands of them,' said Ryll quietly.

And only two dozen human and lyrinx defenders to hold them back until the opening could be sealed. The javelard operator began winding his apparatus up so he could fire over the defenders' heads.

An inflowing current of air ruffled Nish's hair, and round knobs of green ice were forming around the inside edges of the opening, condensing layer by layer like pearls around grains of sand.

'How are we going to raise the platform?' said Nish.

'That's easy,' said Aimee, who was standing on tiptoes whispering to Clech.

'At least they can only come straight on,' Clech said in a low rumble. 'Imagine if they could attack from all directions.'

'Nothing is fixed in the void,' said Nish. 'In five minutes there could be a dozen paths leading this way. What's your idea, Aimee?'

'We sew the opening up, like a tear in the knee of your pants.'

'Fire!' said Stibble, the burly, hairy smith who was Nish's acting sergeant. He did not deign to carry a blade, but wielded his long-handled blacksmith's hammer with deadly force. Crossbows snapped.

'Direct hits.' Nish recognised the voice of Lym, the stocky little archer, then she said, 'Beyl, Beyl, they're not falling.'

'It's hard to kill atatusk with a chest or belly shot,' said Ryll. 'They've got six ells of blubber there. Aim for the throat or the head.'

Neither would be easy to hit, for the nearest atatusk were at extreme range, but the archers fired again. 'Got one,' said Zana.

'He's not falling, though. He's pulling the arrow out of his neck,' said Lym, her voice rising. 'That was a killing shot for any other beast, and the atatusk is still moving.'

'Hold firm,' said Beyl, the grey-haired veteran, who also sounded panicky.

Nish turned away. He had a job to do and he was wasting time. 'Sew it?' He realised he must sound like a fool.

'We worked it out while you were scratching your arse,' said Clech rudely. 'You'll run around the edge of the platform, burning little holes with the flask of distilled fire and knotting ropes through them, while Aimee and I make matching holes in the wall around the opening. Then we attach your ropes to arrows, shoot them through the holes in the wall, and heave the platform up.'

'Let's get it done,' said Nish.

He smoothed the shadow web down with the perilous dimensionless glove, dropped it into the black box, screwed it up and shoved it into his pocket. Pouring a dribble of fire onto the end of his sword, he passed Aimee the stoppered flask. Now Nish tilted the sword blade to allow a single drop of the pink fire to fall near the edge of the platform. It burnt a hole through it, but it kept expanding until it reached the edge – one drop of distilled fire was too much.

He touched his sword tip to the platform, which was better; his second hole was only as wide as a saucer. Once the fire had gone out, Nish hastily threaded a rope through, tied it securely, coiled it beside the hole and ran to do the next.

There came a fearful roar from his militia, and a shout of 'Hold! Hold!' from Ryll. An atatusk let out a triumphant barking bellow but Nish restrained the urge to look around; he continued burning holes and tying ropes to them.

After finishing the last hole, he darted to the opening and looked in, but the view ahead was blocked by a furious melee. Three of his troops were down and one, unidentifiable from his blood-covered back, had been maimed by a savage blow.

Another, the archer, Lym, bore no apparent injury, though her head now faced backwards and her eyes were wide open, as if astonished at what had happened to her. Stibble the hairy blacksmith appeared to have been gored through the skull with two tusks – three more of Nish's loyal Gendrigoreans gone.

Two lyrinx were also down, though one kept trying to rise, purple blood streaming down his left thigh, his right hand reaching out to Nish as if for aid.

It wrenched him to turn away, but he had his own work to do and if he failed their deaths would be for nothing. Aimee was twenty spans up the barrier wall, hanging from sticky pads of shadow web bound around hands, knees and feet. Clech was below her, trying to climb, but the shadow webs weren't sticky enough to support his weight, which was not greatly lessened at the barrier.

Nish began to sweat, for the plan depended on them raising the platform quickly and it was taking far too long. If the atatusk broke through first, as seemed probable, the opening could not be sealed.

Aimee unfastened her rope and crept across the barrier, above the curve of the opening. Being so small and light, the sticky pads held her easily. She shook the flask, withdrew the stopper with her teeth – Don't! Nish thought, if you get any pink fire on you, it'll eat through your face – and pressed it against the barrier until a neat hole formed there.

Bellowing like a walrus, a huge atatusk burst through the line, sending guards and lyrinx flying, and before the javelard operator could bring his weapon to bear, the beast had leapt three spans in the air and was falling towards him from above.

The operator tried to drag out his sword but the atatusk landed right in front of him and snapped its head down, plunging the twin tusks into his back on either side of the spine. It tossed its head from side to side and the operator went spinning across the track, pouring blood from twin lemon-sized punctures, then over the edge into the nothingness of the void.

The atatusk slammed one of the heavy metal spears into the groove of the javelard and wound the cranks so fast that they were just a blur. No dumb beast this – it had understood how to use the javelard in an instant.

Nish reacted without thinking, knowing that if the creature was not stopped it would wipe out the defenders in seconds. As he sprang for the back of the javelard's box-like wooden frame, the atatusk pulled the lever and the spear, fired at point-blank range, passed straight through a massive lyrinx and into the spine of the smaller one in front of him, bringing it down as well. Was it Ryll? No, it had wings.

Letting out a roar of approval for the ruinous weapon, the atatusk took another spear. Nish climbed the frame one-handed and went for the creature from behind. It could not have heard him over the clamour of battle, so it must have smelt him, and it was spinning around in the seat as he swung.

He drove hard for the junction of the atatusk's neck and right shoulder, and the blade cut deep into a blubbery layer before stopping on bone. Such a blow would have killed any human, and disabled most lyrinx.

Green blood poured out; the atatusk emitted an explosive snort, but went for the blade and Nish whipped it out of the wound; another second and it would have been snatched from his fingers. But then, as he watched, the gash pulled itself together and the flesh knitted across, leaving a dark brown, seamed scar across the thick grey skin.

No wonder atatusk ate the lyrinx for breakfast — not even a master healer could heal that quickly. How was he supposed to kill such a creature? Nish wasn't game to get close enough to strike that steep, angling and desperately risky blow up into the heart.

He slid backwards, then feinted, going for its eyes. The atatusk did not even blink; it threw its left arm around the frame upright next to it, swung around it and launched itself at him before he knew what was happening.

Such a heavily-built creature ought to be slow and lumbering, but in the void it was desperately fast, and Nish couldn't get out of the way in time. He hurled himself backwards off the javelard from a height of a span and a half, a fall which, on Santhenar, would have risked a broken neck.

He landed on his head, bounced, flipped over backwards and ended up on his feet again, but the sword jarred out of his hand and went skidding across the track.

Pink fire still flickered near the tip. He leapt for the sword, steadied himself, and waited. He had to stop the atatusk and he'd better be quick. It took a little jump forwards and bared its teeth at him, but its eyes rolled upwards; it was looking at Clech and Aimee. Could it spring that high? Nish rather suspected that it might be able to, in the void, and they were unarmed.

'You're not touching them,' he gritted. 'You're mine, atatusk.'

Letting out a barking sneer, it snapped its tusks up and down, and moved towards him. He ran at it, weaving a wall of steel in front of him, and got in a slash to its lower left arm. The wound was a minor one but the creature seemed to be expecting him to follow through, so Nish did not, and only just evaded a blow that would have torn his head from his neck.

He struck again, trying to probe its weaknesses, but he wasn't seeing any. In the past he'd defeated lyrinx by diving between their legs, but the atatusk's legs were so much shorter that it wasn't an option.

It sprang, soaring high above him then down, the way it had attacked the javelard operator. He swiped at it and rolled well out of the way, or thought he had, but it flipped sideways in the air, a movement he would not have thought possible, swung at his head and a claw tore through the top of his ear, ripping it like parchment.

Nish threw himself the other way, but too far; being close to weightless here, he was having trouble controlling his movements. As the atatusk landed in a crouch he saw an opening, spun on his left foot, bounced upwards and took an almighty slash at its face.

It swayed backwards and he missed, but several motes of the pink fire must have been flung off his blade into the creature's eyes, for it made a harsh squealing sound and rubbed furiously at them.

Yes! Pink fire was glowing in its eyes and it couldn't see, though it continued to fight, turning its head from side to side and sniffing the air to locate him by smell. Since its eyesight was poor, the loss of vision probably wasn't a great handicap.

Nish back-pedalled, thinking furiously. Surely its sense of smell, no matter how acute, could not locate him as accurately as sight, especially if he came at it front-on. That's it, he thought: I'll try to confuse it, make a furious front-on attack, and if I'm wrong, I die.

He rubbed his left hand in his sweaty armpit then raised it high to the left, to spread a false scent trail. As the atatusk swung at his hand, he closed his fist, ducked to the right and darted in under its upraised arms. For a fraction of a second it hesitated, unsure where he was, because the Nish smells were coming from two different directions.

It located him and lunged to take him in a bear hug, but Nish threw himself against its lower belly and struck up, under the hump at the top of the chest, and levered inwards. He felt the tip of his sword slide between the bones into solid, thumping muscle, the heart, and twisted. The atatusk stiffened, emerald blood exploded from its mouth, and before he could free his sword the creature fell on top of him.

On Santhenar the impact of an atatusk eight times his weight would have crushed him to death, but here he was merely trapped beneath it, its scalding blood flooding over his face until he could barely breathe. Its internal organs churned and bubbled deafeningly; its punctured heart gave a last ragged thump, then stopped.

Nish tried to push it off but could not get a grip on the blood-slick skin. His nose was squashed and with every strangled breath he blew gory green bubbles. Each breath was harder than the last and he was close to drowning when the atatusk was heaved off and Ryll stood there, his armoured chest heaving.

Long claw marks across his right shoulder had torn through his armoured outer skin to the soft inner skin beneath, but lyrinx could take a lot of punishment and he did not seem troubled.

Ryll shook his head, wonderingly. 'That was a mighty stroke for a little pink grub,' he said, lifting Nish to his feet. He tore the shirt off the dead javelard operator and Nish scrubbed the green blood off his face with it.

'We can't hold them, my friend,' Ryll said to Nish's unasked question.

Six of Nish's twelve had fallen, plus four lyrinx, and the enemy was regrouping not far away. Nish looked around. 'Where's Clech and Aimee?'

'Outside, trying to shoot your ropes through the holes. Better give them a hand.'

Ryll bounded back to the defenders. As Nish stumbled out, Clech fired an arrow and it shot up towards the wall, trailing the rope, only to fall short.

'Can't get it near the hole,' Clech said disgustedly as he hauled it back.

'The rope's much too heavy,' said Nish, 'and we're running out of defenders. Aimee, you'll have to climb up and pass the ropes through each hole.'

'Have we got time?' said Aimee.

'I'll make time. I've had an idea. Give me the flask!'

She handed it to him. 'Don't use all the pink fire up – I need some to stick the platform back in place.'

Nish ran in and leapt up into the high seat of the

604

javelard – he was getting the hang of the low gravity now. He fitted a spear into the groove and spun the winding handle with one hand while he swung the sights back and forth, looking for a target.

A pair of atatusk were advancing, about fifty spans off, but three lyrinx were in the way. He pointed the javelard to the left, where Ryll was in furious combat with another atatusk, and put a spear through its middle. The impact took the creature over the edge of the track and out of sight. Its blubber layer might stop an arrow but only the heaviest steel armour could keep out a javelard spear.

Ryll raised a thumb in acknowledgement. Nish was looking for another target when Liett flashed though the air above his head, her outstretched wings an iridescent glory. She was pointing further down the track.

'What is it?' said Nish.

'The void is changing, *or they're changing it.* Paths are forming everywhere.'

Nish squinted into the distance. His eyes hurt from the atatusk blood and his vision was a trifle fuzzy, but something did seem to be forming down there. Yes, more paths were extending slowly this way, one curving in from the left and another down from the right, while two more were snaking up from the unseen depths.

On every path he could see atatusk, and once they reached the opening they would wipe out the defence in moments.

'Hurry, Aimee!' he yelled. 'Can you help, Liett?'

Liett flitted through the opening then came racing back, shooting over Nish's head to attack the atatusk from above, going for the eyes and nose. It was a perilous manoeuvre, since they could leap many spans, and Liett, being delicately boned and unarmoured, was far more vulnerable than the other lyrinx, but it had worked so far. Her claws were stained with green blood and she had blinded and torn the noses of two atatusk, enabling the other lyrinx to finish them off.

Nish took down the last two atatusk of the troop with spears, but it only gained a minute, for another small troop of the creatures was not far behind. This battle was like the fight at the pass all over again, only this time there were an infinite number of the enemy.

There had to be a better, cleverer way to attack them. Frantically scanning his surroundings, Nish noticed the thick ice accumulating around the opening. Chthonic fire would feed and grow on ice; could he fuel the fire enough to burn through the track with it? It was worth trying.

Lifting off the leather catapult bucket, he bounced to the opening and hacked off a bucketful of ice. He could barely have lifted it outside, but in the void he could carry the bucket one-handed.

He heaved the bag up, fitted it over the hooks of the javelard, wound the crank and looked for a target. Five atatusk from the next troop had run ahead and were heading for two lyrinx, but Nish had a clear shot this time. He poured a few drops of pink fire onto the ice and stirred it with his sword until the ice began to burn. Aiming at the track in front of the atatusk, he fired.

The ice chunks shattered and pink fire went everywhere, spreading along the track for spans and flaming up around the atatusk's feet. It did not affect the track but the atatusk leapt out of the way, emitting screeching cries and beating at the flames that speckled their feet.

It kept them back for another minute or two, giving Nish time to gather another bucket of ice. By the time he'd run back with it, they were clearing the path with sweeps of their long arms and he knew the ploy would not work a second time, but he had thought of another way to attack them.

Tying a length of rope to the shafts of two spears, he coiled it neatly in the middle so it would not tangle and fitted both spears into the firing groove, their heads slightly diverging.

Aiming at the band of atatusk, he fired and the spears shot out, one angling to the left of the atatusk, the other to their right. The rope pulled taut between the spears, struck the leading two atatusk at neck height, and the momentum of the heavy spears slammed them backwards into the ones behind, knocking them off their feet.

Three of the creatures got up, looking shaky, but the other two lay still, as if their necks were broken. It had gained the defenders another minute, but they were few now. Beyl and four more of the militia were still fighting, though the other seven were dead. Five lyrinx had fallen while another lay on the track, kicking feebly.

'Clech?' Nish yelled. 'We can't hold them much longer.'

'On the last rope,' said Clech.

The three surviving atatusk had waited for the rest of their troop and now formed a phalanx, armed with large rectangular shields and long five-pointed spears, that would be almost impossible for the lyrinx to stop.

Nish roped up another pair of spears and fired again, but the front line of the phalanx raised their shields together and the spears glanced off, deflecting the rope over their heads. Only three javelard spears remained and he could not afford to waste them.

'We're ready!' Clech yelled.

Aimee was coming down the last rope. Clech had hold of the other four and was heaving mightily, trying to raise the platform into place, but his feet kept slipping on the soft track.

'I need the flask,' called Aimee.

Nish poured a few drops of pink fire into the catapult

bucket in case he got the chance to fling more ice, then leapt down and bounded towards the opening, for he'd found that to be quicker than running here.

Clech threw his weight against the ropes but it had little effect. 'I'm too light this far in,' he rumbled. 'Never thought I'd say that.'

'You'll be heavier closer to the opening,' said Nish as he took hold of the ropes behind Clech.

'The angle is too steep there; the ropes won't pull through the holes.'

Nish passed the flask to Aimee, who darted out to smear fire around the edges of the platform.

'Don't forget to leave a gap for us to get out,' he yelled.

She whirled and gave him the look, hands on hips, then tossed her head and went to work. Clech chuckled.

Even with the two of them heaving, they could not raise the platform, and Nish could feel the heavy breath of failure on the back of his neck. 'Ryll?' he yelled. 'Can you give us a hand?'

'When we go through the little hole,' said Clech casually, 'what happens?'

'We hang onto the rope until Tiaan comes to pick us up.'

'What if she doesn't?'

'We fall to our deaths, eventually.'

'Good-oh,' said Clech. 'Just so's I know. I'd better make some footholds, then, otherwise you landlubbers will fall off real quick.' He began to tie loops in the rope on the lower left-hand side of the opening.

Ryll and another lyrinx came running and took hold of the ropes. Their toe claws gave them a much sounder grip yet, even with all their strength, the platform rose slowly.

'We need another two on the ropes,' said Ryll, panting.

'That would leave us almost undefended,' said Nish.

'If we don't get it closed, we've lost.'

'I'll see what I can do.' Nish bounded back to the javelard.

The other paths were extending from all directions, steadily converging on the opening, and each carried troop after troop of atatusk, determined to take Santhenar. At their current rate of progress they would arrive well before the opening was sealed.

FORTY-SEVEN

The atatusk were now close enough that Nish could fire over the top of their shield wall, and with his last spears he took down three of the enemy, but it made no difference. What else could he do? He couldn't take on the phalanx with a sword.

The surviving guards had come to the same conclusion, evidently, for they were retreating to the entrance and heaving on the ropes.

Aimee was clinging to the barrier twenty spans up, applying smears of pink fire to the two edges as the platform was pulled into position, and cutting the dangling ropes. While Nish watched, the curved rent through the wall began to smooth out and fade like a healing cut. *If a breach is made, the barrier yearns to repair itself*, Lilis had said.

The lyrinx ran back to the defence, wrenching used javelard spears out of dead atatusk and gathering up their five-pointed spears. As Aimee scrambled down, the flask swinging by its thong, the phalanx broke into a run. Despite the atatusk's short legs and huge bodies, in the void they could move rapidly.

Why had he delayed? Nish fired the burning ice in the

catapult bucket, but it was turned harmlessly aside on their shields.

'Get moving!' he bellowed, running back. 'Through the opening and onto the rope.'

The phalanxes on the other paths were also running now, racing the leading troop to victory. The five lyrinx on the path made a wall with their bodies, with Ryll in the centre, and Liett swooped down at the leading phalanx, trying to hold them back. An atatusk in the middle pointed a white mace at her, she wobbled in the air and shot off.

'Come away,' Ryll said hoarsely. 'You know their mancers can bring us down in flight.'

Liett ignored him, as Nish had known she would, for she was the best flier among the lyrinx and, despite her lack of armour, she never held back. She attacked again, striking recklessly between the spears at the red-eyed atatusk with the mace.

The air around it shimmered; her wings missed a beat, she fell sideways and three points of a spear plunged into her thigh. The atatusk converged on her but she broke free and flapped away, trailing blood.

Ryll was staring at her, his chest rising and falling. 'Liett!' he said in an anguished voice.

Nish's Gendrigorean troops were at the opening but it was a slow squeeze through, and they had to be careful moving onto the rope. We'll never make it, Nish thought. The atatusk were too close, and coming too quickly. And after they've killed us they'll tear the barrier open again. We've failed.

Liett must have thought so too, for she whirled in the air, cried, 'Fly, Ryll!' and headed for the face of the phalanx.

Red jags burst from her fingertips, for she was an accomplished mancer, and several shields burst apart. Momentarily the spears pointed in all directions; she swooped on one of the atatusk, caught its head in her toe claws and, though it

611

must have been twice her weight, dragged it upwards. It struck at her but she retracted her claws and dropped it onto the front of the phalanx, which collapsed.

'Go through, Nish!' cried Aimee.

Only Aimee and Clech remained, and the lyrinx, but Nish hesitated, watching the phalanx.

'I'm leading this force,' he said. 'I'm not leaving anyone behind.'

The phalanx swiftly reformed and, as Liett flapped away, clearly exhausted, the red-eyed atatusk pointed its mace at her. Her wings collapsed; she fell onto the track ten spans in front of them, hit hard and struggled to get up.

'Liett!' Ryll roared, and ran towards her, swinging the heavy javelard spear in both hands.

'Haaiii!' barked the red-eyed atatusk, and they all surged forwards.

'We can't hold it open,' someone shouted through the hole, which was narrowing of its own accord.

'You'll have to,' snapped Nish, as the lyrinx and atatusk clashed furiously. Ryll was standing over Liett, whose purple blood had puddled on the track. Green atatusk blood began to mix with it.

'Go, Aimee,' said Nish, and raised his useless sword.

'Hey, what about that pink crystal Yulla gave you?' said Aimee.

He'd forgotten all about it. He dredged it out of his pocket, half embedded in the screwed-up dimensionless box. 'I'm not sure how –'

Aimee shook her head at his stupidity, then poured the last of the pink fire over the realgar crystal. Fire spilled down towards his hand; Nish hastily tossed the crystal, now trailing white smoke, over the heads of the lyrinx, at the closest atatusk. It bounced off one of its tusks and landed behind Ryll and Liett.

The atatusk doubled over, coughing white smoke out of its mouth and nostrils, then took a tentative step forwards, but fire enveloped the crystal and white fumes belched up from it to hang in the air above the track, then slowly spread across it, enveloping Liett, and Ryll up to his knees. The other atatusk checked, but came on more slowly.

Ryll bent and lifted Liett, though before he could get back to safety with her, the leading atatusk thrust and caught her in the belly with the points of the spear. She convulsed and went limp.

Nish froze. 'Liett?' he said softly. Was she dead?

Ryll laid her down then, moving faster than the eye could see, tore the spear from the atatusk's grip and drove it through its open mouth and out the back of its head. He wrenched it out, leapt at the enemy like a berserker and, swinging the spear back and forwards like a club, knocked down the creatures behind it, then hurled it at the next row.

Turning his back contemptuously, he lifted Liett and walked into the white fumes with her, one hand pressed against the spear wounds in her belly. As he emerged, the lyrinx separated to let them through, then bowed as they passed, for Liett was a great favourite as well as their brave and noble Matriarch. Her hand moved, her eyes fluttered; she was alive, but grievously injured.

Nish glanced over his shoulder. Aimee was standing by with the flask, for she would have to go through last and seal the hole. Or would she? Clech was struggling to hold the gap open – the breach, yearning to repair itself, was pulling closed and sealing.

'Lyrinx, come through!' Nish shouted.

Before they could follow Ryll to the hole, the phalanx pushed into the cloud to attack. Nish held his breath; would the fumes do their job?

The leading atatusk broke through the clinging white fumes.

The crystal had failed. But then an unseen atatusk let out a deep, shivering squeal and suddenly the rest were choking and dropping their weapons and shields as they scrambled backwards to safety.

A wisp of white fume coiled Nish's way and he caught an overpowering smell of garlic, followed by an acrid pungency that stung his nose and eyes.

'Keep away from the smoke!' a lyrinx shouted.

Nish ran back to Ryll. Liett's soft skin had gone transparent, her bent wings had lost all colour and blood was still running from her leg and belly. Ryll had his hand on her belly and was speaking words of mancery, presumably a wound-sealing spell, but it did not seem to be working. She was pale as snow and her lips were blue.

Nish went with them to the barrier. It was taking all Clech's strength to hold the opening, and he was straining upwards with all the power of his legs to stop it from sealing itself.

'Go through, Aimee!' he choked. 'I can't hold it.'

'Not without you,' she said, unmoving.

There was no way out for him, or the lyrinx, for as soon as he let go, the gap would snap closed. Now, beyond the fumes, the atatusk from the rear of the phalanx were tramping over their fallen fellows, advancing with spears held low and sweeping them from side to side across the track. Once they knocked the crystal into the void the poisonous fumes would thin and there would be nothing to stop them. And the atatusk on the other paths were only a minute away.

'Go!' cried Clech to Aimee. 'You too, Nish.'

Tears flashed in her eyes and she headed towards the opening. Ryll followed, bearing Liett, but there was no way he could squeeze through the hole before it closed.

The smoking crystal was knocked over the side and the atatusk moved gingerly into the fumes, holding their breath. Their spear tips appeared through the fumes. It was all over.

Only then did Nish think of the black glove and know that it was time for the most desperate of measures. He shook it out of the dimensionless box, carefully slid the fingers of his left hand inside, then took up his sword with the right.

'Pull the hole open as far as you can,' he said. 'I'll hold them off.'

It was, undoubtedly, the most reckless of the many reckless things he had ever done, but Nish felt no fear this time. The enemy had to be held back and he was the only one who could do it – if it could be done at all.

As two lyrinx took hold of the hole and heaved it open a little further, Nish headed for the phalanx, gloved fist clenched at his side and sword up. An atatusk leapt for him, swinging a club. He parried it with his sword then thought, here goes.

Springing forwards, he swung, opening his hand so the dimensionless glove's surface was flat. He couldn't reach as high as the atatusk's head; instead he slapped it open-handed in the groin.

The very dimensions gave forth a shrill wailing as they collapsed on contact. The atatusk screamed, dropped the club and tried to clutch at its concealed organs, but they were drawn out of its body into the surface of the dimensionless glove, progressively flattening into a gory sheet, a skein of dripping threads, then disappearing completely.

Then the creature's groin followed, and the belly and thighs were pulled after. As its chest was drawn down the atatusk let out a despairing bark and tried to pull itself out, but nothing could prevail over the dimensionless glove. Within seconds the atatusk had been sucked inside it and disassembled as though it had never existed.

The glove swung from Nish's hand, hot and heavy now,

and he could feel it yearning towards his thigh as though the urge to consume him was irresistible. He hastily jerked it away and pointed it towards the remaining atatusk, who had frozen, staring at it.

They were brave creatures and did not fear death, but the uncanny dissolution of their comrade had unnerved them. The other phalanxes had kept coming, though. They were too far away to have seen.

A second atatusk stepped forwards, a giant at least two-and-a-half spans tall, hefting a double-edged war axe. He was watching Nish carefully, sniffing the air all the while. Suddenly he swung, so fast that Nish could barely see the axe head. Unable to raise the sword in time, he flung his gloved hand into the path of the blade.

It struck the glove with a shocking impact, and Nish expected it to shear right through his hand, but with a shrill shriek the axe's dimensions were stripped from it and it vanished. The giant, who had not let go in time, was drawn in after it.

The glove was far heavier now, and so hot that it was glowing, though Nish's hand was barely warm. All the atatusk stood frozen, staring at it.

From the corner of his eye he saw a lyrinx run to the javelard, smash one of its timber uprights with his fist and bound back to the opening with it. He jammed the jagged end into the floor and forced the smooth end into the gap. The top of the gap snapped down, but the prop held and the remaining lyrinx began to squeeze through.

The other paths were almost close enough to join with the main track, and a troop of atatusk stood at the front of each path, making ready to leap the gap and seize the prize and the glory for themselves.

'Together!' said the leading atatusk on the track, and the front rank of its troop went for Nish.

Nish hurled the dimensionless glove at the leader's smooth grey belly and ran without waiting to see what happened. *Slap!* The dimensionless glove wailed again as it did its work and grew brighter; Nish could feel its smouldering heat behind him.

'Well done, everyone,' he gasped, and scrambled through the opening onto the rope, taking a firm grip of a loop.

Clech was hanging from another loop on the other side of the rope, waiting anxiously. The last lyrinx followed, and everyone moved down the loops, one after another. Only Aimee was outside now.

The five paths joined into one broad track; fifty atatusk ran at them. Aimee scrambled through, one-handed, holding the unstoppered flask ready to seal the gap, but slipped and nearly fell.

'I don't think you're going to need that, little one,' said Clech, catching her in an arm as muscled as Nish's thigh.

'I'm making sure!' Aimee snapped.

She smeared fire across both edges of the gap and, as the enemy lunged with a wall of spear points, Clech punched out the prop. The gap snapped closed and vanished as though it had never been.

And let's hope Stilkeen can't make another one, Nish thought as he rotated on the line to look for the sky-galleon.

FORTY-EIGHT

'You were close to Kandor once,' said Yggur, 'were you not?'

Yalkara looked haggard now, and defeated. Clearly, after losing everything, life had become unbearable for her and she wanted it to end. Maelys felt a trace of pity for her; though only a trace.

'Before we escaped from the void we were the best of friends,' said Yalkara, 'but on Santhenar Kandor changed, and we became ever more estranged.'

'Could he have seen you find the chthonic fire?'

'It's possible. That was thousands of years ago, in the dark days when we were trying to survive in the void, *and failing*. Clever, powerful and tenacious as we Charon are, our competitors were more cunning and more ruthless, and our numbers were dwindling. The best and most brilliant among us sought a way out of the void, and – despite what the tales say – I was the first to do so.

'I saw Stilkeen hide its chthonic fire in the core of a burnt-out comet and, while it prepared to move to another set of dimensions, I snatched the fire and fled. Fire is a marvellous and subtle force, capable of opening the passage between dimensions for us just as easily as it makes a

618

humble portal, if we know how to use it. I found a way out of the void and we took Aachan.'

'And Kandor?' pressed Yggur.

'He might have seen me take it. Or,' Yalkara mused, 'he might have discovered chthonic fire much later, after it had begun to work its evil on us. It rendered most of us sterile, and then drew molten magma up from deep in Aachan's core to ruin the planet in ten thousand eruptions.'

'Could he have taken the true fire and hidden it during the Clysm, leaving you with the corrupt version?'

'He might have,' said Yalkara. 'Despite all that has been said about him, Kandor was more principled than I, and always looking to make amends.'

'Did you know he was my father?' said Yggur, who still seemed bemused by this revelation.

'I did not, though it does not astonish me to hear it. Clearly, he protected the secret of your identity with his life.'

'Kandor made the taphloid for *you*,' said Maelys, looking at Yggur and thinking aloud. 'He put the lost lessons into it and fashioned a shield to protect *you*. The taphloid has to be the key. And it . . . it's always been a mystery to me.'

'How so?' said Yggur.

'I've never understood how it works. Even after we took Father's little crystal out, the taphloid still concealed my aura. How could it do that without a source of power?'

'There may be another crystal inside it,' said Yggur, 'hidden there long ago.'

No one spoke for ages. Maelys thought about that, but for some reason she could not fathom, she was sure there wasn't another crystal inside the taphloid. Yet if that was the case, what did power it?

'What if it isn't a crystal?' she said suddenly. 'Could chthonic fire be its hidden power? What if Kandor hid fire inside a corundite compartment so it would be ready for Yggur once he'd learned his lessons?'

'That would be ironic indeed,' said Yggur thoughtfully. 'Yet, many people have checked the taphloid, I among them, and no hidden compartment has been found.'

Yalkara stood up straight. 'Ah, but you don't know how Charon think, nor the cunning way we design our most precious devices. And for such a vital purpose, Kandor would have designed the taphloid *most* cunningly.'

She held out her hand and Maelys gave her the taphloid.

Yalkara clenched her hands around it, shook it, then held its ends and curves to her ear, and her brow. 'Kandor was a clever maker of such devices, but *I* was a brilliant one, and I think I see what he has done.'

She passed her hands over the smooth, shining metal, tapped, twisted, and pulled, and it separated into two halves. Inside the smaller half, where there should have been solid metal, sat a tiny bottle made of sapphire-coloured crystal.

Maelys let out a great sigh. 'Is that –?'

'Corundite,' said Yalkara. 'And there's fire inside; I can see it.' She held up the bottle. 'It has died to the tiniest flicker, incapable of growing by itself, but I can tell from its glistening platinum whiteness, jewel-like and perfect, that this is the true fire I found in the core of the comet.'

'Now I understand,' said Yggur, his craggy features lit up as though by a newly risen sun. 'This tiny fire must have been the source of my great and mysterious power all along. *That's* why my power did not fade when the nodes were destroyed and almost everyone else lost their Arts. *That's* why I've lived so long, my life force protected by the ever-lasting fire. And *that's* how I came to do the impossible and shoot that blast across the Way between the Worlds long ago, to save Maigraith. Pure chthonic fire dissolves the barriers between the worlds and nothing can stand in its way, save

620

corundite; it's how Stilkeen could roam the eleven dimensions of space and time for half an eternity.'

'And will do again after it destroys Santhenar,' said Flydd, 'if we can't stop it. So how do we stop it?'

'The fire is almost dead,' said Yalkara. 'It must be fed before it can be used, by Stilkeen *or anyone else.*'

'We . . . we wouldn't want to use it,' said Maelys. 'Not after what happened when Flydd had it.'

'I've a feeling you might have to use it,' said Yalkara.

'But if it's fed in our world it'll become corrupt like all the other fire, won't it?' said Maelys.

'It will if you feed it like any normal fire, with *material* fuel.'

'How else can it be fed?'

'Pure fire was the binding force between the physical and spirit aspects of Stilkeen,' said Yalkara, 'and it can only remain pure if it's fed on another spirit – someone's life force.'

Her eye was fixed on Maelys as if planning to feed the fire on her. Maelys edged away.

Yalkara smiled thinly. 'Have no fear, little one. I wouldn't feed it on *your* spirit.'

Whose, then? Maelys thought. Flydd's? Yggur's?

'I was meant to keep watch for Stilkeen,' said Yggur. 'It's the only connection I have with my father, and you can't imagine how much that matters after all this time. I've lived long enough for any man; I'm prepared to make the sacrifice, if it's the only way.'

'We don't know that it is,' said Flydd, who had been unaccountably quiet, 'and we can't take the risk. If Stilkeen gets the true fire and rejoins with its revenants, it'll be a hundred times as powerful and no longer in pain. It will be invincible, and Santhenar will be doomed.'

'If we do need to use the true fire, as Yalkara has hinted,' said Yggur, extending his hand, 'first we have to feed it.'

After a momentary hesitation, Yalkara held out the corundite bottle.

'No,' said Tulitine, struggling to her feet. 'I'm dying, and the pain is unendurable. I'll gladly feed the fire with my spirit.'

'Stilkeen, *here*!' shouted a woman from high above Yalkara.

Maelys, recognising the voice, looked up. It was the Numinator and she was standing at the edge of the third level of Morrelune, pointing down at them.

'There she is, Stilkeen!' cried the Numinator. 'It's Yalkara, the Charon who stole your chthonic fire. She knows where the true fire lies, and she's kept it from you just to torment you.'

Claws scraped on marble, then Stilkeen came lurching out between the flame-covered columns onto the open edge of the tower's third level, and looked down. It was shaking and shuddering with pain, moving forwards then jerking back as if being so exposed to the real world was more than it could bear, but it had to have the fire.

As Tulitine's fingers touched the corundite bottle, Yalkara whipped it away from her. Was she planning to betray them all? Maelys groped for her knife, but did not draw it, for that was not what Yalkara was up to. On the contrary.

'There must be a reckoning,' she said. 'The time is long overdue.'

Flicking out the stopper with her thumb, Yalkara tilted the bottle, allowed the little tongues of fire to slide into her mouth, and swallowed. Within seconds, platinum fire exploded out from her middle and grew into a conflagration all around her as it began to feed on her life force.

'This –' Yalkara gasped, bent double but forced herself upright, clearly determined to meet her end with dignity, 'this will be my atonement,' she said over the brittle hiss of the flames, 'for all that my folly has cost the Three Worlds, and my own, Charon, kind. I will have peace at last.'

Taking a small flat package from her gown, she passed it back and forth through the true fire enveloping her. She groaned, stifled it and hid the pain, then tossed the package to Maelys. 'A gift for – the grandchild I will – will never see. We Charon, once so great, are finally – extinct.'

'What is it?' said Maelys, catching the package absently and stuffing it in her pocket.

'A little treasure made long ago – now cleansed by pure fire.'

Yalkara fell to the floor, writhing, and the chthonic fire rose ever higher as it consumed her fleeing life force. Maelys walked away, unable to watch her death agonies.

High above, Stilkeen had wrapped itself in webs of flame, the only protection it could make against the pain of exposure to the material world, and was staring down at the white fire, hungering for it. Why didn't it jump? Was it waiting for the true fire to reach up to the third level, while enduring the pain as best it could?

Maelys kept walking, and was facing the main entrance to Morrelune when the gateway to the shadow realm reappeared halfway down the broad hall, and Vivimord was standing just inside the black gate, enchanted sabre in hand. To one side, the revenants were drifting in a red- and black-streaked circle.

Had Vivimord decided that remaining in the shadow realm was too great a price, even to save the world he loved? He must have – he must be planning to come back from death.

Maelys ran for the gate, knowing that there was but a minute to lure the revenants out, and after that it would be too late. Once Stilkeen held the fire, it could rejoin with them at its leisure and they could not be harmed. But how *were* the revenants to be attacked?

Again she had that flash of memory – the rain, the caduceus steaming on the hillside, and Yggur falling down –

but now she remembered what had happened next. Skidding to a stop outside the gate, hidden by a pillar where Vivimord could see her but the revenants could not, she hissed his name.

He approached the gate. 'You're too late, Maelys. I'm coming back from death.'

'The true fire has been found,' she said softly. 'It's just outside. You must convince them to come out *now*, else Stilkeen will take the fire and Santhenar will be no more.'

Vivimord looked over her head and his eyes widened.

'But I can be the only dead man ever to return from the shadow realm, to life,' he said softly, yearningly. 'How can I give that up? How can I give up *life*?'

'What would be the point?' she said. 'If Stilkeen isn't stopped, there won't be anything to come back to.'

He knew it, too. Vivimord stalked back and forth; he groaned, he clawed at his hair and rubbed the egg-shaped excrescence on his cheek, but nothing could rearrange the facts. It was a choice between his life and the fate of the world.

Finally, the tension eased in him, and he seemed to come to a resolution that must have offered him some sense of inner peace, for the lines on his face smoothed and he let out a small sigh.

Vivimord bowed to Maelys. 'I salute you, for you have beaten me, over and again.'

Thrusting out his right arm, sabre extended, he cried the spell he'd made long ago to cut open the black gate. The sabre blazed blue and brilliant, the lock sagged, the gate swung open and he spoke, using all his rhetorical Art.

'The way is clear, revenants. The true fire you have been seeking all this time lies within reach, and now Stilkeen comes. Fly, fly to Stilkeen. Complete yourselves at last!'

Maelys glanced the other way. Outside, the white fire was raging upon Yalkara's dying body, calling to the revenants across all the dimensions of space and time, and such was the *voice* in his words that they burst forth, so desperate for the ecstasy of rejoining with Stilkeen that they were blinded by it.

Maelys ducked aside as they rushed the gateway, passed through, and hurtled towards the fire. Vivimord ran after them, raising the sabre to hold open the gate so he could return from death, but the sabre flowed like water in his hands and vanished.

The gate slammed and she saw his anguished face as he understood that his choice was irrevocable, then the shadow realm disappeared. He too had atoned for his crimes, but unlike Yalkara he regretted it bitterly.

Maelys ran after the revenants, unheeded. They had no interest in consuming spirits now, living or dead. But she did, for Maelys thought she knew the one way to destroy them.

Like red-streaked moths around a fire, they began to circle the conflagration feeding on Yalkara's spirit.

Maelys ran up to Flydd and Yggur. '. . . *and burn them to nothingness!*' she panted.

'What?' cried Flydd.

'It's the one phrase we recovered from Kandor's lessons in the taphloid.'

'But what does it mean?' said Yggur.

'Burn the revenants with chthonic fire,' Maelys guessed. 'Stilkeen ordered them to stay in the shadow realm until it called them, because outside they were in peril.'

'Then why don't they rejoin with it?'

'Chthonic fire is the force that binds flesh and spirit together. Until Stilkeen holds the fire, the revenants can't rejoin with it.'

He looked up at the trembling, flame-shrouded *being*. 'All it has to do is jump down onto the fire, snatch it up, and call them to it. So why doesn't it?'

'It can't bear the pain, I suppose,' said Maelys.

'It'll soon find a way to protect itself,' said Flydd.

'Nadiril said there was one single way the revenants could be destroyed, and it must have to do with pure fire – Yalkara said we'd have to use it, remember? If Stilkeen doesn't personally hold the pure fire, it must burn unbound revenants to nothingness.'

'I'm sure you're right,' Flydd said ruefully. 'But *how* do we use it? They aren't going near it.'

'Go back to the shadow realm! Fly!' choked Stilkeen from the third level, but the revenants did not look up. It was as if they hadn't heard. They continued to circle, hungrily eyeing the pure fire, yet wary of it.

Maelys whispered, 'Yggur, I think you're the key. You've got to use the fire.'

'I don't know how,' he said.

'Nadiril said revenants are blind in the real world,' Maelys remembered. 'And they can barely hear. He said we might be able to fool them.'

'How?' cried Yggur.

Stilkeen shot inside, then reappeared, wrapping layer upon layer of its ragged shadow webs about it. It was twitching and shuddering with pain, but it must have been bearable now, for it began to clamber onto the rail of the third level.

'It's going to jump,' hissed Maelys, and suddenly she knew there was only one way. 'They can't see you, Yggur. Act as though *you're* Stilkeen.'

Without a word, Yggur leapt into the pure white fire roaring up from Yalkara's body, wrapped it around himself and it flared even higher. Cloaked in white fire, he looked enormous, powerful, eternal. Yggur looked like a *being*, and he extended his long arms to the revenants as if to envelop them.

'Come, my spirits, it is time.'

Letting out ecstatic cries, they whirled around him like black and red dervishes, spiralling ever closer.

Stilkeen was on the rail now, teetering there in agony. And it jumped.

The revenants circled Yggur, closer, faster, until they were no more than streaks – and then they touched. Yggur enfolded them in his arms and drew them within the fire.

Too late, as Stilkeen came hurtling down, they realised that they had been tricked. The revenants tried desperately to burst free but Yggur crushed them to him and ran with them. White fire exploded out for many spans in all directions as it fed on their pure, spirit selves and seared them into annihilation.

As Maelys scrambled out of the way, a tongue of fire touched the back of her left hand and a sizzling pain shot across it; her hand blistered, went numb, and she fell down.

Stilkeen was screaming as it hit the promenade beside Yalkara's smoking remains, enormously lengthening its arms towards Yggur and the last fading wisps of its revenants, but they burned away just as it touched the fire.

Yggur collapsed and Stilkeen let out a shriek of uttermost agony, a shrill, ululating scream that went on and on as if it were trying to split Santhenar apart, down to its very core.

Maelys blocked her ears but the sound gouged through her head until it boiled and the backs of her eyeballs throbbed. Flydd's nose was bleeding; a trickle of blood had started from Tulitine's right ear; and even the men and atatusk fighting on the paved plain had clapped their hands over their ears, but no one could keep out the dreadful sound.

It cut off as suddenly as it had begun, for the severing of Stilkeen's physical and spirit aspects was now permanent, and it was forever lost, forever abandoned, never to be free of the agony of separation.

It tore the last wisps of the dying fire from Yalkara and Yggur, wrapped them around itself like a shroud, and whirled up and up, and the fire grew until it formed a twisting column more than a league high.

Other tongues of white fire were drawn to it, including a vast streak that came from the Antarctic south, the fire that had been eating the ice there. All formed into a prodigious white javelin racing up towards the celestial sphere. At its very apex the fire burst apart, punched a white-starred hole through into unknown dimensions, and then the hole healed itself without a trace.

A colossal boom thundered down, shaking the palace and echoing and re-echoing off the mountains.

'It's done,' said Flydd when the last echoes had faded. 'Every trace of white fire, all across Santhenar, is gone.'

Shortly, a faint flush began to spread across the eastern sky. Dawn was breaking. Yalkara's body formed an elongated pile of ash and Yggur lay not far away, his arms and body smoking and most of his hair burned off. Tulitine stumbled across and crouched over him, cradling him in her arms.

Maelys did not see how he could still be alive, but Yggur sat up painfully, his charred garments falling to pieces.

'I hoped my Art would come back if Stilkeen was defeated and the caduceus was destroyed,' he said hoarsely. 'But it's not going to, is it?'

'No,' said Tulitine, 'and your long life is also going to end, for both must have come from the pure fire Kandor put in the taphloid when you were a baby. As long as it lasted, so would you. Now it is gone, your Arts will fade to nothing, and you'll soon be an ageing, ordinary man.'

'An ordinary man!' he said softly. 'Me! And yet, when I'm nursed by the most beautiful woman in all Santhenar, how can I regret it?'

'Hush your foolishness,' said Tulitine, but she was smiling, and she did not seem to be in as much pain as before.

She bent over Yggur, put her hands on the worst of his burns and began to heal them, as well as chthonic fire burns could ever be healed.

FORTY-NINE

'Where's Nish?' Maelys said quietly, for battles still raged all across the plain as the soldiers hunted down the surviving atatusk, and the other creatures from the void; several humans were dying for every beast dispatched. 'I haven't seen him in ages.'

She rubbed her blistered left hand, feeling very afraid. Thousands of soldiers were dead, and hundreds of the mighty lyrinx. How could one small man have survived against such terrible foes?

'I don't know,' said Flydd, pacing anxiously.

With Stilkeen's disappearance, the barrier between the world and the void had also vanished and the caduceus, which was still embedded in the marble at the front of the palace, had sagged and run like molten iron. Maelys had felt the power drain from it as it became a cooling puddle of lifeless metal.

The tongues of yellow and orange flame wreathing the palace slowly went out, and underneath, the beautiful white and golden stone of Morrelune had gone a dingy brown, like the smoke stains around the top of a chimney; the stone had been eaten away like decayed teeth.

Yellow fumes still oozed from the deepest and most rotten cavities, to fall in slow coils down the fluted columns and spill across the pitted floors. Maelys caught a whiff and choked, for the fumes reeked as though all the dead from Mazurhize had been interred below the palace.

As the sun rose over the distant ocean beyond Fadd, Morrelune began to shake. The needle-tipped tower swayed back and forth in ever increasing arcs and waist-high waves formed on the Sacred Lake.

'We'd better get to safer ground,' said Flydd.

Maelys helped Tulitine down from the promenade and two soldiers, from the few surviving Imperial Guard, lifted Yggur between them. The broad steps were cracking by the time they reached the bottom and, only moments after they laid Yggur on the paved plain, one of the corroded columns of the grand entrance cracked and fell.

'The foundations must have been eaten away,' said Flydd. 'The palace is coming apart.'

Its base shifted, the nine levels grated against one another, distorting its beautiful symmetry, and several stones toppled, but Morrelune remained intact, as if some greater binding force held it together. However the paving surrounding it broke in a ragged circle and began to slip downwards, ell by ell, until, after twenty minutes or more, it formed a deep trench around the palace, like a dry moat.

Now the palace began to subside as well, in a series of small but wrenching jerks, as though cavities were continually forming and collapsing beneath it. It settled slowly, floor by floor. The stone edge of the Sacred Lake cracked and spilled part of its contents into the moat; steam rose in wreathing clouds.

The palace settled a little further, leaving only the spire standing above the paved plain, and then, as if satisfied that it had demonstrated its superiority over the tyrant and all his works, the ground gave a faint, satisfied grumble and all went still.

Maelys felt so worn that she could barely stand up, but she tottered ten steps to the brink and looked down. The rickety palace was surrounded by a circular, steaming trench at least forty spans deep, bounded by steep walls of fractured rock.

'It doesn't look as though it's going to last much longer,' she said faintly.

'And good riddance,' said Flydd, coming up beside her. 'When it's gone we'll fill the hole with rubble to form Jal-Nish's tombstone – a fitting memorial to a monster.'

The sky-galleon came sideslipping in, the wind whistling through its lines.

'And look who turns up when all the work is done,' Flydd said loudly as *Three Reckless Old Ladies* settled beside them, Tiaan at the helm. 'Where the blazes have you been, Nish?' But Flydd was beaming.

'Oh, you know,' Nish said airily, and vaulted over the side like a true hero, though the grand gesture was marred when he landed hard on his bloodstained leg and would have fallen had Flydd not caught him. Nish was filthy, soot-stained and covered in green blood. 'Going up to the void opening, mopping up the last of the atatusk. Nothing special. Do it all the time.'

Flydd burst out laughing, and Maelys could not restrain her joy as she stepped out from behind him.

Nish's eyes met hers and the most extraordinary expression of longing crossed his dirty face. His eyes took on a liquid shine; he whispered her name, staring at her as though she was a precious, lost jewel that had finally, after years of wild goose chases, been found.

Maelys couldn't move; she had lost control of her legs. She looked into his eyes, not understanding even when he held out his arms to her. She started, blushed, then went slowly to him.

'I heard what you did,' Nish said, embracing her and stroking her dusty hair. 'Going into the shadow realm, all alone – it was the bravest thing.' He kissed her on the tip of her nose.

Maelys didn't know what to think. 'Almost as brave as flying up there to try and seal the void.'

'Try!' he cried in mock outrage, taking a step backwards but still holding her by the shoulders. 'We *did* seal the void. It's over – look out!'

He whirled her out of the way as the ground groaned and a finger-wide crevice snaked out from Morrelune, almost under their feet.

'It doesn't go deep,' said Maelys, too distracted to worry about anything outside of them. 'Nish –'

She wanted to tell him about the baby, but was afraid to. The revelation was too new, too raw, and she had not come to terms with it herself. And also, she was afraid of how he would react.

The ground kept shaking and they moved away from the edge of the pit. Rock tore deep underground, and clouds of dust boiled up on the other side of the palace.

They scrambled onto a boulder to see what was happening. 'That crevice is *huge*,' said Nish, pointing to a broad crack that was zipping across the plain towards the underground prison, half a league away. He and Maelys stared at each other, the realisation taking a while to sink in. 'Mazurhize could collapse as well.'

'And my family are in there,' cried Maelys. Now, finally, she could go to them, but how could she race the crevice? 'At least, I hope they are . . .' She set off at a run.

'This way,' called Nish. 'It's quicker.'

He scrambled up the side of the sky-galleon. Maelys climbed

the rope ladder. 'M'lainte isn't here,' said Nish, looking around, 'and neither is Tiaan.'

'I saw Chissmoul a minute ago,' said Maelys. She yelled, 'Chissmoul?'

'What?' She was sitting glumly on the ground on the other side of the sky-galleon, staring at her feet. Chissmoul had been called to fly earlier, but she had not heard the call, and now it was too late. The battle was over and she might never fly again.

'Pilot!' yelled Maelys. 'We need you.'

Chissmoul bounded to her feet and scrambled up the rope ladder. 'Where to?'

'Mazurhize, and make it snappy.'

The sky-galleon hurtled away, racing the crevice across the plain. After overtaking it halfway, Chissmoul landed near the dark, grimy steps that led down to the prison.

'Get clear, in case it falls in,' said Nish. 'We won't be long. *I hope.*'

The prison was dark save for a few guttering lanterns, for the guards had fled hours ago. The God-Emperor's silent watchers – the wisp-watchers, loop-listeners and snoop-sniffers which, when linked to the tears, could detect a creeping mouse in darkness – hung still and lifeless.

Nish ripped two lanterns off the wall, handed one to Maelys and they ran down the wet steps into the reeking gloom, letting the prisoners out as they went. There weren't as many as she would have thought. Most of the cells were empty and there was no sign of her family. They must be dead.

'What a horrible place,' she said, pressing up against him. 'Do – do you mind if I hold your hand?'

'I don't mind at all. You can't imagine the memories Mazurhize brings back.'

The smoky lantern glasses allowed out only a feeble brown

light which made the prison look even more grimy and oppressive. It was miserably cold and the smell grew worse the further they descended.

They reached the lowest level, the ninth, which consisted of a short corridor leading to a single cell whose large brass key hung from a hook. She took it. After splashing through festering sullage, they approached the cell which had been Nish's home for ten years.

'You spent ten years down *here?*' Maelys said, crushing his hand. 'I wonder that you didn't go mad.'

'There were times I thought I had.' Nish shuddered. 'It's as if no time has passed since my escape,' he whispered. 'I might be being led in now to begin my sentence. Go on.'

Maelys had been hanging back, afraid to look in, but she swallowed and peered around the edge of the cell. In the dim lantern light she could just make out something huddled against the wall at the far side of the cell. Her hand shook as she turned the key.

'They look dead, Nish.'

'So did I, half the time I spent in there. Be brave.'

She crept in, appalled at the smell, which was far worse than it had been in the corridor. The stench was distantly familiar, for Nish had smelled just like this when she had helped him to escape last autumn.

Something moved on the bench and Maelys, thinking about the shadow realm, put her hand over her mouth. What horror was she going to discover?

A tall, bony figure sat up stiffly, focussed on her and snapped, 'You took your time, girl. You always were a lazy slattern.'

The woman was tall and skinny with an eagle's beak of a nose – Aunt Haga. Trust her to survive – she had always been the tough one. Maelys threw her arms around her

635

aunt, overcome to realise that at least one of her family had survived, sour and cranky though Haga was.

'Get off!' said Haga, pushing her away. 'What's the matter with you?'

Maelys turned to the crumpled figures in the corner. 'Are they . . .?'

'Your mother died five days ago and they've taken her body out,' said Haga briskly. 'Lyma always was the weakest.'

Tears pricked at Maelys's eyes. Her poor mother had never recovered from the destruction of Nifferlin Manor and the dispersal of her clan, and the loss of Maelys's father had broken her. It was a wonder she had lasted this long.

'What about Bugi?'

'*Aunt* Bugi!' said Haga, slapping her face. 'You may have been swanning around the world with all manner of villains and reprobates, but you're not yet of age. You will show respect, girl!'

Maelys met Nish's eyes, and he looked shocked at her reception, but she could have hugged Aunt Haga for joy. The world hadn't been completely torn apart after all – Haga was the same cranky old martinet she had always been, and Maelys didn't want her to change one iota. Haga *was* Clan Nifferlin now, and Nifferlin survived!

'Bugi passed this morning,' said Haga. 'Seneschal Vomix tortured her cruelly after we were taken, and she was glad to go in the end, but Fyllis clings to life. She might be saved, if you know a good healer . . .'

Vomix again! He was the cause of all the clan's misfortunes, and it had all come about because of a thoughtless remark Maelys had made when passing him on the road, as a child. No wonder her mother and aunts had treated her so badly and lavished all their love on Fyllis.

'I know a very good healer,' said Maelys. 'The best there is.'

She bent over Fyllis, who lay in the filthy straw, panting, soiled, and terribly thin. Her eyes were dull and empty; a thin band, studded with jewelled knobs, encircled her forehead. 'What's this?' said Maelys.

'The scriers put it there to stop her from using her gift,' said Haga. 'It's linked to the wisp-watchers and can't be removed.'

'The God-Emperor is dead, and so are the wisp-watchers,' said Maelys, easing the band away and tossing it into the corner. It had been on so long that Fyllis's brow was scarred underneath.

Fyllis's eyes sprang open. 'Big sister,' she said softly. 'I knew you'd come,' and fell asleep.

Maelys wept.

FIFTY

The prison began shaking as Maelys carried Fyllis up. Nish came behind bearing the body of Aunt Bugi, and Haga hobbled up the stairs by herself, refusing all offers of aid. They gained the sky-galleon as the broadening crevices approached Mazurhize, and lifted off without looking back.

'I never want to see this place again,' cried Maelys, sitting on a bench beside her sleeping sister and stroking her filthy blonde hair.

'What *do* you want?' Nish said quietly, watching her from the corner of his eye and wondering what she was going to do next, though he had a feeling he knew. And the worst of it was, he had nothing to offer her – at least, nothing she would value above Nifferlin.

'Just to bathe the stink of Mazurhize away and go home,' she said. 'I've got to have a home *now*.'

'I understand. You have your family to look after.'

She looked as though she was going to say something important then, oddly, Maelys blushed. 'My *family*, yes. But . . .'

'What is it?'

'They'll never be safe while Vomix survives. He'll destroy

them just to make me suffer. I'm really afraid of him, Nish; so afraid that I've got to go after him. I couldn't bear to think of him out there, just waiting for the chance –'

'You don't have to worry about Vomix ever again.'

She turned, clutching his bloodstained shirt with both hands and looking into his eyes. 'Are you sure? Is he –?' The sudden relief in her eyes was replaced by doubt. 'He's slimy as an eel, Nish. He can survive anything.'

'Not this time. We spotted him from the sky-galleon on the way down from sealing the void. His personal guard fled down the ridge below Mazurhize but they were ambushed by a troop of atatusk and wiped out. Vomix got away and ran for his life through the woodland with a handful of his officers – abandoning his men yet again.'

Nish shook his head in disgust. 'How could Father have raised a man like him to high office? We hunted him from the air for half an hour, dropping flares to light the way, but with all the trees we couldn't get close enough to corner him. Then Tiaan spotted a band of those lyrinx-like hunters; the ones that came through the opening first. They were just over the hill, and she drove Vomix towards them, letting him think he was getting away.'

'I hope they ate him,' Maelys said fiercely.

'You don't feel as though you should forgive your enemies,' Nish teased, 'now they've been defeated?'

'Not after what he did to my clan. Vomix hasn't got a single redeeming feature.'

'He certainly hasn't now. The hunters pulled down his officers one by one and left them lying where they fell, but they held Vomix down and ate him from the feet up, while he was still alive. He threatened them, begged them, then wept and whined like the cur he is when he finally realised that there was no way out, but it made no difference. It wasn't a pleasant way to go.'

'But he's definitely dead?' Maelys was still holding him. 'We thought he was dead before, yet he came back.'

This was one gift Nish could give her – he could relieve her of the burden of Vomix forever. 'Had he survived, we would have finished him off, but I watched until the last gulp. He's dead and gone, Maelys. There won't be any tombstone for Vomix, just a stinking pile of manure between the rocks.'

She sagged against him. 'Then we've won; we've finally won.'

'Yes,' said Nish as they landed. 'It's over.'

He helped her to climb down with Fyllis, then added quietly, 'but at a terrible cost. Only ten of my faithful Gendrigorean militia are left, of the five hundred I set out with – and they never wanted to fight in the first place.' He shook his head at the futility of war. 'I talked them into it.'

They weren't the only losses; far from it. With the last of the invaders mopped up, the allies gathered on the upthrust boulders between the Sacred Lake and sunken Morrelune to count the grim cost of the day and night.

Garthor had fallen, and more than half of his thousand Aachim with him. The red-haired Aachim of Clan Elienor had fared even worse, losing three-quarters of their number in less than an hour when several large troops of atatusk had come down right in the middle of them, though Yrael had survived.

The Faellem had lost only a quarter of their three hundred and fifty, but both Galgilliel and Lainor were among them, and, being a small and slight people, many more had been badly injured.

The Whelm had also suffered grievously; of their original eighty, only seven remained and none were unscathed for,

640

though they were doughty and tireless fighters, they were slow and awkward compared to their opponents.

'More than two hundred of my people have fallen,' said Ryll, who was haggard and bloodstained. His armoured skin flickered white and grey, the colours of unbearable grief. 'Almost half. And Liett . . .' His deep voice cracked. 'My one, my only Liett will soon join her ancestors.'

Nish had been afraid of that. It seemed impossible that Liett, who had always been so magnificent, so brave and bold and full of life, could be dying. And yet the lyrinx, for all their toughness, were as mortal as any other species. 'Is there nothing that can be done for her?'

'Our healers have been working on her since I brought her down,' said Ryll, 'and I was by her side the whole time, but her belly wounds are too many and too deep. The mancer who speared her must also have damaged her inside. I have little hope now.' He bowed and withdrew.

After the toll of battle had been completed, everyone stood in silence for ten minutes, remembering their dead. Nish tried to count his own, from the time when Fyllis had taken him out of Mazurhize, but the number was too great.

The faces flashed through his inner eye: hundreds of the Defiance killed in that fruitless battle with his father's army; faithful Zham, that gentle giant at the top of Mistmurk; more than three hundred men and women of the militia he'd fought beside at Blisterbone Pass, Taranta, the monastery, and since; and half of Yulla's hundred; not to mention wild, rebellious, beautiful, brave and loving Liett. He remembered all the faces, but he could not always put a name to them, and that was the worst of all.

'Nish, you'd better get on with it,' said Flydd abruptly.

Nish roused, with an effort. 'Er, what?'

'Take command of the survivors, before they get restless.'

'Yes, I suppose so. How many *are* left?'

'Hackel's mercenaries have fled but some three thousand of Vomix's and Lidgeon's troops remain, plus their injured, and they'll swear to you if you demand it.'

'All right,' said Nish, 'but I'll not take their oaths as God-Emperor, only as commander-in-chief of the empire's forces.'

'Whatever!' snapped Flydd. 'Just get on with it.'

Nish took their oaths, then distributed Vomix's enormous war chest equally to every surviving man and woman, excepting himself and his allies. The coin was tainted in his eyes and he wanted none of it.

'I'd advise you to put your troops to work at once,' said Flydd. 'Idleness will allow them to brood upon their terrible losses, and we can't afford that.'

There were thousands of dead soldiers, far too many to be buried in the thin, stony soil, so Nish ordered that they be carried to the cracked and crumbling sump that had once been Mazurhize Prison and placed in a pit there. When it had finished settling, the pit would be filled with rubble and the huge slabs that had roofed the prison would be placed on top, a permanent memorial to the slain.

The lyrinx gathered their own fallen, then dragged up dozens of dead trees and built a pyre on the far side of the plain, near the forest. The bodies were carefully arranged on the pyre and the sacred rites said over them, after which Ryll sent a runner for Flydd, Nish, Yggur, Malien, Tiaan and Maelys, plus those surviving members of the militia who had fought beside Liett.

'Is it the worst?' Nish asked.

'I'm afraid so,' said the lyrinx messenger, a big, heavily armoured female with a battered green crest. 'Our beloved Matriarch has fallen; Liett is dead.'

They stood by the pyre, at a respectful distance to one side of the mourning lyrinx, while Ryll carried Liett's limp body to the top of the pyre and gently folded her beautiful wings for the last time. He kissed her brow and her crest, knelt beside her for several minutes, gazing at her, then backed down.

'Thank you for coming, my friends,' he said when he reached the bottom. He embraced them one by one. 'Liett would have been proud to see such a gathering.'

'I'm so sorry,' said Nish, so choked up that he could barely speak. 'She was one of the greatest of all the lyrinx, and I'll never forget her. I'll miss her more than I can say.'

'There was no lyrinx like her,' said Ryll. 'I may remain as Patriarch, for a while, but I will never take another mate.' His eyes shed thick tears. 'And yet, if she had to die young, Liett would have wanted to go this way, in battle defending her friends and everything she cared about, and this beautiful world. She loved Santhenar more than any of us.'

The sacred rites were spoken, then Ryll carried fire to the four sides of the pyre and within minutes it had enveloped all the bodies, the flames roaring higher than the treetops as if to carry their spirits away to their own special corner of the shadow realm.

When the bodies had become ash, Nish and his friends trudged silently back to Morrelune. The Aachim and Faellem had gathered their dead to be taken through the portals to their own lands, while the Whelm were bearing theirs into the forest, though they would not permit anyone to help them, or to witness their rites.

'What are you going to do about your father?' Flydd said quietly, for Jal-Nish's body remained in the crumbling palace.

'I plan to bury him myself, when it's safe to go into Morrelune. Despite all that he did, I owe Father that much.'

But not today. Nish could not face it.

He went looking for Maelys and found her in one of the healers' tents, sitting beside Aunt Haga, who was confined to

643

a stretcher and cursing everyone in sight, though she broke off the moment he entered.

'Prince Cryl-Nish,' she said, pasting on a sickeningly obsequious smile and trying to rise and bow at the same time. 'Or should it be Emperor?'

He grimaced. Last autumn, Haga and her two sisters had required Maelys, as a family duty, to lead Nish away from Mazurhize and try to become pregnant by him, so as to save Clan Nifferlin and restore it to its rightful position. Though he understood why they had imposed that duty on Maelys, he had not forgiven Haga for it. And yet, she was Maelys's only surviving adult relative, so he could not spurn Haga either.

'Call me Nish,' he said. 'I'm no prince nor emperor, and never will be; I'm just an ordinary man.'

'Of course, Prince Cryl-Nish,' said Haga.

Fyllis was on Maelys's other side. She took after her mother and aunts and looked nothing like Maelys, being tall for her age, slim, blonde and blue-eyed. Fyllis had recovered more quickly than anyone had expected and now, though as pallid as a long-term prisoner, and with a hacking cough, she was sitting up, smiling as she played with a little wooden toy.

Nish knew nothing about her save that she was an obedient, somewhat simple child with an astonishing gift – she could hide people from the God-Emperor's scriers and wisp-watchers. Last autumn, when she had only been eight, the aunts had sent her into the horrors of Mazurhize to get Nish out and, incredibly, Fyllis had done so. He would never forget it, nor forgive the dried-up old women who had put such a burden on her.

'Hello, Fyllis,' he said, shaking her pale hand. 'I'm Nish. Do you remember me?'

'Of course,' she said softly. 'I rescued you from Mazurhize. You were very smelly.'

Aunt Haga choked. 'Fyllis, how dare you speak –'

Nish cut her off with a gesture. 'Yes, I stank, and I'm sorry. You saved my life that day, and I want to thank you with all my heart.'

'And you and Maelys saved mine,' said Fyllis. A shadow crossed her face. 'But not poor Mummy, or Aunt Bugi.'

'We didn't get here in time; I'm sorry.'

'Aunt Bugi was tired; she went to sleep and didn't wake up. And Mummy just cried and cried. She was always crying, ever since Daddy had to run away. Mummy is at peace now.'

'Yes, she is. Are you hungry?'

'I'm starving. The food in your prison was horrible. I couldn't eat it.'

'Neither could I,' said Nish. 'But that's all over now, and as soon as you're better we're going to have a feast.'

'A feast!' Fyllis clapped her hands. 'I'm better already.'

Nish smiled and stood up. 'Rest a while. I'll come for you when it's ready.'

'The last feast I remember was at the end of the war,' said Maelys, going with him to the flap of the tent. 'I was only her age.'

'What are you going to feast on?' said Flydd, walking slowly by with Yggur, whose arms and chest were swathed in bandages, and his face and hands shiny with balm.

Tulitine had not been able to heal his burns completely and he was still in great pain, and yet, he looked more at peace than Nish had ever known him. Yggur's carbonised hair had been shaven, revealing a long, bony skull, which made him look rather severe even though he was smiling.

'Army rations, for the most part,' said Nish. 'Supplemented by delicacies from Hackel's personal supply wagons. Call it a victory dinner, if you prefer, in recognition of all that our friends and followers have done . . . especially those

645

who gave their lives on the way. And to serve as a marker between the past and the future – between the God-Emperor's brutal reign and . . . whatever comes next.'

Flydd gave him a keen glance from under his single, snake-like eyebrow.

'But also,' said Nish, 'thinking about the last victory feast we had ten years ago, and – and the way it ended so abruptly, so terribly, I wanted to do it properly this time.'

'We all wish we could have that day over again,' said Yggur.

The tables were set up on the other side of Morrelune, away from the battlefield, in the triangular space between the edge of the plain, the pit surrounding the palace, and the Sacred Lake. The head table was placed closest to the jumbled rock at the edge of the pit and had a pleasant view, for those facing away from Morrelune, across the lake to the mountains beyond.

Nish had set it up so the ten survivors of his militia could be seated together. Clech and Aimee were to his left and the rest of the militia occupied that end of the table. Having no happy memories of Morrelune, he had seated himself so his back was to the palace.

Maelys was on his right, with Fyllis beside her, playing with some little wooden figures she'd brought from Mazurhize. Haga sat next to her, and Nish noticed her secreting a basketful of large golden fish under the table. She must have caught them in the Sacred Lake, and good luck to her. Clan Nifferlin had lived on the verge of starvation for years and the fierce old bird never missed an opportunity to feed her family. She would always survive.

Opposite Nish sat Flydd and Persia, who was laughing at something Flydd had said, then Flangers and Chissmoul, Yggur and Tulitine. She looked much better since the

646

caduceus had been destroyed and did not seem to be in such pain. Further down sat M'lainte, Yulla and Lilis, who wore a feather in her hat and a brown patch over her left eye and looked more piratical than ever, though she had been subdued for some time after Maelys told her of Nadiril's fate.

Malien, Tiaan and Ryll were at the end. Ryll's huge figure would ordinarily have dominated the table but he was slumped on his bench, silent and lost in his grief. Clearly, he did not want to be here.

'Well done, Nish,' said Flydd, raising his goblet so that the wine glowed in the afternoon sunshine. 'After last night, this is just what we needed.'

'I wanted our "feast" to be as close to the one we shared at Ashmode, at the end of the lyrinx war, as I could manage,' said Nish. 'And the food is on that low par, though the wine . . .' he took a deep sniff, 'is surprisingly good.'

'I confiscated Vomix's private stores before they could be looted,' said Flydd.

'How come you didn't share it out among the troops?' Nish said with a sly grin.

'That would have been like washing my filthy feet in it. There are limits!' Flydd took a sip and said quietly, 'I know why you've organised the feast this way.'

'I hoped, if we could have it again, that it might lay one of my demons to rest,' said Nish, thinking of Irisis's death.

'I hope it does.'

'And what does the future hold for Xervish Flydd, ex-scrutator?' said Nish, changing to a more cheerful subject. 'Are you going to write your Histories of the war again?'

'They were the great work of my life, when I had nothing else to do for nine years in my amber-wood hut, but I'm not planning to write them a second time.'

'Then it must be the little cottage and the flower garden,' Nish said teasingly.

'Nope,' said Flydd. 'Had a garden for a while at the top of Mistmurk Mountain. Wasn't as interesting as I'd imagined. Plants don't do anything; they just sit there.'

'Then what?' said Nish. 'I can't believe you're going to fade away like some decrepit old pensioner.'

'You've got a damned hide,' cried Flydd. 'We're going on a long holiday. I'm planning to catch up on all I missed in my years on the mountain, and since that time at Fiz Gorgo when Ghorr's torturers . . . you know.'

Nish did know. 'Where are you going?'

'To Roros, of course, the centre of the civilised world. The weather is warm, the people friendly, and the food and wine are magnificent. We're leaving on *Three Reckless Old Ladies* as soon as things are sorted out here. Tomorrow, I hope.'

'Tomorrow?' cried Nish, feeling abandoned to a task that he had never wanted and which he felt was way beyond him. 'But . . . what about the empire?'

'I'm sure it's in good hands.'

'After all the months of trying to manipulate me to become God-Emperor, you're just going to walk away?'

'Learned the error of my ways,' said Flydd airily. 'It's time for a new generation to take over.'

Nish did not believe Flydd could let go that easily, but he let the absurd statement lie. 'You keep saying *we*. Who are you going with?' How could he have met someone so quickly? But then, women had always been drawn to the ugly old scoundrel.

'He's going with me,' said Persia, taking Flydd's battered hand in her smooth brown one and looking extremely satisfied with the arrangement. 'My seven years with Yulla are up, and my indenture has been fulfilled. And, now that you've seen to Vomix, Nish, I'm free at last.'

Flydd will give you the security you crave so desperately, Nish thought. He won't let you down. 'I wish you the very best,' he said, and meant it. 'Yggur, I don't need to ask what you and Tulitine will be doing in your retirement.'

'My Art will be gone within days – maybe hours. I'm just an ordinary man with not long to live, and I can't say that I'm sorry about it.'

'All things must pass,' said Tulitine. 'But not for a few years yet, I hope.'

'What will happen to the Regression Spell now?' said Maelys.

'I don't know,' said Tulitine. 'The pain in my bones began to fade when the chthonic fire disappeared and the caduceus died, though the spell could still harm me in other ways. But whatever happens, Yggur and I are going to live our lives as though each day were our last.'

'What about you, Maelys?' said Flydd.

She was sitting back with her arms wrapped around her stomach. She glanced at Nish, who realised that he was staring at her and looked away.

'Aunt Haga, Fyllis and I are going home,' said Maelys. 'We're taking Mother's body with us, and Aunt Bugi's, and Father's bones if I can discover where he was buried. Once they've all been laid to rest I'm calling home the surviving cousins of Clan Nifferlin, and we're going to rebuild Nifferlin Manor just as it was before – only better.'

'That's the best way to heal the empire,' said Tulitine. 'For everyone to get on with their ordinary lives.'

'And so to you, Nish,' said Flydd. 'At our last feast, you didn't say what you wanted for your future, but the heir to the empire can't get off so lightly.'

'Don't dare say that you're going to tear it down,' said Yulla from the end of the table. 'That would only set off worse violence, and it would last a lot longer.'

A piece of rock broke away from the pit wall behind Nish and went tumbling down the slope, making a small splash as it landed in the water. How long before the whole palace crumbled? How long before he had to face the grim task of burying his father? He clung to the hope that the collapsing palace would entomb the body for him.

'I think *you* should be God-Empress, Yulla,' Nish said irritably, for people never stopped telling him what to do. 'I'm sure you'd be a lot better at it than I would.'

Yulla's little eyes gleamed with greed, but she shook her head. 'Every realm requires an able administrator, and few were better than I was, when I was Governor of Crandor. But that was long ago and my time has passed. The empire needs youth, and vigour – and heirs. The stability of the realm must be maintained.'

Gravel crunched behind Nish, the song of the tears rose and fell, and he smelt a foul, decaying odour. Someone gasped; opposite him, Tulitine's eyes widened, and Yggur cursed. Flydd thrust himself to his feet, his mouth agape. Finally, reluctantly, Nish rose, already knowing, though it was quite impossible, what he was going to see.

'Indeed it must,' said his father, Jal-Nish, emerging from between the rocks at the edge of the pit, 'and clearly, since you've all underestimated me *yet again*, none of you have what it takes to maintain my empire.'

'But . . . we saw your body,' said Nish. 'You're – you're not . . .?'

'I'm not reanimated, if that's what you're worried about,' said Jal-Nish, 'for I was never *completely* dead.'

He looked it, though. His skin still had that hideous green-purple tinge, like a long-dead corpse; his flesh was bloated and shiny; slimy, stinking muck was oozing down his chin and he was limping badly on both feet. The God-Emperor's imperial robes were draggled with dust and mud, yet the mask was back over his face and the Profane Tears

650

hung from his neck, and Nish knew that all the agony of the past half year had been for nothing.

'Stilkeen slew me,' said Jal-Nish, who spoke thickly, as if his bloated tongue filled his gluey mouth, 'the moment he discovered that I knew nothing about chthonic fire. And I would have died instantly – had I not already taken precautions.'

'Then what we saw up on the ninth level . . . your . . . corpse –'

'It was real,' Jal-Nish said with a shudder. 'My body *was* a rotting corpse, and you can't even imagine what a horror that was. There can be no worse feeling on this side of death than to live on – in a dead body.'

'How?' Nish croaked. 'How could you live?'

His father smiled thinly. 'The instant I saw Stilkeen, even before it caught me, I withdrew part of my life force into Reaper and, as long as a single living cell remained in my corpse, *I* clung to life. Weeks passed in that ghastly state, until finally, late last night, faithful Klarm brought me the tears. Once I had them, Reaper revived me and repaired the worst of the damage. Now here I stand – somewhat decayed, and with much work to do to slough off the rotted flesh and restore myself, but very definitely alive.'

He favoured Nish with a grotesque smile. Through the half-mask his gums were grey; his good eye oozed a sticky fluid and even from five spans away his breath was foul.

Nish opened his mouth, but closed it again. There were no words for what he was feeling, and there was nothing he could say to his father.

'I'm particularly disappointed in you, Son,' Jal-Nish said. 'I'd thought, after your mighty deeds since the Range of Ruin, that you were fit to succeed me after all. Clearly, I *overestimated* you.'

'I don't want to be God-Emperor,' said Nish. 'I never did.'

'Which proves beyond doubt your unfitness for the throne, in the unlikely event that it should ever become vacant. Had you been fit to succeed me, you would not have stopped until you had burned my body to ash and taken the tears for yourself. But what do *you* do? Sit down to a picnic without taking the slightest precautions!' Jal-Nish's voice dripped contempt.

And he was right. How could Nish have come so far, then failed so badly in the final moments? Because he could not bear to go near his father's corpse and do what had to be done.

'You set up this feast to be as much like the last one as possible,' Jal-Nish went on. 'Did it not occur to you that it might also end the way the last one did – in *every* particular?'

That had not occurred to Nish, but it should have, for Jal-Nish had turned up to ruin the feast at the end of the war as well. And since he'd had the tears for more than half a day, he must have timed his appearance to coincide with this feast.

He glanced at Maelys, whose brows were knitted; she hadn't worked it out yet. But then, she had been just a kid ten years ago; and she had not been there.

'How did you get here?' Nish said dully. His stomach throbbed with jagging pains, as if he had swallowed fish-hooks and someone was trying to pull them out.

'Did Maelys not tell you that she'd encountered faithful Klarm in the lower levels of my palace, and that he was looking for me?'

Jal-Nish beckoned and Klarm hobbled out from behind the rocks, walking on one foot and the knob-ended rod bound above the stump of his amputated leg. The dwarf looked dreadfully haggard.

Nish glanced at Maelys, whose small hands were raised

now, as if to hold back the horror of Jal-Nish. 'We haven't spent much time together lately,' said Nish.

At the tables further off, people were talking, laughing, clinking their mugs and celebrating the victory as though nothing had happened, for they could not see Jal-Nish.

'Clearly,' said the God-Emperor, 'since she didn't give you the one piece of information that should have set your alarm bells ringing instantly.'

'It would have made no difference,' said Nish. 'We'd all seen your rotting corpse.'

'Then you're a bigger fool than I thought.'

The militia scrambled out of the way as Jal-Nish approached. He clambered up onto the left-hand end of the table, pallid and blotchy and reeking like the corpse he had been, but utterly determined to take back what was his.

'The God-Emperor has returned,' he said in a ringing voice. 'All hail the God-Emperor!'

The revelry broke off instantly, and Nish heard someone throwing up. A shocked silence spread across the banquet tables like a ripple across a lake, then everyone began to shout at once. Jal-Nish raised the tears above his head until their churning quicksilver shimmer was reflected in every eye.

'The God-Emperor has returned,' he repeated, more commandingly. 'All hail the God-Emperor!'

Many soldiers rose to their feet, some eagerly, most slowly, and began to chant and bang their swords on their shields. 'All hail the God-Emperor! Hail, Hail!'

'Imperial Guard, you have sworn to me and me alone,' called Jal-Nish. 'Your God-Emperor needs you. Come forward and renew your oaths.'

The surviving Imperial Guard, eleven white-clad, battered and bloodstained men, came forwards.

'Only eleven?' said Jal-Nish. 'Out of eight hundred?

653

Still, eleven of my loyal guards are worth three times as many common soldiers.'

They renewed their oaths, not entirely without hesitation and, once they had, Jal-Nish gestured them to stand around Nish's end of the table.

'This time I won't be bothering with an heir,' he said with a meaningful glance at Nish, and a darker look at Maelys that sent another jagging pain through Nish's belly. 'I don't need one, because neither my flesh nor my powers will ever wane!'

Klarm dropped his knoblaggie but did not pick it up. Maelys gave a muffled cry, reached for Nish's arm, then drew back, and he knew what she was thinking.

Months ago at the Pit of Possibilities, after she had seen into Jal-Nish's mind when he'd been using the tears, she had said, *He needs only three things to become invulnerable for all time: perfect knowledge of the tears; complete mastery of himself; and a clear understanding of the Art by which he uses Gatherer and Reaper. And he's close to gaining all three.*

'I learned a lot from Stilkeen,' said Jal-Nish. 'I now know enough to master the tears and leap further than any other mancer can dream. I'm going to become an immortal *being!*'

And we can't stop you, Nish thought, for they had never found what they had originally gone all the way to the Tower of a Thousand Steps for – the antithesis to the tears, the one power, process, spell or device that could unbind them forever.

But then it got worse – so terribly, agonisingly worse that Nish wished he could die, anything to escape the agony renewed a thousand times over.

'You lied to me, didn't you?' Jal-Nish said to Maelys.

'I – don't – I . . .' she said.

'You told me that you gathered up my son's spilled seed when you nursed him in his delirium,' Jal-Nish grated. 'And

654

inserted it within your virgin body so as to become pregnant to him. Do you deny it?'

Aunt Haga was staring at Maelys, so astonished that for once she was speechless.

'No,' whispered Maelys. 'I said that –'

'And I believed you, because, fool that I was, I was desperate for a grandchild. But it was a lie, wasn't it?'

'Yes.' Her voice was barely audible.

'Worse than a lie – it was a monstrous insult to the majesty of the God-Emperor, one that requires the most dreadful punishment. Then, subsequently you became pregnant to Emberr, son of Rulke and Yalkara, the two Charon who, together and separately, brought ruin upon Santhenar many times.'

'Yes,' said Maelys.

Now Aunt Haga's mouth was opening and closing like a stranded fish.

'So you fully understand what I must do now,' said Jal-Nish.

Maelys didn't answer. Clearly she did not know what he was talking about, though she feared the worst. But Nish knew, with a shrieking, scalding horror worse than anything he had ever felt, exactly what Jal-Nish was planning to do. He'd already said so.

Did it not occur to you that it might also end the way the last one did – in every *particular?* Jal-Nish had said, but Nish hadn't fully taken it in at the time. Now he understood, and the horror was magnified a hundredfold because he already had the entire scene in mind. He'd been replaying it for more than ten years and the agony never grew any less.

'Guards,' Jal-Nish said to the nearest Imperial Guardsman. 'Drag Maelys out between the tables and bare her neck. You,' he said to the second man, 'raise your sword and do the business.'

'Nooo!' shrieked Nish.

FIFTY-ONE

The two guards hesitated, but only for a second, before the closest man took hold of Maelys. She was just sitting there, her eyes staring – she finally understood what was going to happen. Everyone did, with the exception of Fyllis, who was moving her little wooden figures about on the table and talking to them in a range of voices, totally immersed in her world of make-believe.

'Hold them,' cried Jal-Nish, pointing to Nish, Flydd, Clech, Flangers and especially Ryll, and the other nine Imperial Guardsmen, who had so recently sworn allegiance to Nish, sprang to obey. 'Bind the lyrinx – he's the one who maimed me thirteen years ago and I have a special punishment for him.'

Before Nish could draw his sword he had been taken from behind, and so had Flydd and the others. Three guards held Ryll, a naked sword across his throat, while a fourth bound him. Clearly, Jal-Nish knew exactly who had power and who, like Yggur, was no longer a threat.

The people from the surrounding tables were on their feet, staring, but many had already hailed the God-Emperor and, while the Profane Tears sang their dreadful threnody, none dared to oppose him.

He clambered down, directing the first two Imperial Guardsman to take Maelys to the open space between the table and the edge of the Sacred Lake. They held her tightly and she put up no resistance. She must have known it was futile.

The guardsmen were heaving her from her chair, under Jal-Nish's gloating, oozing eye, when little Fyllis set down her toys, picked up a long serving fork, turned around and plunged it bone-deep into his left thigh.

He let out a sharp cry, staggered a couple of steps and bellowed, 'Guards!'

The guards behind Nish and Clech turned to defend Jal-Nish but Clech knocked the first down with an elbow to the nose, while Nish thrust his sword between the legs of the second, gashing him badly on both thighs and sending him reeling to the ground in twin sprays of blood. The rest of the guards, save those holding Ryll, ran around the end.

Jal-Nish wrenched out the bloody fork, dropped it, and turned to face Fyllis, slowly moving his hand towards the churning surface of Reaper. 'You're going to die for that, little girl,' he said viciously. 'Guards, seize her as well. You can take both heads off with the one stroke.'

Now Maelys began to struggle desperately, but she was powerless in the hands of the guardsmen. One carried her away while another went for Fyllis.

As he lifted her from her chair, Aunt Haga, a tall, stringy mass of fury, sprang up, swinging one of the large golden fish by the tail, and smashed Jal-Nish across the face so hard that it lifted him off his feet.

He fell backwards, the mask went flying and Nish's gut tightened, for beneath the mask the wounds that had refused to heal for thirteen years were gone. That side of his father's face showed no rot at all – it was baby-smooth, and in his empty eye socket silvery flames flickered, as if the surface of Reaper was reflected there.

The guard let go of Maelys and stared at the God-Emperor. Little Aimee came out from under the table as if there were springs under her soles and rammed her fist into the throat of Fyllis's captor. He collapsed, gasping for air, and Aimee pulled her away. The other guards froze, swords in the air.

Nish slipped free, slid between Maelys and her guard, and held up his bloody blade. 'If you want her, Father, you'll have to kill me first.'

Jal-Nish shakily climbed to his feet, and Nish could see how the father who still cared, in his own twisted way, for his one remaining child was struggling with the monster who had been obsessed with power for so long that no depravity was beyond him. Would he give the order?

He almost did; Jal-Nish's lips framed the awful words, *Kill him!* but he could not speak them.

'Guards,' he said softly, 'Take the girls and kill them.'

The Imperial Guardsmen shook their heads and backed away. They had sworn allegiance to the God-Emperor, but clearly that oath did not include this flame-eyed version of him.

'Then I'll do it myself,' said Jal-Nish, reaching for Reaper.

There was nothing Nish could do this time; nothing anyone could do.

'Leave my sister alone, you nasty man,' cried Fyllis, raising her right hand.

Jal-Nish spun around, staring at the blonde-haired child, so thin and pale, yet so determined. Her little chin was pointed and her oddly blank eyes met his unflinchingly. His arm quivered, his fingers twitched, but he could not move his hand down the fraction of an ell required to touch the yearning surface of Reaper. Incredibly, the gift Fyllis had used to protect her family from the scriers, by preventing the wisp-watchers and loop-listeners from talking to the tears, had blocked the God-Emperor from using Reaper.

'Klarm,' Jal-Nish said over his shoulder. 'Take her down.'

'I don't harm children,' said Klarm, picking up the knoblaggie.

The flame in Jal-Nish's eye flared. 'Just months ago, you swore a sacred oath to me, dwarf.'

'I swore to the man you used to be,' said Klarm, 'because Santhenar was in peril and you were the only man with the strength to stop it – or so I thought.' He glanced at Nish, thoughtfully. 'But that peril is gone now, and I did not swear to the power-crazed monster you've become.'

'No one breaks their oath to me,' grated Jal-Nish. 'Especially not the only man I've ever trusted with the tears.' He punched his fist into Reaper and a silver flash lanced towards the dwarf, who threw himself backwards over the edge of the pit.

'You'll keep,' said Jal-Nish after a long pause. 'All of you.' He dropped his hand onto Gatherer, then both he and the tears faded and disappeared.

After a considerable hesitation, the allies went to the edge of the pit and looked over. An uncanny flame was slowly spreading across the corroded stone of Morrelune again, though this time it had the same silvery shimmer as Nish had seen in his father's empty eye socket.

'We've got to find out what he's up to,' said Flydd that night. 'And I can only think of one way to do so.'

The allies, except for Ryll, had gathered on the rim of the pit, near where they'd had the banquet and, save for Maelys, were looking down at the rising and falling lights of Morrelune. Maelys had not joined them; she was sitting on a rock, well to one side, gazing up at the mountains.

She could only think of home and family now: her poor mother weeping in that terrible cell until she died of grief; her beloved father, Rudigo, seized years ago and tortured, though it had taken him months to die; and crusty old Aunt Bugi, who had held out almost to the end.

The memory of cranky Aunt Haga, whom Maelys had always thought hated her, slapping down the God-Emperor with a fish pilfered from his Sacred Lake brought a smile to her lips, but when she thought of her little sister it faded again.

What kind of a monster imprisoned a child in that stinking hell-hole, and how had she survived it? Maelys suspected that Haga, Bugi and Lyma had starved themselves so Fyllis would have enough to eat.

And her sweet, simple little sister, who had always been frail and who would not step on an ant, had saved Maelys's life. Fyllis's blind loyalty brought tears to Maelys's eyes. Where had she found the courage to stab the mighty God-Emperor, and how had she managed to deny him the use of Reaper at the most critical time?

It had been too much for her. Fyllis had collapsed the moment Jal-Nish disappeared, and she was now back in the healer's tent with Haga watching over her anxiously. Maelys wished she was there too.

She shook her head, slowly realising what Flydd was talking about.

'You want to go back into Morrelune?' cried Nish.

'No, I don't,' said Flydd. 'But we've got to get into Jal-Nish's mind while he's using the tears, to see how close he is to mastering them. Once he succeeds it will be too late.'

'Of all the dangerous things you've done –' began Nish.

'No, *I* can't do it. That would be far too perilous for all of us.'

'Then who?' said Nish.

'Only one person has seen into his mind since he's had the tears,' said Flydd.

'Who?' said Nish, frowning.

'No!' cried Yggur. 'This time you're going too far, Flydd. I can't allow it.'

Maelys leaned back against the rock and closed her eyes. She couldn't care less what they were plotting. She'd done her bit, and now that she had her family back, all she wanted was to go home; to *make* a home for them, and for the baby.

'You must,' said Flydd. 'Indeed, Yggur, you're the only one who can make it happen – *if* you've got any power left.'

'It's on its last gasp,' said Yggur. 'I already told you that.'

'All the more reason to get on with it. Maelys, come here, please.'

She stood up, her mind still on Fyllis, and Nifferlin. 'Yes?'

'You're the only person to ever see into Jal-Nish's mind –' said Flydd.

'What?' The memories came back so sluggishly that for half a minute Maelys did not realise what he was on about. 'Oh yes, it was when Nish and I went down to the Pit of Possibilities, months ago. My taphloid woke for a moment and I saw Jal-Nish using the tears. He was gloating that he would soon master them, and would then be invulnerable for all time . . .' Realising that everyone was staring at her, she said, 'No! Definitely not. Don't even imagine –'

'No one else can do it. You must get back into his mind and see how close he is, so we can find a way to stop him.'

'I couldn't do it again if I wanted to,' said Maelys. 'It happened by itself. I didn't plan it.'

'The taphloid was the critical factor,' said Flydd. 'And it was originally Yggur's. Therefore, if anyone can make it duplicate what it did in the Pit of Possibilities, he can.'

FIFTY-TWO

The tent had been set up on the narrow strip of paving between the curving edge of the pit of Morrelune and the oval sweep of the Sacred Lake, and Maelys was sitting cross-legged on a folded blanket, on the floor. The hour was late and it was almost pitch-dark inside the tent – to see with the taphloid she had to block out her natural sight completely.

It did not block her other senses, though – Maelys could hear waves lapping against the stone edge of the lake, and every so often a marshy odour drifted across from the fringing reed beds. Once or twice there came a hissing sound from the pit, or the tumble of a dislodged pebble down its sides.

She blanked out the sounds and smells and, holding the taphloid lightly between her clenched hands as Yggur had instructed her, closed her eyes. All sounds from outside faded, and shortly she made out the distant, hackle-raising song of the tears.

Almost immediately she envisaged the faint outline of a tear, though she could not tell which one. They were made of nihilium, she recalled, the purest substance in the world and one that held the print of the Art more tightly than anything else could. The tear was floating above a pedestal that had been rough-sawn from black meteoritic iron; it resembled the iron from which the caduceus had been made.

Jal-Nish was not looking directly into the tear this time. From the way the dark background was moving, he must have been walking around the pedestal, watching it from the corner of his eye.

He was in the topmost level of Morrelune, which was open on all sides. The ceiling was supported by intersecting circles of slender columns made from a golden stone polished to waxy smoothness, though unlike the rest of Morrelune the stone here was hardly stained at all, and only slightly corroded.

The ninth level was still a beautiful, sparsely furnished space, but thickly coated in dust now and with hairline cracks running across the ceiling. A large brown stain marred the floor beneath a hook mounted in the ceiling, where Jal-Nish's decaying body had been hung up by his toes.

'I thought I understood the tears,' he mused as he walked. 'Once they would do exactly as I ordered, but since Klarm has held them they've become capricious. Is that because I allowed him to use them – or can it be the wilful nature of the tears themselves? Or can they only have one master?'

He made several more circuits, the good hand and the replaced one clasped behind his back.

'Thirteen years I've spent prying into their secrets,' he murmured, 'and yet, full understanding still eludes me. I've got to know how they were formed from the destruction of the node at Snizort, but only two people ever knew. One is dead and the other, Flydd, will never tell me.'

Jal-Nish paced between the columns agitatedly. Across and

back, as if trying to steel himself for something he'd never had the courage to do. Abruptly he turned, strode to a blue curtain and wrenched it aside.

Dust sifted to the floor and Maelys saw a rectangular coffin, made from crystal as clear as glass, standing on its end. Inside was the naked body of a beautiful, tall and curvaceous woman; she had eyes of the most brilliant blue and hair as yellow as corn. Had it not been for the thin line running around her throat she might have been asleep.

It was Irisis, and not only had she been beautiful, clever, brave and loyal, she had also sacrificed her life to try to save Nish. No wonder he had loved her so much; maybe he still did. How can I compete with that? Maelys half-rose, embarrassed and wondering where that thought had come from. She had been over her infatuation with Nish for months; she still cared for him, but only as a friend. Definitely no more than that.

'Dare I commit the ultimate, forbidden crime?' Jal-Nish was saying when she sat down again. 'Irisis was with Flydd in Snizort when the tears were created. Can I raise her from the dead long enough to rip the secret from her lying tongue?'

He began to pace again, back and forth, back and forth.

Maelys couldn't bear to watch him any longer. With a shudder, she dropped the taphloid onto the floor, and instantly she was back in the tent by the lake.

'Flydd?' she said softly.

He drew the tent flap open and she made out Yggur behind him, moving painfully because of his many half-healed burns. Nish was further back, pacing as anxiously as his father. She went out into the starlight.

'The tears are acting oddly and Jal-Nish can't work out why,' said Maelys to Flydd. 'He believes something strange happened when they were formed and, since he knows he'll never get it out of you, he's planning to ... do the other thing.'

'What other thing?' snapped Flydd. 'Speak plainly, girl! We don't have time.'

'He was looking at Irisis, in the crystal coffin,' said Maelys, avoiding Nish's eye. He made a keening sound and she went on, desperate to get the words out while she still could. 'He's thinking about ... about raising her from the dead so he can question her about the tears.'

Nish choked, stumbled away and she heard him throwing up over the edge of the pit.

'What did happen when the tears were formed, Flydd?' said Tulitine.

Flydd gestured her near and the others followed. 'It was a long time ago, at the battle for Snizort,' he said quietly, sitting down at the nearest table and picking up a half-full wine glass abandoned during the interrupted feast. 'The lyrinx had excavated a city into the tar pits there. They put in a node-drainer to prevent us drawing from the *field* of the Snizort node to power our clankers and air-floaters, and to take that power for themselves.

'The Council of Scrutators made a device to destroy the node-drainer, and ordered me to take it into Snizort, but the order was a disguised death sentence from my enemy, Chief Scrutator Ghorr. He didn't believe anyone could get into a city of a hundred thousand lyrinx, and out again, and to make absolutely sure of me, the device he gave me was booby-trapped. It was designed for an artisan, not a mancer, and if I had tried to use it, it would have killed me.'

He gulped the wine and continued. 'Irisis was an artisan, of course, so I had her work the device instead. Unfortunately the booby-trap failed and all the power of the node flowed the wrong way, destroying the node itself.'

'But not utterly,' said Yggur.

'No – the blast distilled the essence of the node into two nihilium tears, which Jal-Nish stole, and because he killed his own men to conceal that he had them, and ever since has used them for debased purposes, they became the Profane Tears.'

'What doesn't he know about them?' said Yggur. 'What's he trying to find out?'

'I don't know,' said Flydd. 'But if he succeeds he'll be impregnable *and* immortal, so we've got to strike soon, and hard. Maelys, you must find out what he's up to.'

'What if he sees me watching him?' Maelys could not stop thinking about the narrow seam around Irisis's neck. Had Haga and Fyllis not acted so quickly, she, Maelys, would now be preserved in another crystal box with an identical seam around her throat, where her severed head had been reattached. 'You can't imagine how much he hates me, Xervish.'

'I can imagine it, but if he gets what he's looking for it's the end for us all,' said Flydd after a long interval. 'And you're the only one who can do it.'

'All right!' She crept back to the tent.

When Maelys located Jal-Nish a few minutes later, he was crouched over the iron pedestal. Now both tears stood on it, but the uncertain, pacing God-Emperor of before was gone; he was confident and commanding again. What had he seen in the intervening time? Could he have raised Irisis, and wrung the truth out of her so quickly? It hardly seemed possible – and yet, with the tears, anything might be possible.

Plunging both hands into one of the tears – Gatherer, surely – he said cajolingly, 'Cryl-Nish, my son, I was in pain earlier – the most terrible pain from the torments Stilkeen had inflicted upon me. A madness came over me, and for a few minutes I was out of my mind, but I've come to my senses now.'

Lifting the tear, he held it up before him, and momentarily Maelys thought she saw Nish staring at his father, but Jal-Nish moved the tear closer and the image disappeared.

She shivered in the cool night. Could that really be happening? No, Nish wasn't in Morrelune; he was just outside the tent.

'Join me and become my lieutenant, beloved son, and all will be forgiven,' said Jal-Nish to Gatherer. 'I give you my word that I will restore Irisis to you, whole and unblemished, and never threaten her again as long as I shall live.'

Another figure appeared within Gatherer, but this time Maelys saw it clearly. It was Irisis, wearing a flowing gown of blue silk. There was no seam around her throat; she was gliding gracefully around a large chamber, looking back at someone and smiling, and her smile lit up the room. No wonder Nish can never get over her, she thought. Maelys wanted to wish them well together, but the thought nearly choked her.

'No!' cried Flydd from outside the tent. 'Nish, he sent that image to us deliberately. He's manipulating you, as he's done so many times before. You can't –'

So Jal-Nish had sent the image of Irisis to the others. Did he know she was watching him? Suddenly Maelys felt exhausted, and so cold that the taphloid could not warm her. She allowed it to spill from her fingers, breaking her envisioning, and crawled to the flap.

'Let me go!' hissed Nish. 'It's nothing to do with you. This is between me and him.'

'Don't be a fool,' said Flydd. 'It's exactly what he wants you to do.'

'And I'm still going to do it.'

Maelys scrabbled out of the tent and saw Flydd wrestling with Nish in the starlight. He fought Flydd off, scrambled over the edge of the pit and she heard him going down the steep slope like a madman, heading for the palace.

'Isn't anyone going to stop him?' said Maelys in a small voice.

'We'll never catch him,' said Yggur.

'He spent ten years in prison, brooding about Irisis,' said Flydd, shaking his head, 'and I've often wondered if the experience had turned his mind. No wonder he isn't interested in becoming emperor. He's totally obsessed; he's got to have her, no matter what it costs. He can't think about anything else.'

'What *is* it going to cost?' Maelys whispered.

'More than I can bear to think about,' said Flydd. 'Would you wait here, please?'

He drew Yggur and Tulitine aside, leaving Maelys standing by the tent, wondering how everything could have fallen to pieces so quickly.

She made out a low, furious argument, and shortly they returned.

'This *can't* be allowed to happen,' Flydd was saying. 'Whether Nish joins his father, or even takes the tears for his own, they can't be allowed to exist any longer. That was our original aim up on Mistmurk Mountain, if you recall – to find the antithesis to the tears and use it to destroy them. We lost track of that purpose after Stilkeen came, but we have to get rid of the tears, and surely, with the best minds on Santhenar gathered here, we can find the way.'

'Suppose you do find the way,' said Maelys, trying to

think through the implications. 'What if Nish is near the tears when they're destroyed?'

'The conflagration that formed them laid waste to everything within half a league. I can't imagine their destruction will be any less violent.'

'But Nish would be killed, Xervish!'

'I expect he would be,' Flydd said evenly. 'Yet the tears *must* be destroyed, or Santhenar's oppression will never end. Surely we agree on that?'

'Yes,' said Yggur slowly, and so did Tulitine, and Malien, whom Maelys had not realised was there.

'And if Nish has gone over to his father's side, to get *her* back, he's made his choice,' said Flydd, sounding more like his old, hard self every minute. 'Well, let's see what our collective minds can do. Come away – we're too close to Morrelune. Who knows what spying devices Jal-Nish might be able to activate, now he holds the tears again.'

They headed out into the middle of the plain, but Maelys did not follow; she was too stunned. How, after all they had done together, could Flydd be talking about sacrificing Nish? She sat on a boulder and stared across the Sacred Lake, feeling helpless and trapped. Even if Nish *had* gone to Morrelune for a woman raised from the dead – an abomination Maelys could not bear to think about – she wasn't giving up on him. He meant too much to her and she had to do something.

'Maelys?' Flydd had come back. 'Get a move on; there's no time to waste.'

'No!'

'I beg your pardon!' he said in the famous scrutator's voice that few people dared to defy.

'I'm not going with you. You can all go to hell.'

Flydd raised the right half of his continuous eyebrow. 'Very well. I don't expect you'd have had anything useful to contribute, anyway.'

'Probably not. Go away.'

As soon as he was out of sight, she returned to the tent and took up her taphloid, fuming. Nothing to contribute, indeed! Maelys had also been thinking about the antithesis to the tears, and the search that had taken them all the way to the Tower of a Thousand Steps.

The Numinator had said that she hadn't heard of the antithesis but, when Maelys had asked the question for the second time, the Numinator had replied, *All knowledge collected by the God-Emperor's spies passes through Gatherer. Look within the tears.*

Look within the tears. It had seemed such a useless answer at the time, but the more she dwelt on it, the more she thought that the Numinator had been telling the truth.

Dare she use the taphloid one final time, to peer into the tears themselves? If she was to do anything for Nish, she had to, but what if Jal-Nish was waiting? He had tailored Gatherer to be the perfect spy, and if she looked, he must surely catch her, and kill her.

Nonetheless, Maelys had to try. If Jal-Nish wasn't stopped, the empire would be in his thrall, as it had been for the past ten years, and no one would suffer more than the surviving members of Clan Nifferlin.

She used the taphloid as she had done before, and saw Jal-Nish at once, which was worrying. Yet even if it was a trap, she had to go on.

He was sitting at a circular table carved from green stone, writing in a journal. The tears must be to his left, on their pedestal, though she could not see them from here. She could not see Nish, either, and her heart gave a hard thump, but settled; he would not have reached the palace yet. It might take him half an hour to clamber down the steep walls of the pit, cross the water and climb up to the ninth level.

Over the past ten years, Jal-Nish had written in a beautiful copperplate hand, *I have absorbed all captured powers, forces and Arts into the tears, to strengthen them even further, but I did not understand what I was doing. That was always my failing, as Flydd told me many years ago. I was greedy; I snatched at the power without troubling to understand it.*

The nihilium tears were created with no power nor Art of their own, but an infinite ability to absorb the Art from elsewhere, and I was so eager to make them the mightiest artefacts on Santhenar that it did not occur to me to only absorb compatible Arts. Is that why the tears are increasingly unstable? It's a lesson my study of the Histories should have taught me.

But not just unstable, Jal-Nish wrote. *I worked so hard to make each tear different that I enhanced Gatherer and Reaper's intrinsic antipathy to each other, and it grows worse each day. They cannot trust one another. They no longer talk to each other, nor cooperate unless I force them, and whenever I carry them about my neck I can feel their churning rage. If not for their mutual repulsion, which is far more powerful than trying to hold two north poles of a magnet together, I believe they would have attacked each other by now, and what would happen if they did? It does not bear thinking about.*

He scattered fine sand over the page to absorb the surplus ink, tapped it into a bowl and closed the ledger.

'No matter,' he said softly, 'Once I know exactly how they were created, I will be able to resolve their mutual antipathy, and then I will have the power to become a *being.*'

As he spoke, all the clues Maelys had been puzzling over slid together and the answer sprang into her mind – *the tears must be their own antithesis.* Gatherer and Reaper would have to be forced together so powerfully that their mutual repulsion was overcome and they would merge into one roiling mass which, overburdened with self-antipathy, would be annihilated.

She wasn't planning to tell Flydd that, though. He was so determined to end the power of the tears that he might act without care for the consequences. But Maelys cared very much, and she was going to save Nish, if she could, then annihilate the tears – assuming she could find a way to overcome their resistance without killing herself and everyone around her.

It was time to go into Morrelune.

FIFTY-THREE

Nish had come to Morrelune because the matter had to be ended, once and forever . . . even if he must commit the worst crime of all.

He paced slowly across the floor of the ninth level, struggling to control the panic he always felt before a confrontation with his father, for in the past Nish had lost every one of these battles. He wiped sweaty palms on his pants and took several deep, slow breaths, trying to steady his racketing heart. I can do this, he thought. I've got to, else Maelys and all her clan will die.

His father was sitting at the circular greenstone table, though he no longer wore the platinum mask that had concealed his mutilated face for thirteen years. A closed journal lay in front of him, and a quill beside it. He appeared healthier than he had at the feast, less decomposed, though there was still a tinge of green to his complexion and a dribble of thick fluid from his eye sockets.

When Jal-Nish looked up, Nish wished he had put the mask back on, for he could not come to terms with the baby-smooth skin on the right side of his father's face, nor the quicksilver flicker in the empty eye socket.

'I hoped you would come, Son. We have had –'

Nish's palms were sodden. Again he wiped them, then met his father's eye. 'What do you want?'

Jal-Nish's face hardened, but he forced a smile and slowly it broadened and became genuine. 'At last you're growing more like me.'

'I'm nothing like you,' Nish grated. 'Get on with it.'

'All right. I need your help.'

'Beg for it, then.'

Jal-Nish ignored that, with an effort. 'My plan to master the tears and become a *being* – a true god, if you like – is thwarted by one obstacle. I can't fully understand the tears until I know how they were created, but only two people know precisely what happened in the tar cavern in Snizort before the node exploded: Flydd and Irisis –'

'And Ullii,' Nish said coldly, for that strange, troubled child-woman had once fallen in love with him, a love he had not been able to return, and he could not forget that it had cost her her life.

'Ullii would not have understood,' Jal-Nish said dismissively, 'even if she had been paying attention. And Flydd will never tell me.'

'Neither will Irisis, and you know it. She was prepared to die for her principles; how can you hope to compel her from beyond the grave?'

'I can't,' said Jal-Nish. 'I have many failings, Son, but misreading people is not one of them.' He thought for a moment, then said softly, 'But if *you* asked it of Irisis, she might tell you out of the love she holds for you.'

'If there's one thing I know about the dead, they see more clearly than the living, and Irisis always saw through you.'

'I can bring her back, Cryl-Nish. I would do that for you –'

The temptation so burned Nish that he had to use rage to fight it. 'Don't lie to me, you stinking, maggot-eaten mongrel! You don't give a damn about me, and never have. The

674

only thing you care about is your obscene obsession with power, and what for? What has it ever given you?'

'You'll never understand,' Jal-Nish said scornfully. 'You're truly pitiful, Nish. Power is its own reward, and the most seductive of all life's pleasures.'

'Only an impotent man would say that,' said Nish pointedly. 'I prefer my pleasures a trifle more physical; more *real*.'

'I'm sure you do,' said Jal-Nish. 'You always were shallow, superficial, common. Do you want to see her, or not?'

Nish's throat seemed to have swollen, and for several breaths he had to fight for air. 'I want to see her.'

Raising Irisis seemed to take an eternity. He watched, barely able to breathe, while Jal-Nish stroked the surface of Gatherer in one motion after another, teasing it into patterns and reading them, then shaking his head and dissolving the patterns back into an amorphous glister and starting again.

'She will need clothing,' Nish said. Nakedness had not bothered Irisis while she was alive, but he could not bear the thought of her coming out that way before his vile, sneering father.

'I have already laid garments to hand.'

Finally Jal-Nish put his hand deep into Reaper, drew it back to Gatherer, and Nish heard something stir on the other side of the dusty curtain. On the day his ten-year sentence in Mazurhize had been up, Jal-Nish had drawn back that very curtain to show him Irisis's body, and forced him to relive her death, over and again.

A sharp pain grew in the centre of his chest and a hot flush ran up his throat until his face glowed. What was the matter with him? He was blushing like a schoolboy.

Her heart gave a slow thump, and another; Nish *felt* the air being drawn all the way down her dry throat and into lungs that strained to expand after not knowing air in ten years. She swayed, suffering a momentary dizziness, and he felt that too, as if his father had linked him to Irisis in some way; he also felt her knees wobble as she took a step, and for a second Nish wasn't sure that they would bear her weight.

'Leave us, Father!'

Jal-Nish nodded and went across the floor of the ninth level, out of sight. As he did, the iron pedestal faded, and the tears with it. He was taking no chances.

The lid of the coffin whispered open, silk rustled, and Nish heard her bare feet on the floor. His mouth went dry. The curtain was pulled back and tears prickled his eyes, for Irisis stood there, alive! `

Or at least, restored to life.

He felt an overpowering urge to run and sweep her into his arms, but held back. Apart from a slight pallor, and a faint blueness of the lips that was already changing to pink, she looked just as she had done the moment before she died. Even the thin seam around her throat was gone . . . no, not gone completely, though it had faded to the faintest, thread-like scar. No doubt Jal-Nish had left it there deliberately, as a reminder to them both that he had killed her, and then raised her again.

Irisis looked at Nish, did not seem to recognise him, then her eyes widened.

'Poor Nish,' she said in the deep, throaty voice that had always sent a thrill up his spine. 'You've aged shockingly. What you must have been through.'

It had not occurred to him that he would look so different. Most of the time he felt like a young man – well, youngish – though he'd never regained all the flesh he'd lost in prison, his hair had thinned at the front, and he bore many recent bruises and battle scars.

'It's been ten years, and nearly another half,' he said. 'Do you know, in the shadow realm, what goes on in the real world?'

'The shadow realm is *my* real world,' Irisis said quietly. 'Yet, should one take the trouble, it is possible to see a little of what is happening on Santhenar. As time goes on, however, it becomes harder to understand *why* you mortals do the things you do.'

Did she mean that she could have watched him from the shadow realm, but had not bothered? Did she no longer care? This wasn't going at all the way Nish had expected. 'You look as beautiful as ever,' said Nish. 'Oh, Irisis –'

'Why should I not? My body has been *preserved*, frozen in time by your father's vile Arts.'

'But you're alive again? You really have come back?'

'I've been dragged back from death, forced into the body I was torn from long ago, and the spark of life so violently extinguished has been relit. Yes, I'm alive, but I'm not the Irisis you knew, any more than you're the Nish you were when I died. Why have you brought me here?'

Maelys was struggling down the steep, broken face of the pit in the darkness, terrified that she was already too late, when she heard someone not far behind. Jal-Nish must have sent the Imperial Guard to do what they had failed to do last time.

Drawing her knife, she moved behind a slab of rock, though if he was directing the attack with Gatherer he could probably see her wherever she tried to hide. She peered around the side; a shadow was creeping down, following her path. She raised the knife, but lowered it again when he vanished. Where was he? Had he sensed she was here?

'Maelys, what the blazes are you doing?'

On recognising Flydd's voice, her knees went weak with relief. 'I'm looking after Nish,' she snapped. 'Someone's got to.'

'What are you talking about?' he said irritably.

'You're planning to destroy the tears, even if that destroys Nish at the same time.'

Pulling her close, he hissed in her ear. 'You little fool, I said that in case Jal-Nish's loop-listeners had picked us up. Do you really think I've encouraged, cajoled and driven Nish all this way, all this time, only to abandon him now? Besides, we haven't worked out how to destroy the tears. We've no idea what their antithesis is.'

Maelys started, but fortunately the darkness concealed it. She had never been good at keeping secrets, while Flydd had been an expert at extracting them. Had he been able to see her face, he would have known that she was holding something back.

And I'm not going to tell you, she thought. To distract him, she said, 'I'm going to Nish,' and headed down the slope.

'What do you expect to do when you get there?' he said conversationally as he followed. 'Save him from himself?'

'I don't know,' she muttered. 'But I'm still going and you can't stop me.'

'I can,' Flydd said equably. 'But I'm not planning to.'

They were almost to the bottom now. The moon had come out and there was just enough reflected light from the palace for them to pick their way across the broken rock partly filling the watery moat. It took ages to reach the steps surrounding the palace, and Maelys was afraid they were already too late.

'How long would it take?' she said as she clambered onto the once-magnificent promenade, now fractured and with its tilted paving stones covered in gravel and grit, making it impossible to move quietly.

'To do what?'

'Raise Irisis from the dead.'

'How would I know?' Flydd said. 'I'm no necromancer. Besides, as far as I know, it has never been done.'

'Keep your voice down. The guards –'

'He knows we're coming, Maelys.'

'He knows?' she whispered.

'Of course. Jal-Nish is a show-off; he *wants* us there so we can all see how brilliant he is. Surely you didn't think you could sneak in undetected?'

'Oh!' she said, feeling like a foolish little girl. 'Then what are we going to do?'

'We'll have to make it up as we go along.'

They went inside, and up the floors one by one, though Maelys saw no one until they were climbing the dusty stair to the ninth level. Two Imperial Guardsmen stood at the top, the pair who had been going to kill her at the feast. She froze on the steps, too afraid to move, but Flydd took her arm and the guards silently stepped aside to let them enter.

'Jal-Nish no longer has any fear of us,' said Flydd. 'That's bad.'

As they moved across the polished floor, the dust squeaked beneath their feet. Maelys could hardly breathe; there was a swelling in her throat the size of a lemon and she felt a sharp pain in the region of her heart.

They turned around a column together, and stopped, staring.

'He's done it,' said Flydd in a strangled voice. 'I never thought it was possible, but Jal-Nish has brought her back!'

Nish was about thirty paces away, looking up at a tall, beautiful woman who had the most extraordinary yellow hair. He appeared to be straining forwards, and there was an odd, yearning expression on his face. Irisis was standing side-on and Maelys could not read anything from her features, but she did not need to.

'How can I compete with that?' she muttered, her small shoulders slumping.

'I wasn't aware that you wanted to,' Flydd murmured.

'Neither was I until Jal-Nish mentioned raising Irisis,' said Maelys. 'I loved Nish once, after we fled from Mazurhize last autumn, but that was just a silly, girlish hero-worship. And after the way he treated me when he was playing at being the Deliverer, I almost hated him for a while. But since we met again at the Range of Ruin he's been really thoughtful and kind, and brave and true, and I knew I was seeing the real Nish at last. And, silly girl that I am, I even imagined . . .'

'But you can't possibly compete with the risen dead,' said Flydd, going ahead.

'No, I can't.' Maelys followed, keeping behind him, for she did not want to be seen. She felt sure that Irisis would judge her and find her wanting. 'I'm still going to save him, though.'

'I would expect no less of a true friend,' he said over his shoulder.

Irisis turned suddenly, smiled and reached out to Flydd. 'Xervish!' She took a step towards him, stopped, frowning, but came on again. 'What happened to your renewed body?'

Maelys tried to hide behind him and knew it wouldn't work, since her hips were considerably wider than his scrawny frame.

'It never suited me,' said Flydd, laughing in delight, 'so I went back to the old one.' He clasped her hands in his.

'No, it never did,' said Irisis.

'I thought you said it was too much trouble to look back to Santhenar?' muttered Nish, somewhat piqued.

'I didn't *say* that,' said Irisis, her smile fading. 'I merely allowed you to think it.' She turned back to Flydd and it flickered on again. 'You're not *quite* the old Flydd,' she said, looking him up and down. 'Poor Nish has aged fifteen years in ten, while you've taken five years off. You look very well, old friend.'

'I feel it. I'm fully restored to the man I was when we first met.'

'Fully?' she said with a roguish smile.

'Oh yes.'

'Then I'm glad.' She stepped around him and approached Maelys, who had no idea what to say or do. 'Hello, Maelys. I'm so pleased to meet you at last.' Irisis reached out and took her hands.

She seemed even taller and more beautiful close up, and yet again Maelys found herself flushing. 'What do you mean, *at last*?'

'I've been watching you ever since you saved Nish last autumn. You'll do perfectly.'

Before Maelys could ask what she meant, Jal-Nish appeared fifty or sixty paces off, on the far side of the ninth level. As he came across, the pedestal reappeared, with the tears standing on it.

Flydd had seen them too; Maelys could tell by the slight stiffening of his posture, and the gleam in his eyes that he could not entirely conceal. Did he still yearn for them the way Nish yearned for Irisis? Was he obsessed by the ultimate power they could give him?

'You can finish the reunions afterwards,' said Jal-Nish, striding towards them, his replaced arm hanging limp, the other swinging vigorously and wafting out that faint corpse smell. 'Irisis Stirm, I brought you back for a reason, and I'm sure Nish has told you what it is.'

Maelys moved well back, for she could not bear to be near Jal-Nish.

'You want to know what happened at the node-drainer,' said Irisis, 'to cause the Snizort node to explode in such a way as to create your Profane Tears.'

'That's right,' Jal-Nish said eagerly.

'And you're terrified that, when Tiaan made all the nodes

681

explode at the end of the war, one or two of them might also have produced nihilium tears.'

'I'm not terrified –'

'Of course you are,' said Irisis, and laughed scornfully. 'You never had it in you to be a great mancer, Jal-Nish, and despite all your boasting, you still aren't one. You owe everything you have to the tears and you're terrified that, if another set should be found, a truly great mancer like Flydd would soon cast you down and undo everything you've achieved with them.'

'All right!' he snapped. 'You've had your fun. Tell me what happened at the Snizort node.'

'No,' said Irisis.

'What?' he roared. The old side of his face crinkled up, while the restored side barely moved.

'I'm not going to tell you,' said Irisis.

'But . . . but that was the price,' he cried, flustered, then his face hardened. 'If you don't tell me, I'll send you back to the shadow realm.'

FIFTY-FOUR

Maelys clenched her fists helplessly. Irisis would have to tell him now.

'Good,' said Irisis. 'I want to go back.'

Jal-Nish stared at her in incomprehension. 'But . . . you can't. No one chooses death over life.'

'I do.' She laughed in his face. 'How does it feel to be as powerless as the least of your subjects, *God-Emperor*? There's absolutely nothing you can do to compel me.'

'I could kill Cryl-Nish,' said Jal-Nish.

'Then we'll be together in the shadow realm,' said Irisis, and momentarily such a wistful look crossed her beautiful face that Maelys felt tears form in her own eyes. It was only right that they should be reunited, and yet it felt so wrong. 'But not even you could kill your only son.'

'I *could* kill Flydd, though,' said Jal-Nish.

Flydd took a small step closer to Jal-Nish.

'Go ahead,' said Irisis, not smiling now, 'if killing is your only answer. Flydd's had a good life, and he'll be wonderful company for me in the shadow realm. Kill him or not, I'm not telling you what you want.'

'Then I'll kill Maelys,' snarled Jal-Nish.

'Why should she have your son, if I can't?' said Irisis.

She moved to her left, and Jal-Nish's eyes followed her, but Maelys noticed her make a tiny, wiggling gesture of her fingers to Flydd.

He sprang, punched Jal-Nish in the face, knocking him down, and ran for the tears. Jerking them from their pedestal by their chain, he slid his gnarled fingers above the roiling surfaces of Gatherer and Reaper.

'Xervish!' Maelys cried. 'The tears are their own antithesis. If you crush them together, I think they'll annihilate each other . . .' But how was he supposed to do that without killing himself and everyone else? Or was that the only solution?

Jal-Nish rolled over, spat out blood and a broken tooth, and snapped his fingers. The surface of Reaper seethed and bubbled; Flydd's hand began to smoke and he was hurled ten spans across the floor, where he lay on his back, rolling from side to side and holding his head.

'*You've* always been predictable, Flydd,' said Jal-Nish, 'and it was worth a tooth to have you take the tears, because I'd set my trap earlier. The moment you touched Gatherer, it drew from you the memories of what you did and saw and felt in Snizort and, now I have them, I will finally understand the tears.'

He went to the pedestal, laid his good hand upon Gatherer, and stood for a minute or two, head down.

'I see it,' he said. 'The process that created the tears was unique and none of the other exploded nodes would have reacted that way. There are *no* other tears on Santhenar. No one can hope to match my power.'

He closed his good eye, and momentarily the shimmer in his empty eye socket died as well, though when he looked up it was back, brighter, deeper, and darker. 'Finally I understand the tears, and I have everything I need to turn myself into an immortal *being*. It will be good to escape the shackles of this feeble, fragile world – I've finished with it, and all of you.

'You did discover the antithesis to the tears,' he said mockingly to Flydd and Maelys, 'but you could never have done anything with it. No human save me can withstand the touch of the tears, and even if anyone could, no human has the strength to overcome the repulsion between Gatherer and Reaper and force them to coalesce into one. The tears can never be destroyed; they are *my* chthonic fire and they will last forever, just as I will – once I become a *being*.'

He closed one fist and Maelys staggered, for it felt as though he was squeezing her heart like a lemon. He opened it again and the pain was gone, yet she felt so weak and breathless that she could hardly stand up.

'Your clan has been a burr under my saddle far too long,' said Jal-Nish. 'And I've reserved a special torment for you, Maelys Nifferlin – after I become a *being*. All that time in Stilkeen's thrall taught me much about pain and I can't wait to put my lessons into practice.'

He hung the tears about his neck, put one hand into each, and for a moment Jal-Nish looked almost serene. Then he withdrew his hands and closed his fist again.

Maelys gasped, for the squeezing pain in her heart was far worse this time. The room swam before her eyes, her knees gave, and Nish just caught her before her head hit the floor.

Jal-Nish didn't look at them. Through her daze, she saw that he was moving his hands in complicated patterns above the tears, his movements lifting silvery tendrils off the surface of Gatherer and sending them streaming out towards Reaper, further each time.

What was he doing? She struggled to think, knowing she had to, and fast. Ah, yes! Once he overcame the antipathy of the tears to each other, the antithesis would no longer exist and he could no longer be stopped. They had to act now but Flydd was still twitching on the floor, and there was nothing Maelys could do either. She was as weak as a newborn infant. Had Nish let her go, she would have collapsed.

Nish was staring at her, not even looking at Irisis, and to her amazement his face was wet with tears.

'I'm sorry; I'm so sorry it's come to this,' he said, holding her tightly and smoothing her sweat-damp brow. 'Everything you and your clan have suffered has been done to you by Father, or by me, yet everything I have I owe to you.

'From the moment we met you've stood by me, not because I deserved it, for I did not, but because you could not do otherwise than keep your word. When you give, you do so without reservation and, no matter what I've done, you have always remained steadfast. No man has ever had a *better* friend, yet I can do nothing to help you when you need it most.'

'Your being here is a great help,' she said, clinging to him. Maelys felt someone's eyes on her and looked up. Irisis was watching them, and she was smiling.

'I lied, Nish,' Irisis said softly. 'Of course I've been watching you. I've been aching for you, in your terrible grief, ever since my death, for it's not the one who dies that loses, it's those who are left behind. Not a day of your imprisonment went by without my checking on you, and it wrung my heart that I could do nothing to ease your pain. Now, at last, you have set me free – and I can do no less for you.'

What did she mean? How was Irisis going to set Nish free? Horror churned Maelys's insides, for she could only think of one way to do that.

Irisis came to them. She kissed Nish on the lips, and Maelys on the brow, then flashed a savage warrior's smile, just as the tales said she had done when going recklessly into battle, back in the days of the lyrinx war.

'Thank you, my love,' she said softly to Nish, and strode across to Jal-Nish.

He looked up at her indifferently, then bent to his work again, knowing that, while he had the tears, no one could harm him. But she took him by the arm, spun him around and caught him from behind in a bear-hug, squeezing him against her breast.

Jal-Nish went for the tears but she clasped his wrists so tightly that he could not touch either Gatherer or Reaper and, though he struggled furiously, neither could he break her grip. Irisis was half a head taller than him and had always been strong; she was far stronger than a man of Jal-Nish's age.

'Reaper!' he gasped. 'Burn her from the inside out. Destroy the yellow-haired bitch!'

'You can't,' said Irisis with a mocking laugh. 'You made a fatal mistake when you raised me from the dead, Jal-Nish.'

Flydd rolled over, came to his knees and got up painfully. The squeezing pain around Maelys's heart faded and she felt the strength returning to her legs, but she still clung to Nish. It felt wonderful when he held her; for the first time since she had been a little girl and Clan Nifferlin had been attacked, she felt safe.

'What's that?' Jal-Nish's good eye bulged; his face twisted in the first vestiges of unease.

'You forgot a fundamental law of nature,' said Irisis.

'What law of nature?' he sneered, jerking his arms fruitlessly.

'The law that says no one can be killed twice. You had me slain ten years ago and you can't do it again. There's nothing you can do to stop me, *God-Emperor*, but I'm going to stop you, forever.'

'Your pathetic artisan's Art was never a patch on my mancery,' sneered Jal-Nish. 'You can't hope to use the tears against me, and as for taking them from me –'

'Your big mistake,' said Irisis, holding him without any visible strain, 'and the one *you've* never learned from, is the assumption that other people want the same things as you. I have no intention of attacking you with the tears, and neither do I want them for myself.'

'What do you want?' There was a tremor in his voice now.

Irisis pulled his wrists closer, and closer yet, until the tears were shuddering with antipathy as they tried to repel each other. 'Can't you guess?'

'No!' he cried. 'It can't be done, anyway.'

'*No human has the strength to overcome the repulsion between Gatherer and Reaper and force them to coalesce into one,*' she quoted mockingly. 'Aren't you forgetting something? You raised me from the dead, Jal-Nish – I'm no longer human.'

Irisis pushed the tears another ell closer and, though Jal-Nish strained with all his strength, he could not stop her.

'Besides,' said Irisis, 'I was always stronger than you – mentally *and* physically.'

The repulsive forces between the tears grew ever stronger, and they shook ever more wildly, but she continued to thrust them together until they touched.

Instantly they flared so bright that Maelys could see the outline of Jal-Nish's bones through his skin, and suddenly the façade of calm and control the God-Emperor had maintained all this time sloughed from him like a carapace shed by a cockroach.

'Reaper, unbind her soul from her body!' he raged. 'Hurl the slut back into the shadow realm where she belongs.'

The quicksilver surface of Reaper boiled, and shining globules burst forth from it, but were drawn back at once and Irisis was unaffected. The tears no longer had the power to affect her in any way.

'I can't be killed twice,' she reminded him. 'Nor can any spell designed to attack a human touch me.'

He froze and the tears went still. 'You can't do this to *me*!' cried Jal-Nish. 'I'm the God-Emperor – I'm going to become a *being*.' He twisted to look up at her, and his voice took on what he imagined to be a cajoling tone. 'Irisis, will – will you come with me? I've always admired your beauty, your courage –'

'You impotent little turd,' she said. 'It's too late to suck up to me now. Your son is ten times the man you were. He's a real man, and that's the only kind I ever cared for.'

'No! I'll give you –'

Irisis's slender forearm muscles knotted, then she forced Gatherer and Reaper into each other until they coalesced into a two-lobed spheroid of liquid metal that brightened until it appeared to outshine the sun. Maelys was forced to look away, but she had to see. She let go of Nish and peered through her slitted fingers; sweat burst from her forehead; her heart thundered like a great drum.

'You can have the world,' cried Jal-Nish, trying to twist around to beseech her. 'The universe! I'll make you into a *being* too.'

Irisis laughed in his face. 'There's no coming back from annihilation, Jal-Nish. Not for you, nor the tears either. You're going to the fate you've been trying to avoid all your life.'

'No, I won't! I can't.'

'It's a beautiful irony, don't you agree, that the very objects you killed for, and stole to stave off death, should be the ones to drag you, whining and whimpering, through the worst death any human can suffer, and beyond it to the ultimate oblivion.'

'I'll hunt you down in the shadow realm. I'll make you pay –'

'You're not going to the shadow realm, Jal-Nish. Haven't you worked that out yet? The shadow realm is too good for you. You're going all the way to eternal nothingness, and I'm delighted to take you with me. Oblivion is all I've craved since you slew me so brutally.

'Goodbye, dearest Xervish,' she said, 'and you, beautiful Maelys. Farewell, sweet Nish, the love of my life, but not beyond it. I'm taking Jal-Nish where no one in the Three Worlds, nor the shadow realm, can follow.'

He struggled furiously, and for an anguished moment Maelys thought he was going to free himself after all, but Irisis tightened her crushing grip on him.

'I'm afraid,' said Maelys, clinging to Nish for comfort and never wanting to let go. 'What's going to happen if the tears do annihilate each other?'

'I don't know,' he said, holding her.

'They'll destroy the whole palace. And us. They've got to. All that power has to go somewhere.'

'At least we'll be together.'

'I don't want to die with you – I want to live with you!'

Irisis crushed the coalesced tears, now an almost perfect sphere, tighter to Jal-Nish's chest, squeezing it until it passed through his ribs into the region where any normal man would have had a heart. Jal-Nish shrieked as Gatherer gathered the very life and soul out of him, then slumped bonelessly as Reaper brutally reaped it.

'Farewell, false God-Emperor,' Irisis cried. 'Annihilation, take him!' and she tossed the revolving sphere into the air.

The single tear drifted upwards and flared so brightly that Maelys, squinting through the slits between her fingers, could see nothing but a molten ball of fire whose heat made the stone floor fume underfoot. With a shrill wail, the fire and light were sucked into the ball, and the rag-doll remnants of Jal-Nish too, until he disappeared like smoke drawn back into a pipe.

Irisis opened her hands and the tear settled and floated in front of her in mid-air, slowly rotating, but quiescent now. She stood there, gazing at Maelys, Nish and Flydd, then gave him a fond, parting smile. 'I told you that I had a destiny after death.'

'I never believed you,' said Flydd, and there were bright tears in his old eyes. 'But you were right. You were always right. And I can say it now . . .'

'Yes?' she said.

'That day ten years ago was also the worst day of my life, for you were the only woman I ever loved.'

'Don't be ridiculous,' Irisis said, looking ever so slightly uncomfortable for the first time. 'You must have been with thousands of women.'

'I've had my share,' he conceded, 'but only one mattered. You were the only one I cared about, and even after you cast me aside and took up with Nish, I never stopped loving you.'

'You're a good man, Xervish,' she said wistfully, 'but this has to stop.' She cupped her hands around the tear and pressed gently, and it brightened again, and swelled.

'Wait!' cried Maelys. 'What happens when Gatherer and Reaper annihilate each other and explode?'

'The coalesced tear doesn't explode, it implodes,' said Irisis. 'And all that power doesn't have to go somewhere. It has to go nowhere. Farewell, my friends.'

She crushed the tear between her palms. The dazzling globe shrank to a pinpoint and she was drawn into it, smiling at them, shrinking until she and the tear could no longer be seen. With a little pop, it vanished, and Irisis had gone to a place from which there could be no returning.

Nish stared after her for a long time, then gave Maelys a

small, uncertain smile and took her hand. 'Irisis *was* always right,' he echoed. 'I'm glad she's found peace at last.'

'Ah, Irisis, Irisis,' said Flydd, rubbing his eyes. The ceiling gave a creaking groan and cracked from one side to the other. 'We'd better go.' He continued to stare at the point where she had disappeared, then shook himself and took Maelys's free hand. 'Morrelune was built with the tears, and now they're gone there's not much holding it up.'

With an almighty crash, the metal spire toppled and fell. They ran out to the edge of the ninth level and saw that the spire had crashed across the gap and its tip now rested in the Sacred Lake, which had begun to spill down into the moat surrounding Morrelune.

'Do you think we can walk across?' said Flydd.

'We'd better,' said Maelys. 'There won't be time to run all the way down, then climb up.'

They teetered along the flattened spire in the moonlight, and clambered down onto the cracked paving next to the abandoned feast tables. A mass of people were running their way.

'What did Irisis mean about her destiny?' said Maelys.

Yggur and Tulitine were coming towards them, and behind them were several other people who could not be identified in the dark, apart from Lilis's slender figure and Yulla's sack-like form.

'Nish and I talked about it that night we camped in the mountains,' said Flydd, 'after we stole the Seneschal of Taranta's best wine.'

'I remember,' said Nish. 'You said Irisis had come to believe that her destiny could only be fulfilled after her death.'

'That's why she never expected to survive the war; she didn't think her destiny allowed it. And if Jal-Nish hadn't killed her, she would never have been able to bring him

692

down, *or* destroy the tears, because no human could have done it.'

Nish did not reply, and after a long pause Maelys said, 'She must have been a wonderful woman. It's no wonder . . .' She glanced at Nish, then away hastily.

'She was a beautiful, warm, wonderful part of my life,' said Nish, wiping his face.

'Of all our lives,' Flydd added.

'And I'll never forget her,' Nish added, 'but she's gone, forever.'

'It's over,' says Flydd. 'It's finally over.' He looked around, sniffing the air like a dog on the hunt and added, 'That's strange.'

'What?' says Maelys and Nish at the same time.

'Just for a moment, I thought I sensed a faint, distant *field*.'

'A *field*?' said Maelys.

'It was the force created by nodes, and the source of most mancers' power.'

'But with Tiaan's destruction of the nodes at the end of the war,' Nish explained, 'all the *fields* disappeared, leaving Father, with the tears, in command of almost all the Secret Art.'

'And now the tears are gone, the fields are coming back,' said Flydd. 'It will happen slowly, I suspect, and they probably won't be as strong as before, but even so, they'll be available to all who can master the Secret Art – not just to one corrupt man.'

'And just in time,' said the Numinator from the darkness, 'to complete *my* project.'

FIFTY-FIVE

Maelys had no chance to run, for the Numinator, now right behind her, grabbed her wrist.

'Don't worry,' she said. 'I'm going to take very good care of you – and your unborn child.'

'It won't do you any good, *Maigraith*,' said Tulitine, her granddaughter.

'Don't call me Maigraith!' snapped the Numinator. 'It is a Faellem name and I won't have it.'

'Numinator is equally inappropriate,' said Tulitine coldly. 'The Numinous One indeed! You're no more a *being* than Jal-Nish was a God-Emperor. You were frauds, both of you – and Maigraith it is.'

'Well, I'm having the child,' Maigraith ground out. 'Two hundred and twenty years I've worked on my great project and I'm not giving it up now.'

'You won't find what you're looking for here,' said Tulitine. 'If you recall, and I'm sure you were watching, Yalkara held the same view until the moment she touched Maelys's belly. She seemed to age a hundred years, and then she said, "I have nothing left." As you of all people know, Charon don't give up lightly.'

'I don't *ever* give up,' said Maigraith, 'and having the *field* back will make it so much easier.'

With a flick of her fingers she conjured up a hollow dagger of fuming ice, much like the stiletto she'd used to test Maelys's fertility in the Nightland, save that the core of the dagger was as green as atatusk blood and its point as narrow as a needle. Before Maelys could move, Maigraith had pressed the tip through her shirt into her belly. Maelys felt a burning, freezing pain, then the point was withdrawn and inside was a small thread of blood.

She drew the blood up into the green core, which slowly changed to grey. Maigraith went the same colour. 'No! It isn't possible.'

'Yet it's happened,' said Tulitine, 'and there's nothing you can do about it.'

Maigraith studied the grey core again, and her shoulders slumped. 'It's certain. No wonder she gave up.'

'What's the matter?' cried Maelys, clutching at her belly. 'Is there something wrong with the baby?'

'Terribly wrong!'

'What? Tell me!' She took Maigraith by the coat and shook her. 'You've got to tell me.'

'It's entirely *old human*,' said Maigraith.

Had Yalkara also said that? At the time, Maelys had been so shocked at being told that she was pregnant that she hadn't taken it in. 'It can't be. Emberr is the father, and he was a full-blood Charon.'

'I've been studying the mating business for more than two hundred years,' said Maigraith wearily, 'and there's no doubt. But how can it be?'

She thought for a minute or two, while all the people gathered around stared at her. 'I think I understand – when you and Emberr lay together in the Nightland, the chthonic fire that killed him must have stripped his seed back to its essence – and the essence of all four human species is the one they sprang from in the deeps of time, *old human*. The child was worth nothing to Yalkara. That's why she gave up, and it's no use to me, either. You're free, Maelys . . . and I must start again, from the beginning.'

'Surely it's time to abandon this fruitless obsession, Grandmother?' said Tulitine.

'I *never* give up,' Maigraith repeated. She double-clapped her hands and vanished from Morrelune.

That afternoon, after the last of the soldiers' bodies had been interred in the sump of Mazurhize, the allies gathered at the tables by the Sacred Lake for a final meal. The palace had collapsed and the army was making ready to go down to the garrison at Fadd, under Flangers's command.

'Well, Nish,' said Flydd, when everyone had settled at the table, 'you swore that oath ten years ago, you fought the God-Emperor all the way, and you've prevailed. No one could argue that this is your hour, so what are you going to do about the empire, and your people?'

'You were right all along,' said Nish, who had given the matter much thought. 'The empire can't be torn down, for civil war would surely follow. But neither am I going to become God-Emperor, or *merely* a humble emperor.' He gave Maelys a twisted smile, and went on.

'For most of my life I've yearned for power, authority, and the respect of all who knew me. Yet now I have all those things, what I want most of all is peace and an ordered world, where ordinary people can live their lives as freely as possible. Unfortunately, peace isn't so easily maintained, and I know nothing about maintaining it.'

'Nish,' said Flydd warningly.

Nish held up his hand. 'I've spent most of my life either in the manufactory, in warfare or in prison. I wouldn't know how to run a household, much less rule an empire. Any of you would do a better job.'

'Your father was an able administrator, if nothing else,' said Yulla. 'He might have been an evil scoundrel, but he knew how to control his empire. You could learn –'

Her words were gall in Nish's mouth, but she was right. 'Anything that was good about Father's empire must be maintained; and all that was evil will be torn down and remade. But not by me.'

'Nish!' snapped Flydd.

'No, Flydd. I've had enough of war, empires, dictators and universal rule. The hundred nations of Santhenar should be free to live according to their own laws and customs, rather than having them imposed from above.'

'You can't tear down the empire, and you can't walk away,' said Yggur.

'I wasn't planning to,' Nish said mildly. 'I'm going to replace it with something better.'

'Better!' cried Flydd. 'What are you talking about?'

'I plan to use my authority, as the heir of the God-Emperor and a hero of the wars, to set up a parliamentary council to advise, *and constrain*, the elected leader of the confederated nations of Santhenar, when Santhenar is ready for such a leader – *and it won't be me*. I swore that I would not become my father, and I will not, but neither will I leave Santhenar to anarchy. Yulla, you will advise me as to the permanent members of the council, and what its statutes should be. You'll be a member, of course – at least for the first term.'

Yulla was playing with another of her crystal specimens, a mass of intergrown golden cubes as shiny as metal. 'Thank you,' she said, staring into the distance, and a greedy gleam came and went in her small eyes.

'Don't get any ideas about having your monopolies back,' Nish added, then smiled. 'At least, not all of them.' One had to be realistic – it wouldn't do to try and change the world too quickly. 'Flydd, you'll be on the council, of course, so you'll have to postpone your holiday. I'll be its head at first, since the people must have continuity of leadership, but my vote will be worth no more than anyone else's, unless the issue is tied.'

'Very well,' said Flydd. 'I suppose it's the best I could hope for. It's good enough, for the moment. But don't think I've given up on you,' he said darkly.

Nish shrugged. 'I didn't expect you would.'

'You'll need an interim council,' said Yggur, 'to maintain order and authority until the parliamentary council can be established.'

'And I propose that everyone at this table be on it,' said Nish. 'At least, all those who care to.'

'Thank you,' said Ryll, who had been sitting silently, head bowed. 'But this is not our affair and we have our own world to look after. I will see you again before we depart.'

He bowed and turned away, his shoulders hunched. Lyrinx rarely partnered more than once and his grief for Liett might take the rest of his lifetime to fade.

The members of the council were agreed upon: Flydd and Yggur, Yulla and M'lainte, Lilis and Malien, Tulitine and Nish, Chissmoul and Flangers.

'Maelys?' said Nish.

She had that faraway look in her eyes again. Maelys shook her head, and he understood that she could think of nothing save going home, and all the work it would take to raise Nifferlin Manor from the ruins. Not even her unused gift for the Art, nor the fact that she was too old to begin learning it, mattered any more.

'That's enough,' said Nish. 'I'll take your oaths now. And once the council's statutes have been agreed, I'll have them carved into the largest fragment of Morrelune, as a perpetual reminder of what the new realm stands for. Smaller stones will be taken from the palace and also engraved with the statutes. They will be set up in every city, town and village, at the places where the God-Emperor's wisp-watchers once stood, so the people may know who rules them, and the principles by which they are ruled.

'And now,' he added, 'since I can't remember when I last had a good night's sleep, I'm going to bed.'

Maelys was exhausted but, zigzagging back and forth between the anticipation of finally going home and her dread of tomorrow's farewells, she slept badly and woke late, feeling more tired than when she'd lain down in her blankets.

'There's one last thing we must do before we separate,' said Yggur as Maelys joined everyone at the long table for the last time, for breakfast. 'A great injustice has been done to two dear friends of mine, Karan and Llian, and it must be righted.'

Maelys's weariness vanished, for she had often thought about them, and particularly Karan. Maigraith had pursued Karan, too, but relentlessly, and Maelys would forever feel linked to that unknown woman whose life had ended so tragically two hundred years ago.

And why *had* Yggur, Lilis and Malien, the only people here who had actually known Karan and Llian, grown so angry when their names were mentioned?

'Dear friends of *ours*,' said Malien. 'I never believed those lies, either. I can't believe that the scrutators were taken in by them, Flydd.'

'We obeyed the Chief Scrutator, who took his orders from the Numinator,' said Flydd. 'And as I may have mentioned previously,' he rubbed his scarred and twisted hands, from which most of the flesh had been gouged off decades ago, 'asking questions was strongly discouraged.'

'The Numinator decreed that my friends be called Karan Kin-Slayer and Llian the Liar,' said Yggur, 'and I believe that to be a vile slur on their names; a terrible injustice. It would please me greatly, Nish, if the first decision of your council was to right that wrong.'

'The council will be happy to review the matter,' said Nish, 'once it has heard all the facts.'

To Maelys, sitting beside him, he sounded overly formal, even a trifle pompous. But then, she reasoned, Nish had never wanted this position, nor had he done anything like it before. What mattered was that he had a good heart; he was bound to grow as leader of the council, in time.

Yggur looked at Flydd. 'Will you do it, or shall I?'

'As the only former scrutator here, I believe it's my responsibility,' said Flydd. 'Let's begin with Llian's case, since it's the clearer. The scrutators called him *Llian the Liar, the man who corrupted the Histories*. His Great Tale was banned, withdrawn and all known copies burned, and a new version was subsequently written. To clear his name, strong evidence will be required that the charges were false.'

'Llian was a Master Chronicler of the Histories, an honour awarded to few people,' said Malien, 'and I knew him as well as anyone still alive. He was an honourable man and a brilliant Teller of the Great Tales, though,' she added wryly, 'he was pretty useless at practical matters. He had a head full of stories.'

'He got better in the end,' said Yggur. 'He was willing to learn, unlike some others.'

'And Llian loved the Histories for their *truth*,' Malien went on. 'When it came to writing the chronicles of the times, or crafting the tale that he hoped would become a Great Tale, he was scrupulous – Llian would permit no relevant omission, no exaggeration and, absolutely, not the least hint of falsehood. Besides,' Malien said, fixing Flydd with a cold eye, 'his tale was read by everyone who survived the Time of the Mirror, including myself and Yggur, and no one found any fault with it.'

'Do you agree with these statements, Yggur?' said Flydd. 'I do.'

'In that case, we must accept them as truth,' said Flydd.

'You weren't so accepting when the matter was first raised,' Maelys said mildly. 'I recall you getting angry with Colm and pompously standing on your scrutatorial dignity.'

'So I did,' grinned Flydd, 'but the renewed me wasn't as clear-headed as I am –'

'What does Colm have to do with them?' said Persia. 'Wasn't he the fellow who went over to the enemy?'

'He was,' said Maelys, remembering the good times and the bad with him, 'and he drowned in the flood on the Range of Ruin. Poor Colm. He was a descendant of Karan's cousin,' she said to Malien, 'and heir to her estate, or would have been, had it not been for the war. He was bitter about his loss, and about the stains on Karan's and Llian's names.'

'As I was saying,' said Flydd, 'Maigraith – when she was the Numinator – ordered that Llian be called "the Liar" so as to take revenge on Karan, though this was long after her death.'

'Where did you hear that?' said Malien.

'It was in the Tower of a Thousand Steps,' said Maelys, 'though Maigraith didn't actually admit it.'

'She didn't bother to deny the accusation,' said Yggur. 'And she definitely gave the order to Chief Scrutator Ghorr, didn't she?'

'No question about it,' said Flydd. 'And that's all I know about the matter.'

'The case seems perfectly clear,' said Nish. 'Does the interim council agree to clear Llian's name?'

'*And* have his original Great Tale restored,' said Yggur.

701

The council agreed to both.

'Now, to the matter of Karan Kin-Slayer,' said Nish, 'which, from what I know of it, is rather more complicated. I don't see how we can get at the truth after all this time. What are the facts, Yggur?'

'After Maigraith's lover, Rulke, was slain,' said Yggur, 'and she found that she was with child, she became obsessed with creating an eternal monument to him, by breeding her *triune* children and Karan's to create *quartines*: that is, children with the blood of all four human species. She hoped that these quartines would have all the strengths and none of the weakness of their progenitors, particularly the Charon, whom she believed to be extinct.'

'Karan, rightly, would have none of this terrible scheme,' said Malien, 'but Maigraith pursued her relentlessly. She kidnapped Karan's firstborn daughter, Sulien, when she was just thirteen, and gave her to her thuggish son, Rulken, the twin who most resembled his father – in looks, if not in nobility.'

'Karan managed to steal Sulien back,' said Yggur, 'and the family fled Gothryme in secret; they spent more than a year on the run, pursued by Maigraith all that time. They were penniless and hungry, while she was wealthy and powerful by then. She made sure that Llian could never *tell* again, then destroyed his reputation, and finally Karan could take no more; she was driven out of her mind.'

'They were hiding in Shazmak at the time,' said Malien. 'She hurled her children, then Llian and herself, off the top of a tower into the River Garr, where they all drowned.'

FIFTY-SIX

'At least, that is the *tale*,' said Yggur meaningfully.

'But is it true?' said Nish. 'Or is it falsehood?'

'Everything is true up to the point of Karan's madness,' said Yggur. 'We all knew it at the time; it was no secret. And Maigraith did not bother to deny it, either. Indeed, at the Tower of a Thousand Steps, she attempted to justify her wickedness on the grounds that Karan had three children and Maigraith only wanted one.'

'Madness is the curse of *blendings* and *triunes*,' said Flydd thoughtfully. 'Perhaps Maigraith also lost her wits.'

'It was an evil, cunning madness if she did,' said Yggur.

Someone let out a pained grunt from the jumble of rocks behind the table. Maelys jumped, then saw that it was the dwarf, who was covered in dust. He limped towards them, slowly and exhaustedly, as if it had taken him hours to struggle free of the ruins.

'What are you doing here, Klarm?' she said.

'Coming back to my own,' he said, tentatively.

'You assume too much, little man,' snapped Flydd. 'Treachery is not easily erased –'

'It wasn't treachery, since there was nothing left of our

alliance to betray. Swearing to Jal-Nish was a mistake, and I've paid dearly for it.'

'Not dearly enough!'

'Would you think better of me if, after swearing that sacred oath to Jal-Nish, I chose to break it?'

'Ahem!' said Nish. 'That'll do, Flydd. Since I've been pressed into service as leader of this council, I hereby declare my first amnesty. Klarm, your past is wiped clean – under sufferance!'

Klarm bowed a trifle awkwardly, and Maelys saw that his stump was causing him great pain.

'Thank you, Nish,' he said. 'I always knew *you* were a man of honour.'

'Don't push your luck! Getting back to the matter we were debating,' said Nish, 'there must have been justification for Karan's crime, in her own mind at least. Driven beyond endurance and with nowhere else to turn, she may have seen this terrible act as the only way out. We may feel sympathy for her, even understanding but, on this evidence, the council cannot clear her name. If she killed her family, Karan Kin-Slayer she must remain.'

'How do we know she did?' said Maelys, feeling for that poor, tormented woman, harassed far more unrelentingly than she, Maelys, had been.

'It was about fifteen years after the Time of the Mirror, as I recall,' said Malien. 'Karan and Llian were still famous, and the news of their deaths even reached me at my lonely eyrie inside Mount Tirthrax, the highest peak in the Three Worlds.'

'Who witnessed the deaths?' said Nish.

'I don't remember,' said Yggur.

'The witnesses weren't Aachim,' said Malien. 'Few of my people had returned to Shazmak by that time.' She turned to the other end of the table. 'But Lilis might know.'

'It was one of the first important matters that dear old

Nadiril entrusted to me after I became a fully fledged librarian,' said Lilis, 'because I had known Karan and Llian.'

'And the names of the witnesses were?' asked Nish.

'Two Whelm, called Idlis and Yetchah.'

'I remember them,' said Malien. 'It's almost unheard of for Whelm to form friendships outside their own kind, but there was a deep bond between Karan and Idlis, despite their differences. He was the healer who put her shattered bones together after the Way between the Worlds was opened, and I was there when he left to go home.

'*I will come to Gothryme on this day once a year, in case you need the drug hrux*, he said to Karan, because nothing else could relieve her pain. *There is no other way of getting it, for no one else knows how it is made.*

'And Karan told him and Yetchah to come to Gothryme, if ever *they* needed help,' Malien added.

'Extraordinary,' said Yggur. 'But Karan was extraordinary, and if anyone could befriend the friendless Whelm, it would have been her.'

'Are Whelm long-lived?' said Nish.

'They can be, though not so long that they would still be alive two centuries later. The Whelm keep their own Histories, of course, but I very much doubt that they would allow us access to them. They are a secretive people at the best of times.'

'Then we can't take the matter any further,' said Nish, rising.

'Wait a minute,' said Maelys, who had been thinking through all she'd ever heard about Karan. 'There's something else, isn't there, Xervish?'

'I don't know what you mean.'

'I mean Karan's heritage, left to her as reparation by her enemy, Faelamor. It had once been hidden in that cave we visited in Elludore.'

'Elludore!' cried Yggur, clinging to Tulitine for a moment. Maelys eyed him curiously, but he said no more.

'Colm said that Karan had spurned that gift,' Flydd reminded her.

'Yet years later, in desperate need, she might have gone back for it. Remember that the mimemule had been dug up and replaced – *and* it had been used, twice.'

'Why would anyone use it, then replace it?' said Nish, frowning. 'Why not keep it?'

'To convince Maigraith that Karan had never touched her heritage, perhaps,' said Maelys.

'Again I ask, why?' said Nish.

'We'd have to go to Elludore to find out,' said Flydd. 'Unfortunately the mimemule has died and, without the caduceus –'

'That reminds me,' said Nish, scowling at Flydd. 'How come you didn't make a portal with the caduceus at the Range of Ruin? You could have saved the lives of most of the militia.'

'Do you have to ask?' snapped Flydd, who had never liked being questioned.

'Well, yes I do.'

'You still had to take the pass, and hold it. That's why you were there, remember? To stop your father's army.'

'But you could have made it easier. You could have taken us behind the enemy lines at the pass, for instance.'

'If you'd had an easy victory you wouldn't be here now.'

Nish opened his mouth, but closed it again.

'Besides,' said Flydd. 'I didn't know how to make a portal then. *If you recall*, at the time I didn't even have the strength to make light with my fingers, and if I had, I had no idea that the caduceus could make portals. At that stage, we still thought it was a trap. Have you finished interrogating me?'

'For the moment,' said Nish, unfazed.

'Splendid!' Flydd said sarcastically. 'You were right not to become God-Emperor. Power is already going to your head.'

'You wanted me here,' said Nish, grinning. 'It's too late to complain now.'

'Anyway, as I was saying,' said Flydd loftily, 'without the caduceus I no longer have the capacity to make portals.'

'Ah, but I do,' said Klarm, who seemed eager to impress them, or perhaps to make amends.

'Really?' said Flydd darkly. 'How?'

'During the weeks I spent travelling through the shadow realm,' replied Klarm, 'I found cause to reconsider my allegiance to the God-Emperor, after I discovered that he was not the man I'd thought him to be.'

'And yet you saved him,' snapped Flydd.

'I'd sworn an oath. I had to fulfil it; but I also had to take precautions for the good of the empire, in the event that my worst fears about Jal-Nish were realised. I took the liberty of siphoning some of the power of the tears into my knoblaggie, just in case.'

'No wonder he couldn't get them to work properly,' said Maelys.

'Well, get it out, man,' said Flydd, 'and take us to Elludore without delay.'

Klarm's eyes flashed at his former friend, but he made a portal and minutes later they were standing at the entrance to the cave on that steep, forested slope above the field of bones.

'I know this place,' said Yggur, looking over his shoulder, and again he swayed and clung to Tulitine for support. 'My skin crawls at the memory of Elludore, for it is the scene of my most devastating defeat. In the Time of the Mirror, Faelamor lured my entire army over the cliffs above us, in a fog. Two thousand men met their deaths in that hour, and it took me a good fifty years to recover from it.'

707

Flydd gripped his shoulder. 'We saw the bone field when we were here last time. Would it help if you went down?'

Yggur shuddered. 'I don't think so. Let's get on with it.'

The ebony bracelet Ketila had worn just a month and a half ago lay outside in the short grass, cast away as useless. Malien used it to break the perpetual illusion, and when she moved the bracelet about, the shadow figures Flydd and Maelys had seen with Colm and Ketila came and went.

'Many people dwelt in this cave over the years,' said Malien, 'though we won't see any before Faelamor created the perpetual illusion to hide her treasure. Nor any who came afterwards, save those who possessed enough Art to imprint their shadows on the illusion.'

'That's Faelamor,' said Yggur, pointing to the outline of a small, slender woman bent over something on the floor. 'She's burying the treasure, more than two hundred and twenty years ago.'

A pair of scriers, armed with wisp-watchers, came and went. 'Why are they next?' cried Maelys. 'Did they get it?'

'They did not,' said Malien, smiling. 'Visitors are not shown in order of appearance. The scriers would have been here within the last few years, as were these villainous-looking reprobates.'

Maelys saw herself and Flydd excavating the little wooden box, and then her finding the mimemule and Flydd taking it. Ketila was a fleeting shadow near the entrance but Colm did not appear at all.

'Where's Colm?' she said.

'He had no Art,' Flydd said curtly. 'He created no shadow.'

'Is that Ketila?' said Nish. 'I remember telling her stories long ago, when her family sheltered me in their hovel. She was a pretty, eager girl, and she so loved to hear tales of the outside world.' He sighed. 'And now she's dead.'

'She did not have a good war, poor child,' said Flydd.

'There's Maigraith!' said Yggur. Her shadow was standing by the entrance, watching people digging under the direction of a robed and hooded Whelm, though they did not appear to find anything.

Finally a small, curvaceous woman appeared by herself, limping slightly.

'Karan,' said Malien.

Karan's shadow dug up the box, took the mimemule from it and put everything else back, then faded. She re-appeared, dug a hole near the cave entrance and buried the mimemule in it.

'So Karan came here twice,' said Yggur. 'She used the mimemule, then put it back so there would be no evidence that she'd ever touched the treasure, because Maigraith was hunting her and Karan didn't want her to know what she'd done with it.'

'Is there any way to discover what she used the mimemule for?' said Nish.

'Not as far as I can tell.' Flydd was turning the stained, knobbly wooden object over in his hands. 'It's completely dead now; whatever power it once held has been exhausted and cannot be replenished by any Art I know about . . . wait a minute! Remember how we escaped from here? When the mimemule touched the virtual construct, it opened a gate instantly.'

'Instantly?' cried Yggur. 'But when you used the virtual construct to leave the Nightland, it took ages to open a portal, didn't it?'

'A good hour and a half,' said Flydd. 'Even though the virtual construct was *live* –'

'So the mimemule had encountered the virtual construct previously,' said Yggur. 'I think I see where this is going.'

FIFTY-SEVEN

'Be so good as to explain,' said Nish irritably, 'for I haven't the faintest idea.'

'When I found the virtual construct in the Nightland it was still live,' said Flydd. 'But who could have used it? Rulke was long dead, and neither Yalkara nor Emberr had touched it – I asked Yalkara before she died.'

'Who else knew about it?' said Flydd.

'No one,' said Yggur, 'because I begged Llian to leave all mention of the virtual construct out of his Great Tale. I told you that at the Tower of a Thousand Steps.'

'So you did,' said Flydd. 'Therefore, the only other people who knew it was there were Karan and Llian – because they'd *been* to the Nightland.'

'I'd say Karan used the mimemule to return to the Nightland,' said Yggur, 'then brought it back to the cave so Maigraith would never know she'd had it. And while in the Nightland she must have used the virtual construct – that's why it was live when we got there. Portal us to the Nightland, Klarm, and let's see what we can read from it.'

'Unfortunately I took the virtual construct with us when we left the Nightland,' said Flydd. 'And it was subsequently destroyed.'

'The virtual construct could never be removed from the Nightland,' said Yggur, 'because it was built from it. You must have inadvertently made a copy, but Rulke's original will still be there. Klarm, let's go.'

Klarm was looking unsteady on his mismatched feet, but he made a second portal which took them directly to the room where the virtual construct – Rulke's three-dimensional model for the real construct he'd subsequently built in Carcharon – floated above the floor.

It was about the size of a large covered wagon, though very alien in appearance. Its exterior shell appeared to be made from a dark metal, but was shiny smooth and shaped in perfect curves that no smith on Santhenar could have duplicated, even using the Art. The construct curved up towards the rear, to a high platform, then cut sharply down at the back.

It was not metal, of course: just a model that could be walked through to see the insides, as Maelys had done the first time she was here. Now she sat on the cold floor, weary and wanting to go home, while Nish walked in and out, studying every detail. It was the artificer coming out in him, she supposed, and of course he'd worked on constructs and the flying version of them, thapters, during the war.

'It's an earlier version,' Nish was saying. 'Rulke made many changes and improvements to his real construct. But even so – it's *marvellous*.'

'What can you read in it, Yggur?' said Flydd. 'Can you tell where it went?'

Yggur and Malien were standing inside the structure, and Maelys could just see their shadowy outlines.

'It doesn't seem to have been used here at all,' said Yggur.

'Then it must have been used in Elludore,' said Malien.

'So Karan used the mimemule to mimic a portal and came here,' mused Flydd. 'And then she mimicked a copy of the virtual construct and took the mimemule back to the cave. It all seems rather complicated.'

'But necessary, if she was to conceal her tracks from Maigraith. What did she do then?' said Yggur. 'Klarm, you'd better take us back to the cave.'

'I can't keep doing this,' said Klarm, who was pale and sweating now, and clearly in tremendous pain. 'My knoblaggie doesn't protect me from aftersickness, you know.'

'Think of it as reparation for your crimes,' snapped Flydd.

Klarm staggered; Maelys ran to him and held him while he renewed the portal, and she could feel the agony he was struggling with all his mighty heart to conceal from them, and especially from Flydd.

'You're killing him, Xervish,' she said softly.

'I'm all right,' said Klarm, pulling free. 'I believe in paying my debts. I can do it.'

They returned to the cave and Flydd used the illusion-dispelling bracelet again. Outside the entrance, where he had not looked previously, five shadows appeared, walked into a construct, and vanished.

'That was Karan, Llian and their three children,' said Malien.

'Where did they go?' said Maelys.

'If I had to guess, I'd say Shazmak, and the top of the tower from which, it's said, she hurled them into the Garrflood.'

'Can you direct us to the place?' said Flydd. 'Neither Klarm nor I have ever seen Shazmak.'

'Nor I for some time,' said Malien, 'though I love it most of all our cities. We'll go the scenic way. I'd like to see Shazmak from afar – for the last time. Klarm, if you would make the portal like this . . .'

She bent and whispered in his ear. Klarm nodded weakly and created the portal, but she had to support him all the way.

Maelys, watching the little man anxiously, could hear the roar of the river before they arrived, for this time the portal became transparent while it was carrying them above a mighty gorge, some distance from the city. The walls of the gorge plunged hundreds of spans to the raging River Garr, and the cliffs extended above them almost as far.

Ahead the river swirled around a rocky pinnacle, and from it Shazmak soared up to the heavens, a profusion of slender towers, aerial walkways and looping stairs all connected to each other. A pair of gossamer bridges, crossing the gorge, led to the paths in and out of Shazmak.

'The gale rushing down the great river never ceases,' said Malien as the portal drifted closer.

The wild wind shook the towers and howled around the stairs and walkways, setting Maelys's teeth on edge. 'It seems a sad place.'

'It is now. Shazmak was sacked by the Ghâshâd – formerly Yggur's Whelm – just before Rulke escaped from the Nightland, and much of the damage they did inside has yet to be repaired. Few Aachim dwell here any more, and most of those are from Clan Elienor – or were. The flower of my clan's youth went to Morrelune to defend their adopted world, but few of them will come home to Shazmak.'

Malien turned away, wiping her eyes. She studied the towers, then pointed to the one tower which stood directly above the river. 'That must be it.'

The portal deposited them on the flat roof of the tower and faded out. Klarm flopped down on his back, panting. His face had gone blotchy and his lips were drawn back, baring his square white teeth. Maelys could not imagine how he bore aftersickness on top of the agony of his severed foot, though he was famously tough, brave and determined.

Malien went to the edge, which was enclosed by a chest-high wall, and looked down at the river. 'It is a sad place for me,' she went on, 'for my son, Rael, drowned in the Garr down there while helping Karan and Llian to escape – the first time they came here.' She turned away. 'To business!'

After walking back and forth a number of times, she borrowed the knoblaggie, used it, and another series of shadow figures arose, though they looked clearer than the ones in the cave. There were seven of them – Karan and Llian, the three children, and two taller folk, an emaciated man and a gauntly pretty woman with huge eyes and long dark hair.

'Whelm!' said Maelys, shivering, and not just because of the icy wind on the back of her neck.

'Idlis and Yetchah,' said Malien. 'Karan knew she could rely on them, utterly and forever. Watch!'

Karan's shadow embraced the two Whelm, then Idlis and Yetchah headed down an internal stair. Karan, Llian and the children went inside the virtual construct and it vanished.

'So she didn't kill them,' said Maelys.

Malien did not answer for some time. She was walking back and forth, moving the knoblaggie about, and frowning. What could be the matter now?

'Of course she didn't!' said Malien, but Maelys could see the relief in her eyes. 'I never believed that story for a second. Besides, Karan was scarcely bigger than you, and Llian wasn't a small man. She could never have thrown him over such a high wall. She faked their deaths so as to put the family beyond Maigraith's reach.'

'I've seen enough,' said Nish. 'Well, council, are we happy to clear Karan's name and restore her to her rightful place in the Histories?'

'No,' said Malien. 'It can't be done.'

'Why ever not? They disappeared more than two centuries ago. They must have died long since; Maigraith can't threaten them now.'

'Unfortunately, I think she can.'

714

'Why?' said Maelys. 'Where did they go?'

'I don't know where she took them,' said Malien, 'but I do know *when*.'

'*When?*' cried Flydd. 'There is no *when*, with portals.'

'There is now,' said Malien, 'for I have just read the echoes left by her last portal, as clearly as you can see their shadows. The other treasures Faelamor left in the cave must have included the secret of moving a portal forwards in time, and that's what Karan did. She took her family,' Malien frowned and concentrated hard, her lips moving as if she were reading something dim and distant, 'two hundred and ten years forwards, to a time when she must have thought Maigraith could no longer be a threat.'

'If they were here . . . fifteen years after the Time of the Mirror, plus two hundred and ten . . . that's five years from now,' said Nish. 'And Karan's name can't be cleared in case Maigraith finds out.'

'Which she will,' said Yggur. 'Now that we all know, the secret is bound to get out.'

'What are you suggesting?' snapped Flydd.

'I'm not suggesting any of us would reveal it,' Yggur said. 'But Maigraith is both brilliant and determined, and given time she'll follow in our footsteps.'

FIFTY-EIGHT

'I don't see why she should,' said Flydd.

'Maigraith was suspicious the very first time she saw the mimemule, if you recall,' said Yggur. 'She spent many years in Faelamor's thrall and must have recognised it, and known where it came from.'

'And she knows about the virtual construct too,' said Maelys, 'because I mentioned it when she questioned us in the Tower of a Thousand Steps.'

'Well,' said Nish, 'there's nothing we can do about it now. And who knows, in five years, Maigraith may have changed.'

'She never changes,' said Yggur, 'and never gives up, either. Let's go back. I'm weary unto death and my burns hurt abominably. *Klarm*?'

He was still lying on his back and his crusted stump was oozing blood in several places. 'I can't do it,' he said listlessly. 'Can't take any more.'

Flydd squatted down beside him. 'It's a long walk back to Morrelune, comrade.'

'Too long for me,' said Klarm. 'I'm sorry, Xervish, I really am. Sorry for everything. Do you think you can find it in yourself to forgive all I've done?'

Flydd studied him coolly. 'You're not planning to die on me, are you?'

'Isn't that the only form of atonement you'll accept?'

'You stupid old fool!' Flydd exclaimed. 'What makes you think I want you to die?'

'I've never known you as a forgiving man.'

'People change. All right! I forgive you, you stupid bastard – as long as you never mention it again.'

Klarm smiled faintly, the pain lines relaxed and he let out a little sigh. Maelys thought he had died, but he opened his eyes again.

'I don't suppose, if I loaned you my knoblaggie, you could –?'

'You're going to lend *me* your precious, precious knoblaggie?' cried Flydd in astonishment.

'Just to make a portal or two. Don't get any ideas, you devious old sod.'

'But if you were to die while I still had it,' said Flydd with a cunning leer, 'it would be mine, wouldn't it?'

'You've always lusted after it, you greedy swine,' said Klarm, 'but you're not going to get it.'

'I don't see how you can stop me, if you're –'

'*Dead!*' said Klarm. 'I'm not going to die, no matter how much I want to. I'm going to outlive you, just to spite you. Now take the damn thing and get us out of here.'

Grinning, Flydd made a portal, and they returned to Morrelune, where the army was ready to depart for Fadd. The healers attended to Klarm, and managed to relieve his aftersickness and some of the pain of his severed foot, after which everyone prepared to leave for their separate destinations.

Maelys stood some distance away, an enormous lump in her throat. One part of her just wanted to go home, but the rest couldn't bear the parting –

'It's farewell, then,' said Flydd, 'and for some of us it must be for the last time. I doubt that we'll ever all be together again.' He shook Yggur's hand.

'I don't expect I will,' said Yggur with a weary sigh. 'I haven't many years left.'

'Nor I,' said Malien, 'and I plan to spend them on Aachan. Now that we have a world to go back to, and the *field* gives us the power to do so, many of my people will join me, and I don't plan to return to Santhenar.'

'All things must pass,' said Flydd. 'And all people too, even the oldest of friends. I'll miss every one of you.' His eye caught the dwarf's and he said, 'Even you, runt!'

'I'll miss you equally, scarface!'

Flydd shook hands with Klarm, each trying to crush the other's hand, then they both laughed.

Flydd embraced Malien and turned to Yggur. 'There's a certain irony in Maigraith so desperately hunting those few people with Charon blood for her breeding program, and yet she rejected you, her half-Charon first lover.'

'I'm glad I've found my true heritage at last,' said Yggur, carefully putting his bandaged arm around Tulitine's waist. 'And equally glad that I'm powerless now. She would no longer want me, any more than I would have her back.'

'Before you go,' said Maelys, 'can anyone explain to me why I didn't appear in any of the futures we saw in the Pit of Possibilities? I always thought it meant I was going to die.'

'It must have been the taphloid,' said Yggur, 'hiding you from your enemies, just as Kandor had set it to conceal me from mine. I'm glad you have it, Maelys, and long may it look after you and yours.'

Maelys suspected that its power had gone when the hidden bottle of pure fire had been removed, yet the taphloid would always be a comfort to her. She was embracing him when she felt the little parcel, Yalkara's gift, in her pocket, and drew it out.

'I wonder what this is?' The wrapping was pitted and charred. 'I hope it's still all right.'

Inside she found a small rectangular metal mirror, highly polished, with glyphs arranged around all four sides and a symbol in the top right corner.

'It's the Mirror of Aachan!' Malien exclaimed. 'Where did you get it?'

'Yalkara gave it to me, for the baby.'

'I'm astonished! I don't think you should keep it – it was a terrible, corrupting device –'

'She said it had been cleansed of the past by the pure fire,' said Maelys.

'Yalkara took it to the void with her at the end of the Time of the Mirror,' said Yggur. 'I wonder why she kept it?'

'Why does anyone keep keepsakes?' said Malien. 'To remind them of happier times, I suppose.'

They said their last goodbyes and Flydd created a final portal with the knoblaggie. The lyrinx came marching up, then Ryll stooped and embraced them one by one. Maelys, remembering all the tales she'd read about lyrinx when she was young, found his hug alarming, though she thought she'd managed to conceal it.

'Someday, when things are better,' Ryll rumbled, 'I would have you come to Tallallame. I would like everyone to see what we've made of our new world, and Liett would have wanted that too.'

His eyes grew wet at the memories, then he sketched a farewell and went through the portal without looking back.

Flydd diverted the portal north to Faranda for the Aachim, to Shazmak for Malien, Yrael and the surviving

Aachim of Clan Elienor, then finally to the south for Tiaan, the Whelm and the Faellem.

The portal closed for the last time, and faded away. Flangers and Chissmoul shook everyone's hands.

'Well, General Flangers,' said Flydd, 'until we meet again.'

'Not so much of the general, if you please,' said Flangers. 'I've only taken the command because someone had to, and once I've trained some officers up, I'm leaving the army.'

'But you've been a soldier all your life,' said Flydd, taken aback. 'It's a bit late to change now.'

'If Nish can change, so can I. Besides, now that the field is back . . .' Flangers looked fondly at Chissmoul.

'What?' said Flydd.

'We thought we might go into the business of flight,' she said, grinning broadly and rubbing the scar where her ear had been. 'And if monopolies are being handed out to the unworthy, I don't see why I shouldn't have one too.'

'Be off with you,' said Flydd, laughing, and they waved and turned away to the army.

Tulitine helped Yggur to climb aboard *Three Reckless Old Ladies*. Flydd, Persia and Lilis followed them, and finally Klarm was helped up. He sat on the side, clinging to a rope and looking wan. Eight of Nish's militia were already aboard, going home to Gendrigore at last, yet there was no sign of Clech or Aimee.

'Where the blazes are they?' muttered Flydd.

'I said if they weren't here by ten I was going without them,' said Yulla, and gestured to M'lainte, who was at the helm.

'Aren't you forgetting something, Flydd?' said Klarm coldly.

'What?' said Flydd.

'My knoblaggie, you larcenous scoundrel. Hand it over.'

Flydd pretended he did not know what Klarm was talking about, then patted his pockets and reluctantly brought it out. 'How did that get there? Sorry. Must have slipped my mind.'

'I'll bet,' said Klarm, snatching it. 'Once a thieving scrutator, always a thieving scrutator!'

'You'd know!'

They were still bickering cheerfully as the sky-galleon lifted off, circled twice then headed south, for Roros and Gendrigore.

Maelys was left standing among the tables by herself, dreading what was coming next. Nish was at the other end of the main table, staring into the pit at the ruins of Morrelune, while Haga and Fyllis were a little way off, watching the craft dwindling into the northern sky.

'I suppose you'll be going to Fadd too,' she said.

'Fadd?' said Nish. 'Why would I go to that dreadful, mosquito-ridden hole?'

'That's where your army is going.'

'It's not my army. Why would I want an army?'

'You're the head of the council. You're a great man now; the most powerful in all the empire. You've got to have an army.'

'No, I don't.'

She was staring at him, more confused than ever, when there came a high-pitched peal of laughter, followed by a deep, good-humoured bellow, and Clech and Aimee appeared from the Sacred Lake, where evidently they had been bathing together. They were both drenched; Clech had a huge splatter of mud in the middle of his chest and Aimee was aiming another mud ball at him.

'Where have you been?' said Nish in schoolmasterly tones.

'You're behaving like children, and now they've gone without you.'

'We know. We're going with you,' said Aimee. 'Someone's got to look after you and keep you out of trouble.'

'And the leader of the council has to have an honour guard,' Clech said seriously, scraping the mud off his chest and flicking it at Aimee, who ducked just in time, then ran back to the lake for more.

Nish scowled at the two dripping figures, Clech the giant and Aimee like a little bird, barely coming up to his breastbone, then smiled. 'And I could never wish for a better honour guard. Well,' he said to Maelys, 'it's over. Let's go home.'

She couldn't speak for a minute. What was he talking about? 'I don't . . . I can't possibly . . . where is your home, Nish? I don't think you ever told me.'

'My home is wherever you are.'

'But . . . w-what? You can't come with me. You're the son of the late God-Emperor; the leader of the council. You can't live at Nifferlin.'

'Why ever not?'

'It's just a pile of rubble. There are only two rooms left standing, and one of them has no roof.'

'Then we'll live in the one with a roof while we rebuild Nifferlin Manor, and make it as beautiful as it ever was.'

'But I'm going to have a baby – to another man.'

'A good, kind and decent man, by all accounts,' said Nish, 'and I'm sure I would have liked him. Besides, poor Emberr is dead and his *old human* child needs a father as well as a mother.'

Maelys couldn't take it in. She kept searching for reasons why it wouldn't work. 'But . . . but Aunt Haga is really cranky. You couldn't possibly put up with her.'

'I'm the son of the late God-Emperor,' grinned Nish,

putting on a pompous voice. 'And the leader of the council. Not even Aunt Haga would dare be cranky to me. Besides, she sent you away from Nifferlin to get me, remember?'

Maelys had the grace to blush. 'And now I have you,' she said softly, extending her hands to him. 'So she can't be cross with me, either. Call your honour guard, Nish, and let's go home.'

The End of the Song of the Tears Trilogy

The fate of Karan, Llian and their children
will be explored in a future
Three Worlds Trilogy

Glossary of characters, names and places

Aachan: One of the Three Worlds, the original world of the Aachim and, after its conquest by The Hundred, the Charon. It was recently rendered uninhabitable by massive, and mysterious, volcanic eruptions, and some tens of thousands of Aachim fled to Santhenar through a portal, in a fleet of constructs.

Aachim: The human species native to Aachan, but now also numerous on Santhenar; they are a long-lived, clever people, great artisans and engineers, but melancholy and prone to both hubris and indecision. Many were brought as slaves to Santhenar in ancient times, but later the Aachim flourished until they were betrayed by Rulke in the Clysm, after which they withdrew from the world to their hidden mountain cities, principally Shazmak and Stassor. The Aachim who came from Aachan after the eruptions mainly dwell on the arid island of Faranda.

Aftersickness: Sickness that people suffer after using the Secret Art or a native gift or talent.

Antithesis: The one object (or power or force) that can break the power of the Profane Tears and bring down the God-Emperor.

Bladder-bat: A flesh-formed aerial attack beast. An internal bladder can be inflated with floater-gas, enabling it to lift heavy objects.

Blending: A child of the union between two of the four different human species – Charon, Faellem, Aachim and *old human*. Blendings are rare, and often deranged, but can have remarkable talents.

Boobelar: Captain of the Rigore militia, a malicious, addled drunk and drug user.

Calendar: Santhenar's year is roughly 395.7 days and contains twelve months, each of thirty-three days. Every tenth year is a Dearth Year, where the calendar is adjusted, the midsummer month that year having only thirty days.

Charon: One of the four human species, once the master people of the world of Aachan where, mysteriously, the Charon were practically sterile. Though they had enormously long lives, few children were born, until the race was almost extinct. At the end of the Time of the Mirror, the few survivors went back to the void, to go to their extinction with dignity. The greatest of the Charon were Rulke, Yalkara and Kandor, all of whom came to Santhenar at some stage.

Chissmoul: A thapter (flying construct) pilot during the lyrinx war, shy but known for her reckless verve. She is the long-time partner of Flangers and was held with him by the Numinator.

Chthonic Flame, Chthonic Fire, White Fire, White-ice-fire, Rancicolludire: An elemental force that can feed on ice, chthonic fire has the power of *binding* (it once bound the *being* Stilkeen's physical and spirit aspects together), and *unbinding*, i.e., it is capable of opening dimensions that would normally be closed. It was stolen from Stilkeen by Yalkara in ancient times and used to find the Charon's escape route from the void to Aachan.

Clanker: An armoured war cart which moved via pairs of mechanical legs and was powered by the *field*. All were rendered useless by the destruction of the nodes at the end of the war.

Clysm: A series of wars between the Charon and the Aachim beginning around 1500 years ago, resulting in the almost total devastation of Santhenar.

Colm: Once the heir to Gothryme, he lost both clan and heritage during the war and resented it deeply. He accompanied Maelys to Mistmurk Mountain and once nurtured an affection for her but later became estranged. Embittered by his sister's death, and feeling betrayed by Flydd, he accepted Klarm's amnesty and went over to the enemy.

Construct: A war machine at least partly powered by the Secret Art, invented by Rulke in the Nightland as the virtual construct, a kind of three-dimensional blueprint for the real one that he built on Santhenar after his escape. His construct was capable of creating portals, though the constructs later modelled on his by the Aachim, and brought to Santhenar through a portal thirteen years ago, were not. All were rendered useless by the destruction of the nodes at the end of the war.

Council of Santhenar: An alliance of powerful mancers. The Council helped to create the Nightland and cast Rulke into it, but was later overthrown by the Numinator.

Crandor: A wealthy, tropical land on the north-eastern side of Lauralin. Its capital is Roros.

Cryl-Nish Hlar: Generally known as Nish, he started out badly but grew to become one of the greatest heroes of the lyrinx war, though at the end of it he was cast into prison for rebelling against his father, Jal-Nish. He was freed by Maelys a few months ago and has been on the run ever since. At the end of the war Nish vowed to overthrow his father and relieve the suffering of the people of Santhenar, but has not been able to keep his promise, for he is stricken with self-doubt and afraid that he will take the same corrupt path as his father. He has always been tempted by power and what it can bring. And Nish never got over the death of his beloved Irisis, slain on his father's orders; Jal-Nish lures him by offering to bring her back from the dead and, though Nish knows this is impossible, he is unbearably tempted.

Nish was twice held in thrall to Monkshart (Vivimord), who wanted to turn him into the Deliverer to overthrow Nish's father, but escaped both times, latterly in the distant land of Gendrigore, and is now leading a small militia from that rain-drenched land to the Range of Ruin to defend the high pass of Blisterbone against his father's mighty army.

Cursed Flame: A mysterious flame in the caverns below the Charon obelisk on Mistmurk Mountain. It has somewhat ambiguous healing properties.

Defiance, the: The Deliverer's supporters and army, initially controlled by Monkshart, but now fallen apart after his and Nish's disappearances.

Deliverer, the: The one person (or so the common folk believe) who can overthrow the God-Emperor, i.e. Nish.

Dry Sea: Formerly the Sea of Perion, it dried up in ancient times but began to flood at the end of the lyrinx war a decade ago and is now the Sea of Perion again.

Elludore: A large forested land, north and west of Thurkad on Meldorin Island. Flydd found the mimemule there, in a cave where it had been hidden as part of Karan's reparation to Faelamor.

Emberr: The son of Yalkara and Rulke, born in the Nightland and therefore unable to leave it. He sensed Maelys on her first visit there and she became infatuated with him; on her second visit they made love but a trace of chthonic fire on her skin killed him.

Faelamor: Leader of the Faellem species who came to Santhenar soon after Rulke, to keep watch on the Charon and maintain the balance between the worlds. She was Maigraith's liege and kept her in thrall for most of her life.

Faellem: The human species who once inhabited the world of Tallallame. They were a small, dour people, forbidden to use machines and magical devices (though they sometimes did), but were masters of disguise and illusion. Faelamor took most of her people back to their world, Tallallame, at the end of the Time of the Mirror, and there they self-immolated. A few remained on Santhenar, living deep in the cold southern forests.

Flangers: A soldier and hero in the lyrinx wars, he is stricken by guilt for following orders and shooting down a Council thapter, and desperate to atone. Taken prisoner by the Numinator seven years ago, along with Yggur and Chissmoul, and held at the Tower of a Thousand Steps, he was recently released by Flydd.

Flappeter: A large flying creature flesh-formed by Jal-Nish, it has a pair of feather-rotors growing from the middle of its back. Flappeters are controlled by bonded riders, using enchanted amulets, and any harm to either flappeter or rider causes harm to the other.

Flesh-forming: A branch of the Secret Art invented by the lyrinx but now used by Jal-Nish to create creatures such as flappeters and bladder-bats.

Flydd, Xervish: See **Xervish Flydd**.

Forbidding, the: When Shuthdar's golden flute was destroyed over three thousand years ago, the resultant cataclysm sealed Santhenar off from the other two worlds until the Way between the Worlds was opened at the end of the Time of the Mirror.

Garr, Garrflood: The largest and wildest river in Meldorin. It arises to the west of Shazmak, flows around the island on which Shazmak is built, and runs to the Sea of Thurkad east of Sith.

Gate: A structure powered by the Secret Art which permits people to move almost instantly from one place to another. Also called a portal.

Gatherer: See **Profane Tears**.

Ghâshâd (also **Whelm**): The ancient, mortal enemies of the Aachim, they were a race born to serve unquestioningly. They were corrupted and swore allegiance to Rulke in ancient times, but when he was imprisoned in the Nightland they took a new name, Whelm, and served Yggur for a time. When Rulke escaped, they became Ghâshâd again, but upon his death swore to take no master ever again. However they subsequently broke that oath and went to the Tower of a Thousand Steps to serve the Numinator. Their nominal leader is the sorcerer, Zofloc.

Ghorr: The corrupt former Chief Scrutator of the Council of Scrutators, and Flydd's bitter enemy, now dead and in the shadow realm.

Gilhaelith: An eccentric, amoral geomancer and flawed tetrarch, he died by self-crystallisation at the end of the lyrinx war.

God-Emperor: The title assumed by Jal-Nish Hlar some time after he took control of the world using the Profane Tears.

Gothryme: An impoverished manor near Tolryme in Bannador, on Meldorin Island. In the Time of the Mirror it belonged to Karan. Colm is now the nominal heir but his family fled during the war and it was occupied by people in the favour of the God-Emperor.

Great Library: Founded at Zile by the Zain in the time of the Empire of Zur, it lasted for thousands of years but disappeared from the Histories during the lyrinx war.

Its greatest librarian was the sage, Nadiril, who died two hundred years ago.

Great Tales: The greatest stories from the Histories of Santhenar. A tale can only become a Great Tale by the unanimous decision of the master chroniclers. In four thousand years only twenty-three Great Tales were made, the twenty-third being acclaimed by many as the greatest – Llian of Chanthed's *Tale of the Mirror*. More tales were written during the lyrinx war but they do not have the same standing, as they were written as propaganda at the Chief Scrutator's behest.

Histories, the: The vast collection of records which tell more than four thousand years of recorded history on Santhenar. The culture of Santhenar is interwoven with and inseparable from the Histories and the most vital longing anyone can have is to be mentioned in them. Families and clans also keep their personal Histories.

Human species: There were four distinct human species: the Aachim of Aachan, the Faellem of Tallallame, the *old humans* of Santhenar, and the Charon who came out of the void. All but *old humans* could be very long-lived. Matings between the different species rarely produced children (see **Blending**).

Hundred, the: The one hundred surviving Charon who escaped from the void, led by Rulke, then took Aachan from the Aachim and held them in thrall for thousands of years.

Irisis Stirm: A heroine of the lyrinx war, and Nish's lover at the end of the war, she gave her life to try to save him from his father's vengeance. She has been dead for ten years but her perfectly preserved body is held in a crystal coffin at Morrelune.

Jal-Nish Hlar: Nish's father. He suffered massive injuries from a lyrinx attack during the war and begged to be allowed to die, but Nish and Irisis saved his life. Now hideously maimed and unable to repair himself even with the power of the stolen Profane Tears, he controls the world as God-Emperor and plays malicious games with his enemies, though he has long had a secret fear that the world is under threat, once again, from the void. This fear was proven right when Stilkeen appeared at the Range of Ruin, took him hostage and demanded chthonic fire in return.

Karan: During the Time of the Mirror, two centuries and more ago, she was a young woman of the house of Fyrn, but with blood of the Aachim from her father, Galliad, and *old human* and Faellem blood from her mother. This made her *triune*, though she did not know it. A sensitive whose home was Gothryme, Karan was the heroine of the *Tale of the Mirror* and wedded Llian at the end of it. She is now reviled as Karan Kin-Slayer, for killing Llian and her children, then herself, though no one can understand why.

Kandor: One of the three Charon who came to Santhenar, and dwelt at Katazza, in the Sea of Perion. He was killed at the end of the Clysm.

Klarm: The former Dwarf Scrutator is a great mancer and a handsome, cheerful, brave man. He was one of Flydd's greatest allies during the lyrinx war, but after Jal-Nish became God-Emperor, Klarm took service with him and became such a trusted ally that Jal-Nish made him a general, and even entrusted him with the tears after being captured by Stilkeen. Klarm and Flydd are now bitter enemies.

Knoblaggie: A magical device with the appearance of three brass balls partly fused together. It has much the same function as a wizard's staff or wand.

Lauralin: The main continent on Santhenar.

League: About 5000 paces, three miles or five kilometres.

Lilis: A street urchin in Thurkad at the Time of the Mirror who was taken on as an apprentice librarian by Nadiril at the Great Library.

Liett: A lyrinx with unarmoured skin and no chameleon ability; a talented mancer and brilliant flier who has a turbulent relationship with Ryll. She became Matriarch of the lyrinx as they went to Tallallame.

Llian: An ostracised Zain, he was a master chronicler, a teller of the Great Tales, and one of the heroes of the *Tale of the Mirror*, which he wrote and which became the twenty-third Great Tale. He is now reviled as Llian the Liar, the master chronicler who dared to corrupt the histories and write a Great Tale that wasn't true.

Lyrinx: Massive winged humanoids, some of whom are great mancers, who escaped from the void to Santhenar at the end of the Time of the Mirror. See also **Lyrinx War**.

Lyrinx War: The one-hundred-and-fifty-year-long war between the winged lyrinx and the peoples of Santhenar, which ended ten years ago when the lyrinx were defeated and were given the alien-infested world of Tallallame for their own.

Maelys Nifferlin: A shy, demure girl of nineteen at the beginning of the tale, one of the last of her clan, who was compelled by her mother and aunts to rescue Nish (whom she has idolised since childhood because he was a hero of the war) and get pregnant to him, so as to restore the clan. Maelys has little experience of any kind of action but is very determined, brave and loyal. She did rescue Nish, and accompanied him on many adventures, though he, still obsessed with his beloved Irisis, repudiated her tentative advances and Maelys was so mortified that she was not game to try again. She then accompanied Flydd on various journeys, met Emberr in the Nightland, they made love and she unwittingly caused his death. Now Yalkara and the Numinator are both pursuing Maelys in case she became pregnant to Emberr.

Maigraith: An orphan brought up and trained by Faelamor, she was a master of the Secret Art. She became Yggur's lover, briefly, and at the end of the Time of the Mirror she fell for Rulke and became pregnant to him not long before he died. It has recently been revealed that Maigraith became the **Numinator**.

Malien: An Aachim, and once one of their leaders, she was a heroine of the Time of the Mirror and an ally of Flydd and Yggur during the lyrinx war, but has not been seen since it ended.

Mancer: A wizard or sorcerer; someone who is a master of the Secret Art.

Mazurhize: The most brutal prison in the empire. Nish was held in its deepest and dankest cell for his ten-year sentence.

Mendark: A great mancer from the Time of the Mirror, he took renewal on many occasions but was killed at the end of the Time of the Mirror.

Mimemule: A small wooden object, shaped like several intergrown balls, which can be used to create something else by mimicry. It was a great treasure left to Karan by Faelamor, in reparation for her crimes.

Mirror, Mirror of Aachan: A powerful and capricious ancient artefact (aka the *twisted mirror*) which held a deadly secret, and gave its name to the period of history ending two hundred and twenty years ago (the Time of the Mirror), and also to Llian's Great Tale (the *Tale of the Mirror*).

M'lainte: Flydd's mechanician from the lyrinx wars, the genius who built the first air-floater.

Monkshart: The name taken by Jal-Nish's former ally and friend, Vivimord, after renouncing his allegiance. He was a charismatic zealot and mancer, but corrupt, and attempted to use the Deliverer to bring down the God-Emperor because Vivimord believed that for any man to take such a title was blasphemy. Vivimord was convicted of murder in Gendrigore (in a trial by ordeal), where he was taken by a sea leviathan and has not been seen since, though the leviathan died soon after, rather ominously.

Morrelune: Jal-Nish's palace, near the prison of Mazurhize and not far from Fadd in eastern Lauralin.

Nadiril: The greatest librarian of the Great Library; he died two hundred years ago.

Nightland: A place, distant from the world of reality, where Rulke was kept prisoner for a thousand years. Tensor made a portal into the Nightland to revenge himself on Rulke, but only succeeded in letting him out, and shortly the Nightland collapsed into nothingness, or so it was believed, until Flydd, Maelys and Colm ended up there recently. In fact, the Nightland was recreated before its total collapse by Yalkara, because her son Emberr was born there and could never leave.

Nish: See **Cryl-Nish Hlar**.

Nodes: Rare places in the Three Worlds where the Secret Art worked better because the node was surrounded by a *field* from which power could be drawn by a mancer or certain enchanted objects. The Profane Tears were formed by the destruction of a node. All nodes were destroyed by Tiaan at the end of the lyrinx war.

Numinator, the: A mysterious figure who dwells at the Tower of a Thousand Steps, on the Island of Noom in the frozen south, and secretly controlled the Council of Scrutators. The Numinator turned out to be Maigraith, who for more than a hundred and fifty years had manipulated the whole world for her breeding program, seeking to breed people together to create quartines, a new species, as a perpetual memorial to her dead lover Rulke. She is Yalkara's granddaughter and Tulitine's estranged grandmother.

Old Human: The original human species on Santhenar and by far the most numerous; the only short-lived human species, they typically have the meagre life-span of around seventy-five years.

Phrune: Monkshart's acolyte, healer and perhaps lover, a sadistic killer whom Maelys slew at the Cursed Flame. Vi-vimord's black arts gave Phrune life from death for a while, but Maelys forced him into a column of chthonic fire at Mistmurk Mountain. He came back as five Phrune spirits, then was drawn into the shadow realm.

Portal: See **Gate**.

Profane Tears: Two grapefruit-sized, tear-shaped objects made from nihilium, a quicksilver-like substance which holds the print of the Art more tightly than any other material. The tears were created by the implosion of a node of power thirteen years ago and stolen by Jal-Nish, who has poured all his knowledge of the Art into them, but corrupted them and turned them into the Profane Tears. Gatherer is a collector of information and coordinates all Jal-Nish's spies and spying devices. Reaper is used to enforce Jal-Nish's will, for it longs to bring ruin upon all it touches.

Quartine: See **Tetrarch**.

Reaper: See **Profane Tears**.

Regression Spell: A dangerous and painful spell to make oneself temporarily younger, though the after-effects are extremely unpleasant.

Renewal: A desperately dangerous self-administered spell through which a mancer may replace his old body with a new one, though more mancers die during the attempt than succeed.

Revenants: Stilkeen's severed spirit aspects, now trapped in the shadow realm.

Reversion: A dangerous and difficult spell employed to turn back the effects of another spell, even long after it has been used.

Rulke: A Charon and the greatest of The Hundred. In ancient times Rulke was imprisoned in the Nightland until a way could be found to banish him back to Aachan. When Tensor opened a portal into the Nightland, Rulke was able to escape into Santhenar, but he was later killed by Tensor. He was the father of Emberr.

Ryll: A once ostracised wingless lyrinx; a hero of the war and an honourable male, he rose to become Patriarch of the lyrinx as they went to Tallallame.

Santhenar, Santh: The least of the Three Worlds, home of the *old human* peoples.

Secret Art, or **Art:** The use of magical or sorcerous powers (mancing). An art that very few can use and then only after considerable training. The Art was greatly weakened ten years ago, after Tiaan destroyed all the nodes of power, thus concentrating virtually all mancery in Jal-Nish's sorcerous Profane Tears.

Shadow realm: An uncanny, and very deadly, place where spirits and other non-mortals dwell after death. Stilkeen's revenants are trapped there.

Shazmak: The forgotten city of the Aachim, in the mountains west of Bannador. It was sacked by the Ghâshâd after they were woken from their long years as Whelm and is now only partly occupied by the Aachim Clan Elienor.

Skeet: A large, vicious bird used for carrying messages long distances.

Snizort: A locale in eastern Lauralin where there are vast underground tar deposits and seeps. The lyrinx had an underground city there during the war, and the destruction of the Snizort node led to the formation of the Profane Tears.

Span: The distance spanned by the stretched arms of a tall man. About six feet, or slightly less than two metres.

Spying Devices: The God-Emperor has many spying devices, such as wisp-watchers, loop listeners and snoop-sniffers, all relaying information back to the Profane Tear called Gatherer.

Stilkeen: An immortal shapeshifting *being*, originally composed of physical and spirit aspects (revenants) bound together by chthonic fire. For half an eternity it roamed the eleven dimensions of space and time, until Yalkara stole its chthonic fire. Now Stilkeen is trapped in one physical form, and is in great pain, especially in the physical worlds. It yearns desperately to be reunited with its revenants, which are in the shadow realm, and burns for revenge for the mortal insult done to it, but before it can do either it has to have its chthonic fire back.

Talent: A native skill or gift, usually honed by extensive training.

Tallallame: One of the Three Worlds, once the world of the Faellem. A beautiful, mountainous world covered in forest but now, in a cosmic irony, infested by alien creatures from the void, though the ferocious lyrinx are gradually exterminating them.

Taphloid: A small egg-shaped object made from yellow metal which was given to Maelys by her father, and which protects her by concealing the aura created by her untapped gift for the Art. It has other, unknown powers and is said to contain an important secret.

Tears: see **Profane Tears**.

Teller: One who has mastered the ritual telling of the tales that form part of the Histories of Santhenar.

Tensor: The proud, flawed leader of the Aachim for thousands of years, he let Rulke out of the Nightland. Tensor was killed at the end of the *Tale of the Mirror.*

Tetrarch: A person bearing the blood of all four human species, and (hopefully) free of their individual frailties. The Numinator's great breeding project aims to create tetrarchs but after two hundred years all her efforts have failed. Also called quartine.

Thapter: A flying construct. Tiaan and Malien created the first one during the war.

Three Worlds: Santhenar, Aachan and Tallallame.

Tiaan: A brilliant but troubled artisan who became a heroine towards the end of the lyrinx war, but she could not bear to see all the ruin brought about by mancery and destroyed all the nodes of power at the end of the war, taking most of the world's Arts with it. This had the unintended consequence of allowing Jal-Nish, who held the Profane Tears, to seize ultimate power.

Time of the Mirror: The interval spanned by the *Tale of the Mirror*, roughly 224 to 220 years ago.

Tower of a Thousand Steps: The Numinator's tower on the frozen Island of Noom, in the far south. It was made of ice, but she recently destroyed it in an explosion of distilled chthonic fire after Emberr died, and Flydd and his allies escaped through a portal.

Triune: A double blending – one with the blood of all Three Worlds, three different human species. They are extremely rare but may have remarkable abilities. Karan and Maigraith were triune.

Tulitine: A mysterious old woman, healer and seer, who helped to bring together the Defiance, and then encouraged and aided Nish on the way to the Range of Ruin, even using the perilous Regression Spell on herself so she could reach him to tell him that he had been betrayed. She is the Numinator's granddaughter but has been repudiated by her.

Vivimord: See **Monkshart**.

Void, the: The endless space between the real worlds. A Darwinian place where life is more brutal and fleeting than anywhere. The void teems with the most exotic life imaginable, for nothing survives there without remaking itself constantly, and everything there longs to escape to one of the real worlds.

Vomix, Seneschal: Jal-Nish's seneschal in Fadd. A vicious brute who destroyed Maelys's clan because of something she said about him as a child. He pursued Nish and Maelys relentlessly after Nish's escape, until she nearly destroyed him with the touch of her taphloid, which gruesomely inverted his aura.

War, the: See **Lyrinx War**.

Whelm: See **Ghâshâd**.

Xervish Flydd: A great mancer, former scrutator (i.e. spymaster and master inquisitor) and military commander during the lyrinx war, and one of the architects of the peace that ended it. Flydd went into hiding after Jal-Nish took over at the end of the war, and ended up trapped by old age and infirmity at the top of Mistmurk Mountain for nine years, until Nish and Maelys found him there. Maelys convinced Flydd to take renewal so they could try to find the antithesis to the tears, but the renewal went wrong. He is slowly recovering but seems colder, harder and less trustworthy. Subsequently, fleeing from the God-Emperor and Vivimord, he discovered the chthonic fire and used it to make a portal and escape, though they ended up in the Nightland. After visiting a cave in Elludore, where Flydd obtained the mimemule, he took Maelys to the Tower of a Thousand Steps in search of the antithesis, precipitating the fall of the tower, Maelys's second visit to the Nightland, and finally their escape with Yggur and others to the Range of Ruin.

Yalkara: one of the greatest of all the Charon, she took the surviving, sterile Charon back to the void, to extinction, at the end of the *Tale of the Mirror*, but then returned to Santhenar, trying to find a way to get her son Emberr out of the Nightland. It has since emerged that Yalkara stole chthonic fire in ancient times, so the Charon could escape from the void, but that fire made most of them sterile on Aachan, caused the volcanic ruin of Aachan and then, most ironic of all, her own son's death. Now she is hunting Maelys, thinking that she could be pregnant with Emberr's child. If she is, Yalkara plans to take it. She also appeared in Flydd's mind, after his renewal, as the *woman in red*; and as Bel she helped he, Maelys and Colm to escape from Plogg, on their way to Elludore.

Yggur: A great mancer who has lived for far more than a thousand years. No one understands the reason for his incredibly long life, nor his unusual powers which, unlike almost all others', were not lost when the nodes were destroyed at the end of the war. He was held prisoner by the Numinator for seven years but has recently been freed by his old rival, Flydd.

extras

about the author

Ian Irvine was born in Bathurst, Australia, in 1950, and educated at Chevalier College and the University of Sydney, where he took a PhD in marine science.

After working as an environmental project manager, Ian set up his own consulting firm in 1986, carrying out studies for clients in Australia and overseas. He has worked in many countries in the Asia–Pacific region. An expert in marine pollution, Ian has developed some of Australia's national guidelines for the protection of the oceanic environment and still works in this field.

Ian's three fantasy series, The View from the Mirror, The Well of Echoes and Song of the Tears, have all been bestsellers in Australia and the UK and are being published in many countries and languages. He is currently completing the fourth book of his Runcible Jones fantasy quintet for younger readers, *Runcible Jones and The Backwards Hourglass*, after which he will begin a new fantasy series.

Ian Irvine has his own website at www.ian-irvine.com and can be contacted at ianirvine@ozemail.com.au

Find out more about Ian Irvine and other Orbit authors by registering for the free monthly newsletter at www.orbitbooks.net

if you enjoyed
THE DESTINY OF THE DEAD

look out for

THE DWARVES

by

Markus Heitz

PROLOGUE

Northern Pass,
Stone Gateway to the Fifthling Kingdom,
Late Summer, 5199th Solar Cycle

Pale fog filled the canyons and valleys of the Gray Range. The Dragon's Tongue, Great Blade, and other peaks towered defiantly above the mist, tips raised toward the evening sun.

Slowly, as if afraid of the jagged peaks, the ball of fire sank in the sky, bathing the Northern Pass in waning red light.

Glandallin Hammerstrike of the clan of the Striking Hammers recovered his breath. Leaning back against the roughly hewn wall of the watchtower, he cupped his hand to his bushy brown eyebrows and shaded his eyes from the unaccustomed light. The ascent had been grueling and his close-woven chain mail, two axes, and shield weighed heavy on his aged legs.

There was no one younger to stand watch in his stead.

Only a few orbits previously, the nine clans of the fifthling kingdom had been attacked in their underground halls. Many had lost their lives in the battle, but the young and inexperienced were the first to fall.

Then came the sickness. No one knew where it had sprung from, but it preyed on the dwarves, sapping their strength, clouding their vision, and enfeebling their hands.

And so it was that Glandallin, despite his age, was guarding the gateway that night. Two vast slabs of solid rock erected by Vraccas, god and creator of the dwarves, stemmed the tide of invading beasts. For some the sight of the imposing gateway was not enough of a deterrent; bleached bones and twisted scraps of armor were all that remained of them now.

The solitary sentry unhooked a leather pouch from his belt and poured cool water down his parched throat. A few drops spilled out of the corners of his mouth, flowing through his black beard. Elegant braids, the work of untold hours, hung from his chin and rested on his chest like delicate cords.

Glandallin replaced the pouch, took his weapons from his belt, and laid them on the parapet. The steel ax heads jangled melodiously against the sculpted rock, carved like the rest of the stronghold from the mountain's flesh.

A ray of sunlight glowed red on the polished inscriptions, illuminating the runes and symbols that promised their bearer protection, a sure aim, and long life.

Glandallin turned to the north, his brown eyes sweeping the mountain pass, thirty paces across, that led from the watchtower into the Outer Lands. No one knew what lay there. In times gone by, human kings had dispatched adventurers in all directions, but the expeditions were rarely successful and the few who returned to the gateway brought orcs in their wake.

He scanned the pass carefully. The beasts learned

nothing from their defeats. Their vicious, choleric minds compelled them to throw themselves against the dwarves' defenses. They were bent on destroying anyone and anything in their path, for their creator, the dark lord Tion, had made them that way. The raids were conducted in blind fury. Raging and screaming, the beasts would scale the walls. From the first tinges of dawn light until the setting of the sun, armor would be cleaved from flesh, and flesh from bone. A tide of black, dark green, and yellowy-brown blood would lap against the impregnable gates, while battering rams and projectiles shattered as they hit the stone.

The children of Vraccas suffered casualties, deaths, and crippling injuries too, yet it never occurred to them to quarrel with their fate. They were dwarves, Girdlegard's staunchest defenders.

And yet we were almost defeated. Glandallin's thoughts turned again to the strange beings that had invaded the underground halls, killing many of his kinsfolk. No one had seen them approach. Outwardly they resembled elves: tall, slim, and graceful, but as warriors they were savage and ruthless.

Glandallin was almost certain that the creatures were not elves. There was no love lost between the dwarves and their pointy-eared neighbors. Vraccas and Sitalia, goddess and creator of the elves, had ordained the races with common loathing from the moment of their birth. Their differences had resulted in feuds, the occasional skirmish, and sometimes death, but never war.

Then again, he thought critically, *I might be wrong. Perhaps the elves hate us enough to draw arms against us —or maybe they're after our gold.*

A bitter northerly wind whistled round the mountaintops,

gusting through Glandallin's braided beard. Suddenly, his brow furrowed angrily as his nostrils detected a stench that offended the core of his being: orcs.

Spilled blood, excrement, and filth — that was the perfume of orcs—mixed in with the rancid odor of their greasy apparel. They basted their armor with fat, believing that the dwarves' axes would slither over the metal and leave them unharmed.

No amount of fat will save them. Glandallin did not wait for the ragged banners and rusty spears to appear over the final incline of the path. Standing on tiptoe, he placed his callused hands on the coarse wooden handles of the bellows. A low drone vibrated through the shafts and galleries of the fifthling kingdom.

The dwarf worked two bellows in rotation to produce a constant stream of air. Gathering in volume, the drone became a single piercing note, loud enough to rouse the soundest of sleepers. Now, as so often in their history, the fifthlings were being summoned to fulfill their noble duty as Girdlegard's protectors.

Sweating from the exertion, Glandallin glanced over his shoulder.

Tion's beasts had formed a wide front and were marching on the gateway, more numerous than ever before. Elves would have fled to the woods and a man's heart would have stopped at the sight of the monstrous hordes. The dwarf stood his ground.

The attack on the gateway came as no surprise to Glandallin, but the timing was unsettling. The coming battle would stretch the dwarves' resources more than usual. *More bloodshed and more death.*

*

The defending warriors lined up on the battlements on either side of the gateway, their movements slow, some lurching rather than walking, weak fingers wrapped loosely around the hafts of their axes. The band of dwarves stumbling to the defense of the gates numbered no more than a hundred brave souls. A thousand would have been too few.

Glandallin's watch was at an end; he was needed elsewhere.

"Don't forsake us, Vraccas. We're outnumbered," he whispered, unable to wrest his eyes from the stinking stream of orcs that poured along the path. Grunting, shouting, and jostling, they headed for the gates. The bare rock cast back their bestial cries, the echo mingling with their belligerent chants.

The strident noises jangled in his mind, and it seemed to him that the beasts had somehow changed. There was a palpable air of confidence about the raging, shouting mob.

For the first time, he was afraid of the beasts.

What he saw next did nothing to ease his mind.

Scanning the ranks of the invading army, his gaze fell on a cluster of lofty fir trees. Since childhood he had watched them thrive and grow on the otherwise barren slopes.

Now they were sickly and dying.

The trees are faring no better than we. Glandallin's thoughts were with his wounded and ailing friends. "What strange forces are these? Your children need you, Vraccas," he prayed briefly, gathering his axes from the parapet.

With growing dread, he pressed his lips to the runes. "Don't abandon me now," he enjoined the blades softly, before turning and hurrying down the steps to join the small troop of defenders.

He reached them just as the first wave of beasts struck the wall. Quivering arrows rained down on the dwarves. Ladders were thrust against the walls, and orcs hastened to scale the wobbly rungs, while others set down their catapults and launched burning projectiles to reinforce the bombardment. Leather pouches, filled to the brim with paraffin, spluttered through the air and burst on impact, covering everything around them in an oily liquid and setting it ablaze.

The first salvo was aimed too low, but the dark hordes were undeterred by the sight of their front line burning in a storm of fire. Nothing, not the battery of stones nor the torrent of molten ore, could check their rapacious zeal. For every orc that was slain, five new aggressors scaled the walls. This time they were determined to breach the defenses. This time the gateway was destined to fall.

"Look out!" Glandallin ran to the aid of a dwarf whose shoulder had been pierced by an arrow. One of Tion's minions, a stunted creature with thick tusks and a broad nose, had seized his chance and squeezed through an embrasure, hauling himself over the parapet and onto the battlements.

Dwarf and orc stared at each other in silence. The clamor of voices, the hissing of arrows, the clatter of axes faded to an indistinct buzz.

Glandallin's ears were tuned to his opponent's heavy breath. The red-veined eyes, buried deep within the head, flicked nervously from side to side. The dwarf knew exactly what was going on inside the creature's mind. The orc was the first of its kind to have set foot on the battlement and could scarcely believe its good fortune.

A foul odor rose from the thick gray layer of tallow that

coated its armor plating. The smell filled Glandallin's nostrils, drawing his attention back to the battle.

Shrieking, he threw himself against the beast. His shield jabbed smartly downward, shattering his opponent's foot, while he lunged with his ax from above. The blade smashed through the unarmored flesh around the armpit. The orc's arm, sliced cleanly at the joint, fell to the stony floor. Dark green blood sprayed upward from the open wound.

The orc let out a high-pitched scream, for which he was rewarded by a mighty stroke perpendicular to the neck.

"Tell your kinsfolk I am anxious to make their acquaintance!" Glandallin gave the dying brute a final shove and sent him tumbling against the parapet, where he took the next invader with him as he fell. They vanished over the side and plummeted to the ground. *With any luck, they'll crush half a dozen others,* thought Glandallin.

From then on the enemy gave him no respite. Running from one end of the parapet to the other, splitting helms, cleaving skulls, ducking arrows, and evading firebombs, he felled orc after orc.

Darkness was descending on the Stone Gateway, but Glandallin was untroubled by the fading light; even the thickest gloom could be penetrated by sharp dwarven eyes. But each blow and every movement took its toll on his weary arms, shoulders, and legs.

"Vraccas, grant us a moment to gather our forces," he coughed, rubbing his braids across his face to free his eyes of blood.

The dwarven deity took pity on his children.

A fanfare of horns and bugles bade the hordes cease their assault, and the orcs complied, pulling away from the walls.

Glandallin dispatched a lingering assailant and sank to the stone floor, fumbling for his drinking pouch. He tore off his helmet and poured water over his sweat-drenched hair. The cool fluid trickled over his skin, revitalizing his will.

How many of us remain? He stumbled to his feet and went in search of survivors. Of the hundred-strong army, seventy were left, among them the formidable figure of the fifthling monarch.

Nowhere were the enemy corpses stacked higher than at Giselbert Ironeye's feet. His shiny armor, made of the toughest steel forged in a dwarven smithy, gleamed brightly, and his diamond-studded belt caught the flames that licked from pools of burning oil. He climbed atop a stone ledge to speak to his folk.

"Stand firm!" Steady and true, his voice sounded across the battlements. "Be as unyielding as the rock from which we were hewn. Nothing — no orc, no ogre, no creature of Tion—will break us. We will cut them to pieces as dwarves have done for millennia. Vraccas is with us!"

The speech was met with low cheers and grunts of approval. The dwarves had been dealt a blow, but already their confidence was returning. They had grit and pride enough to stop the enemy in its tracks.

The warriors replenished their weary bodies with food and dark ale. With every sip and mouthful they felt stronger, more alive. The worst injuries were treated as time and circumstance permitted, gaping wounds sewn hurriedly together with fine twine.

Glandallin found himself a space on the floor beside Glamdolin Strongarm. The two friends ate in silence, watching the mass of orcs that had retreated a hundred paces from the gates. To Glandallin's eyes it seemed the enemy had formed a living battering ram, intent on smashing down the gateway with their flesh.

"Such persistence," he said softly. "I have never seen them as dogged as they are tonight. Something has changed." The thought of the dying trees sent a chill down his spine.

All of a sudden an ax clattered to the floor beside him. Turning just in time, he saw his companion slump forward. "Glamdolin!" He caught hold of the dwarf and was dismayed to see delicate beads of sweat glistening on his forehead, drenching his face and his beard. His reddened eyes were glazed and unseeing.

Glandallin knew at once that the mystery illness had claimed another victim, finishing what the enemy had left half-done.

"Get some rest. The fever will soon be over." Hauling Glamdolin's heaving body to one side, he settled him as comfortably as he could, knowing full well that the illness was probably fatal.

The long wait sapped the strength of dwarves and orcs alike. Fatigue, the warrior's enemy, set in. Glandallin dozed on his feet until his helmet hit the parapet with a thud. Awaking with a start, he looked around anxiously. Yet more of his kinsmen had fallen prey to the sickness. Fortune had turned her back upon the children of the Smith.

A bugle call rent the air, setting his heart racing.

In the cold light of the moon he watched the approaching rows of colossal silhouettes, four times as tall as the orcs. There were forty of them. Their hideous bodies were clad in poorly wrought armor and their monstrous hands clasped fir saplings, roughly fashioned into clubs.

Ogres.

The dwarves' defenses would crumble if the giants were to scale the walls. The cauldrons of molten slag were empty, the cache of stones depleted. For a moment Glandallin's doubts returned, but a glance at Giselbert's gleaming figure assured him that evil would be defeated in the time-honored way.

The mass of orcs stirred and a cheer went up as the ogres approached.

Marching to the head of the army, the enormous beasts, uglier and more oafish than even the orcs, deposited their grappling irons, the four prongs of which were the length of a fully grown man. They attached long chains to the stem of each hook.

The apparatus is ill suited to climbing, thought Glandallin. *The beasts intend to topple the walls.*

Whistling through the air, three dozen claws buried themselves in the stonework. A shouted order summoned the watching orcs to join the ogres in their tug-of-war. A crack of whips sounded and the jangling links pulled taut.

Glandallin heard the wall groan softly. The stronghold, built many cycles ago by his kinsmen, was no match for the beasts' raw power.

"Quick, bring the wounded to safety!" he bellowed.

The party of dwarves responsible for tending the cauldrons left their stations and carried off Glamdolin and the other ailing warriors.

Masonry crumbled as a section of crenellated battlement ripped from the wall. The grappling hook went into free fall amid the showering stonework, killing two ogres and ten orcs. The enemy forces held their ground. Soon the hook was ripping through the air again, poised to sink its claws into the wall.

This time the dwarves retreated, abandoning the parapet just in time. They took up position in the barbican above the gates.

Glandallin listened as a large section of wall crashed and shattered on the ground below. The earth quaked and the invading army howled in triumph.

Good luck to them, thought Glandallin, endeavoring to stay calm. *I hope they dash their brains out on the doors.* The gateway was built to withstand more than a few paltry grappling irons.

He peered cautiously over the steel-plated wall. More reinforcements were on their way. Horsemen mounted on jet-black steeds galloped to the head of the army of ogres and orcs. Glandallin instantly recognized the pointed ears of the tall, slim creatures.

A red glow shone from the horses' eyes and their hooves struck the ground in a shower of white sparks. Two riders thundered to the gateway and gave orders to the troops. The orcs and ogres set about clearing the pathway of fallen masonry so the assault could start afresh.

Wheeling round on their horses, the riders found safe quarter from which to watch. One of the two creatures unshouldered a mighty bow and nocked an arrow against the woven bowstring. The marksman's gloved fingers held the weapon loosely as he bided his time.

Hastily, the fifthlings pushed boulders over the parapet and onto the beasts below. The enemy flinched, jostling to evade the projectiles, and three of the orcs turned to flee. The archer raised his bow. Before the deserters could take flight, the first arrow, too fast for Glandallin to follow, sang through the air and an orc fell to its knees.

Already a second missile, uncommonly long for an arrow, sped from the archer's bow. The second beast perished, shrieking, followed a moment later by the third. The remaining minions took heed of the warning and resumed their work on the pathway. The orcs did not venture a protest at the murder of their kinsmen.

By the coming of dawn, the path had been cleared.

The fifthlings marveled at the scene unfolding before their eyes. The sky had brightened in the east, heralding the rising of the sun, yet a thick bank of fog loomed in the north. Its luminous center, a maelstrom of black, red, and silver, flickered with coursing light.

In defiance of the wind, it rolled toward the gateway, sweeping over the beasts below. The raucous orcs fell silent, huddling nervously together and shrinking away from the fog. Stooping, the ogres allowed it to pass. As if hailing their leader, the riders bowed their heads and saluted the vaporous mass. The shimmering mist lowered itself gently to the ground and hovered in front of the horses.

Then the unthinkable happened. With a shudder, the first of five bolts on the doors shot from its cylinder. The gateway quaked. Someone had spoken the incantation, delivering Girdlegard into the clutches of the invading hordes.

"No!" bellowed Glandallin, turning his back to the enemy and leaning over the inner wall to seek the culprit below. "No dwarf would ever . . ."

Glamdolin Strongarm. Alone, the dwarf was standing by

the doors, lips moving, hands raised in supplication.

"Silence!" Glandallin bellowed. "Can't you see what you're doing?"

His shouts fell on deaf ears. The second lock glowed brightly, illuminated by the runes. The bolt creaked back.

"He's been bewitched," muttered Glandallin. "The fog has infected his mind."

The third bolt left its ferrule and shot free.

At last the custodians of the gateway stirred. Springing to their feet, they darted down the staircase, racing to put a stop to the treacherous magic before it was too late. The fourth bolt drew back. With one bolt remaining, Glamdolin was still standing unchallenged on the pathway.

Time is against us, Glandallin thought grimly. "Forgive me, Vraccas, but I have no choice." He gripped his ax and hurled it with all his might and fury at his comrade-in-arms.

The blade sliced through the air, spinning, then plunged sharply toward the ground. Glandallin's aim was unerring and the ax drove home.

Glamdolin groaned as the weapon struck his shoulder. Blood spraying from the wound, he stumbled to the ground. Watching from above, Glandallin sent a quick thanks to Vraccas for guiding his blade.

His relief was short-lived. Death had come too late to prevent the traitor from achieving his terrible purpose. The final bolt shot back.

Slowly, the colossal gateway opened. The vast slabs scraped and dragged across the ground, as though reluctant to obey the treacherous command.

There was a grinding noise of stone on stone. The chink became a narrow channel, which widened to fill the breadth of the path. Time slowed to a crawl as the gates swung open. One final creak and for the first time in creation the path into Girdlegard was clear.

No! Glandallin stirred from his paralysis and hurtled down the steps to join Giselbert and the remaining warriors defending the gates.

He was the last but one to take his place in the doorway. Already the others had closed ranks and were holding their shields in front of their bodies, their axes held aloft.

Shoulder to shoulder they formed a low wall of flesh against the tide of orcs, ogres, trolls, and riders. Forty against forty thousand.

The enemy hung back, fearing an ambush. Never before had the gates opened to allow their passage.

Glandallin's gaze swept the front line of monstrous beasts, shifting back to survey the second, third, fourth, fifth, and countless other grunting rows, all poised for the attack. He glowered from under his bushy eyebrows, forehead furrowing into a frown.

Giselbert lost no time in reversing the incantation. At the sound of his voice, the gates submitted to his authority, swinging back across the pathway but moving too slowly to stop the breach. Giselbert strode behind his troops, laying a hand on each shoulder. The gesture was a source of solace as well as strength, calming and rallying the last defenders of the gates.

Trumpets blaring, the riders ordered the attack. The orcs and ogres brandished their weapons, shouting to drown out their fear, and the army advanced with thundering steps.

"The path is narrow. Meet them line by line and give

them a taste of our steel!" Glandallin called to his kinsfolk. "Vraccas is with us! We are the children of the Smith!"

"The children of the Smith!" the fifthlings echoed, feet planted firmly on the rocky ground beneath.

Four dwarves were chosen to form the final line of defense. Throwing down his shield, the king took an ax in each hand and led the surge toward the enemy. The dwarves, all that remained of Giselbert's folk, charged out to slay the invaders.

Ten paces beyond the gateway, the armies met. The fifthlings tunneled like moles through the vanguard of orcs.

With only one ax with which to defend himself, Glandallin struck out, slicing through the thicket of legs. He did not stop to kill his victims, knowing that the fallen bodies would hinder the advancing troops.

"No one gets past Glandallin!" he roared. Stinking blood streamed from his armor and helm, stinging his eyes. When his ax grew heavy, he clasped the weapon with both hands. "No one, do you hear!" His enemies' bones splintered, splattering him with hot blood. Twice he was grazed by a sword or a spear, but he battled on regardless.

The prize was not survival but the closing of the gates. Girdlegard would be safe if they could stave off the invasion until the passageway was sealed.

Until this hour his ax had defended him faithfully, but now the magic of its runes gave out. Glancing to his right, Glandallin saw a comrade topple to the ground, skull sliced in half by an orc's two-handed sword. Seething with hatred, and determined to fell the aggressor, Glandallin lunged once, twice, driving his ax into the creature's belly and cleaving it in two. A shadow loomed above him, but by then it was too late. He made a last-ditch attempt to dodge the ogre's sweeping cudgel, but its rounded head swooped down and struck his legs. Bellowing in pain he toppled against an orc, severing its thigh as he fell, before tumbling onward through the army of legs. He lashed out with his ax until there were no more orcs within his reach.

"Come here and fight, you cowards!" he snarled.

The enemy paid him no attention. Fired by an insatiable hunger, they streamed past him toward the gateway. They had no need of stringy dwarf flesh when there were tastier morsels in Girdlegard.

Trembling with pain, Glandallin rose up on his elbows. The rest of his kinsfolk were dead, their mutilated bodies strewn on the ground, surrounded by scores of enemy corpses. The diamonds on Giselbert's belt sparkled in the sunlight, marking the place where the fifthling father had fallen, slain by a trio of ogres. At the sight of him, Glandallin's soul ached with sorrow and pride.

The sun rose above the mountains, flooding through the gateway and dazzling Glandallin with its light. He raised a hand to his sensitive eyes, straining to see the gateway. *Praise be to Vraccas! The gates were closed!*

A blow from behind sent pain searing through his chest. For the duration of a heartbeat the tip of a spear protruded through his tunic, then withdrew. He slumped, gasping, to the ground. "What in the name of. . . ?"

The assassin stepped round his body and knelt beside him. The smooth elven face was framed by fine fair hair that shimmered in the sunlight like a veil of golden threads. But the vision bore a terrible deformity; two fathomless pits stared from almond-shaped holes.

The creature wore armor of black metal that reached to its knees. Its legs were clad in leather breeches and dark brown boots. Burgundy gloves protected its fingers from grime, and its right hand clasped a spear whose steel tip, sharp enough to penetrate the fine mesh of dwarven chain mail, was moist with blood.

The strange elf spoke to the dwarf.

At first the words meant nothing to Glandallin, but their morbid sound filled him with dread.

"My friend said: 'Look at me: Sinthoras is your death,'" a second voice translated behind him. "'I will take your life, and the land will take your soul.'"

Glandallin coughed, blood rushing from his mouth and coursing down his beard.

"Get out of my sight, you pointy-eared monster! I want to see the gates," he said gruffly, brandishing his ax to ward away the beast. The weapon almost flew from his grip; his strength was ebbing fast. "Out of my way or I'll cut you in two like a straw, you treacherous elf!" he thundered.

Sinthoras laughed coldly. Raising his spear, he inserted the tip slowly between the tight rings of mail.

"You are mistaken, my friend. We are the älfar, and we have come to slay the elves," the voice said softly. "The gates may be closed, but the power of the land will raise you from the dead and from that moment on, you will be one of us. You know the incantation; you will open the door."

"Never! My soul belongs to Vraccas!"

"Your soul belongs to the land, and you will belong to the land until the end of time," the velvety voice cut him short. "Die, so you can return and deliver Girdlegard to us."

The spear's sharp tip pierced the flesh of the helpless, dying dwarf. Pain stopped his tongue.

Sinthoras raised the weapon and pushed down gently on the battered body. The final blow was dealt tenderly, almost reverently. The creature waited for death to claim its prey, watching over Glandallin's pain-ravaged features and drinking in the memory.

Finally, when he was certain that the last custodian of the gateway had departed, Sinthoras left his vigil and rose to his feet.